ANGEL

by

Alex Kurtagic

London
Spradabach Publishing
2022

Spradabach Publishing
BM Box Spradabach
London WC1N 3XX

Angel

First paperback edition published 2022

ISBN 978-1-9993573-8-2

British Library Cataloguing-in-Publication Data:
A catalogue record for this book is available from the British Library.

To Volcano Head

Chapter I

'Sir?'

The word could've been tweeted by bird. The barman carried on with his tasks, wiping surfaces and lining up glasses, apparently deaf. Angel kept his orbs pealed, anxiously leaning over the counter, reedy arm slightly raised, index finger timidly soliciting attention.

'Sir?' he piped.

Still no acknowledgment. Amelia secured a strand of hair behind her ear, regarding Angel with a kindly smile. His bladder urged attention to nature.

'Sir!'

The barman turned towards him, but his face was down and registered no change. He tossed the cubes around the icemaker with the shovel.

'Sir? C-Could I have two Cokes?'

No effect.

'Sir? Could I have two Cokes?'

No effect.

The barman's inability to hear now seemed impossible. His ears were scarcely a foot and a half from Angel's larynx. Were the acoustics poor behind the counter? Was the wall-mounted TV to blame? Even the latter seemed improbable; though it was blaring a football match, it was mounted on an upper corner at the far end of the bar.

'Sir!'

Amelia glanced at the barman and then away, suddenly fascinated by the cornices around the ceiling. Angel performed an involuntary dance, the tune set by his bladder, before he caught himself.

'Sir!'

The barman turned and disappeared into the kitchen, only to re-emerge ten seconds later, his head turned towards the opposite end of the bar.

'Sir!'

At the farthest end of the counter, a middle-aged man with grey stubble, who'd just seated himself, caught the barman's attention. The latter dashed towards Grey Stubble, who'd not had to open his mouth, nor even modify his facial expression, to summon polite service.

'Sir! Sir!'

Flung like feathers, Angel's words failed to catch him. The incoming order usurped the barman's ears—now certainly out of reach—securing a nod of acknowledgment and a promptly-filled pint of ale.

Angel's eyes fixed on the occiput between those ears, awaiting their rotation. The rotation came, and the barman, now facing him, eyes even possibly seeing Angel for the first time, moved in his direction. Angel again raised his index finger, and, for good measure, the folded ten-pound note he'd been holding in his other hand.

'Sir?'

The barman remained impassive, and again walked past to disappear into the kitchen.

Angel hid his face under his collar-length hair, deflating.

'Never mind,' said Amelia, putting her hand on his forearm. 'It's very noisy tonight, Angel. He's rushed off his feet and probably can't hear half the customers. Let's give him a few minutes.'

'O-Okay.'

'So tell me. What's the occasion?' She smiled, arching her eyebrows.

'Um . . . I . . . I wrote this poem for Madison. I-I wanted to hear what you think before I post it.'

'Oh. Okay.' Amelia's smile faded for an instant, but she perked up. 'Well, you know I love poetry.'

'Er . . . yes, yes. That's why I wanted to ask you.'

'So you're still together?'

'Yes, yes, of course. I'm going to visit her in America in December.'

Amelia tilted her head and put her hand on her considerable bosom. 'Aw, how sweet.'

'Yes. Um . . . so I hope I can find a job soon. That's . . . um . . . why I've pleaded poverty.' He held up the tenner and made to return it to her.

Amelia did not take it back. 'Can you not ask your mum for money?'

'Er . . . no, no. I . . . er . . . I want to do it myself. You know . . . um . . . it's the proper thing to do.'

'What a gallant gentleman you are!'

'So . . . c-c-can I read you the poem?'

'By all means, Angel. I'm all ears.'

Angel reached for the folded sheets in his jacket pocket but his bladder again made him a dancing marionette.

'Um . . . sorry. I-I have to go to the lavatory. Do you mind?'

'Of course not!' She took the tenner from him. 'You go and I'll see if I can catch the barman for us. Okay?'

'Yes . . . er . . . thank you. Thank you.'

No sooner was the tenner in her hand than the barman reappeared, immediately noticing her and stopping, his smile like a Cheshire cat's. 'What will it be?'

'Could I please have a Coke and a pint of cider?'

'Coming right up!'

Like a punctured arm float, Angel looked askance at Amelia, uncomprehending her barman-summoning power. How did she do it? Her voice barely left her body. And the teeming London pub was, at that moment, a storm of joyous, post-work, post-class, tradesmen and student decibels. Was it her sex that gave her the advantage? She was, he supposed, easy to notice; not only did her snowy skin contrast against her dark hair, not only was she much wider than him, but her bouffant turned her head into a STOP sign.

Whatever the reason, he was glad to be relieved of command. Or, rather, of the need to appear in command.

'Oh, Angel. Don't feel sad. There's a reason Troy was about a woman,' Amelia said, batting her long lashes.

Angel steepled his eyebrows. Unable to think of a reply, he hurried off before the barman returned.

A group of brontosaurian men, laughing and conversing, pint in hand, blocked the door to the toilets. Assuming they wouldn't hear him, he moulded himself around the one nearest to the door, hoping the he would notice and move. When this failed to occur, Angel grabbed the handle and opened the door as far as he could without it touching the man's shoe. The fissure was too narrow even for Angel to slip through, leaving him no choice but to get the man's attention. Angel tapped his shoulder. The man kept cracking jokes at the group, now roaring with laughter. Another problem was the man's fluorescent coat: its thick, waterproof material presented an undentable barrier against Angel's noodle finger. Angel tried opening the door further until it touched the obstructing shoe. This still proved futile. The group of shining, red, cackling faces remained unacknowledging. Angel applied pressure, first gently and then almost yanking at the handle. Still nothing.

'Excuse me, sir,' he said, but his voice was lost in the din.

Angel applied pressure once more, this time leaning against the man's endless back.

This did the trick. The man's head turned, eyes puzzled. 'Oh. Sorry, mate.'

As Angel entered the lavatory a burst of laughter followed a jocular remark that might have been at his expense.

The door gave way to a small antechamber, beyond which emanated angry bellows and crashing sounds. As he opened the second door, two rubicund young men, each clamping the other's hoody, tumbled past and onto the floor. The one who landed on top began pounding the other's face, emitting a Tom Warrior 'uuuhh!' as each punch extracted blood from a breaking nose. Angel recoiled a bit, hesitating, then stepped carefully past the brawlers and into the toilet stall, where he hurried to unbuckle and unzip while his right blue orb, open wide, tracked developments behind him.

Uuuhh! landed three more punches before a third hoodie burst in and got to work on Uuuhh!'s face. Uuuhh! attempted to stand but lost his balance and landed on his backside, knocking his parietal on the sink. Grabbing a handful of Uuuhh!'s hair, his assailant slammed Uuuhh!'s cranium repeatedly against said sink until it detached from the wall. Meanwhile, the initial floored hoodie, shaking his head, got back on his feet and joined the others, kicking Uuuhh! repeatedly in the stomach, his cruentous visage blighted by inflammation and rage.

Angel's water could not pass fast enough. Hiding under a curtain of hair, he pushed to accelerate the evacuation. Steady banging, grunts, and heavy breathing continued to bounce off tiled walls for many seconds, until his bladder finally emptied. Keeping his arms close to his body, he yanked his belt all the way down to the last hole and tried to keep his hands steady as he inserted the prong. Even after buckling up, his jeans dropped several inches upon release. He kept his gaze averted as he slipped past the brawlers on his way out, opening the door just enough to squeeze through.

A large, bearded man he'd never seen before had appeared next to Amelia, sporting a grin and a black leather jacket. To his confident jocularity the squirming Amelia responded with a guarded laugh. Angel's Coke stood on the counter, midway between Beard and Amelia. Access to them blocked by angry middle-aged men standing around a table, Angel skirted them and took position next to the intruder, hoping the latter would take his presence as his cue to leave. But Beard carried on as before, allowing no lull in the conversation. Amelia fidgeted awkwardly and darted at Angel a succession of glances, pleading intervention. The passing seconds kept mounting, however, without her silent pleads instigating action; Angel stared at Amelia, goggle-eyed, at best intermittently looking at Beard's leather jacket, but never at his face.

'Excuse, me. Here's your Coke, Angel,' Amelia said, finally, holding an index finger up at Beard and offering Angel the glass.

Angel grabbed it, but as Beard brusquely turned to see whom the Coke had been handed to, bumped Angel's hand, which wobbled wildly, spilling beverage on the intruder.

Amelia, startled, stepped back. 'Oh, Angel, you poor thing!'

Beard looked down at his soaked, cold shirt, momentarily perplexed.

'Oh, dear!' Amelia said, quickly wiping Angel's hand. 'It's everywhere. I'll go and get some paper towels.'

As soon as Amelia had left, Beard's snapped at Angel. 'The fuck are you doing?'

Piercing dark eyes glared. The expectation of a response.

'Oh, sorry,' Angel said.

'What you standing there for?'

'Sorry, it was an accident. I-I'm with . . .' Angel pointed weakly to where Amelia had stood.

Beard mocked him with an impression in a silly falsetto, then gave him his marching orders: 'Fuck off.'

Angel stood paralysed.

'I said: FUCK OFF!'

Angel's adrenalin produced tremors. 'Sorry, I-I'm just with h . . .'

Beard got in his face. 'You fucking little cunt! What? WHAT???'

'No no no no no,' said Angel, taking a step back and waving his palms, before pointing vaguely to Amelia, 'It's just . . . I'm just with her. I'm just with her.'

A dull sound. Pain in his face. The sensation of falling and landing on floorboards.

It took a moment for Angel to realise what had happened. His face numb, he found Beard standing over him, legs apart, body tense, fist ready to redeploy.

Now back with paper towels, Amelia, flung her hands to the sides of her head. 'Oh, Angel!'

The forgotten paper towels wafted their way down.

But before Beard could do anything else, one of the middle-aged men from the adjacent table interposed himself and calmly addressed the attacker. 'Okay, mate. Go on. Let's get some air.'

Amelia gave Angel a hand up. He was so light she nearly flung him into the ceiling.

'Oh, your poor eye!' she said. 'Are you okay?'

'Um . . . yes,' replied Angel, in a high tremolo. Crapulent faces in the vicinity leered with amusement.

Beard was walked out. Amelia held Angel's face in her hands and looked at him in the eye, her eyebrows sky high, 'Are you okay?' she said, speaking fast. 'Does it hurt? Oh, my God. You're so brave! You're so brave!'

'Yes, yes, I'm fine, I'm fine,' he said quickly, still in a trembly squeak, hoping to reassure Amelia so that the scene would be over. He kept an eye on the door as it swung shut, putting his attacker's leathered back out of view. He wondered whether he was local.

Amelia got the barman's attention. 'Could I have a glass of ice?'

While the barman got to work, she turned back to Angel and caressed his head.

'You're so brave, Angel!'

He blinked. 'Um . . . w-w-who was he?'

'Don't know. He just came and started chatting.' She grabbed an ice cube from the glass newly plonked on the counter and gently applied it to his eye. 'Here . . . aw, your precious eye . . . This will keep the inflammation down. You're so brave, Angel.'

'Um . . . thank you.'

Angel wondered about Amelia's cider, only now registering she'd changed his original order. The shards of glass from his Coke were being swept up by the barman into a long-handled dustpan. Angel looked for cuts on his hand, still trembling, but only found it wet and sticky.

'Do you want to go to A and E?' asked Amelia.

'Er . . . no, no.'

'I'll call an ambulance.' Amelia got her phone out.

'No! No! Please! No need!'

'Are you sure? Do you want to go back to the dorm?'

'No no no. L-Let's stay. Let's stay.'

'Let's get you back to the dorm.'

Angel hesitated.

Amelia smiled. 'Don't worry. I'll protect you!'

Chapter II

'The reason I teach the classics is because I *hate* the classics.'

Jaw tense, gaze defiant, the professor stood before her students, as if daring them to contradict. Angel briefly caught her eye, but she didn't linger. The non-lingering he'd only felt, because he'd quickly looked down at his notebook, worried she might have caught him staring at her blue Mohawk.

'I'm going to *change* how you think about them,' she went on, 'and you'll learn to *hate* them too.'

Angel had signed up for the 17th-Century English Literature course with enormous anticipation. He favoured the prose and poetry of that period. Or at least his perception of it, because he had not read as much as he would have liked. Just snippets here and there. Enough to give his own, humble efforts in that direction, always designed to impress Madison, something of their rhythm and style. The idea was to sustain and indeed increase her admiration.

> *Studying inventions fine, her wits to entertain,*
> *Oft turning others' leaves, to see if thence would flow*
> *Some fresh and fruitful showers upon my sunburned brain.*

He'd sat in the front row, eyes wide, ears open, pen ready. But the professor had arrived looking unlike anything he had expected, sporting Doc Martens and fat arms covered in old tattoos. Along with her had come a sense of foreboding, and the hope that, the real professor being ill that day, this was but a grumbling substitute. Yet, the more the person in front shouted, the more it seemed she was, indeed, the professor for that module.

'And, unlike *a certain professor* at this university, whom you may have come across, I will also *not* allow you to *privilege* canonical voices . . .'

Stapled sheets outlining the course material, copies of which had been handed to a sleepy student at the end of the row, now reached him. Angel grabbed one, mindlessly passed the rest along, and browsed through the contents. The professor's name, shown at the top of the first page, matched that enunciated earlier by the woman facing them. Professor George Hynd. Nothing like William Shakespeare in appearance, which is what he'd imagined—at least before he found out the professor's name, after which he had thought of Samuel Johnson, because 'Hynd' made him think of hind quarters, and therefore of a bull, which accorded better with Dr Johnson's build. Which, in the end, had proven not far off.

The reading list, both mandatory and optional, was no less confounding. Aside from Milton, there were no authors he recognised. Numerous women he had never heard of, and quite a few names of exotic provenance. He checked once again the name of the course, in case he'd erred, but, no, this was not a women's studies or a colonial history module; he was in the right place.

'You will be taught how to *analyse* and *deconstruct* the canonical texts,' Professor Hynd announced, almost as a threat, 'but we will not *unduly* focus on them; you will be exposed *mainly* to subaltern voices . . .'

No canonical texts? Given his aim, and his scant readings, he worried about being found ignorant of the basics after completing the course, and, caught like a rabbit in headlights, having to deflect awkwardly in conversation. But in the absence of a choice, he sought the positive side of it. He liked the idea of becoming a repository of obscure knowledge, of largely unexamined literature, and talking about it with confidence and aplomb. The basics he could read up on his own. Thinking about it, in fact, the course material was actually very clever; anybody could look up Wikipedia for the main authors; this is what university was for: exposing one to different texts and perspectives! His arcane knowledge Madison would find even more impressive. But he hoped that they were not teaching the same in American universities, and that Madison would not have signed up for a similar course. The thought of boring her with things she already knew made him anxious. And her not having yet told him what courses she'd be taking that term did so even more. She had not even told him whether classes had already started at her university. He assumed yes. Nothing indicative of it in her social media, however.

'. . . so you will not restrict yourselves to *English* writers,' Professor Hynd continued, showing a missing pre-molar as she grinned, 'or Scottish, Irish, Welsh, Cornish, or colonial American writers—you'll be marked *down* if you do that—you will be expected to cover the whole *depth* and *breadth* of 17th-century English literature . . .'

'But isn't his course supposed to be about English literature?' interjected a male student in a wispy voice.

The professor ignored him and carried on.

That missing pre-molar . . . Angel grew weirdly uncomfortable. He scanned his classmates, to gauge them for clues as to optimal attitudes. Most were foreign students. He unconsciously ignored them because they were from unfamiliar cultures, at odds with his aesthetic. Of the rest, he examined the females first; their faces registered nothing useful. Many had multiple tattoos. One had already tattooed her entire arm with flowers and scorpions. The male students were three: the face of the sleepy one, ginger, chinless, and chubby, was blank; the face of the American, whose provenance was obvious from his attire alone, was nearly invisible, sunken into a hoodie and buried under a baseball cap; and the face of the questioner was cadaveric, a skull with grey skin stretched over jutting cheekbones. As a result, Angel felt out at sea, unsure of how to act, what to do with his face, what body language to adopt, where to put his arms, how to arrange his legs. He imagined Madison observing him and grew unsure of whether to stay or drop the class and sign up for a different one. His classmates had not been what he had envisioned. He had envisioned girls in dresses and guys in shirts and jackets, lace-up shoes with leather soles and heels. And this had proven a foolish vision; no one at the university ever dressed like that.

After three years, he ought to have known better.

Angel awoke from his trance. Professor Hynd had kept blasting at them and moved on to the evaluation policy.

'Unfortunately I have to mark your course work. If it were up to me, there'd no marking, because marking perpetuates *hierarchies.* But that's not my decision. So I'll be marking you as per the guidelines. 55% is an *A . . .*'

Lower than last year! An A was therefore certain. No way he could get less, even while working part time, as he planned to do until Christmas. Angel decided he would stick with the course. He would not tell Madison about the grade boundaries; he would only tell her about having earned As in all his modules.

'. . . and 15% is an *E.*'

He wished he'd arrived early and taken a selfie sitting at his lecture chair. With hair like Charles I, velour jacket, and the beginnings of a Van Dyke beard, he thought he looked the part. He could imagine the photograph on Instagram, posted for Madison to see, but ostensibly just recording a moment. He wouldn't have been looking at the camera; he would have been looking past it, to the front of the classroom, maybe with a slight frown, concentrating on the lecture, on the poetry, on its clever allusions and alliterations. Next time, he resolved. Or, rather, when his black eye healed. He would come fifteen minutes early, stage the shot, experiment with different camera angles, set up his mini tripod, adjust the ambient light. He would order a leather notebook, one with either a clasp or a leather bind—why hadn't he thought of it before?—and a pen worthy of the name, a quill ball pen, if he could find one (a real quill would be too slow, sadly). He look for it online as soon as the lecture was over.

'Any questions?'

Silence.

Chapter III

His roommate had again left his bed unmade. He had also left empty Dorito bags on the sheets and added to his collection of Coca-Cola cans on the bedside table. They were only a few days into the term but said table had already run out of space. So had the rubbish bin, which had proven from day one a testament to his roommate's inaccurate aim. Shoulders drooping, Angel sighed, carefully grabbed the bin, so as not to topple the mountain peak of cans and plastic bottles rising precipitously above the rim—all of it his roommate's work—and placed it outside the room, so that the cleaners could empty it in the morning.

'Angel, my friend. What happened to your eye?' asked Saïd, who was about to enter the room across the hall.

'Um . . . er . . . I fell.'

'Ah, okay. How's your roommate?'

Angel just gestured at the rubbish bin, eliciting Saïd's cackles. The latter asked, 'What happened to single room?'

'Um . . . I missed the deadline with the forms,' Angel said.

'Why?'

He sighed. 'Er . . . they're so long and confusing.'

'But they're easy. You fill in the information.'

'Sixty pages . . . w-why so much detail?'

'Don't know, man. Good luck with your roommate!' More cackles.

Saïd disappeared behind the door, Angel retreated behind his.

Angel dropped himself onto his bed, phone in hand. Not that he made much of a dent on the mattress; the bed stayed made.

A WhatsApp message arrived.

AMELIA: How was your first class?

Angel thought of replying, but it seemed too much effort and, instead, he scoured Madison's social media. No new posts since he'd last checked this morning. Anywhere. The last Instagram post dated still from August, and it showed only her face, laughing, wearing oversized, heart-shaped shades. 'Love summer,' was the caption. No punctuation. No emojis. No tags. The other posts were equally informative. Some had no captions at all. Her Facebook was a morgue; the last post from two years ago; just a profile picture update, in which hair hid most of her face. Her Twitter was empty. Her Goodreads had not been updated in a year. Last book marked as read: Jackie Collins' *The Bitch*. He flinched. It seemed so out of place, so far from the Madison he'd dated during the Spring and Summer terms that he suspected it had been a gift from a relative she had felt obligated to acknowledge. And her TikTok? A catacomb. In times like this, he lost his trust in heaven.

But the voice of Madison
In his ear would seem to say—
'O, be patient if thou lov'st me!'
And the storm would pass away.

He put the phone down and grabbed the book on this bedside table. A Penguin Classics edition of *The Faery Queene*, by Edmund Spenser. His grip wasn't strong enough to hold it with one hand, so he had to enlist the other to prevent dropping the 1248-page tome. He'd not made it past the tenth stanza of the first canto, despite having had the book beside him for several weeks. He put the bookmark aside and picked up from where he'd left off. No sooner had he read the first line, however, his mind began wandering, and, before he knew, an hour had passed, the entirety of which he'd spent re-combing through Madison's social media, this time going all the way back to the beginning, daydreaming all the while and holding imaginary conversations with his paramour. The WhatsApp message he'd sent her in the intervening time had gone unanswered. The status showed two grey ticks.

Hunger eventually brought him to. His slight frame required little sustenance, but he had missed breakfast and only eaten a banana for lunch. With icy hands, he took off his jacket to slip on a thick, turtle-neck jumper. It hung loosely from his shoulders. He hitched up his jeans and made his way to the university canteen.

Chapter IV

Angel switched the empty tray hanging from one hand to the other; it was heavy, the queue slow. He was finally close enough to the serving counter to see what was on offer. Cheesy pasta. Baked potatoes. Cold (and paper-thin) turkey slices. Cheddar cheese, also sliced. Two places in front of him, a girl with short blonde hair wrinkled her nose at the selection, and eventually chose, albeit not without throwing her arms in the air, the turkey and the cheese. The slim Jamaican man behind the counter took her plate, put on it a slice of each, and handed it back with a steady gaze and expressionless visage.

'He freaks me out,' Angel heard her say as she turned to her friend standing by.

Angel selected pasta and potato. The server stared at him with the same enigmatic visage, which, up close, struck Angel as condescending and vaguely mocking. The server splashed a glob of cheesy pasta and placed the smallest of the available potatoes on Angel's plate. Upon getting it back, Angel noticed the potato was black on one side.

'Um . . . sir?' he said. 'The potato is rotten.'

But the server was already attending to the next person, an immense girl with green hair, one of the American students, who now moved along the serving counter, bumping him off balance.

The girl looked at him, her face hard. 'I didn't consent to being touched,' she said.

'I was just standing—'

'I *do not* consent. Step away!'

'Sorry, it's just that there's a problem w—'

'I said, STEP AWAY, YOU CREEP!'

The sudden amping up of aggression took him aback. The girl's voice had reverberated across the canteen, sweeping through it like the shockwave of a hydrogen bomb. Surrounding faces had turned in his direction. Hostile female ones glared. Male ones, kept strictly neutral, observed the unfolding scene, forks midway between plate and mouth. Angel's impulse was to explain, but, seeing that all the faces had turned into ramparts of suspicion, he deemed it best to make himself scarce.

'Sorry . . . sorry,' he muttered, then retreated, head down.

Avoiding eye contact, he loaded up with bread and butter portions from baskets mercifully away from the serving counter and slipped into the safety of the upper level, which he disliked, because always freezing, but found presently appealing, because always empty. The time horizon imposed by the weight of his phone pulling down his jeans accelerated his flight.

He found a remote table and sat down, heart still pounding. As he thought of taking a sip from his drink, he realised he'd forgotten to get one. However, as the fizzy drinks dispenser was downstairs, he chose to eat his meal dry. The pasta would have been the logical way to start, but now, though starving, he couldn't stomach it. He broke off a tiny piece of his bread and put it in his mouth, to at least stave off the hunger pangs; yet, the bread would not move from that station: he could chew, but not swallow. It would be a good twenty minutes, spent in a vacant daze, before he could pick up knife and fork, by which time the food might as well have been snow.

He thought of Madison and pulled out his phone. No updates. His WhatsApp message to her now displayed two blue ticks, but no reply. She'd been online ten minutes ago. He decided to scroll through his Instagram and Facebook feeds, in case she'd posted. Another twenty minutes passed this way.

The scrape of a chair on linoleum jerked him out of his stupor. It was Amelia, sitting down at his table, smiling at him. A sight for sore eyes!

'Hello, Angel,' she said.

'Hello,' he replied.

'You look upset. Is everything okay?'

'Um . . . I-I'm just tired. I-I-I didn't sleep well last night.'

'Oh, no! What happened?'

'Um . . . my roommate came in smelling of lager and cigarettes. He made a lot of noise in the dark and then spent all night snoring.'

'Oh, dear. Maybe you can ask to be moved.'

'No, I . . . er . . . I-I can't be bothered. He'll quieten down.'

'But what if he doesn't quieten down?'

'I-I'm sure he will. He's already boasted he's gone through a thousand pounds. He-He'll run out of money soon and won't be able to get drunk.'

'A thousand pounds! The term only started a week ago!'

'Yes . . . so . . . he'll run out of money, I'm sure. And . . . er. . . his parents will probably stop sending more when he starts failing his classes.'

'That's assuming he tells them.'

'Um . . . i-it can't go on forever.'

'I think you should still ask.'

'No, n-no. I'll be fine.'

'Still, Angel. You can't live like that.'

'I . . . um . . . c-can we talk about something else?' he said, waving his hands.

Amelia gestured at his plate with her eyes. 'Didn't you like your dinner?'

'It got . . . it got cold really fast.'

'You can always order a pizza later.'

'I-I'm saving my money for the flight to see Madison in December. I'll have a Coke later.'

'Have you heard from Madison today?'

'Um . . . I sent her a message, but she's not replied yet. Probably busy. You know . . . um . . . it's mid-day there, so she's probably in class.'

'So when are you going to show me that poem?'

'Erm . . . not tonight. I-I-I decided I need to change a few things.'

'Of course. Better safe than sorry. But don't let the perfect be the enemy of the good!'

Angel did not acknowledge her gentle tease. He couldn't think of anything clever to say.

'Do you want to see a film this weekend?' said Amelia, adding, 'I'll pay.'

'Um . . . w-what's playing?'

'Let me check . . .' Amelia pulled her phone out of her brown suede backpack.

With a shivery breath, Angel crossed his arms, tucking his hands under his armpits as he hunched over the table.

'There is . . .' Amelia began, then stopped, concerned. 'Are you alright? You look cold.'

'This r-room is freezing,' he said, noticing, as he said it, that all the windows were, in fact, closed.

'Doesn't feel cold to me. Actually, it's rather warm. Why don't you get a coffee from downstairs?'

'N-No. I-I-I don't feel like c-c-coffee,' he said, without looking up.

'I'll get it for you.' She made to get up.

'No, no . . . I-I-It's okay. It's fine.'

Amelia hunched her shoulders and began listing various films. Angel barely listened, his ear attuned, rather, on the noise coming from the lower level. There were still students there. The dining room was now maybe a quarter full.

'What do you think?' said Amelia.

'Sorry, w-what was t-that?'

'*Ad Astra* . . . *The Goldfinch* . . . *The Farewell* . . .'

'Er . . .' The titles might as well have been in Bengali. His funds depleted, and not desiring to spend what few pennies he might get, he'd ignored film releases. Eyes still on his tray, he got distracted by a margarine portion he'd picked up by mistake.

'Don't stress. I'll let you think about it,' Amelia said, smiling kindly while putting her phone away.

'Y-Yes . . . I-I'll l-let you kn-know.'

'Let me know when you've decided, okay? In your own time.'

Silence.

'Alright,' Amelia said, cheerfully.

Silence. Shivers.

'How about a hot chocolate?' Amelia said.

Downstairs was now probably an eighth full. Angel frowned and shook his head. 'N-No, no. I-I don't feel like ch-chocolate.'

'You sure? Yummy with sugar.'

'It's fine.'

Amelia ate her dinner. Angel noticed she'd been given a large baked potato, to which she'd added a side of salad. And bread. And fruit. And carrot cake. And tea. She said things, but he was only half listening; he replied peremptorily, monosyllabically. He imagined himself inside Scott's tent, on the Ross Ice Shelf, in Antarctica, in March 1912, and wondered how it was possible to survive forty degrees of frost, when twenty degrees above freezing still felt like freezing.

'Do you want my carrot cake?' asked Amelia, holding out her portion.

'Er . . . no no . . . I'm not hungry.'

'Okay.' She took her slice back, a bit sad.

An eternity later, Amelia had the last mouthful of cake and the last of her tea.

'I'll be in the library if you want me,' she said smiling invitingly, as she stood up, tray in hand.

'O-Okay. I-I-I m-m-might j-join y-you l-l-later.'

'That'd be lovely.' She turned and went, but threw him a friendly backward glance and a wave while descending the stairs.

Still hunched over, Angel acknowledged with his eyebrows: he'd pulled his turtleneck over his nose.

The hubbub downstairs had died down completely. Only the pressurised hiss of hot water and the brusque clatter of trays, plates, and cutlery being washed up in the kitchen. He tracked the sound of Amelia's heels as she finished going down, stopped in front of the niches adjoining the washing up room, and made her way out. At that point he became the last straggler in the dining room. Safe for him finally to leave. Hopefully, the coffee dispenser had not yet been switched off.

Taking a deep breath, he braced himself and made his way down the stairs, swift and silent like a cat, wide eyes scanning the landscape. What if the big American girl hadn't left after all? Or come back unexpectedly because she'd left something behind? But there were no students left. All the tables were empty. The Jamaican was inverting chairs and placing them on tabletops. The coffee machine had already been switched off. Never mind. The niches for the dirty trays were all empty. Beyond them he could glimpse uniformed under-scullions, furiously washing, drying, and throwing the crockery around, as if their intention were to smash it all rather than stack it in piles. The washing-up room blasted its din like a wall of Marshall cabinets. His tray was greeted with a 'Fuck's sake! *Another* one!' in a cockney voice. It was yanked away so violently that its contents nearly flew off. Angel saw a heavily tattooed arm, bursting with muscle, shaking as its shaven-headed operator dumped his untouched dinner into an oversized composting bin. Angel made a move before the skinhead looked up.

He was nearly at the exit, just past the swing doors that gave access to the kitchen, when he heard:

'Pssst!'

Chapter V

'Are you still looking for work?' The woman's uniform differed from the kitchen staff's.

'Erm . . . y-yes. How d-did you know?' Angel said, lowering his turtleneck.

'I overheard you talking about it yesterday evening. While in the queue.'

'Okay,' he said.

'Can you get up early?'

'Er . . . y-y-yes, I suppose so . . .'

'You suppose or you can?'

Realising where this was going, he said, 'Yes, I c-can.'

'We could use an extra pair of hands during breakfast.'

'W-W-What w-w-would b-be the job?'

'Washing up room.'

Angel thought of the skinhead, who was still in there but may be about to come out and see him. He decided the skinhead couldn't have got a good view of his face from inside. The niches were only tall enough for a standing paper cup.

'Okay,' Angel said.

'Nothing formal. Just a bit of extra cash.'

'O-Okay.'

'It's a lot of red tape otherwise,' added the supervisor, rolling her eyes.

'Okay.'

'Can you come in at 6 tomorrow morning?'

'Er . . . yes.'

'Alright. Let me show you.'

The woman led him to the washing up room. The clatter there had given way to chatter. He found Skinhead ripping off his apron, cracking a joke at a tanned man with hairy arms and a unibrow. One look at Skinhead's face and Angel knew he would be trouble. Unibrow didn't appear to speak much English. The warm area smelled of washing up fluid.

'This is . . .' the supervisor told Angel their names. Angel forgot them as soon as he heard them, too distracted by how the two men were sizing him up. Angel offered a weak smile. The men didn't alter their serious expressions. More than anything, they seemed eager to leave.

'Emmanuel,' the supervisor now called out.

'Yeh,' Angel heard.

After long seconds, the Jamaican appeared at the threshold.

'And this is Emmanuel. He mostly serves, but sometimes he joins the boys here too.'

'Okay,' Angel said. 'H-Hello.'

Emmanuel didn't return his greeting; he simply stared at Angel with the same enigmatic visage as before. Angel decided he might not be Jamaican after all. When he thought of Jamaicans, Angel saw dreadlocks, Bob Marley, ganja. Emmanuel didn't strike him as one of those. Maybe he was Nigerian. Or Ugandan. Or Congolese. It didn't matter. Such places were a mystery to him. He only knew there were students from some of them at the university. Angel scratched his temple, looked away, at the floor, at the woman.

'Okay,' she said. Only now Angel noticed her name tag said SUPERVISOR. 'So six o'clock tomorrow.'

'Um . . . six o'clock . . . okay,' Angel said. That was six hours before his normal waking up time, but Madison was worth every sacrifice.

'Six o'clock. *On* the dot.'

'Okay.'

'I'll get you a uniform ready.'

'Okay. Th-Thank you.'

'Oh—What's your name?'

'Angel.'

'Angel. Okay.'

The supervisor walked him back into the kitchen. Two seconds later, Angel heard a cockney voice uttering a short phrase, to which followed an explosion of rough laughter in the washing up room. Angel pretended not to hear it.

'See you tomorrow, Angel,' the supervisor said, stopping near the door.

'Okay,' Angel replied.

The shivers were gone.

Chapter VI

The Arts and Humanities Library, with its Gothic architecture, labyrinthine layout, and Tudor furnishings, was Angel's favourite campus building. Tonight, his least favourite librarian womaned the reception desk. Her face was hidden, because she was short and the reception desk built like a turret, but the top of her head was unmistakable. Sight of it made him fleetingly wish he would not find what he was looking for—even though he didn't quite know what it was—as this would be easier than dealing with that brick wall of strict deadlines and inflexible rules. Over the past three years she had mercilessly and even, he would say, *vindictively*, wrung money out of him with fines for overdue returns. However, the desire to lose himself in the book hoard, to discover obscure literary gems from the Jacobean and Stuart eras, to revel in lyrical poetry and elegant prose, was greater than his dispirited aversion to that member of staff. He checked the time on his phone, hoping for an imminent change of shift, but he knew better, because it was past six o'clock and the last one for the day had already occurred. His archenemy always worked nights.

With an inward groan, Angel went to the collection of Early Modern English literature. While *en route*, he glimpsed Amelia sitting at a table on the upper level, prompting him into an abrupt, winding diversion so as not to be seen. Alas, his desire for solitary enjoyment would be frustrated all the same, for, standing before his target shelves, he found Jae, who held him in contempt.

'Good evening,' he muttered, without enthusiasm.

The towering blonde briefly looked down at him, registering no emotion, and carried on studying the book in hand.

Angel had no option but to browse close to her. Without moving a millimetre, she again glanced at him with icy disapproval. This he pretended not to notice. Jae slapped her book closed, blowing air and dust into his face, and slid the volume back in place, her elbow an inch from his temple. It was an edition of *Pierce's Supererogation* by Gabriel Harvey. Precisely the first title he'd wanted to explore. His mistake was not to pull it back out right away, because, before he had a chance even to twitch, Jae swung her heavily laden backpack, one of whose steel buckles grazed his cheek, and dropped it noisily on the floor in the narrow space between them. He was forced to step back quickly to avoid it landing on his foot.

He got the message, and, after standing paralysed for a few seconds, observing the ponytailed blonde as she, with perfect equanimity, slid free another volume, pretended to be interested in something else, and moved to the shelves opposite. These, however, covered boring topics, so he was reduced to wiling away time, faking interest in random titles, until Jae moved on.

But Jae stayed, an immovable ivory column. And she was not wasting time either: every furtive glance Angel threw in her direction found her scanning indexes or tables of contents, photographing pages or volumes, or making notes on her tablet. She was, in fact, relentlessly productive. There was substance to the jokes circulating about her android origins.

Many minutes passed, and Angel grew faint, calories from the lunch-time banana having long fizzled out. He rummaged in his pocket, where he found a smattering of coins. Enough for a Pot Noodle—if he bought it at Tesco, which was twenty-five minutes away on foot. Depletion prompting action, he got moving. He'd come back later. However, no sooner had he turned the corner that he saw Amelia thirty feet away, walking towards him. As her head was down, Angel quickly avoided detection by reversing course. He absconded to the section dedicated to 18th-century drama, which allowed him to observe, crouching behind a low shelving unit, Jae and perhaps Amelia, if she joined the android.

And Amelia did, indeed, join the android. 'Hi, Jae. Could I just get a book from that shelf?' she said.

Jae picked up the backpack, slung it over her shoulder, and moved aside, saying not a word.

'Thank you,' Amelia said.

Jae nodded in acknowledgment, then carried on with her research.

If Angel thought Amelia would be brief, she soon disabused him; after grabbing the book she'd come for, she sat cross-legged on the floor, pulled a laptop out of her bag, and opened it on her lap. Angel sighed in exasperation. To exit the library, he would have to pass near the two women; it would be impossible for Amelia not to see him, however slowly or quietly he tip-toed. He asked the gremlins *why*.

He yanked out his phone. Still no reply from Madison. No updates on her social media. He had a new follower on Instagram, however, but the owner had zero in common with Angel; a guy with Brylcreemed hair smiling on a sunny beach, showing off his six-pack, which he guaranteed could be obtained in three minutes; another follow-unfollow idiot.

'Please come to reception,' he heard.

Angel looked up and found the librarian two feet away,

That crafty demon and loud beast
That plagued him day and night.

Short she was, but built like a tank—arms like Popeye, torso like a barrel, calves bulging like aviation bombs.

Her fists were on her hips, signalling she meant business.

'I-I-I'm researching,' Angel said.

'Please come to reception.'

Angel stood up with ill grace and followed the librarian. Amelia of course noticed him and waved with a smile. He barely returned the gesture. Jae glanced at him momentarily with a raised eyebrow and went back to her tablet.

At the reception desk, the librarian got his details up on her screen. Angel wondered what he had done wrong now.

'You have a book that has been overdue since the 24th of June,' she said.

'A book?'

'Yes. *The Faery Queene* by Edmund Spenser, which you took out on loan on the 17th June.'

Angel slapped his forehead. 'Oh, balls!'

'Keep your voice down.'

'Okay. Sorry, sorry. I'll return it tonight.'

'You were given three reminders,' the librarian said.

'I promise I'll return it tonight.'

'As you well know, because you were told, the book is set reading for some of the courses . . .'

'Yes, I know. I am really, really sorry. I'll defin—'

'. . . so we had to replace it before the beginning of term. You will be charged the overdue fines, plus the cost of the replacement. There is also an administration fee.'

'An administration fee!'

The librarian opened a drawer, took out a booklet, found the appropriate page, and placed it in front of him to read, pointing with her finger at the relevant paragraph.

'You know what the rules are. We've been through this before.'

'But I had no warning . . . I-I should have been given a warning bef . . .'

'You were given three reminders by email. All the information is there.'

'When was the last email?'

'The last email was sent on the 8th of July.'

He vaguely remembered the email now, stunned that so much time had passed.

'So you've had plenty of time to rectify and avoid the surcharge.'

One of the maintenance staff entered the library and claimed a spot by the reception desk. Baby-faced, with light, bulging blue eyes and curly auburn hair, the new arrival had ordinary features, taken individually. But there was something deeply unsettling about his manner and mien; he walked around campus with his head tilted back, a tendency to stare mutely, and the ever-present hint of a mocking smile. Angel couldn't remember having ever heard his voice.

'How much . . . how much do I owe?' Angel said, trying to blank him out.

The librarian checked her screen. 'You must pay £247.82 by the 8th of October.'

'Two hundred and forty-seven!' Angel darted a glance at Babyface, the latter's visage unchanged, but somehow oozing amusement.

'Yes.'

The librarian then broke down the total: a charge for the book becoming overdue; the rising charges for each week the book remained overdue; the cost of replacement; and the administration fee.

'T-That's a lot,' said Angel, faintly.

'You will not be allowed to take out books until you pay the full amount. You've got 14 days to pay.'

'Fourteen days? Not thirty?'

'If, after 14 days, you haven't paid, there will be a further penalty. If, after 28 days you still haven't paid, interest will start being added to your debt. You will also be excluded from the library.'

Angel's hand was still on his forehead. He'd have to message his mother. And figure out what to tell her.

'Okay. Okay. Um . . . I'll look into it. Fourteen days.'

'Good.'

Chapter VII

It was drizzling.

Georgian terraced houses, inappropriately disrupted by modernist office blocks, flanked the walk to Tesco. The clamour and hiss of cars tearing past on wet asphalt almost drowned out his thoughts. Anyone else would have been reminded of a cityscape from *Blade Runner*, but Angel preferred to think of *Night Time in Paris* by Amédée Marcel-Clément, a 1909 painting he'd seen in an art book.

It occurred to him that he might in the end avoid asking his mother for money, since he was starting work at the canteen the following day. He realised, however, that he hadn't asked when and how much he would be paid. He hoped daily or weekly. And he assumed minimum wage, whatever that was. Probably £10 an hour. Two hours a day would make it £20 a day. That would be enough to settle his debt before the deadline, and still leave him extra. On the other hand, his sole purpose for getting that job was to pay for his flight in December and to have dollars while visiting Madison. And flights became ever more expensive closer to the departure date. And, around Christmas, flights cost an arm and a leg. But maybe he'd be paid more. Yes, he'd be paid more. He had a university education, after all, so it was bound to be more than minimum wage. Perhaps he'd be getting as much as £40 a day. And if he arrived half an hour early, as much as £50!

He reached this conclusion just as he passed the Harrington, a pub frequented mostly by Australian expats and local tradesmen. Several girls had congregated outside. From their attire he guessed they were from the newly arrived crop of American students at the university—not a welcome sight, since this year's appeared even more easily offended than last's. He was about to let his floppy hair fall over his face, in case they'd witnessed the altercation in the canteen, but then realised there was no need: the ones standing had rubber legs, whereas of the two who weren't, one was on all fours, throwing up profusely, while the other lay sprawled on the pavement, near her own pile of vomit.

'Tonight was *so much fun!*' he heard one of the barely standing ones squeal; she had flowery script tattooed above her eyebrow.

'My boyfriend's gonna be *so mad!*' said another.

'Fuck him. Need to know, baby!'

'Yea, you're right. Fuck him. We're in *London!* Wooooooooo!'

Angel felt grateful Madison was not at all like that. He pulled out his phone to check for messages. Nothing. Battery at 8%.

He arrived at Tesco with his head low. The curtain of warm air blowing down at the entrance offered relief, however, and he lingered momentarily to hitch up his jeans. And he would have completed the operation had it not been for an arriving shopper who, taking exception to his stoppage, rear-ended him with an iron shoulder, sending Angel tumbling like a spinning top.

'Watch where you're going,' the shopper said, looking back as he passed. Adding, mostly to himself, 'Fucking plonker!'

As Angel recovered his balance, he saw at once the man's work boots, tattooed arms, and high-visibility jacket, and thought it best not to reply. He was, Angel told himself, blocking the entrance, after all.

Angel had not been there since June, and in the intervening time the branch managers had decided to upend the layout. Where he expected to find the Pot Noodles, he found tinned sausages, meatballs, and chili con carne. Had he been in funds, or with cooking facilities, he would have firstly, gone to Waitrose, and secondly, been tempted by the sun-dried tomato pesto, the antipasti, and the penne rigate, but poverty and romantic goals had made him a bad customer.

When he found the Pot Noodles, he selected the chicken and mushroom flavour. It was fortunate that a price reduction had the pots going for £1, because the low-denomination coins in his pocket amounted to just a penny over.

At the self-checkout till, he found himself directly across from the charity book table, where he spotted, amidst a sea of Jackie Collins, Danielle Steel, Catherine Cookson, and 1970s microwave cookbooks, a set of three fat Penguin paperbacks. He immediately left the Pot Noodle, which he had already scanned, and went to examine the volumes. His heart jumped: Marcel Proust's *Remembrance of Things Past*! Now he was in a conundrum. Eat . . . or get the books. He'd been wanting to read that novel for years, but other priorities had got in the way and since June he'd not been able to afford books at all. Yet here he had a 1980s edition, with beautiful covers, up for grabs—Western civilisation given away *literally for pennies*. The sign on the table said the minimum donation was £1 per book, but Angel reasoned that the three volumes constituted a single work, and therefore the minimum donation would suffice. He threw a glance at the lone Pot Noodle and back at the volumes, one in his left hand, public access to the remainder possessively restricted by his right. What to do? In the end, the self-checkout till made the decision for him by asking, 'Do you wish to continue?' He dug up his coins, put the equivalent of £1 into the charity tin, and walked away in a hurry, not bothering to cancel his purchase.

His stomach protested, but it protested in vain. He waved it off with a smile.

He would eat another day.

Chapter VIII

First things first. His find merited a proud Instagram post. Back in his room at the dorm, Angel lovingly lined up the three Proust volumes on his bed. As he pointed his phone camera at the prize—battery at 3%—he noticed the blue blanket spoiled his aesthetic. The blue carpet was no better. Egyptian blue. The worst blue imaginable. He looked around for a usable surface, but the bland Formica furniture, half-heartedly imitating pine, offered nothing suitable. He poked his head out into the hallway, but it was all blue carpet and scuffed white walls. Terrible. He considered going to the library, but he could not be bothered to go out again for another long walk, or have the librarian smirk at him, knowing she had him captive. Still, he grabbed his Proust and went out searching. All he needed was a small patch of background, and this could be anywhere.

As it turned out, the anywhere he was hoping for was nowhere near. He was forced to venture even past the university gym—through whose glass windows he caught sight of Johannes training deadlifts, more plates than he could count—and as far out as the Junior Common Room of the School of Social and Political Science, in the outer fringes of the campus, to find something he could use. There, seated at a table, playing dominos with a random student, was Saïd's roommate. They knew each other by sight, but they had never spoken; he only knew his name was *Camaro*, of all things, because Saïd had referred to him in conversation, usually joking about Camaro's laziness or, what was even more remarkable, Camaro's wardrobe.

Angel hesitated to interrupt, intimidated by Camaro's obstreperous opponent, a French-speaker, possibly from Haïti. But he could not take his eyes off Camaro's jacket, which boasted a profuse gold rococo pattern. That would work well, with the right set of filters. Angel walked up to the players. All the noise was coming from Haïti; the coffee-coloured Camaro played in silence, staring back at his opponent with beady eyes and cheeks raised in smiling insolence.

'C-Camaro?' Angel said.

Camaro looked up at him, recognition on his face.

'Um . . . c-could I . . . er . . . take a photo of your jacket?'

Camaro exchanged an amused look with his opponent and, shrugging his shoulders, stood up and straightened himself with evident satisfaction, ready to be photographed.

Angel scratched his temple. 'Um . . . can you take it off?'

Another exchange of looks with Haïti, who observed the unfolding scene with a broad, white smile.

'Don't let him stain it!' said Haïti.

Camaro gestured for Angel to take a step back, then carefully removed the garment, buttoned the front, and held it in front of him by the shoulders, ready to be photographed.

'Um . . . could you . . . er . . . could you lay it down on that armchair?' Angel said.

Camaro looked at the armchair and shook his head. No.

'No?' said Angel, perplexed.

Camaro then pointed at a nearby sofa.

'Ah, okay,' said Angel.

The two of them went to the sofa. Haïti came along.

'Careful, Camaro. It could have crumbs!' shouted Haïti, exploding with laughter.

Camaro acknowledged the warning with a glance and inspected the sofa thoroughly for anything that could stain or pollute the precious jacket. He wiped the cleanest part of the cushions as completely as he could, picking off any crumbs, lint, or particles of dust. Haïti got involved by gleefully pointing out the pollutants Camaro had missed:

'Look, look, look, Camaro, look! There's a crumb there!' Roars of laughter. 'And there! Look! There's lint there! Quick, pick it off!'

Not until Camaro was fully satisfied did he deign to lay down the jacket, as reverently and as straight as possible. He stepped aside and gestured with his hand, to indicate the garment was ready to be photographed.

Angel scratched his temple again, then pointed at the three volumes he'd been holding under his other arm.

'Um . . . d-d-do you mind if I put these on your jacket? I'd like to use it as a background,' Angel said.

Camaro gestured to hand over the books. Angel did as told. Camaro checked the volumes quickly, not reading the blurbs but instead inspecting all sides; he shrugged and placed the books on his jacket side by side, with the same care as Angel would have done, but for a different reason. He stepped aside.

Permission thus given, Angel got to work. He changed the order of the volumes (Camaro had placed them out of sequence), adjusted their individual alignment, and experimented with different placements. Once happy with the composition, Angel pointed his phone at the still life. Sadly, the photograph was never taken, for the moment he touched the button his phone shut down. Battery status at 0%.

Chapter IX

He was awakened by the clatter of a key hitting the door lock but persistently missing the hole. The room being pitch black, Angel guessed it was the wee hours. He rolled over to face the wall, pulled the blanket above his ear, and pretended to sleep. After about two minutes, his roommate succeeded in gaining entrance. Angel heard him stumble in and throw the door closed behind him with a bang. The oaf tripped on a chair and crashed onto the floor, bringing down with him textbooks, pens, and notebooks. He appeared to lie on his back for a while, until he pushed out a prodigious burp. The reek of lager intruded on Angel's nostrils.

After another minute, interrupted only by weak moaning, the roommate managed to stagger back up and remain on his feet long enough to topple onto the other bed. Angel heard him fumble into what he guessed was a sitting position, because a moment later followed the thud and tumble of shoes being dropped.

'Shhh!' the roommate said to himself.

More thuds, heavy breathing, the shush of fabric. Then the sound of plastic bottles and cans falling off a bedside table, the crackle of empty packets of crisps, the rustle of a plastic bag, the zip of a zipper, the rumble of flatulence being forced out into a mattress, hiccups, sighing, and more heavy breathing, until these finally died down, giving way to rumbustious snoring.

Angel waited until he could be sure, stretched his arm behind him to reach for his phone. He checked the alert banners on the screen.

Madison had messaged. Yes! A surge of adrenalin. He sat up. Battery at 100%.

The message said only, 'Hey', but that was enough. Angel saw she'd been online at 2:35. An hour ago.

Angel begun composing a reply. It seemed best to keep it brief. Maybe a line. Maximum two. But how to phrase it exactly, what words to use, how to sound, what tone to adopt, was difficult to figure out. Madison hadn't given him much to work with. Consequently, he found himself phrasing and rephrasing his message, editing and re-editing, adding and pruning back, re-adding and re-pruning, until the syntax was so awkward and unnatural, that he had to start all over again.

Before he knew it, it was 5 o'clock and he was nowhere near decided on what to say. Even the shortest messages felt wrong. 'Greetings' seemed trite. 'Hey back' childish. 'You there?' needy. 'S'up' stupid. 'Chat?' desperate. 'Howdy' American. 'Good evening' prissy. 'Yo' lowbrow. Eventually, he got the idea of sending her a coded message with just emojis, but, although clever, it still required him to know what he wanted to say, so after another forty minutes composing ever more fanciful combinations, he was back to square one.

By six o'clock he realised it would be getting late where Madison lived. With time running out to catch her awake, he finally settled on 'Art thou available to converse?'

He pressed Send—although gathering the courage to do even that took a further five minutes—and waited for the single grey tick to become a double grey tick, already doubting his choice.

He waited for those ticks to turn blue.

And waited.

And waited.

And waited.

But Madison never came back online.

Chapter X

Angel woke up with a jerk. The canteen! He checked his phone. Seven thirty.

'For God's sake!' he whispered, jumping out of bed and scrambling for his clothes. Legs into jeans, torso into jumper, feet into shoes, and he was off—although not before also grabbing his phone.

Like a kayak down a waterfall, Angel shot down the stairs, into reception, into the freezing morning air, and ran to the canteen, jumping over, squeezing in between, and moulding himself around all obstacles. He had to keep the waistband of his jeans in his fist to prevent them from falling down.

It took him eight minutes to reach the canteen, and another thirty-five seconds to get past the queue and into the kitchen. He was surprised at how many people got up early enough to have breakfast. Crazy!

The supervisor confronted him the second he walked in.

'What happened, Angel?'

Angel had an excuse ready. 'Er . . . there was a medical emergency with my family—I was up all night on the phone with them.'

'We agreed you'd be here at six o'clock, *on the dot.*'

'I know, I know. I'm really sorry. It won't happen again. I promise!'

'If we say six, it means you're here at six.'

'I know. I'm really really sorr—'

'We can't be running a kitchen with staff that shows up, what, an hour and forty-five minutes late?'

'No, of course not. I really did the best I could.'

'Then you'll have to do better.'

'I know. I'm sorry.'

'This is your first verbal warning.'

'Yes. Of course. I underst—'

'It's *imperative* that you be here on time.'

'Yes. And I will fr—'

'This is the real world, Angel. Actions have consequences.'

'Yes, absolutely!'

'So tomorrow, I want you here at six o'clock in the morning. No reasons or excuses. The kitchen can't stop no matter what's happening in your life. Six o'clock: you're here.'

'I understand.'

'And you're here *on the dot. Every day.*'

'I understand.'

'Otherwise, you're out.'

'Of course. Thank you.'

'Now quickly get your uniform on and run to the washing-up room. The guys are *raging.*'

'Where's the uniform?'

'There, hanging from that hook on the wall.'

'Okay. Thank you.'

Angel moved quickly. He was in the washing-up room in less than twenty seconds.

'Fucking 'ell, mate!' shouted Skinhead above the din the instant he saw him. Unibrow looked Angel up and down and shook his head.

'W-What do I wash?' Angel said.

Skinhead and Unibrow ignored or didn't hear him; they were too frantic trying to keep up with the unrelenting stream of dirty crockery, cutlery, and trays.

'Uh . . . sorry . . . w-what do I wash?' Angel said, a bit louder, but the steaming hiss of running hot water, the clatter of crockery and utensils thrown about, the background murmur of vociferated student conversation in the dining hall, and even the smell of washing up fluid and eggs and bacon still overwhelmed his voice. Angel looked around for something to do, confused as to what cog he was to play in that machine. After twenty seconds, Skinhead glared at him, blue eyes like lasers, and shouted:

'What are you waiting for, mate? *Do* something!'

'It's just that . . .'

'JUST DO SOMETHING! DON'T JUST STAND THERE LIKE A FUCKING IDIOT!'

This jolted Angel out of his paralysis. He went to the niche and pulled in a tray piled up with dirty crockery, cutlery, cups, and napkins that had just been slid in. He located the different bins—paper, general, containers, composting—and got to work.

'*Fuck's* sake!' shouted Skinhead, scrubbing with red-headed, vein-bursting vigour. '*Fucking* useless!'

Chapter XI

‘. . . Now, Chinua Achebe was born in 1930 in the Igbo village of Ogidi . . .’

‘. . . the poet Christopher Okigbo also went there . . .’

‘. . . early gothic, which lasted from the late 12th to the late 13th century; decorated gothic, which . . .’

‘. . . In the *Futurist Manifesto*, which was published in 1909, Marinetti . . .’

‘. . . some of the subsequent events could not have been even imagined at the time . . .’

‘. . . collage and pastiche, irony and play, scepticism towards metanarratives . . .’

‘. . . one of my colleagues at this university, who would have you believe we’re filling your minds with rubbish . . .’

‘. . . in the Allegory of the Cave, he contrasts this

against the intelligible realm . . .'

Silence.

Long silence.

Angel jerked himself awake.

The professor was gone.

The classroom was empty.

He checked his phone (no banner alerts); 1:17 in the afternoon.

'Oh, my God!'

He'd slept right through his 9 o'clock Postcolonial Literature lesson, and then right through whatever followed in that same classroom.

Which meant, he'd missed his 12 o'clock.

'Damn it!'

Why did they have to put his classes *in the morning?*

Angel snatched his notebook and pen and flounced out in a huff.

Chapter XII

Amelia sighted him on the staircase.

'Hello!' she said, stopping with a radiant smile. She was with her friend, the bespectacled Vera.

'Hello,' Angel mumbled, not stopping.

'Have you decided on the film?'

Amelia had yanked his handbrake, mid stride. 'Er . . . the film?'

'Yes. The film we're going to see on Saturday.'

'Um . . . a-are we going to see a film on Saturday?'

Next to Amelia, Vera arched a critical eyebrow at him, a gesture made more dramatic by her tight bun, thick black-rimmed glasses, and noir make-up on permafrost skin.

'Yes. You were going to decide which one you're taking me to. Have you decided?' Amelia leaned on the wall, getting comfortable. Vera sighed.

Angel scratched his temple. 'Erm . . .'

'It will be fun,' she enticed, playing with a strand of hair.

Angel's brain short-circuited; he could not remember any of the films she'd listed yesterday evening.

'Don't worry, Angel. As I said, I'll pay,' she added, her eyes extra friendly. Vera tsked and gave an eye-roll.

'I-I . . . er . . . I haven't had chance to . . . um . . . think about it yet. You know, classes all morning.'

'I tell you what. I'll book it, but you lead.'

'Lead?'

'Of course, we're friends, but you're still the man.'

'Of course, yes. Er . . . I'm happy with whatever film. I'll take you.'

'Excellent.'

'I've got to g—'

'Where are you headed?'

'Um . . . I'm just going to lunch.'

'I'll join you.'

'No, it's alright. I-I'm just going to grab a Mars bar.'

'I'll come with you.' Amelia peeled herself off the wall and made ready to walk with him. Vera, giving another, exasperated sigh, resumed her ascent up the stairs, disdaining a farewell.

'Um . . . I'm in a real rush, actually, my mother is going to call me in twenty minutes.'

'Oh, okay. Never mind, then.'

'I-I've got to go . . .'

'Have a good rest of the day.'

'Yes . . . er . . . thank you. You too.'

Angel descended a couple of steps.

'Angel,' Amelia called out behind him.

He stopped again, 'Yes?'

'Will I see you at dinner?'

'Er . . . yes, I-I'll be there.'

'What time?'

'Ouff . . . er . . . seven?'

'I'll see you at seven, then.'

'Okay. See you.' Angel got going again.

'And Angel?'

Angel stopped for a third time. 'Yes?'

'I'll book us in. Let you know tonight.'

'Okay. Thank you . . . er . . . I-I-I've really got to . . .'

'See you tonight, Angel' said Amelia, sweetening her smile even more.

'Um . . . o-okay . . . See you tonight.'

Chapter XIII

It appeared the most repulsive students had thronged outside the canteen. They held, Angel saw, flags depicting an hourglass inside a circle, as well as placards and banners screaming slogans. Many bodies undulated to the tune of drums and whistles. One shouted apocalyptic imprecations into a megaphone.

Angel didn't care about any of that. That lot were always screaming and outraged and offended. Worse, they had a bad aesthetic, which alone was sufficient justification for turning his nose up at them. On this occasion, however, it seemed that, if he was to have his lunch, he'd have to go through their protest, whatever it was about this time.

Though he avoided eye contact and hid behind his floppy hair, he was confronted the moment he reached the edge of the mob. A clean-shaven youth with pink hair screamed in his face; Angel winced at his bad breath. Another, with blond dreadlocks and piercings, shoved a hand-written sign in his face; Angel cringed and changed direction. A chubby frizzy-haired girl with a 'NO MEANS NO' t-shirt shoved him back with gleeful aggression; Angel bounced against another protester, hair flying. In the commotion, the impact of the girl's hands still burning on his chest, Angel caught sight, between his flapping strands of hair, of a grey head and a chanting couple who, though chaotically dressed in every colour of the rainbow, were too old to be students. But he had no time to ask himself where they'd come from, because he felt a yank from behind that catapulted him onto his backside. The protestors nearest to him laughed and cheered, then carried on dancing. The presumed yanker, a ragamuffin with long greasy hair and a scruffy beard, rejoined the rabble, before similarly assaulting another incomer.

Angel got back up, aching from the impact of sharp bone on meagre gluteal flesh, and, impelled by hunger, having only been given cold left-over toast after his early morning shift, looked left and right, seeking a way to circumnavigate the protest and sneak inside the canteen. But, when he attempted this, he found the entrance blocked by a line of protesters holding a banner that said something about an emergency. The glass walls had been defaced with painted slogans and the word 'MURDERERS'. Beyond, the catering staff stood behind the counter, observing and otherwise idle. The burger patties they'd made—for once, no cheesy pasta and potatoes—lined the serving trays, untouched. Security staff and a couple of Metropolitan Police constables were inside, one with his mouth to the radio. The canteen was empty of students.

Angel retreated. He walked to the other side of the building, hoping he could gain access through the kitchen's back door, but he found that blocked too. There were fewer protesters, but they had formed a barricade with the commercial rubbish containers, which doubled as a stage for those given to undulating and haranguing through the megaphone. The male protesters were all slight in build, so the containers' plastic lids could easily support them.

The arrival of patrol cars disgorging more police constables, some in high visibility jackets, gave Angel some encouragement. But, instead of unsheathing their batons and getting to work on protesters' skulls, they simply took position at a calm distance and got to work as passive observers. Next to arrive was a Met Police van. Another source of encouragement. But, instead of throwing tear gas canisters or shooting rubber bullets, the constables threw unperturbed glances and shot the breeze.

Angel began sulking his way back to the dorm. But not three paces nearer, he was faced with a gaggle of incoming students. Judging by their smiles, wild hair colours, and the holes in their clothing, they'd come to join the protest. A girl with glasses and a bright yellow bobble hat approached him and said, 'Not joining us?'

Angel hesitated, then, waving her off, replied 'No . . . er . . . I-I just came for lunch.'

'Since you're here, why don't you join us,' she said, still smiling.

'I-I-I'm not into protests, I just . . .'

'You don't think the planet is important?'

'Y-Yes, yes, of course it's important.'

'Then why don't you join us?'

'W-What's this about?'

'The planet.'

'Yes, but . . . um . . . why the canteen?'

'They're serving beef.'

'Beef? W-What's that got to with the planet?'

'Beef contributes to climate change.'

'Does it?'

The girl's smile faded. 'Yes. Have you not been reading the news?'

'Um . . . n-n-not really, I've had . . .'

'Cows fart and build up greenhouse gases.'

'Do they?'

'Yes, so if you eat beef, farmers grow more cows, and their farts fuck up the atmosphere.'

Angel said, incredulous. 'I-I thought it was cars that did that.'

'Yes, it's cars, it's factories, it's coal, it's the consumer society, it's everything, but they are also burning down the Amazon forest, right now, to make room for cows so that people like *you* can eat burgers.'

'They're burning down the Amazon?'

'It's being talked about all over. Javier Bosolrano or whatever his name is. Have you not been paying attention?'

'Er . . .'

'You don't care?'

'Er . . . yes . . . of c—'

The girl's temperature seemed to be rising. 'This is the number one issue of our time! Can't you see? There's a planetary emergency!'

'Er . . . is there?'

'Oh, for fuck's sake! Have you been living under a rock?'

'No, no . . . I-I just didn't know there was an emergency. W-What's the emergency?'

'The PLANET! The EARTH! The temperatures are *rising*. The sea levels are *rising*. We're all going to *die* in twelve years if we don't do something about the climate!'

'In twelve years!' Angel put his hand on his forehead. He would not enjoy Madison past his early thirties!

Another of the incomers, a lad with a chinstrap beard and green dreadlocks, joined them.

'What's this?' Chinstrap said.

'He's a beef-eater,' the girl replied.

'Are you eating fucking beef?' Chinstrap demanded.

Angel took a step back and held up his palms. 'N-N-No, I just came for lunch.'

'You came for the fucking burgers, didn't you? You fucking murderer!' Chinstrap's eyes bore into him like two Milwaukee drills.

'No no no no no! I don't even know what's on the menu! I just came for lunch. I promise!'

'We have a denier beef-eater!' screamed the girl, addressing the throng of protesters, raising her arm to point at Angel's head.

Dozens of angry faces turned in Angel's direction. A couple of protesters, including the one with the megaphone, jumped off the containers and began swaggering towards him; they were immediately joined by others who detached themselves from the throng. These were, in turn, reinforced by yet more.

Angel turned to the girl, pleading with his palms. 'Please . . . no! I just came for lunch! I don't know what's on the menu! I just came for lunch!'

The megaphone wielder, an oily-haired hoodlum with black-rimmed glasses and a wispy beard, came right up to him, aimed the megaphone directly at his face, and began shouting. 'How dare you! Stop denying! The earth is dying! Tell the truth! Declare a climate emergency! We don't want to go extinct! System change, not climate change! Stop being a fossil fool! Stop mass extinction! Stop habitat loss! Time's up! Wake up! Open your eyes! Act now!'

A circle formed around Angel, which closed in as protesters massed to make him the centre of attention. Yellow Bobble Hat, having lost all composure, was now screeching like a banshee, at first hurling accusations, and then just insults and epithets, pressing a double fist with raised middle fingers against his cheekbone. 'Fuuuuuuuuuucccccckkkkk yoooooouuuuuuuuuuu!!!!!!!' she shrieked, over and over. In his utter discombobulation, Angel's eyes shot in every direction, his heart beating like cylinders in a dragster's engine. He searched for and caught sight of the constables, but these restricted themselves to passive observation.

Angel's panicked attempt to push his way through the crowd was met with rude hands shoving him back into the centre of the circle. The latter closed in even further, the screaming and leering protesters' faces centimetres from his own. Yellow Bobble Hat spat at him. Thrown fluids began splashing on his head and jumper. He could no longer make out what anyone said; the clamour of drums, whistles, shouts, screams, and megaphonic vituperation had reached saturation point. Though his fluttering curtain of hair barely allowed him a clear view, with pleading eyes he tried again to make eye contact with the nearest constables. Angel even raised his arm, more obviously to signal his urgent need for rescue. And the constables saw him alright, but remained high-visibility statues.

Chapter XIII

A sea-change amidst the turmoil. Faces suddenly switched direction and, like expanding gas, the crowd extended as its density decreased. Angel turned to seek the cause. From behind rows of dreadlocks, beanie hats, blue hair, hoodies, and woolly hats, he glimpsed a bald head approaching like a shark's fin above the ocean's surface. Some of the heads immediately adjacent to the bald one appeared to fly away from it or abruptly sink. The protesters retreated, their fury suddenly ceding ground to doubt and fright. Seconds later they had cleared sufficiently for Angel to see the angry, bearded, Swedish face fronting the ever-approaching bald head.

It was Johannes.

The strongman marched towards him, swatting, and effortlessly hurling or knocking down—for he was three times their size—the few protesters remaining in his way who were not already running scared. The rabble all retreated to their barricade, leaving Angel standing alone.

The tattooed Swede walked straight up to him and stood bearing down with a terrifying visage while he recovered his breath. Angel stared wide-eyed, having forgotten the existence of his body.

A moment later, and gesturing with his chin, Johannes said, 'Y'alright, buddy?'

Chapter XIV

That evening, the canteen was still blockaded by protesters. With a lone penny to his name and Saïd and Camaro across the hall having just taken delivery of pizzas, Angel thought it opportune—or, more accurately, urgent—to call his mother for funds, but he could not bring himself to dial the number. So instead, he checked Madison' social media.

And, at long last, the weeks of excruciating patience had been rewarded!

There was a new Instagram post.

But, alas, it was rather surprising.

Madison—clad in jeans and a jumper, her honey blonde hair cascading down her front, her soft, classical features embellished with a prim, timid smile. The Madison he knew and loved. But—in her hand: an object; a type of object that was anomalous; that contradicted their shared values; that sullied and besmirched the damsel's purity.

Angel put his hand to his forehead, rubbed the skin, and stared at the image for a long time.

Confusion. Apprehension. Perplexity.

He zoomed in to take a closer look. The object was indeed what it looked to be. Rude and incongruous in her delicate hands—hands with slender and well-groomed digits—no fake nails or fancy polish with elaborate designs; just elegant, simple, clear polish.

How did that object get there?

What were the circumstances that led to its appearance?

Where had it come from?

Where had she obtained it?

Why had Madison accepted it if it had been given for her to hold?

Searching for answers, Angel noticed and examined for the first time the two girls standing next to Madison. Typical American college girls, with jeans and jumpers. None as pretty as Madison, of course. One laughing and the other pulling a silly face. Most unbecoming, that. Worse, each of them was holding an object like the one in Madison's hand. Clearly, a bad influence, those two. Bad company. Women of a rougher sort. Of coarser provenance. Not ladies of delicacy and refinement, like Madison.

Or perhaps Madison had found herself there against her will—but then why would she post it on her Instagram? The Madison he knew would have been ashamed. Maybe she was holding the object for someone else, or to be polite, then forgot herself, and the photo was taken before she remembered to dispose of the object or return it to its rightful owner—whose presence there, in any case, augured ill. But, if so, why hadn't she asked for another photo to be taken, following corrective action? And who, which was an equally important question, took the photo? And why had she allowed another person to take it? Because the image lacked Madison's careful artistry. Maddeningly, but as so frequently was the case, there was no caption below the image. No clarifying emojis. No indicative hashtags.

Angel wanted to comment. To send her a private message. To WhatsApp her. To find out more. But it seemed a bad idea. He would sound insecure, or controlling, which was the same. Therefore, it was best simply to wait for her to reply to his message from the previous evening, which she had since seen.

Restlessness impelled him to leave his room and find distraction in company. As he grabbed his jacket, he cast another, disapproving glance at his roommate's mess. Josh or Todd or Brad or whatever his name was had not even bothered to pick up the empty cans, plastic bottles, notebooks, pens, and dirty sandwich box he'd knocked down the night before. Smelly socks, plastic bags, and a couple of t-shirts also lay on the floor. How could anybody live like this? Absolutely no standards!

CHAPTER XV

Angel spotted Vera sitting at a table at the Departure Lounge, one of the university's various cafés. She was reading a book—back like a rod, chin high, head slightly tilted. Though he knew he was not her favourite person, he was desperate. He approached her table without receiving an acknowledgment, even after hovering for long seconds. During this interval, he observed she had disdained the café's student-proof mug in favour of her own fine china cup and saucer. They appeared to be antiques.

'Can I join you?' he said, finally.

Vera looked up and glared at him with affronted disbelief. 'How *dare* you?' she said, in Queen's English.

The lenses of her glasses were so polished they might as well not have been there at all.

'Sorry? . . . I-I didn't mean to . . .'

'I *beg* your pardon? *Can* you *not* see that I'm *reading*?'

'Er . . . yes, I'm sorry . . . er . . . I just . . .'

'*What* makes you think you have *licence* to talk to someone when that person is *reading*?'

'Er . . . I didn't . . .'

'*Of course* you did. Otherwise, you wouldn't be standing there, *would* you?'

'Well . . . er . . . I didn't think because . . . er . . .'

'*Exactly*, you *didn't* think.' Vera arched an eyebrow.

'I-It's just that normally people don't . . .'

'But I am not "people", am I? I am a *person*.'

'Yes, of course you are . . .'

'So don't apply "people" standards if you choose to appear before me. If you must address me, find a *suitable* moment.'

'Of course. I will! It won't happen ag—'

'And that means, *specifically*, a moment when I'm *not* reading.'

'Absolutely. Never again.'

'Very good.'

Silence.

'Now, if I *may* . . .' added Vera, holding up her book, an old hardback copy of *The Castle of Wolfenbach* by Eliza Parsons.

Angel made to leave, but just as he turned to do so, Vera said.

'Oh, and . . . Angel.'

'Yes?'

Vera regarded him again with that same disapproving arched eyebrow. 'Amelia deserves a greater degree of respect from you.'

'Oh?'

'*Your* behaviour around her leaves *much* to be desired.'

'Oh . . . really?'

'Yes. Really. You should brush up on your etiquette.'

'M-My etiquette . . . ?'

'Yes. Your *etiquette*. Are you *deaf*?'

'No, no, I hear you, it's just that . . .'

'And you should also educate yourself in the ways of women, so that you know when a *lady* is trying to *tell* you something.'

Silence again, Angel at a loss as to where this was coming from and where it was going.

Vera continued, 'If you wish to be a *gentleman*, you *ought* to know the basics.'

'I'm sorry, I don't kn . . .'

Slowly and in an emphatic half-whisper, Vera said, 'Open your eyes,' opening oversized eyeballs for effect.

Angel stood, mouth agape.

Vera snapped. 'That *sweet* girl . . . !'

But she stopped when she noticed that Angel twitched as if suddenly on high alert.

'I'm very sorry, but I've got to go . . . very sorry . . .' he said, as he ran away.

He imagined Vera staring, aghast.

With eyes on the back of his skull, he saw the a gaggle of American girls, one of them extraordinarily obese and with green hair, walking towards the café.

'The *cheek*,' he imagined Vera muttering, still watching him recede, tiny in the distance, before getting back to her book.

Chapter XVI

To the gremlins' delight, given Angel's continued famishment, the following morning's lesson was for Food and Literature in Early Modern England.

The lecture theatre was the grandest in the Jenni Murray Hall. A wood-panelled half-funnel with a blackboard and wooden desks, it also had the most antique furnishings, all other classrooms having gone the way of Formica and PVC. Professor Mastropasqua was yet to arrive, and collective apprehension at the impending event electrified the air. Everything Angel had heard about this faculty member, be it from the other academic staff or fellow students, had not been just negative—it had been vituperative. All other professors peppered their lectures with scornful or aggressive remarks about their colleague, and the students complained about his modules being impossible to pass—crushing workloads, intricate reading, ruthless marking, persecutory class participation, and terrifying final exams, which almost everyone failed. Of those who signed up, half never finished. Of those who finished, less than a tenth came back for more. And *that* had been precisely the reason for Angel signing up. Because, were he to obtain an A from Mastropasqua, that A would truly mean something; a 55% from Mastropasqua was said to be the equivalent of 95% from anyone else, so a perfect score would confirm his superior intellect. Madison would no longer doubt it; she would proclaim it and call him 'My Lord'.

Hunger or no, Angel looked forward to the challenge.

The door opened and a tall, elegant, fierce-looking man with dark flamelike eyebrows silenced the murmuring students upon entry. He wore a black frock in the late Victorian style, but his capillary arrangements reminded Angel of the Cavaliers. He stared at the students as he made his way to his desk and put his leather briefcase on the tabletop. He stood in the centre of the dais, saying nothing for long seconds, scanning the students' faces from left to right. As he scanned, the students' necks wilted like flowers.

He filled the hall with a manly and sonorous voice. 'Good morning. My name is Orlando Mastropasqua. I'm your professor for this course. If you are not here for Food and Literature in Early Modern England, please leave.'

Silence. Paralysis.

'Too bad.'

Mastropasqua opened his briefcase and extracted a stack of photocopied paper, held together by a black ribbon. He threw it at a student in the front row, a bespectacled boy with a Harry Potter face that screamed to be punched, on whose desk it landed with a crash. The shockwave blew Harry Potter's hair into further disarray.

'You know what to do,' the professor said, dismissively.

Harry Potter blinked, startled for a moment, then untied the ribbon, saved a set of stapled sheets for himself, and passed the rest along.

When the photocopies reached Angel, he did likewise. The stapled sheets contained an outline of the course. The difference between this outline and other courses'? This was three times as long; the breadth and depth of the material they were expected to cover was immense; and it was also much better organised, each sentence in the most tightly compressed language imaginable. The outline shouted defiance, confrontation, exclusion. This was as expected. However, not all of it was, for at the end of the outline Mastropasqua had written:

> If you find the material easy and enjoy hard work, you are encouraged to leave the university immediately.

'Does everyone have a copy?' said the professor.

The students held up their copies and nodded in the affirmative.

'Very well. We won't bother going over the course outline because you should have received, and read, the email copy I sent you last week. Now that you also have a physical copy, you can't say you weren't warned. Does anybody want to drop the course?'

Silence.

'Are you sure?' More than a question, a threat.

Silence.

Mastropasqua shook his head. 'Fools. All of you.'

Silence.

'Or maybe not. We'll see.'

Mastropasqua returned to his desk and retrieved from his briefcase an ancient, leather-bound volume.

'I asked you to have read Ben Jonson's *The Shepheardes Calender*. Let's see how badly you've done it.'

Angel swallowed. He hadn't read it, having been too preoccupied with the vile object in Madison's hand.

'You,' the professor said, pointing at a doughy boy with a French crop. 'Thoughts on the poem.'

'Uuuuuuuuuuuuh . . . well, yea, uuuuuuuuuuuuuh, like, uuuuuuuuuuh, you know, uuuuuuuuuuh, so the author, like, uuuuuuuuuh, talks about the calendar, and, like, uuuuuuuuuuh, you know, the months, and, like, uuuuuuuuuuh . . .'

'Okay, okay.' The professor waved him to be silent. He pointed at the next student on the right, a scruff with a stubbly double chin. 'You. Thoughts.'

'Me?'

'Yes, you.'

'Oh . . . um . . . okay . . . well . . . um . . .'

The professor moved on. Re-scanning the classroom briefly, hand on one hip, he selected yet another student—a girl in the front row, with oversized glasses and a mass of curly black hair exploding out of a white woolly hat.

She jumped right in, gesticulating with her hands. 'Yea, uh, so, the poem is about, you know, the calendar, and, like, you know, the different months of the year, and, you know, like, farming, and like, you know . . .'

'No, I don't know,' cut in the professor, causing a wave of laughter. 'Please tell me.'

The girl smiled and carried on, a bit louder this time. 'So, yea, so, uh, like, the poem is by, you know, Ben Jonson . . .'

'Yes, we *know* that,' said the professor. 'What are your *thoughts*?'

'Well, my thoughts are, like, you know, uh, so, like, you know, uh . . .'

'*Say* something!'

More laughter from the other students.

This time the girl took it badly and, with a frown, said, 'I don't have any, like, thoughts.'

'You don't have any thoughts.'

'Like, no. I don't.'

The professor moved on and once again scanned the classroom in his quest for articulacy. Coiled from stomach cramps, Angel observed the offended girl make a note on her phone and start videoing Mastropasqua with vengeful determination.

'You,' the professor said.

All faces turned to Angel.

Snapping out of distraction, Angel found the 'you' had been hurled with a finger pointed at his face.

'What's your name?'

'A-A-Angel.'

'Okay, Angelino. Thoughts.'

Angel had only one: that the others had sounded like idiots. So he opted for honesty.

'I'm sorry . . . er . . . but I haven't read it.'

'Angel has not read the poem,' Mastropasqua announced to the classroom, enunciating slowly. 'Has anybody read it?'

Silence.

'Anybody?'

Silence. Averted eyes.

'So, *not a single one of you* has read the poem.'

More silence. Absorption into notebooks.

'Do I just fail you and get it over with?'

No effect.

'Because I've got better things to do than throw pearls at swine.'

Still no effect.

'Aha! You back there,' said Mastropasqua, pointing at someone in the last row. 'What's your name?'

'My name is Vera.'

Angel turned to the voice behind him. Indeed, Vera was in his class. She stared back at Mastropasqua, chin high, eyebrows raised, a look of snooty satisfaction.

Mastropasqua: 'You've read the poem.'

Vera: 'Of course I have.'

'In its entirety?'

'I *beg* your pardon?' Vera said, suddenly indignant. 'When I read, I read thoroughly.'

'Oh, so you must know it well, then! Perhaps you can save me the trouble. Please come to the front and enlighten us.'

'Certainly.'

Vera walked to the front and faced the students, her black velour dress without a wrinkle, her hair lined up with mathematical precision, her flat shoes shined to a mirror polish.

She clasped her hands together and began, in the tone of a primary school teacher. 'It's evident from the start that in this work, which was the first one he published, Jonson owes a great deal to Chaucer. Indeed, you would have seen, if you had read the text, that Spenser mentions him in his address to Gabriel Harvey, who was his friend, along with Sir Philip Sidney, to whom he dedicated the poem. This accounts for the Mediaevalising archaisms used throughout . . .'

Mastropasqua sat on the edge of the tabletop, arms crossed, and listened with a subtle air of amusement.

Angel, in turn, could not but marvel at Vera's eloquence. Her intellectual clarity. Her impeccable enunciation. Her superhuman recall of the material. They inspired him to cultivate that level of skill, to have Madison marvel at him in the same way. Remembering his paramour, however, only worsened the stomach cramps. That accursed Instagram post had infected his psyche. The uncouthness! The degradation! The defilement! Had Piot, in his *Woman with Blossoms*, painted, instead of blossoms, a toilet seat, the effect would still have been nobler, more sublime. And the injury was seemingly self-inflicted, with no apparent self-awareness or explanation. Worse, the post was still up this morning, refuting the possibility of error and affirming Madison's contentment with dangling the image out there for the world to see. His chest tightened at the implication. Angel filled his cheeks with air and exhaled slowly. He hid his face under his hair.

'Any questions?' Vera had concluded her presentation.

Silence.

'Angel?' Angel found Vera looking at him, with a wide-eyed squint.

'I-I-I don't have any questions,' he said.

'Of course you don't,' she said.

Vera cast a glance at the professor, eyes half-lidded with eyebrows raised, seemingly awaiting his applause.

Mastropasqua stood straight. 'Bravo!' He clapped.

Vera acknowledged with arched eyebrows and a slight tilt of her chin.

Mastropasqua pointed at Vera. 'Now *this* is what you should aspire to.'

As the clever student made her way back to her lecture chair, Mastropasqua addressed her. 'Since I see you are far above your fellow students, it seems proper that I give you assignments far above what's prescribed by the syllabus. So, by the next seminar I'll expect you to have read all the supplementary texts and all the optional texts, plus some additional ones that I now deem important. You will receive the list in your student email this afternoon.'

'Of course.'

'But if I were you, Vera, I'd drop out of the university and become an independent scholar. You're wasting your brain here.'

Vera glanced at him, askance.

Mass of Hair recorded it all faithfully on her iPhone.

CHAPTER XVII

By the time Angel entered the library his archenemy was back on duty. Spying behind his curtain of hair, Angel noticed her eyes, just visible above the parapet of the reception desk—indicating she was standing. The eyes bored into him from behind thick-lensed spectacles. He walked past without acknowledging.

'Twelve days,' he heard her say behind him.

He stopped and turned to reply. 'Um . . . I'm sorry?'

'Twelve days remaining.'

'It's thirteen, no?'

'Twelve.'

'I-I'll pay. I'll pay.' Angel made to go.

But the librarian had other plans. 'I can take your debit card now, if you'd like.'

Angel scratched his temple. 'Um . . . sorry, I don't have it on me.'

'You do have your phone. I can give you the bank details. Or you can use Apple Pay.'

'No, it's okay, I'm expecting a call from my mother.'

'Then you shouldn't be in the library.'

'I-I-I'm just popping in quickly to get some books.'

'Then you'll be passing through here again and you'll have time to make a payment.'

'I'm sorry, um . . . I can't right now.' Angel's eyes darted around to see if anyone was within earshot.

'You can also pay by cash. Even a partial payment would reduce interest in the event of a default.'

'Um . . . I don't have anything on me.'

'No cash at all? Nothing in that backpack? You had plenty last term.'

'Er . . . sorry, nothing. J-Just a penny in my pocket.' Angel took it out.

'It will be cheaper if you pay now.'

'I'm-I'm really sorry, but I really can't right now.'

'Okay. How about later when you check out your books? Which you won't be able to do for much longer.'

'I'm-I'm . . . really sorry, b-b-but I really really can't tonight.' He made to go.

'How about tomorrow? Can you do it tomorrow?'

Angel stopped again. 'I-I . . . um . . . I-I won't be here. I'm going to see a film.'

'Ah, so you have money to pay for a film—and no doubt popcorn and nachos and a hotdog and a drink and chewing gum and all that—but no money to pay your library fines.'

'Um . . . I-I'm not paying for it.'

'Oh, so your date is paying for it? I see. Will she be paying your library fine too?'

Angel felt a hot, prickly blush making its way down his face. 'I-I'm sorry?'

'You need to take responsibility.'

'B-But I *am* taking responsibility. I promise! It's just that can't pay right this second.'

'I'll leave a note in the system saying that you will pay on Saturday.'

'On Saturday?' He frowned.

'Yes. I'll be here. Or do you not plan to study on Saturday?'

'Er . . .'

'Do you plan on avoiding the library?'

'No, no, er . . .' Angel started forward a bit, and showed a placatory palm.

'Because the library will not be avoiding you.'

'No, I-I will pay, I promise.'

'Very good. Twelve days.' The librarian turned to face her computer screen.

Angel stood there for a long moment, at a loss for words.

'You may go,' the librarian said without looking at him.

Angel shook his head and went.

For the 17th Century Lit class, he'd been assigned Aphra Behn's *Oroonoko*, plus related essays by Margaret Ferguson, Isobel Armstrong, Ruth Nestvold, Sarah Klein, and others. Inspired by Vera's presentation, he thought it best to get to work right away. Nothing less than an A with Distinction would do—especially since only 60% was needed for one of those. Because she'd been a student during the Spring term, Madison already knew about the stupidly low grading thresholds, and back then she'd told him that at her university, less than 60% was a fail. Imagine if she'd got wind of the fact that they'd lowered the thresholds even more this year! A plain A would not make him brilliant; it would make him a failure.

Angel selected a seat on the upper level and dug out of his bag his copy of *Oroonoko* and the photocopied required essays by feminist authors. He opened the book, and, hoping for extra credit, began with the introduction by Janet Todd.

As a famous woman author, the introduction began, *Aphra Behn was unique—*

Unique. Just like Madison. He picked up his phone and checked her Instagram. The offending photograph was still up; moreover, it had amassed eleven likes. Also, two comments had appeared, both emojis: one with heart eyes and the other the devil's horns. What did they mean? His stomach cramped, his chest tightened, his knees bounced. What *could* they mean? One suggested the commenter liked what she saw—reinforcing low instincts and bad taste. The other appeared to offer encouragement—the commenter must have thought the girls looked 'badass,' or their activity was 'badass.' He puffed out his cheeks with a slow, controlled exhalation as he scrunched his eyes shut, his whole body vibrating from rapidly bouncing knees. It was exasperating! Both the possible meanings and attitudes behind them. He opened his eyes and stared into the distance, playing out in his mind a sickening scenario based on the post—sickening because they involved Madison's degradation, or worse, self-degradation, and his own impotence to stop it.

'Will you stop *staring* at my *tits!*' A voice hissed, amidst heavy breathing.

Shaken out of his stupor, Angel found, standing right by him, tiny fists on enormous hips, the big American girl with the green hair. The one from the canteen.

'Sorry . . . er . . . w-what?' he said, dazed.

'Will you stop *staring* at my *tits*, you *creep!*'

Stunned, Angel's wide eyes could not help but wander for a millisecond to the aforementioned body part. His whole head, plus more, would have fit into one cup of the girl's brassier. He realised he had absent-mindedly been staring at her chest area from afar, subconsciously because of the vastitude, but mostly because they'd happened to have been in his line of sight.

'Oh my *God!* Will you *stop!*'

'S-S-Sorry! I didn't mean to . . . ! I-I-I wasn't staring. I swear! I-I-I was just thinking . . .'

'Please leave the library, you *pervert!* I don't feel safe here!'

'P-P-Pardon me?'

'Please LEAVE!'

Jolted by the rapid escalation and fearing the girl would scream and cause a scene, Angel quickly shoved his study materials back into his bag. Before leaving, however, he could not resist the impulse to explain.

'I-I-I swear to you,' he pleaded, showing placatory palms, 'I wasn't staring.'

'*LEAVE!!!*' she finally shrieked. '*JUST LEAVE!!!*'

All eyes turned towards Angel and the big American girl. Female foreheads registered frowns. Angel bowed his head, hid his face behind his hair, and scurried off.

Chapter XVIII

The library temporarily out of bounds, Angel retreated into the dorm. There, however, he found the door to his room open, blasting out foolish music, idiotic screams, raucous laugher, cigarette smoke, and alcohol fumes. His roommate, Todd or Josh or whatever his name was, had brought round some of his fellow American chums. Todd or Josh, clad in khaki shorts, college hoodie, and backward baseball cap, was seated in Angel's chair, holding a can of Karpackie—presumably the strongest beer he'd been able to find thus far; one of his chums was lying down on Angel's bed, boat shoes on, smoking a cigarette and, because drunk, missing the can he'd set up as his ashtray, dumping the ashes on Angel's £248 copy of *The Faerie Queene*; yet another, his back curved like a Pringle, sat on the edge of the aforementioned bed, unconscious, while a fourth lout successfully added, amidst obstreperous cheers from the rest, an empty can to the top of the tower he'd been building on the sleeper's cranium; two more sprawled on Todd or Josh's bed, one, with eyes too close together, messily devouring a Subway foot-long sandwich, which dripped sauce and fillings onto the carpet; the other, like his bed-fellow, equipped with a can of Karpackie. Empty cans of this beverage were distributed on every surface, including Angel's bedside table, shelving, floorspace, and bedding. Somehow they'd all found it funny to have their iPhones blaring out different songs simultaneously at maximum volume.

'Angel!' shouted his roommate, apparently glad to see him. 'Join us!'

Todd or Josh grabbed a full can of Karpackie and threw it at him. Angel, not expecting it, had to duck at the last instant to avoid being hit in the head. The can flew past and bounced off the door across the hall.

'Ooohhhh!' screamed everyone, in cheerful relief.

'I can't, I have to study . . .' Angel said. But nobody heard him.

Before Angel could say anything else, Camaro appeared behind him. He'd come out of his room to find out what the knock was about.

'Camarooooooo!' cheered everyone, except Angel, in a roar of crapulous delight.

Todd or Josh grabbed another beer and threw it at Camaro. 'Come and join us, dude!'

The can flew past Angel's head, where it was caught by Camaro amid more cheers. Angel swivelled to look at his smiling neighbour, and the latter stepped inside to stand next to a chest of drawers. Camaro was dressed in his idiosyncratic style: pointed crocodile loafers, burgundy velvet trousers, flowery shirt, necktie with a metallic pattern, and a snake print jacket. He opened the can and took a sip, then looked at Angel, gave him a smiley nod, and pointed at his jacket, thus silently asking if he wanted to photograph it. Angel shook his head.

'Time to crank it up, bitches!' shouted his roommate.

Todd or Josh produced a bottle of vodka and, standing in the middle of the room, held it up high amid yet more cheers.

'Chug! Chug! Chug!' chanted the others—except Angel, who didn't know what to do; the passed-out American, who carried on sleeping; and Camaro, who simply smiled and observed the scene with beady, calculating eyes.

Todd or Josh opened the bottle, put it to his mouth, tilted back his head, and began gulping down the vodka.

'Chug! Chug! Chug!'

The clear fluid bubbled down faster than rocket fuel during a launch.

'Chug! Chug! Chug!'

The bottle emptied and Todd or Josh held it up high again, roaring in triumph.

'Yeeeeeeeeaaaaaaahhhhhhh!' screamed the others—except Angel, the sleeper, and Camaro, who silently laughed and deftly swiped something from the chest of drawers into his pocket.

Todd or Josh then grabbed yet another Karpackie and, seemingly needing something extra to wash down the vodka—because, as Angel had heard him say, 'liquor and beer, never fear; beer and liquor, you'll never be sicker'—opened the can and chugged that down too, after which, amid continuing cheers and shouting, he crushed the empty can against his head, knocking off the baseball cap, and staggered towards the chest of drawers, scattering the empty cans and bottles populating the top. A moment later, with a tremendous heave, he vomited between the chest of drawers and the wall behind.

'Ooooohhhhhh!' exclaimed the other louts, before collectively exploding with laugher.

Camaro, worried about his outfit, stepped back quickly and retreated into his room. Angel stepped back too, but he, seeing the party was set to continue, left the scene, in search of a more tranquil venue for study.

Chapter XIX

The Departure Lounge café, which Angel loved because it was decorated like an airport, and therefore recalled his forthcoming flight to visit Madison, was sufficiently quiet at that hour for study, but the décor presently gave him nausea, so Angel walked past it, curtaining the sight of it with his hair. Twenty yards past the reminder of his torment, however, Angel felt his phone vibrate. He pulled it out and stopped abruptly: Madison had replied to his message.

The event making The Departure Lounge instantly attractive again, he boomeranged back, took a table in its deepestmost depths, and readied to privately delectate in the anticipated exchange.

'Hey, I forgot you messaged. S'up?' She'd written.

First and foremost on his mind was her Instagram post. But, however burning this topic, he sensed it would be counter-productive to bring it up straightaway. Perhaps, she'd explain it without him having to ask. Or, rather, he fervently hoped she would.

He typed a reply.

ANGEL: I am enraptured by the appearance of a message from thee on my device.

However, he thought it contrived and deleted it. He tried again.

ANGEL: I have been immersed in literary pleasures

He'd begun, but he thought it silly and deleted that too.

ANGEL: I have withered into a desiccated wraith awaiting thy most anticipated reply.

But this third attempt made him wince, so he deleted.

Fourth attempt:

ANGEL: Oh, beauteous damsel of my dreams, what a balm thy words are for this depressed and lonely soul.

Ridiculous; deleted.

And so it went for twenty minutes, until, finally deciding a proper reply required meditation, he settled on 'I am sorry, I am unable to converse at present.' But ascertaining the optimal wording even for that, and whether to add 'I shall message you later,' and then whether to end with a period or without (because correct grammar was important), took another twenty minutes, following which, fearing the message sounded abrupt, or maybe even hostile, no matter how he tinkered with it, he deleted it as well. Inspiration would come, he reassured himself.

Madison had long gone offline anyway.

The urgent issue of her Instagram not resolved, The Departure Lounge once again became the inducer of stomach cramps. He stood and made his way to the exit.

But Vera had camped out at a table, with an ancient book, her antique china cup and teapot, a leather-bound notebook, and a Montblanc fountain pen. Such elegant taste was worthy of emulation, and he resolved to pay the same attention to detail. Notwithstanding, Angel thought it best to avoid looking at her directly, and kept his sights focused on the exit. Alas, he miscalculated his trajectory; as he passed, his backpack dragged her teapot off the edge of the table; it's explosive landing producing thousands of singing pieces. Instinctively, Angel turned towards the noise, not yet realising what he'd done, only to be faced with Vera's horrified eyeballs and laser-thin lips.

As if having beheld Medusa and turned into stone, Angel saw her stand ominously before him, almost in slow motion, her hands clawed like a tigress. She looked at the broken teapot and then at him with snowballing fury, taking a menacingly deep breath.

'FOR GOODNESS' SAKE, ANGEL!'

Wide-eyed, Angel flinched, and, wanting to apologise but fearing what Vera might do if he lingered, quickly fled the scene.

CHAPTER XX

The Junior Common Room of the School of Arts and Humanities seemed the next logical destination. Like any common room, it was less than ideal, since it was always teeming with students, who used it for purposes of mindless jabbering, pointless arguing, clamorous joke-telling, malicious gossiping, chaotic snooker, rambunctious board games, vociferous card-playing, the fruit machine, crisp-munching, gobbling of chocolate bars, guzzling of fizzy drinks, projectile burping, selfie taking, chatting on the phone, hang-over recovery, and updating employer-disappointing social media accounts, among other activities. Moreover, the giant television screen, set to full brightness and volume, was perennially on.

Angel arrived at his new location only to find it transformed into a flickering dark cave, thundering with

Mad Max: Fury Road. The TV was so deafening, and the action scenes so relentless, that hair, clothes, and cheeks rippled in the decibel storm. By the entrance he almost felt as if standing, angled forward, arms spinning, in a wind tunnel reproducing a category five hurricane.

Unable to think of other places to go, however, Angel told himself that maybe the cacophony, being constant, would in fact help him concentrate. After all, silence was hardly ever perfect anywhere, and the occasional thud or cough or sneeze or sniffling or whispered conversation, whose participants sooner or later ended up laughing or snorting in the attempt to it, often proved the worse distractions. He found a vacant spot at the edge of a sofa and got out his study materials. Then, he pulled out his phone and, careful to shield it behind his open copy of *Oroonoko*, switched on the torch.

Unfortunately, for all his care, the shielding proved inadequate. The student on the adjoining cushion instantly turned to look at him and, pointing irritably at Angel's circle of light, said:

'Do you mind?'

Angel's exile continued.

Chapter XXI

In desperation, Angel repaired to the girls' dorm, knowing Amelia would always gladly receive him. He didn't bother, for that reason, to forewarn her.

His appearance in the building was greeted with frowns, scowls, and dirty looks. It was only then that he realised he'd made a huge mistake. What if the big American girl had gone back to the dorm? He prayed she was still in the library. And the eco-terrorist? Hopefully, she had superglued herself to a Burger King somewhere. He kept his head down and walked a little faster.

He knocked on Amelia's door.

'Angel!' she said, predictably pleased to see him. 'What a surprise!'

'Hello. Are you busy? May I come in?'

'But of course, Angel!' She stepped aside to allow him entry.

To his disappointment, Amelia was not alone. Jae was visiting. He found the tall blonde seated on Amelia's chair with her legs crossed at the knee. She regarded him expressionlessly, did not bother to greet him, and immediately returned her attention to her host. Angel thought she looked oddly out of place amidst Amelia's homely decorations.

'Please sit,' Amelia said to him, pointing at the bottom of her bed. She had a single room, so there was nowhere else for him to rest his glutes.

Angel did as instructed.

'To what do we owe the honour?' said Amelia, beaming.

'Er . . . I couldn't find anywhere to study. I was hoping you'd let me study in your room for a little while.'

'Oh.' Her shoulders fell.

'I hope you don't mind.' He adopted a more amiable manner as he realised his error.

'Of course not, Angel. Stay as long as you need.'

Jae now turned to him and said, 'You should show more respect to your friend.' Her speech was, as always, matter-of-fact, without tonal or volume modulation.

'Pardon?' He feigned perplexity, but knew full well what she meant.

'You didn't come to visit Amelia. You came here because she's convenient.'

'Oh, Jae, come on,' said Amelia.

'No, no, I came to visit. It's just that I thought we could study together,' Angel said.

'If you need a place to study,' said Jae, 'there are plenty of places at the university. If you can't find one that suits you at this hour, plan better next time. Don't make your problem her problem.'

Angel looked at Amelia, eyes asking for help.

'Don't be cynical, Jae,' she said, adding, as she turned to Angel with a mildly flirtatious wink, 'I know Angel secretly wanted to visit, but he didn't want to be obvious.'

'He's rude,' said Jae.

'He's a *gentleman*,' said Amelia, smiling at Angel.

Jae stood to leave. Sky-scraping over Angel, she addressed him without emotion. 'That sweet girl likes you. Show some respect.'

Amelia pretended not to hear. Rolling her eyes, Jae bid her goodbye and left the room.

'Don't mind her,' said Amelia. 'She's feeling fed up.'

'She . . . um . . . doesn't like me very much.'

'Of course she does, Angel. She just had a bad day.'

'I didn't know you were friends.'

'We're in the same module this term.'

'Er . . . really? Which one?'

'Theatrical Cultures in Early Modern England.'

'Okay.'

'How was your day?'

'I found Vera is in my Food and Lit class.'

'Oh, dear!' Amelia giggled, a hand over her mouth.

'I . . . I think she's angry with me. I-I broke her teapot. It was an accident.' He described the incident, omitting his panicked flight.

'Oh, dear, dear!' Amelia bulged her eyes, pressing her lips to suppress a smile. 'In that case, if I were you, I'd drop the module tomorrow morning and see if you can still switch.'

'Really?'

'She'll never forgive you. The teapot was a Victorian antique.'

'Oh, no . . .' Angel rubbed his forehead.

'Or you could offer to replace it.'

'Ouff . . . it'll cost a lot . . .'

'Maybe your mum can help.'

Angel sighed and looked at the wall.

'Don't worry, Angel. I'll speak to Vera.'

'Will you?' he said, his eyes pleading.

'I will. But stay clear all the same.'

'But . . . but what if I see her?'

'Then say you're really sorry again and will try to replace the teapot. Did you apologise when it happened?'

'Er . . . yes . . . yes, of course I apologised.'

'Did you really?'

'Er . . . no. The truth is . . . no. She was too angry. I-I-I didn't get the chance. Will you please explain?'

'I will, Angel. But I can't promise anything. You know what she's like.'

Silence. Angel filled his cheeks with air and exhaled slowly, eyes wide.

'Anyway. How's Madison?' Amelia said, seemingly to move onto pastures more pleasurable to her guest.

'Not so good. I'm . . . I'm worried about her.'

'Oh, why? Did she say something to you?'

'Um . . . Her messages have been opaque . . . a-a-and then she posted this yesterday evening.' Angel took out his phone and showed Amelia the Instagram post he'd been preoccupied with.

Amelia sat beside him, depressing the mattress deeply and tilting Angel in her direction—for she was much heavier than he—to the extent that his arm came to rest against her soft, round shoulder. She made no attempt to separate them.

'What is it?' she said, leaning towards him to look at the image. Angel felt a large breast press against him.

'Um . . . you see that?' said he, tapping at the object in Madison's hand. A part of his mind registered Amelia's pleasant perfume. 'She's holding an open . . . beer bottle. She's drinking lager out of a bottle. And look at those two other girls.'

'Oh, Angel. Is that it?'

'But—can't you see?'

'So she's having a drink. She's at uni, Angel. Of course she's gone to the pub.'

'But . . . beer is what people drink at night to get drunk . . . especially that brand—Miller Lite. I looked it up. Pfff! Maybe Peroni, if any! And she posted this on a *week night*. When she was here, we'd go to a restaurant on a Saturday and have red or white wine over an Italian meal, but . . . but this . . . this is grotesque!'

'Come on, Angel. Maybe she adopted more European tastes when she was here. And now that she's gone back to America she's reverted to her normal tastes.'

'No! She's not like that! She's better than that!' Angel gesticulated with tensed arms.

'You can't control what she does,' Amelia said, easy-going and gentle.

'I-I-I'm not trying to control anything!'

'Have you discussed this with her?'

'No, no. I-I haven't had the chance.'

'Maybe you should, if it really bothers you.' Amelia put her hand on his arm.

'Maybe,' he said, suddenly distant.

'Send her a message. Let's see what she says.'

'Er . . . no, I-I-I think that would be a bad idea.' Angel rubbed his forehead.

'Why? Isn't honesty the best policy?'

'I-I-I . . . er . . . I just . . . um . . . er . . .' Angel's knees began bouncing.

'Come on. I'm sure it's completely innocent.'

'Er . . . I . . . just . . . er . . .'

'Communication is vital for any relationship, Angel. Especially a long-distance one.'

'Yes . . . of course . . . I-I-I . . .' Angel was now rubbing his forehead hard enough to push the skin out of place.

'Come on,' Amelia coaxed, gesturing towards his phone with her eyes.

Angel's mind had ceased to function, overwhelmed by white noise.

'No?' Amelia said.

Silence. Angel shook his head.

'Okay. But think about it.'

'Er . . . okay.' Angel exhaled, in a daze.

'Do you want me to make space for you on my desk?'

'Um . . . sorry?' Angel was slowly coming to.

'You wanted to study . . .'

'Er . . . yes . . . I did.'

Amelia went to her desk and began moving her books aside. 'Here,' she said.

Angel looked at the desk, then at Amelia, and finally said, standing up.

'You know . . . um . . . I'm feeling a bit fatigued. I probably won't retain anything. I think I'll study in the morning. I have to get up early anyway.'

Amelia made only a partial effort to conceal her disappointment.

'Okay. That's probably sensible.'

'Er . . . yes. So . . . um . . . I'll see you tomorrow.'

'See you tomorrow, Angel,' Amelia said, smiling and playing with a strand of hair.

Angel nodded and left, hair over his face.

CHAPTER XXII

Amelia's room having thus failed, Angel's last resort was the lavatory in the male dorm. He would lock himself inside a stall, sit on the toilet with the lid down, and read as much as his skinny coccyx would allow. At least the neon light would be bright.

The first five minutes were unproductive. He was unable to concentrate. His eyes went over the same lines again and again, reading without comprehension, his mind fully preoccupied with the implications of Madison's choice of beverage and friends. How was she not embarrassed by them? Did they photobomb? Yet, if so, why would she not crop them out? On the upside, her heedless, reckless post gave him a heads-up. It provided vital information, which would otherwise have remained hidden. But although knowledge was better than ignorance, knowledge gave him abdominal cramps—and, he recalled from his Classic Lit module of two years ago, it did Oedipus no favours. These reflections increased his intracranial pressure, his head a gas boiler about to explode.

Angel's paroxysm of stress was interrupted by the slam of an opening door reverberating against porcelain, linoleum, and tile. Angel heard heavy breathing, shuffling, trousers being unzipped by the urinals, and a long exhalation, followed by piercing, tuneless whistling. He sighed impatiently while he waited out the familiar sequence of sounds: trousers being zipped; running water; hand drier blasting; door to the lavatory being yanked open, then closing gently.

Angel got back to his book.

As a famous woman author Aphra Behn—

The door to the lavatory burst open again. The incomer seemed in a hurry. He entered the stall next to Angel and slammed the door shut with enough force to shake the stalls. The sound of jeans being yanked down. An explosion of flatulence. Stools hitting water. A sigh of relief.

Angel waited again, looking at the stall wall adjoining his neighbour. The foul smell of kebab food poisoning reached his nostrils. The rattle of toilet paper yanked by the mile. Wiping. The action repeated two hundred and fifty times. Finally, jeans yanked up. Zipping. Flushing. Loud unlatching of stall door. Muted singing. Running water. Hand drier. Lavatory door yanked open, then closing gently.

The hum of ventilation.

The lull gave Angel opportunity to move into a different stall, as far away from the defecator's as possible.

He got back to his book.

As a famous woman author Aphra Behn was—

Voices with American accents suddenly approached and crashed into the lavatory, as Josh or Todd's chums—but not the aforementioned—entered, one of them seeming to fall and land face-first on the floor.

'Duuude!' said a voice, possibly Boat Shoes', who then burst out laughing.

More crashes, which caused the stall walls to vibrate. One of the showers across from the stalls was turned on. Collective laughter.

'Don't do it, man!' another voice said in drunken amusement.

'Oooohhh! He's showering fully dressed! He's shampooing his hair!' Boat Shoes shouted, followed by more gales of laughter.

From the ensuing crash against the stalls and the splash of water on the floor visible through the narrow gab below the stall door, Angel deduced the fully dressed showerer had stumbled out. A wet arm became visible, sporting a spiderweb tattoo on the elbow. Then, a red, dripping, chubby face with eyes too close together appeared in the gap. It belonged the lout with the drippy Subway sandwich he'd seen earlier in his room. Subway's eyes rolled and focused on him momentarily, then the face pulled away and disappeared. Angel remained perfectly still, quiet as a mouse.

'Hey man, there's a motherfucker in the stall,' Subway said.

Angel mouthed an expletive.

The others, however, were too busy shouting and laughing to hear Subway, who, in a thoroughly annoying way, re-stated his observation three or four times.

'What are you talking about, man?' said Boat Shoes, who'd finally heard him.

'There's a motherfucker in there,' insisted Subway.

Angel heard a crash that caused his door to shake and, looking up, saw a pair of hands appear along the top edge. Boat Shoes' face followed, his coiffed hair messy, his cheeks as red as Subway's; his curious expression gave way to a broad smile.

'It's that guy, Angel!' he proclaimed, turning to the others, before disappearing.

'Who?'

'Angel! The guy who came to the room earlier!'

'Chad's roommate?' asked a third voice.

'Who's Chad?' asked Boat Shoes.

'What do you mean who's Chad? We were in his room just now, dude.'

'His name is Brad, you moron,' said Boat Shoes.

'Woah, woah. What the fuck, man? He told me his name is Josh,' said Subway, perplexed.

'No, man, his name is Brad,' replied Boat Shoes.

A fourth voice intervened: 'Fuck dude, this is weird! He told me his name is Todd!'

'What?' said Boat Shoes.

'You fucking serious?' said Subway.

'I've known him as Chad since orientation.'

'And I've known him as Todd.'

'The fuck . . . ?' said Subway.

'Holy fucking shit . . .' said Boat Shoes.

Puzzled silence, heavy breathing.

Angel waited. He couldn't remember what name his roommate had given him. One of those four, but he hadn't cared to remember since he'd had no intention of ever making friends with the oaf.

'We gotta go talk to him,' said Boat Shoes. 'Mother-*fucker* . . .'

They had all sobered up—or so it seemed.

'Let's get the *fuck* out of here,' said Subway.

Collective agreement, followed by noisy exits.

Angel sat still, listening out. However, his and Chad or Brad or Josh or Todd's room was too far from the lavatories for him to hear anything significant; the only sounds to reach him were the hum of ventilation and students walking past in the corridor.

He shook his head and got back to his book.

As a famous woman—

Thuds of a person running, the crash of the lavatory door opening, a roaring heave, the sound of vomiting. Sniffling. Spitting. Heavy breathing. Many minutes of the last three.

Then, the approaching squeak of rubber shoes on linoleum. A brief pause. Subway's frowning face appearing in the gap under the door of Angel's stall.

'And what the fuck is your name?' Subway said.

CHAPTER XXIII

The advantage of having had to spend the night in the Junior Common Room was that, sleep-deprived due to the constant traffic of boisterous students, what with their drunkenness, noisy *Parcheesi* games, English billiards, jabbering on the phone, virulent gossip, idiotic jokes, rollicking banter, and constant laughter—not to mention the ever-blaring television—Angel had every incentive to show up for his kitchen shift right on the dot; even the hiss of pressurised tap water, the sizzling of bacon, the clatter of crockery, the clang and scrape of pots and pans, and the roar of extractor fans set at maximum, offered a less disruptive environment.

'Angel,' said the supervisor as he walked in.

'Yes?'

'Emmanuel has not shown up this morning. You will be serving at the counter. Can you manage?'

'Er . . .' Angel looked at the counter. How embarrassing! At least in the washing-up room he couldn't be seen by fellow students. But now he, a student of literature, in love with the most exquisite princess the world had ever seen, would have to serve students of inferior accomplishment—inarticulate ones who didn't know the classics, received low marks for their course work, and didn't know their theirs from their they'res; who used swearwords instead of adjectives; who dressed inelegantly; who had no standards; and who thought Nike was only a brand of sportswear. Yet, what choice did he have? Visiting Madison was far more important. Did knight errants not undergo trials and perils to earn the love of their damsels? That decided it. He said firmly, 'Yes, of course.' Although his words might as well have been notes from a piccolo flute.

'Good. Follow me then.' The supervisor took him to the serving counter and pointed at the various trays in turn. 'So, no more than *one* bacon piece per student—no arguments—*less than half* a scoop of scrambled egg—again, no arguments—up to *two* tomato halves, and up to *two* slices of mushroom. Is that clear?'

'Er . . . yes.'

'No matter how big the student, the portions are *always* the same,' she told him, with a raised index finger.

'Okay.'

'And the vegan sausages are only for the vegans. Up to two per student. You must always ask them to confirm. Not vegan, no sausages. Is that clear?'

'Y-Yes, yes. It's clear.'

'Good. Put on your uniform and I'll get you the rest.

'Okay.'

'You'll have to wear a hair net.'

'Okay.'

Angel did as instructed.

With a moment by himself, Angel had opportunity to start realising the implications of the job he'd just accepted. First and foremost was the big American girl; she would certainly not miss breakfast; and she would want multiple rashers of bacon, plus a mountain of scrambled eggs, a hill of tomatoes, and a bucketload of mushrooms. No doubt about it. How would he be able to serve her, let alone argue against excess portions, without looking at her and thereby giving her reason to accuse him of sexual harassment? He hoped she'd caught a virus and woken up that morning with a fever high enough to keep her in bed. The student protesters he was less worried about, for the reason their blockade of the canteen had ended was that they were not early risers; they would almost certainly be missing breakfast—or so he prayed. His roommate, whatever he was called, would likely still be unconscious, and the penis his chums had drawn on his cheek with a permanent marker before they left would, when he awoke, keep him occupied; he too was unlikely to show up. Amelia was an early riser and would take her breakfast, but she would always be friendly to him no matter what he did. Vera was another matter altogether. He hoped Amelia had had a chance to talk to her, to explain. But what if she hadn't? With luck, since Vera lived in off-campus accommodation, she'd take her breakfast in her own kitchen, or at The Wolseley.

Once the canteen opened, the first students in the queue were Jae and Johannes. She recognised Angel but made no comment. However, her sphynx-like visage betrayed a hint of contemptuous amusement when she asked for her bacon and eggs.

'Anything else?' said Angel.

'No.'

Jae walked away.

'Angel!' Johannes was glad to see him.

'Hello, Johannes.'

'You're working here?'

'Er . . . yes. Er . . . just part-time.'

'Cool!'

'Um . . . w-what would you like?' said Angel.

'Ten bacon, five scoops of egg,' Johannes said. The strongman knew the rules—everybody did—but something in his manner suggested to Angel that, having saved him from being ripped to pieces by the climate change protestors, the strongman now felt he had moral leverage.

'Er . . .' Angel hesitated. He noticed the student after Johannes was paying close attention.

'Please, buddy,' said the giant Swede.

'I can't . . .'

'Please?' Johannes put on puppy eyes.

Angel cast a backward glance towards the kitchen and, seeing the supervisor's attention was focused elsewhere, quickly scooped as much bacon as he could with his tongs and piled on the eggs.

'Can I also have sausages?'

'Um . . . they're vegan . . . t-t-they're for vegan students.'

'Sure. I'm vegan too. Give me five!'

'Um . . .'

With no rebuttal, Angel added the sausages to Johanne's overflowing plate.

'Thanks, buddy!' Johannes said, giving him a thumbs up and walking away with a smile.

The next student said the inevitable:

'Three bacon, one full scoop of egg, two sausages.'

Angel dared not deny him. And even if he'd dared, he lacked the volubility to contrive a reason to do so. Therefore, the cheeky student got what he asked for.

'Four bacon, two scoops of egg, three sausages' said the next student, who, with every reason, assumed the portion rules had changed.

He too got what he asked for.

And so on it went, until the bacon, egg, and vegan sausage trays were empty.

With no immediate replacement in sight, Angel went into the kitchen in search of more.

'Is it all gone already?' said the flummoxed supervisor.

'Er . . . yes . . . erm . . . the queue moved really quickly.'

'But it's only ten past six. Normally the first trays last until half past.'

'I-I-I don't know . . . er . . . it's just that. . . the queue moved really quickly today . . .'

'Did you stick to the rules, Angel?' The supervisor had twigged.

'Yes, absolutely!'

'Are you sure?'

'Yes, yes, of course!'

'Okay. I'm afraid the next tray is not due until half past.'

'W-W-What do I tell the people in the queue?'

'Well, we can't keep them waiting for twenty minutes, Angel, do we? So, move them along.'

'Ah, so no breakfast?'

'Direct them to the continental table. There's toast and cereal.'

'Okay.'

Angel went back to the counter and informed the queue of the situation.

'Aw, for fuck's sake!' said the first one.

'Fucking useless,' said the next one.

'Ran out of bacon and eggs,' said the one in third place to the one in fourth.

'Fucking hell!' said the latter.

Moans and grumbles all the way down the line. An exodus to the continental table.

For the next twenty minutes, Angel had to deny food and explain the situation to every student who arrived at the counter.

And he also had to deny and explain to Professor Mastropasqua, not one he would expect to ever eat there, nor to take the bad news well.

'Pah! This wretched university!' he said, without seeming to recognise Angel.

'There's the continental table,' said Angel.

Mastropasqua turned to look in its direction, then looked back at Angel.

'Do you expect me to eat furniture?'

Angel turned to look and discovered a further knock-on effect of having favoured his friend: the swarm of locusts had left only dry carafes and empty baskets.

Mastropasqua left in disgust, and Angel went back to the kitchen to inform the supervisor.

'Tell them to wait,' the supervisor said.

'Okay.'

At that point, the big American girl entered the canteen. Angel's heart stopped; she approached the counter with two companions, both big girls, but not as big as the green-haired virago. Their faces were uniformly unpleasant, albeit for different reasons. Companion number one had narrow eyes and wavy, bright pink hair in a ponytail. Companion number two had dark locks, a long mouth, and epic eyebrows that arched ever higher as they moved to the sides of her face. Breaking into a cold sweat and trembling, he immediately pulled his hat down as far as it would go to avoid recognition.

Just before they reached the counter, the supervisor stepped out of the kitchen and affixed a laminated sign on the customer-facing side of the glass. It read:

STRICTLY ONE BACON RASHER
AND HALF A SCOOP OF EGG
PER PERSON.

The American girls joined the back of the queue. The latter moved fast, as Angel could only offer tomatoes and mushrooms, which not even the vegans wanted on their own (fried in the same hot plate as the bacon), or the continental table, which had since been replenished, complete with its own vegan options.

New bacon, egg, and vegan sausage trays arrived just as the American girls reached the front of the queue. Angel was torn between fear and relief; so much could go wrong in the ensuing minutes. Pre-emptively, Angel averted his gaze from the big American girl.

'Three bacon, one full scoop of eggs,' said Pink Hair.

'I-I'm sorry,' Angel said, shielded by the supervisor's sign. He pointed at it. 'I can only give you one rasher and half a scoop of eggs.'

Pink Hair was instantly angry.

'We've been told that we can get as much as we like!'

Angel shrank. 'I-I'm sorry,'

'Then why do those *men* there have multiple slices of bacon?' She pointed at a group of male students sharing a table near the counter. 'And look at Mr. Toxic Masculinity over there,' she pointed at Johannes, who'd since cleared his plate and was leaning back in his chair, perspiring and exhausted from so much eating. 'I bet he had *mountains* of bacon *and* egg.'

'I-I-I'm really sorry. It's just that I'm not allowed . . .'

'Is it because I'm a *woman?*' Pink Hair's blue eyes blew up into gas giants, her lips thinned into a razor's edge.

The big American girl glared at him with hatred. Angel got the impression she hadn't recognised him, but even though thought to be a different person, he had already incurred her wrath all the same. Behind her, Epic Eyebrows stared at him with a disbelieving sneer.

'No, no, no. Of course not!' said Angel, his voice jumping an octave. 'It's just the rule. There's a sign. It's just the rule!'

'I don't *care* about the stupid sign!' Pink Hair said, raising her voice. 'You gave those men there all the food they wanted. We *expect* and *demand* the same treatment!'

'He's looking at your belly,' Epic Eyebrows said, addressing Pink Hair.

In fact, Angel had looked at the back of the sign when he pointed at it a moment earlier, but, upon hearing Epic Eyebrows' comment, he noticed the sign was in the line of sight of Pink Hair's mid riff, which was exposed to the air by a cropped top.

'I-I-I'm sorry, I-I'm really sorry, I-I really really can't,' said Angel.

While he said this, Pink Hair looked at Epic Eyebrows, realisation washing over her face. Pink Hair turned to Angel.

'Is it because I'm FAT?'

'No, no, no, no—It's just the rule. You're not fat. It's just the rule!'

'Well, we're big *beautiful* women and we don't measure our *worth* by the size of our *pants!*'

'No, it's, it's nothing to do with size. It's just the rule!'

'And stop looking at my belly, you *pervert!*'

'No, no, I'm not looking . . . I only looked at the sign! I promise!'

'Men here are *disgusting,*' said the big American girl. 'We want another server.'

'I'm sorry, I-I-I . . .'

'I *SAID*: WE WANT ANOTHER SERVER!'

The supervisor came to the counter.

'Angel, go wash the dishes,' she ordered.

All too happy to do as told, he stepped back. As he changed into the appropriate version of his uniform, he listened to the supervisor arguing with the American girls. The two camps battled back and forth, all parties shouting at each other, but there was no overcoming the supervisor's defences, and with verbal bucketfuls of urine and boiling excrement, the supervisor brought the raiders to heel. As the latter received their portions, they complained incessantly. They promised to report Angel, to go to the newspapers, and to sue for a million dollars.

Back in the washing-up room, Angel was relieved to stay out of sight until the end of his shift.

Afterwards, the supervisor came to see him.

'Follow me,' she said.

The supervisor led him into a tiny office where on a desk was a computer screen showing CCTV feeds. She pointed at a portion of the screen showing an overhead view of the serving counter.

'You didn't follow the rules.'

'I—'

'As a result—'

Chapter XXIV

With time before class, Angel returned to his room to assess the damage. The canteen supervisor had given him his second verbal warning; one more and he was out. She'd also docked his pay. If only the university were as strict with his roommate!

The aforementioned was gone. The room stank of alcohol, vomit, and cigarettes. Empty beer cans, some crushed, some not, some with ashes, and glass and plastic bottles, all empty, claimed space on every surface. Litter and debris coated the carpet, now irregularly patterned by stains, burns, and rotting sandwich fillings. The vomit, not quite dried up, stained the top and back of the chest of drawers, forming a parabola on the wall behind it, and a semi-circle on the carpet below.

Angel opened the window and kicked the rubbish over to his roommate side. He picked up his copy of *The*

Faerie Queene and, not without satisfaction, was careful to blow the ashes covering it onto his roommate's bed. Also on the latter went any can or bottle he found polluting his shelves, desk, bedding, and bedside table.

To discuss having the room cleaned, he went to Student Services in the main building. He was directed to the Accommodation Team, at whose door Angel knocked several corridors later.

'Come in!' The sharp voice augured trouble.

Angel entered the cramped office and found a matronly woman with grey hair tied in a bun so tight that her eyebrows were on the back of her head. Coloured binders filled wall-mounted shelves above her desk. The accommodation officer swivelled on her chair to face him. Any smile must have been an illegal migrant long deported from her countenance.

'Good morning,' said Angel.

'What is it?'

'Um . . . there's been an incident in my room.'

'What kind of incident?'

'My . . . erm . . . roommate vomited on a wall.'

'It's the students' responsibility to keep their rooms tidy.'

'Yes, but . . . er . . . he's made a mess of the room. I-I think it needs a professional clean.'

'The cleaners come on Saturday mornings. So just wait until tomorrow.'

'Yes, but . . . um . . . they only hoover the carpet. W-What about the wall?'

'It's the students' responsibility to keep their rooms tidy.'

'B-But it stinks.'

'Well, then you boys shouldn't have been drinking in the room.'

'I-I didn't drink. It was him. He had a party in there.'

'Well, then you should have laid down some rules.'

'But I didn't expect it! I-I was in the library and . . . it had already started when I arrived.'

'Well, then ask him to clean it up.'

Angel sighed. 'I don't think he will. Um . . . he's really messy.'

'Have you spoken to him?'

'Er . . . no.'

'If you're not going to lay down your rules, you're going to have to live by his.'

'He . . . um . . . doesn't seem to have any rules.'

'Then lay down yours.'

'He won't listen.'

'Then get a bucket and sponge and get scrubbing.'

'Um . . . can I change rooms? I'm graduating in the Summer and I am entitled to a single room.'

'It's too late to change accommodation. We would only ever do that in cases of a vulnerable student with special needs or medical reasons.'

'B-But I'm entitled.'

'Did you not fill out the form at the end of the Spring term?'

'I filled it out, but I-I missed the deadline.'

'Then you're not entitled anymore.'

'B-B-But I only missed the deadline by a few days! Can you not . . .'

'Sorry. You snooze, you lose.'

'I-Is there no other way . . . ?'

'No.'

'Erm . . . alright then,' he said, crestfallen, and made to leave.

But the accommodation officer stopped him. 'By the way . . .' she said.

Angel turned to face her again.

'Any permanent damage will come out of your deposit. So get whatever chemicals you need and scrub hard.'

Chapter XXV

Silence.

Long silence.

He opened his eyes; the classroom was empty.

'For God's sake!' he whispered, leaping up from his chair and checking the time on his phone.

Quarter till two in the afternoon.

'Bollocks!'

The canteen served lunch until two and it was ten minutes on foot. Angel yanked his bag off the floor and walked fast.

His phone vibrated.

Madison had messaged. It again just said, 'Hey.'

Angel stopped and, for a moment, resembled a malfunctioning robot, trying to walk, but unable to take a step, torn by the indecision between heart and stomach. In the end, stomach won, and he joined the queue at the canteen before replying—or, rather, before attempting a reply. To ensure correctness of approach, he took one more look at her disturbing Instagram post.

And, lo—there was a new one!

The image showed Madison smiling next to a dark-haired girl, with the description, 'I made a new friend,' followed by a heart emoji. Angel flinched. His stomach cramped. His head swarmed with bees.

He quickly put the phone back in his pocket, filled his cheeks with air, exhaled slowly, and rubbed his forehead while staring into space.

'Oi!' said someone behind him, tapping him on the shoulder.

Angel turned.

'The queue's moved,' said the student, pointing with his chin.

'Oh. Sorry.' He caught up.

Angel dug out his phone again. Looked at Madison's post. Put the phone in his pocket.

His chest tightened. Air became thick water.

Yet again he dug out his phone and, bracing himself, studied the post.

Madison's new friend. Somehow, she triggered instant revulsion, even though not necessarily ugly. Her long black hair was a rat's nest; her thick eyebrows wide arches; her eyelids blackened with bold eyeshadow—individually, none of these elements would have been disturbing. But then her mouth was way too wide; it might as well have been the M1. And her closed smile, devoid of lipstick, on a face tilted back with half-lidded eyes, appeared crassly smug. More alarmingly, she seemed amused by her own crass smugness. But one should not judge so hastily, Angel self-admonished; it could simply be that the wide mouth created a false impression, or perhaps that, not being privy to the context, the humour escaped him. Such things did happen. Take Jae, for example; she was always judging him—one misunderstanding after another, seemingly without a solution.

Nevertheless, the negative first impression of Madison's friend was buttressed by her t-shirt. White, which was bad enough, but also bearing a word in cherry-pink capital letters, which was worse. Only the top of the last three were visible, and Angel had the ominous feeling they spelled something rude. Did it really say BITCH? No. No way. Madison would not make friends with someone that vulgar. Maybe the girl was a computer science major and the t-shirt said GLITCH. Computer nerds were not known for their sartorial skills and they did have an occult sense of humour. Yet, Angel knew full well this explanation was incongruous. Computer nerds were brainy and harmless. This girl looked neither. She looked nasty.

And Madison?

She looked the same and she didn't. Something in her physiognomy had changed. At least in that photograph. No sign of discomfort or embarrassment. Had she not chosen to *publicise* this new friendship? Indeed, she appeared entirely relaxed. Standards had slipped another notch. Her beer-drinking friends from the earlier post had possibly introduced her to theirs, who were worse. The earlier post could no longer be dismissed as a fluke. It was the beginning of a slippery slope.

What was happening?

Something was going awry there in America. The Madison he knew would have *never* associated with girls of that *ilk*. The Madison he knew read Mediaeval romances and 19th-century novels. She enjoyed walks in the park and fine Italian and French restaurants. She appreciated letters on parchment-like paper, with good calligraphy. She swooned at roses and smiled when a gentleman held open a door. She wore Cartier and Louis Vuitton. She liked William Boguereau and John Waterford, Frank Dicksee and Jean-Léon Gérôme, Gustav Doré and Maxfield Parrish. She listened to Berlioz, Chopin, Beethoven, and Lintz. She spoke with modesty and elegance, and she *never* swore.

Whereas her new friend . . . she looked as if she might do that frequently. Could it be that she was, in fact, from a well-to-do Catholic family and was going through a rebellious phase?

It occurred to Angel he could maybe find out. He scoured through Madison's Instagram followers and, soon enough, found the girl's profile. Her name was 'Syd.' Even the name was tawdry. Although, to be fair, Sydney was classy; it reminded him of Sir Philip Sydney, a Knight of the Realm. She was a student at Madison's university. But the way she expressed it her profile! 'Studying the fuck out of shit,' she had written. So revolting! And, what was worse, her account was gross. No style, no theme, no colour coordination, bad lighting, erratic filters. There were pictures of her walking around town *in flip-flops*, of her drinking beer out of a bottle, of her reading in a bra with greasy hair, of her showing off her tattoos, of her eating pizza with one foot on the backrest of a chair, of her at Walmart in pyjamas, of her smoking on a public toilet, and even one of her proudly showing an unshaven armpit with a Billy Idol grin. Then there were selfies galore, all pulling ugly faces. And memes. One, for example, said,

'Uh oh someone sent me a box of masculinity again,' above a parcel sealed with tape inscribed FRAGILE. The descriptions were replete with boorishness, attitude, and expletives. And her choice of books? All aggressive modern paperbacks—*Resisters* by Lauren Sharkey, *Rude* by Nimko Ali, *Women Don't Owe You Pretty* by Florence Given, and *Rage Becomes Her* by Soraya Chemaly. Not a single classic novel, hardback, or book of art.

Bafflement and perplexity paralysed him.

'Oi!'

The queue had moved again. He caught up.

Angel checked whether Madison was following this Syd. And she was. Openly. On her *public* profile. This he couldn't compute. Had Madison not browsed through Syd's content before following? The Madison he remembered had curated her follows carefully; she had wanted to keep her feed aesthetic and inspiring. The only explanation was that maybe Madison, having somehow been bewitched by the gorgon, had followed impulsively during their first meeting, and, too polite to unfollow after sampling the pestilential cesspit, had simply muted the account.

But still—how on earth could Madison, *his* Madison, ever find things in common with someone so . . . base . . . so . . . full of hate? And yet, Madison had hearted their friendship!

It was so incomprehensible, so offensive, so hurtful, even, as to be exasperating. What was he going to do? He was thousands of miles away, whereas this Syd was a probably right next door. Syd could talk to Madison face to face, invite her for drinks—*beers*—and lend her some of those horrible books, every day, any time; whereas he only had pixels via WhatsApp—pixels that often arrived late, were stopped by Wi-Fi or signal dropouts, and which she didn't even always see because her girlfriends were constantly messaging.

His bowels lose, his forehead corrugated, and a wave of nausea rising up his oesophagus, by now Angel had reached the front of the queue. He looked up to find Emmanuel, slotted turner in hand, staring back at him with his enigmatic visage. The serving trays had only dried-up scrapings of mashed potatoes and cheesy pasta. The pandemonium of babbling students, coffee machines, screeching chairs, clattering trays, and extractor fans agitated the bees in his brain to a fever pitch.

Angel dry heaved and ran away.

Chapter XXVI

In a slough of despond, black clouds of confusion and despair weighing over him, Angel burrowed himself deep into the library. By doing so in the early afternoon, he had, for once, caught the gremlins slumbering, for his archenemy was not due to go on duty for several hours yet; however, this supplied no relief, since his mind still reverberated with what she was sure to say later: 'Ten days, Angel'; 'Could I have your debit card number?'; 'I can also take cash'; 'How about PayPal?'; 'Will you pay tomorrow?'; 'What about the next day?'

He'd had to find his way to the farthermost desk with hair over his face, in case the big American girl was on the premises. As a result, having miscalculated his trajectory, he had injured his knee by colliding with an oak bench covered in angular carvings. Set against the accumulation of petty misfortunes, this had brought tears to his eyes.

Having sat in a way that barred wandering eyes, Angel launched WhatsApp and typed his reply to Madison:

ANGEL: Greetings, most beloved damsel. I apologise for not writing earlier. I have had a most troublesome few days.

He was in luck. The single grey tick immediately turned double and then blue.

MADISON: Apology not accepted. When I write, you must reply immediately! lol

ANGEL: I promise to do better next time.

MADISON: Not better. I want your best

ANGEL: I will do my best.

MADISON: We'll see. You're on probation, mister. I might not have the patience to suffer another infraction

ANGEL: I am penitent.

MADISON: So you should be

ANGEL: I saw you have a new friend.

MADISON: Which one? I made a few this semester

ANGEL: The one on Instagram.

MADISON: Oh, Syd. Yea. She's wild

ANGEL: Wild?

MADISON: Yea. Funny. Feisty

ANGEL: She seems unlike other friends you have

MADISON: Definitely. I like her. She's free and refreshing. She has flair

Angel's finger hovered over the digital keyboard for five seconds, ten seconds, twenty seconds, forty seconds, eighty seconds, a hundred and sixty seconds, three hundred and twenty seconds . . .

MADISON: Angel?

Angel's finger vibrated nervously. His knees began

bouncing. He typed, then deleted. Typed. Then deleted. Typed. Then deleted.

MADISON: Cat ate your phone?

Angel rubbed his forehead, ever harder, eventually nearly ripping off the skin. He typed. Then deleted.

MADISON: Listen. My friend has just arrived. Gotta go. Later

Chapter XXVII

The buzzing beehive in his brain negating cognition, Angel couldn't sit still. He left the library and headed towards the Estate Office in the main building. Perhaps Domestic Services would be willing to send a cleaner to his room that same afternoon, so he could sleep in his bed tonight.

As he approached, he saw Professor Mastropasqua chatting to Babyface, of the Estate Maintenance Services. It was an odd scene: the tall and elegant Mastropasqua, clad all in black with a frock coat; the shorter Babyface, in jeans and hoodie, covered in plaster, light blue eyes as disturbing as ever. Babyface stared at Angel and Angel looked away.

Once in the Estate Office, he was directed to an outhouse and told to ask for 'Barry.' At the site, a stocky man in a high visibility vest operating a pallet trolley was pointed out to him.

'Sir?' Angel called out, approaching.

Barry didn't hear.

'Sir?'

Barry still didn't hear.

'Sir!' Angel was now six feet away.

Barry kept pushing the trolley without acknowledgment.

Angel raised his voice a bit more. 'Sir!'

Finally, Barry, when only three feet away, turned to look.

'Um . . . are you Barry?' said Angel.

'Aye.' the man said, stopping.

'I . . . um . . . I have a small problem . . .'

Barry stared at Angel, silently weighing him.

Angle continued, 'Um . . . my roommate has made a mess of the room. I think it needs a professional clean.'

A fleeting wave of amusement passed through Barry's eyes, then his bushy eyebrows went up. 'He's myed a mess?'

'Er . . . yes . . .'

Barry chuckled and shook his head, 'Divvint gerrus wrang, lad, but if yor roommate is a mess yee nee't tuh sort him yeut.'

'Er . . . I'm sorry?'

'If yor roommate is a mess yee nee't tuh sort him yeut.'

'Er . . .'

Silence.

Barry said, 'Wot's the mess, like?'

'Um . . . there's vomit on the wall and on the carpet.'

Barry laughed. 'He wes propah mortal then!'

'No, he didn't prop up the molehole . . . sorry what was that?'

'He was propah mortal . . . drunk.'

'Ah, yes. He was,' Angel gave an awkward laugh.

'Soz, lad, nee way. Yas ganin tuh hev tuh sort that yeut yersel.'

Angel noticed there were three other workers standing nearby, observing the exchange. One with his body half turned, the hint of an expectant smile on his face; another, bearded and serious, arms crossed and sleeved in tattoos; and a third, near a pallet sealed in clingfilm, as if about to cut it open, but frozen in mid task, Stanley knife in hand.

'Gunning?' Angel frowned, confused. 'You mean a pressure gun?'

'Haddaway and shite. Are yee deaf, man, like?' Barry threw up his arms.

'Er . . .'

'Nar na one's comin owor tuh clean up yor mess, laddie.'

'I'm sorry, what was that?'

'Yas ganin tuh hev tuh git a bucket an' a sponge and git scrubbin'.'

Angel heard a trumpet-like note—the air release of a suppressed guffaw. He noticed Half-Turned's face had gone red and looked like a baloon about to explode. Tattoos had his face down, also reddened, and was pinching the bridge his nose between the eyes while convulsing with that same high-pressure look. Stanley Knife was openly grinning, tool still hovering in mid-air.

Angel said to Barry, 'But . . . are you not with Domestic Services?'

'Aye.'

'But my room needs a professional clean . . .'

'Divvin' be daft, lad. Wuh are Domestic Services, dee ah lyeuk leek yor fucking skivvy?'

'Er . . . but . . .'

'Nar. Neet me job, that.'

'But Domestic Services is responsible for the cleaning . . .'

'Am neet ganin tuh stand heor shooting and bawling wi' yee, lad. Stop faffin aboot. Eithor git scrubbin or sort the gadgie yeut.'

'Er . . . okay . . . thank you, anyway.'

As Angel walked away, he heard an explosion of rowdy laughter behind him. He was sure it had something to do with the conversation he'd just had, but he pretended not to hear.

Chapter XXVIII

Angel walked back to the dorm. Thankfully, his roommate was still gone. But then of course he was: it was Friday afternoon and doubtless he was already out drinking; the lout wouldn't be back until the wee hours.

As much as he disdained cleaning up the American's mess, sleeping in a skipful of rubbish, smelling of stale ashes, lager, and vomit, appealed to him even less. He went to the back of the canteen to find a large cardboard box and brought it back with him. He filled the box with all the empty bottles and beer cans, the latter of which proved so numerous that he had to crush them first to be able to fit them all in. This proved difficult because he was too light to do so by standing on them, forcing him to jump up and down repeatedly. Then, with a Bic pen, Angel scrapped the dry vomit and sandwich fillings off the wall and carpet—dry retching and silently cursing the vomiter all the while. First, he'd had to enlist the help of Saïd to move the Formica chest of drawers that had stood in the way, as he could not do it on his own. With a sheet of paper ripped from a notebook and partially folded lengthways to form a groove, Angel collected the vomit shavings and tipped them into an empty lager can. Deodorant took the duties of disinfectant, and with it he sprayed the wall and carpets. Finally, he attempted to conceal the cigarette burns on the carpet by using Typex and then colouring it blue with a highlighter marker. After two hours of arduous and stomach-churning labour, the room was tolerable once again.

Next, Angel took the open cardboard box with the discarded containers to the recycling centre, which was a five-minute walk. The box's contents effectively consisted of 99% air, but even so the weight was at the limit of his strength. While *en route*, since he had to pause several times to rest, he remembered being told some eighteen months prior of a bottle and can return scheme, which was in force in Germany and which the UK was hoping to emulate, through which one could get money vouchers against recyclables. He thought he'd overheard somewhere that the scheme had already been implemented. Good! He could raise funds to see Madison!

When he reached his destination, he found the usual row of coloured recycling containers, but no indication of how one obtained the money vouchers. He saw two students, one with green dreadlocks, the other with a khaki parka, stuffing plastic bottles into a container, and decided to ask.

CHAPTER XXIX

'Hello. Um . . . do you know how we get the money from the recycling?' said Angel.

The student with the dreadlocks turned to look at him; when Angel noticed his chinstrap beard he thought he looked familiar. The student also seemed to have recognised him.

'What money?' Chinstrap sounded vaguely hostile.

'The-The-The money for cans and bottles brought in for recycling.'

Chinstrap chuckled with incredulity. 'Are you fucking joking?' he said, while Khaki Parka stopped what he was doing to observe the interaction.

'No, er . . . it's just that I read . . .'

'Are you fucking retarded?'

'What . . . why . . . er . . .' mumbled Angel, taken aback.

'Saving the fucking planet is your payment.' Chinstrap came face to face with him.

'I'm sorry . . . it's okay . . . it's just that I'd heard . . .'

'You're the climate change denier, aren't you?'

'Cl . . . no . . . no . . . I'm not a . . .'

Now Khaki Parka took a step forward also to get in Angel's face. 'Found the Tory!' he snarled.

'It's because of Tories like you that we'll all be dead in twelve years!' said Chinstrap, giving Angel a little shove through his box of recycling, which Angel was still holding against his chest.

'I-I'm not a Tory . . . I'm sorry . . . I-I'm not a Tory . . .'

'Fuck off!' Chinstrap's eyes burnt holes into Angel's face.

'I'm sorry . . . I'm sorry . . .' Angel mumbled, taking a step back, heart thumping.

He turned and left the site, taking his box with him.

CHAPTER XXX

Back at the dorm, Angel searched for a place to hide the recycling. He'd think of a way to dispose of it later. Or perhaps the cleaners would find it first and save him the trouble.

After much walking up and down the corridors, trying locked cupboards, and going up and down the floors, he settled on leaving the box in a nook under the stairs in the basement. For good measure, he took a discarded copy of *The Guardian* he'd found in one of the bins and, separating and opening its sheets, used them to cover up his deed.

All the while, he thought of Madison. Or, more accurately, of her new friend. Was she the one who had suddenly arrived, interrupting his and Madison's WhatsApp chat? What were they doing now? Where had she taken her? The thought of that Syd girl taking

Madison to a bar to drink beer out of a bottle and pump Madison's head with angry feminist ideas was maddening. Even more so was the idea that Madison might be enjoying this and allowing herself to be nefariously influenced. How could he stop her? What could he write in a message subtly to slay this dragon?

The anxiety induced by these meditations made him aware of his long, greasy hair. As it was still pointless trying to read, he decided to shower instead; maybe hot water would help cleanse his mind. He changed into a bathrobe and flipflops, went to the bathroom with a towel, and, keeping the flipflops on, stepped into the shower.

Far from dissolving his anxiety, however, being in close quarters with it turned it into a concentrate. What if the bottled beer led to tequila shots? That would be the lowest of the low. And what if this Syd introduced Madison to even worse people? That seemed, if not just likely, almost certain. But perhaps, exposure to such a person would, in fact, prove salutary, and cure Madison of unromantic illusions. An aim of university education was exposure to different ideas; but transformation by them was not a given; equally possible was a reaffirmation of one's correct values through becoming better informed. This offered a modicum of reassurance.

Now somewhat calmer, and his stomach settling down at last, Angel stepped out of the shower and turned towards the wall, where he'd left his towel and bathrobe hanging from a hook.

'Oops!' said a voice behind him. 'I'm sorry, miss, I think you're in the wrong ba—'

Angel turned to look and saw one of the Indian students, Sanjay, clad a bathrobe and holding a towel, his hair dry. As soon as his face was revealed to Sanjay, the latter, taken aback a second time, muttered, 'Oh, sorry,' before leaving the bathroom altogether.

Angel put on his bathrobe, pretending he'd not heard what he thought he'd heard. He had lost weight since summer, after all. Yet, secretly, he decided to grow his Van Dyke as long as it would go; he could not afford ambiguities while visiting Madison.

Chapter XXXI

The financial situation had become an ever-growing problem. The canteen supervisor had docked his pay, and he'd yet to find out when he'd get the money and how much. He hadn't dared ask after the cock-up at breakfast. Now he discovered he'd run out of clean clothes, and he had not even a tenner for the cash-operated launderette. He picked up his mobile and launched WhatsApp. However, he could not bring himself to message his mother, even though she was still waiting for his reply to her question of two weeks earlier, so he closed the app.

A cursory sniffing of his laundry confirmed that every item was past social acceptability. The clothes he had on remained passable only at a distance. This would not do. Therefore, desperate times demanding desperate measures, he knocked on Saïd's door.

'Angel, my friend!' said his neighbour. 'What's up?'

'Hello. Um . . . d-do you think you could lend me a tenner?'

'Yes, no problem, my friend. Let me get my wallet.'

While he waited at the threshold, Angel saw Camaro lying in bed, glittery suit and pointy shoes still on, playing JellySplash on his tablet.

'Here,' said the Sudanese when he came back.

'Thank you. Um . . . I'll pay you back,' said Angel, as he made to leave.

'Angel!'

'Yes?'

'When can you pay me back?'

'Er . . . next Friday?'

'Next Friday. Okay.'

'Um . . . okay.' Angel made to leave again.

'Angel?'

'Yes?'

'Friday, yes?' Saïd stared at him steadily, with a warning index finger.

'Yes, Friday.'

'Okay. I'll be waiting.'

'Um . . . okay. See you later.'

'And see you Friday.'

'Yes.'

'Definitely on Friday, yea?'

'Yes, definitely.'

'Okay, my friend.'

'Okay.'

'But Friday, yea?'

'Yes, Friday.'

'Okay.'

'Okay.'

Angel grabbed the bin liner with his laundry—

everything he owned except his current attire— and took it to the laundrette, a ten-minute walk. He brought along his copy of *Oroonoko*, determined to use his time well.

Sadly, the on-campus laundrette was flooded. Therefore, he was forced to walk to the one down the road. As a result, while the on-campus laundrette would have merely taken a bite out of the borrowed tenner, this other one, with its money-sucking detergent dispenser, would gobble up everything he had, minus the penny still in his pocket.

He found the laundrette nearly deserted, which was a welcome change. At times, it had been packed like a tin of sardines (the on-campus facilities were out of order on a semi-regular basis, so Angel had been there at least a dozen times). After obtaining change, Angel shoved his exiguous but stylish wardrobe into a washing machine, started a cycle, carefully folded his bin-liner into a square, and sat down to read.

The harsh neon light afforded optimal illumination, and the hum of driers provided soothing background noise, which helped his fragile concentration as long as the laundrette's front door remained closed, muting the hiss and trundle of passing vehicles. However, whether because of customers exiting or entering, that front door was opened far too frequently, and once again he found himself re-reading the same lines over and over again. After half an hour, he was still on the second page of the introduction. From where he was sitting, the front door was in his peripheral vision, and customer traffic was always accompanied by a gust of air and urban noise. Angel switched to the other side of the steel bench bisecting the shop floor and sat with his back to the machine washing his clothes.

A bearded man in a black leather jacket came in, carrying a large sports bag. A chill swept over Angel as he recognised him from the pub: the thug who'd punched him the other night in front of Amelia. Angel immediately sat forward, elbows on his knees, head tilted down, and hair covering his face. Beard had entered staring straight ahead, so he'd failed to notice his victim; he'd then chosen the washing machine next to Angel's, throwing in his clothes and slamming the door. When he finally dropped himself down onto the bench, quaking it with the impact, the two of them ended back to back: Angel, hunched over; Beard, sprawled with his arms spread across the backrest. Heart thumping, head throbbing, breathing shallow, Angel pretended to read, his mind wholly focused on every nuance of movement, smell, or sound emanating from behind him—the creak of Beard's leather jacket, his lager breath, his potent body odour.

Angel realised that, to avoid detection, he'd have to wait for Beard's washing to end. And, depending on what drier Beard chose afterwards, that he might need to wait out Beard's drying cycle too. But what if the thug had chosen the longest cycle on the washing machine? He, Angel, could maybe leave the shop and come back later. But what if his clothes, having been left unattended for too long, were taken out and dumped on the floor? It'd happened once before. It seemed that his only recourse was to remain where he was, as inconspicuous as possible, and wait however long was necessary, until the thug left. He put his phone on silent.

Twenty minutes passed.

During this time, Beard entertained himself mostly by chatting on the phone. The raucous conversation did nothing for Angel's nerves. It seemed Beard was into boxing and something called 'MMA', and his circle of friends were all gym goers, hyper-focused on fighting—in and out of the ring—and, likely, given Beard's voice, well-versed in performance-enhancing drugs. If only Johannes would come in now to do his laundry! But the Swede was likely at the gym himself.

Angel's washing machine beeped, marking the end of the cycle. Venturing a furtive peek between strands of hair, he saw that Beard's cycle had still a long way to go. He also noticed that Beard's arm, which was still on the back rest, ended in a huge, callus-knuckled, heavily tattooed hand, with possibly the word 'EVIL' across frankfurter fingers. He wondered whether the other hand also spelt 'evil'; he could not imagine it saying 'good.'

Meanwhile, two new customers had come in, followed soon after by a third, with their attendant gust of air and traffic noise. Each arrival meant added pressure for Angel to free his washing machine. He launched WhatsApp and began composing a message for Madison, mainly to distract himself, but, after much typing and deleting, he gave up. However, Amelia had sent him a message ten minutes ago, so he composed a reply:

ANGEL: Here sit I languishing at the Atlantis Laundrette, the university's having gone the way of that continent. Attempting have I been to read *Oroonoko* ere Monday, but boisterous churls my concentration persist in dashing. Surely Corry omnibus or a critical football match are available to keep the mob away. But no! A tidal wave of urges to do laundry has swept the eventide! Hast thou parleyed with Vera?

Amelia did not immediately reply, so, after waiting for five minutes, Angel browsed through his other contacts, hoping to initiate conversations, but he could not think of anything to say to anyone. His stomach warned him against Instagram. Facebook was a graveyard. And Twitter replete with vociferous, offended activists he had no time for, due to their incivility and poor aesthetics.

Yet another customer came in—much more cacophonously than previous ones and leaving the door wide open. Warm air hurricaned out and a racket of idling diesel engines exploded in. Through his curtain of hair, Angel cast a glance in its direction. As luck had it, the newly arriving customer was the big American girl. Pink Hair and Epic Eyebrows waddled in behind her. Another chill ran through Angel's body, and, hunching over even more, he buried his head as deep into his cold hands as their bone structure would allow.

A cockney cab driver hauled in the big American girl's immense bag of laundry and plonked it down. 'Alright, love?' he said. She dragged her bag by the strap to the washing machines facing Angel, selected, of the two available, the one directly opposite to him, and began loading it, huffing and puffing all the while, and occasionally stopping to recover from the exertion. Through his hair Angel saw she'd come with an extra-wide foldable chair of solid construction. Her companions followed immediately after, Pink Hair finding an empty washing machine, Epic Eyebrows complaining that there were no more available.

'Oh, wait. There's one that's just finished here,' said the latter.

Pink Hair said, 'Maybe it's his.'

Angel could not think of a way to make himself smaller.

'Excuse me. Is this your washing,' said Epic Eyebrows.

Angel was relieved her voice had moved somewhere behind him and appeared to address someone else.

Beard momentarily stopped his phone conversation. 'What was that?'

'Is this your washing?'

'No.'

Epic Eyebrows sighed and came around to Angel's side of the bench.

'I bet you it's some *man* who left his clothes there,' said Epic Eyebrows.

'Fucking *men*,' said Pink Hair, adding a moment later, 'Wait. What about him? He seems to have fallen asleep.'

Angel knew she was referring to him. He didn't move a muscle. His nose, on the other hand, refused to cooperate, deciding, at that moment, to leak snot.

'Excuse me . . .' said Epic Eyebrows, addressing him. 'Excuse me . . .' Pause. She tried again, louder. 'Excuse me . . .'

Beard ended his conversation and Angel heard him get up.

'Hey, luv. My cycle's almost done. Five minutes if you want to use the machine.'

'Oh. Thanks,' said Epic Eyebrows.

But Beard didn't leave it there. 'You from the university?' he said. He was standing two feet away from Angel. Like a leaf hanging by a single fibre, Angel trembled. His chest felt so tight he could barely get air. Tickly runny snot exited his left nostril.

Pause. 'Yea,' said Epic Eyebrows.

'No,' said Pink Hair, firmly, hackles raised.

'Oh, you're American too?' said Beard.

Pink Hair didn't reply.

'Yea,' said Epic Eyebrows.

'I have a relative there. Where from?' said Beard, his voice fake friendly.

Angel imagined Beard and Epic Eyebrows having sex later in the evening. The fat girl moaning, breasts and belly jiggling, while the heavily perspiring tattooed thug angrily pounded, her legs making a slapping sound, her head slamming the headrest rhythmically against the wall in some grotty bedsit. But Angel doubted Beard would get his wish.

Pink Hair addressed Angel again. 'Excuse me . . .'

Angel remained still, inwardly cursing. The snot kept travelling down the hair on his upper lip. It was difficult to resist the urge to sniffle. His hands had become ice.

'Excuse me!' repeated Pink Hair, loudly, tapping him on the shoulder.

Yet another customer came in.

'Arizona,' said Epic Eyebrows.

'Oh, what are the odds! That's where my relative lives. What town?' said Beard, fake surprised.

Pink Hair sighed and said, presumably to the big American girl, 'He won't wake up.'

The big American girl replied, 'Just shake him!'

'Excuse me!' tried Pink Hair once more, louder than ever.

'I'll do it,' said the big American girl.

However, the shake didn't come. It seemed their attention had been diverted, although not by Beard, who persisted in chatting up their companion, monosyllabic replies notwithstanding. Footsteps approached Angel, then stopped to reveal two female feet in ballerina flats, toes pointing towards him. *What now?* he thought, scrunching his eyes, his head about to explode with the stress.

'Angel?'

Angel flinched.

Amelia.

He hesitated for just a second, then bolted and fled into the street, head down, leaving his book and clothes behind.

Chapter XXXII

Angel holed up in his room for the next six hours—long enough, in his estimation, for all the laundrette customers to have washed and dried their clothes, even assuming the longest cycles, meticulous folding, careful packing into bags, and delayed hailing of cabs by those unfit for long walks. The first hour he spent cold and shivering in bed, under the blanket, partly due to nerves, partly due to lack of calories. He had missed lunch and dinner, after all. The other five hours he spent listening to music—'Stay High' (Hippy Sabotage Remix) by Tove Lo, even though he disapproved of the drugs and alcohol; 'Sadeness' by Enigma; Liebestraum by Liszt—or watching YouTube videos. Towards the end, he found the courage to open Instagram; he stayed away from Madison's page, for once, and instead browsed through his sister's, whom he didn't follow; she had added many posts since the last time he checked—all powerlifting-related—the most recent being a video from a squat session, posted an hour ago: '200 kg/440 lbs x 3'. Angel had no concept of such numbers or what they implied; he only knew she was stupidly strong. In the intervening time, Amelia messaged several times, but Angel was careful not to open WhatsApp, so that the status of her messages remained unread. She eventually came round to his room and knocked on the door, calling out his name a couple of times, but Angel sat quietly, holding his breath, pretending he wasn't there.

In the wee hours of the morning, he walked back to the laundrette, hoping not only to recover his book and clothes, but also to miss his roommate's inebriated arrival. The streets gleamed from the drizzle, amplifying the fizz of passing vehicles, although now there were few. The tungsten streetlamps lent everything a jaundiced colour, casting expressionist shadows on his dejected solitude.

As Angel approached the laundrette, he found it dark.

'What?' he murmured, and stepped up the pace.

The laundrette was supposed to be open twenty-four hours. But when Angel reached it, he found a sign on the door indicating that it now closed at 10pm.

'Blast!' he whispered.

Angel got close to the glass and, cupping his hands around his eyes, peered inside to scan for his clothes. It was difficult to see from where he was standing, but the door of the washing machine he'd used was open, as were the others'. Empty. Aided by his phone torch, he searched every surface for a basket with his laundry, waiting to be claimed. But all the surfaces were clear.

He muttered a series of expletives.

As things stood, he presently only had the smelly clothes on his back.

Angel let out a long sigh.

Nothing to do but return to the dorm. He'd have to come back in the morning to learn of his wardrobe's fate.

'I'm sure they put it in a back room,' he said to himself.

As he turned to leave, however, he noticed a dark sock on the pavement. Its coloured rhombuses looked familiar. Angel went to it and got on his haunches, to take a closer look. Burlington. He did own three pairs of those, and one with that pattern, given to him by his mother two Christmases ago. It could have been his, it could have not.

Heart pounding, Angel stood and looked around, carefully searching the surrounding pavement, the gutters, and the road. At some distance, he found a pair of cotton trunks. Soiled with mud. But M&S. Navy blue. Those also matched a pair he owned. Again, they could have been his, they could have not.

He rubbed his forehead, emitting another long sigh.

He shook his head. 'No. It . . . er . . . probably fell out of someone's bag. Bound to happen.'

But still, he had an ominous feeling. One item, okay, but two matching his wardrobe?

Angel felt hollowed out. He wondered if he would ever see his clothes again. There was nothing at that moment he desired more. What was he going to do? He could not wear the same outfit for the rest of the term, even if he washed his underwear every day! And what would he wear while they dried on the dorm's radiators? Staring into the distance with bulbous, haunted eyes, he hoped he wouldn't have to waste money on new outfits; that would upset his plans with Madison.

His clothes *had* to be in the laundrette! Yes. They *had* to be. Yet, to find out, he'd have to wait until morning.

Chapter XXXIII

Angel was awoken by clumsy fumbling and falling objects. He opened his eyes to find daylight and his confused roommate searching for something.

Hearing Angel stir, the nameless American, Josh or Chad or whatever, turned to face him. 'Dude—have you seen my watch?'

'Um . . . no . . . I haven't.' Angel didn't care.

'My fucking Rolex!'

Angel rolled over.

Then, remembering, Angel grabbed his phone and checked the time.

Two o'clock in the afternoon.

'Fuck!' he whispered.

Todd, Josh, Chad, Brad, or whatever his name was, grinned at him. 'So he finally wakes up!'

Angel gave him no reply, instead jumping out of the

bed and into his clothes as fast as he could.

'Dude, calm down. It's Saturday!' said the American, chuckling.

Angel still said nothing. The moment he was dressed, he darted out of the room, out of the dorm, off campus, and into the Atlantis laundrette.

He found the attendant.

'Um . . . I accidentally left a load of washing here last night,' Angel said.

The Asian man pursed his lips and shook his head, 'I'm sorry. No. I didn't see anything.'

Angel's heart sank to his feet.

'D-Did anybody leave a basket?'

'No. No. Nobody left anything.'

'Is there nothing in the back room?'

'No, there's no laundry there. Did you bring a bag or a basket?'

'N-No. I brought a bin liner.'

'There was a bin liner. For the rubbish. Someone left it on the bench.'

'B-B-But no clothes? They were in that machine over there. N-Number six.'

'No. No. Nothing. Maybe someone took them out.'

'W-What happens in those cases?'

'If clothes are left in a washing machine, we put them in the drier and we charge the customer when he comes back.'

'A-A-And there was nothing in-in the drier?'

'No. No. Nothing at all. All the machines were empty when we closed last night.'

It occurred to Angel that Amelia might have taken them. She could—he hoped!—have thought there'd been an emergency and, recognising his clothes through the glass door of the washing machine, took them with her back to the girls' dorm. They could be waiting for him there!

'Um . . . my friend was here last night. A girl. Big, curvy. Big dark hair. Could she have taken it?'

'I'm sorry, I don't know. I can't remember. Lot's of people come and go.'

'Um . . . you sure?'

'Wait . . . *big* girl you said? I remember a very *big* girl coming in last night. *Very* big. Big, big, *big* girl.'

'Yes!' Angel pepped up. 'My friend came in soon after. They were standing next to each other.'

'I'm sorry . . . so many people . . . I can't remember . . . just the big girl. I saw her on the monitor. Big, big, *big* girl,' said the attendant, stretching his arms as far out as they would go, for emphasis.

'The monitor? You have CCTV? C-Can I see the video?'

The attendant shrugged. 'Yea, yea. No problem. You can look.'

They went to the back of the shop. A rack of dry-cleaned clothes—coats, suits, and the like—hanging under protective plastic, a dry-cleaning machine, a Hoffmann press, an ironing board, irons, a desk with a phone, binders, paperwork, an old computer, a screen showing the CCTV feed. The attendant sat down at the desk, behind the computer, grabbed the mouse.

'What machine? Six you said? Six?' said the attendant.

'Er . . . yes . . . er . . . number six.' Angel bent down and looked intensely at the screen.

With painful slowness and hesitation, the attendant selected the appropriate camera and went through a series of menus, finally summoning the previous day's video recording.

'What time?'

'I . . . er . . . left around eight o'clock.'

The attendant clicked the appropriate point on a segmented bar along the bottom.

'Okay. You watch,' he said, getting up and taking position by the kettle in the opposite corner of the room. There was a click followed by a rising rumble.

The screen showed Angel, the three girls, and Beard getting up to talk to one them. Then Amelia arriving and Angel fleeing. Then Amelia looking perplexed and leaving shortly afterwards—at a normal pace. Then Beard chatting up Epic Eyebrows and eventually being slapped by the big American girl. Then Beard stepping away with palms in the air, collecting his laundry, and stepping out of sight, while the girls carried on with their laundry. Then someone claiming Beard's washing machine before Epic Eyebrows could get to it. Then Epic Eyebrows seemingly asking around, pointing at washing machine number six, without getting a reply.

There! thought Angel, leaning further forward.

The video now showed Epic Eyebrows angrily pulling all of Angel's laundry out of the machine, dumping it on the floor, and kicking it towards the entrance, until she was out of sight. Then coming back into view thirty seconds later and loading her laundry into number six.

Angel fisted his hands and swore silently.

The attendant re-joined him by the screen, holding a mug of steaming tea. 'Found what you looking for?'

'Yes . . . um . . . I'm afraid I have.' Angel straightened up, his shoulders slumped with the realisation that his clothes—all his shirts, his ties, his socks, his trunks, so carefully selected at the time—were forever gone.

'Anything else?'

'No . . . um . . . that's it . . . thank you.'

'No problem.'
Angel hung his head.
'Good luck.'
The formulaic well-wish brought a tear to Angel's eye.

Chapter XXXIV

Back in his room and having thought of an excuse, Angel opened WhatsApp.

ANGEL: Greetings! Please accept my profoundest apologies about last night and for not replying to thy messages. My sister had a catastrophic medical emergency and a velocious exit was imperative. We spent much of the evening at A&E. Unfortunately, I was unable to return for my laundry before the laundrette closed (no longer 24 hours, apparently). Didst thou, out of kindness for this wretched soul, rescue my laundry?

The single grey tick turned double and then blue.

AMELIA: I'm so sorry to hear that, Angel! Is she OK? What happened? I was so worried about you.

ANGEL: She injured herself at the gym.

AMELIA: OMG! Is it serious?

ANGEL: She tore a ligament while squatting monstrous amounts of weight. But she'll be alright. Now hist!—Dost thou have my clothes? I repaired to the laundrette and they shrugged their shoulders in ignorance.

AMELIA: Oh my goodness! Will she need surgery?

ANGEL: No, the doctor declared that it will heal itself.

AMELIA: Really? My cousin tore a ligament once and it definitely needed surgery. They had to put a screw in his knee

ANGEL: I can only relay the doctor's verdict. Apparently this injury will heal itself.

AMELIA: Maybe ask for a second opinion

ANGEL: I will suggest it. But I'm certain the doctor knows his profession. She had a scan and this was his assessment.

AMELIA: Okay. But I still would get a second opinion. She could end up crippled

ANGEL: I will suggest it. What about my clothes? My frame requires them.

AMELIA: I don't have them, Angel. When you left, I thought something urgent had come up, but assumed you'd be back. I started to worry after you didn't reply to my messages

ANGEL: Didst thou not return to the establishment?

AMELIA: I only came to visit you, so when you left, I went back to the dorm. Are you without clothes?

ANGEL: No, all's well. No worries. It was only a piddling load. Old items, easy to replace. And besides—

Who, with a little, cannot be content
Endures an everlasting punishment.

AMELIA: Oh, Angel, you poet. I'm glad you're taking it so well. At least the damage is minor. Phew! Are you looking forward to tonight?

ANGEL: Tonight?

AMELIA: Yes, we're going to the cinema, remember?

ANGEL: Oh, of course! What time is the showing?

AMELIA: 8.30. Why don't we meet at the Departure Lounge at 7?

His stomach cramped.

ANGEL: Yes, that seems suitable. I will appear at the designated hour and locale.

AMELIA: Please send my well-wishes to your sister

ANGEL: I will.

AMELIA: Actually. Do you have her address? I'd like to send her a card

ANGEL: She moved recently and I don't have her new address. But I'll relay your message.

AMELIA: I can send her a digital card. Do you have her email address?

Angel rubbed his forehead. He inflated his cheeks and released the air slowly.

ANGEL: She doesn't use email. I know, it's weird and bizarre. But she is like that.

AMELIA: Oh. Okay. Well, send her well wishes on my behalf for a swift recovery

ANGEL: I will. I shalt see thee tonight.

AMELIA: See you tonight, Angel

Chapter XXXV

Angel's plan was to wash his clothes in the sink and dry them with a blow-drier, provided he could find someone in the dorm in possession of one. Before that, however, he needed his roommate to get lost—the indignity of his plan was bad enough without a witness. Yet the anthroponymically indeterminate American, Brad or Todd or whatever, having either found or given up the search for his Rolex, appeared in no hurry to go anywhere. He lay in bed, sockless feet in boat shoes, legs in khaki shorts, torso in a college hoodie, head in a baseball cap, watching *Aliens* on his laptop. Surely, he planned to 'hit the booze' again tonight, no? Unless he was planning another party—but, if so, he would have already left to buy the booze from the nearby off-licence or been back from there laden with cans and bottles.

While Angel waited, he found an audio version of *Oroonoko* on archive.org, so he put on his headphones and pressed PLAY, hoping this time he'd make some progress. The loss of his book may well have proven a blessing in disguise; it would be much easier to concentrate with the audiobook. But his mind was too preoccupied with the American's immobility, worries about drying his clothes on time, the prospect of wasting money on a new wardrobe, the seemingly intractable debt with the library, the rumbling of his stomach, and the fact that it would soon be time for dinner, which would force him to choose between eating—for the first time since yesterday morning—or washing and drying his sole remaining outfit. Consequently, though Elizabeth Klett read Aphra Behn's text for him, the words went into one ear and sailed out the other.

After having had to re-wind and re-listen several times, without ever being able to follow the story, Angel stopped the audio. He looked at his roommate, and said, finally:

'Um . . . a-are you not going out tonight?'

'No, bro. I'm taking it easy.' The American kept his eyes on the screen.

'Er . . .'

Angel inwardly cursed him, scrunching his eyes shut.

'You alright dude?' said the American, who had turned to look at him just at that moment.

'Er . . . yes, yes. I'm-I'm fine.'

'Cool.'

As soon as his roommate got back to his film, Angel jumped out of bed, put on a jumper, his velour jacket on top, and headed out.

He went into the bathroom, considering stepping into the shower fully dressed and then drying his clothes with the hand dryer. But with fellow students coming in and out, the procedure would look ridiculous, particularly since he would have to monopolise the hand dryer for at least an hour, if not two or three, and step aside and wait whenever someone needed to use it—which would be often. So that idea was discarded. He could make the long walk to one of the other on-campus laundrettes, but (a) he was already 30p short of what he needed and (b) it was not as if he was going to stand around in his underwear while he waited out the cycles. So that idea was also discarded.

But wait! He still had a fiver on him. He could get deodorant from the nearest corner shop or petrol station and hide in a bush while he sprayed himself all over. Angel marked the eureka moment with a snap of his fingers and, with a spring in his step and Era's 'Ameno' in his ears, walked to a petrol station twenty-five minutes away,

The walk, however, burnt well over a hundred calories, of which, at this point, he was in a deficit by the tens of thousands. Therefore, when he passed the sandwiches, Angel, concave with hunger, could not resist picking one up. The deodorant and the prawn sandwich combined came up to £5 exactly, so he was back down to the one penny in his pocket.

The route took him past a small area of wooded parkland, which, albeit only a couple of trees deep, was sufficient for his purposes, so Angel entered via a footpath and immediately deviated into the shrubbery. He hung his jacket and jumper from a branch, got out his deodorant, and began thoroughly spraying his clothes, including socks and underwear.

Two minutes into the operation, two familiar voices approached above the road noise. Paranoid about detection and enveloped in a nimbus of Lynx, Angel froze and looked through the shrubbery by the iron fence separating the park from the pavement. Just on the other side, he found, to his alarm: Beard. This time the thug was clad in a camouflage t-shirt, which displayed the legs hanging from his shoulders. Said legs were sleeved in tattoos. And even his neck had one. Angel felt the familiar chill run through his body. A gremlin hit his heart like a gong. With shallow breath and alert eyes, Angel sought a view of Beard's companion. And who would have imagined it? It was Professor Mastropasqua!

Wha . . . ? thought Angel, blinking.

The two men walked past, absorbed in grave conversation, and turned to enter the park by another, nearby gate. From his place of concealment, Angel observed the duo stop a few feet into their footpath. Beard's body language, cocky and menacing as it was generally, suggested deferral to the professor. Yet, at the same time, the professor's face was no less menacing. What the subject of their conversation was, Angel could not discern. The men spoke quietly amid too much road noise. Could they be relatives? wondered Angel. His search for a family resemblance, however, proved inconclusive. After forty seconds, the two men laughed, rather hideously, and carried on walking.

Angel rubbed his forehead and stared into the distance.

Whatever. Once sure he was out of hearing and olfactory range, he resumed his spraying in a hurried manner. The nerves, however, had upset his stomach. If the thug was Mastropasqua's criminal nephew or younger brother or what have you, then it was likely that he, Angel, would encounter him again, possibly even on the university campus . . .

CHAPTER XXXVI

Angel made it back to the university just in time for dinner. But still nauseous from the encounter at the park, and, burping prawn sandwich, he left the canteen while he was still in the queue. It was a pity, because for once they weren't serving cheesy pasta and potatoes.

With an hour and a half to kill, and no desire to be in his room with the American, Angel installed himself in The Departure Lounge. He plugged headphones into his ear canals and gave *Oroonoko* another go, once again starting from the beginning.

An explosion of female laughter startled him.

Entering the café were Jae and Alba, a girl he'd had in his 19th Century Novel class. Alba had aced that module, despite arguing vehemently against the Freudian interpretation of Kate Chopin force-fed by the professor—an achievement he could never understand, for people who questioned Freud's validity in literature were typically failed. But the truth was, Alba, the curvy and fiery redhead, got a 100% A, whereas he, who did everything right, got a 60% A.

'Oh, hi Angel,' said Alba, passing him with a radiant smile.

Jae looked at him coldly and said nothing. The two women sat at the neighbouring table.

And that ended his nth attempt at getting through *Oroonoko*, because Alba was a boisterous, cheerful, and constant talker. Moreover, her periodic bursts of laughter sent shockwaves across the café, knocking over glasses, blowing people's hair out of place, and sending paper napkins flying.

Although annoyed, Angel couldn't stop himself from shyly smiling on occasion. This Alba had in warmth what Jae had in frostiness.

'*Angel* was so boring—not you Angel, the novel,' said Alba, talking to Jae. 'I gave up after a hundred pages.'

'Why?' asked Jae.

'I knew what was going to happen from the first sentence.'

Alba gave Jae a summary of the novel, with all the reveals.

'I wouldn't know. I only read classics and non-fiction.'

'That's the opposite of me. I like modern fiction. But I can usually tell the whole novel from the first page, classic or modern,' said Alba. 'That's why it's hard for me to find one I can stick to. Most are so predictable.'

'Let's test that,' said Jae, raising her chin with an air of intrigue. "Have you read *The Castle of Otranto* by Horace Walpole?"

"No."

Jae removed her tablet from her backpack, and using Amazon's Search Inside feature had Alba scan through the first page.

It took but seven seconds.

'Yea. That's about this Lord Mandred, whose sickly son dies before his weeding day. Manfred will want to marry the bride, Isabella, and will divorce his wife because she gave him a sickly son and thus failed in her so-called duties, but Isabella will flee with the help of what will almost certainly be a peasant, who will hide her in a church or somewhere like that. The bride's father will show up, wanting his daughter back and Manfred's castle, which will be the castle of Otranto, of course, to which he will have a stronger claim. So they'll both want to find Isabella. Manfred will end up locking up the peasant, but I bet Manfred's daughter Matilda will in turn end up meeting Isabella in secret and freeing the peasant. Isabella's father will fall in love with Matilda and he and Manfred will agree to marry each other's daughters, but then Manfred will accidentally kill Isabella, maybe because she's disguised and he confuses her with someone else, and the peasant will turn out to be the true heir to Otranto. Manfred will give up and retire to a life of prayer with his ex-wife and the peasant will of course marry Isabella. Easy.'

Jae blinked with understated amazement. 'Correct. Okay. How about *Zanoni* by Edward Bulwer-Lytton. Have you read it?'

'No.'

'Here.'

Alba read for five seconds.

'Yea. That's about . . .' Another summary.

'Correct,' said Jae. 'But you could be lying about

not having read them. So let's find something less well known.'

'Go. *Any* English-language novel,' said Alba, completely confident.

'How about *The Orphan of the Rhine* by Eleanor Sleath.'

'Haven't read it.'

Jae swivelled her iPad. Alba read for six seconds.

'Yea. That's about . . .' Yet another summary.

'Impressive,' said Jae. '*Horrid Mysteries* by Carl Grosse.'

Alba read for eight seconds, and again summarised the novel with ease.

And so it went on for three quarters of an hour, Jae finding ever more obscure titles to test her friend's genius for plot divination; Alba effortlessly accomplishing the task, stumbling only with a couple of penny dreadfuls, *The Mysteries of London,* a 4.5-million-word mammoth written by four different authors, being one of them.

Angel, who had observed the scene in disbelief, suddenly had an idea and butted in. 'Um . . . Alba? C-Can you do *Oroonoko*?'

Alba inhaled to give her reply, but before she was able to speak, Angel heard a happy, high-pitched greeting from behind.

'Oh, hi! We seem to have a literary convention!'

Amelia had just walked in fully made up, perfumed, and in heels.

CHAPTER XXXVII

'Wooooooooooooowwwwwwwwww! You look amaaaaaaaaaaaaaazing!' Alba's face lit up with planet-sized orbs and a Milky Way smile.

Amelia gave a coquettish twirl, showing off her ample figure, hugged in a tight black dress, which pressed her J-cup bumpers into a cleavage. All but the top two inches of pale flesh were covered. Alba further complimented her with a long whoop.

Jae simply stared at Angel, critically evaluating his reaction.

Angel watched Amelia with surprise but said nothing. Students from nearby tables turned to look, the males briefly curious, some females with smiles, others with jealousy.

'So where are you two going?' said Alba, almost announcing it to the whole café.

Amelia said, 'Oh, just to watch a film.'

'Oooooooooooooo! A film, ehhh?' Alba gave her an exaggerated wink.

Amelia laughed. Surrounding students chuckled. Angel stood up, bumping his thigh against the table, sending his phone on a parabolic trajectory to the floor. He bent over to pick it up but moved too quickly and knocked a chair down, adding a crash to the phone's clattering. Jae watched him in frosty silence, lasering him with blue irises.

'Careful, Angel!' said Amelia.

Angel picked up his phone and the chair, his stomach protesting.

'Are you alright?' Amelia put a hand on his shoulder.

'Yes, yes. All good,' said he, quietly, straightening his jacket and combing his hair with his fingers.

'Look, you nearly knocked him flat on his back!' Alba exploded with laughter.

Surrounding students quietly joined in the laughter. All except Jae, who carried on staring at Angel with scorching disapproval.

Smiling from ear to ear, Amelia said. 'Angel, Vera's going to join us. Do you mind?'

'Oh. Really?' he squealed, his eyes nearly falling out of their sockets.

At this, Jae suppressed a laugh, shaking her head. It was the only time she'd been amused.

'No, I'm joking,' said Amelia, against Alba's gales of laughter. 'It's just you and me tonight.'

Alba grinned with raised eyebrows. 'Uh-oh. Someone's upset Vera!'

'Just a tad,' said Amelia.

'What did he do?'

'Apparently . . . he broke her teapot. You know, the

antique one she carried around.'

'Oh, dear!' Alba flapped her hands dramatically. 'Well, Angel, it was good knowing you!' More laughter.

'Any news from your sister, Angel?' asked Amelia.

Angel scratched his temple and shifted. 'Er . . . she's fine.'

'What happened?' said Alba with alarm.

'Angel's sister tore a ligament while training. Angel spent the night with her at A&E.'

'Blimey! Really?'

Angel's blinking accelerated. 'Yes. But she's fine.'

'Not with a torn ligament,' said Alba. 'She'll need surgery for that. Wait, is she in London?'

'Oh, yes, she lives up north, right?' said Amelia.

Angel shifted again. 'Er . . . sh-sh-she was just doing a training session with another powerlifter.'

'And is she still in London? I'd like to go and see her,' said Alba. 'I met her when she stopped by last April,' she added, turning to Jae, 'and man, I tell you, that girl can *eat!*'

'Er . . . no, she's back up north,' said Angel.

Alba frowned. 'Will she need surgery?'

'N-No, the doctor said the ligament will heal itself.'

'That's bollocks,' Alba said. 'She needs to go back to A&E and speak to a proper doctor. Call her now.' She gestured at Angel's phone.

Angel put his phone in his pocket. 'No, no, it's okay. I-It's very minor. The doctor said it won't be necessary.'

'Well, then he doesn't know what he's talking about. Call you sister and tell her to go back to A&E.'

'I-It's fine, it's fine. She had a scan and the doctor said to just rest.'

'If you won't do it, I will,' Alba said, getting her phone out of her bag. 'What's her number?'

'Um . . . I don't have her number,' said Angel, hunching his shoulders, his irises darting furiously between Alba's phone and her face. 'She changed phones recently.'

Amelia frowned. 'Wait, how did you know she was injured then? Did she not call you?'

Angel scratched his temple again. 'Y-Yes, yes, she called, b-but it was a number I didn't know. She called from the gym.'

Jae steepled her fingers. 'Then the number will be on your recents. Check your phone log.'

'Um . . . y-yes, but I won't recognise it.' He pressed his phone down into the bottom of his pocket, as if more firmly to keep it there.

'You don't get many calls. You can work it out from the time stamp,' said Jae.

'Give me your phone, I'll find it,' said Alba, clicking her fingers.

'I-I-I've got to go to the lavatory. I'll be back in a moment,' said Angel, hurriedly making to leave.

'Wait! Leave me your phone. I'll find her number while you go poopies,' said Alba, causing a new wave of laughter.

'I-I-It's okay. I'll be back. I'll be back.'

Angel fled the scene and locked himself in the toilet. He rubbed his head, filled his cheeks with air, and exhaled slowly. After five minutes, he re-joined the girls at the café.

'Better?' said Alba, loud as ever.

'Yes, much better. Thank you.'

'So. Let's contact your sister.'

'Um . . . I've already done it.'

'Oh, so you found her number?'

'Yes, it was in the log, as Jae said.'

'What did she say?'

'She'll go to A&E.'

'Good. *Finally!*'

'Is she on WhatsApp?' Amelia said, 'I'd still like to send her a message.'

'Um . . . I need to check.'

'She'll be on Instagram.' Alba unlocked her phone screen. 'Is she under her real name? Destiny? Let's see.'

Alba launched Instagram and went to the search page.

'Um . . . no . . . she's . . .' said Angel, taking a step towards her, then stopping himself, his eyes zeroed-in on her phone.

'I found her. "84+ kg British and IPF powerlifter". Wow, she's *strong!* Look at that,' said Alba, showing Jae the 200 kg squat for reps video Destiny had posted the previous evening.

'I'm going to send her a DM.'

'Um . . . she never checks her messages on Instagram!' said Angel, speaking high and fast.

'Well, I'm sending her one anyway,' said Alba.

Angel sighed, rubbed his forehead.

'Why are you so stressed, Angel? She only means well,' said Amelia.

'You should have confronted the doctor at A&E last night,' said Jae, without emotion. 'She's stronger than you but you are still her older brother.'

'Don't embarrass him, Jae. He's not a doctor,' said Amelia.

'He should know better,' said Jae.

'Well, he ran straight to her and was with her at A&E the entire evening until they did the scan,' said Amelia. 'I'm sure he was very worried and was focusing on supporting his sister.'

'All the more reason.'

'Oh, Jae. You're so unforgiving sometimes.'

Jae rolled her eyes and turned to Alba, who now wanted to show her one of Destiny's photos.

'Look at that,' said Alba. 'When she was here last April, she did a food challenge with that Beard Meats Food guy. She wiped the floor with him!'

Jae raised an eyebrow.

'Can I see? Angel has never shown me her account,' said Amelia, walking over to the table where Alba and Jae sat. 'Wow,' said Amelia. 'I wish I could get away with eating like that.'

'Well, you know what to do, Amelia,' said Alba, 'Hit the weights!'

Amelia laughed, then looked at Angel. 'Angel, you'd look even sexier if you did some bodybuilding. Ooh, my!'

Angel shifted, 'Um . . . I just don't have time . . . you know, with uni . . .'

'Of course you have time,' said Jae. 'It's not as if you're studying twenty-four hours a day.'

'It's just that . . . er . . .'

'*Listen* to what she's telling you,' said Jae.

'Yea, *listen*. Open your ears,' said Alba, elongating the last three words for emphasis while tugging on her ears and golfballing her eyes.

'You're so funny, Alba,' said Amelia.

'You'll need muscles to face Vera, Angel,' added Alba, instigating yet more laughter.

'Oh, let him be,' said Amelia. 'He's clever. He'll come round.'

'This shouldn't even be an issue, Angel,' said Jae. 'You should have already been building muscle without having to be told.'

'Jae. Come on. Enough,' said Amelia.

Chapter XXXVII

Angel burped into a fist. Prawn and mayonnaise. The sandwich was still brawling with his stomach, a malignant refusal to capitulate.

Chapter XXXVIII

As they stepped out of the building, Amelia grabbed Angel's arm and bent it to a ninety-degree angle, playfully reminding him to offer support, something he had always done for Madison.

'Oh, sorry,' he said.

Angel only half-registered Amelia pressing herself against him while they walked; her soft plushness was pleasant, like her perfume, but he felt like a flimsy raft dragged along by a luxury ocean liner. Exacerbating this feeling were unwashed jeans in constant need of hitching up and a jacket that, though expensive, he could no longer fill. Madison was shorter and slight in build, and, back in the Spring, he had been a bit heavier and yet to spend all his money on their dates and her presents.

'How's Madison?' asked Amelia, in a casual tone.

Angel sighed, 'Er . . . not so good. She's met a new friend.'

'Oh. Who is he?'

'No, not like that. A female friend.'

'A female friend. Like she's experimenting?'

'No. Not like that. She's just horrible.'

'How so?'

'Just . . . vulgar and crass and full of angry feminism.'

Amelia laughed. 'You think she's going to turn Madison into an angry feminist?'

'No, I hope not. But you've seen what her other friends managed to do already. She's drinking beer out of bottles!'

'Oh, Angel,' said Amelia, squeezing his arm.

'They've probably introduced her to this girl, and now this girl is going to introduce her to even worse girls.'

'Do you think Madison is easily influenced?'

'Um . . . I-I hope not. B-But you know what it's like, with peer pressure and all of that.'

'Have you noticed any change?'

'Er . . . no . . . er . . . not in her messages. Only in her Instagram posts.'

'Is she posting angry feminist memes?'

'Um . . . no. Just the picture I showed you the other day and a picture of her new friend.'

'Can I see?'

'Er . . . maybe later.'

'Go on, let me see.'

'Er . . . no . . . it's okay . . . later . . . I'm not in the mood. It's too upsetting.'

'Well, I'm not a feminist,' said Amelia, offering a smile.

Angel said nothing.

'You can always talk to me, Angel.'

'Er . . . yes. Thank you.'

'I mean, you can always talk to me, about Madison or anything else.'

'I-I know. Thank you.'

The prawn sandwich insisted on being inconvenient, and the fresh nocturnal air supplied no relief. Even the vibration from humming taxis aggravated his condition. Angel discretely burped prawn and mayonnaise gas into his free fist, realising a mild malaise had taken possession of his body.

'Are you alright, Angel?'

'Y-Yes, I'm fine.'

'You don't look so good.'

'No . . . yes . . . I'm fine.'

'Are you looking forward to the film?'

'Yes . . . it should be good.' The truth was, Angel had no idea of what film they were going to see; if Amelia had told him, he couldn't remember.

'I loved the book.'

'I'm sorry?'

'The book. Donna Tartt's book. The one on which the film is based.'

'Ah, yea, of course.'

'You might like it. She tends towards maximalism. Doesn't that author you like, Alexander Theroux, write in that style?'

'Er . . . yes. *Darconville's Cat* is a masterpiece.'

'So you keep saying. I need to read it. So much to read, Angel!'

'Yes . . . more books than there's time.' His voice trailed off.

As they descended into the London Underground,

the corridor reverberated with the oscillating drone of a busker's didgeridoo. The long-dreadlocked musician wore an elegant pinstriped shirt in brown and navy blue, clashing with his grimy and ripped combat trousers, slouchy knitted hat, and decrepit Doc Martens.

'Angel? Did you see the shirt that man was wearing?'

'Er . . . no. W-What about it?'

'It's just like a shirt you have.'

'Oh, really?' Angel turned to look behind him.

The shirt could well have been formerly his. He remembered adding one like it to his laundry bag yesterday evening. Seeing it again on someone else was a stab in the heart. Less because he'd chosen it with great care when he bought it—although that mattered too—than because Madison loved it, had caressed it, and even buttoned it on one occasion. He had fond memories of strolling through Kensington Gardens while wearing it in her company some five months ago; they had walked all the way to Guste Remo, the Italian restaurant in Porchester Road, not far from Khan's, where they had dined on another occasion. He pushed the memory away, rejecting the thought of food.

'Yes. W-What an amazing coincidence,' he said, feigning relaxed detachment.

He felt violated.

They made their way to the platform. It was packed with humans. To get a seat on the next train, Amelia suggested they squeeze their way to the edge of the platform. The next train was in seven minutes. Amelia fused herself to his side, clinging tightly to his arm, which was by now going numb; she was so much heavier than he, however, that he was being pushed off balance, and constantly having to press in the opposite direction was serving the war aims of the rotten prawns.

'You look hot, Angel,' said Amelia, 'Why don't you take off your jumper?'

'Um . . . I'm actually cold,' he replied.

'But you have a sheen on you.'

'I-I-I don't want to carry the jumper.'

'Do you want me to carry it for you?'

'No, no. No need.'

'Because I will, if you need me to. It's not a problem, Angel.'

'No. Really. No need.' Angel's legs were turning into polystyrene; a mild headache, which had kicked in during their walk, was also gathering momentum.

'You sure?'

'Yes, yes, I'm sure,' he said, distant, his focus shifting ever more towards his symptoms.

A gust of warm air blew across the tunnel and Angel's hair flew across his face. The clattering train shot towards the platform with a tremendous downward whine.

'Blimey. Look at that old train!' said Amelia.

Angel pushed his hair aside with his free hand and witnessed the approach of a grimy train of unpainted aluminium alloy, fronted by three small windows, the middle of which was part of a door, and above which was a back-lit black and white sign in an outmoded sans-serif font. Its two headlights were on the side farthest from the platform. The train stopped with a screech. A deafening hiss and rumble followed as the doors opened, revealing a dimly illuminated interior with windows about a quarter of the size of the normal trains'. The high-pitched whine and low, rapid chugging of the air compressors reverberated along the platform.

'Wooden floors,' said Amelia, as they stepped into the carriage. 'How quaint! This is exciting! she giggled, tugging at his arm.

But there was no time to dwell on details, as the marabunta on the platform flowed into the carriage like a mud slide, pushing the couple into the middle, where they were fortunate to find a pair of adjacent seats. People kept hopping onto the carriage for what seemed an eternity, compressing the ones standing ever tighter and blocking whatever little ventilation the crack-opening windows allowed. Air molecules already accelerating due to rising temperatures were turbo-charged by a gaggle of skinny girls who took position in front of Angel and his date; said girls, dressed for a hen night in pink and white, with hairbands sporting springed-mounted penises, the bride-to-be wearing a fake veil and a learner's plate, and every other hand holding open bottles of prosecco, emitted a cacophony of chatter, squeals, laughter, whooping, and strident banter, all of it enveloped in a cloud of perfume and alcoholic fumes.

'Look, Angel, a hen party! How cute!' said Amelia, giggling.

'Er . . .' Angel mumbled.

To the mounting headache, chills, heat, and nausea were now added stomach cramps. Angel tilted his head forward to seek refuge in his hair. Amelia fastened her hand around his arm even more firmly.

Angel imagined Madison turning up at their wedding marred by an arm tattoo that he'd been unaware of, and Syd being one of the bridesmaids, ringing another discordant note with her Doc Martens, constant swearing, and vocal fry, and prawn cocktails being served and a wedding cake being displayed that was, in fact, made of prawn sandwiches and pink champagne.

The hen party girls grew rowdier by the second, drowning out the relentless clattering and creaking of the train once in motion. Punctuated by swigs of prosecco, their banter moved to commenting on each other's cleavages. One of them, with little more than mosquito bites, was targeted by the others, who were displaying mangoes of varying sizes. Flinty-eyed Mosquito Bites gave as good as she took, however.

'Well, I'd rather have bites than carry boulders on my chest like that *fat* girl there!' she said, pointing at Amelia.

Although Amelia continued to stare into space, her dropping jaw registered her shock. So did her hand, which, clamped around Angel's meagre bicep, nearly ripped it off the bone as her cheeks turned into halogen heaters.

Angel, however, did not respond, having the more immediate concern of holding on to his stomach's contents. In fact, attributing Amelia's vicelike grip to the bouncy train ride, he seized on the localised pain to distract himself from his gastric issue.

But the gremlins were only getting started. Two stops away from their destination, the train halted, mid tunnel. The hen party carried on unabated; the catatonics around them carried on staring into space; Amelia: same; Angel carried on with his capillary seclusion.

Long minutes passed.

'What time is it, Angel?' said Amelia, speaking into his ear.

Digging his phone out of his jean's pocket required disproportionate effort; his arm moved like a sloth's. Rather than speaking, he showed Amelia the time displayed on his lock screen.

'We're going to be late,' she worried.

Angel said nothing. He dropped his phone into his breast pocket.

'Are you okay, Angel?'
'Uh?'
'Are you okay?'
'Um . . . yes . . . I-I'm fine . . .'
'Are you sure?'
'Yes . . . I just . . . need fresh air.'
'But are you sure?'
'Yes . . .'
'Because we can go back and do this another day if you want.'
'N-N-No . . . I'm sure.'
'You don't sound like it.'
'I-I'm . . . fine. I promise.'
'You're *sure* sure.'
'Y-Yes . . .'
'Okay.'
Pause.
'But you're sure?'
'Yes . . . I'm sure . . . I just . . . need . . . a bit of air . . .'
'Okay, Angel. But let me know if you change your mind.'
'Okay . . .'
The crackle and rattle from the public announcement system—'This is your driver. I apologise for the delay. I have not been given a reason yet, but there appears to be a signalling problem ahead of us. I will give you an update as soon as I know more. I hope it will be a matter of minutes. Thank you.'
'Oh, dear,' said Amelia.
Angel groaned inaudibly.
More minutes passed.
The hen party remained unaffected by the delay, the announcement having simply served as fuel for

a raft of banter and jokes; the girls were too drunk to have an accurate sense of time. Down the carriage, male voices exploded with their own excitement, banter, and jokes peppered with loud and regular detonations of laughter.

Angel rubbed his head, which had become a cauldron of fever and strange imaginings. The multiple vectors of discomfort were getting to the point where, if the train failed to get moving again soon, his brain would explode like in a scene from *Scanners*. He could imagine the veins on his nape getting fatter and fatter.

Yet more minutes passed.

Crackle and rattle from the PA again. 'Just an update on the delay. It seems the signalling issue is now being dealt with, but it will take five to ten minutes for the engineers to resolve it. We'll get moving again as soon as we're given the go ahead.'

'Oh, dear . . . we're going to be so late' said Amelia. 'What's the time, Angel?'

Angel showed her the lock screen of his phone again; 8.35pm.

'Well, at least there's twenty minutes of ads,' Amelia said.

It wasn't until ten minutes till nine that the train resumed its journey, and another eight before it reached the station. By this time, Amelia had become agitated about their film showing. Holding on to Angel, she led the way out of the station and into the cinema theatre, which was five minutes away on foot. Angel had grown so torpid and sluggish, and Amelia in such a hurry, that he was practically flown like a kite. The forced pace didn't help to appease his stomach. Nevertheless, no film date being complete without food, Amelia still joined the queue at the snack kiosk.

'Please get me a large nachos, a large hotdog, a large cherry Icee, a medium popcorn, and whatever you like,' she said, as if trying to break the world record for words spoken per minute. 'I'm going to pop over to the ice cream counter. I'll be back.'

Angel's rubber legs could barely hold him aloft. The food counter appeared to move sideways—or the floor to spin, he wasn't sure.

The man in front paid for his and his date's snacks, grabbed them, and moved on.

'HowcanIhelpyou?' said young man serving, apparently after Amelia's record.

'Er . . . could I have . . . er . . . a-a large . . . er . . . . hotdog . . .'

'Anythingelse?'

'. . . er . . . a large nachos . . .'

'Cheeseorsalsadip?'

Angel could barely understand him. 'I-I'm sorry?'

'Cheeseorsalsadip?'

'Oh . . . er . . . um . . .' Angel turned to look for Amelia, but she was too far and with her back to him. '. . . er . . . cheese . . .'

'Jalapeños?'

'Um . . . er . . .' Another look towards Amelia. She was still queuing, and, for all that mattered, a lightyear away. 'No . . . er . . . no.'

'Anythingelse?'

'Um . . .' Angel frowned, trying to remember. 'A . . . a . . . um . . . a large Pepsi.'

'Anythingelse?'

'A-A-A large popcorn . . .'

'Anythingelse?'

'Um . . . a-a small popcorn . . .'

'Cheaperifyouorderalargedrinkandpopcorntogether.'

'Oh . . . er . . . um . . .' Yet another glance at Amelia. Still out of reach. 'O-okay. I'll have a . . . large popcorn and . . . Pepsi.'

'Anythingelse?'

'Ah . . . no.'

'Thatwillbefortytwopoundsninetyfour.'

'Um . . . oh, balls . . .' Angel cast a fourth glance at Amelia, his brow corrugated with worry. He nearly fell over due to the speed of the floor's spin. He sighted Johannes traversing the food court on his way out, having come out of a film. Johannes saw Amelia, though he didn't speak to her, and then him; surmising that Angel was on a date with Amelia, the Swede' beard split with a grin as he gave him a thumbs up.

'Sir?'

'Ah . . . um . . . just a moment . . . um . . . my friend . . .' Angel said, feebly pointing a finger towards Amelia.

'Cashorcard?'

'Er . . . um . . . um . . .' Angel's heart was now racing. He rubbed his forehead. A fifth glance at his date, finally ordering her ice cream. Johannes had gone.

'Sir? There'speoplewaiting.'

'Ah . . . yea . . . just a moment . . . my friend . . . my friend . . .' Angel pointed again, barely able to raise his arm to do so.

Angel heard sighs and tuts behind him.

'Doyouwanttocancel?' The kiosk assistant seemed suddenly fed up.

'No . . . ah . . . just a minute . . .'

'Sir, Ican'tkeepcustomerswaiting.'

'J-J-Just a minute . . . please . . . it won't be a minute . . .' A sixth glance at Amelia as she watched her scoops being pressed into a cone.

'Sir, doyouwanttocancel?'

'I-I-I just . . .'

At last, Amelia returned. She put her ice cream on the counter and stared at angel with a smile, waiting.

Hyper-aware of the people behind him, Angel spoke in a soft voice that barely left his body.

'Do you mind . . . paying . . . you said . . .'

'I'm sorry, what, Angel?' said Amelia.

'Do you mind . . . paying . . .' Angel pointed weakly at the mountain of snacks and drinks on the counter.

'Oh, of course, Angel! Of course I'll pay!' said Amelia, loud and clearly enough for everyone to hear.

Angel heard snorted male laughter behind him. In turn, the kiosk attendant smiled contemptuously and shook his head, his attention already diverted to Amelia while she dug up her card.

'Thankyouenjoythefilm,' He smiled at Amelia, but ghosted Angel.

Angel was tasked with carrying one of the popcorns, the nachos, the hotdog, and one of the drinks, while Amelia carried the rest. To accomplish this, Angel had to balance the nachos and the hotdog on top of the bucket of popcorn, and then hug that with one arm, while holding the drink in his other hand. His gorge rose at the smelly hotdog steaming under his nostrils. The interaction with the kiosk assistant had drained most of his energy reserves, so he barely had enough strength left to reach their seats. The film had only just started. Amelia had selected the two seats nearest to the isle.

Sitting down was a delicate operation, particularly as Amelia filled her seat completely and had to manoeuvre with her handbag and snacks, and then receive the food Angel was holding for her, before she could settle down, bumping Angel's left elbow numerous times in the process, which nearly caused spillages and loss of food. Just as they'd managed to settle down, however, two women arrived requiring access to seats further down their row, necessitating Angel and Amelia to stand to get through. Alas, one of the women, bumped Amelia's hotdog-holding hand, which dumped the hotdog, sauces first, onto Angel's jumper.

'Oh, I'm so sorry, Angel!' whispered Amelia, all shock and alarm. 'Oh, dear! Oh, dear!'

'Oopsies!' said the woman, quietly, putting her hand to her mouth as she realised what'd happened.

Angel looked down to find his last remaining jumper and the lapel of his velour jacket covered in ketchup, mustard, mayonnaise, and crispy onions; the sausage, which had remained attached to his lapel via the sauces, rolled off at that moment, spreading the damage onto his jeans and suede shoes.

'Oh, no!' said Amelia, momentarily paralysed.

Angel, too, was paralysed, despite having only partial awareness of the incident; he was mostly concerned with not collapsing on the floor.

'Here, let me clean you up!' said Amelia, searching her handbag for a packet of tissues.

The clumsy woman who'd bumped her, and who was mostly indifferent, used this as a cue to move on.

'Oi, cunts! Sit down!' shouted someone two rows behind.

Amelia and Angel sat down.

Once she'd dug out the tissues, she wiped Angel's clothes as quickly as she could.

'Are you okay, Angel?' she whispered.

'Yea . . .' he breathed out; he was only mildly conscious.

'I'll wash your jumper when we get back to the dorm. And I'll pay for your jacket to be dry cleaned. Just leave it with me, okay?'

Angel only managed a nod. His saliva production had ramped up. He tried to suppress the stomachal insurrection with what little might he had left. Maybe the prawn sandwich would give up, finally broken down by digestive acids. Growing hot, he took off his jacket and his jumper, folded the jumper, placed it carefully by his feet, and put his jacket back on.

The film passed before his eyes in a confused jumble of brash colours and noise. He only caught snippets of dialogue, disjointed and instantly forgotten. But his mind could not stop focusing on Amelia as she munched through her ice cream, her nachos, and her seemingly bottomless bucket of popcorn. He couldn't touch his and wondered why he'd ordered anything at all. Autopilot. God knows what would've happened if the kiosk had offered prawn canapés. And Amelia was also at the wedding, but she had invited Vera and Vera was still angry about the teapot, objecting to the wedding on the grounds that Angel would break all the crockery, while Jae also stood to object that Angel had treated Amelia badly and therefore shouldn't be allowed to marry Madison, while Madison's hair was suddenly dyed green and Epic Eyebrows was her maid of honour and his parents disapproved of his vulgar marriage and guests.

'Ready?' said Amelia.

'Eh?'

The screen was running the credits. The lights were on and people were leaving the projection room.

'Poor Angel, he fell asleep.' Amelia reassured him with a smile. She was standing and people were waiting behind her to get out.

'Oh, sorry . . . I . . .'

Angel stood.

But he nearly collapsed, his flubber legs unable to support him.

'Oops!' said Amelia, grabbing hold of him. 'Are you alright?'

Before he could reply, however, his stomach expelled the insurgency of chewed prawn, bread, and mayonnaise, forcefully and unexpectedly, along with the Pepsi he'd been sipping throughout the film. The bilious torrent of projectile vomit splashed the front of Amelia's dress.

She screamed.

Chapter XXXIX

A crunch.
Crunching.
Crackling.
A crunch.
Crunching.
Crackling.

Angel opened his eyes to a white ceiling.

He turned. Todd or Josh or Brad or Chad or whatever, lay in bed, YouTube-playing laptop on the belly, crunching his way through a bag of Doritos. He was watching LA Beast 'chugging' down a giant glass of beer aided by a power drill. On the floor near him, the American had already managed to build up a pile of empty bags, sandwich boxes, wrappers, and discarded bottles of water, Lucozade, and Coca-Cola.

Angel checked the time.

Three o'clock in the afternoon.

As he sat in bed, he became aware of the ephemerality of his body, as if it were made of air and polystyrene. Hollowed out. A headache hammered the top of his head. His throat felt like pumice stone.

'Dude . . . you're skin and bones! It's fucking freaky!' said his roommate. 'Here,' he added, tossing him a bag of crisps.

Angel was too slow to catch it and the bag hit his chest, collapsing his ribcage and knocking the air out of his lungs. Chad or whatever went back to his YouTube.

Amelia.

Oh, God! Angel thought.

Images of his friend screaming, a parabola of vomit on her black velvet dress. Of her, coming out of the ladies looking like a panda bear. Of her, sobbing all the way home. Of her, bidding him goodbye with a kindly but hurt and shy half-smile, pink cheeks still running with tears.

The poor girl!

Elbows on knees, hair over the face, he held his head for a long time.

He could not get Amelia's sobbing and wounded expression out of his mind. She had, he had to admit, the sweetest, warmest, kindest face imaginable—not classically beautiful like Madison, of course; Madison would always be the goddess; but Amelia was always pleasant and reassuring to look at—with her big eyes, round cheeks, and open smile. The picture of innocence. And vomiting all over that, even if accidentally, was like stomping on a rose. Nowhere in literature had there ever been an errant knight behaving as he had, even when mortally wounded or under a spell.

What a *pillock* he was.

He had to make things right.

Angel stood up gingerly, put on his shirt, pulled up his jeans, and fastened his belt. Said jeans, however, fell straight down to the floor. The belt would require further perforation. He used a tack and a Bic pen to punch a new hole, although the strength required was almost beyond his capabilities. Thankfully, the leather was lambskin. He looked for his jumper, his jacket being fit only for the bin. But the jumper was nowhere to be seen. It was not over his chair, nor by the foot of his bed, nor on the floor, nor in the chest of drawers, nor in the armoire.

Where is it? he wondered, his frowning eyes darting around the room.

The cinema.

He'd left it at the cinema.

On the floor.

Angel sighed.

He grabbed his jacket and examined the lapel. The crusty, dried up red, white, and yellow stains stood out disgustingly against the hickory brown velour. He'd have to scrape them off with a Bic pen and wear the ruined garment until he could fund a professional dry clean. Which would be another expense he could have otherwise avoided, because Amelia would certainly not pay for it now. It looked as though his first wages, and maybe several after, had already been spent before he'd received them.

But for now, there was a more important matter to worry about.

His heart was committed to Madison, but it would be unseemly and most ungentlemanly not to right the wrong of the previous evening. Not doing so would send a bad signal to Madison anyway. And it would make him feel base, uncouth, and unworthy of his American damsel.

So, prompt and splendid corrective action was imperative.

Deciding to go just in his shirt, though he felt woefully underdressed for the occasion, Angel made his way to the girl's dorm. But in the gardens, walking in the opposite direction, he encountered Jae. She stopped him.

'Amelia doesn't want to see you,' she said.

'Um . . . I just wanted to apologi . . .'

'Amelia doesn't want to see you.'

'But . . .'

'Leave her alone.'

'B-But . . .'

'Leave her.'

Chapter XL

At dinner time, Amelia didn't show. From the moment they started serving to the moment they closed, Angel sat at the table with the clearest view of the entrance, his eyes blue and white 12-inch vinyls, scanning every face that came in. He barely touched his pasta and cheesy potatoes; even if his stomach had not still been delicate, even if he'd not been ready to bolt in case the big American girl walked in, nerves had clamped it shut.

He'd sent a few WhatsApp messages, expressing his desire to discuss the previous evening and meet to offer his apologies in person, but the messages had been read without a reply.

He had looked for Alba, but not found her anywhere on campus. At least he had not come across Vera. That was a level of terror too exquisite to contemplate.

If Amelia had barricaded herself in a fortress of closed doors, calculated absence, ignored messages, and angry friends, his only recourse, he reasoned, would be the battering ram of poetry. Angel collected from his room a notepad and a sheet of parchment-like paper out of a ream reserved for epistles to Madison—he hesitated, even then—and went to the library, hoping to find inspiration in the classics. He planned to construct an intricate web of clever allusions and swooning metaphors, knowing that Amelia would respond, as she was an avid reader of verse. And it was better, he also knew, to do it the old-fashioned way, with pen and paper, and physical books, complete with their dusty scent, yellowed paper, and old fonts, rather than sterile laptops and online sources.

'Time's running out, Angel,' said the librarian as he entered her kingdom.

'Yes . . . yes . . . I'll pay soon,' he said, trying to get past without paying the toll.

'I can take your debit card now.'

Angel stopped. 'I-I-I'm sorry, I don't have it on me.'

'Cash?'

'I-I'm sorry, I only have a penny.'

'I'll take the penny.'

'M-M-Maybe later.'

'The longer you leave it, the worse it will be.'

'Yes, I know. I promise I'll pay.'

'It will go to debt collection otherwise.'

'Um . . . um . . . that won't be necessary. I promise!'

'And you'll be banned from the library even if you later pay in full.'

'Eh?'

'If you repeatedly fail to pay your fines, and we are

forced to collect payment, then you can't be trusted and you get banned.'

'But . . .'

'No buts. You know the rules.'

'Okay. I'll pay soon. I promise. I promise.'

'I'll be waiting.'

Angel made to resume walking.

'*And* the debt collection agency is just an email away,' added the librarian. 'Remember that.'

'Yes, I know, I know.'

'And you don't want bailiffs at your door with a court order.'

'No, no, I really don't. I'll pay. I really promise.'

'Okay.'

Angel waited.

'You may go,' ruled the librarian, getting back to her computer.

Angel found a remote desk and surrounded himself with volumes of poetry. Edmund Spenser, John Hoskins, Ben Johnson, Christopher Marlowe, Alexander Pope, John Donne, William Blake, Lord Byron, Samuel Taylor Coleridge, John Keats, Percy Bysshe Shelley, William Wordsworth. Also rhyming dictionaries, dictionaries of archaic and obsolete words, a word thesaurus, an emotion thesaurus, and *The Compact Oxford English Dictionary*, which compressed all twenty volumes into two and came with a magnifying glass. With Debussy's *Claire de Lune* playing on his headphones, Angel laboured on his apologia, forgetting bladder and stomach, ignoring coughs and conversations, disdaining clock and phone. His head swirled with words, similes, metaphors, syllables, rhymes, prosody, allegories, allusions, alliterations, transliterations, anaphoras, metonyms, and synecdoches. He revised and polished his verse, obsessively, compulsively, altering and improving, constructing and reconstructing, adding and cutting back.

Hours flew by.

By the time he was ready to write the definitive version—in swirly calligraphy—the sky outside was growing light. Angel completed the transcription and headed for the girl's dorm. His plan was to sneak in and slip his poem under Amelia's door. Along the way, while traversing the gardens in the crisp morning air, he picked a white rose from a flower bed. The rose he later attached to Amelia's door handle by wrapping it with the long stem. He pricked his fingers with the thorns, but he welcomed it as part of his penance, a form of self-flagellation. Fortunately, though some of the girls were up for their morning classes—the ones who saw him, who were in bathrobes with their heads wrapped in towels, all treated him to scowls, frowns, and disapproval—Amelia was still in her room, and none of her angry friends were around to bar him access.

Chapter XLI

'Angel. What evidence can we find of Manfred's repressed homosexuality?' said Professor Turner.

'Um . . .' Angel rubbed his forehead. He'd completely forgotten about his assignment for The Gothic Novel.

'Yes?'

'Er . . . um . . . I'm sorry, I didn't read the book. I was really busy . . .'

'Ah of course, with the board meetings and all that.'

The classroom burst out laughing.

But at that moment Angel could only think of Amelia. During breakfast, he had spied into the canteen from the washing-up room and not seen her at all. He worried she may have slipped past him, contriving to stay out of his line of sight and eat her breakfast in the upper level. Proof, if true, that his efforts had failed.

Then, after only managing two bites of dry toast (all his co-workers had left him), he had encountered Alba on his way to class.

'How was your date, Angel?' she had said.

'Oh . . . um . . . not so good. I had food poisoning.'

'I see.'

'Um . . . Amelia doesn't want to see me,' Angel had said.

'Try bringing some flowers and not vomiting next time,' Alba had replied.

'I-I did bring flowers!'

'No, I mean *before*. To the *date*. Not after you've vomited your guts out.'

'Oh . . . it's just that we were only going to the cinema . . .'

'What? Are you blind?'

Angel had not known how to reply.

'You're gonna have to do *a lot* more than just write a poem and steal a flower from the garden. And I mean *a lot* more,' Alba had said, pealing back her eyelids for emphasis.

'C-C-Can you speak to her?' he had said.

'Are you joking?'

'No . . . why . . . er . . .'

'Angel: if you want to be forgiven, you're going to have to go there and beg on your *knees!*'

'But she won't see me.'

'Oh, for goodness' sake. *Think!*' she had said, tapping her forehead. '*Think!*'

'. . . so the crumbling castle and the prophecy about a Lord grown too large to inhabit it could symbolise rampant financial speculation and the inevitable bursting of economic bubbles . . .'

Yes, and on the financial side, because of his poetry

and subsequent excursion to the girl's dorm, he'd been late for his morning shift, which had resulted in his pay being docked again. At least the supervisor had not sacked him altogether. Angel wondered if he would *ever* see any money again, besides that remaining penny.

'. . . more problematic still is the women's devotion to their husbands and fathers . . .'

Angel's phone vibrated in his pocket.

CHAPTER XLII

A message from his sister.

DESTINY: What's this about you telling people I'm in hospital with a torn ligament?!?

Angel closed WhatsApp without replying.

After his class, he went to the canteen and searched for Amelia, but again failed to find her. Was she not eating?

He again seated himself where he could monitor all arrivals and departures. And he again stayed for the duration. The butterflies in his chest, and the cramps in his stomach, however, kept him from ingesting more than a bite of potato and a forkful of cheesy pasta. And even that modest portion made him sick.

On the way to the girl's dorm, Angel stopped by the library. No Amelia. He scanned the gardens. No Amelia. He swung by The Departure Lounge. Still no Amelia.

But Vera was seated at a table, reading. She had a new china teapot and a matching cup and saucer. Angel reasoned that, since she was Amelia's friend, apologising to her in person would be a step in the right direction. He braced himself and approached her, heart pounding.

'Hi, Vera. I-I-I'm r-really s-sorry about the other d-d-day,' he said, hands freezing in his pockets, head bowed in penitence.

Vera carried on reading, as though he weren't there.

'I-I-I'm really s-sorry,' he insisted.

No change.

'I'm r-r-really, r-really s-s-sorry.'

Vera turned the page and carried on reading.

'Um . . .' Angel hesitated, hardly able to breathe, his body swaying, operated by two virtual strings, one pulling him out of the café, another pulling in the opposite direction, forcing him to stay.

Vera remained unacknowledging.

'I'm so s-sorry,' he mumbled.

No change.

Angel left, feeling one inch tall, and headed for the girl's dorm.

He knocked on Amelia's door, softly.

Silence.

He knocked again.

Silence.

He knocked a third time, a little louder.

Silence.

He put his ear to the door.

'Oi! What are you doing?' said an angular brunette with a tattooed upper arm.

'Er . . . I'm just looking for my friend.'

'You're not allowed in here. Piss off.'

'It's just that . . .'

'*PISS OFF!*'

'No, she's my friend! It's just that . . .' he said, speaking quickly.

'I'm calling security.'

'No, no, no need. She's my friend. Amelia is my friend . . .'

The girl started shrieking at him at the top of her lungs, bending over with the vehemence, veins swelling on her neck, face turning red, phone held to her ear: 'PIIIIIIIIISSSSSSSSSSSS OOOOOOOFF!!! PISSSS OOOOOOFFFFFFF!!!'

Angel ran.

Chapter XLIII

Angel retreated into his room.

The American, Todd or whatever, was thankfully gone.

A knock on the door.

Amelia?

He opened fast.

Saïd.

'You pay me back on Friday, right?' Saïd asked.

Behind Saïd, the Brylcreemed Camaro walked out of their room, wearing a metallic patterned jacket, a tiger-print shirt, and a money-print tie; he was carrying a box and seemed to be headed for the post office. Camaro noticed Angel and lifted his chin at him.

'Ah, yes . . . on Friday,' said Angel.

'Alright, my friend. See you on Friday.'

'Yes . . . see you on Friday.'

Angel closed the door.

Another knock. Angel opened a crack.

Saïd: 'Friday, yes?'

Angel: 'Yes, Friday.'

'Okay, my friend.'

Angel closed the door.

Saïd's visage made him think of the cover illustration of the Penguin Classics edition of *Oroonoko*—a detail showing the head of King Gaspard from *The Adoration of the Magi* by Hieronymus Bosch.

'Oh, balls!' he whispered.

His 17th-Century Lit class was the following day, and he was yet to even begin the book.

He pulled out his phone, intending to read the online version. He would start now, and if he read nonstop, he'd be able to finish it and arrive prepared.

But before doing that, lying down in bed, he checked Instagram. To calm down.

Or so he told himself.

And that was the end of his good intentions, because Madison had posted another image. The caption read: 'I did a thing.' In the image, it was Madison, except she was putting on an Instagram kissy face, three quarters turned, and her hair was green.

Green!

Angel winced and his arm jerked as if from electric shock. His phone fell on the bed.

He covered his face with his palms and bent over, eyes scrunched.

He remained in that posture for a long time.

When he sat up, he rested his forearms on his thighs and let his head hang like loose fruit, hair covering his face.

He remained in that new posture for even longer.

It was that Syd! *She* put her up to it!

Angel felt nauseous.

He needed money *urgently*. He needed to cross the Atlantic and stop the madness before it got worse! He needed to rescue his paramour from that bewitching sorceress, that succubus, that Circe! To right that wrong and prise Madison from the ogress's claws before she was lost. To fill the coffers quickly and move forward his departure.

He picked up his phone, closed Instagram with a flick, launched WhatsApp, and found his mother in the contacts.

Extreme conditions demanded extreme responses.

His finger hovered over the digital keyboard, ready to type.

But, instead of typing, seconds passed.

Then more seconds.

And yet more seconds.

Until, finally, his finger pressed the home button to close the app.

Chapter XLIV

At dinner time, Angel went to the canteen, less to eat than to find Amelia.

But, as before, Amelia never showed up.

O dearest Amelia, whither hast thou gone,
That I sit in this dreary canteen alone?

It had been two days.

If only he had money! He would have bought her a box of chocolates or, if the girl's dorm were out of bounds, ordered her a pizza. On the other hand, it seemed likely she had been ordering them herself, or been eating out, in order *not* to see him.

His archenemy was on duty at the library by then, so he sat on a bench outside until the cold forced him to move. He'd hardly touched his potato and cheesy pasta dinner, so movement was needed to keep his body temperature above freezing.

The Departure Lounge contained only strangers.

Thus, the only place to go was his room. At least it would be warm there, thanks to the university's wasteful policy of running the central heating at maximum. Perhaps he could make a last-ditch attempt at getting through *Oroonoko*. If the average reading speed for a university student was three hundred words per minute, he would only need one hundred minutes to read the whole novella—provided, that is, he somehow managed to concentrate for that long.

Angel lay down in bed and pulled up the online version of the text on his phone.

A hundred minutes passed.

But rather than having finished the novella, he had just finished going through the whole of Madison's Instagram history (minus the last three posts), and the whole of Amelia's. Madison's account was as sporadic, elegant, and cryptic as Amelia's was profuse, homely, and regular; Amelia's content consisted of park and woodland scenery, home-made food, antique books, cute animals, flowers, bullet journaling, crafts, and a smattering of selfies, typically reading a book. Her last post had been from Saturday, showing off her dress.

He shook his head, coming out of self-hypnosis, and, berating himself, closed the app, sat up, and maximised *Oroonoko* on his screen. He frowned hard and opened his eyes wide, as if to aid his concentration.

Two lines into the first chapter, however, he was rudely interrupted by Josh or whatever entering the room, followed by two others. His roommate had a stack of four large pizzas in his arms. The two other guys were not the ones from the previous week, but they were of a similar type: reversed baseball caps, American college hoodies, shorts, and either boat shoes or loafers. A cloud of beer fumes came in with them.

'Angel!' said Brad or whatever with alcoholic effusiveness. 'Here. I got you a present!'

Todd or whatever flung one of the pizza boxes at him, spinning it in the air. Angel had to duck to avoid it hitting his face. The pizza box hit the wall shelving in such a way that it opened and the pizza fell upside down on his pillow.

'Ooooohhh!' Josh or Todd or Chad or Brad's companions chorused, while the former looked stunned.

'Oh, shit! Sorry bro!'

Angel rubbed his forehead, his brain short-circuiting. For about ten seconds, he sat looking at the mess, paralysed, while his roommate's chums roared with laughter, bent over and almost unable to stand.

The lout put his stack of pizza boxes on his desk and went to Angel's bed.

'I'm so sorry, bro. Here. Let me help you.'

Todd or whatever lifted the pizza from the pillow as carefully as his inebriation would allow, flipped it around, put it back in the box, scooped up the pepperoni, mushroom, and mozzarella that had been left behind, and dropped them in a clump on top of the pizza.

Angel observed the procedure without saying a word. The other two, one of whom had landed on his backside, carried on laughing.

'There,' said Chad or whatever. 'Eat up!

Chapter XLV

Angel, however, had an idea.

He fixed the toppings as best he could, and, instead of eating, left the room.

'Bro! Where are you going?' Todd or Josh or Chad or Brad or whatever called out after him.

Angel walked to the girl's dorm and stood outside the building for many minutes, in his mind waiting for the flow of girls coming and going to cease, but in reality not daring to go in at all, even when the coast was clear. It then struck him that he could reach Amelia by other means. He went round to the back and counted the windows, trying to work out hers. Once satisfied, he put the pizza down and collected a few pebbles. These he threw at Amelia's window. Sometimes he'd miss, sometimes he'd hit it, but when he did hit it, the impact seemed too slight to be heard. His arm hurting after a dozen attempts, he collected slightly bigger pebbles and tried again, this time throwing harder. After having the same results, he upgraded to stones. Lacking the strength to make these airborne, most fell well short of the target, until, frustration and adrenalin supplementing what was missing in muscle fibre, he hit a window. But, alas, he'd miscalculated, and the stone flew faster than it ought to have into a window from the storey below, shattering it with a crash. Noisy shards of glass rained onto the pavement below.

'Bugger!'

Panicking, Angel ran into the building. Quicker to disappear that way than into the open gardens.

He slowed down as soon as he was inside and hid behind his hair, hoping he'd be taken for a pizza delivery boy. Which the girls in the lobby seemed to do. He headed for the staircase and paused briefly on the third landing to compose himself before resuming his ascent to Amelia's floor.

But on the second floor he collided against a large, soft obstacle moving fast in the opposite direction; his thin wrists bent downwards, flattening the pizza box against his thighs, and the pizza slid out to land toppings down onto a pair of white canvas sneakers.

'You fucking idiot!' screeched a familiar voice.

Angel opened his hair curtain and found the big American girl glaring back at him, red-faced, wild-eyed, thin-lipped, alternately looking at Angel and down at her ruined shoes. He noticed she had a few shards of glass in her hair.

'YOU!' she screamed in recognition.

One more time, Angel ran.

Chapter XLVI

He was still running across the gardens when his phone rang.

Angel slowed to a brisk walk.

'Hello?' he said, with a high, expectant voice.

'Hi, Angel. It's Madison!'

Angel stopped.

'Oh, my goodness! Oh, my goodness! It's so good to hear from you!'

'I know, right?' she said, then burst out laughing.

'How are you?'

'I'm good. I-I was thinking about you. And you?'

'I've never been better!'

Pause.

'So. Tell me.'

'I-I'm sorry?'

'Tell me.'

'Tell you what?'

'What's up?'

'I saw you . . . er . . . er . . . um . . . er . . .'

'Yes?'

'Coloured your hair . . .'

'Ah, yes. I signed up for a play and I'm playing a mermaid.'

'Oh, I see!' Angel smiled, exhaling with relief.

'Are you exhaling with relief?'

'No, it's just windy here.'

'Ah, okay. How are your classes?'

'Er, yea, they're great. I-I'm going to ace all of them.'

'I should hope so. With 60% As, if you don't get straight As, I'm gonna have to break up with you,' Madison teased. 'What are you reading?'

Angel stumbled and fell.

'What was that? Are you alright?'

'Sorry, just a moment,' he said, getting up.

'Okay.'

He had torn his shirt sleeve and scraped his elbow, which was bleeding. Looking down, he saw that the paving slabs in front of him were two inches higher than the ones behind him, which appeared to run through a depression on the ground. He didn't remember it being there earlier.

'Sorry,' he said. 'I slipped on ice . . . I'm reading *Oroonoko* by Aphra Behn.'

'On ice? In September? How cold is it there?'

'Er . . . we've had an Arctic front. The . . . er . . . result of global warming.'

'Ah, okay. What did you think of *Oroonoko*?'

'Um . . . it was interesting. I finished it in an hour. And-and you? What are you reading?'

'*In Search of Lost Time* by Marcel Proust.'

'Oh, excellent.' Another sigh of relief. Angel made a mental note to hurry and read that as soon as possible. At least he had the complete set!

'Do you miss me?'

'Er . . . yes.'

'How much?'

'Um . . . A lot.'

'Is that all?'

'Um . . . I-I miss you immensely.'

'Is that all?'

'I-I miss you like a limb.'

'Prove it.'

'Er . . . How?'

'Come and see me.'

'I'm coming in December.'

'No. Sooner. Can you come in October? During the Fall break?'

'Um . . . we don't have a break in the Autumn.'

'Come and see me anyway.'

'Um . . . I'd love to. I'll . . . er . . . I'll look up some flights.'

'Get on your laptop and do it now.'

'I-I-I'm not in my room at the moment.'

'Go to the library.'

'I'm sorry . . . um . . . I'm off campus at the moment.'

'You going out without me?'

'No, no. I just went for a walk.'

'Because I haven't gone out at all. I'm not going anywhere without you, Angel.'

'Oh? But I saw on your Instagram that . . .'

'The picture with the girls?' Madison laughed. 'I'll tell you a secret. It's an inside joke we've got going on. We've decided to make people think we are dumb boozers so that they underestimate us, and then we're going to ace all our classes.'

'Oh, I see! Very clever.' Angel silently looked at the heavens to thank God.

'Alright Angel. I'll let you get back. Find a flight and come and see me pronto!'

'Will do.'

'Let me know as soon as you've booked. I can't wait to see you. I can't wait until December.'

'I-I'll let you know the moment it's booked.'

'Awesome. I'm sure it's been great hearing my voice.'

'Yes . . . er . . . it's been music for sore ears!'

'So do you love me?'

'Yes, yes, of course! I love you intensely!'

'So why did I have to ask?'

'Er . . . um . . . I'm sorry?'

'Kidding. Speak to you soon.'

'Bye.'

'Bye.'

Angel walked back to the boys' dorm, but this time, instead of depressed or nervous, euphoric and with a spring in his step.

Chapter XLVII

Professor Hynd addressed a third female student. 'Janet. How does the female voice operate in *Oroonoko*?'

Janet, a girl with ruby red lipstick, frizzy brown hair, and pointed glasses said, 'Okay, well, basically, the female voice, you know, operates, like, you know, I guess, um, like, you know, in the, you know, so, like, you know, um, er . . .'

The professor moved on to the next student. 'Amy. How does the female voice operate in *Oroonoko*?'

'Okay,' said Amy, 'so, the female voice, basically, operates, like, you know, like, er . . . shit. . . er . . . wait . . . fuck . . . okay, okay, so, basically, it operates, like, you know, like, basically, like, the female, the female voice, like, in the, text, and, so, basically, the narration, you know, like, the narrative, like, you know, the female voice . . .'

There were two male students with their hands up, as well as a trans person who used female pronouns, but Professor Hynd persistently ignored them, seemingly only interested in students who were biologically female. Angel, yawning incessantly, hid under his hair, praying he wouldn't be asked all the same. He'd had to wait until his roommate's chums had left before he could sleep, and even then, the room had smelled of booze and cigarettes. And even after that, he could not stop thinking about his telephone call with Madison.

'Angel. Same question.'

Angel lifted his head, allowed his fair to fall back.

'Ah. Okay. Not you. Liz. Same question.'

Angel was relieved to be given a miss.

Liz got started on her own litany of crutch words, but, four seconds in, there was a knock on the door. Liz stopped. Professor Mastropasqua poked his head into the classroom and pointed at his colleague.

'Don't believe a word she says. It's all rubbish. Poison!'

'Leave my class alone,' Hynd snapped.

But Professor Mastropasqua ignored her. 'If I were you, I'd drop the class and drop out of university altogether. Trust me. You'll be better off.'

'Get out!' Hynd shouted.

'Yes. Do that,' said Mastropasqua, still addressing the students. 'Do it before they take your *soul.* Do it while you still can!'

And with a villainous laugh, he disappeared. Professor Hynd rolled her eyes, then said: 'I hope *none* of you are taking any of the *dreadful* classes taught by that *man.* If *I* find out that you are, you'd better *drop* it, or I will *fail* you!'

Angel couldn't tell whether she was serious or joking, so he put it out of his mind.

Chapter XLVIII

A giant in a hoodie intercepted Angel as he exited the building. He had the hood up, a baseball cap pulled down low, and mirrored wraparound sunglasses; because the mouth, cheeks, and chin were covered by a beard, only the nose was visible.

'Angel, buddy. I need to talk to you,' the man said. It was Johannes. The Swede's voice was anxious, urgent.

'What is it?'

'Follow me.'

'Um . . . okay.'

They went inside the building, Johannes leading the way. The Swede walked the length of the corridor. When he found an empty classroom, he went in and said, 'Close the door behind you.'

Angel did as told.

'Some bitch has falsely accused me of raping her

and the university has suspended me. I'm banned from campus. I'm not supposed to be here.'

'Oh . . . really? W-Who was it?'

'They haven't told me.'

'W-Why would anyone accuse you?'

'Who the fuck knows. Maybe she's confused me with some other guy. Listen, I need your help. She claims the incident took place on Saturday at nine o'clock here on campus. I need you to tell them that I was at the cinema. You saw me there.'

'Yes, I-I-I saw you there.'

'I need you to write and sign a statement telling them that. As soon as possible.'

'Er . . . w-what about Amelia. Didn't she see you too?'

'I haven't seen her.'

Angel scratched his temple.

'Um . . . I-I-I think a statement would be more powerful coming from her, don't you think?'

'Yea, definitely. But I need both your statement and her statement. Please.'

'D-D-Do you still have the cinema tickets? Because that could be proof.'

Johannes sighed. 'It isn't. It only proves I bought a ticket. Not that I was in the theatre when the fake rape took place.'

'Oh . . .'

'Will you write out a statement? And ask Amelia when you see her?'

'Erm . . . er . . . yes, yes . . . er . . . I'll write a statement.'

'Today?'

'Um . . . yes, today.'

'Cool. And ask Amelia?'

'I-I-I haven't seen her since Saturday.'

'I know. You fucked up. But you have to find her. I can't go into the girls' dorm—for obvious reasons. And I can't be seen talking to girls right now.'

'B-But surely, if you're innocent . . .'

'It doesn't work that way, buddy. With this type of accusation, nowadays, you're fucked the moment it's made. It's very difficult to prove your innocence. Guys who were innocent have gone to prison.'

'H-How do you know?'

'Because it was in the news a few months ago.'

'Oh.'

'So apologise to Amelia and ask her to please write a statement.'

'Er . . . okay,' Angel said, rubbing his forehead, 'I will ask her as soon as I see her. I haven't had much luck on that front.'

'Oh, come on, man. It's easy. Send her flowers, a box of chocolates and you're good.'

'I-I'm afraid haven't been able to get flowers or anything else. I'm skint.'

'You haven't even done that?'

'Er . . . no.'

'But your date was four days ago!'

'I-I know.'

Johannes looked at the ceiling in exasperation. 'Here,' he said, pulling out his wallet and removing a twenty-pound note. 'Go to Tesco, right now, buy Amelia a dozen roses and a box of chocolates, heart shaped, if they have it, and then go straight to the girl's dorm and give them to her.'

'Erm . . . it's just that . . .'

'Look, Angel. Don't argue. You need to do this right fucking now. Get the flowers, give them to Amelia, *fucking apologise*, and then ask her to write a statement.'

'Um . . . um . . . okay . . . but . . . b-but what if she doesn't forgive me?'

'Then you beg on your knees, Angel. Look, I don't know. You need to work that out. And you need to do it fast. The window is closing.'

'Um . . . okay. I'll get the flowers and chocolate.'

'Okay. Good.'

Angel stared at him like a rabbit before headlights.

'Go, man. Now!'

'Oh, sorry. Okay.'

Chapter XLIX

Armed with a bouquet of (white) roses and a box of chocolates, Angel made his way back to the university campus. He had, however, a tenner left over, and it occurred to him, as he neared his destination, that, to pre-empt his falling short of Amelia's standards for an apology, and to apologise, in addition, for the lateness of this act, he could stop by the off-licence, Arnude Windera Merchants, to get her a bottle of wine.

Once inside, however, he was instantly intimidated by the wood panelling, antique furnishings, and subtle illumination; by the variety of wines with names he'd never heard of; by his lack of knowledge as to their appropriateness to any given occasion; and, most importantly, by the prospect of choosing one within his limited budget. He had taken Madison to quite a few expensive restaurants during the Spring and Summer terms, and always ordered good wines, but these were either paired in the menu or he—or rather *she*—had gone by price, choosing always the most expensive ones. The ensuing poverty had since made him unused to that environment and undermined his confidence. And oenophile he was not—although he aspired to become one, as it would impress Madison.

Half an hour passed without a decision, other than the thought that Amelia might like a sweet dessert wine.

'How can I help you?' the shopkeeper said at last.

Noticing the man's suit and tie made Angel even more acutely self-conscious of his current sartorial deficiency. The sting in his scraped elbow prompted him to use his hand to cover up the torn shirt sleeve. 'Um . . . er . . . I'm looking for a sweet dessert wine.'

'Certainly, Sir. What type do you have in mind?'

'Er . . . what types are there?'

'Well, you could have sparkling or non-sparkling; white or red; lightly sweet, very sweet, fortified . . .'

'Er . . . red, yes, red. But the sweetest.'

'And what is it for?'

'Um . . . it's for a friend . . . a girl . . .'

'Ah, a girl! And why a sweet wine, if I may ask?'

'Um . . . er . . .'

'Maybe she's sweet and she likes sweet things?'

'Um . . . yes, yes . . . that's it.'

'Okay. I can certainly help you with that, Sir. What sort of occasion is this for? Is it to be had over dinner, is it to be had after dinner . . . ?'

'Um . . . on its own.'

'So, maybe a fortified wine. Like port or sherry . . .'

He remembered a dessert wine his parents enjoyed. 'Do you have Málaga wine?'

'Yes, we do. But I'll have to get it from the cellar. We've had a delivery this morning and it's yet to go on display.'

'O-Okay,' said Angel, encouraged that things were going well.

'If you bear with me for a moment, Sir, while I go and get it.'

'Okay.'

The shopkeeper disappeared into the back of the shop.

While waiting, Angel found the fortified wine section and, laying the bag with the flowers and chocolates on the floor, looked at the bottles that most drew his attention, based on their shape or the decorativeness of the labels.

Then he noticed the prices.

'Oh, balls!' he muttered, casting a glance behind him, fearful someone may have heard.

Dreading potential embarrassment, Angel quickly decided to chase after the shopkeeper, to tell him, while he was out of sight and out of hearing range from the shop floor, that he needed something within a ten-pound budget.

At the back of the shop, Angel found an open door that led to a flight of stairs. He descended with rapid steps into a narrow, frigid tunnel, which he followed. The shopkeeper could not be seen, as the tunnel bent and a section had recently subsided, leaving dirt and some of the Victorian brickwork on the ground—albeit without blocking access. Along the wall leaned spades, shovels, picks, camping lanterns, and stacks of masonry buckets. At the end of this tunnel Angel found the cellar, a vaulted space, with columns and more Victorian brick work. Enormous casks lined the walls, while islands of stacked-up crates and racks of wine bottles populated the floor. From behind one of the racks Angel heard low voices engaged in conversation. As he rounded the corner, he once again encountered Professor Mastropasqua, and, again incongruously, Babyface. The men stopped talking and turned to look at Angel. Both appeared surprised and displeased to see him there. In turn, observing him up close for the first time, Angel noticed the ferocity of the professor's features. Absolutely demonic. Not what he would expect from an academic.

'Who the fuck is he?' said a familiar voice behind Angel, who turned to find Beard, holding a crate.

A chill passed through Angel.

'He's leaving,' said Mastropasqua. 'Right?'

The shopkeeper appeared behind Beard and looked at Angel. 'Sir? I'm terribly sorry, but you're not supposed to be here. Can you please go back to the shop and wait for me there?'

'Oh, um . . . I'm so sorry. I-I just wanted to say . . . I don't want to spend more than ten pounds.'

'Give him whatever he wants from the shop floor. I'll pay the difference,' said Mastropasqua.

Angel turned to glance at his benefactor, but the latter was looking past him to the shopkeeper, gesturing with his hand to make haste and clear Angel out.

Chapter L

Angel was almost at the girl's dorm when, noticing a flower bed, he realised the plastic bag he was carrying contained only the £40 bottle of tawny port he'd been allowed to get for his tenner; he'd left the roses and the chocolates at the off-licence.

'Oh, for goodness' sake!' he mumbled.

He turned around immediately and made his way back at a brisk pace. When he arrived, however, he found the shop closed. The early hour gave him hopes the shopkeeper might still be inside. He put the bag down and cupped his hands around his eyes as he pressed his face against the glass, hoping to see the shopkeeper and get his attention, or to at least locate his other bag. But neither could be seen. He knocked a few times, with no effect. He rang the telephone number displayed on the fascia, also with no effect.

Angel rubbed his forehead and looked around, racking his brain. But with nothing else he could do for the moment, he took a picture of the shop's telephone number, and walked back to campus, unsure of whether he could get away with delaying the additional apology to Amelia until the following morning. What if he saw her before then? Would anything he said be good enough? And what if she didn't accept his apology?

At least he had the port, so he had a chance.

The port!

Angel had been walking empty handed. No wonder he'd felt light!

He ran back to the off-licence, praying the bag would still be where he'd left it.

But it was already gone.

'Oh, for God's sake!' he muttered through gritted teeth, punching his thighs.

Chapter LI

Angel took his tray to the canteen's upper level, hoping to dine unseen—unseen by Amelia, by Johannes, by the big American girl, by Saïd, by Jae, by Alba, by the climate change activists, and by his archenemy, the librarian. All the same, and despite days of starvation, he was too nervous to eat more than a mouthful of potato and cheesy pasta. Angel sat hunched over, forearms resting on the tabletop, fork playing with his food.

'Hi Angel.'

Angel looked up to find Amelia standing before him, a shy smile on her face and a tray in her hands.

'Amelia!'

That smile had blown away his fears in an instant—it was the gladdest sight he'd seen in days!

Amelia pulled back a chair and sat down. To Angel the scene unfolded in slow motion.

'I heard about what you tried to do last night,' she said.

'Uh? W-What I tried to do last night?'

'How sweet of you to bring me pizza.'

'H-How did you know?'

'There was commotion at the dorm last night, after you dropped the pizza on Betsy.'

'Betsy? Is that her name? D-Do you know her?'

'No. But she described you. I knew it was you.'

'Um . . . I . . . I accidentally bumped into her while I was bringing up the pizza. She was making her way down the stairs really fast.'

'I know, Angel.' Amelia put her hand on his. 'You don't need to explain.'

'I-I just wanted to say how sorry I was about Saturday.'

'I know you are. I know you didn't intend it. I read your poem.'

'I'm . . . so sorry about your dress.'

'Don't worry,' said Amelia. 'It was getting a little tight anyway.' She giggled and tucked a lock of hair behind her ear.

'I was . . . um . . . going to bring you flowers and a box of chocolates, but I accidentally left it at the off-licence while getting you a bottle of wine.'

'Oh, Angel. You did all that for me?'

'Er . . . yes.'

'You sweet, sweet man. I know how poor you've been lately. And still you spent what little money you had, and probably delayed booking your flight, just to make amends.'

'Er . . . yes, yes. It-It seemed only fair.'

'But Angel, why did you lie to me about your sister?'

'W-W-What do you mean?'

'She replied to my message on Sunday and she said

she'd not been injured, or been in hospital, or been in London, or even seen you since the beginning of January.'

'Um . . . er . . . ufff . . . I'm . . . sorry. I had a panic attack,' he lied. As much as he disliked being thought of as someone who had them, he disliked the truth even more.

'Angel . . . I didn't know you suffered from panic attacks'. She tilted her head and squeezed his hand.

'Um . . . yes . . . occasionally.'

'Poor Angel. But it's okay, you don't need to be ashamed.' She squeezed his hand again.

Angel saw Jae climb up the stairs, notice them, and very deliberately walk past to sit at a vacant table.

'Jae! Come and join us,' said Amelia.

Jae stopped and, upon turning, glared at Angel momentarily before accepting the invitation without a word. Even sitting, she towered over the other two.

'Don't be rude, Jae. Say hi to Angel.'

Jae said nothing. Instead, she turned her attention to her plate and picked up her fork.

After an awkward silence, Amelia pressed on. 'How was your 17th-Century Literature class?'

Angel observed the blonde. He didn't know Jae was also in his class.

'I've dropped it.'

'Oh, Jae. What was the problem this time?'

'Pure feminist propaganda. I've switched to Occult Philosophy in the Elizabethan Age.'

Angel hadn't taken that module.

Amelia said, 'That sounds interesting. Who teaches it?'

'Mastropasqua.'

'I keep hearing about him. He seems unpopular with the academic staff. But some of the students love him.'

'He's the only good professor here, that's why.'

'You're taking a class with Mastropasqua, aren't you, Angel?' asked Amelia.

'Um . . . yes.'

'How do you find him?'

'Erm . . . he . . . er . . . doesn't like students who say *you know* a lot.'

Jae said to Amelia, 'They're studying for English Lit degrees. If they can't even speak their own language properly, they shouldn't be there.'

'You put it so brutally,' Amelia said.

'If people don't hear the truth, they won't learn.'

'And are you learning from Mastropasqua's classes, Angel?'

'Um . . . y-yes, but I'm worried because Professor Hynd said that if she caught us taking one of Mastropasqua's classes, she'd fail us.'

Jae didn't look at him, 'Of course she'd say that. She's jealous of his intellect.'

'How so?' said Amelia.

'He's original. She's a conformist.'

'But have you taken a good look at her?'

'Feminist? Tick. Fat? Tick. Blue hair? Tick. Hates men? Tick. Tattooos? Tick. Doc Martens? Tick. She's a conformist.'

'But so what if she fits into a type? Lots of people conform to a subculture.'

'Her subculture is ideological. Ideological professors don't teach; they indoctrinate.'

'You must have dropped maybe five or six modules since I've known you, Jae, so you must realise by now that a neutral professor is like a needle in a haystack. Can't you just sit through the course? Take it with a pinch of salt?'

'I've come here to learn, not to sit through lies.'

'What you call lies they might call reasoned conclusions backed by evidence. Isn't the whole point of uni to be exposed to different points of view? You don't have to agree with them.'

'An academic develops theories to advance knowledge. An activist deploys propaganda to proselytise. Hynd is activist.'

'But activists are the *opposite* of conformist.'

'Activists are the *ultimate* conformists. They've conformed to an ideology and they want everyone else to do the same.'

'Aren't they rebelling against social institutions?'

Jae scoffed. 'They are not rebelling against anything. They *are* the social institutions. If they were rebels, they wouldn't be running universities, they'd be serving time in prison.'

'Some of the student activists *have* been arrested at times.'

'They do their professors' dirty work. They're not the rebels they think they are.'

'Well, it's true that most of the students here are involved with some form of activism. I do feel like the odd one out. They make it clear.'

'They perpetuate a toxic culture at this university and outside on social media. And their professors never condemn them. On the contrary. Which is why I'm against them.'

'I do have my own issues with the activists here, including the feminists. They mock me for my feminine interests. They check up on who I follow on Twitter, even though I never tweet . . .'

Jae snorted and shook her head.

'. . . And they call me a traitor because I don't join in with their man-hating.'

'Of course they do. Activists are haters. Their ideologies are negative.'

'Now, don't get me wrong, I am all for equal rights, and there are issues that affect women that make me very angry, so there is an argument for feminism. Betsy is a good example—'

A chill ran through Angel. He pricked his ears.

'Betsy is a perfect example of why activists are toxic. She has mental health issues. She's not emotionally able to handle the fear and paranoia of their shitty worldview.'

'Betsy had a rough childhood.'

'She needs to stop listening to their rubbish, take responsibility, and own the outcomes in her life.'

'But she's not responsible for her childhood.'

'She's not a child anymore. She's a big girl.'

'But how can she fix her mind if it's broken, Jae? She needs her mind to fix it!'

'First she needs to realise she needs to fix it. But she's in a fog of outrage and grievance porn, looking outwards instead of inwards. So she thinks anger and victimhood are the only ways to respond.'

'She was also treated badly by previous boyfriends.'

'And you weren't? Do you make that your whole identity? Do you hate all men?'

Amelia looked at Angel and smiled. 'Okay, fair enough.' She reached for the carrot cake.

'Most women have dated creeps in their teens. That's when you learn about relationships. And in the past, hardly anyone had an ideal childhood. Yet they didn't end up a quarter tonne of screaming green-haired feminist.'

'Yes, but instead they were forced to hold it in and took it out on other people.'

'It's not the past anymore. It's the present. People don't bottle anything up. They put it on YouTube.'

'Besides, we don't know what it was like for her. Each person experiences things differently.'

'And each person is responsible for how their life turns out. You can either moan about the past and blame other people, or you can fix your problems.'

'Not everyone has the will power.'

'If they won't do what they need to do, then they shouldn't complain.'

'Professor Hynd would say it's the system.'

'The system didn't make Betsy fat. She's fat because she overeats. If she can't get a job at an oil rig it won't be because of the *men*; it will be because she's fat and you need to be fit to work in oil rigs.'

'Well, there goes my ambition to be an oil drill roughneck,' said Amelia. 'But you have to admit few of them are women and not all applicants are unfit.'

'Women don't generally apply for those jobs.'

'I'm sure some do.'

'And Alba knows one who works in an oil rig. So women can get those jobs if they're qualified.'

'But what about the hundreds of other ways our world is designed with only men in mind? Crash test dummies were based on the average male body.'

'A female version has been introduced.'

'But only after forty plus years. And it looks like a child. That won't help you. You're well over six feet tall; the dummy is four eleven! And it's still based on the male body type. *And* it weighs *seven stone!* Look at me, that's not going to help *me* in a collision.'

'Crash dummies were also based on the average American male body. In Germany they were bigger. In Italy they were smaller. So there's equal reason to complain about Americanism. Where are the anti-American activists?'

'I don't understand your point.'

'Engineers need better data, not better feminists. The solution is technological.'

'So we just let computers take over?'

Jae arched an eyebrow. 'Ideally.'

Amelia laughed. 'But seriously, Jae . . .'

'We need logic, not emotion.'

'So your prescription is—We are Borg. Resistance is futile?'

'Too many feminists are overemotional extremists who focus on stupid things and discredit their cause.'

'And yet, surely, it's not all of them.'

'Exceptions are irrelevant. The extremists pretend to speak for all women. By doing so they make women look stupid. That's the diametrical opposite of feminism. Which is why I am an anti-feminist.'

'But aren't you allowing yourself to be defined by extremists? And thereby becoming an extremist yourself? It's like equating Islam with Isis!'

'Isis is shunned by most Muslims.'

'Alright. Saïd does say they're crazy.'

'By contrast, feminists don't shun their extremists. If they want to be taken seriously, they should shun them categorically, not give them professorships.'

'Ay! It's impossible to argue with you!'

'That's because I'm good at it.'

Amelia turned to Angel and put a hand on his to draw him out of his daydream. 'What do you think, Angel? Would you rather I teach you instead of Profeesor Hynd?'

Angel's head jerked up, his startled eyes darting in all directions. 'Er . . . um . . . um . . .'

'I'd be good at it.' She winked. 'I'd give you *top marks!*'

Jae rolled her eyes and looked away. Angel stared, paralysed.

'I'm only joking. Here, have an apple. You need vitamin C.' She put her gala on his tray. He stared at it but left it untouched. She said to Jae, 'I wonder what Mastropasqua's wife is like.'

'Was like. He's divorced.'

'Oh, really?'

'But I'm sure she was clever and read loads of books.'

'From what I've heard, I can't imagine him going back to a normal house. He probably lives in an Elizabethan manor out in the country. I can imagine big oil paintings on the walls and ornate gilt frames and suits or armour and hunting trophies and a large gothic library.'

'And coal smoke coming out of his seven chimneys.'

Angel imagined the plumes of black smoke blotting out the sky above, and Mastropasqua seated on a leather armchair by the fire, angrily burning the coal.

Amelia said, 'I've heard some of the other professors say in class that he was once in prison and made his money through crime.'

'I've heard that from Turner. He's a communist.'

'And Professor Albert said he dabbled in the occult and was a member of a secret society.'

Jae laughed with scorn. 'They're all mad.'

'Is it true his daughter committed suicide?'

'Yes. I found two old articles online.'

'What happened?'

'She was a student here years ago. But other than that, no one will say.'

Chapter LII

Johannes again intercepted him outside the Jenni Murray Hall, disguised as before. His sunglasses reflected the flowerbeds and waif-like students passing by. He'd been hiding behind an oak tree.

'Angel! Did you write the statement?' he hissed. 'I need it, man!'

'Um . . . yes, I've written it.'

'Can I see it?'

'Er . . . it's in my room.'

'Can you show it to me now?'

'Um . . . I have a class in two minutes.'

'Can you show it to me after?'

'Er . . . Yes, yes . . . but I need to go over it.'

Johannes frowned. 'You mean you haven't finished it yet?'

'Um . . . no, yes . . . it's finished. It's just that I need to check it one more time. I just want to make sure all the details are correct.'

'Okay. Can you show me what you've written anyway? After class?'

'Erm . . . do you mind if I show you the finished version?'

'Today?'

'Er . . . yes, today. In the evening.'

Johannes' voice rose an octave. 'In the evening!'

'No . . . er . . . I meant, in the afternoon.'

'Straight after lunch?'

'Er . . . yes, fine, of course.'

'Okay. I'll wait for you.' Johannes checked his surroundings.

'Okay.'

'See you at one.'

'Erm . . . see you then.'

Johannes made to leave but stopped himself abruptly. 'Oh and, Angel—did you see Amelia?'

'Er . . . no, no, I haven't seen her.'

'You didn't give her the flowers and chocolates?'

'Er . . . er . . . um . . . yes, yes, I did. I knocked on her door, but she didn't open, so I left it there for her to find.'

'Okay. So she should have forgiven you by now. Can you send her a message?'

'Um . . . yes . . . er . . . she should have seen the flowers by now. I-I-I'll send her a message.'

'Now?' Johannes pointed at Angel's phone.

'Um . . . I've really got to run. My class is about to start.'

'Okay. After class then. Please.'

'Yes, of course, I-I . . . er . . . I will. I just want to do it right.'

'I'll type it for you if you don't know how.'

'N-No, no, it's okay. I can manage.'

'Okay. But don't forget. It's vital. I need this shit resolved fast.'

'Er . . . yes, absolutely.'

'Okay. See you at one.'

'See you later.'

Johannes walked away, quickly and checking his flanks.

Before turning to go into the building, Angel saw Mastropasqua's gleaming 1959 black Silver Cloud pull up by the kerb opposite the front lawn. Out of the front passenger door came out Josh, or Todd, or Brad, or Chad, or whatever his name was, wearing the inevitable shorts and college hoodie.

Angel frowned. 'Whaa . . . ?' he mumbled.

The American cheerfully bid goodbye to the professor in what might have been a *Kent* or a *Sussex* accent, but there was too much ambient noise to hear properly. Angel shook his head. Maybe he's taking an Elizabethan drama class with Mastropasqua, he thought, before entering the building and letting the incident slip out of his mind.

Chapter LIII

Angel spent his class coiled with hunger. As usual, his co-workers had only left him cold, dry toast. Now, with the classroom emptying and his classmates happily heading for the canteen, he had to find a way to leave the building unseen and a place to lay low while Johannes was about.

Angel left the classroom and searched for the fire exit. While in the corridor, however, he caught sight of Johannes entering the building. Fortunately, the Swede had his head turned in the opposite direction, although obviously looking for him. Thumped in the heart, Angel leaped into the lavatory. The latter was empty. Fearful that Johannes would look for him there, Angel yanked open the door to the first toilet stall, intending to hide inside. But the stall wasn't vacant and, worse, he'd entered the female lavatory. Seated on the toilet, jeans pulled below the knees, upper arms touching the walls, Betsy screamed. It was the loudest, most piercing noise he'd ever heard.

As if hit by lightning, Angel jumped back and searched for a way out, while Betsy continued to scream, first in horror, then to attract attention. The door being out of the question, Angel opted for the window. And although the window only opened a crack along the top, thanks to metal stoppers, Angel was sufficiently emaciated to fit through. But his escape was not smooth, for he managed to break the glass, rip his jeans, and re-scrape his elbow as he landed on the concrete paving outside. Worse, as he ran away, he saw, perambulating on the grounds nearby, several witnesses to his flight.

Chapter LIV

Angel hid behind a hedge and thought hard. He couldn't run to the canteen or the library, because Johannes would find him there; he couldn't go to Amelia's room, because it meant passing through Betsy's floor; he couldn't hide in his room, because if the American was there and if Johannes knocked on the door, the American would open; he couldn't hide in the main building, because Betsy was probably headed there finally to report him; he couldn't sit in The Departure Lounge, because it had floor-to-ceiling glass windows and he would be easily seen—besides, Vera would likely be there; he couldn't find safety at the pub, because Beard would almost certainly be having a pint; he couldn't absquatulate at the laundrette, because he didn't have any clothes—and, besides, it also had floor-to-ceiling glass windows and he would be easily found;

he couldn't lock himself up in a toilet stall, because Johannes could take a peek over or under the door; he couldn't walk to Tesco, because he was too hungry and didn't have money; he couldn't disappear into the shop at the petrol station, because the cappuccinos there smelled too good; he couldn't climb a tree, because he wasn't strong enough; he couldn't be at the gym, because Johannes would be standing outside, pressing his sad face against the glass windows, longing to train.

It occurred to him, however, that now was a good time to visit the off-licence and see if he could get back the flowers and chocolates he'd left there the previous afternoon. Before making a move, he checked the rip in his jeans: it was on the back of his right thigh, high up, near the glute. Thankfully, the jeans had become so loose that the rip, if it showed while standing or walking, opened into a black chasm.

When he reached the off-licence, he found Mastropasqua's car parked in front, behind a skip filled with rocks and dirt. Angel imagined that the professor had wine with his meals, so it made sense that he would be a frequent customer; in fact, he was likely an oenophile—otherwise, why would they allow him into the cellar? Mastropasqua, however, was nowhere to be seen on the shop floor. Angel went to the shopkeeper, who was occupied dusting the bottles behind the counter.

'Sir?' said Angel.

The shopkeeper kept dusting.

'Sir?'

No response.

'Sir.'

No response.

'Sir.'

The shopkeeper moved on to the next bottle.

'Sir!'

No acknowledgment.

'Sir!'

The bottle in the shopkeeper's hand kept receiving a very conscientious and thorough polish.

'Excuse me! Sir!'

A customer came to the counter with a bottle, ready to pay.

The shopkeeper turned around and addressed him with a smile. 'Wonderful wine. Is there anything else you'd like, Sir?'

'Yes. You wouldn't happen to have a bottle of gluten-free Szicsek plum pálinka somewhere, would you?'

'We might have. I'll need to check in the cellar. If you bear with me for a moment while I go look for it.'

'I'll wait.'

Angel stared at the customer. A balding middle-aged man in a grey suit, which made him self-conscious of the fact that he, Angel, was virtually in rags, with a bleeding elbow to boot. The middle-aged man noticed Angel's stare and gave him, through the corner of his eye, a brief, disapproving look.

After a few minutes, the shopkeeper returned, carrying three small, dark bottles.

'Good news! We have a bottle of Szicsek,' he said, putting in on the counter. 'And we also have two others, which are not gluten-free, but which I thought might give someone a chuckle. One bottle of Immortal, and another of Spirit of Dracula.'

The two men laughed at the names.

'With a name like that, I really can't resist. I'll take the Szicsek and the Spirit of Dracula,' said the customer.

'Certainly, Sir. That will be £89.98.'

The customer handed over a Centurion American Express, the sight of which made the shopkeeper obsequiously tilt and bow his head. Angel had never seen the black American Express; his parents were wealthy, but he had only ever seen them use gold or platinum cards. And they were very sceptical of them. So that was what a Centurion Amex looked like. Such opulence! The thought of it made him think of fine dining with Madison, which at once saddened him and sharpened his hunger pangs.

It was only after the transaction was over that the shopkeeper, about to go back to polishing his bottles, finally acknowledged him, albeit almost as an afterthought.

'I know what you're going to ask,' he said, fake amiably, as he bent down to pick something up from the floor behind the counter. As he straightened, he lifted Angel's Tesco bag, holding it between his thumb and index finger, as if it were a distasteful object beneath his dignity.

'Oh, thank you,' said Angel, relieved.

'My pleasure,' said the shopkeeper with a plastic smile and both hands on the counter, now signalling with his body language, in a subtle yet pointed way, that Angel should clear out directly.

Angel did as indicated.

Chapter LV

While standing for a moment outside the off-licence, admiring Mastropasqua's car, it occurred to Angel that, since Amelia had forgiven him, there was no need to waste the flowers and chocolates on her; he could, instead, send them to Madison.

> *Of praise deservèd, unto Thee I give,*
> *A wreathèd garland of deservèd praise . . .*

Unfortunately, there was still the matter of the postage and he was yet to be paid, despite the end of the month having come and gone, so he would have somehow to obtain the funds.

He pulled out his phone, opened WhatsApp, and found his mother in the contacts. But, when it came to typing the message, his finger once again hovered over the digital keyboard for numerous seconds, until the sting in his scraped elbow offered an excuse to re-pocket the device.

Hunger urged him to move on. Thinking they might have penny chewing gum at the petrol station, he headed hither; admittedly, the chewing gum wasn't food, but a bit of sugar mixed with aspartame was better than nothing.

Once at the petrol station, however, he found that, while they did have penny chewing gum, it was sold in minimum quantities of a quarter of a pound, rather than in single units, so, at £1.97, it was well beyond his budget. Head bowed, he walked out.

An American voice beside him shouted, 'Hey, Josh! Can you fill it up?'

Angel turned right to find a brown-haired man with white shirt, blue jeans, and white high-tops, who had exited the shop almost at the same time as he. The American had addressed a fat teenager in a white t-shirt standing by a pump across the forecourt.

'Americans are *so loud!*' said a loud female, who then burst out laughing, not far from him on the left.

Angel saw the American turn towards the voice with a serious visage. But before Angel could follow the American's gaze of hate, he heard the female voice say:

'Angel! What are you doing here?'

Alba—in an above-knee floral dress and black tights.

The American walked on.

'Um . . . I just came for some chewing gum.'

'I see you got flowers! Are those for Amelia?'

'Er . . . no . . . er . . . they're for my Food and Lit class tomorrow.'

'Oh, I see.'

Angel stood there, not knowing what to say or where to go.

'I'm going to meet my sister for tea,' Alba said, 'Do you want to join us?'

'Your sister? I-I didn't know you had a sister.'

'Of course you did, Angel. Vera!'

Angel's eyes widened as his eyebrows shot up.

'V-Vera is your sister?'

'Angel! Don't you ever pay attention?'

'Yes, no . . . er . . .'

'So will you join us?'

'Um . . . no, that's alright. I've got to—'

'Come on. It'll be fun!'

'No, no, I've really got to—'

'Is it because of Vera? Has she emasculated you?' Alba smiled with teeth and gums.

'Er . . . no . . . it's just that . . .' Angel used his thumb to point in the general direction of the university.

'Let's go. I know you apologised already, so she'll just have to get over herself.'

'She's mentioned it?'

'Yes, and said you fell *well short*.' Alba cackled, as usual: explosively. The Americans at the pump turned to look, two pairs of eyes lasering out hate. The fat teenager pressed the pump trigger so tightly his knuckles had gone white.

'You know, I'm really busy . . . I've got—'

'You're coming with me,' Alba said, grabbing Angel's sleeve and yanking him along.

Until there was a rip.

'Oh, no!' she said, staring at the dilapidated sleeve, eyes like basketballs, mouth like an O, hands clutching her chest.

Her action had added twelve inches to the rip along his elbow.

'Oh, well, you might as well cut off the sleeve!' said Alba.

Stunned, Angel examined the rip, trying to pinch the separated flaps of cloth together.

'Okay,' said Alba suddenly, 'Now you're really coming with me.' She grabbed him by the belt and yanked him along.

Outmassed, Angel stumbled and had no option but to follow.

Chapter LVI

The taxi left them at The Lanesborough, in Hyde Park Corner. A palatial, white, neo-classical four-storey building.

Angel had been there once, during the late Spring, when he took Madison for a themed afternoon of tea with champagne, just before she'd returned to the United States. The experience had cost him £166. At the time, though his funds had been largely depleted, he'd still been a well-dressed young man. Now he feared he'd be denied entry; but, with her outgoing charm and aplomb, Alba secured him access.

Angel affected distraction with the Regency style décor during the proceedings.

They found Vera already installed at a table in the Withdrawing Room, which was decorated in pale blue, gold, and saffron, with *trompe l'œil* marbled columns and tasselled, tieback curtains. Predictably, she was clad in black and aghast to see him, eyes like golf balls below a frown, lips forming a wine-coloured asterisk.

Before even taking a seat, Alba said to Vera, 'I've come to broker a truce.'

Vera literally turned her nose at the proposal, her raised eyebrow lanceolate and supercilious.

Alba chuckled and took a seat, gesturing for Angel to do the same. Angel took care to hide his crinkly Tesco bag under the table, holding it between his feet. So concave with hunger was he that it took effort to keep his torso straight.

'Come on, Vera,' said Alba. 'Angel's already shown genuine contrition.'

'I was not planning on spending high tea in this sort of company,' said Vera, still looking away.

'You'll adapt.' Alba smirked.

Vera glanced at Angel and wrinkled her nose. 'He stinks!' she said, with distain. 'Look at him!'

'Don't worry. After tea, we're going to fix him. That's why I brought him along.'

'You can't polish a . . . doo doo,' said Vera.

Angel discretely looked at the faces in the room, hoping they couldn't hear the conversation. He caught one or two casting disapproving glances at him from a nearby sofa.

'I . . . um . . . I took Madison here about four months ago,' he said. 'W-We sat at the Cél—'

'I'm surprised they let you in,' said Vera, giving him an up-and-down look. 'You might have broken something valuable.'

'I-I'm really sorry about—'

'And so you should be. But sorry doesn't put antique china back together.'

'Um . . . k-kintsugi?' suggested Angel.

'I'm surprised you even know about that.'

'It was only a teapot, Vera,' said Alba.

Vera's jaw dropped. 'Well, and I suppose if someone accidentally burnt a Jane Austin manuscript, you'd say, it was just paper,' she said. 'Clearly, I'm surrounded by savages!'

A waiter came to take their order of tea, of which there were forty choices available. Alba selected green tea and Vera Earl Grey. The waiter made to leave without taking Angel's order. Angel was relieved, because Alba hadn't offered to pay.

'Oops! Sir! You forgot to take the gentleman's order,' said Alba.

'My apologies,' said the waiter, his polite mask barely concealing contempt.

'Uh . . . er . . . um . . .' Angel looked at Alba with pleading eyes.

'He'll take Earl Gray,' decided Alba, putting a hand on his arm.

'Certainly, madam,' said the waiter.

'Don't worry, Angel. My treat.'

'Huh! Chivalry is dead!' said Vera, her lips curving downwards.

The waiter's face registered the subtlest of twitches, a possible inward smile. Angel made sure to speak the instant the waiter moved to leave.

'I brought Madison here some months ag—'

'I think you need to forget about Madison,' said Alba.

'Er . . . I-I'm sorry?'

'You need to forget about Madison.'

Angel stared, perplexed.

'Poof! Out of your mind,' Alba added.

'W-Why do you say that?'

'She's not good for you.'

'But w-w-why is that?'

'You'll end up *disappointed,*' said Vera.

'Oh?'

'You need a nice, sweet girl who'll look after you,' Alba added.

'A-And you don't think Madison is sweet?'

Both Alba and Vera looked at each other, then burst out laughing. Alba so loudly she nearly shattered the neighbouring fine china. By contrast, Vera's laugh was quiet and derisive.

'Mark my words, young man. If you don't wake up,' said Vera, 'she's going to *eviscerate* you.'

'You spent all your money on her,' said Alba. 'Look at you now. If that isn't a sign, I don't know what is.'

'It's . . . um . . . a sign of my devotion,' he protested.

More laughter from the girls.

'Devotion to a *sorceress,*' said Vera. 'She's *bewitched* you and you're *deluded.*'

'Trust me. You'd be better off with someone else,' said Alba.

'Um . . . um . . . I saw Mastropasqua at the off-licence just yesterday,' he said.

'You must think us *fools* changing the topic like that!' said Vera.

'Have you read that mega assignment he gave you for the Food and Lit class?' asked Alba, addressing her sister, before Angel could reply. Angel bowed his head.

'Of course I did.'

'I'm taking his Occult Philosophy class,' said Alba.

'Oh, um . . . Jae said she'd signed up for that,' said Angel.

'In that case, Mastropasqua will pass *two* students this year. Wow, that must be a record!' said Alba, sending another shockwave of crystal-splitting cackles, jolting a lady into spilling her tea.

The waiter arrived with a three-tiered tea stand containing finger sandwiches, pastries, cakes, a plate with scones, clotted cream, and various fruit preserves.

Angel wanted to grab one of the sandwiches immediately, but knew he had to wait. He was dizzy.

'Have you heard about Johannes?' Alba asked Vera.

Angel re-bowed his head, lower than before, to avoid eye contact.

'That *tattooed* brute? What's he done? Broken another chair?'

Alba leaned forward, her voice low for the first time. 'He's been accused of rape. Summarily suspended and banned from campus.'

'Oh, goodness gracious!' said Vera, lowering her own voice. 'Now we have *rapists* at the university. What next! Eating out of a *trough?*'

'It was one of the American exchange students. You know Elise?'

'I have no idea who you're talking about,' said Vera, a little louder.

'Well, of course. You wouldn't *deign* to live on campus.'

Vera again raised an eyebrow.

'There's this big girl, Betsy, and I mean *big* big, huge,' Alba continued, holding her arms as far apart as they would go. 'You've seen her, right? Well, Elise is her friend. They're always together. She's the accuser.'

'Well, good. I hope justice is served.'

Alba lowered her voice to a whisper. 'It seems he accosted her at the pub on Saturday evening.'

Vera whispered, 'Then there will be witnesses.'

'Apparently no. He shoved her into a car after following her into a dark alley.'

Angel knew that Johannes didn't have a car. All his money went on food and steroids. Outside of university, all he did was train, eat, and sleep. He didn't even drink, because, he said, it inhibited 'protein synthesis'. However, Angel said nothing. He hadn't remembered to write the statement for Johannes, but now, with that Betsy about to accuse him, Angel, of harassment, he couldn't afford to.

'Pah! Animal!' said Vera.

Alba leaned forward even closer and whispered more softly still. 'She said he sodomised her.'

'Alba, for goodness' sake! We're in a *tearoom!*'

Alba paid no heed. 'Elise said the incident took place at around nine in the evening, so it could have been any of us.'

'What's the world coming to? Soon they'll be attacking women in broad daylight. And so close to the campus! We're going to have to start walking in pairs.'

'Exactly. And Vera, there's no way I'm letting you walk back to your flat alone. I'm coming with you.'

'And what about *you*?'

'I'll get a hunting knife. Stuff it in the leg of my boot.'

'And where are you going to get one today, Alba. From the reception desk?'

'We'll take Angel, and I'll walk back with him. I'm a two-minutes away from campus.'

Vera scoffed at the idea. 'What good is *he* going to be?' She poured some milk into her tea.

Angel's knees started bouncing under the table. He could only half-hear the women's whispers but was equally preoccupied with the matter. He disliked the idea of betraying his friend, who was clearly innocent, but he'd have to if he wanted to save his own skin. Why did that Betsy have to come to London?

'Well, good. But enough of this scabrous matter,' he heard Vera say.

Angel hid under his hair, and hoped they'd expel Johannes quickly so that he'd not have to face him when he came around asking again for the statement.

'She's given a description of his penis,' said Alba, grabbing a cheese and pickle sandwich.

'Alba, please!'

But Vera's stiff discomfort brought a glint to Alba's eye. With her powerful lungs hurling her voice far and wide, she said, 'She said his penis is about this long, very hairy, and has a pier—'

'Alba, *really! Must* you?'

Chapter LXVII

After tea, Alba hailed a taxi and took Angel to the Marks and Spencer on Kensington High Street.

'Okay. Choose one,' she said, standing before a rack of pastel-coloured shirts.

'Er . . . is there something dark? Like navy blue or brown?'

'I think you'd look great in a pink shirt.'

'Er . . . n-no, it's not really my style. A dark shirt would be better.'

Alba grabbed a pink shirt from the display. 'Here. Why don't you try it on at least.'

'Um . . .' Angel looked at the shirt and didn't move.

'Go on,' Alba prompted, waving the shirt at him.

'Um . . . erm . . . um . . . no, really, I don't need a shirt. I can sew this one back together.'

'Argh, okay, mister moody, let's find a dark one.'

Alba rolled her eyes and put the shirt back on the rack.

It took half an hour of humming and hawing, with Angel never satisfied with any of the choices available. The colour was the wrong shade. The stitching too low density. The cuff circumference excessive. The buttons too thick and not mother of pearl. They also lacked shanks.

'Angel!' snapped Alba. 'We're not in Saville Row! This is just so you're not in *rags*. Make a choice and let's go!'

Eventually, they found something that Angel could live with. They took it to the till.

'That will be £9, sir,' said the shop assistant.

'Erm . . .' Angel looked at Alba.

Alba, however, was on her phone.

'Um . . . Alba?'

'Just a second,' she said, lifting her index finger. 'I'm just typing a message.'

'Cash or card?' asked the shop assistant.

'Er . . . um . . .' Angel looked at Alba again.

But Alba's reply to whomever seemed never-ending.

'Sir? Cash or card?'

'Ah . . . um . . . just a moment. Alba?'

'Yea. Just a minute. Jeepers!'

She kept on typing, and typing, and typing, and typing, and typing.

Angel heard a tut behind him.

'Um . . . Alba?'

'Okay, okay, okay! I'm almost done!'

Alba kept on typing, and typing, and typing.

Angel now heard behind him a shuffling and a sigh.

'Sir? Could you please stand aside so I can take care of the lady behind you?'

But Angel didn't move because Alba was done.

'Ready?' she said, smiling at Angel.

'W-W-What do you mean ready?'

'Ready to go?' She then noticed the shop assistant was waiting. 'Oh, have you not paid?'

'Erm . . . I thought . . .'

'Angel, but it's only nine pounds. You don't even have nine pounds?'

'Um . . . no . . .'

Alba reached into her handbag with a sigh. 'Ay ay ay, Angel. Madison really did a number on you, didn't she?'

Angel stepped aside so that Alba could pay. He gazed into the distance, feigning thought.

The transaction complete, Alba very visibly handed the bag to Angel. 'Here you go, Angel. Follow the washing instructions, don't forget the softener, and more importantly, don't rip it!'

Angel moved swiftly, eager to leave the shop.

Outside, Alba hailed a taxi, which took them back to campus.

'Alright. I've got to head to the flat and do some reading. See you later.'

'See you later . . . and . . . thank you.'

'Now you go back to your room, change into your new sh—' Alba stopped, her mouth open and eyes wide.

'What?'

'Angel? Where's the other bag?'

Angel lifted his hand and saw he was only carrying the Tesco bag with the flowers and chocolates.

'Oh, balls!' he muttered, turning to find the taxi far down the road and rounding a corner.

Chapter LVIII

The threat of Johannes ever present, Angel thought it best to disappear somewhere the strongman wouldn't think to look for him. The video editing suite seemed optimal: if it was available, he could book it for a block of time, lock himself in, and sit there reading his assignment for Food and Literature until it was dark. Of course, darkness wouldn't guarantee his safety, but if it served to disguise Johannes, it would also serve to disguise him.

At the Film, Music, and Media building, Angel found he was in luck, for the suite was unbooked. Before going in, he grabbed a stapler from one of the print media rooms.

The suite was as sterile and barren a space as it was possible to find. Every material was artificial. A sharp-cornered Formica desk, harsh neon lights, and various objects of polyvinyl chloride and polyethylene terephthalate taking the form of speakers, a keyboard, an editing console, screens, prickly low-pile carpeting, and stiff swivel chairs, plus acrylic polymer wall paint. There were zero decorations.

After closing the door and ensuring it was fully and firmly locked, he sat on a swivel chair and took off his shirt. He turned the ripped sleeve inside out and stapled the fabric back together at one-centimetre intervals. He then turned the sleeve the right side out and examined his work. It was less than ideal, but, the shirt being navy blue and nowadays fairly loose, the new seam would be disguised by the folds. Or so he told himself. Upon re-donning the shirt, he found the mended sleeve decidedly heavier and stiffer along the forearm than the other.

While he was at it, he also stapled the rip in his jeans.

The course reading materials for Mastropasqua's class were in his room, or in the library, but Angel thought he'd read whatever he could find online about early modern cookbooks, which was what they were going to cover the following day.

Before doing that, however, Angel checked Madison's Instagram.

She had posted a new image.

The image showed the now green-haired Madison seated at a Formica restaurant table, facing with determination an enormous meat and cheese sandwich, sitting alongside a mountain of chips and a bucket of Coca-Cola. The sandwich was on a metal tray lined with a white-and-red-checker sheet of paper. '5-lb philly cheesesteak challenge,' her description said.

Angel winced.

So vulgar!

No tablecloth, no crockery, no cutlery.

Worse, eating like that, she was going to get fat!

Angel rubbed his forehead.

Maybe it was part of her secret plan to make people underestimate her. But he remembered the deception involved making people think she was a drunken party person. What did gross food challenges have to do with it?

Angel pressed the home button twice and swiped Instagram up into the stratosphere.

Moving his visit forward seemed increasingly urgent, despite her reassurances. Maybe her asking him to fly over this month was a cry for help. He opened WhatsApp, located his mother in the contacts, and got ready to type. And this time he got as far as typing the letter 'H'. But beyond that he was unable to proceed, and, once again, he closed the app.

Too nervous to read now, he sought calm in music. But everything in his iTunes reminded him of Madison in some way or another, no matter the genre or the tempo. Arcangelo Corelli's 12 Concerti Grossi reminded him of a date at St Cuthbert's Church in Earls Court back in April, when he took Madison to a baroque music concert. *Der Graf von Montecristo*, the German musical adaptation of Dumas' novel, reminded him of an afternoon they spent in Hyde Park, jointly reading the novel. Jean-Henri D'Anglebert's harpsicord transcriptions of works by Jean-Baptiste Lully reminded him of their first dinner date, at Le Gavroche, in Mayfair—£580 he'd gladly spent to make her swoon.

As a last resort, he tried to get at least some of the information he needed for his class by watching YouTube videos. But there was hardly anything remotely useful and he was barely able to concentrate anyway, his brain having turned into a buzzing beehive.

Chapter LIX

Angel left the media building and, careful to keep himself hidden behind hedges, fences, statues, and other structures, travelled a circuitous route to the dorms. In the gardens he was seen by Amelia, who was on her way back to her room.

'Angel!' she said, smiling broadly, 'Where have you been all day?'

Angel quickly put the Tesco bag he was carrying in the rubbish bin he'd just passed. 'Er . . . um . . . I . . . I bumped into Alba and she took me to The Lanesborough for tea with Vera.'

'Oh, so you two have made peace? Excellent!'

'Um . . . er . . .'

'Well, at least you made it out of there in one piece, which is something, no? How brave of you to go. I'm very proud of you.' Amelia nodded with approval.

Angel's smile was wan at best. 'Yea . . . it was good.'

'Come to my room. We'll chat.'

'Er . . . are you sure that . . . um . . .'

'Don't worry about Betsy. She has more serious things to worry about, to be honest. And I'd like to talk to you about something that's happened.'

'Oh? Okay.'

Angel followed Amelia to her room, keeping, all the same, a wary eye out for Betsy when they passed the second floor. He noticed, as Amelia offered him a seat next to her on the bed, that a large, empty, heart-shaped box of chocolates was sticking out of her bin. From the rubbish that had accumulated around it, the box had been there for most of the week. The flower he'd left her was in water, in a tall glass, and she'd pinned his poem on her corkboard.

'Have you heard about Johannes?' said Amelia.

'Er . . . yes, Alba and her sister were discussing it in the tearoom.'

'What do you think?'

'Um . . . wasn't he at the cinema at the time?'

'What—do you think she's made it up, Angel?'

'No, no . . . um . . . it's just that maybe the victim made a mistake . . . you know, erm, mistook him for someone who looked similar.'

'Angel, what are you saying? This is very serious.'

'Um . . . it's just that I thought I saw him there on Saturday, while I was queuing to get the snacks. Didn't you see him? He passed right by you.'

'No, I didn't see him. Are you absolutely sure it was him?'

'Yes, yes . . . he saw me and waved at me on his way out. It looked as though he was coming out of a film.'

'Angel, if you're sure it was him, you need to come forward as a witness.'

'Oh, well, it's just . . . um, the thing is that . . . um . . . I'm not really sure . . . I wasn't feeling well, you know? Er . . . there was a lot of people . . . and . . . the person was far . . . and he could have been waving at someone else near me . . . or behind me . . .'

'But Angel, all the girls are scared now. And if Johannes really was at the cinema, then the man who did it is still out there.'

'I-I-I . . . um . . . um . . . I just can't . . . I-I-I can't be sure . . . I can't be sure. I wasn't feeling well . . . I was dizzy. You . . . er . . . you sure you didn't see him?'

'Angel! Listen to me. If you saw him there, you're a witness and you must come forward to make a statement. If you don't, they'll expel Johannes, but the man who did it will still be out there. He could hit any one of us next, including me.'

'D-D-D-Do do do y-you . . . er . . . do you, er . . . think Johannes could have done that?'

'I don't know him that well. He never gave me a bad impression, but a woman can never be sure. There are many dangerous men out there no one would suspect.'

'B-B-But there are also dangerous-looking men who are . . . er . . . you know, gentle giants.'

'I don't know the answer. But, if you saw him, and you're absolutely certain it was him, you must make a statement. Otherwise, you could be putting all the girls on campus in danger.'

'I-I-I just can't be sure.'

'But there's CCTV at the cinema, right? So if you make a statement, the police can check it, and we'll know.'

'I-I-I don't know . . . thinking about it now, I'm almost sure it wasn't him.'

'Well, think really hard, Angel. Try to remember. And do it soon. If there's a rapist loose out there, he'll do it again unless they catch him. And they won't catch him if the police won't look for him.'

'I-I-I really don't think I saw him.'

'Think about it. Please. I'm scared. We're all scared. And you could make a difference.'

CHAPTER LX

On the way back to his room, Angel collected the Tesco bag from the rubbish bin. He now had ten pounds and one penny in his pocket, having borrowed a tenner from Amelia, whom he'd led to believe he would use it to get some food.

Now he had the funds required to send the box of chocolates to Madison—plus the flowers, once he'd pressed them. They would serve as a suitable stopgap, to remind her of him and of the romantic and elegant values they shared, until he scrounged the money to fly to the United States of America.

The room was like a sauna, thanks to the blazing radiators. Chad or Brad or whatever, was thankfully gone. At the pub, drinking, no doubt. His mess, on the other hand, had grown, and had covered most of the floor; the bin had overflowed on Sunday, and surfaces had been fully colonised by bottles several days ago. Angel kicked the rubbish that had invaded his half of the carpet towards his roommate's.

Able now to walk unimpeded, Angel propped the box of chocolates between the Marcel Proust volumes on his bedside table, and the windowsill directly behind it, so that the box was sitting at an angle.

He then put four of the roses, minus the stems, between two sheets of his parchment-like paper and pressed them down. This procedure he repeated with the remaining roses. Finally, he stacked every book he had on top of the three rosen sandwiches.

A knock on the door.

'Angel?'

Johannes.

Angel jumped from his seat and, stepping gingerly, so as to make as little noise as possible, moved towards the door, intending to lock it by turning the skeleton key as quietly as he could. He was only part way to his destination when there was a second knock.

'Angel? Are you there?'

Angel resumed moving at a sloth's pace, but Johannes opened the door and poked his head in. He was disguised, as before.

'Angel! Finally!'

'Johannes! Um . . .'

Johannes stepped inside and closed the door behind him. 'What happened earlier? You never came out of your class.'

'Um . . . er . . . I-I had, I had more than one class.'

'Never mind,' said Johannes, lowering his hoodie and removing his sunglasses. 'Did you give them your statement?'

'Er . . .'

'For fuck's sake, Angel! I asked you yesterday!'

'No . . . it's just that . . . I-I-I had classes and I wanted to go over it and show it to you first.'

'Fuck, Angel! I really need you to do this. Show it to me now.'

'Erm . . . um . . . er . . .'

A noise behind Johannes.

'So Friday, yes Angel?' Saïd's voice.

Johannes turned, revealing Saïd standing at the threshold of the open door.

'Um . . . yes. Friday,' said Angel.

'Okay, my friend.'

'Okay.'

Saïd went back to his room, leaving the door open.

Johannes returned his attention to Angel. 'Right. The statement.'

Angel went to his desk, walking slowly, then began moving binders and papers around. 'L-L-Let me look for it.'

Angel could hear Johannes' heavy breathing behind him.

'Come on, Angel. Let's go! I'm not supposed to be here. You know that. Hurry up!' said the Swede.

'Y-Y-Yes . . . yes . . . I know . . . I'm just looking for it. I put it here on my—'

'Sir, I'm going to have to ask you to leave,' said a voice behind them.

Both Angel and Johannes turned. Two stern-faced campus security men were at the door, staring at Johannes.

Johannes turned to Angel, 'Fuck's sake, Angel. Fuck you!'

'I-I-I . . .'

'Sir? You must leave *now*.'

Johannes waved at them. 'Yea, I'm coming.' He again turned to Angel. 'Give them that fucking statement. Fucking tomorrow morning, Angel!'

'Um . . . um . . . er . . . yes, yes, I will, I promise.'

The security men grabbed Johannes by the arms in order forcibly to remove him. But the strongman shook them off and sent them tumbling like bowling pins.

'Fuck you!' he shouted at one of them with his terrifying, deep voice. 'I'm leaving, okay? I'm fucking leaving.'

A wooden baton rang as it hit the Swede in the head, hard. At first it was as if the baton had done nothing, Johannes' neck being the thickness of an average man's leg, but Johannes faltered in momentary confusion, allowing the security men to grab hold of him again and force him out of the room. Johannes threw them off a second time as if they were rag dolls.

'I said I'm leaving!' he shouted again, touching his skull where the baton had hit.

He began walking and the security men, knowing they were no match, but wanting to be seen doing their jobs, led him out.

Angel leaned out of his door to look down the corridor at his receding friend. Angel's entire body trembling, heart pumping, breath shallow, stomach churning, he caught the red-faced Johannes throwing a glance back at him, emitting lightning bolts, the rage in which hit him in the heart like the hammer of Thor.

Chapter LXI

Angel sat on his bed—hands still shaking, heart still stomping, Johannes still filling his mind—and stared into space for a long time.

Then, he noticed the rich, pleasant aroma of warm chocolate. Like a camera on a tripod, his head swivelled on a pencil neck, his nose sniffing the air. Was Saïd standing in the corridor with a mug of hot chocolate, waiting to accost him the moment he left the room? But this chocolate smelled like good Swiss chocolate, not the vegelate powder dissolved in water they dispensed at the canteen. Besides, coffee seemed more Saïd's taste. Same with Camaro. Angel had only ever seen him drink coffee. Never mind. He wasn't opening the door, no matter what happened outside or who knocked. For good measure, he locked it firmly and laid in bed to look at his phone.

He'd lose himself in old photographs of Madison. The one he knew, with the lustrous long hair. That would calm and soothe him. But the aroma was stronger, he found, lying down.

Angel turned his head.

'Oh, my goodness!'

Angel jumped out of bed and grabbed the box of chocolates. He'd momentarily overlooked, when he first laid it down, that the gap in between his Proust and the windowsill was filled by the blazing radiator. The chocolates had all melted and, by thus moving the box, the brown liquid poured over his bedside table, the carpet, his caseless pillow, his jeans, his suede shoes.

Angel stood for a moment looking down, arms apart, box in one hand, fingers brown. He scanned the room for something to clean the mess, but nothing was usable. His only choice being toilet paper from the lavatories, he made to head in their direction.

But his phone rang, stopping him in his tracks.

It was Madison.

Angel spun his wheels for a few seconds, head turning from side to side, whirling his hands in the air, weight of his body shifting from one foot to another, until he finally made the radical decision to wipe his hands on his sheets, lest by delaying further he missed Madison's call.

'Hello?' he said, in a high, flustered voice.

'Hello, Angel. It's Madison!'

'Hi. Hi. So good to hear fr—'

'Yea. Isn't it great to hear from me again so soon?'

'I'm-I'm-I'm utterly delighted!'

'Good. That means you are a man of discerning tastes.' She chortled.

'To what . . . er . . . do I owe the pleasure?'

'Have you booked your flight?'

'Er . . . um . . . no, no, I haven't had the chance. I've been so busy with uni . . .'

'What—with 60% As? You can get by with just half-remembering what you heard in class, Angel.'

'I've had a tonne of reading to do. I . . . um . . . I want to get 100% As.'

'Well, you're getting an F from me right now, mister. Come on, Angel! Aren't you *dying* to see me?'

'Yes, yes, of course! In fact, I was . . . um . . . going to look for flights tonight.'

'Cool. Why don't you open your laptop and look for it while we're on the phone?'

'Um . . . er . . . I-I-I . . . um . . . I was going to do it later because I still have reading to do.'

'I see. Well, in that case, I expect a message from you before you go to bed.'

'Y-Y-Yes, of course. I-I-I will look for flights after I'm done.'

'Alright. Everything good there?'

'Yea . . . um . . . I . . . er . . . saw your Instagram post.'

'That was *insane!* Right?'

'Um . . . but . . . don't, don't . . . um . . . don't y-you w-w-worry that . . . um . . . you might have to . . . er . . . end up buying new new new jeans afterwards . . . ?'

'Why? I didn't spill any.'

'Um . . . I mean . . . it's a lot of food . . .'

'I'm kidding, Angel. You worry I might get *fat.*'

'Er . . . um . . . no, no . . . not necessarily . . .'

'Well, I've decided to get fat on purpose.'

'Oh, really?'

'Yes. I've decided I'm going to let go and get really fat. Will you love me still?'

'Um . . . yes, of course . . . but-but-but what about your health?'

'Don't you know you can be healthy at every size?'

'Um . . . b-b-but why?'

'Because why not? Besides, it will make you look more manly.'

'I'm sorry?'

'Yea. Don't you see? The things that distinguish a female body from a male one are more pronounced when the female is fat. So, if you only like skinny women, you could well be a closet homosexual. Not that there's anything wrong with being gay, by the way, it's just a reality. And so, if I'm fat, and you love me, people will think you're more manly.'

Silence.

'So, will you still love me?'

'Um . . .'

'Because I'm craving McDonald's right now.'

Angel's voice leapt up into a squeal. 'McDonalds!'

'Yes. I'm dying for a big, *greasy* burger with lots of French fries. And a big Coke. And apple pies. Like, maybe five of them.'

'Oh, my goodness . . . oh, my goodness.' Angel rubbed his forehead.

'So you'll still love me, right? No matter how fat.'

'Er . . . um . . .'

Madison cackled. 'Angel, I'm kidding.'

'Oh . . . phew!' Angel only managed a half-hearted laugh. 'I was worried for a moment!'

'I really had you, eh?'

'Ah, yea, yea, you did. I'm so relived.'

'But you would love me anyway, right?'

'Yea, yea, of course I would.'

'What if I weighed two hundred pounds? Would you love me still?'

'Er . . . yes . . .'

'What about three hundred? Would you love me still?

'Three hundred . . . yea, o-o-of course I would.'

'What about *four* hundred? Would you still love me then?'

'Ah . . . yea . . . yea . . . um . . . I'd love you no matter what size.'

'Cool. So I can get fat then.'

'Oh. B-But you said you were kidding.'

'I did. But I changed my mind.'

'Um . . .'

'Ha haaaa! Got ya again!' More cackles.

Angel half laughed.

'Well, the truth is, Angel, that the food challenge was fake,' said Madison. 'What happened is that there are girls in the dorm who are jealous of my figure and me and a couple of friends thought it would be funny to rile them up by making them think I can eat like a pig and still remain slim.'

'Oh, that's . . . er . . . that's so funny.'

'We had a blast doing it!'

'Yes, yes . . . I-I-I'm sure you did.'

'Now those girls are so jealous they don't know what to do with themselves.'

'Yes . . . um . . . I can imagine.' Angel's accompanying laugh was still hesitant, peremptory.

'Well, anyway. I've got to go now. It's been fun chatting with you, Angel. Will you send me a message tonight? About the flights?'

'Yes . . . yes . . . I will. Before I go to sleep.'

'Cool. I can't wait to see you.'
'Neither can I.'
'Speak to you soon, Angel.'
'Yes . . . um . . . speak to you soon. Oh wait! Ah—'
But Madison had ended the call.

Chapter LXII

'One of you made a formal complaint to the Faculty Pro-Vice-Chancellor about my allegedly *sexist* behaviour,' announced Professor Mastropasqua. He was clad in his usual black frock and cravat. He paced confidently, scrutinising the students' faces all the while.

'And I'm *glad* the accusation was made,' he continued. 'I'm glad it was made because I don't mind saying that I *hate* women.' He paused for effect. '*All* women.' Another pause. 'In fact, women are *despicable* to me,' he snarled, leaning forward with a gurn and a fist. Then he straightened and stood in front of Mass of Hair, who was pointing her iPhone camera at him, angrily recording. Speaking in a normal voice, he said to her 'Are you offended yet? Because this is going to get a lot worse. Do you need better lighting?' He faced the students again.

'I hate women, gay or straight, trans or otherwise, the same way I hate men, of any description—although there are few proper ones these days—who *do degrees* in English Literature and *cannot* string a coherent sentence together when asked a question.' Pause. 'Most of you would be better off training for a trade—*manual labour*—although I suggest avoiding trades where you have to lift heavy objects, because from the look of most of you . . .'

Having done his manual labour earlier in the day, Angel could only think of food. Once again, at the canteen, his co-workers had left him just dry toast. Angel suspected it was a running joke at his expense, but one look at Skinhead's or Unibrow's face and he knew it was pointless to bring it up.

He remembered taking Madison to the Ritz for breakfast back in March. She'd wanted to taste their £180 caviar omelette in addition to their full English, which, Angel had been disappointed to discover, tasted the same as a normal one, despite the £40 price tag. But money had been unimportant. It was about the experience: the baroque décor, the fine buffet, the grand atmosphere, being among discerning people, being treated with curtesy and deferment, being of a certain standard of refinement and pedigree. He remembered Madison relishing every moment, smiling back at him from across the table, gawking at the Versaillesque fantasy decorations, snuggling up to him as they walked through Green Park, towards the Victoria Memorial and Buckingham Palace, and then along St James Park Lake, before heading for the Household Calvary Museum. He'd been wearing his hickory-brown velour jacket, his suede shoes, and a dark grey shirt by Eton, which he'd bought to be at his best for her. Afterwards,

Madison had wanted to see *Dumbo*, so they'd gone to the Odeon Luxe in Leicester Square, where they had ordered food from their seats at the beginning of the film.

Angel awoke from his daydream at the sound of students getting up to leave. Mastropasqua was standing behind his desk, looking down and frowning as he closed his attaché case. Angel grabbed his bag and headed out.

In the corridor, Mass of Hair bawled her eyes out while comforted by another girl.

'We'll get the bastard, don't worry,' the latter said, as Angel passed by.

He wondered what Mastropasqua had said to upset her thus.

As he approached the entrance up ahead, Angel became conscious again of his safety at the university. So far, he had not received any emails stating that he had been suspended, so perhaps Betsy had decided not to report him—yet. He hoped that the incident with the toilet stall having happened so suddenly and quickly, she'd not recognised him. He had, after all, exited the scene at lightning speed. Still, there remained the problem of Johannes. He had thrice flouted the campus ban and was therefore capable of doing it again. He could, in fact, be waiting for him outside the building right now.

Angel stopped walking mid-corridor, the entrance to the building at some distance ahead. He rubbed his forehead for a moment. Then, he turned around and headed for the lavatories, this time making sure to enter the correct one, and locked himself in the farthermost toilet stall—which was also the cleanest.

He got out his phone and checked Madison's Instagram.

She had posted again.

Occupying the left half of the image, Madison smiled at the camera; next to her stood a woman, who also smiled. Madison's hair was still green, but it was now a foot shorter, ending six inches below her shoulder. Her caption read. 'Freedom! I've always been ridiculously attached to my long hair. No more! And it feels awesome!'

Angel found he'd put a hand to his forehead, so great his shock had been. Her beautiful long hair! It would take years to grow back!

'Why?' he whispered.

The woman next to Madison would be her stylist, the barbarian who'd criminally chopped her locks, who'd defaced his beloved princess. The stylist's big, square jaw and wide mouth he found repellent. A vulgar woman with no appreciation for the pre-Raphaelite aesthetic.

He closed the app and put his phone away. He sat there—coccyx on the toilet lid, forearms on his knees, staples digging into his skin—staring into the floor, thinking.

An hour passed.

He checked the time on his phone. It was well after two o'clock.

Lunch!

Angel bolted out of the stall and made his way to the canteen at a forced pace, all the while checking his surroundings for the possible appearance by Johannes. He reached the canteen undetected, but when he arrived at the serving counter, he found all the display trays had already been removed.

'Oh, for goodness' sake!'

He stretched his neck to see if he could get the attention of the kitchen staff. But the kitchen was mostly kept out of view by a wall. The supervisor caught sight of him and went over to the counter.

'Yes, Angel,' she said.

'Is all the food finished?'

'Lunch hour is over. It's half past two.'

'But is it all gone?'

'I'm afraid so.'

'Is there really nothing left at all? I'm really hungry.'

'We have four onions left over.'

'Oh . . .'

'I can chop them up for you and put them on a plate.'

'Er . . . um . . . oh . . . o-okay.'

'Wait here.'

Angel heard Emmanuel laughing in the kitchen. A few minutes later, he appeared with a plate heaped with diced raw onion. He held it out to Angel with his enigmatic gaze.

Angel took the plate, went to the nearest table, and, taking one of the chairs down from the tabletop, sat down to eat.

Chapter LXIII

Angel. Bent in half. On his bed. Blazing pain. In his stomach. In his liver. Worst agony. Gas. Onions. More onions. All he can taste. All he can think about. Acid. Sour burps. Face contracted. Grimaces. Every second a minute. Every minute an hour. Every hour a day.

Afternoon fades into darkness.

Midnight.

Door opens.

Light floods in.

Human silhouette.

'Angel, my friend! It's Friday. You got my tenner?'

Angel moans.

'What's that?'

Angel mumbles.

'Okay, my friend. But it's Friday. You owe me ten pounds.'

Silence.

'Have you got the money?'

Moan.

'What's that?'

Silence.

'You alright, my friend?'

Silence.

'Okay, okay. I come back later.'

Door closes.

Syd's face. Laughing. A serpent comes out of her mouth. Bites Madison on the neck. Fangs sink into pale flesh. Madison smiles. Enjoys it. She begins to mutate. Hair turns green. Then falls out. She eats burgers. She's fat. Angel pleads. She laughs. She can't walk. Uses frame. Is crawling. Has no leg. Gave it to Syd. Or Syd took it. Syd has a knife. Syd-Demon. Cuts Madison's face. Madison asks for more cuts.

Angel opens his eyes. Darkness. Terror. Chills. Scrunches lids shut. Hides under blanket. Chills pass. Terror fades.

Door opens. Silhouette. Baseball cap. Backwards. Stumbling figure. Darkness. Crashing noises. Bags crinkling. Bottles ringing. Swish of fabric. Shoes dropping.

'Shhhhh!' the shape says.

Chapter LXIV

'Dude. You have to start eating. It's freaking me the fuck out,' groaned Josh or Todd or whatever, still lying in bed, in the stupor of slumber, as Angel pulled up his trousers.

Angel said nothing, and the American rolled over to slumber some more.

'I'll buy you another pizza tonight,' Chad or whatever mumbled.

Angel could barely stand on his pipe legs. He could still taste the onions. The aftertaste would not go away. For once he looked forward to dry toast after his morning shift. He would not be able to stomach anything else. Although even cold margarine and artificially sweetened fruit preserve would be nice.

His phone vibrated.

It was Madison. She'd sent him a message.

MADISON: You never messaged me with your flight details

ANGEL: I experienced a contretemps. I'll look tonight.

MADISON: You don't love me anymore

ANGEL: I do! I just haven't had a chance to go on Skyscanner.

MADISON: If you truly loved me you would have already bought your tickets

ANGEL: I've just been swamped. I promise!

MADISON: Are we dying?

ANGEL: I'm sorry?

MADISON: Should I get another boyfriend?

ANGEL: No! I will look for a flight. Tonight. I promise.

MADISON: Why not now? You're up

ANGEL: I'm on my way to the canteen.

MADISON: Good you can do it over breakfast

ANGEL: I have to eat quickly. I have an early class.

MADISON: At 6 am?

ANGEL: I've got some reading to do still.

MADISON: See? You don't love me. You put your reading ahead of me

ANGEL: It's for a class!

MADISON: I'm not number one for you

ANGEL: But I have to do my assignments!

MADISON: I knew it. It was all a sham.

ANGEL: It was not a sham. I love you passionately. I've just got uni. I promise I'll look for a ticket tonight.

MADISON: I don't know what's up with the delay

MADISON: You go on the website. Choose a flight. Pay with your card. Done.

ANGEL: I'll do it, I promise!

MADISON: All this delay and indecisiveness is very unattractive

ANGEL: I will book boldly.

MADISON: Do it after class

ANGEL: Okay, I'll do it after class.

MADISON: I shouldn't even have had to say that. You should have thought of that on your own! You don't love me! I'm second

ANGEL: No, you're first! Always!

MADISON: Then skip your class and book the flights

ANGEL: I'm really sorry but I can't. I've got to do my reading so I can get top marks.

MADISON: You only care about your marks. You're selfish

ANGEL: I'll skip the class and book the flights.

MADISON: Don't worry about it. It's OK

ANGEL: What do you mean?

MADISON: It's OK. Forget about it

ANGEL: I'll book the flights. I promise.

MADISON: You go to class. Hurry, you're gonna be late

ANGEL: I'm sorry, but I don't understand. Don't you want me to look for flights?

MADISON: No. Go to class

ANGEL: I'll look after class. I promise!

MADISON: Gotta go

ANGEL: I'll send you the details

But Madison had already gone offline.

Chapter LXV

Holding his tray, Angel scanned the canteen for a free table. He noticed Amelia waving at him, bidding him to sit with her and Jae. Angel did as invited, even though Jae looked displeased.

'Hello, Angel,' said Amelia.

'Hello,' said Angel.

Jae looked away.

'You look like death,' Amelia said.

'Um . . . I-I didn't sleep well last night.'

'Poor Angel. Lunch will do you good.'

Angel threw a glance at the entrance, in case Johannes was in the vicinity, then looked at his potatoes and pasta, hoping the latter's cheesy sauce had been made without onion granules.

'We've heard about Johannes. Are you okay?,' said Amelia.

Jae finally looked at him.

'Yes, I'm-I'm okay.'

'How did he get into your room?'

'H-He followed me there.' Angel shrugged his shoulders, wide-eyed.

'Why did you let him in?'

'He just . . . walked in.'

'What did he want?'

'Um . . . he . . . um . . . h-he didn't get a chance to say anything because security came to get him.'

'Did he also ask you to make a statement, Angel? Is that why?'

'Um . . . no, no, no . . . I don't . . . I-I don't know what he wanted. It was the first time I saw him since he . . . er . . . got in trouble, and he didn't get a chance to speak.'

'And did you make the statement we discussed, Angel?'

'No . . . I-I-I didn't get around to it.'

Jae asked, 'What statement?'

'Angel thinks he saw Johannes at the cinema when we were there last Saturday. He told me on Wednesday night that Johannes had waved at him.'

'I-I-I'm not sure it was him,' said Angel.

'I asked Angel to think about making a statement, because if Johannes was elsewhere then the man who raped Elise is still out there.'

Jae asked, 'And did you intend to make the statement?'

'Um . . .'

'That'll be a no, then.'

Amelia said, 'We've heard he got violent.'

'Er . . . yes, he did. He was very aggressive.'

'Well, I'm glad he's been expelled now.' Amelia pressed her lips together.

Angel's eyes widened. 'H-H-He's been expelled?'

'Of course, Angel. With an accusation like that, and then breaking onto campus and getting violent with security, what else could they have done?'

Angel tried to sound surprised and a little shocked. 'Oh.' His knees began bouncing.

Jae asked, 'Did you see Johannes at the cinema, yes or no?'

'Um . . . I can't be sure . . . He was far . . . I had food poisoning.'

'You should make a statement. Tonight.'

'I don't think that's necessary anymore, Jae,' interceded Amelia, 'Johannes has proven to be violent.'

'If Johannes knows Angel saw him at the cinema and Angel, who is his friend, is refusing to come forward, of course he's pissed off.'

'But there's no justification for violence,' said Amelia.

'No. But we also know he's full of steroids.'

'Still not a justification for violence. Besides, he could have just messaged. He knew he was banned from campus.'

Jae turned to Angel, 'Does Johannes have your phone number? Or your email address?'

'Er . . . no.'

'That's why Johannes broke onto campus,' said Jae to Amelia.

'He could still have contacted Angel via Instagram or other social media.'

Jae addressed Angel again. 'Let's see your phone.'

'Um . . .' Angel picked up his phone, but instead of handing it over, he passed it into his other hand, away from Jae. The blonde quickly reached over and snatched it off him.

Angel's stared, eyebrows aloft. 'Um . . .'

Jae tapped the screen, held it before his face to unlock it. Angel made to grab the phone back but the blonde again was too fast. 'Um . . .' he said.

Jae said, 'Instagram.'

Angel's voice rose an octave. 'Um . . .'

'Messages.'

Angel made a silent plea to Amelia, but she was looking at Jae.

'Aha!' said Jae, 'There. He has a request from Johannes. Which Angel has ignored.'

Amelia thought about this for a moment, then said, 'Angel, you must make a statement. However bad it looks for Johannes, if he's innocent, and there's a man out there still on the loose who could come for us, the police need to be informed. Otherwise, you're putting us at risk.'

'Um . . .'

'Tonight,' said Jae.

Amelia put her hand on his arm. 'Will you, Angel?'

'O-Okay, yea. I will.'

Jae scoffed, '*Finally.*'

'Thank you, Angel,' said Amelia.

There was a pause, during which they all ate potatoes and cheesy pasta.

'Mm! Angel, what happened with Mastropasqua yesterday?' Amelia asked.

'Er. . . Nothing. Why?'

'Because one of the female students went on Twitter and started posting about him under the everydaysexism hashtag. A few others joined in. And of course Betsy got in there, even though she's not taking any of his classes.'

'Er . . .' Angel inflated his cheeks, then released the air slowly as he cast his mind back. 'He-He said one of the students had complained about him to the Pro-Vice-Chancellor.'

'And was he sexist towards her in class?'

'Um . . . er . . . H-H-He asked her a question last week and s-she couldn't articulate her answer . . . S-She said *you know* a lot so h-he got impatient and moved on. He . . . um . . . prompted her a couple of times but it was all a word salad.'

'And did he say anything else?'

'Um . . . He said that most of us should get proper manual jobs rather than waste his time.'

Jae laughed—a sound Angel had only heard once before. 'Hands down—he's the best professor at this university.'

'But is he *sexist*?' asked Amelia, looking at Angel.

'Er . . . I-I-I think he hates all the students—except Vera.'

'There. See? His favourite student is Vera. A woman. That's why the hashtag is stupid.'

'It's not stupid. Sexism is a real phenomenon,' said Amelia.

'Being called out for being inarticulate is not sexist. She just happened to be female.'

'Maybe she felt targeted.'

'She *should* feel targeted. She's here to learn, and she won't learn if she's not told when falling short.'

'But if she's treated more harshly than a male student, then it would be unfair targeting.'

'I'm a female student and I've only ever seen him target stupid students, which is the majority.'

'Maybe he targets more females than males.'

'The student body is majority female.'

Angel raised an index finger to get attention. 'Th-Th-The girl was crying after class.'

'But maybe he targets proportionally more females,' said Amelia, speaking to Jae.

Angel piped, 'Th-The girl was crying after class.'

'The girl was crying, Angel?' asked Amelia.

'She's a cry-baby,' said Jae.

'Come on, Jae. You don't know that.'

'I've taken his classes and when he called me out for not meeting minimum standards, I didn't go bawling my eyes out on social media. I studied.'

'I can't imagine you ever not meeting minimum standards.'

'That's because I'm at the library and not the pub.'

'You're so harsh, Jae. Not everyone is as tough-minded as you.'

'Then they should toughen up. The world out there won't soften just because someone can't take it.'

'But tough love doesn't work with everyone. Some people respond better to nurturing and mentoring.'

'Nurturing and mentoring are not always available.'

'Okay, but even if this girl misused the hashtag, it doesn't make the campaign stupid.'

'The campaign has become stupid because too many women abuse it and it's become a hate fest.'

'Alright, *some* women abuse it, but many are also pointing out genuine sexism and misogyny. I'm not a feminist, Jae, but I'd rather be able to walk down the street without getting catcalls.'

'That's not a feminist issue.'

'Oh, Jae. How is it not a feminist issue?'

'Because it's a degeneracy issue. The general loss of manners in our culture.'

'But it only affects women. Angel, you wouldn't catcall a woman, would you?'

'Um . . . no, o-o-of course not. Never!'

'Degeneracy affects both men and women, but it manifests differently depending on sex.'

'And what's the woman version?'

'Exposing themselves while drunk in town centres on Friday and Saturday nights.'

'Okay, yes, that's not very nice, but they're not sexually harassing anyone.'

'The sexes are different, so there's no straight equivalent to anything. But it is throwing something sexual and unsolicited at other people in a public space.'

'But men expose themselves too. What about the drunken louts baring their bums in town centres?'

'They're also degenerate.'

'Still, they don't get criticised for it the same way women do. Haven't you just proven my point by not mentioning them alongside those drunken women?'

'Both represent bad behaviour, both are the result of degeneracy in our culture. That's the deeper problem.'

'But if something disproportionally affects one sex . . .'

'Men are disproportionally affected by other things that women don't have to deal with.'

'Is that so? What do you think, Angel?'

'Um . . .' said he, raising his head; he'd been preoccupied with his cheesy pasta.

Jae said, 'Women are under constant pressure to be beautiful. Men are under constant pressure to be tough.'

'And women aren't?' said Amelia. 'When I go into central London, or use the public transport, I need look tough, otherwise I'll be harassed.'

'The problem is still degeneracy. It's degenerate men who create that pressure, not men in general.'

'But degenerate women don't harass men to the

point they feel unsafe, the way these degenerate men do with women. So if it's a degeneracy issue, it's one that affects women and not men.'

'Men have to be on their guard around degenerate men just as women do. On top of that, men are expected to protect the women in addition to defending themselves; women are not expected to protect men. A woman can scream and use pepper spray; any man she's with would be expected to be physically strong and have combat skills, which take years to develop. Similarly, degenerate women are also a physical threat to other women, and again it falls on the men to protect them. So the issue is still degeneracy.'

'And what about women in office jobs? Unless they're tough, they won't get promotions.'

'Competitive environments require everyone to be tough. If women enter a competitive environment with men, they need to be as tough as the men.'

'And yet, men are praised for it, but women are criticised. They're called viragos and harridans. Surely you know that, Jae. You're criticised for your toughness all the time!'

'They're weak. Their opinion is irrelevant.'

'What about the double standards when it comes to sexual partners? If a man has many, he's regarded highly by his peers, but if a woman has many, she's thought loose.'

'Promiscuous men are unserious and therefore degenerate.'

'But that's what you think, not how our society sees it.'

'Our society is degenerate.'

'And what about the fact that feminine hygiene products are hugely more expensive than men's?'

'Men's Nivea is more than double women's Nivea.'

'Nivea, but certainly not the anti-ageing creams.'

'Men are less concerned with ageing than women.'

'There are still many products that are more expensive for women.'

'When cheaper, buy men's products, problem solved.'

'What, like men's tampons?'

'Tampons are now gender neutral.'

'Oh, Jae. I *know* you don't believe in that.'

'Society does. What I think is irrelevant.'

Amelia laughed. 'Oh, dear. Okay. So you're happy for tampons not to be treated as articles of first necessity and be subject to VAT? You, who hate taxation?'

'The Finance Act 2016 commits the government to zero rate on all women's sanitary products. It will be implemented after Brexit is finalised.'

'And what about the fact women can't wear the same outfit twice in a row, but a man can do so for an entire week without anyone commenting?'

'Since when does a man notice what a woman wears? All they see is: dressed or naked. Any comments come from other women.'

'Ay, Jae! You've got an answer for everything! But now that I think of it, it does seem your theory of degeneration is wrong. It presupposes that there was a time when women were treated better by men—before they began *degenerating*, as you put it—but if anything the *opposite* is true. Women were subject to a great deal more male violence in the past. And as much as I love the aesthetics of the 19th century and the Middle Ages, I wouldn't like to live back then. And I doubt you would either.'

'Chivalry set a good standard that has been lost.'

'But don't we have overly romantic notions of chivalry? Remember these knights we read about in Mediaeval romances were *errant*. Their damsels were abandoned for *years* at a time. I know you would demand a lot more from any man you *deigned* to be with!'

Jae thought for a moment. 'Insufficient data. Further research is needed.'

'Anyway,' said Amelia. 'Angel, now that we are on the subject of knights and chivalry, I have been thinking about our date last week. I feel we need to make it right. Would you like that?'

'Er . . . yes . . . um . . . um . . . of course. I-I'd like to,' he said.

'How about you take me out to dinner,' said Amelia.

Angel looked momentarily stumped.

'Don't worry, she'll pay,' said Jae, without even looking at him. 'As usual.'

'Er . . . um . . . yes . . . sounds good,' Angel said.

'Oh, this is fun!' Amelia squealed. 'How about, then, you find a restaurant and book us a table for tomorrow evening?' said Amelia, smiling at him, and grabbing his hand.

'Er . . . er . . . um . . . yes, yes, I can do that.'

Amelia giggled and clapped her hands. 'Oh, I'm excited!'

Jae gave Angel a pointed look.

'Oh . . . um . . . yes . . . I'm excited too.' He offered Amelia a weak smile, then focused on buttering his cold potatoes some more.

Chapter LXVI

The coast seemed clear of Johannes, so Angel emerged from behind the last hedge before the dorm and walked the distance at a forced pace.

His corridor was deserted, yet it seemed a good idea to tread softly. He reached his door and inserted the key gently, careful not to make a sound; he turned the lock at a snail's pace, his ear tuned for any sound, either from the lock or from the door behind him.

The lock clicked.

Angel's eyelids scrunched.

The door behind him opened in an instant.

'Angel, my friend!'

Angel swore silently, then turned to face Saïd.

'You owe me ten pounds,' his neighbour said, extending his hand.

'I-I-I'm sorry, but I don't have it yet.'

Amelia's ten-pound note burned in his pocket.

'But it's Friday. You said you'd pay me back on Friday.'

'Yes, I'm so sorry. I just don't have it. I-I just don't have it right now.'

'Okay, when? Tonight?'

'Er . . . c-c-could I pay you next week?'

'Next week? What day? Monday?'

'Um . . . y-yes, okay, Monday.'

'No problem, my friend.'

'Um . . . thank you.'

'But you owe me fifteen.'

'I'm sorry, what?'

'If you pay back on Monday, you owe me fifteen.'

'B-But why?'

'Business administration.'

Angel blinked, uncomprehending.

'Interest, my friend. I'm providing a financial service.'

'Oh, I see. But I'm only ask . . .'

'Ten today, fifteen on Monday.'

'But that's 50% interest!'

'Could you have borrowed a tenner from a bank?'

'No, but . . .'

'At short notice?'

'N-No, but . . .'

'But you could from me.'

'Yes, but . . .'

'And you took the money.'

'Yes, but . . .'

'So you stick to my terms. Ten today, or fifteen on Monday.'

'But . . .'

'So Monday, yea? Fifteen pounds on Monday.'

'Um . . . um . . . o-okay.'

'Okay, my friend. Speak to you on Monday.'
'Speak to you Monday.'
'But fifteen pounds, yea?'
'Yea, fifteen pounds.'
'Okay, my friend.'
Saïd disappeared into his room.
Angel disappeared into his.

Chapter LXVII

Chad or Brad or Josh or Todd was gone. However, he'd knocked over a one-litre bottle of Lucozade, most of whose contents had spilled onto the carpet. Capillary action had ensured that surrounding paper, cardboard, socks, and t-shirts had been tinted by the orange nectar.

Angel examined his jacket, although first he had to remove the mountain of dirty hoodies, shorts, underwear, and chinos his roommate had been piling on top. The crusty stains would require tools to remove, not just water and soap.

He took the cap off a Bic pen and got to work.

His phone vibrated.

Destiny had sent him a message.

DESTINY: Hi Angel. It's father's birthday next weekend. Have you booked your train ticket?

Angel hesitated.

ANGEL: Do I have to go?

DESTINY: Yes you do

ANGEL: I haven't booked anything.

DESTINY: Book it now and let me know the details. Mum asked me to collect you from the station

ANGEL: I don't have money for a ticket.

DESTINY: Two ticks

Angel put the phone down and got on with his scraping.

His phone vibrated.

DESTINY: Ticket only £40. Mum asks why you don't have money

ANGEL: Books and daily living. Uni is very expensive!

DESTINY: Mum says it wasn't anywhere near that expensive last year. She wants to know where the money has gone

ANGEL: Lots of small things to do with uni.

DESTINY: Mum not happy. Says she wants you to sit down with her and give her a full account when you're here next weekend

ANGEL: But I don't have any receipts. They were small transactions!

DESTINY: Find them. Mum not happy

DESTINY: Mum has just mentioned how much money she sent you six months ago. Mind: blown. What are you doing, Angel??

ANGEL: I'll do what I can.

DESTINY: She says she's going to book your ticket now

DESTINY: She's seeing red

DESTINY: I won't hear the end of it

ANGEL: I have a lot going on next weekend. I'm swamped with reading.

DESTINY: You'll have 3+ hours to read on the train

ANGEL: I might not be able to go.

DESTINY: Angel you're coming

ANGEL: But we are expected to attend plays and cultural events for the literature modules. I can only go on the weekends.

DESTINY: Mum says you only have one or two classes a day. Plenty of time during the week

ANGEL: But we have to go on certain dates! It can't miss them or they'll fail me!

DESTINY: Give me your Professor's name

ANGEL: What for?

DESTINY: Mum will phone the university

ANGEL: That won't be necessary.

DESTINY: Then find a way. You're coming

ANGEL: I also have a date.

DESTINY: With what money?

ANGEL: I have a little bit.

DESTINY: OK, so you can book your train ticket, then

ANGEL: It's a really cheap date.

DESTINY: Since when do you do cheap dates, Angel? If you have money for a date, you have £40 for a train ticket. So book it now and let me know the details

ANGEL: Sorry, I don't have enough for a ticket.

DESTINY: *Sigh* Wait

Angel waited, then, nothing happening for a couple of minutes, he put the phone down in order to get back to scraping. His heart raced.

His phone vibrated.

DESTINY: OK. Friday 11 October, 19:30, King's Cross. I'll collect you from York

DESTINY: And don't worry, it's direct

ANGEL: But I can't get to King's Cross!

DESTINY: Why not?

ANGEL: No money for Tube.

DESTINY: Wait
DESTINY: Mum will transfer £10
DESTINY: For use in Underground fare only!
ANGEL: Okay
DESTINY: Don't forget!

Chapter LXVIII

Angel remembered that for the 17th Century Literature class he was supposed to have read, by Tuesday, Margaret Cavendish's *The Blazing World*, a work of utopian science fiction. He found it among the tower of books pressing Madison's roses, slid it out, lay down on his bed, and got reading.

But one sentence in, he decided to check Madison's Instagram.

She had posted a new image.

It was another selfie, this time in three-quarter profile, gurning at the camera while holding a clawed hand. 'In for a penny, in for a pound!'

As if convulsing from a grand mal seizure, his arms sent his phone flying across the room. Angel grabbed his head, thumbs, index finger, and middle finger touching his forehead, framing haunted eyes that stared into space.

'What have you done?' he whimpered.

Did he really see what he saw?

Angel got up and, reluctantly, picked up the phone, which had landed by the door, screen-side down. He flipped it, eyelids scrunched up, and slowly opened his eyes, one at the time.

It was true.

Madison had shaved one side of her head.

And were those acrylic nails?

He zoomed in.

Yes. Fake acrylic nails in a green and orange chevron pattern.

So garish! So *vulgar!*

And that animalistic face!

Sick to his stomach, Angel simply threw the phone in the bin.

As the bin was overflowing, the phone slid off to land on the floor.

What was going to happen?

How was this going to end?

He had to save her!

And she was asking for rescue.

The odd way she'd been behaving lately . . . the forces of good and evil, pulling her in opposite directions.

And at the moment, *evil* was winning.

But he was stranded in Britain, thousands of miles away, penniless, unable to reach her.

He resolved to ask the canteen supervisor about his pay. Although it seemed risky. The question could get her hackles up and lead to his being sacked altogether! It would be three weeks still until the end of the month. If he got paid on the 31st, he'd still be able to fulfil his promise to Madison to visit her in October, if he bought a flight for that same day.

But what if the money was insufficient?

What would he do then?

And what if, even if he got paid, and it was sufficient, the library made good on the threat to pass his debt to collection? By then more penalties would have been added. The total would be greater than anything they paid him at his minimum wage job.

They'd come and take away all his money, plus his laptop and his phone.

He'd still be able to use the university computers, but he would not have access to the library.

Which meant: his marks would suffer.

Which meant that Madison would be unimpressed.

Which could mean that she would break up with him.

And even if she wasn't and didn't, even if he evaded the debt collectors and flew to see her on Halloween, there was no telling what else might happen in the next three weeks. Piercings? Mutilation? Amputation? There might be nothing left to save anyway!

Angel rubbed his forehead.

The only thing he could do at present was to keep showing up for work, on the dot, every morning, and read the assigned materials.

Maybe his mother would pay the library fine.

Although that would mean telling her.

Which would mean her telling his father . . . an even worse prospect.

Yet, being reunited with Madison, and saving her from evil influences, was worth every sacrifice.

The knights sacrificed for their princesses.

And their travails were always rewarded.

He picked up his book and lay down in bed to read, determined to see this through.

But instead of reading, he stared into space.

Chapter LXIX

Because he'd only calmed down enough to sleep after it was light, and because he'd only woken up at three in the afternoon, Angel had missed both breakfast and the lunch hour. And because he was hungry, he could not read—*The Blazing World* or any of his other course materials. And because he could only think of Madison, he could not stay in his room.

Angel retrieved his phone from where it'd fallen the previous evening and went into the university gardens. Madison might be far away and under an evil spell, but he could still provide a positive influence via Instagram. Therefore, his plan was to find suitable scenery and take a selfie that could transmit the values of romantic elegance he and Madison had enjoyed when she'd been with him.

But at a short distance from the dorm, he encountered another depression in the terrain. This one was deeper, but very localised and in the middle of a lawn. Angel went over to examine it, although always keeping an eye open for signs of Johannes. Then, it occurred to him that he could prop up his phone with a stone in the middle of the depression, put the timer on, and take a selfie, with himself standing at the rim against the nearby oak tree; the phone thus set up would make him look taller.

Angel found a suitable stone and placed it the depression. He stood to pull out his phone, scanning the horizon in case Johannes was lurking behind a tree or a hedge. The ground, however, softened beneath him, creating the sensation of sinking. Realising what might be about to happen, he turned to leap out of the depression. But the sinking sensation accelerated exponentially and overtook him; with a sonorous crash, he fell through, landing on his back, on a patch of lawn that ended up four or five feet below the surrounding surface.

It took a few moments for Angel to recover. As he stood, clothes muddied, he saw Babyface running towards the sinkhole. His apparent worry was a surprise, as Angel had taken him for a psychopath incapable of emotion. Alas, when Babyface reached him, Angel realised he was not worried about him; Babyface was worried about the sinkhole. Without saying a word, Babyface pulled out his phone, tapped a number, and with the device against his ear walked towards the outhouse near the main building, where the estate maintenance-crew hung around joking and having cups of tea.

Left to his own devices, Angel climbed out of the sinkhole. The students who now approached it ignored him in favour of gawking, taking selfies, and posting pictures on social media. The boys mostly filmed or photographed the hole once or twice; the girls mostly photographed themselves next to the hole, numerous times, doing kissy and other Instagram faces, before airbrushing them, thinning their bodies, and whitening their teeth. Angel took a couple of pictures of the sinkhole, then left the scene.

As he re-joined the paved footpath, Angel noticed there was something wrong with his left shoe. He lifted his leg to examine the sole and found the rubber top piece on his heel had come off.

'Oh, for God's sake,' he moaned in a quiet voice.

Angel found he'd left the top piece behind while climbing out of the sinkhole.

Chapter LXX

The edifying selfie now having to wait until he could wash his clothes, and unable to stand the hunger any longer, Angel headed for The Departure Lounge, careful to ensure the coast was clear before going from hedge to tree, from tree to statue, from statue to bush, from bush to building. He calculated he could get a cupcake and still have enough money left to send the chocolates and flowers to Madison.

'Any tea or coffee with that?' asked the barista, a slender man with a short beard called Julian.

'Er . . . no. Just tap water.'

'Any soft drinks?'

'Er . . . no. Just the tap water.'

'How about a lemonade?'

'No, no. Thank you.'

'Orange juice, freshly squeezed?'

'No, thank you.'

'An infusion—how about an infusion?'

'No.'

'Herbal tea? Very good for you.'

'No.'

'Hot chocolate? Yummy!'

'No.'

'Milkshake?'

'No.'

'Smoothie?'

'No.'

'We have a three-pound meal deal if you choose a drink and a bag of crisps.'

'No, thank you.'

'Wedge of lemon with that tap water?'

'No, thank you.'

The barista snorted but filled a glass from the tap. He made to hand it to Angel, who reached for it, but Julian pulled it back at the last instant.

'Are you sure? Last chance!'

'I'm sure, thank you.'

'You'll have to queue all over again if you change your mind.'

'Um . . . I-I won't change my mind.'

'Alright. I'll be here when you do.'

'Thank you.'

Julian offered a bright, fake smile. 'No, thank *you!*'

Angel chose a table at the deepestmost part of the café, facing the entrance (in case of Johannes), and got started on his cupcake.

His desire for solitude was soon frustrated, for, of all the tables available, two enormous, muscular students with tattoos chose the one beside him. They each had a tray piled with meaty sandwiches, plus tall glasses of cranberry juice.

'So, what's Johannes gonna do?' said the bearded one facing the front of the café.

A chill ran through Angel, who tilted his head forward to hide under his hair. He pricked up his ears.

'He'd like to sue the uni and that American tart,' said the unbearded one. 'For now he's hoping the CCTV video recording at the cinema will show him there.'

'You said there was a witness too.'

'Yea, but the little bitch won't come forward.'

'Why not?'

'Scared.'

'Of what?'

'Fuck knows.'

'Who is it?'

'One of the students here. I'll ask Johannes to describe him. Maybe we can, you know . . . have a word with him.'

'Yep. I'm in.'

Angel attempted to control his trembling by slowing down his respiration.

'You said his bail was revoked?'

'Yea. After they caught him in the dorms the other night.'

'Why was he on campus?'

'Probably to speak to that little cunt who won't come forward.'

'We should ask around at the dorm. They'll know who it is.'

'Yea, yea. Let's do that. After we eat.'

Angel scrunched up his eyes; his knees began bouncing but he immediately stilled them.

He had the urge to swallow, but stopped himself lest the gulping be too loud.

The guys ate in silence for a minute.

'When's your competition?'

'March.'

'What are you aiming for?'

'Three-hundred squat, two-hundred bench, three-fifty dead.'

'Is Luke Richardson gonna be there?'

'Don't know. But Shahlaei might. He's yet to confirm.'

Angel could not finish his cupcake. His stomach had clamped shut and began cramping, his bowels loosened. He decided to wait out his neighbour's meal and only slip away after they'd left.

'Stinks in here, doesn't it?' said the bearded one.

Silence.

Angel speculated that the other guy had pointed at him with his eyes. Angel had, after all, not been able to do laundry in two weeks and repeatedly spraying his outfit with deodorant could only do so much. Clad in feculent rags mended with staples, to his neighbours he probably looked homeless. It occurred to him that, if they identified him, he could maybe feign mental incapacity, like catatonia or schizophrenia, and thus prevent an otherwise certain beating. He imagined himself being held down and one of the brutes laying punches on him until they broke his nose, knocked out his teeth, and detached his corneas, while the other kicked him in the ribs, liver, and kidneys, until they were all mince. He also imagined he would not be able to identify his attackers to the university or the police because doing so would mean explaining their motives and that'd be embarrassing. And, worse of all, he imagined he would be unfit to travel, placing Madison beyond reach. On the upside, perhaps his condition would elicit her sympathy, and yank her out of her self-destructive madness, provided he could tragically explain his wounds.

'There's the American slag,' said the bearded neighbour, *sotto voce*.

Angel peeked through hair curtain to find Epic Eyebrows and Pink Hair approaching a table opposite. Both were holding trays loaded with cupcakes, chocolate sponge, and cappuccinos. Epic Eyebrows had a sad, nervous air. Upon seeing three men, or perhaps two and a half—the two powerlifters and Angel—sitting at nearby tables, she stopped and scanned the surroundings, obviously looking for a deserted space, or at least a space without male company. The presence of the two girls, Angel worried, meant the potential arrival of Betsy, so he hoped they'd move on. Angel directed an eye towards the counter, to see if the big American girl was ordering. But Betsy was absent; Angel exhaled with relief as quietly as he could.

'Which one is it?' asked the unbearded powerlifter.

'The less fat one with the eyebrows.'

'Fucking 'ell. She looks like a right snobby tart, that one.'

Unable to find a table with the desired characteristics, Epic Eyebrows seemed momentarily stumped, but Pink Hair reassured her, and persuaded her to take the table they'd originally aimed for.

Without taking her eyes off the powerlifters, Epic Eyebrows grabbed a cupcake, before putting it back down, unbitten.

'I need to use the bathroom. Will you come?' she said to Pink Hair.'

Pink Hair, wrinkled her nose in a manner that showed her upper gums. 'I'm tired. I've just sad down. I don't want to get back up,'

'Will you please?' Epic Eyebrows cast a glance at the powerlifters.

'They're just students here.'

'I'm scared.'

'You can't let this control you, Elise. You have to live your life.'

'I know. But it's too soon . . .'

'Take your phone. I have mine right here. And I have pepper spray.'

'Okay . . .'

Reluctantly, Epic Eyebrows left, casting a backward glance at the powerlifters, who'd not taken their raging eyes off her.

As soon as she left, Pink Hair grabbed her phone and began photographing her food and herself, multiple times and from multiple angles, deploying a dictionary of smiles and kissy faces.

The two powerlifters carried on eating in silence.

Ten minutes later, Epic Eyebrows returned and rejoined her friend at their table.

Still fearing Betsy's arrival, Angel's eye spied the counter, where he found Beard, clad in a camouflage t-shirt and ordering.

Another chill ran through Angel, whose knees had once again sprung to life. Why was he there? Did he come often? He followed Beard as the latter got moving, tray in hand. And, of course—why would it be otherwise?—Beard walked towards where Angel was sitting. Angel mouthed a silent expletive.

Beard saw the two American girls and, with a cheeky smile and easy-going familiarity, greeted Epic Eyebrows.

'Fancy seeing you here, love.'

But Epic Eyebrows appeared shocked by the sight

of him. Her pale face drained of what little colour there was, and she sat paralysed, eyes bulging, mouth open. She whispered something to Pink Hair.

Beard approached their table.

'You won't mind if I join you, sweetheart?' he said.

Epic Eyebrows' blurted response was, 'We're leaving.'

Both she and Pink Hair immediately rose to their feet, grabbing their bags, and made their way out—but not before Pink Hair backtracked for a moment quickly to grab the slice of chocolate sponge she would otherwise have left behind.

Perplexed by the swift departure, Beard shrugged his shoulders and sat at the adjacent table.

'The fuck was that about,' said the bearded powerlifter, in a low voice.

With pursed lips, his companion shrugged his shoulders and got started on his fifth sandwich.

Angel's phone vibrated.

He flinched.

He pulled out the device and brought it under his curtain of hair.

AMELIA: Shall I meet you at The Departure Lounge at 7pm?

He hesitated. What if Beard recognised him? The longer he stayed, the greater the chances. On the other hand, Beard might leave soon, while Johannes' friends planned to comb the campus with a fine toothcomb to obtain a description of him, Angel, and 'have a word'. It seemed safer to stay put.

ANGEL: Can you make it 6?

Chapter LXXI

'Hello, Angel.'

Angel looked up to find Amelia in a figure-hugging black lace dress, with shawl, elbow-long black gloves, a string of pearls around her neck, and high-heeled pumps.

Angel stared, perplexed by her attire.

Then he remembered.

The date!

He quickly faked a smile and said, 'Oh . . . er . . . you look amazing.'

'Thank you,' said Amelia shyly. 'Do you like my new perfume?' She offered him her neck to smell.

Angel stood and went to inhale.

'Very nice,' he said.

'*J'adore* by Christian Dior.' Amelia pronounced it in an exaggerated French.

'Very good.'

'Oh, Angel! What's happened to you? You're covered in mud!'

'Um . . . I was swallowed up by a sinkhole in the gardens this afternoon.'

'Oh, no! Are you alright?'

'Yes, yes, I'm fine. 'Twas just the shock.'

'Oh, dear. The state of you. Do you want to stop by your room to clean up?'

'No! No, no. I'm fine.'

'Are you sure, Angel?'

'Yea, yea. It's fine.'

'Let me ask the barista for a wet cloth.'

'No, no. No need. It's fine. It's fine.'

'But Angel, they won't let you in anywhere like that. Please let me clean you up.'

'Er . . . o-okay. Okay.'

Angel thought he might as well buy himself a few minutes to think of a restaurant. Maybe, if he could convince Amelia to visit the ladies before they got going, he could quickly phone to make a reservation—or, rather, to see if there was any restaurant that could still take a reservation; on a Saturday evening, in London, that would be almost impossible now.

After a few minutes of wiping and rubbing, Amelia decided there was no more she could do.

'Well, it's dark in these elegant restaurants anyway,' she said. 'And there are many patterned jackets and trousers from designer brands.'

Then, before he could object, she took a small bottle of perfume out of her bag and sprayed him with it all over. Angel pretended not to notice the nearby students who were staring while attempting—not very successfully—to suppress laughter.

'There,' Amelia said.

Chapter LXXI

As they were leaving campus, Amelia holding onto Angel's arm, she asked, with girlish excitement, 'Any hint as to where we are going?'

'Um . . . Hyde Park Corner.'

'Should we hail a taxi? It's a bit drizzly.'

Angel needed extra time to decide on a restaurant. 'No . . . um . . . it's best to go by Tube.'

'Let's take a taxi, Angel.'

'Er . . .'

But he had no time to argue; Amelia had already raised her arm to hail an approaching black cab.

When the car stopped, Amelia stood motionless, holding her small Channel handbag in front of her with both hands, smiling at Angel in expectation.

'Oh, of course,' he said, the penny finally dropping. He opened the door for his date.

'What a gentleman,' she said, 'Thank you.'

'London Hilton at Park Lane,' said Angel to the driver.

'Oo!' said Amelia, all smiles. 'A hotel . . . interesting!'

Amelia slid closer to him, creating contact all long their sides, from shoulders to calves. The car joined the traffic.

'How's Madison?' said Amelia.

Angel moaned, dispirited. 'Um . . . awful . . . really awful . . . she's dyed her hair green and . . . chopped a foot off . . . and now she's shaved the side of her head.'

'Oh, dear.'

'It seems to get worse and worse.'

'Well, Angel, I would never shave parts of my head.'

'She's also wearing fake nails. I really don't like those things.'

Amelia slid off a glove and held her hand up, wriggling her fingers. 'You'll be pleased to find my nails are all natural.'

Angel glanced at them but said nothing.

'Do you think she'll end up getting a tattoo?' asked Amelia.

Angel's eyes nearly popped out of their sockets. 'A tattoo?!?'

'Many girls are getting them these days. And from what you've said, she's heading in that direction.'

'Oh, no!' Angel put his hands to his head and bent over, resting his elbows on his knees, suddenly hyperventilating, feeling the sleeve staples digging into his flesh but not caring.

Amelia turned to him so she could comfort him with a softly squeezing hand on his forearm and a caressing one on his back.

He whimpered. 'At least hair can be dyed and will grow back! But a tattoo!'

'I know, Angel. But if she ends up getting a tattoo, maybe she's not the right person for you. Maybe she never was.'

'No! She is! She's just fallen under evil influences. Met all the wrong people.'

'But, Angel,' Amelia said in a gentle tone, 'if she was the right person, don't you think she'd know better than to spend time with girls with shaved heads and tattoos?'

'Her mind's been poisoned!'

'In just a month, Angel?'

Angel had no answer.

'And if she's so easily influenced, clearly she doesn't have a solid core.'

Again no reply. Just short, rapid breathing.

Amelia continued. 'Do you really want a girl you can't trust because you never know what self-destructive phase she'll embark on next?'

'I need to save her,' he burst out.

'But what will you do? Tell her off?'

'No . . .' Pause. Angel leaned back and noticed the driver's mocking eyes in the rear-view mirror, which he then pretended not to have seen. A moment later he caught sight of the driver's forearm, which was covered in blonde hair and old, faded tattoos. 'I think when I go there, I will take her to classical music concerts . . . That will remind her.'

'That sounds lovely . . . but do you really want to date a girl with tattoos?'

'I must get there before she gets one.'

'What if she's getting one right now, Angel? You couldn't stop her.'

Angel again curled into himself, even more tightly than before, hyperventilating like a steam engine.

'Oh, Angel. Calm down. I didn't mean to upset you. Let's talk about something else.'

Amelia waited until Angel's paroxysm dissipated. When he sat up again, she smiled and said, 'You know I'd never get a tattoo. They're very inelegant.'

The taxi left them in front of the twenty-eight -storey building. Angel got out immediately; Amelia stayed behind to pay. Once she stepped out of the vehicle, Angel offered his arm to lead her into the lobby. She took it, but, before he could get them moving, she craned her head back to admire the high-rise, a 1960s modernist block that, floodlights casting azure onto the façade, could pass for the local administrative headquarters of an android civilisation.

'Wow,' she breathed. 'It's quite a sight when they light it up like that.'

Angel waited until Amelia was ready. No need to rush the inevitable.

'Let's go,' she said, eagerly pointing at the entrance with her eyeballs.

She let him lead them through the revolving doors and, almost in slow motion, he walked towards the lifts ahead, his heart hammering in his throat, knowing every step brought her closer to disappointment.

'Look at that rug,' she gushed, tugging at his sleeve. 'It's like an exploding star.'

She giggled and held on tighter. As did the people around them, her head moved in all directions, her orbs sponging in the marbled floor, coffered ceilings, and wood panelling.

'Um . . . Londoners didn't want the building when it was first proposed,' Angel said, regurgitating something he'd once researched to impress Madison. 'They didn't like the idea that it would overlook Buckingham Palace.'

'I love that you know these things,' she said, grinning.

The restaurant was on the top floor. As the lift doors opened, Angel took a deep breath.

'Are you okay, Angel? You seem a bit nervous,' asked Amelia.

'No, I'm-I'm fine.'

They approached the entrance to the restaurant, the Galvin at Windows, as indicated by the sans serif gold lettering against wood panelling. Angel had taken Madison here on a couple of occasions; the first time, back in March, they had tried the *menu dégustation*, with wine, which had come to over three-hundred pounds; the second time, they tried the *menu prestige*, which, with desert and wine, came to about the same. But money was of no consequence back then—not like now, when maddening scarcity had made it a focus. If they stuck to the cheaper Market Menu tonight, it would be sufficient for the evening's purposes.

The hostess behind the desk smiled at them warmly as they approached. 'Hello, Sir. Good evening.'

Angel cleared his throat. 'Um . . . we have a reservation for—' Angel gave their names.

'Certainly, Sir.' The lady at the desk checked her computer screen.

Angel's ears throbbed with a deafening heartbeat.

'I'm sorry, what time is your reservation for?'

'Eight o'clock?'

The hostess scrolled back and forth with her mouse.

'I'm so sorry, Sir. Do you mind spelling your name?'

Angel did as requested, trying not to shift his weight from one foot to the other. He glanced over at Amelia, but she'd turned to admire the curved wall of mirrors.

The hostess checked the spelling of his name a second time.

Long pause.

Frowns.

Amelia smiled as she watched a well-dressed couple in their thirties leaving the restaurant.

'I'm terribly sorry, Sir. But I can't find your booking. Did you make it online, over the telephone . . . ?'

'Um . . . online?'

Another long pause.

'I'm so sorry, Sir, but I can't find your booking.'

'Um . . . is there a table available anyway?'

'I'm sorry, Sir, we're fully booked tonight.'

'Fully booked for the whole evening?' Angel knew better, and hated feigning such naivety, but he felt he had no choice.

'Yes, I'm afraid so, Sir. It's very busy on a Saturday night.'

'But if there was a glitch on the website . . . ?'

'I'm terribly, terribly sorry, Sir. On another day,

we'd do our utmost to accommodate you, but unfortunately we're fully booked and there's really nothing we can do.'

'O-Of course. W-What a shame,' Angel said. 'Er . . . thank you for your help.'

'I'm sorry. However, there are other restaurants in the area. You may have better luck with one of them if there's been a cancellation.'

'Yes. Will do. Th-Thank you so much for your help.'

'You're welcome, Sir.'

Angel looked at Amelia. He didn't have to affect distress; he'd wrecked the previous date and he'd already wrecked the present one. Amelia's face fell—but only for an instant, her crestfallen expression swiftly replaced with a smile.

'Oh, Angel. Don't worry, as the lady said, there are other restaurants in the area. Why don't we find one? It'll be nice to go for a walk.'

'Yes . . . er . . . let's do that.'

Angel pulled out his phone to find the other French restaurants he knew in the area. There were several, even more expensive than the present one, which didn't seem fair on Amelia, but, at this stage, he reasoned that she'd pay whatever it cost to save the date. Besides, the way she'd dressed suggested this was what she desired. Angel hoped her card would go through.

The nearest and easiest restaurant to get to was the Alain Ducasse at the Dorchester Hotel, about a quarter of a mile away. It had three Michelin stars. Angel had taken Madison for afternoon tea at The Promenade for Valentine's—with its sienna and gold marbled columns, gilded ceilings, brass lanterns, giant mirrors, and damask drapery and upholstery, a much more luxurious experience than the Lanesborough—but not for a meal at the restaurant, since he liked the latter's décor a lot less. Nevertheless, beggars couldn't be choosers, so once disgorged by the Hilton, Angel led the way, heading West down Park Lane.

'Is it very far?' asked Amelia, using her shawl to protect her styled hair from the drizzle.

'Er . . . no, just down the road.'

Park Lane was an eight-lane A-road, which did not make for a pleasant experience; it was wet and noisy with traffic.

'Angel, would you mind slowing down a bit?' She threw the shawl over her shoulder, unable to hold it up any longer.

'Oh, sorry.'

'High heels, you know,' Amelia said, in a good-humoured tone, panting nevertheless.

'Of course, of course.'

They covered the distance slowly and at decreasing speed, with Amelia taking ever shorter steps.

The Dorchester being a step up from the Hilton and more traditional, and also featuring marble and neo-classical wall mouldings, but with warmer décor in white, gold, and jasmine, Amelia's excitement was re-ignited as soon as they walked in.

'Give me a moment to compose myself,' she said, standing close to the famous Promenade.

Her face had reddened and acquired a sheen from the exertion. While her perspiration evaporated, she took in the luxurious yet cosy atmosphere, the silverware, and the live jazz music.

'Beautiful,' said Amelia, grinning from ear to ear. 'I think Vera told me about this place.'

'Yes . . . er . . . I imagine. Th-They've served afternoon tea here since 1931. The Alain Ducasse has a 1940s feel . . . um . . . a modern interpretation of traditional.'

'I'm excited! Okay, let's go.'

At the entrance to the restaurant, Angel cleared his throat again, fearing the worst.

'Um . . .' he swallowed. 'We haven't reserved a table, but I'm hoping you may have had a cancellation.' His heart was pounding.

'I'm sorry, we're fully booked tonight.'

'Maybe at a later time? We can wait.'

'I'm sorry.'

'O-Okay . . . thank you anyway.'

He looked at Amelia. Her face again fell, and this time the smile didn't return as quickly, or as brightly; the latter had acquired a tincture of sadness.

'Er . . . there's two other restaurants here.'

'Okay, let's try them.'

Alas, at both The Grill and the China Tang they obtained identical results.

He said to Amelia, 'Um . . . er . . . I know another one we could try elsewhere.'

'Is it far, Angel?'

'No, no. Just down the road.'

They went back out into Park Lane and again into the drizzly cold. Amelia contracted her shoulders and pressed herself against Angel, who led the way west.

'How far is it?' asked Amelia, her steps even shorter than before.

'Um . . . less far than from the Hilton to here.'

The truth was the opposite—easily double the distance—but Angel didn't have the heart to tell her. He hoped she wouldn't notice.

He also hoped that time passing would increase chances of a cancellation. It was, really, his only option; restaurant websites would not allow him to book at such short notice, and he disliked the idea of telephoning ahead because something in his voice, or the way he spoke, meant he was never treated well.

Midway to the Gavroche, their next destination, Amelia began limping slightly and hunching over. Angel was freezing, having no body fat to insulate him and having had only half a cupcake to fuel him since the previous day. His discomfort was accentuated by Amelia's; even though he'd been walking more slowly than normal, which prevented him from raising his body temperature, Amelia kept holding him back, like a partially released handbrake. She also leaned on him ever more heavily, which continuously destabilised him.

'Are you okay, Angel?' she said. 'You're limping.'

'Um . . . I'm . . . I'm just missing part of the heel of my shoe,' he said, taking it out of his jacket pocket. 'It . . . er . . . came off when I climbed out of the sinkhole.'

'You poor thing. When we get back, give it to me. I'll fix it for you.'

'Oh . . . er . . . really? Er . . . thank you.'

The half mile took them four times as long to cover as the previous quarter.

Before going in, Amelia pulled at Angel's arm to make him stop. They stood under the restaurant's wrought iron canopy.

'Angel, I need another moment . . .' she said, puffing, 'to compose myself.'

Amelia's face had become a gleaming tomato.

'A-Are you okay?' asked Angel.

'No worries. Just big girl problems,' she said, her half-smile faltering.

They gave it a few minutes, alternately hearing vehicles fizzing past on wet asphalt, pizza delivery mopeds buzzing by, or engines idling before traffic lights. Angel monitored Amelia's mood via her facial expression, but he was growing sullen, thus affecting her.

'Okay, let's go in,' she said, finally.

Angel offered his arm, and she took it. The warmth inside offered welcome relief. His soul, however, was in agony, knowing that the main dining room downstairs was small, perhaps even more unlikely than the previous restaurants to contain an empty table.

'Good evening,' came the polite greeting.

'Good evening' said Angel. 'Um . . . we don't have a reservation, but I hope maybe someone's cancelled and there's a—'

'I'm sorry. We're fully booked tonight.'

'Maybe at a later time? We could wait.'

'I'm sorry.'

'Okay . . . thank you for your help.'

As they turned to leave, Angel noticed Amelia's embarrassment. She let go of his arm.

'Where next?' she said, back under the canopy outside the front door. Having cooled off, she was shivering.

'There's . . . er . . . another restaurant a couple of streets from here.'

'Maybe we could find a pizza parlour nearby.'

'Pizza?!?' he nearly shrieked. 'No! I want to take you to a good restaurant,' he moaned. 'I'm not giving up.'

'How far is a couple of streets? It's miserable and my feet are aching, Angel.'

'Not far. Just two turns.'

Technically, it was three, and the distance more than a quarter of a mile again.

'Okay, Angel. I trust you.'

Aided by his phone, Angel led the way to the Hélène

Darroze, at the Connaught, which had two Michelin stars. He'd taken Madison there in April, when she'd ordered from the seven-item menu with the premium wine pairing, a meal that had cost him over one and a half grand, and only because he'd suggested they stop at two glasses; they had sat at the sommelier's table, with a view, via glass walls, to the adjoining limestone wine cellar, with its wall upon wall of racked bottles, and Madison had wanted to try a few more. However, if tonight they stuck to the five-item menu option and chose one seventy-five millilitre glass each of the classic wine, they could keep it under five hundred pounds. Again he prayed Amelia would have the funds, and again he wondered how fair it was to ask her to pay that much; she was a university student, after all.

How he missed the days when money was no object! He sneered at having to consider pecuniary issues; what mattered was living according to his aesthetic. His father had reminded him on a number of occasions that living according to that aesthetic required *a lot of money*—'money doesn't grow on trees'—and that to have a lot of money, one had to *earn it*, and that to *earn* it one had to attain *extreme levels of excellence* at something, and that to attain it and sustain it, one had to work *longer, harder, and more consistently than anybody else*. Angel appreciated and agreed about the excellence, but his father's hectoring obsession with 'reality,' always had a way of sucking the romance out of everything.

When they reached the Connaught, while still under the neo-classical portico, Amelia, for the third time, asked for a moment to compose herself. The weight of accumulated drizzle had partially flattened her hair; her foundation was patchy from perspiration; her eye make-up had begun to run. In full view of the liveried porter manning the portico, Amelia sat on the bench abutting its columns, took off a shoe, and massaged and wriggled her toes through the black nylon; then repeated the procedure with her other foot; it looked to Angel as if she'd lost sensation. All the same, he waited, pretending it was not as bad as it looked; convincing himself that her discomfort would fade quickly.

'Okay. I'm ready,' said Amelia, taking his arm, with neither enthusiasm nor hope in her voice.

'Um . . . Hélène Darroze was a disciple of Alain Ducasse,' Angel said.

'I'd be happy with just being able to sit down,' said Amelia.

The lobby was darker and smaller that the previous venue's, its décor ponderous with oak panelling and wall mouldings. They made their way to the restaurant, which had more wood panelling and ample, comfortable armchairs around its tables.

'Good evening.'

'Good evening. Um . . . we don't have a reservation, but I hope maybe someone has cancelled and you could offer us a table.'

'I'm sorry. We're fully booked.'

'Maybe at a later time? We can—'

'I'm sorry.'

Angel looked at Amelia, who had stepped aside to lean her aching back against a wall.

'Um . . . I'm so sorry,' he said, getting closer, 'We're not having luck.'

They made their way out. Amelia didn't take Angel's offered arm this time. Instead, she stopped before reaching the revolving doors.

'How about, Angel, we go for an ethnic meal. It's bound to be busy everywhere on a Saturday night, but we'd find a table at Wagamama's or at an Indian, for example, if we're patient.'

Angel squeezed his brain for a moment, unwilling to accept such a steep drop in standards.

'Er . . . no . . . er . . . yes, wait, I have an idea,' he said, simulating modest enthusiasm. 'I know this Peruvian restaurant.'

'Peruvian sounds good,' said Amelia, brightening up, although only a notch. 'How far is it?'

'Um . . . not too far. Just on the other side of Oxford Street.'

'Well, I suppose we're not far from there now.'

'I-I'm sure they'll have a table. Not a lot of people think of eating Peruvian,' said Angel, a spectre of doubt behind his smile; he'd made that up on the fly.

They got moving—albeit more slowly than ever before.

And also with frequent stops.

Angel noticed that Amelia had begun gently stamping the ground, keeping her feet flat at all times, rather than rolling them on their balls. After they passed Grosvenor Square, Amelia stopped to scan the street.

'Let's take a taxi,' she said, with an edge to her voice.

'But . . . but it's just up the road.'

'I can't walk anymore, Angel. And it's very wet.'

'Okay.'

She let go of his arm and made to sit down on one of the empty docks in the hire bike docking station. Noticing it was dripping with water, Angel promptly took off his jacket and placed it on the dock, to protect Amelia's dress.

'Thank you,' she said, without emotion.

Sadly, every taxi that passed them—and there were quite a few—was filled with happy occupants. How did all these people find taxis? Minutes dragged by, beaten down by road noise, drizzle, and occasional gusts of wind. When Angel next looked at Amelia, he found her sniffling, with her hands on her lumbar area, her face showing pain. Her make-up was now in full flow.

'Is everything alright?'

'No, Angel. But it's just a pinch. It will pass in a minute.'

Angel stood looking at her, numbed by indecision and depression.

'Angel, would you mind calling a taxi?'

'Yes, of course.'

Angel searched Google and dialled a number.

'Hello? Could I order a cab?' he piped.

'What address?'

'Duke Street, just past Grosvenor Park'

'It's very busy tonight. We're looking at an hour before we get to you.'

'An hour!'

'I'm afraid it will be an hour. Saturday night. Everybody's wanting a cab.'

'Okay. Never mind. Thank you anyway.'

Angel dialled another number.

The conversation went exactly the same way.

Angel dialled a third number.

Same result.

Each time Angel called, it became more difficult to speak clearly. He was chilled to the bone and trembling.

Many more minutes passed.

At last, Angel turned to Amelia. 'I'm I'm s-s-s-so s-s-s-orr-rry. The-the-the-re s-s-seem t-to b-be n-n-none a-available.'

'Try Uber.'

Angel tried Uber.

But, as before, there were no cars available anytime soon.

'I-I-It s-s-s-seem-ms w-w-we're c-c-cu-curs-s-sed.'

'That's okay, Angel. I feel better. Let's keep walking.' She took his arm again, putting almost all her weight on it, which caused Angel to zig-zag and shake with the flexion of whatever meagre muscles he had left.

'Y-Y-Y-You okay?' he asked.

'My feet really hurt,' she said, sniffling.

'W-W-We'll b-b-be the-there in-in n-n-n-no t-t-t-t-time.'

But before they'd taken two steps, Amelia's weight shifted suddenly, her arm letting go of him.

There was a thump.

'Oogh!' he heard, almost simultaneously.

Angel turned and found Amelia face down on the ground.

'Amelia!'

Angel dove down onto his haunches, next to his toppled date.

'A-A-A-Are you h-hurt?' he asked.

Amelia burst out crying.

Angel stared at her for a moment, then looked around him, not knowing what to do, save grabbing her handbag, which had landed some way ahead, and placing it by her ribs. He put a hand on her back, to comfort her. She cried long and noisily, only managing, 'I twisted my ankle,' between sobs.

At last, Amelia temporarily recovered from the shock, she rolled onto her back and held out a hand. Angel noticed her gloves were covered in grime and mud and that one of them had ripped, revealing a scraped hand.

'Help me up,' she said.

Angel grabbed the hand and both he and Amelia pulled, but all Amelia achieved was to pull Angel to the ground. She ended up having to sit up on her own by rolling on her side.

She sat for a while longer, crying some more, her shawl hanging limply from the crook of her elbow, also covered in mud and grime like the front of her dress. Angel saw she'd scraped both her knees.

What a disaster, he thought, getting back on his feet, palm on his forehead.

For lack of tissues, Amelia was forced to wipe her snot on her gloves. These, ruined, she took off and threw aside. In time, she calmed down.

'Help me stand,' she said, again holding out her hand.

Angel grabbed and pulled.

Amelia was too heavy for him, however, so her mass would not budge. Next, she took off her shoes and planted her feet flat on the pavement, holding out her hand for a third time. Angel grabbed and pulled as hard as he could while Amelia struggled to lift herself up, but her backside never left the ground. Her feet seemed too sore for the pressure demanded by the manoeuvre anyway.

At this point, two middle-aged men stopped by the couple. One wore a Barbour jacket and a tweed flat cap, the other a tweed jacket and a roll-up jumper.

'You alright, love?' said Flat Cap.

'Yes. I'm fine. Help me stand,' Amelia said.

Before they could organise themselves, a third man, Afro-Caribbean, wearing an anorak and a beanie, joined the group, taking position behind Amelia. He took charge.

Addressing the other men, Beanie said, with a high voice. 'Okay. You pull, I push. You pull, I push. Okay? Okay. Let's go. Count of three. Ready? Okay. One, two, *three*.'

Amelia's feet slid forward, instinctively guarding against pain, so the attempt failed. Amelia had only moved a few inches closer to Oxford Street.

'Put your feet before her toes,' said Beanie. 'Put your feet before her toes. Don't let them slide. Right before her toes. There. Okay. Let's go. You're ready? Ready? One, two, *three!*'

Amidst a collective groan, this time Amelia went up.

'Yehhh!' The good citizens cheered.

Angel stood looking at Amelia, dumb and numb.

'You alright, darling?' said Beanie.

'I fell,' said Amelia, timidly and getting weepy again.

'Is there anything broken?' said Tweed Jacket.

'No, I don't think so, just a scrape.' Amelia adjusted her dress.

'You with her?' said Beanie to Angel, pointing at him.

'Yes.'

'Okay. You buy her flowers. Okay? You buy her flowers.'

'Okay,' said Angel, automatically.

The good Samaritans got going, all walking towards Oxford Street, just up ahead.

Angel remained frozen, in a daze.

Without a word and with her shoes hanging from her fingers, Amelia walked towards Oxford Street.

Snapping out of his stupor, Angel followed.

Amelia turned right into Oxford Street, then right into the West One shopping centre, which was also the entrance to the Bond Street Underground station. Like a zombie, Angel continued to follow.

A few moments later he looked up to find himself passing under the golden arches of a McDonalds.

Chapter LXXII

The McDonalds was an oversized sardine tin. Informally dressed humans often sporting joggers, hoodies, beanies, and baseball caps stood nose to occiput, holding shopping bags, babbling noisily in a wild array of languages and dialects, exhausted and impatient to reach either the counter or one of the ordering screens. The scarce seating space was occupied by boozers, tourists, and vagabonds, hungrily devouring their meals or in the early stages of a sugar coma, the surfaces before them piled high with burger boxes, paper cups, and crinkly wrappers. At least it was warm.

Amelia stopped, charcoal tears rolling down her cheeks. Angel caught up and looked at her face. She dug into her handbag and produced a debit card, which she held out to him.

'Here. Order something.'

Angel was paralysed, both by Amelia's dejection and the surrealness of ending up there. 'W-W-What should I order?'

'I don't . . . care.'

'B-B-But I don't know your pin . . .'

'It's contactless.'

'Oh, okay.'

Angel became conscious of ears and eyeballs in the immediate vicinity, so he made to head for the counter, feigning equanimity.

'Angel?'

He stopped and turned. 'Er . . .Yes?'

'Please get me two Big Macs, large fries, large milk shake, three apple pies, and whatever you want.'

'Um . . . okay.'

He got Amelia's order and a McChicken sandwich plus a small Coke for himself, although not before queuing for an eternity with snotty customers sneezing around him. With a loaded tray, he wedged his way through the crowd. At one point, however, a boorish elbow bumped his arm, rocking the tray and overturning Amelia's milkshake. The plastic lid came off and the liquid spilled onto the tray.

'Watch where you're going!' Angel heard; he flinched, but ignored the voice and kept plodding, the tray sloshing and dripping.

At the sauce station, Angel used paper napkins to mop up the mess. Fortuna had smiled on him for once, and only the paper lining, the burger and apple pie boxes, and some of the fries were soaked. All the same, it took him endless minutes to make the tray presentable again, after which he couldn't decide whether to rejoin the queue to replace the milkshake, find Amelia to drop off the food before doing the above, or simply join her and offer her his Coke. Fearing that leaving her alone for even longer would make things worse, he chose the last option.

Amelia had found a table and it was obvious she'd been crying the entire time. Angel hovered.

'Where's the milkshake?' she asked.

Angel explained what happened. 'W-Would you like me to get another one? You could have my Coke in the meantime.'

'I can't be bothered. Just stay.'

Angel sat down.

For a while, they ate in silence; Amelia was too miserable to talk, and Angel didn't know what to say. The contrast between the gracious opulence he'd dangled before her and the gross circumstances into which he'd reduced them, however, eventually made it clear that there was only one valid statement he could make.

'I'm . . . I'm terribly sorry about . . . tonight.'

Amelia regarded Angel, sclerae still red. After a long moment, her features softened, the grief of humiliation melting into compassionate sadness.

'I understand, Angel. It's not your fault that the booking didn't go through.'

'E-Everything went wrong,' he said, moping.

'And you tried *so hard* to make it work.'

'I really wanted you to have a good evening.'

'It was stupid for me to wear high heels. That's my fault.'

'I . . . should have listened after The Dorchester. A good pizza would have been great.'

'It was so sweet of you to want to take me to a fine restaurant. You *really* wanted to make it up to me, didn't you?'

'Um . . . it's the least I could've done.'

'What a magnificent man you are.'

'I'm really sorry.'

'I know you are, Angel.' She held his hand.

'I have to make it up to you.'

'It was unfair for me to put the burden on you when you were not at fault the last time. I just knew you felt horrible and I wanted to give you the satisfaction of making it right.'

'I tried to hold it in as long as I could . . .'

'You don't need to explain, Angel. I know.' Amelia looked into his eyes. 'This was all my idea and I should have been paying closer attention, and not been so selfish.'

'You only wanted to see a film.' Angel shook his head, pursing his lips with regret.

'I forced you into these situations. Please forgive me.'

'Um . . . there's nothing to forgive. But I've never had two nights out go all wrong in a row. It never happened with Madison. I know how to take a girl out on a date.'

'I know, Angel. I saw it.'

Angel looked away, wistful.

'Angel? How much does it cost to eat in those restaurants?'

'Um . . . well . . . when I took Madison, it was three hundred and up.'

Amelia blinked, taken aback. 'Oh, dear. Just as well, then.'

'I once paid two grand.'

'Two grand . . .' she marvelled, her jaw on the floor and rolling down Regent Street.

'Yes. The wine can make it very expensive.'

'It's so sweet that you only thought of the very best, but my . . . two grand!'

'I . . . I w-would have suggested we drank sparkling water.'

'Angel, you didn't need to take me to these super-luxurious places—although it would have been nice. I only wanted us to have a good evening. I would have been happy with just a nice, cosy restaurant, even Pizza Express.'

'Oh.'

A moment passed, during which neither said anything, but merely floated like buoys in the sea of boozer hubbub.

'Angel?' she said, finally.

'Yes?'

'Where's your jacket?'

Chapter LXXIII

When he returned, Angel might as well have been thrown into a swimming pool with his clothes on.

'It's gone,' he said, dripping.

'Oh, Angel,' Amelia steepled her eyebrows. 'You loved that jacket. And you wasted it trying to keep my dress from getting wet.'

'It . . . er . . . it was ruined anyway.'

They looked at each other for an instant.

'Let's go back,' she said.

'Okay.'

They squeezed their way out of the McDonalds.

'Let's take the Tube,' said Amelia. 'We'll never find a taxi in the rain.'

Amelia put her right hand around Angel's arm, then lifted his forearm with the hand holding her pumps—to form a supporting horizontal when he didn't respond.

'Oh, sorry,' he said, as they resumed walking.

A few paces later, however, Angel registered that Amelia was ambling barefoot—in a city centre, with all the grime and filth that this entailed. He didn't relish the idea of walking on wet pavement, but he was soaked right through anyway, and in his ill-fitting rags people likely assumed him homeless. More importantly, the thought of him walking comfortably shod, while allowing Amelia to go discalced, to step onto a piece of glass or into a pool of urine, seemed ungentlemanly and likely to incur the wrath of Jae, Alba, Vera, and who knew whom else. And Madison would certainly be disappointed if she ever learnt of it. By a stroke of luck in the lottery of female emotions, Amelia had ended up blaming herself, but the situation was still fragile, and it seemed best to stay in her good books. Angel stopped.

'Um . . . you're not wearing your shoes?' he asked.

'They really hurt to walk on. It's like acid.'

'Er . . . let me give you mine.'

'Oh, Angel! Really?'

'Er . . . I-It's dangerous to walk around barefoot. I . . . er . . . I can't let you do it.'

He went down onto his haunches and began unlacing his right shoe. Amelia, meanwhile, stood, looking down, her hands on the sides of her face, smiling, her eyes tearing up.

'I hope they fit you,' he said, placing the first shoe by her foot.

Amelia slid it into the shoe, and Angel re-tied the laces. He noticed her delicate toes, her pale, angelic feet, swollen, bloodied, dirty, and rubbed raw in parts. It seemed criminal to have damaged them like that. All his doing.

'It's a bit long, but it's fine,' she said, feeling it with her foot and taking a couple of test steps.

'Um . . . okay. In that case, here's the other one.' Angel said, untying the laces of his left shoe.

They went down to the platform, Amelia limping slightly from the rubberless heel, Angel's soft feet stinging from the freezing tiles and the rough concrete. The diminution from his unshod status, both in stature and in standing, he felt as acutely as his awareness of urine, spit, chewing gum, spilled beverages, and Saturday night vomit.

But once again, Fortuna smiled on Angel, for when the train arrived, two seats were available. They took them, and Amelia put her head on his shoulder.

'Oh, it's pointy,' she said, pulling back, rubbing her cranium.

But she found her handbag served as a pillow. Angel chose not to mention that the Chanel logo was digging into his bone.

Chapter LXXIV

At the exit to the Underground station, Amelia hailed a taxi to take them to the university. This was after Angel had tried and four taxis had ignored him. Thankfully, it was easier to find them in the vicinity of the campus because of the absent nightlife.

Angel walked Amelia to the girls' dorm.

'Goodnight, Angel.'

'Goodnight.'

Amelia made to turn and walk into the building, but then hesitated. An instant later, Angel found himself receiving a kiss on the cheek.

He said nothing, did nothing.

'Goodnight,' said Amelia again, sounding a bit happier.

He watched Amelia disappear, still wearing his shoes, and walked back to the boys' dorm in his wet, muddy socks. Before going in, he observed the sinkhole had been encircled with a temporary barrier.

As he approached his room, he found the door open. A great din was blasting out of it, consisting of rock music, shouted banter, and outright screaming. Obviously, Todd or Josh or whatever, was having another of his parties.

But what if the two powerlifters were there too? Chad or Brad or whatever would have asked them to join him and his American hooligans. Angel thought it prudent to creep towards the door, hugging the wall. Once he reached the door frame, he began leaning in slowly to take a peek inside, hopefully undetected.

The door behind him opened suddenly.

'Angel, my friend!'

Angel scrunched his eyelids, then turned to find Saïd standing at the threshold.

'Monday, yes? Fifteen on Monday.'

'Yes, fifteen on Monday.'

'Okay, my friend. See you Monday.'

'See you Monday.'

Saïd retreated and closed his door.

Angel renewed his peeking manoeuvre. As soon as his eyeball crossed the door frame, Josh or Todd or Brad or Chad or whatever saw him. The American was sitting on his chair, clad in his usual khaki shorts, hoodie with printed letters, boat shoes, and reversed baseball cap. On the latter's bed sat two giggly girls, one chubby, one skinny, both American, both holding beer bottles, both drunk. On Angel's bed stood, with his shoes on, one of his roommate's chums from the previous time, also holding a beer bottle, while on the corner nearest to the door sat Babyface, holding a can of Tennent's Super. Babyface pierced Angel with probing yet impertinent eyes.

'Angel, dude!' shouted Chad or whatever, grinning.

Angel straightened and walked in.

'Two big guys came looking for you earlier,' shouted his roommate. 'They looked *pissed.*'

Angel's orbs widened; he knew the American meant angry, not drunk. He said nothing. It was too loud, and he didn't like shouting—particularly since he knew that, even if he screamed at the top of his lungs, no one would hear him anyway.

'I told them you'd be in later tonight.'

Angel's hands shot to his head. He hesitated for a moment, then hurried out.

'Angel! Bro! Where are you going?' the American called out.

Chapter LXXV

Everywhere else being out of the question, Angel headed for the video editing suite. He'd have to sleep on the floor, but, on the upside, it was clean and quiet.

Luckily, booze being students' priority number one on a Saturday night, the suite was available. Angel stole a few yards of bubble wrap and a bagful of shredded paper from the printed media room and used these to fashion a blanket and a pillow. But he neglected to consider the floor temperature, which, with his clothes still wet, felt as if below zero. And no adequate source of heat was on offer; the electric heaters the university had knocking about until last year had been banned and disposed of due to pressure from climate change activists. Neither was he able to find adequate cushioning for below the neck, a matter of necessity given the absence of padding from his own soft tissue; there was a sofa from which he could steal cushions, but he dared not take them in case their absence led to his being discovered.

Angel spent the night shivering, unable to sleep on the hard floor.

Chapter LXXVI

Like a possessed scarecrow, Angel ambled back to the dorm at the crack of dawn. He'd remembered that he was expected to have read Ann Radcliffe's *The Mysteries of Udolpho* for his Gothic Novel class on Monday. The edition Professor Turner wanted him to read was the Oxford University Press', which had 736 pages. But he had bought the edition published by Dover Press on account of the cover artwork; the problem with it, besides the prospect of being unsynchronised with course materials that referred to passages by page number, was that in the Dover edition, the same text had been compressed into 624 pages, with the consequent reduction in leading, font size, and reading speed.

Angel hoped that the powerlifters were not early risers, or so determined to confront him that they would have risen early to do it first thing in the morning. Keeping his orbs on the alert for oversized men with wall-like backs and leg-sized arms, Angel followed his route from hedge to tree, from tree to statue, from statue to bush, from bush to building.

The door to his room was closed, suggesting the party had ended. All the same, the stench of cigarette smoke lanced his nostrils from the corridor. Angel opened the door gradually and peeked inside; his roommate's guests were all gone except the chubby girl, who was sharing a bed with the American. Both were asleep. And both, having thick necks, suffered from sleep apnoea, which filled the chamber with a symphony of snores. The musk of copulation still lingered in the air.

The space between the door and his bed had, overnight, become an obstacle course. Not only the usual empty cans and bottles, the discarded sandwich packaging, the pizza boxes, the messy Subway wrappers, the greasy serviettes, the plastic bags from the off-licence, the smelly socks, the dirty underwear, the shorts, the hoodies, the pens, the pieces of paper, and the highlighter markers got in the way, but also spilled liquids, ketchup, crumbs, dried-up onion rings, limp lettuce, cigarette butts, ashes, a brassiere, women's jeans, a jumper, and several condoms had been added to the landscape. Finding a safe place to put his foot required flexibility, balance, long legs, small shoe size, and good aim. The semi-darkness contributed to slowing him down further. As a result, it took him a full minute and a half to cover the short distance.

Unfortunately, his only reward was an even longer delay to lying down, because he found the blanket, the sheets, and the pillow covered in footprints, ashes, cigarette butts, and beer stains. Angel was forced to flip the pillow and discard the bedclothing to make it tolerable.

With the best of intentions, before lying down, Angel retrieved his copy of the Radcliffe novel from the book pile pressing Madison's roses and took it with him to bed. However, he was unable to finish the first sentence before falling asleep.

Chapter LXXVII

Angel awoke to rhythmic sounds and moaning, the renewed musk of copulation saturating the air. He opened his eyes to find the chubby girl riding his roommate, putting her hair in a bun with the expression of meaning business. The room was boiling hot, with the central heating at full blast, and the jiggly girl had a sheen of perspiration. For a moment, he observed in horrified fascination, after which Brad or whatever, noticed Angel and, with a bright grin, gave him a thumbs up. The crudeness proving too much, Angel rolled over, shoved a finger as deep into his ear as he could, and went back to sleep.

When he next woke up, it was four o'clock in the afternoon. The girl was gone and his roommate dressed. The latter had swapped the pleasures of the flesh for the distractions of the internet; laptop on his belly, he was watching YouTube videos of girls chugging beer, wine, and tequila. Angel sat on his bed, but, unable to put his feet on the floor on account of the rubbish, held them in the air, looking for a clear section of carpet. Unable to find it, he crossed his legs.

Angel stared at the American with annoyance. However, he dared not bring up the mess, much less ask him to clean it up. What if he got angry? Josh or whatever seemed either oblivious or happy to live in such conditions. Or maybe he assumed the cleaners would come and clean it eventually.

There was a knock on the door.

Angel's head whipped towards the sound, and, just as quickly, his legs propelled him up and towards said door, into whose lock still dangled the key. More as a reflex than conscious thought, his hand turned it, to prevent entry.

'Dude, what's up with you,' said his roommate, in too loud a voice and smirking.

Angel scrunched his eyelids, turned towards the American, and, pressing the air down with his palms, his eyelids and eyebrows sky-high and his mouth an asterisk, gestured for him to be quiet.

'What?' said Chad or whatever, still in a loud voice.

Angel rolled his eyes, at once exasperated and panicked.

The knocker knocked again.

Angel dropped onto his haunches, pulled the key out of the lock as quietly as he could, and looked through the keyhole. All he could see was denim.

The uninvited visitor knocked a third time.

'Angel, what the fuck? Open the door!' said the American, putting his laptop aside as he sat up.

Silently swearing, Angel ignored him and kept looking through the keyhole, suddenly aware of the thudding in his chest.

The voice on the other side said, 'Angel?'

It was Alba.

Angel exhaled with relief.

He stood up, turned the lock, and opened the door.

'There you are!' she said, her face taut.

'Hello,' he said.

Alba stepped inside before Angel could invite her.

'Woah. What happened here?' she exclaimed.

'Er . . . my roommate had a party,' said Angel, vaguely pointing at the culprit.

'Yea! It was awesome!' said the American, grinning. 'You should join us next time.'

'What—you guys had a party after you came back from Amelia?' said Alba.

'No . . . no. I-I-I-I found it in progress when I got back,' said Angel.

'You should clean up,' said Alba.

'Nah,' said Todd or whatever.

Angel had no reply.

'Anyway. Amelia told me about your date,' said Alba.

'Oh,' Angel feigned surprise.

'Yes. And you have a lot of work to do. You need to learn how to treat a lady on a date.'

'I . . . er . . . I-I know how to treat a lady.'

'No, you don't. You're lucky Amelia is so nice that she blames herself for it going wrong. Again. But you're to blame, Angel. One *hundred* percent.'

'But . . . the booking didn't go through!'

'Bollocks. You should've had a back-up reservation.'

'Erm . . .'

'No *erm*. You should've also taken an umbrella with you.'

'It's just that . . .'

'And you should have had an Uber on standby just in case.'

'On standby!'

'Yes. On standby. You have no idea what it's like for a big girl to walk in high heels—let alone for miles and miles. Are you out of your mind?'

'But I . . .'

'Weren't you paying attention the other day when I took you to the Lanesborough? Did I not keep hailing taxis?'

'Yes, but . . .'

'And another thing. Amelia tells me you went dressed in *rags*. And that she had to clean you up. What's *wrong* with you? The least a man does when he takes a girl on a date is to shower, put on a smart suit, and splash on some cologne, for goodness sake.'

'It's not . . .'

'That's as a *minimum*. You don't deserve Amelia. She's too forgiving. If I'd agreed to go with you on a date and you'd shown up in rags and covered in filth like that, *believe me* you wouldn't have heard the end of it.'

Angel's voice rose a few notes. 'No, it's just that . . .'

'And what is this about your expecting her to spend two grand on dinner? Two fucking grand! On *your* date that *you're* taking her to. Are you thick?'

'Um . . .' Angel's voice went higher still.

'When a man takes a woman on a date, he pays for *everything*. Like you did with Madison. *Everything*.'

'It's-it's—'

'You didn't even bring flowers with you. You can get a bouquet for three quid at Tesco. *Three fucking quid*. And you couldn't even do that!'

'Yes, but—'

'And Amelia even had to bend your arm so you could provide support while you dragged her through the Underground network, wet, barefoot, and covered in filth.'

'But I gave her my . . .'

'Yes, you gave her your smelly shoes with a missing heel. Great fucking job, Angel. You should have been *carrying* her.'

'I—'

Angel registered for the first time that Josh or whatever had for a while been laughing his head off.

'And you should have seen the state of her *feet!* She was plastering and picking nylon out of bloody blisters all night. She'd be lucky to wear heels ever again!'

'Oh . . . I'm so sorr—'

'There's no excuse these days for a date going wrong. Not with all the resources you have online. Next time watch some YouTube videos so you can learn the basics.'

'But-But—'

'No buts, Angel. Next time, *if* there is a next time, *I'm* going to make sure you don't fuck things up.'

'You're going to—?'

'Too right I am. And I'm going to give you tasks and a list of things to say.'

'Er . . . um . . .'

'And we're going to rehearse a few scenarios, so that you know what to do.'

'Er . . .'

'Okay?

Angel's mouth worked soundlessly.

'Thoughts?'

'Er . . . um . . .'

'Say something!'

'Um . . .'

'Never mind. Look, clean up your room, take a shower, wash your clothes in the sink, ask your parents for money, buy a nice shirt and trousers, and be *really really nice* to Amelia this week.'

'Of c-course, but . . .'

'You should be really nice to her every day, but you should *especially* this week.'

'Yes, yes, um—'

'And I mean, really *focus* and put effort into it.'

'Um, of course—'

'Okay.'

They stared at each other for a moment.

'Alright. So I'll be watching you.'

'Er . . . okay . . .'

'Good. Now you better get started cleaning.'

'Um . . . yes.'

'And here are your stinky shoes.' Alba slammed a plastic bag she'd been to his chest, but he wasn't fast enough, was destabilised, and the bag fell on the floor.

Alba left.

Angel stood by the door, dumbfounded.

Todd or whatever's laughter was still ongoing.

At last, the American said, 'Angel, dude, who the fuck was that?'

Angel looked at him.

'And who's this Amelia? Are you fucking her?'

Angel turned away.

Chapter LXXVIII

Angel calculated that he could easily read the whole of *The Mysteries of Udolpho* before his class at ten o'clock the following day. The 624 pages, divided by 17 hours, gave him just over half a page a minute. Very doable. If he focused. And even if he slept for eight hours, he would still be able to get through the entire volume at a rate of just over one page a minute. The question was—would he read at twice the speed if he slept?

Angel decided to go for the latter option.

However, that meant he could not waste time while awake, because during those nine hours, he'd be faced with interruptions for dinner, to go to the bathroom, to shower, and so on. In reality he might only have seven hours. And, if so, that meant a page and a half a minute. And that was a bit tight. Especially considering how densely packed the print was on each of those 624 pages.

That decided it: he would go with the former option and stay up all night.

Angel grabbed the book and lay down to read.

But one sentence in, he decided to check his phone.

Chapter LXXIX

The phone blared and vibrated on his chest. Angel opened his eyes, which he thought he'd just closed, and picked up the device. It was five thirty in the morning.

Todd or whatever rolled over.

The Mysteries of Udolpho laid next to Angel's hip, his bookmark still on page three.

'Oh, for goodness' sake!'

Angel had forgotten to factor his morning shift into his calculations, so now, with four and a half hours remaining, during which he could still, at the rate of under two and a half pages per minute, read the whole book, he had no chance of doing so.

He was already dressed, so Angel walked to the door, and slowly and silently, opened it a crack, to check that the coast was clear. The corridor was empty. Angel squeezed his way out.

But he hadn't quite completed the manoeuvre when the door across from him flew open with such brio that the air sucked out of the corridor sent Angel's hair flying.

'Angel, my friend!'

Saïd was smiling.

'Good morning, Saïd.'

'You owe me fifteen pounds.'

'Um . . . can I pay it to you later? I've got to go to my morning shift.'

'Later what time?'

'Er . . . after lunch.'

'Okay, my friend. What time after lunch?'

'Um . . . four o'clock?'

'Okay. I knock on your door at four.'

'Okay.'

'See you later.'

'See you later.'

'But at four, yes?'

'Yes, at four.'

'Okay, my friend.'

Saïd disappeared into his room.

Chapter LXXX

When he entered the kitchen, he found the catering supervisor conversing with Emmanuel. Angel went to them and stood in silence, waiting for the two to finish so he could address his employer. The conversation, however, continued for far too many minutes, to the point that Angel began feeling stupid, not knowing what to do with his arms or face. Yet, he persisted.

At long last, the supervisor deigned to acknowledge him.

'Yes, Angel.'

'Um . . . I-I-I was just wondering . . . um . . . when . . . um . . . what day . . . um . . . the wages are paid.'

'End of the month.'

'Um . . .' Angel stared at the supervisor like a rabbit caught in headlights. 'Um . . . um . . .'

'What is it, Angel.'

'Um . . . l-last month . . . I-I-I . . . didn't . . .'

'Angel, we don't have a lot of time.'

'Yes . . . just . . . um . . . l-last month . . .'

'I tell you what—you start your shift and think about what you want to say.'

'Um . . . oh . . . um . . . o-o-okay.'

'Good. Now put on your uniform. And tomorrow don't show up in rags.'

Chapter LXXXI

'What evidence of patriarchal tyranny can we find in *The Mysteries of Udolpho*?' asked Professor Turner.

Sitting as far back and away from the professorial desk as possible, Angel hunched over, hid under his hair.

'Nadia.'

'Well . . . you know . . . like . . . I mean . . . you know . . . er . . . actually . . . like . . . er . . . like . . . uh . . . so . . . essentially . . . uh . . . you know . . . so basically . . . like . . .'

Professor Turner waited, his kindly, phlegmatic visage perfectly equanimous. He gave the student twenty more seconds, hands on his skinny hips.

Not long enough, as far as Angel was concerned.

'Very good,' the professor eventually said. 'Lubna'

'Okay, so—'

The screech of a grinder cutting sheet metal directly outside the classroom blasted out the reply.

As Lubna kept talking regardless, Professor Turner gestured with a hand for her to stop.

The grinder stopped a few seconds later.

The professor gestured for Lubna to continue.

The grinder resumed cutting, sending irregularly oscillating waves of ear-splitting decibels into the classroom.

The professor's inch-wide shoulders slumped, but he still waited in silence. Lubna did likewise.

The grinder stopped.

'Okay, carry on, Lubna.'

Once again Lubna re-started her answer.

But now regular hammering on sheet metal blew away her words.

Professor Turner rolled his eyes and, saying, inaudibly, to wait, left the classroom. The students nearest to the window, which included Angel, looked out, their eyes following the professor as he approached Babyface, who had stationed himself directly below said window to work on corrugated galvanised steel. They watched the two men converse—or rather, they watched Professor Turner say things they couldn't make out to Babyface, who said either nothing or very little. Babyface's shrugging of the shoulders and shaking of the head in negation, followed by Professor Turner's irritation and departure, identified the victor.

The professor returned to the classroom, his face tight, and, after waiting for a break in the hammering outside, addressed the students:

'I'm going to see if we can find another classroom. Wait here.'

Professor Turner left.

Some of the students looked at each other, grinning, before picking up their phones. Others picked up their phones immediately. Within moments, few of them were not on social media, scrolling, posting, commenting, or replying to comments. Several of the girls took selfies, in three-quarter profile with a kissy face, but not before they made sure their hair and make-up were on point. Angel took a nap.

It was twenty minutes before the professor returned, his body language jerky, his movements fast, his face a knot of muscles. He stood before the class and opened his mouth, simultaneously inhaling, to address the students.

But the grinder went back into operation at that precise moment.

The waves of screeching and buzzing bounced against the walls for what seemed like an eternity.

Until, finally, it stopped.

The professor again opened his mouth to speak.

But the hammer resumed banging on steel.

Angel, who'd been awakened by the lecturer's return, noticed that several of his classmates had inflated like red balloons in their attempts to suppress laughter.

The hammering paused.

Seizing the opportunity, Professor Turner at last made his announcement.

'I couldn't find another classroom, so we're going to call it a day. Next Monday we'll be discussing Matthew Lewis' *The Monk*, so make sure to have read the whole book, along with the supplementary materials.'

The students were already on their feet and leaving before the professor had even finished his last sentence. Angel was one of them, as chances were that, if Johannes' friends were waiting for him outside, it would be at the top of the hour, rather than midway. All the same, Angel left via the fire exit.

His chosen route took him past Babyface, who was still occupied with the corrugated sheets. The maintenance guy, however, was not alone, because he had been joined by Professor Mastropasqua, saying something about 'feminist drivel.' After Angel passed them, he heard the two men burst out laughing.

Chapter LXXXII

While on his way back to his room, Angel felt his phone vibrate. He'd received an email from the Estates' Environmental Services Unit asking him to present himself there at the earliest opportunity. Angel course-corrected and headed for the main building.

Once inside, he was asked to go down lengths of corridor to a specified office.

'Um . . . H-Hello,' he said, upon entering. 'I've been asked to speak to the Environmental Services administrator.'

'That's me. Who are you?' The administrator was a small, wiry woman in her forties with murine features.

Angel identified himself.

The administrator went to her computer, searched through various menus, typed in his name, waited for the desired screen to appear, read the information on that screen, scrolled up and down, and finally said:

'Ah.'

Angel scratched his temple.

'Okay,' continued the administrator. 'It's come to our attention that you have been fly-tipping.'

'Fly-tipping?' he said, perplexed.

'Yes. We found a box filled with recycling under the stairs in the basement of the boys' dorm.

'Oh!' Angel said, but now his perplexity was feigned.

'We know it was you because we were able to identify you from the CCTV.'

'Er . . .'

'And as you well know, fly-tipping is a criminal offence. All rubbish must be handed over to a licensed waste management agent or be deposited at a site with a waste management license.'

'Is it a criminal offence?'

'Yes, under Section 33 of the Environmental Protection Act 1990.'

'Oh!'

'So we are going to issue you with a fine of one hundred and fifty pounds.' The administrator rifled through some paperwork on her desk and dug out a sheet of paper. 'Here.'

Angel examined the sheet. It was a penalty notice.

'Are you paying with cash or by card?'

'Er . . . um . . . I-I-I don't have my card with me at the moment.'

'That's fine. You have fourteen days to pay. If you do so before then, you'll pay one hundred and twenty. If you pay on the deadline, you'll pay the full amount. And if you are late, you'll pay double. So it's in your interest to pay as soon as possible.'

'Um . . . yes, of course.'

'Do you want to go and get your card?'

'Um . . . I-I-I can't at the moment, I've got class . . .' Angel pointed vaguely in the direction of the Jenni Murray Hall.

'That's fine. We're open till five today, and nine till five during weekdays. You can come at any time between those hours.'

'Okay.'

'Good. So no more fly-tipping, Angel.'

'Um . . . yes.'

'Our CCTV sees everything, so there's no point. Do you know where our recycling centre is?'

'Er. . . Yes, yes . . . I do.'

'Okay, so next time you have excess rubbish, take it down to the recycling centre.'

'Yes.'

'Are you letting the cleaners into your room on Saturday mornings?'

'Um . . . yes. But they won't collect the rubbish.'

'You mean they don't empty the bin?'

'Um . . . they do empty the bin. They just don't collect the rubbish that's elsewhere.'

'It's your responsibility to tidy up and put the rubbish in the bin. The cleaners won't do that for you. They're cleaners, not servants.'

'Ah, okay.' Angel of course remembered what he'd been told previously on the subject, but feigned ignorance.

'Right. So if you have rubbish that you can't put in the bin, you need to take it to the recycling centre.'

'Okay.'

'Remember: there's CCTV everywhere. We're watching.' The administrator pulled down her lower eyelid.

'Okay.'

'Very good. So bring your card as soon as possible and we'll process the payment.'

'Okay.'

The administrator went back to her desk and sat behind her computer.

Angel stood for a few moments, waiting.

'You may go,' said the administrator, without looking at him.

'Okay. Thank you.'

The administrator made no reply.

Chapter LXXXIII

For his 17th Century Literature class the next day, Professor Hynd had asked students to read Mary Astell's *A Serious Proposal to the Ladies*. This was, thankfully, a short text of just over fifty pages, so Angel thought the task easy to accomplish. Knowing that Saïd would be in class, he headed back to his room.

When he entered the corridor, he saw, up ahead, the two powerlifters from The Departure Lounge knocking on his door. As if hit by lightning, Angel bolted and ran down the stairs, down the corridor, into the lavatory, and into a toilet stall.

Once locked in his hiding place, however, Angel realised his mistake. How would he know when the coast was clear? The only way to be sure would be to wait long enough to make the powerlifters' continued presence unlikely. Thankfully, he'd never seen them in the dorms before, so it was likely their accommodation was off-campus, like Johannes', who shared a flat in the neighbourhood. All the same, if he waited too long, the chances of his would-be attackers returning increased. Angel decided to wait for an hour.

He put down the toilet lid—using his foot—and sat, trying not to think of the skid marks left by a previous occupant.

He got his phone out.

And checked Madison's Instagram.

She had posted a new image.

Madison appeared seated at a restaurant table—no tablecloth, no cutlery—in front of a thirty-two-inch pepperoni pizza. Her face seemed a bit rounder than he remembered it. The description read: 'Loving these food challenges! Man, body positivity is sooo freeing!' The hashtags, Angel noticed, included things like #effyourbeautystandards, #bodypositive, #bodyliberation, #fuckdietculture, and #wouldsellmysoulforpizza.

Angel suddenly stood, opened the toilet lid, dumped his phone into the bowl, slammed down the lid, and flushed. Moments after sitting down, however, he stood again and opened the lid. Fortunately, the phone was still there. He dunked his hand in the water, retrieved the device, angrily yanked toilet paper from the dispenser, and used a large glob of it to dry up and clean his only link to Madison. Yet, it was too late; the screen had sustained water damage, and now a cirrus-cloud-like formation overlaid her post.

Angel swore silently, his head bobbing with the vehemence.

He closed Instagram with a jerk of the finger, put the phone in his pocket, kicked the toilet lid down, and dropped himself onto it, where he sat, slumped over, elbows on knees, staples digging into skin, head in clawed hands. In that posture he sat for a long time, cursing Syd, and almost cursing Madison.

But as the minutes passed, his heart softened, as did his face, and anger gave way to sadness. A tear rolled down his cheek.

My love is as a fever, longing still
For that which longer nurseth the disease.

He pulled his phone out and browsed through his photo album, reliving the Spring of 2019—his life and times with the Madison he knew.

It then occurred to him that this might be another of Madison's prank posts. Didn't she say she wanted to appear dumb and then shock everyone by acing all her modules? And didn't she say she wanted to make diet-obsessed girls jealous by making them think she could eat without ever getting fat? It did speak well of her that she chose pizza—Italian was always good in his book. In fact, it showed him that his influence endured, since he'd taken her to numerous Italian restaurants while she was in London, and some of their best dates had involved delectation of Italian cuisine. As to her face looking rounder, that was probably just the camera angle, or the lighting, or a filter. He'd heard girls say from time to time that the camera always adds ten pounds. Yes, she'd fallen in with a bad crowd, but his beloved Madison was still there, awaiting rescue. If only he could get money!

Chapter LXXXIV

Before he knew it, more than an hour had passed, and Angel, stomach growling, deemed it finally safe to re-emerge. He cracked the door open, an alert eye scanning the world outside, and repeated the procedure before leaving the lavatory altogether. He took a deep breath before exiting the building.

The sinkhole was still proving an attraction, with students stopping by to take pictures or record videos for their Instagram accounts. Using his low-visibility route, from building to bush, from bush to statue, from statue to tree, from tree to hedge, Angel headed for the canteen, hoping that, if the powerlifters had decided to have their lunch there, they would have done so earlier, after failing to find him. Nevertheless, he hid behind a bush to scan the interior through its large windows, in case his would-be beaters were still there. The coast was clear.

A girl with a clipboard and a fluffy mushroom of artificially orange hair intercepted him near the entrance.

'Will you sign our petition?' she said, smiling.

Angel looked around him, eyes wide. 'Erm . . . I-I-I don't have time. Maybe later.'

Angel made to walk past to enter the canteen, but the girl blocked his path.

'It will only take a moment,' she said, still smiling.

'I'm sorry . . . I-I-I really don't have time.'

'You don't have time to save the planet?'

'Um . . . no, it's just that—'

'You won't have any time at all if the planet is wrecked and everybody dies.'

Angel quickly scanned his surroundings again, looking for big arms and broad backs; in passing he noticed a table around which were students holding handmade placards and banners screaming confrontational demands and questions. A student in a khaki parka picked up a megaphone and began shouting apocalyptic statements about the earth.

'Um . . . I'll stop by later. I'll stop by later,' he said, making another attempt to get past.

Again the girl blocked his path.

'Time is running out. We can't delay. We need to act now,' she said, her smile replaced by a frown.

'Er, yes, of course. It's just that . . .'

'Then sign and get it over with. Or even better, fuck lunch and join our die in.' Orange Mushroom pointed at a group of students who had laid down a short distance from the entrance, forming the Extinction Rebellion logo.

But Angel only gave them a cursory look, more worried about the possible presence of big arms and broad backs. His stomach growled its urgent need for food.

'Um . . . I'll act after lunch, I promise.'

'So you're not signing the petition, then.'

'Yes, I'll sign it, of course, it's just that I've really got to—'

'If you're eating, you're going against us.'

'Oh! But why?'

'Because we're asking the university to ban all animal-based products in our food and that's what they're serving.'

'Um . . . I'm just having a salad.'

Orange Mushroom's voice became shrill. 'Look, we need radical action! The planet is dying! Half measures are not enough. If you eat *any* of their food, you're still supporting them!'

Angel looked around again, shifting his weight from one foot to the other. 'But it's just the salad . . . just leaves!'

'What is wrong with you?!?' she screamed. 'Can't you fucking understand?!?'

At this point, the girl's screams drew the attention of nearby students. And this included the green-dreadlocked Chinstrap and his fellow activist, Khaki Parka, who joined the scene.

'I've seen this *fucker* before. He's a denier! A *fucking* Tory!' said Chinstrap.

Khaki Parka just stood by frowning, burning Angel with laser eyes.

Chinstrap's revelation caused Orange Mushroom to switch from arguments to insults, and Angel, paralysed, watched her shrieking at him at the top of her lungs; her face turned red, the veins in her neck stuck out, her body bent over from the intensity. This, in turn, drew in other activists and standers-by.

Angel showed his palms, eyebrows airborne, and said with a high voice, ‘I was going to sign, I was just having salad, I was going to sign, I was just having salad!’

But Chinstrap was beyond words, and his fist collided with Angel’s face, sending him to the ground.

Angel felt the impact on his back and found himself staring at the sky. A second latter, the sky was blotted out by screaming faces. Chinstrap bent over him and grabbed Angel’s shirt, ripping two buttons. But the fist he was about to rain on him never made it to the launch phase, for two men from campus security grabbed his attacker and pulled him away. This diverted everyone’s attention and, the climate activists seeing one of their own violently restrained, massed around their comrade, to shout slogans and imprecations at security.

Left to his own devices, Angel got up and ran.

Chapter LXXXV

And he kept running until he'd left the campus.

Standing by the road, his stomach still concave, he remembered he still had Amelia's tenner. It was originally for the chocolates and pressed flowers he'd intended for Madison, but, since the chocolate had melted, and the flowers would cost less to send, Angel thought he could afford some food. He'd borrowed the money ostensibly for that purpose anyway.

As the route to Tesco would take Angel past the gym, he headed towards the Underground station, knowing of a Pret a Manger nearby. The walk proved uncomfortable as the uneven height of his heels had started cricking his lower back.

Once at the sandwich shop, he picked up a BLT. He scanned the refrigerator for a normal Coke, since he needed the calories, but they'd only offered Diet Coke or Coke Zero ever since the sugar tax had come into force, so he chose a Coke Zero, hoping it would taste better than the hated Diet version.

'Four pounds fifty-nine,' said the barista.

Angel handed over his tenner.

'Forty-one pee change. Thank you. Next?'

Angel, in a daze, made to pocket his change, but then realised that he'd been short-changed a fiver.

Amid the din of pressurised milk, crinkly wrappers and paper bags, cups plonked on metal or Formica surfaces, background music, and people babbling everywhere, he piped, 'Sir?'

The barista was by then serving another customer, moving fast, talking fast, not looking at Angel.

'Sir?'

Now the barista attended to the coffee maker.

Angel waited.

The barista returned.

'Sir?'

'Next?' the barista said, looking at the following person in the queue. The female office worker thought Angel was trying to cut in and gave him a hostile glance.

'Sir? Um . . . I'm missing five pounds.'

No acknowledgment. Instead, 'Next?'

Another office worker, a man in a suit holding a wrap, stepped forward. 'Could I also have a cappuccino?'

'Drink here or take away?'

'Drink here.'

The barista went to the coffee machine.

Angel waited.

The barista returned after long minutes of frantic preparation. The customer paid contactless and moved on.

'Next?' said the barista.

'Sir? Sir!' said Angel, raising a finger, eyes bulging out.

No acknowledgment.

'Sir!'

No acknowledgment.

'Sir!'

'A crème brûlée latte,' said a woman in her fifties, with a loud, piercing voice.

'Sir!'

The woman scowled at him. 'Would you mind joining the queue?'

'No, it's just that—' Angel began, open palm showing his change.

A thirty-something man in a blue polo shirt butted in. 'Fuck you! Join the fucking queue!'

Dumbstruck, Angel noticed other hostile faces in the queue and desisted, walking away to find a stool on which to eat.

Once seated, he pulled out his phone.

It was bursting with social media notifications. Normally he had zero.

'Wha . . . ?'

Angel launched his Facebook app. He had 347 comments and 223 message requests. All hostile, calling him climate change denier, Tory, and less polite terms of abuse. Some were long rants pouring out expletives or threatening violence. Instagram: same story, distributed across 551 comments and 397 message requests.

Heart pounding, Angel closed the apps and scanned his surroundings. No young people with unnaturally coloured hair or XE logos, which was a relief. All the same, he felt exposed in front of the floor-to-ceiling window, so he grabbed his sandwich and Coke Zero and left the shop to seek safety in seclusion.

Chapter LXXXVI

It was one o'clock in the morning before Angel dared return to the campus. Under cover of darkness, and following his low-visibility route, he entered the dorm and went to his room. He'd been shocked at how difficult it had proven to find a spot out there where he could be left in peace; especially since the forty-two pence he had remaining bought him nothing and gave him access to nowhere; on several occasions, being thought indigent or, perhaps worse, *identified as a student* after he'd found a quiet mews or alleyway, he'd been asked to move on.

When he opened the door, the room was dark. The light coming in from the hallway revealed that, for once, Todd or whatever was already asleep. The room stank of alcohol, of course, so Angel deduced his roommate must have incapacitated himself early, likely after having been able to source even more potent liquors than usual.

Closing the door behind him and using his phone torch, Angel navigated the zig-zagging pathway to his bed. The rubbish was calf deep by now, so each day the task became slightly more difficult.

Once recumbent, Angel examined his phone. The social media notifications had kept coming in throughout the afternoon, and he'd amassed 2998 comments and 1470 messages on Facebook, and 3713 comments and 1786 message requests on Instagram. There were also several WhatsApp messages.

DESTINY: What's up with your social media? What have you done now?

AMELIA: Are you okay, Angel?

AMELIA: Angel?

AMELIA: Please, if you see this, send me message so that I know you're alright.

AMELIA: I'm worried about you.

He hadn't dared set his social media profiles to private or to disable comments after the abuse had started coming in because he feared he would anger the mob even more, and, what was worse, prove in their minds that their accusations were true. For the same reason, he didn't dare delete the comments or the messages. As to an explanatory post, he had spent several hours in the afternoon attempting to draft one, intending it to be short, ending up with an epically long paragraph after adding all the pre-emptory context and subordinate clauses, and pruning it back several times, but he'd given up, unable to decide on the exact framing or phrasing. And replying even to just the messages that were not simply expletives or nonsense was too much effort. Looking at the torrent of abuse now, heart hammering once again, he arrived at the only definitive solution: delete his social media accounts.

He did so.

He then started new ones under a modified name and sent Madison follow and message requests.

With that vital task accomplished, Angel sat up to slide out the Astell book from the tower on his desk. He opened and began reading by the light of his phone. Within minutes, however, during which he read the same lines over and over again with zero comprehension, his eyelids kept plummeting and the book falling on his face, so he gave up.

Chapter LXXXVII

When Angel walked into his 17th Century Literature class the following morning, he was surprised to find Jae sitting at the back. Professor Hynd had not yet arrived, so Angel approached his classmate, who was typing something on her phone.

'Hello, Jae.'

Jae ignored him and carried on typing.

Angel waited a few seconds.

'Hello, Jae,' he said again.

Jae glared at him without saying a word.

Angel intuited that she must be angry at him for the date disaster with Amelia. 'Um . . . I thought you had dropped this class,' he said, pinching his shirt together where the buttons were missing.

'Required for graduation.'

'Oh.'

Jae added nothing else. And clearly she was unhappy to be there. She went back to her phone.

Angel walked away and sat at in his usual chair.

Professor Hynd arrived, dropped her studded knapsack on the floor, and began vociferating the lesson. Knowing he'd not be called to share his thoughts on the Astell text, not a line of which he'd managed to read, either the night before or after his breakfast shift, he sat back to listen and observe. But even that he could not manage for long, as his mind wandered, daydreaming about terrible scenarios involving Madison getting fat and tattoos.

'. . . the text continues to be relevant today,' heard Angel, suddenly tuning in again, 'because the same *patriarchal structures* continue to *oppress* women in our society even after three hundred years . . .'

The professor faltered.

'Yes, Jae,' she said.

Angel turned to look at the tall blonde, who had her arm up. It was so long Angel thought a little more and she would touch the ceiling.

'On what basis can anybody argue that women are oppressed in our society?' Jae said.

Professor Hynd threw her hands up in the air. 'Where to begin? Women can't walk around topless in public while men can.'

'That's not oppression.'

'Men being allowed to do something that women aren't *is* oppression.'

'No. It's basic manners.'

'So women are expected to *behave*, but men get can do whatever they like.'

'You assume men and women are interchangeable. They're not.'

'*Equality* means men and women *should* be allowed to do the same things.'

'It's not equality if you're comparing apples and bananas.'

'Men and women *are human*, are they not?'

'Humans are dimorphic.'

'Dimorphic or not, they both have the same *human* rights. Or *ought to have*, I should say.'

'Sexual public display is not a human right.'

'Breasts are not sexual.'

Angel's eye could not help wandering to Professor Hynd's breast area. He looked away quickly, afraid she'd notice.

'They are erogenous zones,' said Jae. 'Therefore they're sexual.'

'Showing your breasts is *not* an invitation to sex.'

'Showing your breasts is exposing an erogenous zone, therefore showing something sexual.'

'I disagree.'

'The male equivalent would be walking around naked from the waist down with the member hanging out.'

'No, the equivalent to that is a woman showing her vagina—*not* that there's anything wrong with that.

'The vagina is mostly internal; one can see little or nothing when a woman is walking around. It's not so with male reproductive organs.'

'Both are still *exposed* to the *air*.'

'But in one case you can see almost nothing. And nothing at all if the woman is overweight.'

'Visibility has *nothing* to do with it. It's *like* for *like* that counts.'

'Visibility offers context and the context changes what like for like is. Like for like is very visible erogenous zones.'

'*This* is why we're not making progress. It's because of *retrograde* ideas like these.'

'What's retrograde about context? Are we not supposed to consider context when we weigh what a person says and does? And if not, why study literature? What's this class for?'

'One of the things we're looking at today is the *oppressive* expectations that have been imposed on women. And *double standards* in what a woman can or cannot do is at the *centre* of this.'

'So we look at a three-hundred-year-old text today as context. Therefore context is important.'

'I *never* said context is *not* important.'

'But you cherry-pick the context that suits you.'

'No. I look at *relevant* context.'

'In that case, human dimorphism is relevant when considering whether a woman walking around topless is the same as a man doing it.'

'These *biological deterministic* ideas are outdated, problematic, and *wrong*. In fact, they're *dangerous.*'

'You might want to ignore human biology, but human biology is not ignoring you.'

'I *don't* understand you. What interest do you have, *as a woman*, in continuing the *subjugation* of our sex?'

'Basic manners is not subjugation.'

'There you go again with the manners.'

'Manners are important because they show discipline. A person with bad manners loses credibility and respect because they show lack of conscientiousness and respect for others.'

'Manners are form of *social control.*'

'Discipline is a desirable trait. We should cultivate it.'

'Discipline is an *oppressive, patriarchal* value.'

'Discipline is asexual. A woman can have discipline without becoming male.'

'They become *co-opted* by the patriarchy.'

'A woman looks after herself out of self-respect and an impulse to signal desirable traits.'

'Self-respect as a function of the *male gaze*. Desire by the *male gaze*.'

'Women are mostly concerned by their own gaze or the gaze of other females. Most men don't even notice when a woman has a new pair of ear-rings.'

'They're competing for *male* attention.'

'Women don't want most of the male attention they get, but they do want all the female attention.'

'These preconceived notions about women are *toxic*.'

'What's toxic is pitting men and women against each other and creating a culture of blame, victimhood, and resentment, rather than taking responsibility and having the sexes complement each other in harmony.'

'Damn right we're resentful! And you think women are *responsible* for their own *oppression*?'

'I think modern feminists are responsible for discrediting their movement.'

'By campaigning for equal rights?'

'By focusing on silly non-issues when there are important things they could focus on.'

'There is nothing *silly* about equal rights for *all* humanity.'

'Man and woman are the foundation of the family, and therefore the foundation of society and of humanity. By destructively pitting women against men, feminism becomes an anti-social and anti-human ideology.'

'Feminism is not pitting women against men. It's demanding men be made *responsible*.'

'Modern feminists are allergic to responsibility. They

want men to be made responsible for everything that goes wrong in their lives because it's easier to blame others than work on yourself.'

'Allergic to responsibility,' Professor Hynd enunciated slowly. 'Now *that's* a new one. I don't know what you've been reading on the internet, but I want to speak to you after class.'

'Allergic to responsibility because—'

'Jae!' the professor shouted.

Angel flinched.

'—by arguing that walking around bare-breasted is a human right—'

'Jae, stop—'

'—or encouraging women to be rude and gross—'

'Jae! Jae!'

'—you're trying to abrogate responsibility for the negative reactions—'

'Jae, stop right now!'

'—you're bound to get due to your being anti-social and not wanting to bother with basic manners.'

'Jae! *Stop!* Just *stop!* I want to speak to you after class.'

Angel turned to see Jae sitting back in her chair, arms crossed.

'Being gross is not a human right,' Jae added.

'Jae! Enough! The human body is *not* gross.'

'But you can be gross with it through the way you behave.'

'Jae, this is my *final warning.*'

'One thing is baring your breasts for a nude drawing in an atelier—'

'Jae!'

'—another is going to a pub with your wares hanging out.'

'Jae! *Enough* of this! Please leave the classroom. *Now!*'

'If I could, I'd drop this class in a second,' said Jae, getting up and calmly winding her way towards the door.

Professor Hynd's mouth opened, but then closed suddenly; she waited until Jae had left, following the recalcitrant student with her gaze, a trembling hand on her hip, her boot tapping the carpet, her face red, her breathing fast.

The professor then addressed the students. 'If any person here needs to leave the classroom to feel safe, please do. It won't affect your grading.'

Two female students left the classroom. The one with lilac hair and tattoos down her arm looked angry and flustered; she wiped away a tear before she opened the door to exit. The one with the jeans and the tall boots followed her very quickly; Angel sensed that she just wanted to head for the pub, and that the professor sensed the same. A third student, male, also left, presumably pub-bound as well. Angel thought about leaving too, but he didn't dare. What if Professor Hynd linked him to Jae and, finding out he was in one of Mastropasqua's modules on top, changed her mind about leaving his marks unaffected?

'Alright,' said Professor Hynd. 'Back to the lesson. *As* I was saying . . .'

Chapter LXXXVIII

Angel left the Jenni Murray Hall via the fire exit and headed for the canteen using his low-visibility route. He'd noticed, when leaving the classroom, that Jae had not bothered to wait for Professor Hynd. Hiding behind a bush, he saw there were no climate change protesters today, either outside or inside the canteen. Neither were Johannes' powerlifter friends in sight. Since, unfortunately, they also ate, and could walk in at any moment, his plan was to grab some bread and run out.

He stepped out from behind the bush and headed towards the entrance.

'Angel! There you are. I've been looking for you. Are you okay?'

Angel turned.

Amelia stood clad in jeans and a striped jumper, her eyebrows a steeple.

'Your eye!' she lamented.

Angel touched his cheek near the socket where he'd been punched the previous day; it felt tender.

'Um . . . I'm in a hurry.' He scanned the gardens.

'I sent you messages. I saw what happened on social media.'

'Um . . . s-sorry, I wasn't checking my phone. I'll tell you later.' He shifted his weight from one foot onto the other.

'Are you having lunch? I'll eat with you.'

'I-I'm just grabbing some bread.'

'But, Angel, you need to eat. You're so skinny.'

'Um . . . I'm not very hungry.'

'It hurts me to see you this way. Look at you.'

'Er . . . I'll have a big dinner.'

'Come on, let's go in.'

'Um . . . I really have to dash.'

'Are you scared, Angel? I'll protect you.'

'No . . . er . . . I'm not scared. I'm fine. I just have a lot of reading to do.'

'I won't let anyone hurt you. And if anyone comes to shout abuse at you, I'll report them to the university. Come on, let's go in.'

Once again, Angel scanned his surroundings. 'Um . . . it's fine. I just want to get some bread and dash off.'

Jae approached the canteen.

'Oh, hi, Jae,' said Amelia. 'Are you going to have lunch now?'

'Yes.'

'Do you mind if Angel and I join you?'

Jae looked down at Angel as if he were an insect.

'He stinks,' she said, then looked away.

'Don't be harsh, Jae. He's had some wardrobe difficulties that I'm sure he'll take care of right after lunch. Right Angel?'

'Um . . . er . . .'

Amelia turned to Jae, 'You see? Angel is on the case. Let's eat.'

Amelia and Jae got moving. Angel hesitated for a second, his limbs moving in opposite directions like a puppet operated by antagonistic masters, but he was curious about what Jae might say about the classroom incident and, more importantly, he felt safe around her, despite her disdain. No one, male, female, or otherwise ever messed with the towering blonde. She was hated by the feminists, the climate change activists, the socialists, the communists, the trans, you name it; but she neither cared nor was afraid to confront them and put them on the back foot with her logic.

Angel followed the girls.

Once sitting at the table, Amelia addressed her companions. 'How was your class?'

Angel inhaled to speak, but Jae was faster. 'I was thrown out.'

'Oh? Really? What happened?'

Jae summarised her argument with Professor Hynd.

'I'm surprised she chose that example. It's very silly! But I do worry she will fail you and you won't be able to graduate. Is it really worth it to be so belligerent, Jae? It'd be better for you if you keep your head down, write whatever she wants in the essays, and collect your degree. That won't mean she'd have changed your mind, does it?'

'Nothing wrong with challenging her lies in class.'

'But what for? You're not going to change anybody's mind. Not hers. Not the students.'

'The students don't have minds to change.'

'Oh, there you go again with your cynicism!'

'They just parrot what their teachers say because their teachers speak from a position of authority and they're not exposed to alternative viewpoints.'

'But you're making my point. It's useless to get into arguments. The only person *that*'s going to hurt is *you*.'

'The truth is important.'

'And yet, aren't you all about discipline? You can think whatever you like, and you'll be able to say whatever you like outside of uni, and even attack the uni if you want to, but while you're here *asking* for a degree, you need to do what they want in order to get one. Otherwise, you're spending time and money for nothing.'

Jae stared at Amelia for a second, then, sighing, started buttering a potato. 'Your point has merit.'

'What do you think, Angel?'

Angel looked up from his cheesy pasta and potatoes, again caught by surprise. 'Oh . . . me? Er . . . um . . . yes . . um . . .'

'You see? He agrees.'

'Don't make me ashamed.'

Chapter LXXXIX

After lunch they stopped outside the canteen. Jae went her own way. Amelia stood with Angel for a moment.

'Angel, you poet . . .' Amelia began gently, 'you really need to do something about your clothes. It's becoming a bit of a problem. You're still wearing the same outfit you wore on Saturday night.'

Angel's mouth opened, as if to say something, but he couldn't think of a reply.

'Which is the same outfit you were wearing on Friday evening,' continued Amelia.

'Um . . .'

'In fact, you've been wearing the same clothes for the past two weeks at least, now that I think of it.'

He bowed his head. 'It's so embarrassing . . .'

'Why don't you ask you mum to send you some money so you can replace those rags? I find them very Romantic. They make me think of an Elizabethan poet. But, honestly, a man of your pedigree deserves better.'

'Um . . .' Angel exhaled and looked at the sky.

'Why don't you want to message your mum?'

Angel shook his head and stared at his shoes.

'Is she nasty to you?'

Angel inflated his cheeks and released the air slowly, his eyes haunted.

'Well, leave it with me. I'll see what I can do,' she said, putting a hand on his shoulder, and trying to look into his eyes.

'Um . . . er . . . there's . . . there's no need.'

'I won't hear it, Angel. Leave it with me. But for now, why don't you go and give those clothes a wash. I can lend you some detergent.'

'Uh . . . no, no. No need. I'll sort it out. Thank you.'

'Let me help you.'

Angel looked across the garden. In the distance, he spotted Saïd walking towards the canteen, accompanied by Hassan and Ibrahim. His lender hadn't yet noticed him.

'Um . . . it's okay. I've got to go. I'll speak to you soon.'

'Angel!'

But Angel was already on his way. He cast a quick backward glance and gave Amelia a peremptory wave before heading for the dorm, using his low-visibility route.

Chapter XC

Josh or whatever was gone, and since he was hardly ever in their room, except to party or sleep, Angel thought he had time. He stripped naked and, wrapping a towel around his waist, put his shirt, socks, and underwear in the sink under hot water. In the absence of detergent, Angel thought of using shampoo, but that was running low and his hair was greasy, so he opted for hand soap instead. When done, he hung the garments on the red-hot radiator.

For his Literary Modernism class on Wednesday he was supposed to read a stack of photocopied excerpts, so, while he waited for his clothes to dry, he lay down on his bed, and got started.

But the heat, combined with the cheesy pasta and potatoes he'd had for lunch, soon made him dozy, and, within minutes, the photocopies were on his chest and he asleep.

He was in an aeroplane, flying to Atlanta, or maybe Chicago, where he was to catch his connecting flight. He'd received information before he left that Madison was going to get a tattoo that evening, but his flight would land just in time to catch a taxi and make it to the tattoo parlour to prevent her permanent defacement. Seven hours into the journey, however, an engine malfunctioned. The captain announced they were going to divert the flight and attempt landing on an island in the Bermuda Triangle. Angel began worrying about the Atlantean technology submerged near Bimini Island, called Bimini Road, which could cause the aeroplane to disappear. In a frantic effort to avoid it, he began WhatsApping the Pentagon in hopes of refuelling mid-air so they could make it to Dulles International airport, but then realised he didn't have the Pentagon's number. The aircraft began losing altitude. Looking out the windows, he could see the malfunctioning engine had burst into flames. Then the fire spread into the cabin, filling it with smoke. The oxygen masks would not deploy. Instead, a portly Afro-American stewardess stood in the isle and kept asking passengers to 'adopt the recovery position.' He didn't know what that was! 'Please adopt the recovery position,' she kept repeating. He hunched over and put his head in his hands, but he couldn't breathe because of the pungent smoke.

Angel woke up with a gasp.

There was smoke in the room.

Then he saw his shirt had caught fire.

'Oh, God!'

He jumped to his feet and yanked the shirt off the radiator, throwing it onto the floor, on top of whatever rubbish was there, and smothered it with his duvet.

Once the fire had been extinguished, he took his socks and jeans off the radiator. They were scalding hot, so he threw them on the floor too.

He inspected the damage.

The shirt was still wearable, but it looked as though it had been barbequed and a hole had appeared near the bottom. A stain had just been acquired from an old sandwich box. Thankfully, the shirt was navy blue, so, provided there was bad lighting, the burnt fabric would be hardly detectable. Unrelated to the heat, further damage was present on the stapled sleeve, where the fabric had partially ripped, loosening the staples and opening a gap.

Angel re-stapled the sleeve, pinching a bit more fabric this time. After the procedure, the affected sleeve was one inch narrower than the other one, but what choice did he have?

There was a knock on the door.

Angel looked at it and went to check his phone on the bedside table. The phone said it was four o'clock. He mouthed an expletive.

'Angel, my friend,' his lender said from the other side.

Angel didn't move a muscle. The most tenuous noise could alert Saïd to his presence in the room.

More knocking.

'Angel, my friend.'

Angel waited, holding his breath.

Seconds passed.

Yet more knocking.

More seconds passed.

The door opened.

'Angel, m— Aha!'

Angel stared at Saïd, holding his towel in place.

'You owe me fifteen pounds.'

'Um . . . I-I-I don't have it yet.'

'You said four o'clock. It's four o'clock,' said his lender, pointing at his watch.

'I'm sorry . . . I . . . er . . .'

'You want extension?'

'Um . . . yes, yes. C-C-Could I pay on Friday?'

'No problem my friend.'

'Thank you.'

'But you owe me twenty-five.'

'Twenty-five!'

'Compound interest, my friend.'

'Why compound?'

'So it's fifteen now, or twenty-five on Friday.'

Angel sighed. 'Okay, Friday.'

'No problem.'

'See you Friday. And, yes, Friday.'

Saïd laughed. 'You know me. But Angel . . .'

'Yes?'

'What the fuck, man?' He pointed vaguely at Angel.

'W-What?'

'What happened to you?

'W-What do you mean?'

'You don't eat?'

'I-I-I just had lunch.'

'Eat more, then. What the fuck?'

'Um . . . I haven't been hungry lately.'

'Your girlfriend eating all your food?'

'Um . . . she's in . . .'

'Come visit tonight. I'll give you food.'

'I-I-I'll have dinner at the canteen.'

'Then come for second dinner. Okay?'

'O-O-Okay.'

'Okay. See you tonight.'

'See you tonight.'

Saïd exited the room and began closing the door. But one inch from closing he stopped and re-opened the crack wide enough to squeeze his head back into the room.

'So tonight, yes?'

'Yes, tonight.'

'To eat?'

'Yes, to eat.'

'Okay, my friend. Because what the fuck?'

Chapter XCI

As Angel got dressed, he realised his clothes didn't smell right. The mixture of burnt cotton and hand soap elicited a wrinkling of the nose. He grabbed the deodorant and sprayed, but within seconds the last of the compressed liquid ran out, allowing the funny odour to survive. Nothing he had available promised a less unpleasant one. His only hope was to displace it by wearing the garments, and afterwards to keep said garments scent-neutral by not perspiring until he could afford detergent and deodorant.

Meanwhile, the stack of photocopied excerpts on his bed had to be read by morning, so Angel grabbed them and laid down to get started.

But first, he checked his phone.

There was nothing to see on Instagram because Madison had not yet accepted his request for a follow, and he'd not followed any other account. He sent a request to Amelia. He then thought about sending a request to Alba, but she was angry with him, so he decided to postpone. Vera, he didn't dare send anything. Johannes—the less he saw of Angel the better, at least for now. Jae would almost certainly ignore him, if not block him altogether; he'd been able to follow Jae from his old account only because at the time she had not yet made hers private. Destiny was out of the question. Thus, he was reduced to following or sending requests to his cousins in Italy, the subset of his acquaintances he felt sure enough were not into climate change activism, and generic inspirational accounts. He then re-uploaded the images he'd previously had, in the original order, as best he could recollect, cursing the water-damaged screen all the while.

By the time he was done re-building what he could of his old account, two hours had passed.

At long last, Angel, realising his mistake, shook his head out of the hypnosis, put the phone down, and picked up the stack of photocopies. Alas, twenty minutes in, most of which he spent reading and re-reading the same lines, he realised that a sheet of paper was missing—four pages from the source book.

Angel sighed. He'd have to photograph the missing pages from a volume in the library (no money for photocopies).

He got up and headed thither.

Chapter XCII

As Angel entered the library, his archenemy was already on duty. He checked the time: 6:29pm.

'Bugger!' he whispered.

Angel tilted his head forward to hide his face under his hair and walked past the front desk as silently as he could. He'd just passed it when he heard:

'Will it be cash or card, Angel?'

He stopped and turned to find the librarian's head visible above the parapet. Which meant she'd stood up.

'Um . . . I don't have my card on me at the moment'.

'It's after end of business today, so you now owe two-hundred and eighty-four pounds and ninety-nine pence'.

'Two eighty-four?' Angel squealed.

'Yes. There's a fifteen percent penalty for missing today's deadline'.

'B-But the day's not ended!'

'It was by end of business today, which was half an hour ago. If I'm here, it's already end of business, because I come in for the night shift'.

'I thought it was midnight'.

'Angel, I've explained the rules to you on numerous occasions. You know what they are. If you take out books and don't return them on time, or don't return them at all, then you have to pay—'

'Yes, I know but—'

'—and if you don't pay, there are penalties. And if you don't pay those, you get banned from the library. It's that simple'.

'C-C-Can I get an extension? Until next week?'

'This has been going on since June. You've had four months to sort this out'.

'B-But much of that time was Summer. The Spring term had already ended and the Autumn term only started two weeks ago'.

'We're still open during the Summer. And when a book is due, it's due, no matter what term it is. So is it cash or card?'

'I-I-I don't have my card with me and I'm not carrying any cash'.

'What about that penny you had last time?'

Angel hesitated for second. What if he gave her the penny, and he was then a penny short at the post office when trying to send the flowers to Madison?

'I-I no longer have it'.

'So you spent it. You have money to spend on things, but you don't have money to pay your library fines'.

'No, it's just that . . .'

'So now you have fourteen days to pay the two-hundred and eighty-four pounds and ninety-nine pence.

If you don't pay it by the 22nd of October, a further penalty will be added, the debt will be passed to a debt collector, and you will be banned from the library'.

'I-I-I'll pay, I promise!'

'You said that last time'.

'Yes, but—'

'Deeds, not words, Angel.'

'I know, but—'

'Do you want to go to your room to get your card?'

'Um . . . I'm very busy. I have an assignment and—'

'You'll have more than one assignment to worry about if you're banned from the library'.

'Yes, I know, but—'

'So do you want to go to your room to get your card, then?'

'Um . . . I'll come back during the day'.

'Either way I win. If you pay, the library gets money. If you don't, I get to finally ban you. So do whatever you like'.

They stared at each other for a couple of seconds.

'Alright', said the librarian at last.

She sat down and got back to work on her computer.

Angel stood, waiting, for a few moments.

'You may go', she said.

Angel moved on, head low.

Chapter XCIII

The book he required was out on loan, so his visit to the library proved a waste.

It being time for dinner, and also cold, Angel headed for the canteen. But as he spied, shivering, from behind the bush outside the canteen's glass wall, he saw that Chinstrap, Khaki Parka, and a couple of the other climate change activists were inside, eating vegan meals. Consequently, despite his rumbling stomach, he went back to his room to wait in the warmth for half an hour.

After the self-imposed exile, Angel again headed for the canteen. As before, he hid behind the bush and scrutinised the interior. His shirt, like a colander of graphene aerogel, allowed free ingress to the wind, so he was swiftly chilled to the bone. He'd also developed a scratchy sensation in the back of his throat, and no matter how much he swallowed, the sensation would not go away. This time he could not recognise anyone dangerous, so he emerged from concealment and walked towards the entrance, hunched over and with his hands in his pockets. But five paces into the journey he saw Betsy approaching in the distance, accompanied by Epic Eyebrows. Consequently, Angel did a one-eighty and re-absconded behind the bush, wherefrom, amid violent shivering, he waited for the American girls to pass before fleeing back to his room.

After another half an hour next to the radiator, Angel yet again headed for the canteen; the wind snatched all the heat out of him like a robber in the night. From behind the bush, however, he found that Betsy and Epic Eyebrows were still eating, having since been joined by Pink Hair; the latter still had a slice of cake to get through, plus a hot chocolate and a couple of bananas. Their faces were red from raised body temperatures. Angel moaned, eyebrows steepling. Seated at another table, Amelia, Jae, and Alba were chatting over empty dishes, enjoying hot chocolate, tea, and coffee, respectively. By this time the canteen was about to stop serving, and he could see Emmanuel already withdrawing the empty serving trays. Consequently, it seeming pointless to wait any longer, he retreated into his room, comforting himself with the thought of Saïd's offered second dinner. He hoped it would be hot.

Back in the dorm, still shivering, swallowing constantly, nearly bent over with hunger pangs, he knocked on Saïd's door.

Silence.

He knocked again.

Dead silence.

He pressed his ear against the door.

Not a sound.

Saïd must be having dinner at the canteen, he thought. Nothing to do, then, but to wait and try again a couple of hours later.

It took another half hour kneeling next to the radiator in his room, up to his hips in rubbish, before the shivers subsided.

To pass the time, he picked up the photocopies he'd left on the bed, and laid down under the duvet, intending to continue with the assigned reading, missing pages notwithstanding.

But first, he checked his phone.

Amelia had posted on Instagram.

Her picture showed balls of rich brown wool and knitting needles. She said in the description it was for a secret project.

Madison had finally accepted his follow request and posted on Instagram.

The post showed two images, visible through the nimbus of his water-damaged screen: one of her face, in profile, and the other a close-up of her ear, showing that she'd had the conch pierced.

Her conch!

Angel threw the phone across the room. It landed unharmed among the empty packets of Doritos on Chad or whatever's bed. Angel then pulled the duvet over his face and curled up into a ball, teeth bared, eyelids scrunched, brain screaming. In that position he remained for a long while. But eventually anger gave way to sadness as he visualised looking through her ringless ear and seeing the sky, a little piece of her hearing organ forever gone.

Tears welled up in his eyes.

Of course, Syd was to blame.

Because before she met that demon, Madison had never, nor would she have ever, mutilated herself.

Angel made a mental note to check Syd's Instagram account later to confirm her culpability. For now, however, polluting his vision with her content seemed unbearable. Too hideous. Too maddening. Too revolting.

Minutes passed, the anxiety and horror of Madison's mutilation cramping his stomach and vibrating his foot.

Then, his phone buzzed.

Angel got up and retrieved the device.

Madison had sent him a message.

It consisted simply of a question mark.

Obviously, asking for the flight information.

Angel began drafting a reply, scouring his brain for a non-embarrassing deflection. And, as so many times before, the glib and elegant remark he aspired to grew uncontrollably into an enormous paragraph that he then unsuccessfully and counter-productively attempted to prune back to a single phrase, the process only inspiring additional edits, adjectives, and qualifying phrases.

He only stopped at half past eleven, when he heard Saïd returning to his room. Angel got up and knocked on Saïd's door.

Camaro opened.

'Oh. Um . . . is Saïd not there?'

Camaro shook his head.

'Angel, my friend!' Angel heard, coming from his right. 'What's up?'

He turned and saw Saïd and Hassan approaching. His lender wore a shirt, a velvet jacket, and polished shoes. The tall Hassan's attire was equally smart.

'Oh . . . hello', said Angel. 'Y-You you you said to come by to visit tonight'.

Saïd tilted his head, smiling, now remembering. 'Ah, yes. We went to Maroush in the end'.

'Oh . . . okay'.

Saïd slapped him in the shoulder.

'Next time, eh?'

'Okay'.

'And . . . twenty-five on Friday, yes?'

'Yes'.

'And did you eat?'

'Um . . . yes, yes, I ate'.

'Good. Because what the fuck, man'.

Chapter XCIV

The torments of starvation kept Angel awake most of the night. His throat didn't help. In desperation, finally, he rose at five and headed for the canteen, which he knew Emmanuel opened at quarter past, thirty minutes before the supervisor arrived and forty-five minutes before everyone else's shift. Angel hoped to steal sliced bread while Emmanuel had his back turned.

But when he arrived, he found Emmanuel conversing with Professor Mastropasqua. The two of them fell silent as soon as Angel walked in, subtly surprised at his early arrival. Angel was both taken aback and annoyed; this would complicate his plan. Feigning complete normality, however, Angel put on his uniform, although much more slowly than usual, while keeping an eye on the two men.

The latter had, meanwhile, resumed conversing. What was said between them Angel was unable to hear, as they kept their voices low. Except that every now and then Emmanuel would say 'Yehhhhhh, yehhh, yehhh', each 'yeh' a note lower than the previous one. Once in uniform, and at a loss as to what else to do, Angel headed for the washing up area; he'd bide his time with a pretended inspection of the sponges, brushes, and washing up liquid. However, the professor stopped him and said:

'Doing manual labour, eh?'

'Um . . . yes.'

'Good. Good. You'll benefit. But you need to build some muscle.'

'Er . . . I've been scrubbing a lot.'

'You need to eat.'

'Um . . . yes.'

'And if you see the sense of doing manual labour, you should see the sense in dropping out of this university.'

'Oh?'

'Do you like this university? What they teach here?'

'Um . . . yes. Er . . . I like it.'

'Too bad.'

Emmanuel chuckled.

Angel looked at him, perplexed.

'Well, because you've listened and taken up manual work,' said Professor Mastropasqua, 'I'll do you a favour. You'll thank me later.'

'Okay.'

'Drop out and study on your own. You don't need me or those clowns from the academic staff. Not for what you're studying.'

'Okay.'

'If you stay, you won't learn anything useful. Nothing.'

'Okay.'

'And most importantly, you won't get a degree anyway.'

'Oh, really? Why?'

The professor hesitated for a moment, then said, 'Because you're not made for this world.'

'Oh!'

'So find work on a building site or with a moving firm, eat so you can build some muscle, and study on your own. Get real life experience.'

'Okay.'

'If you stay, they'll poison your mind, if they haven't already, and then you'll be gone.'

'Okay.'

'Yeh. *Listen* to him,' said Emmanuel, still chuckling.

Angel frowned, ever more confused.

'Must go now,' said the Professor to Emmanuel. 'So . . . you know how I want those eggs, right?'

'Yeh, yeh, yeh' came the reply.

'Very good.'

The professor left.

Angel stared at Emmanuel, who was grinning at him. Emmanuel said, '*Listen* to him, okay?'

'Okay.'

Emmanuel left to get on with his chores.

Angel went to the washing up room, stood there for thirty seconds, and then came out, keeping an eye on his co-worker. The fridge, where the bread was kept, was two paces to the left. If only Emmanuel would leave the kitchen for thirty seconds! Angel visualised himself opening the fridge, opening the plastic wrapping, and taking out two slices of white bread before Emmanuel returned.

But no such luck, because the supervisor arrived early.

'Oh, what a pleasant surprise! You're bright and early this morning,' she said.

'Um . . . yes.'

'In that case, help Emmanuel. He'll tell you what to do.'

'Okay.'

'And, Angel?'

'Yes?'

'Please wash your hair every day. Hairnet or no hairnet, we need to maintain standards of hygiene in the kitchen.'

Chapter XCV

After his shift, Angel went to the Jenni Murray Hall to read his Literary Modernism assignment ahead of the class. He knew the classroom was empty at that time and thought the quietude would allow him to get through the photocopied material.

On his way to the classroom, he passed the faculty kitchenette, which offered tea- and coffee-making facilities. From the hallway, he caught sight of Professor Mastropasqua, standing like a giant raven in front of the coffee machine, alone, humming a melody with his back to the door. The professor's briefcase was open on a chair; inside were papers and a box of Zimovane 7.5 mg tablets.

Once in the classroom, Angel sat in his usual chair, got out the photocopies, and located the point where he'd left off. If he concentrated he'd be able to get through the whole lot in less than twenty minutes.

But first, he checked his phone.

Madison had no new updates. But the picture with the conch piercing had thirty-four likes. Angel rubbed his temple. Why? And who *were* these people? When he went to check, the few that weren't private aggregated into a freak show. The facial expressions of the girls alone told him any sensible person would run for the hills.

Amelia also had no new updates, but her page was an oasis of warmth, sanity, and pleasant aesthetics. Far from comforting him, however, it only reminded him of the urgency of rescuing Madison from her influencers. If only the canteen would pay him early!

When Angel finally began reading the class materials, students had already begun to arrive. Professor Albert, a tatterdemalion in his sixties with wild grey hair and a messy goatee, then entered at five minutes to the hour, carrying his tote bag and a mug of coffee. The tatterdemalion sat behind his desk, got his notes out, and waited for the remainder of the students to arrive, sipping his steaming beverage.

At five minutes past, Professor Albert closed the door and locked it, trying the lever handle to confirm tardy arrivals had been barred entry. He stood in front of his students, resting his glutes on the edge of his desk, and said:

'Good morning.'

No one answered.

But there was a knock on the door. Angel saw a student with poor time-management skills peer pleadingly through the vertical window above the door handle. Professor Albert turned to look and, with a dismissive wave of the hand, made a show of ignoring him. A second knock followed, before the student's face disappeared.

'Alright, so today . . .' Professor Albert began before trailing off, his speech giving way to gargantuan yawn.

'I apologise for that', he said, as he reached for his coffee.

He took another sip.

'Okay, so today we're going to be discussing examples of . . .' Another yawn.

The professor shook his head and blinked fast several times.

'Sorry. Just a moment', he said.

A few more sips of his coffee.

'Okay, so as I was saying, today . . .' More yawns.

The professor now detached himself from the desk and rubbed his face. 'Come on, wake up', he muttered, before addressing a student many rows behind Angel. 'Erm . . . can you open the window there at the back?'

Angel turned and saw an Asian girl stand to do as instructed. The window only opened a crack.

'Will it open more?' said Professor Albert.

'Yes, it's open.'

'But will it open more?'

'Yes, it's open.'

'Okay, never mind'.

Professor Albert opened the door and looked up and down the corridor, to ensure there were no tardy students hoping to squeeze in. It seemed there were none.

'Alright, so if you look at . . . erm . . .' he resumed, rubbing his eyes, but he was interrupted by yet another, epic yawn.

'Wait here', he said, at last.

The professor left the classroom. Angel looked around. Some of the female students took the opportunity to chat amongst themselves; others to take selfies; yet more to go on social media. The few male students, it seemed, were as somnolent as the professor, and completely inert.

Professor Albert returned with wet patches on his jumper and the edges of his hair.

But he seemed no more awake than before. Indeed, he seemed *sleepier*.

'Alright, let's see if we can get started finally . . . so today we're discussing . . . examples . . . of . . . of . . . erm . . .'

Wobbling, Professor Albert took a seat behind his desk. He closed his eyes for a moment. Yet, the moment never ended and the professor's neck turned to plasticine, dropping his head until only hair was visible.

The students watched and waited.

Seconds passed.

Then more seconds.

Then yet more seconds, without a change in status.

Angel heard tittering.

Some the students' faces now either registered unconcealed smiles or turned red as they suppressed laughter. Many had deployed their phones as video recorders.

Professor Albert began snoring.

The students waited, amusement and confusion in the air.

Eventually, an Afro-Caribbean girl in the first row stood, walked to the professor, and gently shook his shoulder.

But her effort proved fruitless.

'Professor Albert?' she said.

No response.

'Professor Albert?'

Again, no response.

The girl shook him again, more firmly, causing his head to swing from side to side.

Still he would not wake up.

'Professor Albert', said the girl, more firmly.

No response.

'Professor Albert!'

No response.

The girl threw her hands in the air.

'Dead to the world', she announced.

'Should we call the nurse?' said a red-headed girl with Pippi Longstockings braids.

'Has he had a heart attack?' asked a Muslim girl in a hijab.

'He seems to be just sleeping', said the Afro-Caribbean girl.

'Let's find the nurse', said Longstockings.

The three girls agreed and left the classroom.

'Let's go to the pub!' said one of the male students, suddenly standing, reanimated from his stupor.

The proposal was greeted with cheers by three-quarters of the students, who exploded out of their seats and left in a hurry.

Angel sat in his chair, waiting, along with a few others, too shy to leave and too at a loss to do anything else.

But after ten minutes, the laggards began leaving, one at a time, until Angel, feeling a bit feverish, concluded there was no risk in joining their exodus.

Chapter XCVI

Angel left via the fire exit, but, as he rounded the Jenni Murray Hall and headed for the dorm via his low-visibility route, he saw that students, including a number from his class, had thronged in front of the building. They were chatting, laughing, and telling jokes. Professor Mastropasqua then emerged, like a vampire out of his castle, sight of the students eliciting a chuckle before he left the scene.

Back in his room, he found Brad or whatever, sitting at the edge of his bed blowing his nose with a box of tissues between his feet.

'S'up, dude,' said the American, less cheerfully than usual.

Angel stared at him briefly without responding.

'I feel like *fucking shit!*' added the roommate, before blowing his nose again, so hard he bent over.

'I don't feel good either,' Angel moaned, during a pause in the nose-blowing. That probably doubled the number of words he'd said to the lout since the beginning of term.

'I gotta go to class, though,' said the roommate.

Angel silently hoped Todd or whatever would clear out fast, regardless of how he felt. With luck, he'd collapse and be flown back to the USA.

The American stood and spent aeons rummaging through his desk, then his bedside table, then the chest of drawers, then the floor, looking for something, knocking cans and bottles off surfaces and making a racket, while Angel lay in bed, impatiently waiting for the upheaval to subside.

'Where the fuck are they?' mumbled Josh or whatever.

At last, he found what he sought: paracetamol. He put four 500 milligram tablets in his mouth and washed them down with lager.

'*Alright!*' he said, rallying. 'Let's do this, *bitch!*' He paused and, turning to Angel, said, 'Not you; bitch in general.'

Chad or whatever grabbed his notebook, a pen, a packet of tissues, and a large bottle of water, and headed out. After the door closed, Angel eyed the paracetamol, weighing whether to steal a couple of tablets, but he worried Brad or whatever would notice and get angry, so he refrained. He searched his iTunes for music and selected Franz Liszt's Liebestraum, which always made him think of Madison. The *good* Madison, not the Madison she was metamorphosing into, thanks to that dragon, Syd.

The feverishness intensifying, he grew sleepy, drifted in and out of consciousness as his iTunes moved onto Beethoven's *Moonlight Sonata*, Claude

Debussy's *Clair de Lune*, and the rest of his playlist.

When he came to, it was already black outside. The only light in the room funnelled in from the corridor, travelling under the door and through the door lock. Angel's throat now felt as if he'd swallowed a golf ball; his forehead as if supporting a boulder; his skin tender to the touch; his muscles aching and even weaker than normal.

He checked the time on his phone.

Midnight.

He'd missed lunch and dinner. No wonder he had no energy.

Angel sat up, his twig-like arms barely able to support him, and cast a glance at his roommate's bed. He was gone. Unbelievable. Out drinking, flu or no flu.

Within moments, his nose began blocking up with snot. He had no tissues, of course, so this time he was forced to steal one from the American. Getting to the box of Kleenex, however, took him close to an hour, half to summon the will to leave the bed, and another half to crawl on all fours towards his target. And in the end, it seemed counter-productive, because despite being able to blow out some snot, the inflamed tissue inside his nose, producing ever more mucus, had since blocked it solid. That nose-blow, in fact, sucked the last of his energy, and he was forced to rest on the floor, amidst a layer of rubbish averaging six inches in height. Even the wet patch on which he'd collapsed proved insufficient to induce motion.

At least the radiators were hot.

Yet, even this provided no relief, because with no calories consumed since early morning, those he had consumed having been few and of fast-digesting carbohydrates, and his body working overtime trying to fight the virus, a short while later he got the chills. Unable to move, Angel grabbed whatever plastic bags were within reach, but these were not enough to fashion himself a blanket, and one of them was wet. He scrunched his eyes shut, trembling uncontrollably.

His phone vibrated.

But even if it were Madison, he didn't care.

It was then that Chad or Todd or Brad or Josh or whatever decided to walk in. From the silhouetted figure at the door, Angel saw that the American was bringing in yet another plastic bag. The clinking of glass betrayed its contents before the overhead light's being switched on confirmed the Windera branding. He also saw that the American had arrived with companions.

'Party time!' he announced before he noticed Angel. 'Yo, why are you on the floor?'

Angel moaned, unable to respond.

'How can you be cold, man? The radiators are fucking hot!' added the roommate, coughing and sniffling as he towered over him.

Todd or whatever's companions laughed as they filed in, also carrying plastic bags and claiming seats on Angel's bed, chair, and desk. The one who sat on the desk, Boat Shoes from a couple of weeks ago, who'd obviously made peace with Brad's indeterminate forename, accidentally knocked over the tower of books Angel was using to press the flowers for Madison. Boat Shoes was untroubled by the mishap and made no attempt to fix it.

Chad addressed one of the guys who'd sat on Angel's bed—the one with the curly hair. 'Hey, can you toss me that blanket?'

Curly grabbed Angel's duvet and did as requested. Brad caught it in the air and dropped it on Angel.

'There', he said. 'Sweet dreams, bro. Hope you don't mind a quick party.' He chuckled, triggering another bout of coughing.

Angel frowned and groaned unintelligibly.

The hope that neighbouring students would complain seemed futile, since none had ever given signs of minding the noise. On the contrary, they held their own parties from time to time, although not as frequently.

'Cool,' said Josh, taking a bottle of Tennent's Extra out of the plastic bag. 'Let's gooo!'

Brad opened the bottle and gulped it all down. He then pulled out his phone, connected it to portable speakers, and had it play Run-DMC's 'Walk This Way' cover at full volume. This quickly revved everyone up, except Angel, whose roommate now grabbed a second bottle.

Disrupting the din of music, cackling, and shouted banter, Angel heard a collective cheer. From the floor, he saw two girls enter the room. One was skinny with long black hair, olive skin, and a big smile full of teeth; the other, also skinny, had blonde hair and bitchy eyes.

Thus, to the shouts and roars of the boys were added the squeals, whooping, and screams of the girls as they all guzzled their way through the alcohol. Angel's fever kept on rising, the agony of the racket and his symptoms aggravated by the stench of lager and cigarettes. With so many convergent vectors of discomfort, Angel felt only seconds away from exploding, every second a year, every minute a millennium, every hour the age of the cosmos.

Unable to make heads or tails of what anyone was saying, firstly because of the music and secondly because, although they threw words about, the interlocutors were so inarticulate that even cavemen communicating in grunts would have conveyed more meaning,

Angel's only distraction was the aforementioned music, but he hated the American's taste, so it was more a case of waiting for whichever song was playing to be over, rather than enjoying any part of it. And each song dragged on stridently and repetitively, with vastly more verses, choruses, and instrumental segments than he'd hoped for. Cymbals, screaming vocalists, and shrill guitar soloing stabbed his brain like knives.

After a while, Chad or whatever took something out of a drawer that caused everyone, except Angel, to explode with shrieking jubilation. What it was, Angel only discerned after the partiers began rolling paper money and sniffing whatever it was on his bedside table. The American had trouble hoovering up the white powder because of his congestion, but, where there is a will, there is a way, and the will was not lacking.

The infusion of powder kicked up a frenzy of activity. Everyone's speech grew louder and accelerated. The girls danced. Two of the boys danced with them. Curly jumped up and down on Angel's bed. Brad stood on his chair, spinning as he gulped down yet another bottle of Tennent's Extra. The iTunes playlist had now switched to techno, which convulsed that chamber of horrors with its joyful pulse.

How long this lasted for, Angel could not tell. An eternity. But somehow he fell asleep part-way through the coke-fuelled rave and only regained consciousness after everyone had left, except his roommate and Bitchy Eyes, whom the American had on all fours while in rowdy copulation. The American had adjusted the ambiance to the occasion by throwing a red t-shirt over the lamp on his bedside table. Angel considered crawling back onto his bed, but the air was so pungent with cigarette smoke, alcohol, and sex that it seemed best to stay close to the ground. His roommate appeared to have performance issues, as the thrusting went on and on, without a conclusion anywhere in sight. The girl, however, was loving it, filling the air with crass exhortations and expressions of approval. Angel closed his eyes and wished his life away.

Chapter XCVII

When Angel next woke up, it was light. He caught sight of Bitchy Eyes with her hands on her upper back, trying to clip on her brassiere. Her hands and legs were unsteady, and the task was taking forever, instigating in her a torrent of whispered swearing. Todd or Josh or whatever was snoring away in bed. At last, the girl succeeded, slipped on her jumper, and quietly cleared out, her hair a rat's nest.

Angel went back to sleep.

He was then woken up by Chad or Brad or whatever rushing to get dressed, also on unsteady legs. All around him, he caused noisy avalanches of empty cans, bottles, wrappers, sandwich boxes, sheets of paper, and what not, adding to the ever-growing layer of litter on the floor. The American exited the room slamming the door behind him, although not before returning to grab his baseball cap, which he put on backwards, as was his preference.

Angel slept.

Hours passed.

At last, his phone brought him back to consciousness. It buzzed several times in quick succession. Angel thought about crawling to bed, but when he attempted it, his arms failed. He stared at the ceiling lethargically, his throat feeling as if he'd swallowed a cricket ball, his musculature, whatever little of it there was, aching all over, his nose blocked as if with cement, his head like a hot air balloon constantly heated to never let up the pressure, his stomach a bottomless abyss, emptier than the Great Hall in Mark Danielewski's *House of Leaves*. Not by choice, all further buzzing of his phone went unacknowledged.

Angel slept.

It was already dark by the time he next awoke. From the hubbub in the hallway, Angel surmised the canteen had already stopped serving dinner. Hunger added light nausea to his plethora of symptoms, curling Angel into a foetal position. This, however, made his headache worse, so he returned to lying on his back. He imagined, or felt himself, sinking into the carpet, forming an ever-deeper depression and finally a well, the opening above him receding further and further.

He was nearly asleep again when he heard the door open followed by a familiar voice.

'Angel!'

It was Amelia.

'Oh, dear! The state of this room!'

Clearing a path with her foot, Amelia made her way to Angel and kneeled beside him. 'Angel! Angel! Wake up!'

Angel moaned, semi-delirious.

Amelia's tone softened. 'Angel. You need to wake up.'

Angel heard her voice but was unable to focus.

'Angel, you have to get up. Come on. Let's get you to bed.'

Angel attempted to lift himself but crumbled back onto the floor.

'Oh, dear! Oh, dear!' said Amelia, putting her hands to the sides of her face.

She got her phone out and touched a name on her contact list.

'Hi. Are you busy? I'm in Angel's room. Can you please come here? He's in a bad way. I need your help.'

Amelia put her phone down and caressed Angel's head.

'Everything's going to be alright.'

She looked around the room for something. Moments later, Angel heard the kettle. Then the sound of a spoon tinkling as she presumably stirred sugar into a cup. She was soon back by his side.

'Here. Drink some tea. I couldn't find any milk,' she said, lifting his head as if it were the most precious object on Earth, and putting the mug within reach of his lips.

Angel took a sip, then laid back.

In this fashion they spent the next twenty-five minutes until Alba arrived.

'Oh, my God! What happened here?' she said. 'Look at this mess! It's even worse than last time!'

'His temperature seems very high,' said Amelia. 'Help me move him onto the bed.'

'Phwagh! It's stinks in here!' said Alba, grimacing. 'Grab his ankles; I'll grab his wrists.'

The two women thus carried him to bed.

'Wow! He weighs nothing!' said Alba. 'Is he made of polystyrene?'

'I doubt he's eaten anything. We should get him some food. And a big bottle of water,' said Amelia.

'I'll get something from The Departure Lounge. It should still be open.'

Alba left.

'Angel, where are your sheets? Why is your bed so dirty? There are shoe prints all over! Is your roommate treating you badly?'

Angel could not summon the strength to reply.

Amelia opened the window to allow in some fresh air. Using her foot, she pushed the rubbish covering the floor on Angel's side towards his roommate's. By the time she was done, the rubbish piled up on the American's side was eighteen inches high.

'The state of this carpet! And to think you've been living like this!'

Amelia grabbed the duvet under which she'd found Angel, but, upon noticing the stains, the shoe prints, and the cigarette burns, she deemed it too insalubrious. Instead, she took off her jumper and placed it over his torso, carefully tucking the wool under his sides, and leaving herself in a t-shirt. She then found a packet of tissues in her bag, took one out, wetted it in the sink, and laid it gently on Angel's forehead, taking a seat beside him on the bed.

Alba came back a while later with a BLT, three bottles of water, a hot chocolate, a slice of cake, and a banana. Amelia made space on Angel's bedside table and placed all the items there except the BLT, the sandwich box containing which she opened to extract one of the triangles.

'Here, Angel. Alba has brought you food. Take a bite,' she said, putting the sandwich half against Angel's lips.

Angel took a mousy bite and slowly chewed.

'Shouldn't we give him paracetamol?' said Alba.

'I don't know when he last took some,' said Amelia. 'Too much paracetamol is bad for the liver.'

'Seriously, Amelia? Does he look to you like someone who's taken paracetamol anytime this century? He can't even feed himself properly!'

'Well, I don't see any on his bedside table.'

'Of course he doesn't have any. Since when has he been prepared for anything? Let's give him two tablets. I have Panadol in my bag.'

'Don't be sarcastic, Alba. He's had a lot on his mind lately.'

'La la la, come on!' Alba produced the tablets.

Amelia put them in Angel's mouth and brought the mug with the last of the tea to his lips. He took a sip and swallowed.

Alba sat on Angel's chair, although not without first inserting a plastic bag between her jeans and the stained and shoe-printed polyester.

'The state of this place!' she said, crinkling her nose. 'This is third degree squalor!'

'It's not him. It's his roommate.'

'It's not him? He stinks, he walks around in rags, he has greasy hair. Of course, it's him!'

'He's lovelorn. He wasn't like that in the Spring. You know that.'

'Okay, but this is his room this term. So it fits.'

'Alba, Angel doesn't like drinking beer and he doesn't smoke. Look around you. A lot of the rubbish is cans or bottles of lager. The room smells of cigarettes. The dirty clothes are his roommates—Angel doesn't wear shorts or American university hoodies. It's his roommate.'

'Then he should grow a spine and tell him to tidy up!'

'Oh, come on. I'm sure he has, but people can be stubborn.'

Alba scoffed, but distained to argue further.

After forty minutes or so, the paracetamol dulled Angel's symptoms sufficiently for him to regain awareness, eat the rest of the food, and briefly answer questions.

'What happened, Angel?' asked Amelia.

'Um . . . I felt ill after class . . .'

'What, today?'

'No . . . yesterday . . .'

'Oh, dear . . . you've been here since yesterday morning?'

'Um . . . yes . . .'

'No wonder you didn't reply to my messages. Why were you on the floor?'

'I needed a tissue . . . but then I couldn't make it back . . .'

'So you stole it from your roommate,' said Alba.

'I . . . um . . . I . . . er . . . borrowed a sheet.'

'Okay. So you stole it,' declared Alba.

'Let him speak,' said Amelia, gently. 'Did your roommate not show up last night?'

'Um . . . er . . . yes. He had a party.'

'And he left you there on the floor?' Amelia was horrified.

'Er . . . yes. They were all drinking and doing drugs.'

'And afterwards?'

'My roommate was having sex with a girl.'

'Oh, gross!' said Alba.

'With you there on the floor next to his bed?' asked Amelia.

'Yes . . .'

'Oh, Angel . . . you poor thing!'

'That's it,' said Alba. 'I still think he needs to grow a

spine, but I'm having a word with that yank!'

And just as well, because it was at that moment that Todd or Josh or Chad or Brad or whatever arrived, again carrying a plastic bag filled with bottles, and again accompanied by louts carrying yet more lager.

'Ah, no no no no no no!' said Alba, jumping to her feet and going straight to the door to block access. 'You're not having any parties here tonight.'

'What?' said the American.

Amelia joined Alba to reinforce the blockade.

'Angel is very ill,' said Amelia. 'He really needs to rest. Can you take your party somewhere else?'

'But this is my room! What the fuck? Who the fuck are you?'

'Not tonight and none of your business!' said Alba. 'So take your booze and your chums and *bugger off!*'

Todd or whatever stood at the threshold, momentarily paralysed.

'Where's Angel?' he finally said, craning his neck to look past the women and into the room.

'He's in bed, resting,' said Amelia.

'Ah, so *now* you care?' said Alba. 'Too late! Come on, away you go. Chop chop!'

'But—'

'You snooze you lose! Out or I start screaming!' Alba then opened her mouth and eyes wide to convey that she could, and would, scream until their eardrums burst.

'Jeez! Okay! Alright already!' said the American, raising a placatory hand.

He then turned to Boat Shoes and said, 'We'll go to your room. Do you mind if I crash there, bud?'

Boat Shoes vehemently shook his head. 'No way José. I have to study!'

'Come on, buddy! It's only one night.'

'No way, man. You're gonna trash my room.'

'I won't trash your room, bud. I promise.'

'Okay, but you have to pick up your shit when it's over. I have standards!'

'Cool. Let's go party then!'

Alba didn't wait to see them move. She slammed the door shut and locked it.

Chapter XCVIII

Once satisfied that Angel would be alright, the girls left him to sleep, his bedside table cleared except for bottles of water and two more Panadol tablets, his bed made with the clean floral sheets Amelia had brought from her room.

Amelia came to visit him again at lunch the following day. She seemed relieved to find, as she walked in, that Angel's roommate was absent.

'Hi Angel. How are you feeling?'

'Um . . . not so good.'

'Well, I brought you some supplies.'

Amelia took individual items out of her backpack and carefully lined them up on his desk.

'I got you: a BLT sandwich . . . a chocolate cupcake . . . an apple . . . Earl Grey . . . a pot noodle . . . a spoon . . . Panadol . . . tissues . . . VapoRub . . . lozenges . . . water . . . and . . . a hot water bottle!'

'Oh . . . thank you . . .'

He sniffled, reached for a tissue, and blew his nose.

Amelia opened the sandwich box and handed him one of the triangles as she sat by his side on the bed.

Angel took a small bite and chewed.

'I forgot . . .' she said, taking out a thermometer from her bag. 'We'll measure your temperature when you're done.'

Angel finished the sandwich, which tasted like cold cardboard, and blew his nose again; Amelia then took his temperature.

'Oh, dear! Thirty-nine point eight! It's still very high.'

Angel said nothing, his headache having gathered momentum since the Panadol had worn off hours before. He wiped away some snot that was coming down his nostril. The skin around them was becoming irritated.

'Promise me you'll rest. I've spoken to the canteen supervisor about your shift. You don't need to worry until Monday.'

'Um . . . Thank you . . . really?'

'Yes, so just stay in bed, drink plenty of water, take paracetamol every four hours, and sleep as much as you can.'

'Okay . . .'

'I have to go now, but I'll come and visit you tonight to see how you're doing. Okay?'

'Yes . . . okay . . . thank you.'

Amelia caressed the side of his face, offering him a sweet smile, and left.

Angel blew his nose and drifted back to sleep.

A while later, however, his phone buzzed.

He picked up the device, wiping snot off his nostril with the other hand.

Destiny had WhatsApped him.

DESTINY: Reminder that your train leaves King's Cross at 19:30. Have you packed your bags?

Angel's hand went to his forehead.

ANGEL: Yes, of course.

DESTINY: I'll meet you at the station in York. Stay awake. Don't miss your stop!

ANGEL: No, I'll be there.

DESTINY: OK. Keep me updated

ANGEL: Okay.

DESTINY: Mum has just put £10 in your account so you can get to King's Cross. STRICTLY FOR TRANSPORT!

ANGEL: Okay.

Putting the phone down, Angel rubbed his head, scrunching his eyes, his forehead throbbing. He checked the time: it was 17:31.

'Damn,' he whispered.

The thought of even just walking across the room was daunting. How was he going to make it to the station?

He laid in bed, blowing his nose and feeling weak, until 18:15, the latest he thought he could possibly delay getting up for. Then, at a sloth's pace, he sat up and swivelled to plant his feet on the floor. Minutes passed, all of them in discomfort. Finally, he summoned the strength to stand, which he managed only by pressing his hands against his knees. It felt as if his body had become a dense, viscous material. His muscles ached. His skin ached. His head ached.

Once vertical, he felt light-headed and dizzy, prompting him to steady himself by leaning on the shelves above his bed.

More minutes passed.

It occurred to him that it would be bad to show up at his parents' house without a suitcase, because that would lead to questions, so he dragged his empty Samsonite down from the top of the wardrobe; it fell out of his hand and crashed onto the floor. He set it upright onto its wheels.

At that moment, the chills suddenly hit him. He coiled with uncontrollable shivers. This urged him to get dressed in a hurry. The solution he found for the missing buttons on his shirt was to staple the gap shut, although he fumbled and had to use both his hands to close the stapler, so weak was his grip. His blocked nose spared him the strange smell of his clothes, which probably still stank of cigarette smoke. He hoped that exposure to fresh air and the train's ventilation system would get rid of the odour, and that his mother would not notice the staples in his jeans and shirt, or the missing top piece on the heel of his shoe. She'd likely still comment on the dilapidated state of his attire, but he decided to tell her he chose to wear old and comfortable items for travelling, so as not to mess up his good clothes.

It was now 18:47. Time was running out.

Movement being his only source of heat, Angel left the room, then the dorm, then the campus, dragging his suitcase in the rain. The suitcase, because empty, kept bouncing wildly against every pebble or paving imperfection, which repeatedly toppled it and forced Angel to stop and pick it up. He found it difficult to walk in a straight line, and he continuously tripped over his feet. His eyes watered and his nose ran in what felt like Arctic cold. Worse, the exertion of walking angrily augmented his headache. He also had to stop frequently to blow or wipe off snot; the tissue, however, was wet and had begun disintegrating. He dreaded to think of how much the force of climbing stairs in the Underground station would add to the pounding in his head. He was almost certain his cranium would explode were the suitcase full or the escalators broken.

He entered the station soaked from head to toe. The walk had brought to his attention that the sole of the hitherto undamaged shoe had come unstuck, allowing rainwater ingress to his foot. Thus, his walk became an alternating limp and squelch, limp and squelch, limp and squelch.

After he purchased his ticket, he blew his nose before making his way through the corridors, where he passed a busker playing the guitar. On the foot-tapping, head-bobbing guitar player he thought he recognised another of his lost shirts, which also had a distinctive stripe pattern.

The platform was vacuum packed with humans, sampling every age, sex, race, gender identification, sexual preference, disability status, and mental health condition. Just as well that he was in a tin of sardines, because Angel, once again dizzy, would have otherwise collapsed, his head thumping, his legs no longer able to support him. It was the chest pressed against his back, the back pressed against his chest, and the shoulders pressed against his shoulders that kept him aloft. He could not move his arms to pull out his tattered tissue, so he had to let the snot run ticklishly over his moustache and upper lip.

The platform display said it was 19:14:32. The next train was not due for another five minutes.

'Oh, balls . . .' he mumbled, not altogether consciously.

When the Northern Line train arrived, he was carried into it like driftwood, and compacted into the centre of the carriage so tightly that his arms not only remained pinned against his sides but his ribcage could only expand a millimetre to allow air into his lungs. All he could see around him were ears, noses, lips, cheekbones, occiputs, hair, hats, glasses, and headphones. As he was having to breathe through his mouth, he initially thought the steam around him was coming out of his buccal cavity, but he realised that, his clothes being wet, and the train being hot, the steam was coming from his body.

The train made a number of stops, during which even more commuters came on board, making room for themselves by pressing into the ones inside with their shoulders, wedging themselves into whatever crevice was still available, with just enough clearance for their heads to escape being guillotined by the inwardly-curving closing doors. At one point the train stopped in the tunnel, with no explanation from the driver. In the midst of this, Angel was left with no idea of where he was, or how he would extricate himself when he reached King's Cross. But the latter station's being a major node in the network supplied a solution in the end, for the train, upon arriving there, disgorged most of its passengers, again carrying Angel along like driftwood, first onto and then out of the platform. It was only on the main escalator that the crowd thinned enough for Angel to rely on his own legs to maintain a vertical posture.

He blew his nose and checked the time on his phone. It was 19:24:58. Yet, a lot of walking lay ahead.

Angel's pace upped a gear and, though unsteadily, he made it to the King's Cross railway station, wiping his nostrils raw with his shirt sleeve along the way. The concourse clock said it was 19:29:01. Train doors closed thirty seconds before departure. He had twenty-nine seconds to find out his platform and make it to the train.

'Bollocks!' he whispered, gasping lungfuls of air through his mouth, adrenalin speeding up his aching movements.

He located the departures board, hurried over, and scanned it for the relevant platform information.

The clock now said 19:29:17.

Thirteen seconds.

Angel found the platform information, located the platform, and ran thither, wiping his nose and dragging his suitcase too fast for it to stay on its wheels. Even though empty, it still felt heavy to him, to the extent that his grip kept slipping.

The clock ahead said 19:29:29.

He heard the whistle.

'No!' came his high-pitched moan.

But he had one second remaining, and the door to the first carriage had only just begun closing. With a final and rapid beating of the legs, head ferociously pounding, Angel closed the gap between himself and the narrowing aperture. It was just as well he'd lost so much weight, because he only just managed to squeeze inside the carriage before the doors closed. The latter nearly lopped off his arm, but as they automatically reopened, he was able to heave in his suitcase, a manoeuvre that sent him flying backwards and landing onto the steel floor. His luggage followed and landed on his face. This double collision rendered him unconscious.

Chapter XCIX

Angel only woke up when the train stopped at Stevenage and travellers stepped over him to disembark or come on board. No one acknowledged his presence.

After the train got moving again, he sat up, his back freezing from prolonged contact with the steel flooring. He dug up what was left of his tissue, wiped his nostrils, stood unsteadily, and held onto a handle, swaying from the motion of the carriage, while the dizziness passed. Search for Amelia's Panadol in his pocket proved fruitless: he'd forgotten it on his bedside table. Also gone were the forty-one pence he'd had left from Amelia's tenner; a hole had swallowed them, leaving only the original penny.

His head felt like a hot pressure cooker with a blocked release valve.

In wobbly slow-motion, Angel ambled his way

through the carriage, dragging his suitcase, searching for his seat. When he found it, he saw that his mother had booked one facing forward, next to the window in a bay of four; there was no table in the middle. The other three seats were occupied. In front of him sat an Indian man in a dark business suit. Next to the latter was a lanky teenager in a hoodie, playing video games on his phone. In the isle seat next to Angel's sat a middle-aged woman, reading an old edition of Richard Adams' *Watership Down*.

Angel's suitcase was too big for the space provided overhead, so he left it in the luggage carriage area, returned to his seat, and, stepping over his neighbours' feet, sat down. In the process he aimed his foot incorrectly and briefly stepped on Business Suit's mirror-polished shoe.

'Oh, sorry!' said Angel, showing his palms, eyes wide, and nearly stumbling as he corrected course.

Business Suit gave him a disapproving look, but a moment latter his visage regained its sphynx-like neutrality. Watership Down, casting a disgusted sideways glance at him, leaned away. Video Game remained absorbed in his video game.

The unrelenting build-up of mucus and the absence of a serviceable tissue soon became a problem. He sniffled continuously, ever more noisily, and scoured his brain for ways to contain the upcoming avalanche. His only recourse seemed to get toilet paper from the lavatory. He was about go and find it when he became overwhelmed by a tickle in his nostril. Despite awareness of the danger, and his last-instant effort to stop the incoming sneeze, the latter gained momentum with unstoppable force, leading to the inevitable nasopharyngeal explosion. He ended with his torso bent forward and hands on either side of his nose. When he leaned back and looked down, he noticed a large glob of mucus had landed on his chest. His hands were also covered in mucus.

'Oh, God!' he whispered.

Business Suit's face, he saw, had contracted into a grimace of disgust, and pushed his head back into the headrest, as if to keep himself as far from Angel as possible. Watership Down quickly stuffed her book into her handbag and forfeited her seat, leaving the carriage entirely. Video Game kept playing his video game, either unaware of, or indifferent to, the naso-pharyngeal event.

Angel went in search of a lavatory; along the way, silent faces registered a spectrum of opinions, all negative. He reached the front of the train without encountering a lavatory. The mucus on his chest sliding down his shirt, Angel searched in the opposite direction. He finally found the lavatory right at the back; moreover, it was occupied and barred by a queue. Along it, silent faces again registered a spectrum of negative opinions.

After some fifteen minutes, it was his turn. The lavatory was already filthy, accuracy of aim appearing foreign to some of the travellers. Moreover, the roll of toilet paper was on its last quarter inch. It took a succession of long segments to clean up his hands and the bulk of the mess on his chest, but the toilet paper ran out before the job was done. He was thus forced to rely on tap water, which, being offered cold only, might as well have been liquid nitrogen.

While there, Angel thought it prudent to empty his bladder. But as he unbuckled he saw that his belt had cracked where he'd drilled the latest of the extra holes, so he made a mental note to be gentle when buckling up. Unfortunately, as weak as he was, the crack had made the leather on that spot even weaker, and after he'd completed his evacuation and pulled on the perforated end to fasten, he ended up with a detached length of belt in his hand. Were it not for his holding the buckle in the other, his trousers would have fallen straight down to the floor.

'Oh, balls!' he whispered.

He scanned his surroundings for anything he could use to prick a hole in the remaining belt segment. There was, however, nothing except the prong in the belt buckle, which was very blunt. With no choice but, he got started.

Many minutes passed. All in resultless exertion.

A knock on the door.

Angel swore in silence, and renewed his efforts, the mucus building up in his nasal cavity once again, forcing interruptions to wipe. (For this he only had the cardboard toilet roll cylinder, which, on his raw skin felt like wire brush.) No matter how hard he pressed, however, which wasn't very hard, the leather proved stubborn.

More knocking on the door.

Angel took a deep breath through his mouth and pushed the prong against the leather one more time, shaking with the effort, giving it his all. Yet, the leather would not yield.

Still more knocking, now louder.

'Oi!' he heard. 'Are you done, mate?'

Scared of being told off, Angel released the latch and exited the lavatory, holding his jeans up with one hand, carrying the severed belt fragment in the other.

A tattooed man with a week's worth of beard stared at him as Angel exited. 'Fucking 'ell, mate!' he said, before shoving his way in, slamming the door shut, and angrily flicking the latch.

Angel pretended not to notice the tight faces around him and returned to his seat.

There, he found that Video Game had slid down the backrest, curving his spine like a banana; he'd also put his feet up, pressing the soles of his trainers onto the seat opposite. Angel had to step over the intruding legs, as the teenager was unmoved by his arrival.

Business Suit was typing on his phone; he stopped to inspect Angel's shirt; then, shaking his head slightly, carried on typing. Angel searched his pockets for re-usable tissue fragments. He found two fuzzy ones the size of a fifty pence coin. He rolled them into balls, stuffed them up his nostrils, tilted back his head, and closed his eyes.

Before long, he'd fallen sleep.

He later woke up to new neighbours, an obese family of three. The woman, clad in black, had a Morrison's bag filled with crisps and chocolate bars in every flavour available; her husband, a balding man with a pink polo shirt, slept next to her; and the boy, seated next to Angel, had a buzz cut and Down syndrome.

Due to having slept breathing through his mouth, Angel's buccal cavity was parched. A porcupine had also taken residence in his throat. It took him a full minute of running his tongue over his gum and swallowing to moisten the tissues.

Yet, dehydration not only made the task difficult, but had compounded his headache, demanding action. The only free source of water was the sink in the lavatory. Whether he could trust it not to be full of viruses or harmful bacteria was another matter. In desperation, he looked at the floor to see if anyone had left behind a half-drunk bottle of Pepsi, Fanta, or water he could pour into his mouth. Nothing.

His phone screen told him it wasn't too long to York, however. Maybe his sister would buy him water at the station.

Then he remembered he had a bit left over in his bank account from the £10 his mother had sent him. This knowledge activated his legs, which sent him in search for the Café Bar.

But when he found it, a hand-written sign explained that it was closed due to a payment system failure.

At this juncture, the train began slowing down. Angel stood by a window to watch the train pull in at Doncaster Station. After the train came to a halt, he listened to the doors hissing open, the din of the platforms, travellers disembarking and coming on board. He watched the former as they marched towards the exit until the whistle blew and the doors closed.

Once the train got moving again, Angel, jerked out of his daze, tired, his fever rising anew, returned to his seat.

But when he got there, he found a usurper: a stern middle-aged man in a grey business suit. Angel opened his mouth to speak, but Grey Business Suit didn't notice him.

'Um . . . sir?' Angel said.

No acknowledgment.

'Sir? Excuse me. Sir?'

No acknowledgment.

'Sir?'

The boy with Down syndrome looked at him, but not Grey Business Suit.

'Sir?'

Still no acknowledgment. The boy continued to stare.

'Um . . . sir?'

Grey Business Suit was deaf.

Uncomfortable from the boy's persistent stare, Angel sought a seat elsewhere.

Yet, all the seats were taken. Young and not-so-young women, tarted-up for a night out; young and not-so-young men, clad in jeans and shirts, with plastic hair and litres of aftershave; exhausted office workers; drunken teenagers; football hooligans; hospital nurses.

For the final leg of his journey, therefore, Angel stood.

Chapter C

At 9:31pm, the train rolled under York Station's arched Victorian skylights. Angel had already gone to the luggage carriage area to retrieve his suitcase, aiming to be first to disembark, though less out of assertiveness than of necessity. The sooner he could sit down, the better. But everyone else being faster, more vigorous, and more aggressive, backs, shoulders, and arms got in his way, bumping him, knocking him off balance, spinning him like a spinning top, and preventing him from disembarking until most of his fellow passengers had done so.

His descent onto the platform was also not without incident, for the detached sole of his shoe caught on the step, propelling him face-first onto the concrete surface. He landed with an 'Ooff!', scraping his hands, chin, and nose. His suitcase followed him with a clatter.

Freshly disembarked travellers who'd been in the rear carriages ghosted him as they passed.

A child in a sailor outfit laughed, staring and gleefully pointing at him with a tiny finger while dragged away by his mother. 'Aaah haaa haaa!'

Again with sloth-like movements, Angel got up and inventoried the damage. His front was covered in dust; his hands bleeding; the tip of his nose stinging. The offending shoe sole now hung from the arch like a tongue.

Given the temperature, the platform could well have been in Antarctica; a frigid wind chilled him to the marrow, instigating uncontrollable tremors. As he zig-zagged his way to the iron bridge leading to the concourse, his suitcase rattling behind him, the weight of his shoes probably the only thing keeping him from being blown away, he sniffled to contain the mucus drooping towards his upper lip, but the action proved ineffective, forcing use of his shirtsleeve. It was already caked with snot.

Alas, no Destiny on the concourse. Angel headed towards the meeting point near the entrance, where she could have been waiting for him on a bench, but, again, no Destiny. Neither was there Destiny at the entrance. Nor outside, in the freezing darkness. He moaned with steepled eyebrows; his head throbbing, he could barely hold himself aloft. Every sinew in his body screamed for a warm bed, steaming lemon tea, a hot water bottle, and bushels of paracetamol.

Angel retreated into the concourse as a second, monumental sneeze built momentum. Sighting the W. H. Smiths up ahead, a two-storey rectangular island with sashed windows along its top, he dashed in, aiming for a packet of tissues. But his body exhibited its exquisite timing for humiliation, for no sooner had he entered the shop that he convulsed with the dreaded nasopharyngeal explosion. Customers who heard it turned to find him bent over, slowly pulling his hands away from the sides of his nose, the palms, upper lip, and chin covered in green mucus.

'Woah, that's fucking gross,' chuckled a long-haired man, exiting with a copy of *Metal Hammer*.

The young woman behind the metalhead, a Goth, went '*Euuurghhh*,' her face a portrait of revulsion.

For a moment, Angel was stumped as to how to proceed. He needed his hands to fetch the packet of tissues and pay, but he had no idea of how to wipe them without relying on his clothes, which, given the vast quantity of snot involved, he was averse to do. He thought about buying a contemptible tabloid for the purpose, but he bristled at the idea of being thought a troglodyte with an infant's reading level. In the end, he deemed the first option the lesser evil, since he'd have tissues to wipe his clothes with afterwards. He pretended not to notice the wincing customers around him as he performed this operation.

While at it, he considered also getting Panadol, but the price of the Kleenex multipack left his funds just short. And the self-checkout left his bank balance at a penny. Which was just as well, for the penny in his pocket had since vanished down the hole.

He hid behind the W. H. Smith, next to the large, old-fashioned scale facing the platform, to wipe himself clean. If Destiny saw him, he knew, she'd mock him, tell his parents, tell her friends at the gym, and on and on. By the time he was done, and despite his best efforts, his ripped, burnt, and stapled shirt looked as if it'd been dunked in Irish stew.

All the benches long the front of the W. H. Smith were taken, so once again he had to stand. Still no Destiny. He pulled out his phone in case she'd messaged and held the device to his face.

And in a flash, it was gone.

Angel stared at his empty hand for an instant, then looked around in all directions, mouth agape, eyebrows steepled, orbs fifty percent exposed.

All he saw was people walking.

'Wha—' he breathed.

A hoodie swaggered away at two or three yards' distance, but he couldn't see his phone, so he dared not stop him.

He checked both his front pockets in case he'd hallucinated.

But no, his phone was gone.

He visually scoured the floor, in case he'd dropped the device.

But no, his phone wasn't there.

He looked under the benches, in case it'd bounced to land under one of them.

But no, there was only floor and rubbish.

The inevitable conclusion: his phone had been stolen.

Snatched right out of his hand at lightning speed.

'Bollocks!' he whispered, staring into the distance, sniffling, his eyes fixing on this or that individual among the hundreds coming and going.

He then felt a fast tug in his back pocket.

His hand flew to it.

Empty.

Now his wallet was gone too.

Angel spun round and round, head again jerking in every direction, hair flying, mouth more agape, eyes wider, eyebrows more steepled.

Again, all he could see was people walking.

All walking normally.

Some even laughing and telling jokes.

The only remarkable individual was standing by the flower shop across from him: a blonde man in a raincoat, with shoulder-length hair, which he vainly combed with rapt delectation.

He shoved his hand into his back pocket, pulled it out, shoved it in, pulled it out, and scrunched the loose denim.

It truly was empty.

No doubt.

And the wallet was neither on the floor, nor under the benches, nor anywhere.

It too was gone.

In the absence of thieves, Angel scanned the concourse for a member of the Transport Police. But there was none. In the process, however, he found the door to their station, right next to the Starbucks terrace. He walked up to it and pushed. Yet, the door was locked. A sign asked to ring an 0800 number. What was the point, he thought, sighing, if his phone had been stolen? He rang the intercom.

No answer.

He rang again.

No answer.

Angel waited.

He rang a third time.

Nothing.

Angel walked around the concourse, renewing his search for a police officer, then returned to the door and rang the intercom a fourth time.

Silence.

He knocked on the door.

Still nothing.
He knocked on the door again.
Zero.
He waited.
And waited.
And sniffled.
He knocked a third time and rang the intercom a fifth.
Nada.
He pressed his ear against the door.
Like a tomb.

Angel stared at the door, baffled. After some hesitation, he decided to go back to standing by the W. H. Smith, as from there he could see both his sister arrive and catch sight of any police officer coming out of that door.

Minutes passed.
No Destiny.
No police officer.
The clock above him said 10:23 pm.

It was not like Destiny to be late. She ran her life by the clock. In that sense she was much like their parents: tidy, organised, logical, on top of things. And she'd become more so since she started powerlifting a few years ago. Every meal controlled for macro- and micronutrients. Optimised for athletic performance. As was her sleep, which nowadays required a fan, complete darkness, dead silence, a maternity pillow, a Tempur mattress, and room temperature not above 15° Celsius. All strictures that she adhered to and enforced with android-like rigidity.

More minutes passed.

Angel watched people come and go, drink coffee, eat cupcakes, choose flowers, buy sandwiches, check the departures information board, scan the arrivals board, go into W. H. Smiths, come out of W. H. Smiths, wait, jabber on their phones, chat with one another, push prams, pull suitcases, stand in groups, stroll, run. The aroma emanating from the Cornish pasty shop just across—what little of it made it through his nasal blockage—made his stomach growl. It was strange to blow his nose while concave with hunger.

With each passing minute, the adrenalin from the robbery wore off, leaving him weaker, more feverish.

When the clock read 10:47 pm, he could not bear to stand any longer. The soles of his feet burned. His throat had a cactus growing in it. His muscles ached. His cephalic pressure cooker still had no release valve.

The benches stubbornly occupied, Angel sat on the floor, forearms resting on pointy knees.

Another fifteen minutes passed.

Drowsiness overtook him, its murky waters submerging his consciousness, sapping tension from his neck, and allowing his head to droop forward like melted wax.

The aeroplane was due to land in an hour. If he made it out of the terminal quickly, and if the taxi was fast, he'd be able to reach Madison before she got the tattoo. But then the aircraft started losing altitude, and the engines, he noticed, had grown silent. From his window seat he saw that they were flying over the Himalayas. Weren't they supposed to be flying over the Atlantic? The pilot announced that due to an engine malfunction, they were going to attempt a landing after they'd cleared the mountains. A bossy Afro-American stewardess then ordered everyone to 'adopt the recovery position'. 'Please adopt the recovery position', she kept chanting. Why couldn't the Pentagon refuel the aircraft in mid-air? How long would it take for rescue teams to find them and get him to Madison? Could they get him to her before she arrived at the tattoo parlour? He considered sending her a message to stall her, but he had no signal. The cabin started rattling and shuddering ever more violently. Passengers panicked. There was a hull breach . . .

'Oh my God! Angel? Is that you?'

Angel opened his eyes.

He opened them to Destiny's muscular, football-sized calves. She was clad in black tights, Converse shoes, and a Giants Live hoodie. Her long ginger hair cascaded down her front.

'What *happened* to you?' she said, eyes gas giants.

'Um . . . hello,' he said, slumberous.

'Have you been attacked?'

'Um . . . attacked?'

'You're covered in wounds!'

'Um . . . er . . . no . . . I-I fell.'

'Then are you doing drugs? Is that why you're begging? What's going on?' Destiny hid her alarm with sarcasm.

'Sorry, what?'

'I've walked past *twenty times* while looking for you. I can't believe this is you. You're a wreck!'

'Um . . . sorry . . . I've got the flu,' Angel said, standing up.

'I only recognised you because of the suitcase. Bloody hell. The state of you! And you bloody *stink!*'

Angel looked down at himself.

'Mum's going to kill you when she sees you dressed in rags and covered in filth and wounds. Let's hope father doesn't see you before you've changed.'

'Er . . . is he home?'

'Yes.'

'Oh . . .'

'And do you *ever* eat in London?'

'I-I-I haven't been very hungry lately. I've been busy.'

'You look like a skeleton. People think you're homeless.'

Destiny pointed to the coins that had appeared in front of him while he slumbered.

Angel glanced at them only briefly. 'Um . . . can we go?'

'Why are you holding on to your jeans?'

'My belt broke.'

'Bloody hell, Angel. What's wrong with you?'

Angel grabbed the suitcase handle with his free hand and got ready to pull.

'Um . . . are you in the short-term carpark?'

'Yes. But stay away from me if you've got the flu. I don't want to miss training days.'

CHAPTER CI

Destiny opened the boot of her white Mercedes CLA 200. Immaculate. Not a speck of dust on its carpet lining. Angel slid his suitcase next to her Adidas gym bag, which she'd lined up, leaving space for him.

'Have you got a lot in there?' she said.

'Er . . . just . . . normal.'

'Because it looks heavy, the way you're lifting it.'

'No . . . just normal.'

Destiny pulled the handle and the case flew up.

'Blimey! Is this heavy for you?'

'Um . . .'

She held the suitcase up with one hand and knocked the plastic shell with her knuckle. The case bonged hollow.

'This is empty!' she said. 'Why would you bring an empty case?'

'Um . . . just light summer clothes I won't need.'

'I suppose you have clothes at home. But they won't fit you now, being that skinny.'

'It's really cold . . . can we go?' he said, shivering, arms wrapped around himself.

Destiny quickly eyed him up and down. 'Okay. But wait.'

She put the case in the boot, making sure it was lined up, unzipped her gym bag, and took out a towel. She then zipped the bag close with a single, precise movement, closed the boot, and opened the door to the front passenger seat. While Angel watched, she covered the seat with the towel.

'You can sit now,' she said, stepping aside.

Angel did as bidden.

Destiny sat behind the wheel and they got moving. She manoeuvred the car deftly and smoothly. Not like Angel, who was prone to miscalculation and inciting rage in other drivers.

'Pfuagh! You really stink!' She switched on the fan, set it to maximum, and opened the windows a crack.

'Um . . . sorry.'

'Have you eaten?'

'Er . . . no.'

'Of course you haven't. Look at you. Don't they feed you at uni?'

'Yes, they do feed us.'

'Well, mum'll make you something. Hopefully you'll still be alive when we get there.'

'Okay,' he said, sniffling.

'Have you taken Panadol?'

'Er . . . no.'

'Why not?'

'Um . . . I ran out.'

'Why didn't you buy more at W. H. Smiths?'

'I only had enough for the tissues.'

'It's £2.65, Angel. You didn't have three quid?'

'No.'

'Bloody hell. What a mess!'

Angel didn't reply.

'Mum is still fuming about the money.'

Angel said nothing.

'She's not told father yet. Better brace yourself. *I* still can't believe it.'

Angel swallowed, his gaze haunted as he looked out the window. His knees started bouncing.

'Mum's gonna work it out soon enough. Where the money went. It's pretty damn obvious.'

He sniffled and looked out the window, eyebrows steepled.

'I told you this before, and I will tell you again. She's laughing at you, Angel.'

'Who?'

'That girl. Madison. She's laughing at you. Can't you see?'

Angel regretted having allowed his sister to know about Madison. It had slipped out one day. And of course she had mentioned his beloved to their mother. 'You don't know her,' he moaned.

'She's trouble.'

'Um . . . she pranks people a lot. It's not what it seems.'

'Oh, really? She's convinced you of that too, eh?' She chuckled, shaking her head.

'Um . . . it's not what it seems.'

'If I were you, I'd drop her like a live coal. She's a right psychopath, that one.'

Angel said nothing.

'Up to you. But don't say I didn't warn you.'

'You don't know,' he mumbled.

'I'm a girl. She's a girl. *I know.*'

Silence.

'But up to you,' Destiny continued. 'Although not with mum's money. She'll make that *one hundred percent clear.*'

'Um . . . why were you late?' he asked. 'The train arrived at nine thirty.'

'Didn't you get my messages?'

'Er . . . no.'

'What—you don't check your phone? I'm sure you check it every nanosecond to see what that girl is posting.'

'Um . . . there must have been an outage with WhatsApp.'

'A car burst into flames and the police closed the road. There was no way around.'

'Oh.'

'But they didn't catch me unprepared. I had my food Thermos with me plus protein bars, so I kept up with my meals.'

Angel noticed she was a little bigger than last time.

'Because you know, Angel, *failing to prepare is preparing to fail!*' Destiny laughed.

He said nothing.

'How about some music?' she said.

'Okay,'

Destiny pressed PLAY.

The car speakers exploded with angry decibels. Down-tuned electric guitars, blast beats, growled vocals. Angel flinched and eyed the display. It said, 'Malevolent Creation - The Will to Kill'. She cast a side glance at him, frowning with her lower lip tucked under her front teeth, nodding along with the music.

Re-steepling his eyebrows, Angel said, with a raised high voice, 'C-C-Could you turn it down a little bit?'

'Sorry what?'

'C-C-Could you turn it down a bit?'

She turned it down to a whisper.

'I forgot,' she said, grinning. 'His Lordship likes *elegant* music.'

She sang the beginning of Vivaldi's *Four Seasons* in a mocking falsetto while conducting with her left hand, her thumb and index fingers holding an imaginary baton.

Angel's head sank into his shoulders.

'Well, you're moody tonight,' she said, grinning.

'Um . . . it's just the flu.'

'Then be stoic.'

'Sorry?'

'Be stoic. Act as if you were completely normal.'

'Um . . .'

'Come on . . . let's see it. Pretend you're completely normal.'

'Er . . . I'm really tired.'

'You have to train your mind, Angel.'

'Maybe later . . .'

'There's never a good time to have the flu. That's why you have to be stoic. Come on! *This* is when it counts!'

No response.

'Think about the Antarctic explorers. They had to pull ninety-kilo sledges for hundreds of miles, on sticky ice, at minus forty, blizzard winds blowing in their faces, with half the calories they needed, and all this with their gums swollen out of their mouths from *scurvy*.'

No reply.

'Oh, dear. It looks like you're going straight to

bed . . . like a baby.'

'Um . . . I do need to lie down.'

'Poor wittle baby . . .' she said, pulling a sulky face. 'I'll bring you your dummy.' She laughed. 'Should we stop to get some nappies?'

Chapter CII

They arrived at the manor shortly before midnight. The family abode was a complicated stone house of many gables, the oldest parts dating from the Tudor era. Asymmetrical 17th and 19th-century additions gave the structure a labyrinthine quality. Destiny parked the car in the courtyard, next to their father's black Rolls-Royce Phantom and their mother's Audi RS7.

Destiny opened the boot so that Angel could remove his empty suitcase.

'Do you want help with that?' she said, grinning, 'We wouldn't want you to dislocate your shoulder.'

Angel gave her a sullen look and pulled out the suitcase. Before they headed for the house, he thoroughly blew his nose, made sure his shirt was properly tucked in, and combed his hair with his fingers.

'Angel,' said Destiny. 'Mum's got eyes. She's gonna notice you're a mess.'

Angel said nothing.

'Ready?' she said when he was done.

'Yes, I'm ready.'

'Let's go around the back. Father's likely asleep already.'

They walked towards the house, their footsteps crunching on the gravel. Angel tilted his head back to gaze at the firmament. The Milky Way shone above. He'd missed the country night sky; in London nights were a featureless tungsten orange. He imagined one day bringing Madison here, maybe next summer, to spend the whole season with him. They'd visit the Brontë Parsonage, York Minster, Fountains Abbey, and go for strolls on the Moors. Once his parents got to know her, they'd realise her uniqueness and her worth. He imagined them getting married and living in this house, his parents having bought a castle in Scotland.

An automatic light switched on as they approached the oaken service door. Angel stopped, heart racing.

'Um . . . sorry. I have to go back to the car. I forgot my pack of tissues.'

'Angel, it's in your hand.'

'Oh,' he said.

Destiny inserted a large skeleton key into the lock.

'Wait!' said Angel. 'Um . . . I need a moment.'

'What are you scared of? She's not gonna eat you.'

'I-I-I just need a moment.'

'Okay. You've got five seconds. Five . . . four . . .'

'N-N-Not so fast!'

'. . . three . . . two . . . one. We're going in.'

She turned the lock and, as Angel inhaled to say

something else to stop her, quickly used a Yale key to turn the latch.

She opened the door.

Angel hid behind Destiny.

Destiny stepped inside.

Angel hesitated, then followed.

The familiar scent of cloves and cinnamon, from the scented candles squeezed past a tiny fissure in his inflamed and blocked nostrils. But Angel's eyebrows steepled yet again as he sunk his head into his shoulders. Their mother, Victoria, was ready to meet them in the dimly lit corridor.

'Finally,' said she to Destiny, not in admonishment, but in sympathy for the four-hour errand. She was clad in a grape purple jumper, tweed trousers, and brogues. Her shoulder-length hair was impeccably styled. Still ginger despite being forty-five. Her subtly made-up visage was cold porcelain.

Their mother's expression had been neutral, but when Destiny stepped aside, bringing Angel into view, Victoria's jaw dropped and her hands flew up to her forehead.

'Angel! Is that you?'

Victoria looked at Destiny for confirmation.

'Yes,' said Destiny, 'I passed him twenty times at the station, thinking he was a homeless person. People had even thrown change at him.'

Angel stared at their mother like a rabbit in headlights.

With a frown and intense eyes, Victoria swiftly went to him.

'What *happened* to you?' she demanded.

'Um . . . I-I fell . . . coming out of the train. I-It's just a scratch.'

'You look like death! And you *reek!*'

She put her hand on his cheek and then pushed his hair back to take a good look at his face.

'Um . . . nothing . . . I just have the flu . . .' he said.

'But you're skin and bones!'

She put her hand on his forehead, to feel his temperature.

'You've got a fever.'

'He couldn't afford Panadol at the station,' Destiny said.

'Right. Follow me to the kitchen,' ordered their mother.

They followed, Angel dragging his suitcase.

The kitchen was large, architecturally Tudor but fitted with modern cabinets and appliances that were, nevertheless, stylistically in keeping with the house. It had a natural slate tiled floor, honey brown wooden fittings, black marble tops, and a black four-oven Aga cooker inside of what had once been an inglenook fireplace. Every surface was uncluttered and spotless, gleaming under harsh LED lights.

Said lights brought into relief the state of Angel's attire.

'Oh, my goodness!' said his mother. 'And you travelled like that?'

'Um . . .'

'Dressed in those filthy rags?'

'Er . . . I didn't want to wreck my good clothes.'

'He brought an empty suitcase,' said Destiny, picking it up from the floor with one finger.

'Okay,' said Victoria, 'first, you're going to wash up and change. Destiny, go to his room and find him clothes. Put them in the downstairs shower room.'

'Coming right up,' said Destiny, immediately moving, a glint in her eye.

Their mother then handed Angel a glass of water and two Panadol tablets. 'Take this.'

Angel did as told under his mother's gaze.

'You're lucky it was Destiny who picked you up. If it'd been your father . . .'

'I-Is he asleep?' he asked, eyebrows high.

'Yes.'

Angel sighed with relief, albeit not without sensing the menacing weight of his father slumbering on the floor above—it was like looking at the sky and seeing it covered from horizon to horizon by a planet hurtling towards Earth. His father would wake in four hours. Angel could hardly wait to disappear into his room.

His mother ripped a black bin liner off a roll.

'Take this,' she said, giving it to Angel. 'When you take those off, put them here. Including the shoes.'

Angel took the bag.

Destiny returned. 'Your outfit is ready, Sir,' she said, speaking in the polite tone of an Edwardian butler, albeit with a mock deferential face that could barely hold back laughter.

'What have you done now?' he heard his mother ask as he walked away.

'Nothing!' Destiny said, laughing, 'I just brought down a change of clothes!'

In the marbled downstairs shower room, he stripped naked, putting all his clothes in the bin liner, as instructed. The floor was warm. He showered, enjoying the fragrant bathroom, with not a speck of black mould or limescale in sight, with privacy, without his lung tissue burnt by bleach fumes, without having to wear flipflops in a plastic shower stall with slimy curtains shared with the whole dorm.

Once washed—and it took a good while for the water running off him to go from brown to clear—he found, hanging from a decorative brass hook on the back of the door, a black garment cover. He was greeted, upon unzipping it, by his dinner suit. He sighed. Through the steam, on a marbled top, he now saw that Destiny had also left him a dress shirt, a black bowtie, and his patent-leather shoes. For a touch of added elegance, she had included a pair of gold cufflinks.

Yet, although he didn't appreciate the prank, he didn't mind it too much; it'd be nice to wear something clean and elegant for the first time in months.

But Destiny had forgotten to supply, or deliberately not supplied, a belt, so when he zipped and buttoned up his trousers, they fell straight down to the floor. The jacket, waistcoat, and shirt also had cubic lightyears of excess space. Even the shoes were loose, no matter how tight he fastened the laces.

When he returned to the kitchen, holding on to his trousers with one hand, carrying the bin liner with the other, Destiny burst out laughing.

'That was cruel,' admonished their mother.

'He's back home after many months. I thought he should *rise to the occasion!*'

'Show respect to your older brother.'

'I am respecting him!'

'You're mocking him.'

'Look how smart he looks!'

'Destiny.'

'I'm sorry, mum.'

Victoria turned to Angel, 'You need to eat.'

Angel pulled back a wooden chair and sat down at the round table in the kitchen's adjacent breakfast area. The chair felt harder than he remembered.

'You can have a prosciutto sandwich or chicken and rice leftovers.'

'Er . . . um . . . um . . .'

'Sandwich it is.'

His mother took out a baguette, cut half of it into three equal segments on a wooden board, filled them with prosciutto, pleating it loosely so that it would be aerated for flavour, and brought them to him on an ornate plate—Villeroy & Boch, Burgenland red—along with some paper napkins.

Angel took a bite from the first sandwich. Fresh baguette! Prosciutto! He hadn't had that in months! And after week after week of cheesy pasta and boiled potatoes, the salty flavour played like a symphony in his mouth. However, his jaw muscles could barely manage the bread's crust.

'May I go?' said Destiny. 'It's past my bedtime and I've got deadlifts on Monday.'

'You might as well. It's a busy day tomorrow.'

'Goodnight, mum,' she said.

'Goodnight.'

Then, turning to Angel, raising her eyebrows while tilting her head, Destiny added, 'And a very goodnight to you, Sir.'

Angel mumbled his reply.

Destiny left.

Victoria then brought him lemon tea with honey, in a cup with its accompanying saucer, also from their everyday Villeroy & Boch set.

'Straight to bed after this,' she said, adding, after a pause, 'We have much to discuss over the weekend.'

There was an ominous, subtle emphasis on the 'much'.

Angel swallowed.

Chapter CIII

Angel entered his room equipped with a box of tissues, a packet of Panadol Extra, and a strip of lemon lozenges supplied by his mother. He locked the door and tested the handle to make sure.

He sat on his bed and, noticing his mother had already placed a glass and a bottle of S. Pellegrino on his bedside table, took off his dinner suit. More out of fear than out of discipline, he hung the garment on the oaken standing valet, barely able to stand himself, due to fever and crushing exhaustion.

The simple, forgotten pleasure of getting into a clean bed was pure ecstasy. Crisp, fragrant sheets. A comfortable mattress. Silence and tranquillity. Sweetly scented air. Being among his possessions, knowing they would not be moved, knocked, soiled, damaged, or destroyed.

He stared at his books, his record collection, and his framed posters, depicting paintings from the Romantic era: William Boguereau's *Baigneuse*, Frank Dicksee's *La Belle damselle sans merci*, Friedrich Caspar David's *Wanderer Above the Mist*, Jean-Auguste-Dominique Ingres' *Jupiter and Thetis*, Maxfield Parrish's *The Glen*, and John Waterhouse's *Tristan and Isolde with the Potion*. All paintings that Destiny had mocked him for, even though she liked them herself.

Slumber overtook him.

But he slept badly, the weight of the moon flattening him, and woke up in an aeroplane, seated in the middle seat of the middle block of an Airbus 380. Fellow air travellers had finished boarding. Members of the cabin crew were slamming galley and overheard compartment doors. Others were walking through the aisles, checking that passengers had fastened their seatbelts. Angel was eager for the aircraft to get moving. He kept checking the time on his phone. It was 25:30. Any delay meant he might not arrive in time to stop Madison from getting tattooed.

When a stewardess reached Angel's row, however, she stopped; she signed to a male colleague, who joined her with a serious face.

Addressing Angel, she said, 'This gentleman will escort you back to the terminal.'

Faces turned to observe the scene.

'Oh? B-But why?' said Angel.

'You're sick.'

'No, no. I'm not sick. I'm perfectly fine.'

'You're sick. You must leave the aircraft.'

'But I'm not sick! I'm not sick at all!'

'You're sick. My colleague will accompany you back to the terminal.'

'But I'm telling you I'm not sick!'

'You're sick. If you don't cooperate, I'll ask security to remove you.'

Angel got up.

'But I'm not sick. And I really have to be on this flight!'

'You're sick. It's best if you cooperate.'

The pilot then switched off the engines, somehow to convey to Angel that so long as he remained in the cabin they weren't going anywhere. The cabin lights were switched off too.

'I'm not sick! I'm not sick! Please!'

'You're sick. You must leave the aircraft.'

Neighbouring passengers pierced Angel with stares to make their displeasure known.

'I'm not sick! Please! I promise I'm not sick! I really have to be on this flight! Please! I can't get off. Please!'

'You're sick. You must leave the aircraft now.'

Angel looked down at the passenger seated beside him—a scowling businessman in his sixties.

'Just *go*,' said his neighbour, in a low voice.

Angel made his way to the aisle, hair flopping, eyes everywhere glued to him. He heard a child snigger.

Once in the aisle, he was faced with a portly Afro-American stewardess.

'Please adopt the recovery position,' she chanted, in a bossy voice.

'But I'm not sick!'

'Please adopt the recovery position.'

What was the recovery position?

'Please adopt the recovery position.'

'Please! I'm not sick. Please! I need to be on this flight! Please!'

Recovery from what?

His eye wandered to one of the windows, through which he saw his suitcase being thrown out of the hold and exploding open on the Tarmac. One of the ramp agents was Epic Eyebrows, who proceeded to hurl his clothes all over the parking zone, and stomping on them with her combat boots. Another parking agent was Beard, or Babyface, who began sawing his suitcase in half, gleefully making eye-contact with Angel as he cut. The suitcase then became Madison.

He woke with a jerk, only to feel a chill of terror sweep over his body. Pulling the covers over his face, he scrunched his eyelids shut and waited for the feeling to pass.

When he next opened his eyes, he saw that the lamp on his bedside table was still on.

His bedside clock read 4:13 am.

He heard his father pacing in the corridor.

Faster than the speed of light, Angel's hand darted towards the lamp and switched it off. He closed his eyes and lay completely still, facing the ceiling, not even breathing at first, pretending to sleep.

Chapter CIV

A knock on the door.
Angel opened his eyes.
It was still dark.
The bedside clock said it was 7:05 am.
'Breakfast time, Angel,' said his mother, from the other side.

Angel groaned. Steepling his eyebrows, he switched on the bedside lamp. He blinked and rubbed his prickly orbs, yawning incessantly. The night's sleep, besides thus abbreviated, had left his headache intact.

After five minutes, parental expectation radiating from the breakfast table downstairs, Angel peeled himself off the sheets. Feet on the bedside sheepskin rug, nose already re-occluding, he took Panadol and sat hypnotised by the floor for another five minutes, trying to summon the strength to get dressed.

This, at last, he did, though at a sloth's pace, with a blue shirt, jeans, a brown corduroy jacket, and brown brogues. None of his belts having enough holes, he secured his jeans with a couple of binder clips. Before going downstairs, he stopped by the bathroom to thoroughly comb his hair and hide some of its length under his shirt collar.

At the top of the massive oaken stairs, he took a deep breath before descending to the ground floor. The grandfather clock chimed half past the hour.

In the breakfast room, he found the rest of the family at the table, already half-way through. His father, a muscular man on the threshold of fifty, with a square jaw, a lined forehead, and a buzz cut, seemed completely absorbed by his breakfast, his brow like an overhanging cliff, his temples pulsing as he chewed before a plate piled high with streaky bacon, scrambled eggs, toast, sausages, chips, and pancakes. By this time, Angel knew, he'd already worked out, gone for a jog, downed his protein shake, showered, shaved, gone to the village for fresh bread, caught up with the world's news, replied to emails, done chores, and who knew what else.

'Good morning,' Angel said, approaching.

'Good morning, Angel,' said his mother, turning to him with a restrained smile.

'And a very good morning to you, Sir!' said Destiny, raising and then dipping her chin as she tilted her head in mock deference.

His father greeted him in turn, his voice a low rumble, his eyes carefully examining him.

Angel expected his father would have been apprised on the circumstances of his arrival and was already angry and disappointed.

Angel sat down, keeping his eyes averted. He felt x-rayed.

'Have some toast,' said his mother.

Angel grabbed a slice and started buttering it.

'And some tea,' she added, already pouring some in his Burgenland cup.

'Has the good Sir enjoyed his lie-in?' said Destiny, steepling her eyebrows, her fake-polite mien masking barely suppressed laughter.

His father's dissatisfaction with Angel's tardy arrival fulgurated like a solar corona. Or so Angel perceived it, because the man had not altered his demeanour.

'How are you liking your classes this semester, Angel?' asked his mother.

'Um . . . they're good.'

'Good how,' said Destiny.

'Destiny,' said Victoria.

'Sorry, mum.'

Victoria's eyes remained latched onto Angel.

'Um . . . the most interesting so far is Food and Literature in Early Modern England.'

'And what have your learnt?'

'Er. . . um . . .'

Silence. Expectant faces—including, suddenly, his father's.

'Um . . . er . . . um . . .'

'Well?' said Victoria, with a nod and raised eyebrows.

'Er . . . er . . . um . . . I-I'm sorry. I'm blanking out.'

'But you just came from classes yesterday.'

'Um . . . I-I was sick, so I missed two days' worth of classes.'

'Okay, but you still had other classes on Monday, Tuesday, and Wednesday, didn't you? So what did you learn on those days?'

'Er . . . um . . .'

'Is Food and Literature on Fridays?'

'N-N-No, it's on Tuesdays.'

'Very well. What did you learn on Tuesday?'

'Um . . .' Angel rubbed his forehead.

'Is your professor bad, Angel? Because if you can't remember . . .'

'Oh, n-no, he is . . . er . . . the best one, I think.'

'Are you not paying attention then?'

'Er . . .'

'Because degrees cost money.'

Angel felt his father's eye on him again.

'Er . . . no . . . it's just that . . . um . . . I'm blanking out right now . . . um . . . it-it-it happens to me when I travel sometimes . . .'

'Well, then try to remember. Your father and I want to know.'

'Um . . . c-can we talk about it later?'

'Why not now?'

'I-I'm just not feeling well . . .'

'Alright. We'll ask again later. But think that after you graduate, when you get invited to speak at conferences, you won't be able to postpone your speech because you've been travelling.'

'He could bring it written down,' said Destiny.

'Yes, but then what will he do during the Q and As? Not answer because he was on a train the day before?' said Victoria.

'He could arrive a day earlier.'

'Then he'll have to pay extra nights at the hotel. While everybody else gets on with it.'

Angel buttered his toast.

'You need to build up your stamina. People out there are not going to relent just because you're not feeling well.'

Angel kept buttering his toast.

'Do you want some more bread with that butter?' asked Destiny, offering him another slice.

Angel looked up but said nothing. He did, however, stop the buttering, although not because he was done, or because of his sister's taunt, but because his appetite had died.

'Eat, Angel. You need it,' said his mother.

Angel took a tiny bite.

'And sit straight,' she added.

Angel uncurved his back.

'Right,' said Victoria, when everyone was done. 'So the caterers will be arriving at six. I have to make phone calls and run some errands. Destiny get Andrew and his men to arranged furniture in the great hall as we did in 2017 when we had my book launch. But watch them, because they're a bit clumsy.'

Andrew was their groundskeeper.

'Oh, I'll do it!' said Destiny.

'No. Those tables are too heavy.'

'I can do it. I'm strong enough now. Besides, I like the challenge.'

'No. They're much heavier than you think.'

'Please?'

'You won't be able to budge them.'

'Please, mum, please!'

'Alright, alright. Have a go. But when you find that you can't lift them—'

'I can do it. No problem!'

'*When* you find that you can't lift them, get Andrew and his men. Angel, you go straight back to bed. You'll need your strength tonight. You have until seven to rest and make yourself presentable.'

'Okay,' he replied, without enthusiasm.

'Although you might want to come with me to town to get a haircut.'

If a cricket ball had hit him in the chest at one hundred miles per hour, it would have had the same effect as his mother's suggestion. His mind raced to Madison, and to the 17th-century look he'd so carefully cultivated to impress her. It took effort keep his voice under control. 'Um . . . no . . . er . . . I'm fine.'

'You look like a ragamuffin.'

'Um . . . no . . . er . . .'

'Alright, then Destiny will trim the ends.'

Tucking her lower lip under her upper row of teeth, Destiny suggested with scissoring fingers she was going to chop his locks off.

Angel looked at her and bowed his head, keeping quiet. But beneath his subdued exterior, his heart played Paganini's Caprice No. 5. He resolved to evade the haircut no matter what. Appearing to slough it off and letting the idea be forgotten seemed best. It'd worked for similar situations in the past.

'Yep,' she pressed. 'I'm going to give you a short bob.'

'Destiny. Don't torture him,' said Victoria.

'But you said cut the ends, right? So I'll put bowl on his head and cut around it.'

'Enough of that.'

Angel quietly sighed with relief, glad Destiny was stopped from further growing the topic.

Their mother exchanged glances with their father, and, after the latter's subtle nod of agreement, they all got up, signalling the end of the proceedings. The whole family, including Angel, automatically cleared the table and took everything to the kitchen, where a maid—Caroline, daughter of a local farmer—had begun washing the pans and putting everything else into a Miele dishwasher. Destiny took the tablecloth to the garden to shake off the crumbs and she and Angel, although the latter with trembling hands, folded it with mathematical lines and put it away in a drawer. Their father disappeared into his study. Their mother went to the wine cellar, phone in hand.

'Your Lordship will come with me to the great hall,' said Destiny to Angel, already heading there.

Angel hesitated.

'Come on, your Lordship's assistance is required.'

'But . . .'

'What? Has his Lordship lost his hearing?'

'No, but . . .' Angel pointed vaguely to the upper floor, in the direction of his bedroom.'

'Then come on. It won't be a minute.'

Angel followed in slow motion, dragging his legs, watching his sister's long ginger hair, feeling his own hair on his cheeks. He felt drained. Feverish. Just wanting to be back in his room. To escape, to sleep, to dream of Madison.

In the great hall, three carved oak tables stood along the walls: a shorter one, about ten feet in length, on a dais, which was where their parents and guests of honour would be eating, and two longer ones, running the length of the hall perpendicular to the dais.

'Okay,' said Destiny. 'So help me move the long tables.'

'I thought . . .'

'You heard mum. They're heavy. So your Lordship will assist.'

Angel groaned, his voice barely audible. He sniffled, but the mucus hardly budged.

'Now, we need to both do one end at a time.'

'Okay,' he mumbled. 'Um . . . er . . . let me blow my nose first.'

Destiny waited while Angel attempted to clear his nasal cavity of all possible mucus.

'Come on, Angel! Hurry up!'

'Wait—I'm not done.'

Angel dried up his nostrils with a fresh tissue—very thoroughly, taking his time. Or rather, delaying as much as he could.

'Are you trying to dig a third hole?' said Destiny.

Angel made no reply.

At last, having squeezed that lemon for all it was worth, Angel joined Destiny at the far end of the left-hand table. He slid his supinated hands under the tabletop, ready to pull.

'No. Not like that. You'll detach your biceps if you try to curl the table,' said Destiny. 'Arms straight.'

Angel corrected his arms.

'And brace your core.'

'Um . . . how do I do that?'

'You don't know how to brace your core?'

'No.'

'Tighten all your muscles around your belly.'

Angel did as instructed.

'And don't lift with your back. Rather push the world down with your legs.'

'H-How do I do that?'

Destiny sighed, albeit smiling, and went over to Angel to adjust his posture. 'Okay. Bend your legs slightly. More. More. Okay. Back straight. Tilt it forward a bit. No, no, not that much . . .' It took her a good two minutes to get her brother into the optimal position.

'Now, brace your core.'

Angel tightened his abdomen.

Destiny punched him in the stomach, holding back. 'No. Harder!'

Angel tightened some more.

'More!' Another punch.

His face turned red.

'Okay,' his sister said, laughing, 'Stay like that and wait until I give the signal.'

Angel trembled as if he had Parkinson's, maintaining Destiny's suggested posture being that much of an effort.

She returned to her end of the table. 'Okay. At the count of three. One . . . two . . . three!'

They pulled.

The table stayed put.

'Angel, you have to actually pull.'

'B-But I did pull.'

'Pull much harder, then.'

'B-But you couldn't lift it.'

'Angel, how do you expect to impress your princess if you can't even lift a table?' she replied, smirking with raised eyebrows. '

'Um . . .' Angel scratched his temple.

'Grab the table. Grab the table. I said grab the table! Okay. Ready? Don't snap your spine. One . . . two . . . three!'

They pulled again, Destiny's face turning red with the effort.

The table stayed put.

'Bloody hell! This really *is* heavy,' said Destiny, breathing hard and shaking her hands. As she held them up, Angel saw deep indentations where she'd gripped the table.

Angel stared, dumbfounded.

'Well, never mind. This thing must weigh more than two-hundred kilos.'

Destiny pulled her phone out of her jeans and looked up something online. After a minute, she said: 'Wow.

This table could weigh as much as a tonne. No wonder.'

'Really? A thousand kilos?'

'Yes, if you look at it, it's like a snooker table cut in half lengthways and one half placed after the other. And a snooker table weighs eleven hundred kilos.'

'Oh.'

'But you should have been able to lift it.'

'Me?'

'Yes. You. Angel. You'll be the lord of the manor one day, so you should be strong enough to defend it.'

'But—'

'Oh, I forgot. His Lordship is a refined *gentleman*.' Destiny steepled her mocking eyebrows, 'Muscles are for peasants!'

'I—'

'But you know, Angel, a proper feudal lord not only has to know his way around the court; he also needs to know how to get his hands *dirty*.'

Angel said nothing.

'Because along with his *privileges*, His Lordship has *responsibilities*.' Destiny chuckled. 'And these include getting *in the muck* with the *peasantry* when there's work to be done.'

Angel said nothing.

'Remember Gwydir Castle? They had to put up sand-bags to keep out the river and the owner was there, in muddy overalls, not just doling out tea and cake, but *labouring* with the volunteers.'

Angel looked down.

'And besides, what happens when His Lordship's realm is invaded? Art thou not to wield thy sword?'

Angel crinkled his forehead.

'Agh. Never mind. Let's do the benches at least. Grab the other end.'

Angel did as instructed.

'Okay. Like I showed you. Ready? One . . . two . . . three!'

Destiny's end of the bench went up. Angel's stayed on the floor.

'Come on, Angel! Pull!' she said, guffawing, still holding the bench.

Angel pulled as hard as he could, but neither would the bench move, nor his grip hold.

'Are you being serious?' said Destiny, putting her end of the bench down, her sides splitting with laughter now.

She went over to Angel's end and lifted it with ease.

'See? Weighs the same,' she said. 'Try again. Come on!'

Angel tried again.

Yet the bench wouldn't budge.

'This is bonkers!' she said, cackling.

Angel let go and stood, sullen, head low.

'I tell you what—you go lie down, and I'll ask one of the maids.'

Chapter CV

Angel was all too glad to be back in bed. He lay in full pyjamas. Every tissue in his body ached, it seemed—even his hair. However, he was not allowed to rest long, for, having locked the door to his room, and just begun his descent into slumber, he was yanked out of by his mother's knocking. Groaning, he got up to let her in.

Victoria was carrying a tray of lemon tea with honey and buttered toast. He retreated back under the covers and she, after placing the tray in front of him, sat by his side.

'What's happening, Angel?'

'Um . . . nothing . . . I just got the flu.' He slurped the tea, as quietly as he could, his lips like an anteater's snout.

'Angel. Stop evading. Look at you. You look like a skeleton.'

'Um . . . I-I just haven't been very hungry lately.'

'And why is that?'

'Um . . . I don't know . . . I just have a lot on my mind.'

'What exactly?'

Angel fidgeted. 'Um . . . er . . . just my coursework and the uni.'

His mother sighed. 'You need to tell me what's been happening to you. Your father thinks they've thrown you out of the university and you've been living on the streets, not telling us. He's talking about having you find a trade job. You know—a building site, installing boilers. Things like that. If you don't talk to me, I can't help you.'

Angel sat up. 'Is-Is-Is it because I couldn't remember this morning? I've-I've learnt a lot, I promise! I just blanked out. I blanked out!'

'It's the fact that you arrived looking like a homeless person. The fact that you've lost so much weight. Even you sister didn't recognise you at the station. Are you still enrolled at the university?'

'Um . . . yes, of course!'

'So, if I phone them, they'll confirm it.'

'Y-Y-Yes, of course they will!'

'And do you have accommodation? Or did you forget to fill out the forms?'

'No, no, I have a room!'

'Also you haven't been in touch once since you left in January. You didn't even come home for Summer.'

'Um . . . I-I-I was just really busy.'

'Then what, Angel?'

'Um . . . er . . .'

'Is it that Madison girl?'

'Oh . . . um . . . er . . .' Angel rubbed his forehead.

'What?'

'Um . . . no . . . it's . . . um . . . I'm-I'm-I'm visiting her in December. It's all good.' He offered a fake smile.

'And how are you going to pay for that? Because, as I've already told you, I'm not sending you any more money until you explain what you've done with the fifteen thousand pounds I sent you ten months ago.'

'Um . . . I've-I've got a job at the uni. In the canteen.'

'Okay. That's good. But, is that keeping you from studying? Is that why you can't answer our questions?'

'No . . . um . . . I just blanked out. You know, the flu and travelling and all that . . . I just blanked out.'

'Because if you're not coping, you should focus on your studies.'

'No no no, I can do it. It's-It's just a couple of hours in the morning. That's it. Just a couple of hours. Not even weekends.'

'What do I tell your father, then? Because he's of the opinion that you'd benefit from army training—'

Angel's eyelids retracted and his voice rose an octave. 'The army! B-But what about my degree? I really—'

'—except he knows you'd not pass the physical fitness test and it would take too long to train you, so—'

Angel sighed with relief. But his head still throbbed with adrenalin.

'—instead he'll want to withdraw you from the university and put you on a building site or something like that. "To toughen up," as he'd say. You know what he's like.'

Angel's eyelids retracted further. 'A building site!'

In a flash, he imagined himself labouring out in the cold, his hands hurting from handling rough bricks, surrounded by brutal men with tattoos, crude jokes, and high-visibility jackets, who'd bully him day after day. He'd never survive it. And what would Madison think?

'And I'm thinking of withdrawing you too, because clearly something's gone wrong there and you're not telling me. And, maybe, a year in a trade job, getting away from whatever situation you're in would clear your mind and equip you to deal with it when you go back.'

Angel's voice rose another octave. 'No no no no no! Please! There's no situation. Please! I can do the uni! I can do the uni! I promise!'

'Angel. Control yourself. It's unbecoming.'

'Okay, but—'

'So think about it. Okay? Either that or tell me what's happening so I can help you.'

'No, no, please! N—'

'Okay. So you'll think about it. We'll discuss it again over the weekend.'

Chapter CVI

Left reeling for most of the morning, Angel's mind scrambled for ways to avert the humiliating fate before him. His heart galloped non-stop. The thought of Madison discovering he was to graduate a year after her, or not at all, was horrifying, unbearable, unsurvivable. She'd *never* be interested in a manual labourer, with only a handful of words instead of an immense vocabulary, who drank PG Tips instead of Twinning's Earl Grey, ate fish and chips instead of gourmet food, and with only A levels instead of a doctorate in philosophy. He had to convince his parents that he was on top of his studies, that Madison was emphatically *not* a distraction, that Madison was absolutely worth *every* effort, that Madison, though American, would be a priceless ornament to the family, and that his current appearance was just a blip caused by a bad flu. He decided that, at the earliest possible opportunity, he'd mention Professor Mastropasqua's approval of his canteen job—*that* would obviate sending him, Angel, a refined student, to a building site; he was, after all, already 'benefiting' from manual labour, was he not? He also decided to spend the weekend catching up with the course texts to then demonstrate his mastery of the material—he'd be able to answer all their questions.

That determination made, he wrapped himself in a blanket, sat behind the computer on his desk, and looked for online versions of *Oroonoko* and all the other texts. He lined them up on browser tabs as he found them.

But before he got reading, he checked his social media.

Amelia had sent him several messages on Facebook Messenger, expressing her alarm at not finding him in his room the previous evening, at his not replying to her WhatsApp messages, and at nobody knowing where he might be.

AMELIA: I'm really worried about you. Please, Angel, reply to my messages or answer my calls so I know you are okay!

Angel stared at the messages, uncertain of how to reply, the fading Panadol in a losing battle against his headache.

Then came a knock on the door.

'Angel?'

It was his mother.

Angel opened.

His mother had changed into a maroon tweed suit. She was carrying a tape measure.

'Oh, you're up. Good. I was thinking that the outfits you have here won't fit you now, so I'll need to pick up something for you in York. I need to measure you.'

At any other time, he would have leapt at the chance of a new suit, but the weakness, aches, and fatigue were profound. More importantly, he sensed danger: besides tailors, York also had barbers and hairdressing salons. But what if his mother chose a suit he didn't like? He couldn't risk that either! He was torn. But he calculated that there wouldn't be enough time for a haircut, and the salon he used cut by appointment only. And he could cause delays, or stop hiding his symptoms, if sight of a barber gave his mother ideas.

'Um . . . can I come?'

'No. You need to rest.'

'Um . . . um . . . I'm feeling better. I-I-I can come.'

'Are you sure?'

'Yes! Yes! I'm sure.'

Victoria thought for a moment, eying him.

'Very well, then. I'll wait for you downstairs.'

'Okay . . .'

'But hurry. Time's short and there's lots to do still.'

Victoria left.

Angel closed the door and, with the speed of pitch, he dressed, taking long breaks between one item of clothing and the next. He couldn't have moved much faster even if he wanted to. He took Panadol and combed his hair again with the same lack of celerity.

'Angel!' shouted his mother from the foot of the stairs.

'I'm coming,' he said, but in such moribund fashion that the words hardly travelled in the air.

He heard his mother already climbing the stairs to fetch him.

'We have to hurry,' she said from the top of the stairs as he exited his room, pointing at her Cartier gold watch. 'It's already eleven thirty.'

Angel said nothing, walking down the corridor and descending at a snail's pace, his tubular thighs barely able to support his weight, scant as it was.

His mother didn't wait for him; heels clicking on the rugless areas of floor, she headed for the service entrance and the courtyard beyond. Angel followed. By the time he reached the courtyard, the Audi was already running with his mother inside. He got in and the car moved the instant he'd buckled his seat belt.

Victoria drove through country lanes for a while, during which Angel stared out the window without a word, only half-listening to his mother's 1980s electro-pop.

The journey, however, was abruptly interrupted by a police patrol car parked athwart an A road, in front of which a short queue had already built up. A police officer approached the car and informed them that the road was closed. Victoria turned her Audi around, while Angel cheered inside.

He cheered even more when they found the usual alternative route was also blocked.

'Angel,' said his mother, 'Can you get the Maps app on your phone to find a way around?'

Angel's heartbeat accelerated. 'Um . . .'

Victoria looked at him briefly.

'Come on, Angel. Time is short.'

He pretended to search his pockets—first breast, then jeans.

'I'm coming up to a crossroad.'

'S-Sorry, just a moment.'

'Angel! I've got cars behind me.'

'Er . . .'

'Angel!

'Er . . . um . . . I left my phone at home.'

His mother sighed. 'Okay. Never mind. Can you programme the SatNav?'

Angel instinctively touched the multi-media interface screen. Nothing happened.

'No. Use the controls,' she said, talking fast. 'Here. Behind the gear shift.'

His right hand hovered over the buttons for several seconds, while his left caught renegade mucus with a tissue.

'Um . . .'

Angel felt the car stop.

'I'll do it,' snapped his mother.

She'd stopped in a layby.

Victoria's fingers operated the menus with the dexterity of a concert pianist, screens flashing before Angel's eyes on the MMI display ere he could register their contents.

'Okay. Let's go,' she said when done.

They got moving again. Angel checked the time.

Forty-five minutes later, they entered the Piccadilly car park in York, a weathered brick multi-storey.

'We'll get your shopping out of the way first,' said Victoria after she'd parked.

'Okay.'

'We'll try Marks and Spencer and if not Debenhams.'

Angel cringed. 'Um . . . Marks and Spencer?'

'We only need something for tonight.'

'B-But—'

'—and a couple of things to tide you over until you're back to normal.'

'Um . . . but—'

'No, Angel. We're not getting anything extravagant. It's pointless. When you're back to normal, we can talk again.'

Angel deflated, eyes sleepy. 'Okay . . .'

Mother and son walked towards Parliament Street, Victoria's heels clicking fast on the pavement, Angel having to walk much more briskly than he would've liked or was advisable for a headache that the paracetamol had barely blunted. Out in the cold, his runny nose caused him to pull out a now tattered tissue.

'Angel, please use a new tissue,' said Victoria, after casting a quick side glance at him. 'It's inelegant.'

He did as instructed, inwardly agreeing, but realising how bad habits had become ingrained after months of poverty.

When they reached the Marks and Spencer, they went straight to the menswear section. After much scouring of the racks, humming and hawing from Angel, and trying on the smallest sizes available, the challenge of his current physique proved intractable. The shirts fit him like parachutes, the belts like garden hoses, the trousers like hula hoops. He didn't mind, as it would mean more delays. Victoria suggested that they go to the children's section. But there the trousers were like shorts, the jackets like a matador's, and the shirts like boob tubes. Again, Angel didn't mind; the clock was running and the chance of a haircut decreased while the chance of a tailored suit increased.

They next went to Debenhams, where they encountered the same problems.

They then walked all the way up to Clarksons Menswear, in High Petergate. This was a more traditional shop, with tailored options and prices more in line with Angel's preferences. Not that this made it any easier to choose an outfit that fit or pleased him. It took another hour of humming and hawing before he had something he liked or could live with. Everything had to be tailored, of course, and the same-day service, as a favour to Victoria because of her husband's power and influence in the region, incurred an extra cost. The total came to nearly three thousand pounds—ten times what Victoria had hoped to spend.

'I hope you're happy, Angel,' she fumed.

Angel said nothing.

Inwardly, he hoped this meant less money for a haircut.

'We'll have lunch now,' she announced. 'After that I have a couple of errands and we can pick up your clothes.'

'Okay.'

'Do you have a present for your father?'

Angel's eyes widened, his mouth forming an 'O'. 'Um . . .'

'You forgot.'

'Um . . . I'm so sorry . . .'

Victoria sighed. 'Okay. We'll have to do that too, then.'

Angel's mood improved, but he hid it behind a long face.

She led him into the Café Rouge in Low Petergate. Once at the table, she messaged her husband, telling him she would not be back till five o'clock.

Victoria ordered a *demi poulet* and Angel the breaded camembert.

'And for mains?' said the waiter.

'Um . . . that's all,' Angel replied.

'Is that all you're having?' said Victoria.

'Um . . . yes.'

'You need to order something else. It'll be a while before dinner.'

'Um . . . but—'

'Angel, I just spent three thousand pounds getting you clothes because you haven't been eating. I don't want to have to spend even more on a complete new wardrobe. You need to eat.'

'Um . . .' Angel picked up the menu to scan through it again.

The waiter waited.

'Um . . . c-could I have a *croque monsieur*?'

The waiter looked at Victoria, as if for approval. She nodded.

'*Croque monsieur* it is, sir,' said the waiter, taking note. 'It will be with you shortly.'

The waiter left.

Angel blew his nose.

'Have you thought about our conversation this morning?' asked Victoria.

A woman stranger approached the table holding a book and a pen. 'Excuse me, madam,' she said 'Would you mind signing my copy of your book?'

'Yes, certainly,' said Victoria, suddenly very pleasant.

She signed the copy of her *Social History of the Penny Dreadful*, one of her more popular books.

'Thank you so much,' said the stranger, smiling.

'My pleasure.'

The stranger left with a spring in her step.

Victoria looked at Angel again. 'Well?'

'Um . . . yes, yes, I have.'

'So what's been happening?'

'Um . . . er . . . um . . .'

'Okay. Let's start with your suitcase. Why have you brought an empty suitcase? Where are your clothes?'

'Um . . . er . . . th-th-there was an incident at the laundrette and they were damaged.'

'Damaged how?'

'Er . . . th-the dryer caught fire.'

'And when was this?'

'Er . . . about three weeks ago.'

'So you've been without clothes for three weeks? Is that why you arrived dressed in rags?'

'Um . . . yes.' Angel looked down.

'Why didn't you message me?'

'Um . . .'

'And did you pursue the laundrette about the damage? Because they should be compensating you.'

'Er . . .'

'And if they're refusing, you should be taking action against them!'

'Um . . .'

'What's the name of the laundrette?' demanded Victoria, grabbing her phone. 'Let's see if they will respond to pressure. If their dryers are catching on fire, there are regulations they're not complying with.'

Angel's voice rose an octave. 'Oh . . . um . . . I-I-I-I d-don't remember the name—'

'Well, I'm sure you remember where it is. What's the name of the street? I'll find in on Google maps.'

'Er . . . um . . . um . . .'

'Coke?' said a waitress, who'd just materialised.

'Him,' said Victoria, pointing at Angel.

The waitress placed the drinks in front of them and left.

'Right,' said Victoria, putting her phone away. 'We'll chase this up later. Meanwhile, try to remember the name of the laundrette. You paid a hundred and seventy pounds for each of those Eton shirts you insisted on getting.'

'Um . . . o-o-okay. I-I will.'

'But it worries me that you've been so passive about this.'

'Um . . . it's just uni . . . you know, there's a lot of reading . . .'

'There was a lot of reading last semester and you didn't end up a scarecrow with all your clothes burnt to a crisp.'

'Yes, but—'

'Which makes me think it's that Madison girl.'

'No, no, er—'

'Because that's what's changed.'

'No no no, it's all fine with her, it's all fin—'

'Which makes me think that maybe your father is right.'

Angel's knees began bouncing under the table.

'Angel. Stop bouncing your knees. It's inelegant and makes you look weak.'

Angel did as told, but his mouth still moved like a fish's as he stared at his mother with panicked orbs.

'So give it some thought. I know it seems scary, but you could benefit.'

'B-Bu—'

'Just for a year. To build some character and get real world experience.'

'Um . . . um . . . no . . . er—'

'Think about it, okay?'

Mother and son ate lunch, although Angel barely managed a bite of breaded camembert and a half a bite from the *croque monsieur*, his mind flickering with images of cement mixers, PG Tips, yellow safety helmets, and Madison's sneers. Afterwards, Victoria proceeded with the bulk of her errands, having decided that Angel would select a tie for his father when they went back to Clarkson's.

Once at Clarkson's, Victoria was relieved to see that Angel's clothes fit as if they'd been spray-painted on his body, even though the proportions looked strange—like besuiting a giraffe's neck.

'You look very elegant,' she said to her son, inspecting his suit, front and back.

'Um . . . s-should I keep it on?' asked Angel.

'No. Take it off. We don't want it to get wrinkled in the car.'

Upon his mother paying, Angel grabbed the bag with the three-grands' worth of clothing and followed his mother as she headed back to the carpark, her heels clicking down Parliament Street as rapidly as before. He was relieved she seemed to have forgotten about the haircut.

When the ornate neo-Gothic branch of Barclays came into view, however, Victoria stopped.

'I need to go in for a second,' she said.

Angel followed her inside and took a seat while Victoria waited in the queue. He blew his nose, his mind already flickering again with visions of bricks, hoodies soiled with concrete, and work colleagues with coarse humour, massive forearms, and weather-beaten faces. Rather than graduating simultaneously, with Madison impressed by his academic brilliance, Madison would graduate *ahead* of him—and not by one year but *two!*—finishing her masters before he obtained his BA, finding employment or starting a doctorate, but either way *earning*, while he was still a lowly undergraduate, dependent on his parents for support. Having been left behind, she'd deem him *inferior* and grow icy, distant, and weird.

He cast a glance out the window. The sky was an unsettling shade of grey. He resisted the urge to hide under his hair from his unpleasant thoughts; it could remind his mother of the barber.

'Let's go,' said his mother, phone in hand, jolting him out of his daymare.

They made their way back to the car park, Victoria chatting on her phone as they walked, organising matters relating to the birthday party. When they reached her car, she opened the boot for Angel to put his bag in.

But as she did so, she froze.

'Angel? Where's your bag?

Chapter CVII

They arrived home with Victoria's bollocking still ringing in his ears.

'Find Destiny so she can give you a haircut,' ordered his mother, while getting out of the car.

Angel's heart nearly leapt out of his chest. Yet, he dared not protest. He let his mother walk past him—she had the keys—and followed her into the house, his entire nervous system crawling with ants.

Relief washed over him upon finding that Destiny was nowhere in sight, and prospects further improved when his mother disappeared to doll up for the festivities. The caterers were already in the kitchen, hovering and buzzing like bees in a hive. As the party was starting in fifty minutes, he calculated that if he made himself scarce for the next thirty, his mother's obsession with hair cutting would be frustrated, for Destiny would lack the time to execute her orders. Allowing his sister anywhere near with her scissors was out of the question; she'd ruin his aesthetic, preventing him from posting selfies online for Madison to see. More crucially, it would take months to reverse the damage, which would delay his flight, since he would be unable to face Madison looking less than his best. That would be catastrophic.

The optimal place to hide, he determined, was something close to plain sight: in his bedroom under the bed. Anyone looking for him would cast a glance from the door and, not seeing him, move on.

He stealthily ascended the stairs, eyes and ears acutely alert to approaching family members, glided down the corridor, slipped into his room, leaving the door ajar to allay suspicions, and dragged himself under the bed, facing the door to monitor it for intruders. He would wait out the next half hour and then get ready. If his mother asked, he'd tell her he'd been unable to find his sister.

Ten minutes passed.

'Angel!'

It was Destiny, shouting from downstairs.

Angel scrunched his eyes shut and swore silently. His mother must have instructed her to find him, which meant she'd now be like a foxhound unleashed, sniffing for its prey. He retreated as far back from the edges of the bed nearest to the door as he could and hid under his hair.

'Angel!'

He kept his breathing slow and controlled, eyes on the bottom of the door, which was all he could see.

'Angel!'

The voice was nearer, his sister ascending the stairs. Angel trembled.

'Angel!'

Steps approaching down the corridor. He madly considered running to the window, jumping out into the grounds, and hiding in the woods, but he feared he would not have enough time.

Destiny's trainers visible at the door. Angel braced himself, squinting.

'Not here,' she murmured to herself, before disappearing.

'Angel!'

The shouts were repeated a number of times, each time the sound growing fainter as she explored faraway parts of the house. Angel relaxed a little. Maybe his luck would hold!

If only he had his phone, he thought; he'd be able to check how many minutes he had left!

'Angel!'

Destiny's voice now grew nearer.

'Angel!'

Nearer still.

'Angel!'

At his door.

He swore again, without emitting a sound.

Then silence.

Destiny's trainers crossed the threshold into Angel's domain.

Angel cringed.

They approached the bed.

Heart thumping, Angel observed them as they remained still. He heard his sister breathing and worried she would hear his heartbeat.

Then, her hands appeared. Followed by her face.

'Aha!' she said, grinning.

Angel, stumped, simply stared back, unable to think of an explanation for his being there.

'Come on, Angel, come out. Mum said to give you a haircut.'

Angel remained still.

'Time to chop off your locks!' she said.

Angel remained still.

'It'll be worse if you resist,' she teased.

No response.

'Okay, you asked for it.'

Destiny rose so that again only her trainers were visible. The trainers moved to the foot of the bed. Her fingers appeared, gripping the bottom of the footboard. The bed was pulled forward and lifted above him.

'Come on! Time for your bowl cut,' she said, standing before him, holding the bottom of the bed aloft over her head, leaving Angel fully exposed. Her face was already made up and her hair styled, but she was still in joggers and a t-shirt.

Angel hesitated.

'Mum!' she shouted, pointing her mouth at the corridor.

This, finally, had the desired effect. Angel quickly got on his knees and crawled from under the bed. He stood next to it, head bowed.

Destiny put the bed down.

'Good boy,' she said, cackling.

'I was looking for something,' he moaned.

'Yeh, your spine!'

'Um . . . there's not enough time.'

'Of course, there is. I'll be super quick.'

'If you . . . if you rush, you won't do a good job.'

'I'll just cut around. Five or six inches. It'll be a minute.'

'Five or six inches!'

'All the way around, just below the ear,' she said, underlining her statement with scissor fingers.

'Er . . . um . . . no . . . no.'

'Yes.'

'No . . . no . . .'

'Yes.'

'No!' He grabbed his hair, protectively.

'Yes.'

Angel made to run away, but Destiny blocked his path. He made to squeeze himself around her, but she grabbed his arm and yanked him back into the room, throwing him down onto the bed. The next instant, before Angel could get up again, Destiny jumped and landed astride his hips, pinning his shoulders down with her hands, eyes feral, lower lip tucked under her upper front teeth.

'Blimey! You really weigh nothing!' she said, chuckling.

Angel struggled, to no avail. 'G-Get off me.'

'Now I'm *really* gonna give you a bowl cut.'

'What's going on here?' said Victoria from the door. She was in a forest green towel robe.

Destiny looked back and got off Angel.

Angel sat up, with a sullen frown.

'I was reading him his rights before his bootcamp haircut,' said Destiny.

'There's no time for games now,' said Victoria. 'Do the trim, then finish getting ready.'

'Yes, mum.'

Victoria left.

'You've heard your commanding officer, private. To the bathroom. Off you go,' ordered Destiny. 'One . . . two . . . three . . . four . . . *I . . . love . . . the marine . . . core!*'

Angel reluctantly got up and the two headed for the bathroom, Angel closely followed by his baby sister.

'Wait here,' she said, when they'd reached their destination.

Angel saw her leave and looked at himself in the mirror. The vision of him walking around with short bob, the sides flapping rapidly in the wind, looking stupid, not like a poet, but like an emo or a muppet, and the thought of Madison laughing at him, lit a fire under his fundament.

Angel sprung to the door and looked up and down the corridor.

The coast was clear.

He slipped out and dashed towards the staircase, planning to hide in the barn outside.

To reach the stairs, however, he had to go past his room, and it was as he approached it that Destiny stepped out, pushing his swivel chair.

'I *knew* it!' she said.

Angel made to run around her, but she, again, blocked his path, this time with the chair. He lost his balance and fell on his face.

Destiny burst out laughing.

Angel made to get up, but Destiny planted a foot on his upper back.

'Ah-ah-ah-ah! Don't even think of it!'

Angel relaxed and Destiny, grabbing his hand, yanked him back to his feet. She did it with more force than was necessary, however, and nearly sent him flying into the ceiling.

'I can't get over how light you are,' she said. 'It's awesome!'

With one hand wrapped like a vice around his wrist, she dragged him into the bathroom, pulling his chair along with the other. Once there, she rolled said chair in front of him.

'Sit.'

He sat.

'I hope you're ready!'

Destiny took the battery-operated clippers out of the cupboard and switched it on, lower lip again tucked under upper front teeth.

Bzzzzz!

Angel again made to run, but Destiny caught him and slammed him back down onto the chair.

He steepled his eyebrows and with his eyes, via the mirror, pleaded she desist.

'Do you want me to shave from the forehead back, or from the back to the forehead?' she asked. 'Or go sideways?'

Angel, suddenly exhausted, bowed his head in defeat.

'You know what? I've decided I'd rather give you a bowl cut instead.'

Angel stared at the floor.

'Argh! You're so boring sometimes,' she said. 'Okay, what's this worth to you?'

Silence.

'Angel, wake up.' She snapped her fingers in front of his eyes.

'I-I'm sorry?' he said, at last.

'What's this worth to you?'

'W-What to you mean?'

'What can you offer me in exchange for cutting just a millimetre.'

Angel livened up a bit. 'Er . . . um . . . really?'

'Yes. But hurry.'

He stared into space, irises twitching left and right. 'Er . . . um . . . er . . .'

'I tell you what. You do all my chores this weekend.'

'Erm . . . okay . . . w-what are the chores?'

'You'll be advised.'

'Er . . . okay . . .'

'Good.'

'*And* . . .' Destiny held up an index finger.

'Um . . . what?'

'You also owe me for telling your friends at uni that I injured myself in the gym.'

'Oh, that was . . .'

'That was a *lie*. And for that alone I should shave your head. So you *owe* me.'

Angel rubbed his forehead.

'So in exchange for that reprieve, you will go baby-faced for six months.'

He started. 'B-But—'

'But nothing. You shave.'

His mouth moved without forming words.

'Joking. No, in exchange for that, you'll . . . .'

'Er . . . no . . . no.'

'You'll hoover the inside of my car.'

'Ah . . . well, okay.'

'And clean all the windows.'

'Okay.'

'And I mean, so that they look as if though there's *no* glass. *Total* transparency. I don't want to see a *speck* on them!'

'Okay.'

'And wash the car, by hand, including the alloys.'

'O-Okay.'

'And polish it with wax and buffer.'

'Okay.'

'And wax the tyres too, so that they're nice and black.'

'Okay.'

'Okay. So we have a deal?' She offered her hand.

Angel grabbed it and she squeezed, her callused hand nearly triturating his metacarpal bones. He flinched.

'Come on, not like that!' said his sister. 'Shake like a man!'

Angel squeezed harder.

'Come on, go! Squeeze!'

Angel squeezed as hard as he could, but the pain only intensified.

'Are you going squeeze or not?'

Angel kept squeezing as before, making no dent on her grip, until he tried to pull away.

'Argh! Never mind. Deal.'

Angel let go.

Destiny grabbed a comb, wet it, and combed Angel's hair, straight down. She then lifted his chin with a finger, and, with the scissors, trimmed the tips of his hair, not cutting off more than a couple of millimetres here and there—enough to eliminate the worst of the jagged edges and be able to tell their mother she'd done as told, yet not enough for it to really make a difference to her brother.

After ninety seconds, Destiny dried the scissors and put them away.

'Off you go,' she said.

Slowly, not quite believing it, Angel got up and headed for the door, briefly looking back at Destiny with suspicion.

She stared back at him, hands on hips, chin slightly raised with an insolent half-smile.

Just as he was about to go out the door, he heard her voice.

'Angel?'

He turned.

Finger scissors. 'You *owe* me.'

Chapter CVIII

By the time Angel finished dressing for the party, the guests had begun to arrive. His father was militaristically punctual, and he'd surrounded himself with default-aggressive individuals.

The loss of his mother's purchases in York meant he'd had to perforate one of his belts, help to do which he'd had to request from his sister, since he lacked the strength. He'd also had to bolster his shirt with a thick under-jumper, so that the shirt would not billow like a parachute; accept Destiny's shoulder pads, to give his jacket the necessary support; and use binder clips to hold his trousers neatly pleated at the rear, so that the newly perforated belt would not make an accordion out of his waistband. Alas, little could be done about his cadaverous visage, with its cheekbones projecting for miles below his cavernous eye-sockets; Destiny offered to apply make-up, but Angel refused.

He finally descended the stairs, his mother casting a critical eye over him as she passed him by. He'd tucked his hair under his collar, so it slid under her radar undetected, he hoped. The guests had congregated in the parlour, an oak-panelled room decorated with oil paintings in ornate gilded frames, tapestries, velvet armchairs and sofas, carved Tudor oak furniture, Greek amphoras, and intricately decorated vases in bronze and ceramic. A fire raged in the enormous, stone fireplace.

Among those present were his Italian great-uncle, Ludovico, Ludovico's French wife, Yvonne, their son, or Angel's uncle, Giancarlo, Giancarlo's wife, Rosalia, and Angel's second cousins, Archangelo, Luca, and Vittorio. There were also important-looking men and women—Angel supposed they were captains of industry, politicians, generals, and the odd aristocrat, mainly from his father's circle, plus historians, authors, and academics from his mother's. All terrifying in their seriousness. And then there was his father, the most terrifying man of all; like an iron statue, he towered in the centre of the room, generating a gravity well around himself, clad in a black suit, wearing Edward Green black oxford shoes, and his favourite watch, an Omega Speedmaster Professional. He, Angel's father, liked the fact that Neil Armstrong had worn one on the moon.

Angel approached his Italian relatives, who stood near the drinks and canapés table. He got on best with Vittorio, who played in a Depressive Black / Doom band and was also a photographer. Vittorio was clad in a black shirt, a black tie, and a black velour jacket; his long chestnut hair was in a ponytail. He didn't recognise Angel; neither did the brothers, nor their parents, and much less their grandparents, who were in their eighties and could barely hear or understand Angel's voice.

'Forgive me, but who are you?' said Vittorio, holding a crystal champagne flute.

'I'm . . . I'm Angel.'

'Angelo!' Vittorio put his palm to his forehead. 'I'm so sorry, it's been so long. Have you been ill?'

'Um . . . just caught the flu recently.'

Vittorio's manner now warm, he led the greeting, with kisses on the cheeks, first right, then left, followed by an embrace.

'How have you been? Apart from the flu, of course.'

'Um . . . doing my final year at uni.' Angel subtly twitched, fearing suddenly that this would change after the weekend.

Vittorio turned to his elder brother, Archangelo. 'Look, it's Angelo!'

Archangelo's eyebrows shot up, and the hitherto reserved second cousin reacted like his brother, greeting Angel in the same fashion.

Luca, the youngest brother, becoming aware, did likewise. Angel marvelled at the resemblance Luca had developed, since they'd last seen each other, with a young Leonardo DiCaprio.

The older relatives followed, Rosalia trying to pinch his cheek, but failing for lack of flesh. The great-uncles frowned, still confused as to Angel's identity and therefore sceptical and reserved.

'We'll have a new album out in December,' said Vittorio, referring to his band.

'Ah, okay,' said Angel.

'Vinyl only, limited to 300 copies.'

'Um . . .'

'Let me show you the cover,' Vittorio retrieved his phone and went on Instagram. 'Here.'

Angel saw a black and white photo of Vittorio's bandmate, dressed in a 19th-century suit and made up to look like a decomposing corpse, lying in a coffin, surrounded by flowers. The band logo was completely illegible, a bowl of spaghetti thrown against the wall.

'We borrowed the coffin from a funeral parlour,' said Vittorio. 'Emanuele's father runs one in Palermo. They wouldn't let us use a real corpse, so Emanuele gave his life for the cause.'

'Oh. He . . . um . . . he looks as though he died of a broken heart.'

'No, he committed suicide.'

Angel blinked. 'Oh, really?'

'Yes, he told me to store his body at home for a week and then photograph it for the album.'

'Y-You can't be serious . . .'

'No. I'm completely serious. Afterwards we fed him to the dogs.'

'To the dogs!'

'Yes, it was his last will and testament.'

Angel rubbed his forehead, mouth agape, not knowing what to make of it.

'But we only fed them the head and the torso. The legs went to a kebab shop.'

'I-I don't think you're telling the truth.'

'I can show you!'

Vittorio got his phone out again and showed him a photograph of wild dogs in a back alley over a pile of bloody intestines, organs, and random raw meat. Angel stared, eyeballs nearly rolling out of their sockets.

'B-B-But what if the police find out?'

'Nah. The kebab shop won't tell—they were happy to get the free meat. One hundred percent profit for them. Emanuele must have been eaten completely by now.'

'B-B-But . . .'

'We're putting the pictures in the booklet.'

'B-But you're going to get arrested!'

'No one will take it seriously. You know, it's Black Metal, after all.'

'B-B-But what if someone investigates?'

'Fuck'em.'

Silence.

Vittorio drained the champagne flute and watched Angel, who continued to stare at him, eyes ever-wider loops of alarm.

Then Vittorio exploded with laughter, the peals rising above then hubbub of the party.

'I'm only joking Angelo,' he said, slapping Angel on the shoulder and knocking him off balance. 'Of course he died of a broken heart. But we revived him.'

Angel hesitated and gave a half smile.

Destiny joined them. She wore a black dress with a long skirt that opened to mid-thigh on one side, showing a muscular leg thicker than Angel's torso.

'Do I hear talk about music?' she said.

'I was telling Angelo about our new album.'

'What's it called?'

'*Esequie a un'anima disperata*. Obsequies to a Desperate Soul.'

'Ooh, I like it,' said Destiny.

Vittorio and Destiny laughed together. Angel stared into space.

'It's made him think about his girlfriend,' said Destiny to Vittorio. 'He's the desperate soul.'

Vittorio and Destiny laughed again.

'I-I like the title,' said Angel.

Archangelo butted in saying, as he waved his hands, 'It's all noise. Don't listen to him. Techno! Techno! That's the real music.'

Archangelo got his phone out and showed them a YouTube video of Dario Rossi, a percussionist from Rome, making techno music with pots and pans in central London.

'See? You can even make it like classical. No electronics.'

'That's amazing! You're onto something,' said Destiny. 'What do you think Angel?'

'Y-Yes, he's good, and I do like some Techno, but I prefer something with more atmosphere. M-More Romantic.'

'Well, Archangelo is an archangel and you are just Angel, so his opinion counts more,' said Destiny.

They all laughed, except Angel. Archangelo high-fived Destiny.

'But you're not allowed to say it,' Destiny warned Archangelo. 'He's my brother. Only I can tease him. Sister's privilege!'

Smiling, Archangelo bowed his head and showed his palms at the sassy sister.

Angel went to the table, grabbed a canapé, and shoved it into his mouth. He started chewing while he found a champagne flute.

But the task was rudely interrupted by the intense burning in his mouth and eye-watering fumes exiting his nose. He considered spitting out the canapé, but knew he couldn't, so he accelerated his chewing and swallowed speedily. This, however, proved a bad tactic, as the spicy meat burnt the back of his throat on the way down.

Destiny turned to find Angel nearly bent over, coughing his lungs out, beating his right hand in the air, then blowing air out of his mouth. She burst out laughing and elbowed Vittorio.

'Look, he found your father's *spianata calabrese*!'

They all laughed, except Angel, and carried on with their conversation.

While he recovered, through watery eyes, he saw his father's serious manner transform suddenly into surprise and joy. Angel did a double-take, disbelieving, as his father *never* changed his facial expression: angry, bored, happy, frustrated, proud, tired, fired up, confused—it was always the same. Angel followed his father's gaze to find the cause of this event, and, lo, the cause proved wholly unexpected: the entrance into the parlour of Professor Orlando Mastropasqua.

'Wha . . . ?' breathed Angel.

The professor approached Angel's father with arms outstretched and an equally perplexing facial expression: joy and familiarity. He also uttered Angel's father's given name. The two men converged into a mutual embrace and pats on each other's backs so forceful they would have cracked lesser men's ribs. The professor had arrived in an 1870s frock, but Angel's father seemed unsurprised by this choice. Of all the men present, the professor was the only one who approached his father's intimidating aura.

Angel observed the two men conversing for a while. At one point, his father scanned the room, found him, and pointed him out to the professor, who turned to look. Recognition registered on the academic's face. For a moment, he seemed subtly taken aback at Angel's presence; he thinned his lips and nodded slowly, rather than greeting Angel acknowledging his father.

The two old friends then continued talking.

Intrigued, but also worried, Angel grabbed a champagne flute and drifted in their direction, making sure he stayed out of their line of sight. He took position with his back to his father's, and with ears so focused on the unfolding conversation that, had it been possible, Angel would have rotated the conches.

'He's not done the course work.' said Mastropasqua.

His father said something about wanting to withdraw Angel from the university.

'*Fantastic* idea. If I were you, I would not wait until the end of term.'

The ants in Angel's nervous system sprung into motion. The ventricles of his heart became pistons. The cubic inchage inside his lungs suddenly halved.

Angel drained his champagne in a series of sips and, curtaining his face with hair, left to get more.

His father had never mentioned Mastropasqua before. How did they know each other? Did his father have other spies at the university?

On his way back to the food table Angel collided against a man. When he looked up, he found a chillingly serious, middle-aged face—the empathyless face of a psychopath when he thinks he's not being watched—which, upon making eye contact, abruptly lifted into a smile, as if someone had tugged at strings to make it happen. Angel knew him; the man was a medical doctor by name of Giovanni Fini. His mother knew him from the bridge club, and he was primarily a master raconteur. Angel apologised and moved on. Fini's face fell into its original expression just as quickly as it had previously changed.

Back at the table, Angel grabbed a second champagne flute. He was about to re-join the Italians, if anything to distract himself from his own worried thoughts, when his mother put her hand on his elbow to get his attention. Angel turned to find Victoria standing next to a girl his age. She was blonde, refined, with bland classical features. Her slim body was draped in an elegant golden dress.

'Angel. This is Natalya. She's the daughter of an author friend. I thought you might get on.'

Victoria left to mix with other guests.

'Erm . . . hello,' said Angel, his mind two hundred miles away.

'Hello.' The girl's greeting was flat, her gaze steady, her face blank.

Silence.

'Um . . .'

Silence.

Angel's eyes twitched multidirectionally. 'Er . . .'

Silence.

Natalya continued to stare.

'Um . . . do . . . er . . . you . . . er . . . um . . . know my father?'

'No.'

'Okay.'

Silence.

Angel stared at his shoes, then looked around the room.

Natalya continued to stare.

'Um . . . I-I-I have to go to the lavatory. Excuse me,' said Angel, holding up an index finger.

The girl said nothing.

He exited the room, went to the stairs, climbed them quickly, slipped into his bathroom, and locked the door—checking the handle to make sure.

Leaning against the door, Angel turned his orbs upwards and deflated with relief.

He thought of Madison.

If only he had money . . . He would have flown her in! His parents would have never financed it, however, so he would have had to rely on independent means. He imagined himself and Madison in the parlour, standing in front of each other, discussing poetry and Elizabethan plays with those beautiful crystal flutes of champagne in their hands. He imagined taking a stroll with her on the grounds, away from his parent's somniferous guests. He imagined introducing her to the Italians and having Vittorio prank her with his dark stories of feeding suicidal band members to the dogs. He imagined her pranking the cousin back with her clever reverse psychology. He imagined sitting next to her at the dinner table, eating whatever elegant delicacies his mother had ordered from the caterers, plus whatever Italian delicacies uncle Giancarlo had contributed for the occasion. He imagined his parents noticing Madison's elegance—that she came from a wealthy family—and approving of his choice.

He felt the urge to check her Instagram, though he dreaded what he might find this time. Being at home somehow made it all seem alright; it somehow minimised the import of her derailments—made them seem trivial and temporary. And the thought that he might be pulled out of the university was far worse than anything she had done or might do still—except for getting piercings or tattoos. Anything else could be reversed. If only he had his phone!

Angel thought of dashing into his room and visiting her Instagram on his computer. And, to this effect, he quietly unlocked the door and poked his head out to check the corridor. The coast was clear. Swiftly and silently, he slipped into his room, closed the door behind him, sat at his desk, and took his computer out of standby.

'Angel?'

It was Destiny. She was in the corridor, approaching.

'Damn!' he whispered.

His door opened.

'Mum says to come back down and talk to the girl.'

'Oh, really?'

'Yes. So come on.'

Angel rose from his chair sluggishly and without enthusiasm.

'She's not that bad. She's pretty. *And* elegant.'

He said nothing.

'Argh. That Madison has polluted your brain, Angel.'

He mumbled a protest.

'You're possessed,' she added.

Angel held his tongue. They went back downstairs and into the parlour.

He found Natalya with the Italians. Vittorio was holding his phone against her ear—probably playing her one of his funereal songs about mortality, decay, and oblivion, as the girl was frowning, bobbing her head slowly.

Angel joined the group. Luca and Archangelo were busy chatting in Italian, so Angel stood, listening in silence, without understanding a word. After a minute, Vittorio pulled his phone away from Natalya's ear and the two of them got wrapped up in a discussion about Black Metal. It seemed to Angel the girl had at least a passing interest in the genre, something he would have never guessed from her insipid aspect. If he'd known, maybe they would have had something to talk about, as he'd learnt from talking to Vittorio in the past that his—Angel's—interests overlapped with the more Romantically inclined Black Metallers. Angel tuned in, but neither Vittorio nor Natalya made any effort to include him; in fact, Angel might as well not have been there at all.

His last dose of Panadol wearing off, and the champagne taking hold, Angel wandered away, but fell short of leaving the parlour, as he noticed his mother was watching. The Panadol was in his room, so he now faced a conundrum. He fished for Destiny's attention as she passed him by, but she appeared busy and failed to notice him. Consequently, Angel stood against a wall, head low, thinking about Madison and the university while he waited for Destiny to return.

Half an hour passed, during which more people arrived. As the guests grew in number, Angel grew lonely and dizzy. He imagined flying back from America with Madison beside him, holding his hand, and bringing her to live in the United Kingdom. But even if that were possible, it was presently in jeopardy. If his parents pulled him out of the university, Madison would look down on him, regard him as a 'loser', a failure, *less*. He *had* to stop this *madness* and convince his parents otherwise—graduation was only months away! Just a little bit longer and he'd be through! If only he could slip upstairs and get started catching up with the course reading! He'd then very quickly impress his parents with his command of the course materials, and, in turn, show them he was on top of everything else, and that what they'd seen since Friday night was just the effects of a freak virus and a malfunctioning drier at his local laundrette.

This plan of action—bolstered by the champagne—stilled the ants.

Chapter CIX

Victoria's announcement that guests were to migrate to the great hall yanked Angel back to reality. He consciously lagged until he was the last person to leave the parlour.

When he entered the great hall, the guests were still finding their assigned seats, as indicated by ornate place cards. A long, rectangular table at the far end had been relegated to bottles of wine and water, breads, cheeses, fruit, and other accessory comestibles—a vast, Renaissance still life. The two long tables running the length of the room flanked the one on the dais. The massive benches had been pushed against the walls and replaced by ponderous oaken chairs. The tables were laid out with Wedgwood china with a discontinued Persia design, Royal Scot crystalware, florid golden napkin rings, and the baroque golden cutlery his mother reserved for celebrations. Angel's parents presided from the table on the dais, flanked each by their guests of honour, Professor Mastropasqua being one of them. Angel and Destiny, being the two youngest diners, had been assigned the farthest-most seats of the long tables, opposite each other. Angel found that Natalya, seated to his right, was his only neighbour.

'Hello,' he said, peremptorily.

The girl looked away.

'Do you like Edmund Spenser?'

No acknowledgment.

Angel tapped her shoulder. 'Sorry. Do you like Edmund Spenser?'

'Who?'

'Ed-Ed-Edmund Spenser. The poet.'

'Haven't read him.'

'Oh, okay.'

The girl looked away.

Angel inhaled to ask something else but changed his mind.

Everybody was standing, waiting for the head of the household to sit down. Angel stood with silent impatience, hanging on to the backrest of his chair as his legs slowly liquefied and the room spun, his headache regaining momentum while minute after minute was spent by the guests fumbling about and, among much chatting, joking, and distraction, taking position behind their respective chairs. Just as Angel thought he was about to collapse, his father finally sat down, detonating a deafening rumble as everyone pulled and scraped their chairs against the ancient flagstone floor to follow his example.

The action set the liveried catering waiters into motion. Two trolleys, each with a selection of breads, began making their way down the tables, beginning with the lady guest of honour and moving outwards from oldest to youngest, before the gentlemen were served in analogous fashion. It took many minutes before the trolley reached Angel, he being the very last stop before his father was served, by which time the breads Angel liked best had already been taken. All that was left were seedy varieties that he didn't care for, so he chose the one with the least amount of seeds. Then came the water, which, again, took many minutes, because the crystal carafe and glasses had to be handled carefully. And then came the wine, which took even longer, because guests who had requested something specific had to be shown the labels, the waiters had to receive each of those guests' nod of confirmation (which was often delayed because said guests were all distracted chatting), the liquid had to be poured slowly, sampled, approved, topped up, and the pouring each time had to end with a twisty flourish; moreover, new bottles had to be fetched constantly.

The entire time, Angel and Natalya sat in silence, ignoring each other. Destiny, however, caught his eye and, cheekily grinning, wiggled her eyebrows at him when Natalya wasn't looking. Angel shook his head, annoyed, and looked down at his plate.

At long last came the appetiser. This, too, took an eternity to reach him, by which time it might as well have come straight out of the freezer. Worse, it consisted of garlic butter langoustines, paired with Chardonnay (Côte d'Or), which only made him think of Cineworld, Johannes, and Amelia angry with him. Angel exhaled with a grimace, his gorge rising. Destiny, he noticed, got a double ration, which prompted her to tease him with a thumbs up. Natalya, meanwhile, got started, showing dexterity with the cutlery and impeccable manners. The Italians beyond her, however, were loud, lively, and prone to explosive laughter, which felt like shards of glass going into Angel's brain. Worse still, fuelled by the champagne they had already consumed and now the Chardonnay, they sucked Natalya into their banter, particularly after they discovered she spoke a fair amount of Italian; quiet as she'd been, the florid Vittorio soon got her trachea rippling with laughter too.

The next dish was an onion soup, paired with Beaujolais Nouveau. Once again, Angel was the last one to be served, so it was also freezing. And once again, the dish brought terrible memories, so he didn't even pick up the spoon. Natalya, on the other hand, ate all of it and drank the wine apace, responding to whatever the Italians threw at her with quick-witted gusto and ear-blasting eruptions of hilarity. At first, Angel only winced, but, over time, and without realising it, he adopted a defensive body posture on the outermost edge of his seat.

'Angelo!' shouted Vittorio, finally taking notice of him.

Hunched over, Angel turned to look.

'Parli italiano adesso?'

'Um . . .' Angel felt Natalya's and all the Italians' eyes on him, accompanied by expectant smiles. 'No, er . . . I don't'

'Ancora non parli italiano?'

'No, no . . .'

'Quando imparerai l'italiano, allora?'

'What was that?'

'When will you learn Italian?'

'Um . . . I've got uni.'

His response elicited a collective moan of disappointment.

'It's just that . . .'

With dismissive hand waves, they swatted away his explanation and carried on with their banter, Natalya included.

Angel glanced across to Destiny and found her looking at him, doing a finger purse gesture and Italian facial impressions. He frowned and stared at his plate.

Next came the main dish: canard à l'orange, paired with Alsace Gerwürztraminer. And, for the same reasons as before, there was no chance of Angel tasting it hot. At least it was something he could eat, however, so he picked up his utensils. Peacefully operating them, on the other hand, proved surprisingly difficult, as the bibulous Natalya had become so riled up partaking in the Italians' boisterous energy that she kept bumping his elbow and occasionally leaning into him in fits of cachinnation. Angel ended up with sauce on his cheek and in his hair, after an elbow-bump caused him to miss his mouth, and wine on his hand and sleeve, when the bump was repeated two minutes later.

Angel moved his chair, plate, wine glasses, water goblet, napkin ring, and utensils a few inches further out.

As the party was generating plenty of background noise, Archangelo thought nothing of pulling out his phone and playing his 90s electronic dance megamix. This only energised Natalya even more, who started wiggling her torso and singing, her arms in the air.

'Balla con me!' she said, suddenly turning to Angel, laughing. 'Balla con me!'

The Italians urged him to respond.

'Balla con la regazza! Dai!'

Angel became a deer in headlights. Madison, the Madison he knew, would have never behaved in this manner—although he feared the current Madison would've been slamming the booze even harder.

'I have a headache,' he said, but no one heard him, his voice obliterated by the decibel storm.

Natalya grabbed his hand and lifted it in the air, still laughing and wiggling her torso.

'Balla! Balla con me!'

All the Italians were leaning forward and staring wide-eyed, encouraging the scene with grins and raised eyebrows.

Angel pleaded with his eyes for it to stop and allowed his arm to fall.

At this point, Natalya lost interest, but found a willing accomplice in Luca—he of the slicked-back hair—who, albeit ironically, began wiggling his torso too, much to the joy of the other Italians. The wine and the excitement appeared to have blinded Natalya to Luca's mockery, but nobody cared when there was fun to be had.

Angel caught sight of his mother smiling at the scene from a distance and casually making a comment to her neighbour, who echoed her expression. His father was wrapped in an intense discussion with the professor. Angel thought the latter cast a brief glance at him, before focusing again on his father. Were they talking about his removal from the university? A tsunami of anxiety swept over him, reactivating the ants and turning his knees into pistons. But, conscious of his mother's gaze, he stopped them as soon as he became aware.

The plates were removed, Angel having only managed a quarter of the cold slice of duck. It was aeons before the dessert appeared: crème caramel, paired with Pedro Ximénez. This dish was a win, since it was one of his favourites. But as he picked up the spoon to get started, Natalya burst out laughing yet again and, with a wild swing of her arm, bumped Angel's elbow for the thousandth time. On this occasion, the violence of the collision caused Angel to knock over his sherry glass, which then began rapidly rolling towards the edge of the table. Angel's hand instinctively shot out to catch it. However, in the process, he leaned forward and pressed his shirt and tie into his dessert.

Angel put the glass down and sat back, annoyed with himself. His napkin having fallen on the floor, he picked it up, noticing, in that instant, that his father was staring. The latter's facial expression remained unchanged, as always, but Angel could sense the confirmation in it of a prejudice. He told himself it was just his imagination. Inconveniently, Victoria also happened to glance at that moment. And so did Destiny, who shook her head with benevolent condescension. Angel feigned normality and cleaned up the crème caramel as best he could, but there was little he could do with a linen napkin.

A positive consequence of the stain, however, was that it gave him an excuse to quit the scene.

Chapter CX

Back in his room, Angel changed into a new shirt and tie. But returning to the great hall promptly was never his plan; instead, he sat behind his computer and checked his social media.

There were several alerts on both Facebook and Instagram notifying him of new messages from Amelia. 'Please, Angel, wherever you are, please reply. I'm really worried about you,' she wrote in one. Angel thought of replying, but first he checked Madison's Instagram page.

Madison had posted a new image. It showed her in a tank top, looking at the camera with her arm raised so that it showed her armpit. The armpit hair, Angel saw, had been allowed to grow. The description read: 'I need feminism because my natural hair should not disturb anyone.'

Angel's eyes scrunched shut as his hands shot to his forehead, where they remained for a cosmological age.

In this part of the story I am the one who dies
. . . and I will die of love because I love you

Every day the situation became more urgent. At least Madison had, for now, only grown armpit hair. It could be shaved, and good habits regained. This was, in fact, reason for joy, since the damage was not permanent. As long as she got no tattoos or piercings, there was *hope*. But the danger remained: the way things were going, she would do either or both of those things eventually; she might even do them *soon*; she might, indeed, be already *thinking* about it, and Syd would almost certainly be *encouraging* her to do it sooner rather than later.

He had to get back to London tomorrow night, do his canteen shifts, and amass the necessary funds to fly to Madison before it was too late. He'd already lost several days' worth of wages, but soon October would come to an end and he'd get five weeks' worth. No doubt Ryanair or some exotic airline that would fly him for a low price. Although he'd have to give Madison a fake arrival time, so that she wouldn't find out he'd had to budget. She'd expect him to fly First Class on British Airways, at the very least.

He'd also have to spend tomorrow displaying his profound knowledge of the university course material as a step prior. He should, on that account, get started with the course reading tonight.

'Angel?'

Once again, it was Destiny in the corridor, approaching.

'Um . . . yes?' he said.

Destiny appeared at the door.

'They're about to wheel in the cake. You should come down.'

'Oh. Already?'

'You should hurry.'

'Okay,' he moaned like a child who'd been told to do a chore.

He got up, but almost in slow motion, and made his way to the door with the speed of a viscoelastic polymer.

'Come on! We're going to miss it!' she urged.

Angel accelerated his stride, but infinitesimally. Rolling her eyes, Destiny chose to dash back downstairs without waiting for him.

By the time he reached the great hall, the guests were already singing Happy Birthday. The cake, which Angel now saw for the first time, was large and shaped like a Mediaeval fortress, complete with crenelated castellations, towers, a pull-up gate, and snake-infested moat. Atop the central tower, which was taller than the others, was the number 50. Angel observed his father smiling while the song was sung. Smiling. A facial expression that transformed the man's face—unrecognisably for Angel, since it was reserved for those who earned approval.

After the explosion of cheer marking the end of the song, the fifty-year-old rose and delivered his extemporaneous remarks, cannonading the great hall with his thundering voice. Angel's mind was still filled with Madison, so whatever his father said went out the other ear. But in this he was alone, because both guests and family, and even Natalya, gave their host their full attention, the host's jokes detonating payload after payload of laughter and infusing the crowd with euphoric energy.

Angel was jerked back to reality when his father received a standing ovation.

The distribution of cake slices immediately followed, moving slowly in the same order as before, until it was Angel and Destiny's turn. Destiny, however, received a double helping, while Angel's slice was half the thickness of Natalya's.

Natalya's euphoria continued unabated, stoked by Vittorio's banter and the rowdy contributions of the younger Italians. Luca decided to mirror all her movements and repeat everything she said in a ridiculous falsetto. His stunt only amped up the hilarity. Angel, realising he'd forgotten to take paracetamol while in his room, cringed at the constant cacophony of strident decibels. Natalya's trachea waved with non-stop laughter, her serpentine torso would not stop twisting, and her wayward elbow became a pneumatic drill applied to his side. As he looked across, Angel saw Destiny staring at him, covering her mouth, her face red, as she attempted to contain her cackles.

The minutes could not pass fast enough for Angel. Yet, dinner was by no means finished after the cake, for then came the coffee and the liqueurs, both of which took the age of the universe to pour, and even longer to be drunk, since the guests persisted in their jocularity and conversation.

To numb himself, Angel opted to knock back the thimbleful of grappa before him, having thus far avoided the wines, out of fear of worsening his headache. But this soon proved a mistake, because with his exiguous body mass, the liqueur, primed by his earlier consumption of champagne, hit him like a mallet in the face. The hall became a centrifuge, and Natalya's shouts and shrieks of laugher, the Italians' raucousness, the rumbling of scores of babbling guests, and the innumerable coughs, sneezes, cackles, clearings of throats, scraping of chairs, clinking of glasses, blowings of noses, clappings of hands, and what not, reached him as if through a glass bottle. Deeming it prudent, under the circumstances, to regain alertness, Angel stood, so as to repair to the downstairs toilet. Except that as soon as his legs had straightened, he discovered them to be made of jelly. As he stepped sideways to leave the table, Angel lost his balance and fell on the floor.

Neither Natalya nor the Italians noticed, but, as he attempted to get back on his feet, Angel saw that the opposite had been the case with his mother and father. Aware that he was under their microscope, Angel focused his mind on making slow, controlled movements to conceal his intoxication. Yet his mother and his father's respective visages made it plain that his effort was in vain.

Angel left the great hall, walking as straight as he could; his perception of straight, however, did not conform to mathematical definitions.

Chapter CXI

'I'm getting tired of having to go and find you,' said Destiny, for the third time at his door.

'Um . . . um . . . um . . . sorry . . . I'm . . . not feeling . . . well,' said Angel, lying in bed.

He felt as if trapped inside a washing machine on a fast spin cycle.

'Well, then walk around, splash some water on your face!'

'I-I-I can't . . . I . . .'

'Angel: you need to get back down. Mum says you need to show up in the drawing room. At least for a bit. And she's right. It's father's fiftieth birthday. So come on.'

'B-But . . . no one . . . cares . . . if I'm there . . .'

'Mum does. Father does.'

'They always notice . . .' he moaned.

'And I'm sure Natalya does too.' Destiny grinned, wiggling her eyebrows.

Angel groaned, wrinkling his nose, crinkling his brow, and exposing his upper gums.

'That's the most *disgusting* face I've ever seen,' his sister said.

Destiny pulled his arm, partially dragging him out of bed. 'Come on. Stop whinging. Up!'

Angel made to rise, but, overcome by dizziness, collapsed back onto the mattress.

'Oh, for goodness sake!' snapped Destiny.

She grabbed his left arm and leg, mounted him on her back, carried him into the bathroom, and dropped him in the bathtub. Before he could react, she turned on the tap, blasting him with freezing water from the showerhead. Angel scuttled out of the bathtub like a frightened spider.

As he stood looking down at his wet clothes, Destiny, fists on hips, said, 'Now, go change and get back downstairs. Twenty minutes. Then you can squirm away if you want.'

Destiny left.

Angel did as told, albeit dispensing with the under-jumper and shoulder pads, since he lacked the time.

Back downstairs, he found that the ladies had gone into the parlour, and the men into the drawing room. Instinctively, Angel preferred the former, but fear of encountering Natalya led him to the latter. Besides, it seemed opportune for his father to see him comporting himself appropriately among men of status and pedigree. *That*, he thought, would help sway him against pulling him out of the university.

He found his father standing in the centre of the room, the congregation's axis. His father was still in deep in conversation with the professor. Angel made sure to cross his father's field of vision on his way to a table where the catering staff had laid out trays with fine chocolates. As he passed, Angel overheard Mastropasqua:

'. . . it's a wimp factory . . . a menace to society . . .'

Angel grabbed a chocolate and, desiring to overhear more, again walked past his father and the professor, who now said:

'. . . I'm going to destroy them all . . .'

Before he could hear any more, Angel felt someone grab his hand and tug him away. It was Natalya, who'd decided, for unfathomable reasons, to lead him out onto the grounds.

At some distance from the manor, gathered around a picnic table under the mulberry tree, he found Destiny and the three Italian brothers, champagne flutes in hand, all cheering Natalya's and Angel's return. Archangelo's infamous iPhone had been placed on the tabletop, otherwise crowded with a fleet of bottles of Moët & Chandon, and was still going through his 90s electronic dance megamix. As soon as Natalya released Angel, she turned to face him and began dancing.

'Balla con me!' she said with a drunken voice.

Everyone loudly encouraged him to comply.

Paralysed, Angel stared at Natalya as she undulated to the sound of Gigi d'Agostino's 'L'Amour Toujours'.

'Come on, Angel! Don't be shy!' shouted Destiny.

'Balla! Balla! Balla con lei!' urged Vittorio.

Archangelo clapped, his face lit from below, his closed smile like the Joker's.

Luca jumped in alongside Natalya, mirroring her every movement.

'Balla con me!' he said, in his ridiculous falsetto.

As if to rebuke Angel for his party-pooping ways, Alice DJ's 'Better Off Alone' followed out of the iPhone. Yet, even this was not enough to persuade him, so Destiny decided to join in and, grabbing his hand, forced him into dance. Angel noticed that she was barefoot and her high-heeled shoes had been left on the table.

Angel danced mechanically, in a daze, removing himself from the scene by imagining a slow or, even better, a Renaissance dance with Madison, alone and under the stars. But still better would have been to dance with her in the ballroom of the Westin Paris at the Vendôme, or of the Palais Garnier, or of the Vienna State House, or the of Catherine Palace in Tsarskoe Selo, in St Petersburg. He imagined Madison in a full-length evening gown, and himself in white tie, she looking like Marie Antoinette, he like a taller King Charles I.

But such visions were incompatible with Archangelo's track list: Corona's 'Rhythm of the Night' pushed out the baroque, rococo, and neo-Renaissance splendour in favour of sudorous nightclubs, lasers, and disco balls. Natalya, who was now swigging champagne directly from the bottle, and holding a cigarette in the other hand, was loving it—and so was his sister, who contrived, most of the time by force, to keep him there and moving, as she would a marionette. Vittorio, being a Black Metaller, disdained to dance, but found Luca's open ridiculing of Natalya, and Natalya's lack of self-awareness, so comical that, when not disintegrating with laughter, he rewarded his younger brother's insolence with all manner of cheers and incitement. Archangelo, the beaming mastermind, sat on the tabletop, content to watch with his feet on the bench and his forearms on his knees.

Yet, the hilarity could not last, for Natalya finally twisted an ankle, or lost her balance, and fell on the grass. Luca copied her fall and facial expression, not caring about getting grass and mud on his suit. Everyone burst out laughing, except Angel. However, as Natalya found no way to get back on her feet, Destiny took action: she grabbed Natalya's right hand, slung the girl over her shoulder, and plonked her on the bench opposite Archangelo. Natalya was so inebriated, however, that she might as well have been a string of wet spaghetti.

Angel stood by, observing mutely while Destiny and Vittorio examined the drunkard. Archangelo stopped the music and Luca, back on his feet, brushed the grass off his trousers. Natalya's dress was in much worse shape, as she'd landed on mulberries and the juice had left ruinous stains.

'Angel! Don't just stand there. *Do* something!' said Destiny.

'B-But . . . w-what?'

'I think she's gonna be sick,' said Destiny, not answering him, but as a statement of fact to everyone.

Angel got nearer.

'Angel, my feet are muddy. Take her back to the house and guide her to the toilet downstairs.'

'O-Okay,' he said, hesitating.

Vittorio interjected, 'Why don't you let her be sick behind the bushes, over there?'

'Oh, no way. My parents would hit the roof.' Destiny turned to her brother. 'Come on, Angel! Get a move on!'

Angel stood right by Natalya and Destiny brought her to her feet.

'Take her arm and put it across your shoulder,' she said. 'Hold on to her.'

Angel did as instructed. But his muscles trembled as even the slender Natalya he found shockingly heavy. After a second, he collapsed under her weight.

'Angel, I said hold on to her!'

'She's very heavy.'

'Argh! Okay. I'll help you walk her to the house.'

'Okay.'

Angel, helped by Destiny, walked Natalya back to the house. They opted for the service door, hoping it would avoid detection.

When they got there, Destiny said, 'I'll hold her while you open the door.'

Angel tried the handle. 'It's locked. Do you have the key?'

'I'm wearing a dress, Angel. Where was I going to put it?'

'Er . . . okay.'

'Let's go to the side door.'

They walked Natalya to the sashed doors she'd used when dragging him out of the house. The problem was that it led into a hallway with heavy traffic, since it linked the drawing room, the parlour, and the downstairs toilet.

Angel opened the door and poked his head in. The coast was clear.

'All good?' said Destiny.

'Yes.'

'Okay. I can't go in, so find someone to assist you. I'll go and re-join the Italians. See you later.'

'Okay.'

He brought Natalya in carefully, his back curving under her weight, the girl inexorably slipping, but he couldn't close the door behind them. He needed it for support.

He was pondering how to get her to the toilet when suddenly Victoria appeared. Her eyes widened and jaw dropped.

'Angel! What's happened here?' she hissed.

'Um . . . she fell.'

His mother sighed and looked at the ceiling for a moment.

Angel gripped the door handle, stumped, trembling and barely holding on to Natalya.

'Okay,' said Victoria at last, 'Give her to me.'

Angel not so much handed over Natalya as dropped her into his mother's arms as the latter reached for the incapacitated waif.

'What a mess,' said his mother. 'You go upstairs and clean up.'

'Yes.'

'And, Angel?'

'Um . . . yes?'

'Don't come back down.'

Chapter CXII

'. . . Which reminds me—after breakfast, you and I are going to sit down and go over your bank statements.'

Angel stared at his mother wide-eyed. 'Oh, really?'

'Yes. I want to know *exactly* where the fifteen grand went. So you will print out your statements and bring them to me so we can go over line by line.'

'Erm . . . okay . . .'

His father glared at him, although the paternal visage showed no expression—only seriousness. Anger and disappointment radiated all the same.

'Uh-oh. You're in trouble,' said Destiny, smirking.

'Destiny.'

'Sorry, mum.'

Angel swallowed. His parents were going to hate Madison and oppose his plans to visit her.

He tilted his head forward and hid under his hair.

'Angel—pull your hair back. You're going to get food in it.'

Angel promptly did as told, realising he'd made a potentially fatal mistake.

'Destiny, I thought I asked you to cut Angel's hair.'

Angel scrunched his eyes shut, as if awaiting impact.

'I did,' she said.

'It looks exactly the same.'

'I evened out the ends.'

'I expected you to cut a great deal more.'

'There was no time. The guests were about to arrive.'

'I see.'

Angel prayed for a distraction that would divert from the topic. The ants stirred.

'I think Angel looks good with his hair like that,' said Destiny, winking at Angel.

Victoria turned to her son. 'If you're going to wear your hair like that, you should put it in a ponytail when you eat.'

'I can lend you a scrunchy, Angel. I think I have a pink one upstairs.' Destiny's expression was mock helpful.

Angel frowned but said nothing.

'We'll talk about it later,' declared his mother. 'I still think you look like a homeless person.'

After breakfast, the whole family cleared up, all members, including Angel, plus the maid, working like parts of a machine. The dishwasher was loaded, the tablecloth shaken outside, the pans washed, the counter surfaces wiped. The mass killing of germs was so thorough that those still standing were angry because there was nothing left to nourish them.

'I'll be waiting for you in my study,' said Victoria to her son.

Chapter CXII

Half an hour later, after printing out the statements, moving as slowly as he could, Angel walked to his mother's study. An observer would have thought that time had stopped altogether, for each of Angel's steps took a galactic year.

He knocked on the oak door with the force of a feather landing on a cushion. Unfortunately, when it came to detecting Angel's presence and whereabouts, his mother's hearing was like a cat's.

'Come in,' he heard.

Angel hoped, against all evidence, that he'd find his mother seated at her long desk—reserved for writing—because that would indicate she was to examine his statements in the middle of other business, and therefore spend less time drilling down and pressing him with questions. If he found her behind the short desk, he really was in trouble.

He entered. Victoria was behind the short desk—a 19th-century oak imitation in the Jacobean style, located in a corner of the wood-panelled room, much of which was lined with old volumes in built-in bookcases. Orderly piles of paperwork—invoices, contracts, bank statements, credit card statements, official correspondence, etc.—covered half the desk's surface. His mother had before her a pad of paper, which signalled her intention to take notes, break everything down, and get to the bottommost bottom of his spending.

'Sit,' she said. 'We're going to be here for a while.'

'Would you like tea?'

'No. Thank you.'

'Or coffee?'

'I've got coffee. Please sit.'

Angel did as told. The wingback armchair he sat on

was ancient and low. His head only just rose above the desk's surface.

His mother beckoned with her hand. 'Let me see those statements.'

Angel handed over the stack of A4 printouts he'd been carrying, trying to contain his tremours.

He scratched his temple, fingers like ice, and caught himself bouncing his knees. He stilled them. His chest felt tight. His bowel loose. His brain like a beehive.

His mother got to work, reading every page in silence, using her pen occasionally, tapping on her calculator. To Angel's terror, her frown got deeper, her eyes wider, her lips thinner.

He was never going to see Madison again.

And his mother was going to avenge herself by sending him to the barber and pulling him out of uni.

'Angel—you spent eleven thousand pounds just on restaurants?'

'Um . . . eleven thousand?' he squeaked.

'Yes. Eleven thousand. Are you insane?'

'Um . . .'

'I didn't send you that money so you could blow it taking a girl on fancy dates!'

'Um . . . um . . .'

'Because I *know* you, even if you don't tell me. This is about a *girl*.'

'Er . . . um . . .'

'And your sister has confirmed it.'

Angel blinked fast. 'Oh . . . d-d-d-did she?'

'Of course she did. I should have known. It explains everything!'

'Er . . . erm . . .'

'And who is this girl? This Madison.'

'Er . . . she's . . .'

'Did she ask you to take her to these places?'

'No . . . no . . . um . . . I just . . .'

'So *you* took her. Have you lost your mind?'

'No . . . she's just . . . elegant . . .'

'Elegant!'

Angel flinched.

'Um . . . yes . . . um . . . s-she comes from a very good family . . .'

'She's a university student!'

'Yes, but . . .'

'Yes, but nothing! Students don't go to these places several times a week! Not even billionaires do. Students order *pizza* if they're hungry.'

'W-W-We *did* order pizz—'

'Let me see this girl.' Victoria picked up her phone. 'Is she on Instagram? What's her username?'

'Um . . . I-I-I don't remember . . . it's something with numbers . . . I just follow her . . .'

'Give me your phone, then.'

'Um . . . er . . . it's . . . it's . . . I l-l-left it in my room . . .'

'Go and get it.'

'Um . . . I-I-I-I . . . I-I-I think I mislaid it on F-Friday night . . .'

'Go to your room. I'll ring it so you can find it.'

Victoria didn't wait for him. She dialled Angel's number and pressed her phone to her ear.

Angel got up slowly, hesitantly, eyes fixed on his mother.

'Go, Angel. Go!'

He walked towards the door.

However, before he got there, his mother said, 'Who are you?'

Angel turned, watched paralysed.

Her face became momentarily indignant. Whoever had answered had abruptly hung up. Victoria checked the screen to see she'd dialled the number correctly.

She re-dialled.

This time there was no reply. The phone rang and rang and rang.

Victoria stopped the call, tapped her phone with her index finger in quick succession, then waited.

Angel snapped out of his stupor and reached for the doorknob quickly.

'Angel?'

He turned again. 'Yes?'

'Why does my app say your phone's in Manchester?'

Chapter CXIII

Angel sat on his bed, staring into space, heart pounding, breathing shallow and fast.

The ants were marching.

Everything was up in the air.

The only thing that would convince his parents not to withdraw him from university, or his mother not to insist on a haircut, was to show them that he was put together. On this basis, he thought it would be a good idea to pack his suitcase ahead of returning to London tonight, so that when they checked, he'd be able to tell them he'd already done so.

This reminded him that he hadn't checked his train's departure time. Clearly, not until late in the afternoon, or perhaps the evening, as otherwise his mother would have already asked him to pack. He went on his computer and combed through his emails.

His train was scheduled for 19:49.

This gave him a fair few hours to prove himself.

Angel packed his suitcase, making sure his clothes were folded neatly and arranged with perfect geometry and efficiency. He selected seven pairs of black socks, a pair of blue jeans, a pair of black jeans, a pair of black corduroys, seven shirts, his DaVinci t-shirt, his Rossetti t-shirt, a couple of ties (for the opera or the theatre), a Maya blue V-neck merino wool jumper, a beige cashmere polo neck, and toiletries. He also took out a brown corduroy jacket, and, upon reflection, he packed a navy one, in case of another accident.

After he was done, Angel stood the suitcase by the foot of the bed, making sure it was exactly in the centre and parallel to the footboard.

It seemed likely that his mother would want to take him to York to find a replacement telephone, but that could either be now or in the afternoon. Either way, York meant proximity to a barber, so he brushed his hair thoroughly and tucked it under his shirt collar. The horrid prospect still loomed of a Sunday lunch, flanked by his angry mother and father, so it was imperative he caught up with this university reading fast.

He again sat at his computer and clicked on the browser tab showing *Oroonoko*.

But before reading, he decided to check his social media.

There were now several more Instagram, Facebook, WhatsApp, and email messages from Amelia. The last one was from this morning.

AMELIA: Angel, I'm begging you. Please reply. Answer my calls. I'm really worried and I fear something has happened to you. I've asked everyone and no one has seen you or has any idea of where you might be. Let me know you're okay.

He thought it best to reply, so he began typing.

However, before he got past his greeting, he heard his mother's voice behind him.

'Angel—let's go.'

He turned to find Victoria at the door. 'Erm . . . are we going?'

'I'm taking you to the barber.'

His heart nearly burst through his sternum. The ant armies sped through his nervous system.

'Oh, b-b-but why?'

'Because I say so.'

'Um . . . b-but I thought . . .'

'I haven't got all day.'

Angel saw his mother's face was tight. He realised she'd remain angry for hours—maybe even until he left. If only he could stall until it was time to go to the station!

'I-I'm feeling very nauseous . . . I think I'm going to be sick.'

This was true.

'Have a glass of milk on the way out.'

'I-I-I also have a massive headache.'

His mother sighed.

'Wait. I'll bring you some Panadol.'

Victoria left.

Angel's eyes darted in every direction. He rubbed his forehead, blew up his cheeks, and released the air slowly, scouring his brain for the next delaying tactic. Yet, his brain buzzed with bees. He wished his headache were worse, his fever higher, his symptoms more visible—but not so bad that his parents would then stop him from leaving in the evening. He had to get back to London no matter what!

His mother came back.

'Take this,' she said, offering two tablets.

Angel did as told, washing it down with water from his bedside table.

'Let's go,' his mother said the instant his Adam's apple had returned to its resting position.

Angel grabbed his brown corduroy jacket, put it on with sloth-like movements, spent as long as he possibly could adjusting it in the mirror, and, finally, made his way out.

Victoria led the way to the courtyard and into her Audi. No stoppage in the kitchen for the glass of milk; obviously his mother hadn't bought his claim to nausea.

Outside, the Royce was gone. So was the Mercedes, Destiny having gone to the 'clicker', *i.e.*, her chiropractor.

Angel's hands were like ice. The ants were even in his scalp. He prayed the car wouldn't start.

His mother turned on the ignition.

The engine rumbled to life.

Angel let his head fall forward. He saw his hair form a curtain around his face and lamented that it might soon be gone.

An alert pinged on the dashboard.

'Oh, for goodness sake!' said his mother.

She switched off the engine and got out of the car. Angel observed her as she walked round to the passenger-side front wheel, pebbles crunching rapidly under her shoes, her head low. He saw her stop and look at the sky in frustration. She came back around and, grabbing her phone, said to Angel, 'You've been saved for now.'

Angel got out and, while her mother punched in a number on her phone, he examined the front tyre.

It was flat.

Chapter CXIV

Angel retreated into his room and closed the door.

He was not yet in the clear, because his mother could still take him to the barber after lunch, but, if he found a way to divert her attention, she might forget to ask Destiny or, worse, his father, to take him instead. Options ran through his mind. Perhaps he could photoshop the email confirmation from the railway company and change his departure time to 13:49—he'd have to be put in a cab before lunch, thus killing two birds with one stone. However, his mother was not one to mix up times or dates—she was a historian—nor one not to double-check erroneous information. Perhaps he could tell his mother he needed the hair for a role in a play at the university. However, she'd argue he could wear a wig instead. And if his parents intended to pull him out, it wouldn't matter anyway. Perhaps he could pretend to go for a walk and then tell his mother he'd seen climate change protestors within the grounds. However, his father would find no evidence, leading him to put even less store in anything Angel said.

Unable to think of anything, he weighed writing to Amelia. She no doubt liked him as he was. Perhaps she'd have ideas on how to deflect his mother's determination. He got on his computer and carried on typing the reply he'd begun earlier.

But before he got two more words in, he heard a knock on the door.

'Yes?' he squeaked.

The door opened.

It was his mother again.

'Angel—what's the name of that laundrette?'

'Um . . . I-I-I don't know it . . . I just use it . . .'

'What street is it on?'

'Um . . . I-I-I just walk there, I-I d-don't know it either.'

His mother sighed. 'Pull up Google maps.'

Angel did as instructed.

'Type in the university post code.'

Angel did as instructed and the screen showed the area.

'Okay, where is the laundrette?'

Angel hesitated. 'Um . . .'

He stalled by playing around with the mouse, rotating the map, changing to satellite view, frowning and pretending to look intently.

All along he sensed Victoria's impatience.

Eventually, realising that further delay would only reinforce the perception of his being incompetent, he pointed out the location.

Victoria enunciated the name of the street and then typed it into her phone.

'Aha!' she said moments later.

Angel's knees began bouncing. He stilled them.

'What day exactly did the fire happen?'

'Erm . . .' Angel thought back, blowing up his cheeks and releasing the air slowly. 'I-I can't remember . . . it seems so long ago.'

'Angel, come on. Think.'

'Erm . . . um . . . um . . . I think . . . er . . . I think it was on a Friday . . . a couple of weeks ago.'

'So Friday 27 September?'

'Um . . . yes . . . I think—'

'Okay. Did you take pictures?'

'Um . . . no.'

'Were there witnesses?'

'Um . . . er . . . no, I-I-I was by myself.'

'Was there CCTV?'

'Er . . . um . . . I-I-I don't think so, er . . .'

'Did you check?'

'Er . . . yes, yes . . . I-I did check.'

Victoria sighed. 'Okay. I might have to come down and see for myself.'

'Oh, really? Erm . . . I-I c-could go there tomorrow myself to check. I-I could go there tomorrow.'

'No. I need to see.'

'S-Surely that's not necessary . . . I-I can send you photos when I'm there. W-With my phone.'

'What phone, Angel?'

'Oh . . . um . . .'

'Have you packed your bag?'

Angel immediately brightened up. Finally, something he could say in his favour. 'Yes, I have!'

'Unpack it, then.'

'Oh . . . er . . . really? Why?'

'You're not leaving tonight.'

His voice jumped an octave. 'B-B-B-But why? I've got classes on—'

'Your father and I will discuss it with you later.'

Chapter CXV

Angel spun slowly on his swivel chair, eyes haunted and distant, cheeks blown, the air in them gradually released. The ants crawled in force.

It was real—not a threat thrown in anger. It was happening.

Yet, so long as his parents were yet to tell him, the possibility existed of changing their minds, of stopping their decision from becoming final.

Perhaps it was not so bad that his mother would be taking him to London. It seemed doubtful that the laundrette would have kept the CCTV footage for longer than a week. And in that case, the situation would be diffused, as she would be able neither to prove the incident to the police nor disprove his version of events.

But what if they kept the footage for longer?

Angel went on his computer and googled his query.

He rubbed his forehead.

Thirty-one days was the standard police recommendation. But small premises could retain it for less. For them, fourteen days was the minimum. And it was past that now, so the footage could well have been deleted.

Angel's knees bounced rapidly.

Could well. That was by no means certain.

He wished the laundrette would suffer an arson attack before they went to London.

Angel thought of hiding his mother's purse, demagnetising her debit cards, letting the air out of another tyre, taking the battery out of her car fob, dissolving sleeping pills into her drink—but what if she caught him?

There was a knock on the door.

'Yes?' he said, his voice too high.

Destiny poked her head in.

'I don't know what you said to mum, but she's *fuming!*'

Angel's forehead crinkled under steepled eyebrows.

'What time is lunch?' he asked.

'At one. As always.'

Angel checked the time on his computer. Two hours from now.

'Mum's asked me to cut your hair.'

Angel jerked, as if convulsed by electroshock. 'Again?'

'Yep.'

'Please, no!'

'It's happening.'

'Please!'

'Don't be alarmed. My bowl cuts are excellent!'

Angel rubbed his forehead, bounced his knees, sent his irises ricocheting all over like balls in a game of Breakout.

'Come on. Let's go,' prompted Destiny.

The army ants were racing. 'D-D-Does she want you to do it *right now?*'

'She said *immediately*.'

Angel cast a glance at the window. It was small and high up in the wall. It also only opened partially, so, slender as he was, he would not have been able to squeeze through it even if he'd managed to climb up and jump out before his sister grabbed his ankle and pulled him back down.

'You can't escape. And I won't let you,' she said.

'Can't you tell mum you couldn't find me?'

'She knows you are here.'

'Please. Just tell her I wasn't.'

'Nope.'

'Please, Destiny, please!'

'Nope.'

'I'll do anything!'

'It's out of my hands. Come on. Let's go.'

'But—'

'There's nothing you can do or say. She's determined to see this happen today.'

Angel's lungs inflated and deflated at a rapid pace. His eyes were in fast Breakout mode.

'Come on, Angel. Let's get it over with'

Angel delayed a few more seconds, then stood. But he resisted the walk to his own execution.

'Come on, Angel. I've got other things to do.'

In slow motion, he walked towards the door, dragging his legs, eyes haunted.

'Oh, don't be a baby. It'll grow back.'

He said nothing.

Once in the corridor, however, Angel bolted.

'Oi!' shouted Destiny, taken by surprise.

He ran down the corridor, Destiny in pursuit, and

descended the stairs like a scurrying arachnid, his pursuer's footsteps hammering in his ears.

Destiny's superior strength proved a disadvantage this time, for, with a lot less mass to move, and fuelled by adrenalin, Angel was faster at a lower metabolic cost. His sister lagged and gassed out quickly, allowing him to slip into a broom cupboard unseen.

'Angel!' he heard her shout, panting.

Angel tried not to breathe.

'Angel! Oo?'

He closed his eyes—a hare-brained attempt at invisibility.

'Oo?'

She was closer.

'Oooo?'

Careful not to disturb the contents of the cupboard and availing himself of the light coming through the edges of the door, Angel looked around to see if he could burrow himself deeper, but no depth was available. Behind him were brooms and mops; to the sides were shelves with cleaning products. His only option was to move the buckets and bottles of bleach out of the bottom shelf, squeeze under it, and line-up the bleach in front of him; but space to perform the operation was very limited, so he had to move with extreme slowness and deliberation.

'Oooooo?'

Closer still.

Angel worked with precision and celerity, clearing the shelf within seconds. The problem then became how to crawl under the narrow space without knocking things.

'Angel! Ooooooooooo?'

She was now maybe three metres away—within sight of the cupboard.

He rubbed his head, squeezing his brain for a solution.

Then, unexpectedly, Destiny's voice grew fainter.

'Oooooo?'

He waited impatiently; this could be his chance!

'Oooooo?'

Destiny had moved away far enough for him to attempt a high-risk manoeuvre. He opened the cupboard, slid under the shelf feet first, and, with his hand, pulled the door closed. With equal speed, he lined the cleaning products he'd moved earlier all around him, hiding himself from view.

Then he waited.

And waited.

And waited.

There were no more 'oooooos', which was suspicious.

But no matter, he was willing to stay there for the next seven hours, if that's what it took.

He waited.

And waited.

And waited.

There was only silence.

The floor was cold and granular. His arms and shoulders began to hurt.

Yet he waited.

He closed his eyes. Maybe, if he slept, time would pass quickly, and he could avoid hearing things that would make explaining his vanishment more difficult.

Perhaps another minute passed. Or two.

Then, abruptly, the door was yanked open, flooding the cupboard with light.

'Aha!' exclaimed his sister, before adding a baffled, 'Oh.'

Nevertheless, she didn't walk away. She stood still. He heard her breathing.

Next, her trainer intruded, opening a gap between the products he'd lined up for his concealment.

Once the gap was a foot wide, she burst out laughing. Loud peals reverberated above him.

Angel, all the same, didn't move, didn't make a sound.

'I *knew* you were here!'

Still, he stayed put.

'Alright, time to come out.'

Angel did not acknowledge.

'Come on. Chop chop!'

Silence.

'Alright, you've asked for it!'

Destiny kicked the remaining bottles out of the way, grabbed Angel's wrist, and pulled him out as one would a trout from a lake.

He again made to run, but this time Destiny was ready, and she thwarted him by gripping his belt.

'Ah-ah-ah-ah! You're not going anywhere, mister!'

'Destiny, please!'

His baby sister closed the cupboard with her other hand, and, carrying him like a suitcase, transported him upstairs. Angel tried to cling on to steps, wall mouldings, and columns, but his grip being like melted butter, his effort offered no impediment.

Destiny released him in the bathroom. The second he hit the floor, Angel made to run again, yet one more time his sister grabbed him, preventing escape. Angel struggled in a panic, but the appearance of his father in the corridor, directly outside the bathroom, quelled his rebellion. Although his father took no notice because absorbed in a telephone conversation, his presence was sufficient.

Destiny had already brought in the chair and had the scissors and towel ready. Angel had no choice but to sit, like a condemned aristocrat in revolutionary France putting his head in the guillotine. He imagined himself arriving in the United States, being met by Madison at the airport, looking stupid, a lesser version of himself. Every fibre of his being screamed against that future.

Destiny put the towel on his shoulders.

'I can't believe the narrowness of your neck,' said Destiny, chuckling. 'I can almost wrap my fingers around it!'

Angel stared at the floor, brain buzzing with bees, nerves devoured by ants, eyes blinking like a strobe light, stomach in nauseous ebullition.

Destiny put her face in front of his and, placing her fist just below her eye, pouted her lower lip, steepled her eyebrows, and said in a high falsetto, 'Waaah waaah waaah.'

He frowned and looked away.

'Alright,' she said, grabbing a comb and turning on the tap. 'Here we go.'

Except—no water flowed.

Destiny turned the cold water valve all the way open, then did the same with the hot. Nothing. She checked under the sink, to see that the stop valve wasn't closed. Open.

'Argh, I forgot mum said the groundkeeper would have to shut a pipe this afternoon.'

Angel blinked, hopeful.

'Well, Angel, it seems you've got a last-minute reprieve. The water's been cut off.'

Angel jumped up like a spring and went back to his room.

However, a few minutes later, Destiny was again at his door.

'Mum said to use bottled water,' she grinned, holding up a bottle of Perrier.

'No!'

'Sorry, Angel. You know mum.'

'B-B-But that's sparkling.'

'There is no still water left and she said to use sparkling.'

Chapter CXVI

'It's an improvement, but still not good,' declared Victoria after Angel sat down at the table.

'I don't know how to cut hair,' said Destiny.

His father suppressed a smile.

Destiny had simply taken five inches off all around, leaving him with a bob ending mid cheek—a similar length to Bernini's, but Angel's hair was too straight to achieve the desired effect, so it looked stupid, no matter how he brushed it or what products he used. Not even Lope de Vega or Edmund Spenser, in lieu of Salvator Rosa or a young Shakespeare, but Willy Wonka in Tim Burton's *Charlie and the Chocolate Factory*.

Angel sulked, head down over his plate.

'Well, maybe use the clippers next time,' said his mother. 'A manly haircut.'

Lunch was fried hake with courgette fritters and 'a good salad'. Destiny and his father had double helpings of the fish. Angel managed only a few leaves of rocket, his mind filled with Madison and O'Hare.

'Eat, Angel. You're going to disappear,' said Destiny.

Angel brooded and said nothing.

'At this rate,' she added, 'we're gonna have to attach a string to your ankle when we go out, in case the wind blows you away!'

He stared at his salad, hypnotised by the leaves, the latter becoming a green abyss filled with snakes.

Destiny kept teasing. 'Do you think you'll be able to fit that tomato seed in your stomach?'

'Destiny, enough!' said Victoria.

'Sorry, mum.'

'Angel,' said his mother, 'after lunch, you, your father, and I are going to sit down and have a conversation.'

His head jumped up, eyes bulging. 'Oh . . . really?' The ants got marching again.

'Yes.'

'W-W-What about?'

'The way forward.'

Angel knew what that meant, so he said no more.

This was it.

They were going to tell him.

Nausea clamped his stomach shut. Angel's knees started bouncing and, inflating his cheeks, he released the air slowly.

'Angel, you're vibrating,' said Destiny, grinning.

Angel stilled his knees.

But it was difficult, so he curled his toes inside his shoes as hard as he could.

He felt his head was going to explode.

When dessert came—lime pie—his stomach said no. And not just to dessert, but to anything.

'Come on, have a slice,' said Victoria.

'I'm . . . I'm . . . I'm not hungry,' he said, shaking his head and waving off the slice.

'You need to eat.'

'I-I-I'm just not hungry,' he moaned.

'You have to try.'

'I . . . er . . .'

'Here,' said his mother, putting the slice on his plate. 'You eat whatever you can. But make an effort. You're too skinny.'

Angel stared at the lime pie on his plate. Sensing his father's eyes on him, he cut off a tiny piece, literally three millimetres a side, no crust, and put it in his mouth. It dissolved, but even that felt like too much food.

After they'd finished eating and cleaned up, Victoria said to her son: 'Let's go to the drawing room.'

Heart thumping, hands freezing, respiration shallow, chest butterfly-filled, head a pressure cooker, Angel took a seat at the edge of a sofa, his mother in an armchair facing him, and, a few minutes later, his father in another armchair, also facing him. His father's face was expressionless, as always, but nonetheless savagely stern. Victoria sat with her legs together and her back straight. His father like a monarch on his throne.

Despite the daylight coming in through the windows, the wood-panelled room was gloomy—a cold cavern. The latticed casement windows were too small and the furnishings too dark. The drawing room was only welcoming in the evenings, and even then only when the inglenook's log burner was lit. During the day it was best avoided.

Victoria spoke first. 'Angel, your father and I are of the opinion that you're not benefitting from being at university.'

Angel's eyebrows steepled and he made to speak, but Victoria carried on before he could.

'So we have decided to withdraw you and find you a job locally.'

Angel started, 'No! Please—'

'Meanwhile, I'll take you down to London tomorrow so you can gather your belongings while I deal with the university.'

Angel held out his hands, as if trying to stop an on-coming train. 'No no no, please, no—'

'Your father knows people in the council who can help find you a position quickly, so you won't have to go via the Job Centre.'

'Please, no! Please! I'm doing really well, I promise!'

Victoria glanced briefly at her husband. 'Professor Mastropasqua told your father you're sleeping through your classes.'

'B-B-But the term's only just started. Please! No! Please!'

His father's visage remained ostensibly unchanged, but Angel sensed his displeasure and disappointment.

Victoria continued. 'So empty your suitcase and get another one ready, in case you need it.'

'No! No! Please! No! *Please!*'

'We'll be leaving at six.'

Chapter CXVII

The landing was messy, bouncing the passengers' heads. The engines then spun in reverse, sending torsos forward until the aircraft had lost sufficient speed to taxi its way to the terminal.

The terminal looked like the Jenni Murray Hall. Angel glanced down at his legs and realised, with alarm, that he was wearing blue overalls, stained with plaster. He felt his hair and it was short; his face was also clean shaven.

At the moment of disembarkation, he found the overhead compartment empty. He'd forgotten his bag at the Nero coffee shop at Manchester Airport. On the way out, he found the aircraft heaped with litter—tissues, plastic bottles, beer cans, a flip-flop, bottles of vodka, sandwich and pizza boxes, empty packets of crisps, chocolate wrappers, dirty socks, a bra, blankets, pillows, breadcrumbs galore, and what not, covering every inch of the carpet and seats. In places the rubbish reached his knees.

The terminal's interior was dilapidated, with missing ceiling panels, threadbare or ripped-out carpets, graffitied walls, broken or dark LED boxes, cracked windows fixed with brown tape, untenanted retail spaces, dead neon tubes, dirty or flaking paint, rusting metal columns and beams, letters missing from the signage. Walking ahead of him was the big American girl, who appeared to have been on his flight. Epic Eyebrows and Pink Hair were with her, scoffing down chocolate cupcakes. Chad or Brad or whatever sat at a bar, baseball cap backward, waiting for his flight, slamming back tequila shots. Chinstrap rummaged through a rubbish bin, raging at the presence of non-recyclable items; he stopped and stared at Angel, eyes ablaze.

Stormy weather shoved water into the terminal through broken skylight windows and worn-out sealant. Puddles of sooty rainwater encroached on the chequered floor tiles, along with black chewing gum dots, cigarette butts, fast food wrappers, plastic bottles and cups, empty bottles of duty-free alcohol, discarded magazines and newspapers, and dog-eared airport novels in mass market paperback.

Beard manned a passport control booth, but he didn't recognise Angel and waved him through. Angel sensed he was under an assumed identity because he was wanted for rape.

The sliding doors opened.

Madison was waiting for him.

He realised he was naked.

He used his hand to cover himself.

Madison smiled and waved at him.

She'd had a tooth pulled out. Angel knew it was to look more 'badass'. She also had many tattoos—big, dark ones—and her shorts revealed she even had them on her thighs and calves, besides her arms, shoulders, back, sternum, and breasts. She'd had a finger amputated—because Syd had asked her to do it, and he knew somehow that Madison was thinking of having her arm surgically removed.

Then he noticed her arm was already gone.

Angel woke with a start, covered in sweat.

A chill of terror ran through him, and he scrunched his eyes shut while he waited for it to fade.

He checked the time on the clock on his bedside table. It was 4:12 am.

His father, he could hear, was already up.

He'd arrived too late, he realised, thinking about his nightmare. He'd arrived too late, and Madison had already been permanently disfigured.

Then he remembered what day it was.

The first day of a future not worth living.

He thought about the university, his degree, his friends—Amelia, Alba, Jae, Vera. And most importantly, he thought about Madison.

His hands flew to his face; he pressed his fists against his eyes, crinkled his forehead, and felt his mutilated hair.

A lump grew in his throat, and Angel wept.

Chapter CXVIII

Angel put the empty suitcase down and grabbed his shoulder, steepling his eyebrows.

'What's happened?' asked Victoria, her breath forming a cloud in the morning air. She cut an elegant but imposing figure, clad in a grey tweed suit, woollen black tights, and black medium-heel pumps. Her red hair she'd put up in a tight French twist.

'I hurt my shoulder,' he said.

'The suitcase is empty, Angel.'

'It hurts.'

His mother sighed.

'Okay, hold this,' she said, handing him her handbag. It felt even heavier than the suitcase. Angel's fingers absent-mindedly felt the genuine crocodile skin.

With ease, Victoria put the two empty suitcases in the boot of her car, lining them up. She slammed the lid shut and said curtly, 'Let's go.'

Angel dragged his legs and got in the car as slowly as he possibly could.

After they got moving, Victoria said: 'You need to get your life together.'

Angel looked at her briefly but said nothing, at a loss for a reply.

Instead, he thought of Madison. Each mile they made was a mile closer to the end of his world. Just last week he'd been studying literature and working to pay for his flight; there had been a few mishaps, but things were going well. And now all of that was being snatched away on a pig-headed parental whim—because they thought he was too skinny and his hair too long and he'd taken the love of his life to a few elegant restaurants.

The lump in his throat paid him another visit.

'I really want to study literature,' he moaned.

'You can still study it if you want,' said his mother.

'But . . . y-you're pulling me out of uni.'

'That doesn't mean you can't study what you want.'

'But . . . how?'

'*That*'s why we need to withdraw you, Angel. That's exactly it.'

'W-What do you mean?'

'You can't function on your own. If you could, you'd've known that you can study in your own time.'

'But I won't get the qualifications . . .'

'You're sleeping through your classes, so you wouldn't be getting them anyway.'

'But I haven't slept through my classes!'

'That's not what your professor said.'

'I've been fully awake!'

'I can only go by what I've seen. You don't eat, you don't look after yourself, you don't remember what you've learnt in class, you don't ask for help when you need it, you don't report your phone when it's stolen, you don't tell me about it until after I've found out, you don't make good use of the money we give you, you don't have table manners, you don't behave correctly at social events, you don't read your course material . . .'

'I *do* read my course material!'

'Really? Because since you've been back I haven't found you reading *once*. Not *once*.'

'But I've had no time.'

'Of course. All the business deals keeping you so busy.'

'I've just . . . had no time.'

'Your only task this weekend was to be presentable at your father's birthday party. If you were really serious about studying literature, you would've been reading every spare moment.'

'But . . .'

'Even now, in the car. Where's your book?'

'Um . . .'

'There you go. That's why we need to withdraw you.'

Angel sulked.

'Don't worry, Angel, it's temporary. A year doing honest work will sort you out.'

'It won't . . .' he mumbled.

'Even your professor thinks it will do you good. He was quite adamant about that.'

Angel sighed and looked at the passing landscape through the side window. It was green, but sombre because of the leaden sky and the caliginous half-light.

'What? Is that it?' said his mother after a while.

'Sorry, what?'

'Is that it? You're giving up?'

'W-What do you . . . ?'

'You have no fight in you. If you were really serious about getting your way, you would've argued and done *everything* you could to prove us wrong. You would've taken responsibility for your failures, you would've said "this is what I'm going to do to correct them", and you would've taken *immediate* action—without being asked.'

'But you decided . . .'

'Even after we decided, you had many hours to prove us wrong. But what did you do? You stopped eating and went to sleep.'

'I-I-I was depressed . . .'

'You're not going to get very far in life if that's how you respond to setbacks, Angel.'

'But . . . what do you want me to do?'

'That shouldn't even be a question.'

Angel had no words.

She drove in silence through the A-roads and then down the M1, until they reached the Donnington Park services, off Junction 23a, where she made a stop to rest. The Audi she parked right at the back of the car park, between unoccupied bays, lest a careless motorist dented the doors or scratched the paint.

They walked in silence towards the building, Victoria leading the way, Angel walking with his head bowed, hair flapping nervously against his cheeks. The asphalt was wet, the sky heavy, the cars dirty, the motorists tired and ugly. Although they all had better haircuts than he. As mother and son entered, she stopped by the W. H. Smith.

'Do you want anything?' she asked.

'Um . . . a Coke?'

'Okay.'

He followed her inside and went to browse the book section. Nothing of interest. All misery memoirs, celebrity books, and thrillers. Groaning, he moved onto the magazines. Again, nothing of interest. All motorcycles, cars, home improvement, celebrity gossip, video games, and weight loss.

He gazed at the dizzying kaleidoscope of printed matter, their irrelevance notwithstanding, pondering how the professionals on the covers of most all had university degrees. The lump in his throat dwelled there for a while, convulsing, as his forehead crinkled and tears welled up in his eyes.

Since his mother was already at the checkout, he wiped the tears with his shirtsleeve and went to join her.

'Here,' she said, handing him a plastic bag with 500-millilitre bottles of mineral water and his Coke. The bottles numbered four in total, but the weight of them abruptly skewed his shoulders to the extent he nearly fell over.

As they walked out, Victoria suddenly stopped, her eye catching a newspaper headline from the stand at the entrance. Angel waited next to her and watched the exhausted motorists strolling by.

'Angel?' said his mother, her voice sharp.

'Um . . . yes?' he said, listless.

'What's the meaning of *this*?'

His mother held before him a tabloid with his university ID photograph on the front page and a headline screaming that he'd gone missing.

Chapter CXIX

Sitting with Angel at the Costa, Victoria spent the next hour on her telephone, speaking to the police, newspaper editors, journalists, and family members, or else replying to the hundreds of messages that had built up over the past two and a half hours. From the conversations, Angel, nauseous and crawling with ants, surmised that Amelia, after not hearing from him despite her repeated messages and calls, had gone to the police to report him missing and then to the papers. Amelia had also sent message requests to Destiny via her social media, but, because of the numerous creeps online, Destiny had never bothered checking them. His father hadn't seen the reports until after Victoria and Angel had left; he'd been among those telephoning and messaging her while she was driving. She had remained unaware because her phone had been in her bag, set to silent.

By the time the excitement had died down, Victoria's coffee was cold.

'I'm *very* angry with you,' she said to her son.

'I-I'm sorry, I-I-I didn't know . . .'

'And your father too.'

'Um . . .'

'This girl from uni has been trying to contact you since *Friday*, apparently.'

'Erm . . . I-I-I didn't see her messages . . .'

'What—you don't check your messages on your computer?'

'Er . . . yes, I do but . . .'

'Angel—your father is an important person. And I'm also well known. How you conduct yourself reflects on all of us, not just you.'

'Um . . . yes, but . . . I-I just didn't know . . .'

'You need to take responsibility. This happened because of you.'

'I was feeling sick . . .'

'You took a train even though you were sick. You went shopping even though you were sick. You attended a formal dinner even though you were sick. Sending a message would have taken less effort than any of those things.'

'I . . . er . . . it just slipped my mind . . .'

'Angel—we are in the *papers* this morning. *Think!*'

'I'm . . . I'm really sorry . . .'

'Your father's right. You need a good year of manual labour. Maybe two.'

Angel rubbed his forehead. The ants sped up. His stomach somersaulted some more.

A man of thirty, well dressed, muscular under his suit, with sculpted features and not a hair out of place, approached their table, holding a copy of Victoria's *Social History of the Penny Dreadful*.

'Excuse me madam, would you sign my copy of your book?' he said.

'Certainly,' said the author, grabbing the book but ignoring the pen that was offered. Instead, she took out her Montblanc fountain pen out of her bag. 'What name?'

'Luke,' said the man.

Victoria personalised and signed the book.

Angel observed the man's oxford shoes were shined to mirror polish. He'd only ever seen his father and former servicemen achieve such level of perfection.

'Thank you, madam. Have a good day,' said the reader, taking back his book and leaving.

'You see that young man?' said Victoria.

'Er . . . yes?'

'Take note.'

Angel looked down into this freezing coffee cup and said nothing. He'd not been able to swallow a drop.

Their next stop, after losing an hour to congestion, was the Welcome Break at Newport Pagnell. They sat at Starbucks. Victoria had a café latte and Angel a cappuccino. Both ordered BLTs. Angel was unable to sip or bite, let alone chew or swallow, anything at all. His mother's phone had calmed down, but her lock screen kept piling up alerts.

'It just occurred to me that you shouldn't be out here without money,' said Victoria, grabbing her handbag.

Angel watched his mother get a fifty pound note out of her ostrich leather purse.

'Here,' she said, giving it to him. 'In case of an emergency.'

Angel took the note and, folding it in half twice, put it in his jeans' front pocket.

'Best to put it in your wallet.'

'Er . . . I . . .'

'Don't tell me you left it at home.'

'Um . . . no . . . um . . . I, mean, yes . . .'

'What happened to your wallet?'

'Er . . . um . . .' Angel looked down. The ants crawled, his stomach cramped.

'Angel—what happened?'

'Um . . . I-I don't have it anymore. I was mugged at the train station.'

Victoria sighed, looking at the ceiling, her lips thin. After a moment, she glared at Angel and said, 'You told me it was only your phone that got stolen.'

'Th-They took my wallet first.'

'In London or in York?'

'Er . . . in York.'

'And you only tell me now?'

'Um . . . I'm sorry . . . it slipped my mind . . .'

'It slipped your mind.'

Silence.

'Did you report it to the police?' she asked.

'Um . . . no . . . er . . . they wouldn't answer the door at the station.'

'Did you call the bank to cancel your debit card?'

'Er . . . no . . . my phone was stolen, so . . .'

'You should have told me and called from home *the moment you got in.*'

'Um . . . I . . . was feeling sick.'

Resting her elbows on the table, Victoria held her forehead with her fingertips, and, taking a deep breath, stared at her coffee for a few seconds. Angel felt the ants marching as if electrified, his bowels loosening, his head and neck building up with pressure. Victoria then put her hands on the tabletop and, with tight lips and looking daggers at him, said, 'Angel—what is *wrong* with you?'

Chapter CXX

They pulled into the university car park just before lunch time.

He'd only missed one canteen shift and one class, Angel thought. He could still pick up from where he'd left off, but his parents' minds were set in reinforced concrete. The ants had not ceased marching, nor had his stomach settled, nor his bowels stopped boiling, burning, or cramping.

'That's Mastropasqua car,' said Angel, pointing at the black Rolls-Royce parked in the row in front.

Silence.

'That's Mastropasqua's car,' he repeated.

Silence.

His mother was typing on her phone.

'That's Mastropasqua's car,' he said, yet again.

'I heard you.'

'H-How does father know him?'

'They went to university together.'

'Um . . . father seemed glad to see him at the party.'

'They hadn't seen each other in a long time.'

Victoria finished typing on her phone and turned to Angel, business-like.

'Okay. We'll go to the laundrette first. Then to the Student Support Adviser. Then to the dorm to clear your stuff out.'

The lump in his throat waltzed in.

'I really want to study literature,' he pleaded with steepled eyebrows.

'What for?'

'Um . . . to be a writer.'

'Writing what?'

Angel scratched his temple, 'Um . . . literary novels . . . poetry . . . plays.'

'You need life experience to do that.'

'Yes, b-b-but Bret Easton Ellis wrote two novels while at uni. And they were made into films . . . s-so I-I already have some life experience.'

'You're six months from graduation. Have you written two novels?'

'Um . . .' Angel rubbed his forehead. His knees started bouncing, but he stilled them. 'Um . . . um . . . I've written poems.'

'Do you have enough for a volume?'

'Er . . . no, not yet.'

'Have you been learning about querying an agent?'

'N-No, not yet.'

'So what's your plan?'

'I . . . er . . . I will keep writing and find an agent.'

'Find an agent how?'

'Google?'

'You're not ready, Angel.'

'But I am!'

'Did you call the bank to cancel your card?'

'No, b-but you did, so . . .'

'Exactly. I had to do it. You could have borrowed my phone to do it yourself.'

'B-But why? If you were . . .'

'Because it would've shown me you're willing to take responsibility.'

'Oh . . .' Angel looked down.

He swallowed saliva, close to vomiting.

'You can stop this at any point, Angel. You're in control, not me or your father or anyone else.'

Angel frowned, confused. 'But . . . you're withdrawing me . . .'

'You still have forty-five minutes to turn things around. Get yourself together, show me you can be trusted, and I'll call your father and go home.'

'Um . . .' Angel's knees started bouncing again. He rubbed his forehead as if on fast forward.

Victoria waited, watching him.

'Um . . .'

'Make a decision,' urged his mother.

'Um . . . um . . .'

Ten seconds passed.

Victoria sighed, and this time it was she who dropped her head, momentarily dispirited.

'Come on. Let's go to the laundrette,' she said, getting out of the car.

Angel's eyes twitched in every direction and he stayed inside the car for a few more seconds, heart racing, then jumped out.

'Um . . .' he said, chasing his mother.

But she didn't hear him. Her heels clicked on the asphalt at a steady, inexorable pace.

When he'd caught up with her, she said, 'Which way is the laundrette?'

'Um . . . that way,' he replied, pointing in its general direction.

They walked for five minutes in silence until their destination came into view.

'T-There. It's that one,' said Angel, pointing ahead.

Just before they entered, Angel, touched his mother's elbow to get her attention.

'Um . . . c-c-can I talk?'

She stopped. 'Angel—again, that shouldn't even be a question.'

'Oh . . . b-but why not?'

'Because if you want to take charge of your life, you just do. You don't ask for permission. You do it.'

'Um . . .'

'"*I'll* do the talking", is what you should've said.'

'Oh, okay. I-I'll do the talking.'

'After you,' said Victoria, stepping aside and gesturing with her hand for him to enter the shop first.

Once they were both inside, Angel stood by the entrance, looking around. The laundrette was nearly deserted, except for two depressed and bored individuals, one, a woman in a hijab, another a Chinese student.

'Okay. What now?'

'Um . . .'

Victoria waited, watching him.

'Um . . . there's no one around.'

'So what do we do?'

'Um . . . um . . . I-I d-don't know.'

'Is there an attendant?'

'Um . . .'

'Is there an office in the back?'

'Um . . . I-I-I've never seen one.'

'So what do we do?'

'Um . . .' Angel rubbed his forehead.

Victoria waited and watched his face.

'How do we find out if there is one?'

'Um . . . have a look?'

'Okay.'

Silence.

'Ah, okay! L-Let's have a look.'

As if shackled to a ball and chain, Angel dragged himself towards the back of the shop. The back office became visible; there was no way his mother would not see it. No choice but to go in.

'H-Hello?' he squeaked, poking his head in and knocking on the open door with his tiny knuckle, so lightly that it could only be heard an inch from the point of impact.

The attendant, who'd been at his desk going over paperwork, noticed Victoria and said, 'Yes?'

Angel scratched his temple. 'Um . . . er . . . um . . .'

Victoria stood behind him, silent.

'Um . . . er . . . ah . . . um . . .'

'Yes?' repeated the attendant, his gaze alternating between Angel and Victoria.

'Er . . . I . . . er . . .'

Angel could say no more. His mouth worked without sounds.

The attendant now addressed Victoria, 'How can I help?'

'Tell him, Angel,' she said.

'Er . . .'

But Angel's brain had completely short-circuited, and he'd forgotten every word in the English language.

Both Victoria and the attendant waited for a few more moments, with nothing forthcoming from Angel. Finally, the situation becoming awkward, Victoria took charge.

'My son tells me there was an incident here on Friday the twenty-seventh of September. I'd like to review the CCTV footage.'

'Ah, yes, I remember. Your son was here two weeks ago. No problem.'

Victoria looked askance at Angel, but Angel looked down. His stomach backflipped.

The attendant went to his computer and began navigating menus. He said, while doing it, 'We keep the video for thirty days, so it should all be there. What time?'

'What time, Angel?' said Victoria.

'Um . . . evening . . . um . . . seven?'

'Let's do seven till ten,' said Victoria to the attendant.

The latter fast-forwarded the video from the point requested. 'Tell me when to stop.'

Chapter CXXI

'I-I'll speak to the Student Support Advisor,' said Angel, trying to catch up with his mother.

'Too late for that,' she said, curtly.

Victoria's heels clicked metronomically, faster than before.

'Unbelievable,' she muttered, between her teeth. 'Clothes all over the street.'

'I-I-I'm sorry. I'm really sorry,' he pleaded, for the twenty-third time. 'I was embarrassed . . . I was embarrassed.'

His mother said nothing.

Her eyes were wide, her lips were thin. His window had closed.

He kept wiping the tears streaming out of his eyes with his hands or his shirtsleeve.

They entered the university gardens and headed for

the main building. The lush lawns were now strewn with soggy, brown leaves; the trees clawed at the grey above, the atmosphere not of learning and free inquiry, but of depression, finality, and loss. Victoria knew where to go; Angel's input was superfluous. He walked with his head low, hair flapping stupidly on his cheeks.

'Angel!?'

He turned towards the female voice.

Amelia.

They had reached a crossing in the footpath at the same time, and she stood at ten o'clock, staring at him, gaping, wide-eyed. She wore black jeans and jumper, and a three-quarter suede jacket that flared out from the waist. Alba stood next to her, similarly flabbergasted.

Both Angel and Victoria stopped.

'Angel! You're alive!' screamed Amelia, overcome with joy and relief, as she ran to embrace him.

She enveloped him so tightly that for a moment Angel could not breathe. He felt her enormous bosom unselfconsciously pressed against him.

Victoria watched the scene, mildly perplexed.

As soon as Amelia stepped back, Angel felt the impact of an object against his cheek, followed by a burning sensation.

Through tearful eyes, he saw Alba's face staring angrily at him.

'Do you have any idea of how much *grief* you've put her through?' she shouted, pointing at Amelia.

Amelia gently pulled her back.

'I beg your pardon! Who do you think you are, slapping my son like that!' snapped his mother.

'I'm sorry, madam, but if you knew what he's put her through, you'd be asking me to slap him harder!' shot back Alba.

Victoria, stumped for an instant, looked inquiringly at her son.

Angel, rubbing his cheek, looked at Amelia with steepled eyebrows.

Unable to hold back, Amelia once again engulfed him in her arms and pressed him firmly against her, squeezing all the air out of his lungs. He was a mere sliver between her breasts.

'I'm so happy you're safe!' she said, on the verge of tears. 'I was so worried about you!'

She covered his head and face with a rapid succession of kisses, until, becoming self-aware, she stepped back, casting a contrite glance at Victoria.

'Sorry. I couldn't help myself,' Amelia said to his mother.

'Are you the girl who went to the papers?' asked Victoria.

'Yes. I'm truly sorry, madam. I thought he'd got hurt and no one knew where he was.'

'I see.'

Amelia burst into tears. 'I didn't know his parents were prominent. Angel refused to talk about you.'

Victoria frowned at Angel.

'I found him delirious in his room the other night,' continued Amelia, her voice trembling with emotion, 'and I was nursing him back to health . . . and I worried he might have wandered out . . . and been run over . . . and was dying under a hedge where no one could see him . . .'

'I understand.'

'I'm so sorry for causing trouble, madam.'

'You did the right thing. What's your name?'

'Amelia.' She pulled a tissue out of her backpack and blew her nose, before carefully drying her tears.

'Listen, Amelia,' said Victoria. 'I appreciate your concern. Angel should have replied to your messages. You're not at fault.'

'Thank you, madam.' Amelia was still sobbing.

'I'd love to talk, but we need to get going.'

'Of course, madam. I didn't mean to delay you. But may I have a word with Angel before you go?'

'You may.'

'Angel, will I see you later?'

He rubbed his forehead. 'Um . . .'

Silence.

'Tell her, Angel,' said his mother.

Amelia looked at Victoria, worried.

'Um . . .'

His mother sighed, then said, impatiently, 'Angel's leaving.'

Amelia's jaw dropped. 'Oh? Really? Where?'

'He's leaving the university.'

'Now? But why?'

'He's not benefiting from the course.'

'Is that true, Angel? You've lost interest?'

Angel's mouth worked soundlessly. After a moment, the lump in his throat took possession, his chin trembled, and the tears flowed yet again.

'He's going to get a job up north and come back after a year. Maybe two.'

Amelia was flummoxed. 'Really?'

Angel's tongue had been eaten by a cat. He wiped away his tears.

'We're headed for Student Support now. He'll be in his room later collecting his belongings. You can visit him there in a little while if you want.'

Amelia blinked, paralysed, disbelieving. 'Okay . . .'

Angel saw that new tears had begun welling up in

her eyes. Yet, even if his throat hadn't been blocked by the lump, he wouldn't have found the words.

'Let's go, Angel,' said Victoria, taking a step forward.

This jolted him out of his paralysis. 'Um . . . um . . . I'll . . . I'll speak to you later.'

Amelia's eyebrows steepled, her lip began to wobble, a tear made its way down her cheek. Alba turned to console her.

The last thing Angel heard was Amelia bawling her eyes out behind him.

He cried too.

Chapter CXXII

After speaking to the Student Support Advisor, Victoria remained in the main building to deal with the necessary forms, since she couldn't trust Angel to fill them out correctly. The suitcases were still in his mother's car, and, since she couldn't trust him with the keys either, she'd instructed him to gather his belongings and wait for her in his now former room.

He found Amelia waiting for him seated on a bench outside the dorm.

'Hello,' he mumbled.

'Hello, Angel.' She stood, eager.

'I-I have to go and pack my stuff . . .'

'I'll come with you.'

'Er . . . thank you.'

'I'll keep an eye out too.'

'Um . . . keep an eye out?'

'For Johannes. He's back on campus.'

His voice rose an octave. 'Oh, really?'

'He's been reinstated. Cleared of all charges.'

'Oh . . .' Angel's irises darted like balls on a squash court. 'H-H-Have you spoken to him?'

'He's very angry with you. He said you betrayed him and that he's going to make you pay.'

'Oh . . . erm . . .'

'He's been looking for you all morning.'

'Um . . .'

'Don't worry, Angel. I'll always protect you.' She offered him a wan smile.

Angel looked all around him, eyes like Frisbees.

'It's okay,' she added, flexing her bicep, 'I'm strong.'

Angel dipped his chin and quickened his pace.

'Also, Saïd says you owe him fifty pounds.'

'Fifty!'

'But don't worry, I saw him leave before you arrived. He's not in his room.'

Angel sighed, relieved. 'Okay.'

When they got to his room, however, Angel found, upon inserting his hand into his pockets, that he'd left the key at his parents' house.

'Bugger!' he muttered.

Finding Angel stumped, Amelia tried the door handle. The door was unlocked.

'Oh, good!' he breathed.

But the door didn't quite yield. An obstruction limited the opening to a crack. Amelia pushed, then leaned into it, using her weight to widen the crack.

'Oh, my goodness!' she said, once she could see inside.

She got the door open enough for her to get through and went in, stepping over the heaps of rubbish.

Angel followed, eyebrows levitating.

Chapter CXXII

Even though he expected the room to be filthy, it seemed that Josh or Todd or whatever had gone berserk partying while he was gone, and coming from his parents' spotless house, the present level of squalor boggled the mind. The rubbish was up to their knees in places. Litter covered Angel's bed, together with footprints, stains, crumbs, and vomit on Amelia's sheets, which had also been ripped and burnt with cigarettes. Every surface had been colonised by empty glass bottles or cans—even Angel's laptop and books. Holes had appeared in the plasterboard walls. The curtains were also partially burnt. Angel's chair had lost its back. The chest of drawers was in the middle of the room, with the top drawer open and overflowing with rubbish, the others scattered on the floor. Yet, none of this was worse than the stench of decomposing food, mould, stale cigarettes, alcohol, and sex.

Both Angel and Amelia stood amidst the chaos, unsure of where to begin. Amelia covered her nose with a manicured hand.

Eventually, Angel used his foot to push the rubbish away from his desk, so he could gain access. The noise triggered a groan from Todd or whatever's side of the room.

Angel and Amelia turned to it and saw movement in the roommate's bed. A girl's dishevelled head appeared from under a blanket, then Brad or whatever's, both blinking.

'Dude,' croaked the American, giving Angel a thumbs up, before going back to sleep. The girl did likewise, thumbs-up and all.

Hand on his head and mouth flapping like a fish out of water, Angel saw Amelia gaping at the slumbering lovebirds, her palms on the sides of her face.

He began to gather his books from all over the floor, each and every one of them damaged in some way. If they worked quickly, it occurred to him, perhaps they'd be done before his mother made it there and they could meet her in the corridor, or outside the building, thus preventing her from seeing the room. But the task proved insurmountable, and he slowed down as despair set in. Meanwhile, Amelia moved the bottles and cans that were on and around Angel's laptop to wherever else she could fit them on the roommate's side.

'Angel, I'm very surprised by your sudden decision to leave,' said Amelia.

'Um . . . I don't want to leave.'

'You don't? But then why are you?'

'M-My parents think I'm doing badly.'

'Oh, Angel. So they're forcing you to withdraw?'

He said nothing. The lump in his throat returned.

'Angel, talk to me. What's happened?'

He stopped gathering books and stood with his head bowed, covering his face with his hands.

She caressed his back and prompted him gently. 'Talk to me. You can trust me.'

He looked away, his eyes haunted, tearful.

At this point, they heard the metronomic thumping of heels approaching from the corridor. Victoria appeared at the door seconds later, an empty suitcase in each hand.

'What is this?' she said, her eyes bulging under a frown.

She dropped the suitcases.

Angel and Amelia froze in terror as they observed Victoria slowly inhale as storm clouds gathered over her brow.

'Angel—Don't tell me this is how you've been living!'

'Er . . . no . . . er . . . it's my—'

Chad or whatever, roused by Victoria's shouting, poked his head from under the blanket again.

'Hey, I'm trying to sleep,' he croaked to Angel.

'And who are you?' demanded Victoria.

'I'm his roommate,' said Josh, indignant. 'Who are you?'

'I'm Angel's *mother!*'

'Well, keep it down, lady. We're trying to sleep.'

She gasped. 'How *dare* you speak to me like that!'

'Aw, whatever,' said Todd, dropping his head back onto the pillow.

But Victoria, not one to be trifled with, stepped over the rubbish to reach the roommate's bed, and yanked the blankets off him and the girl. The action exposed the lovebird's nudity.

'Eugh!' Victoria grimaced.

'What the fuck?' said the American, sitting up.

The girl, startled, followed suit, covering her breasts.

'Get dressed and get *out* of here! The two of you. I need to speak to my *son*,' yelled Victoria, pointing at the door with an outstretched arm.

Brad or whatever obviously thought it best not to challenge the raging lioness. Both he and his one-night stand got moving in a hurry. Except that, amid all the rubbish, they could not find their clothes, least of all the girl, so rather than delay they left in starkers.

Chapter CXXIII

Victoria turned to Angel, while Amelia watched the unfolding scene, hands again on the sides of her head.

'What's been going on here?' his mother demanded.

'Er . . . nothing . . . er . . .'

'You call this nothing? Look at this mess!'

'It's not me . . . it's . . .' he whined, pointing weakly at the door.

Amelia deemed it prudent to remove herself from the scene. Putting Angel's books aside, she pulled her sheets off his bed, rolled them up, and headed for the door.

Victoria addressed her before she managed to exit.

'Where are you going with those sheets?'

'Sorry, madam. They're mine.'

Victoria turned to Angel. 'Why have you been sleeping on her sheets?'

'Um . . . I-I-I lost mine.'

A fist on her hip, his mother tilted her head back and stared at the ceiling, releasing a long sigh, before dipping her chin and pinching the bridge of her nose.

'See you later, Angel. Please message,' said Amelia, softly, before swiftly slipping out.

'And is that how you treat other people's belongings?' shouted Victoria.

'N-N-No . . . um . . . she put them on on Friday . . . she put them on on Friday . . .'

'This is *not* how we raised you!'

'But she put them on on Friday, just before I left! I promise!'

'And that there? Is that your laptop?'

'Um . . . yes, but . . .'

His mother stomped towards it, picked it up by the sides with her fingertips, and tilted it to show Angel the lid. A used condom fell off in the process. What was once shiny silver was now brown and covered with rings, muddy gloop, ash, and cigarette burns.

'Look at the state of this computer! An absolute *disgrace!*'

'It wasn't me . . . it was . . .'

'Angel, my friend!'

Angel and Victoria turned. Saïd was at the door, smiling.

'You owe me fifty pounds,' he said.

Victoria glanced at Angel.

'Um . . . I-I-I thought it was twenty . . .'

'Twenty-five on Friday. You defaulted and didn't refinance. There's penalty, so today it's fifty.'

'What are you talking about?' demanded Victoria.

'Are you his mother?'

'Who are you?'

'I'm Saïd. I study here.' He smiled. 'Angel and I are good friends. Are you his mother?'

'I'm speaking to my son, so you will leave.'

'No problem. But Angel owes me fifty pounds.'

'What part of *leave* did you not understand?'

Saïd put his hands up. 'Okay, okay. No problem, madam. I come back later.'

The creditor disappeared into his room.

Victoria turned back to Angel. 'You know what? Forget it. Take the computer and leave everything else here. We're going home.'

'B-B-But my books!'

'They're filthy. I don't want them in my house.'

Angel dared not further infuriate his mother by arguing, even though he wanted to take at least *The Faerie Queene* and the Proust volumes. He took the laptop from her, examined the ruined top, and, after wiping it briefly with a tissue, held it in his hand the way he would have held a book, ready to go when Victoria gave the sign.

This she did immediately, eager to leave that cesspit or vandalism.

Part of him was relieved they weren't lingering—with luck, he'd give Johannes the slip! Encountering him remained a distinct possibility, since the lunch hour had ended and the mountainous Swede, fully nourished and energised, would be at large.

As they made their way back to the car park, Victoria said, 'Your father is going to be *furious* when he finds out what I've seen.'

'Um . . . a-a-are you going to tell him?' he said, twitching like a bird.

'I won't volunteer, but if he asks, and most likely he will, I will tell him. We do not *lie* in this family.'

'B-B-But it was my roommate . . . he's the messy one . . . I . . .'

Halting, his mother turned to face him. 'Angel—*stop*. If your room was like that, it's because *you chose* to live like that. That mess didn't appear over the weekend. If you were unhappy with it, then you would have said something.'

'But I was unhappy! It's just that . . .'

'Then you *should* have said something.'

'But—'

'But you didn't. And instead you *chose* to live like that. So that room accurately reflects *you*.'

'Yes, but . . .'

'And it in turn reflects badly on *me* and your *father*.'

Victoria resumed marching, fast, before Angel could blurt another 'but'. He tried to keep up.

When they reached the Audi, they found the driver's door had been blocked by a black Hummer H1, whose width rudely hogged part of Victoria's parking bay.

'Oh, for *goodness sake!*' hissed Victoria through her teeth. 'Angel, go and find the parking attendant.'

Angel didn't move; instead, he scanned the surroundings searching the parking attendant's hut.

'Go, Angel! Go! I haven't got all day!'

'Sorry . . . sorry!' he said, leaping into action.

About five minutes later, he returned with the attendant, Ali.

Victoria and the attendant exchanged minimum pleasantries, following which Ali examined the situation and got on his walkie talkie. After some back and forth with whomever was at the other end, Ali said:

'The owner is coming now.'

'Good,' said Victoria, one fist on her hip, her other hand holding her phone.

Fifteen minutes later, Angel saw Professor Hynd approaching.

'I'm so sorry, madam,' she said, upon joining the group. 'These bays are so skinny, and the car park was chocka when I got here.'

'I see.'

The professor made to climb into her Hummer but stopped before disappearing behind its huge bulk. 'Wait . . . are you the author of *The Social History of the Penny Dreadful*?'

'Yes.'

'Hi, I'm George Hynd, I teach 17th-Century Literature here.'

'Hello.' Victoria ignored Hynd's extended hand.

'Fascinating book.' Hynd put her hand down.

'Thank you.'

'Although I think it's very male-centric. Too many men. And it needs more LGBT rep. But still fascinating.'

'Okay.'

Professor Hynd hesitated for a moment, then, seeing in Victoria a steep rampart, decided to just do what she'd been summoned to do. She reversed the Hummer noisily and with brusque manoeuvres.

Victoria got into her car. Angel walked around to the passenger side to do the same.

But just as he was about to open the door, he heard his name bellowed by an ogrish voice in the distance. He turned towards the sound.

He saw Johannes at the edge of the carpark, marching quickly towards him.

As if touched by a high-voltage electrical wire, Angel jerked the door open and got in the car. Except his impatience made him clumsy and he dropped his laptop, which clattered on the asphalt.

'ANGEL!!!' he heard, a bit closer now.

He glanced through the windscreen and saw Johannes, beet-faced with rage, approaching at a trot.

Angel grabbed the laptop and whipped himself back inside the car, slamming and locking the door.

'Don't slam the door, Angel!' snapped his mother.

'Sorry sorry!' he said, yanking the seatbelt, repeatedly causing it to lock.

'*Slowly*, pull it *slowly*,' said his mother.

Angel relaxed his arm for long enough to be able to pull the seatbelt and secure it.

Johannes was now weaving his corpulence between the rows of cars in front.

Victoria turned the ignition.

Angel saw Ali walking slowly towards Johannes, having taken notice of him.

The car began reversing out of the bay, but stopped when Victoria saw the strongman shoving his way past Ali and towards her car.

Angel, holding the laptop on his knees, lowered his head, and stared intently at the brown markings on the lid, pretending Johannes wasn't there.

'ANGEL!!!'

Victoria followed Johannes with her frowning gaze as the bearded Swede made it to Angel's window and filled it with his face.

'ANGEL!!!'

Angel attempted to retract his head inside his collar, turtlelike, all along avoiding eye-contact with his former friend.

To get his attention, Johannes slammed the window with his fist.

This proving intolerable to Victoria, she unlocked the doors and exploded out of the car.

'Oi! Who do you think you are hitting my car!'

Ali attempted to grab the snarling Swede, but the latter shook him off with ease, sending him to the ground.

Victoria walked around the front of the car towards Johannes, who opened the door on Angel's side before Angel could depress the lock button.

'Oi, I said! Stop right now!' shouted Victoria.

Johannes turned towards Angel's mother and, taken aback by her ire, faltered for a moment. She went up to him and jabbed him in the chest:

'I said *stop*'—jab—'*right*'—jab—'*now!*'

Ali got up and interposed himself between Victoria and the giant.

Angel used this opportunity to close the door and depress the lock button—although in his panic he missed several times. Safely behind the glass, he observed his mother shouting at Johannes, who, stunned out of his rage, took a step back, having thought better of carrying down the path he'd been. His manner changed and, with his hands, made a conciliatory gesture before taking another step back.

With one hand in the air up against Johannes, Ali gestured with his other for Victoria to get back in her car and leave.

'Go. Just go, madam. I'll deal with this,' he said.

Victoria stared Johannes down for a second and, via Ali, rebuked the university for tolerating unacceptable behaviour. She demanded the thug be charged and expelled.

Ali said conciliatory things Angel was unable to discern amidst the thumping in his head, and, with further conciliatory gestures, persuaded Victoria to get going.

'This university's a *disgrace*!' she said, as she got back in the car.

Then, before reversing further, she turned to Angel and added, 'And *you*—we're going to have a *long* conversation with your father when we get home.'

CHAPTER CXXIV

Getting out of London took an hour, but they made rapid progress on the way north, since the day's events had loaded tension on Victoria's foot and removed any appetite for rest at service areas. Angel vaguely noticed they were passing everyone, but his head was full of the university, his degree, Madison, Amelia, Madison, Johannes, Madison, Alba, Madison, Vera, Madison, Jae, Madison, Mastropasqua, Madison, O'Hare, Madison, Chad or whatever, Madison, Syd, Madison. She was as good as lost now. Everything felt heavy, bleak. He gazed at the grey above and wished he were already old, because then it wouldn't matter anymore and his life would soon be over. By the time they reached Leeds, however, the onset of rush hour ground them to a halt.

Victoria used the time to catch up with the messages that were still trickling into her phone. Angel gazed out the window, his mind far away. He imagined himself driving a classic car, maybe an old Bentley, with Madison by his side. He imagined being a lauded poet, living in Surrey, in a country manor, with Madison. He imagined taking her to the premier of his latest play in London, both elegantly attired, he with mirror-polished shoes, she glittering with jewels. He imagined flying to America to host a book launch party, possibly in New York, with Madison dressed to the nines. He imagined taking Madison to Venice and Milan, to Florence and Pisa, to Rome and the Vatican; to Paris and Strasbourg; to Munich and Cologne; to Bruges and Geneva. He imagined reading poetry to Madison in the moonlight and making her swoon and sigh. The lump in his throat sprung back to life, his nostrils clogged, his tear ducts ran and ran.

If only he'd wake up from this nightmare!

He closed his eyes and desperately yearned to find himself in the humanities library at the university, having dozed off after finishing *Oroonoko* ahead of his class. But no. When he opened them, it was all cars, lorries, and red brake lights. His mother had been too angry to even play her 80s electro-pop on the car stereo, or even classical, so his sonic universe consisted of idling diesel and petrol engines.

Had he still been in possession of his phone, he would have plugged his ears with headphones and played Chopin Nocturne Op. 72 no. 1 in E minor, Albinoni's Adagio in G Minor, Beethoven's Moonlight Sonata, and Berlioz's and Mozart's respective requiems.

Instead, he heard his mother.

'Your father's found you a job,' she declared, putting her phone down.

Angel twitched. 'Oh!'

Chapter CXXIV

'You start tomorrow morning.'

His heart accelerated; the ants got their marching orders.

'W-W-Where is it?'

'Everywhere. You'll be helping install boilers for the council.'

Chapter CXXV

Angel's heart was already thumping when they entered the drive leading up to the manor. His knees started bouncing, but he stilled them. A gremlin had tightened a belt around his lungs, constricting his breathing. The ants crawled over his nervous system. Normally pleasant, the moonlight now lent the landscape a spectral quality. The Audi's headlights cast a grim chiaroscuro of pebbles, grass, and bare branches ahead of them. Every yard closer to the house meant a moment closer to his father's face.

Before he knew it, the car had come to a halt. He twitched as he noticed his mother switching off the engine and grabbing her handbag.

It was 7 o'clock—his father would be fully awake and alert.

Victoria got out of the car without delay. Angel wanted to stay where he was. Nay, he wanted to be hundreds of miles away still, and for a split second he considered snatching the keys from his mother, stealing her car, and driving back to London, to the university, to rescind his withdrawal. But he knew he wouldn't get far: the police would stop him on the motorway, charge him for driving uninsured, and bring him back home to face his parents. Thus, in a vain last-ditch effort, he lingered.

'Come on, Angel. Don't delay. Let's go,' ordered his mother.

With the utmost lethargy he could manage, Angel . . .

pulled the lever to open the door . . .
opened it . . .
put a foot out . . .
swivelled . . .
put the other foot out . . .
stood . . .
bent down . . .
grabbed his laptop . . .
straightened up . . .
stepped aside . . .
closed the door . . .
and pushed to make sure it was properly closed . . .

He made to ask his mother whether they should get the empty suitcases out of the boot, but she'd already done it. Next, he considered offering to carry them to the house, but she'd already slammed the lid shut and begun carrying said suitcases herself. Finally, he checked his shoelaces hoping they'd be untied and, when he found them both tied, thought of untying and re-tying them several times, but by then his mother had already opened the service door and called for him to hurry up.

Angel entered the house, the presence of his father inside like radiation—invisible, deadly. He heard his mother slam the door behind him. The empty suitcases boomed like orchestral timpani when she put them down on the stone floor. Too quickly for his liking, his mother rushed past him and vociferated their arrival. And it didn't end there: she continued to stride deeper into the house, her heels echoing cavernously, making their presence known, stirring the invisible giant within its walls. They found Destiny in the kitchen, clad in black tights and a hoodie, closing the lid of her steel bottle, containing her intra-workout drink. The lid emitted a piercing squeak. Destiny greeted them stridulously and she and their mother exchanged clamorous dialogue, their voices reverberating through even the most remote corners of the manor. Angel tried to gulp some air, but his constricted lungs barely allowed in a few millilitres at a time. At last, he heard the ominous footsteps of his father descending the stairs, with slow deliberation, each leg a piledriver, each footstep an earthquake, shaking the walls, rattling the windows, swinging the lamps from the ceilings. To Angel it felt as if an enormous spherical boulder were rolling inexorably in his direction, unstoppable despite its low velocity because of its colossal momentum. He'd once heard, in relation to the power of momentum, his parents speak of a train crash that occurred when they were young, which caused prodigious wreckage, even though one train was standing still and the other barely crawling along the track.

His father appeared.

His gold cufflinks, depicting Alexander the Great, glinted under the harsh LED lights. He'd taken off his jacket and tie, but not yet changed out of his suit, meaning he'd arrived home not long ago. Meaning, he'd not had time to relax from the day's business. Meaning, he'd still be in skull-crushing mode.

He joined them in the kitchen.

Victoria greeted him and her husband silently reciprocated.

Then they both turned to look at Angel.

'See you later,' said Destiny, walking past them on her way out.

'See you later,' said their mother.

Their father didn't need to say anything; it was understood.

Angel heard Destiny slam the service door shut in the distance.

He was now alone.

'Hand me your computer,' said his father, the latter's hooded eyes in shadow under a heavy brow, lending his granitic visage a skull-like appearance.

Angel spasmed, hesitated, then complied.

His father examined the laptop, flipping it back and forth with his veinous, hairy hands. Despite his father's lack of expression, Angel could somehow sense his mounting rage and disappointment. His father had headphones, Walkmans, and photographic cameras bought in the 1980s that were still as good as new; he still had the instruction manuals and the original boxes. Victoria joined her husband in the examination, her lips a line, her head shaking sporadically as she mentally catalogued and interpreted each form of damage. This done, Angel's father put the laptop on the counter and opened it to check that it still worked. Angel noticed with terror that spilled liquid, possibly Coca-Cola, had during his absence entered the keyboard and dried into a gloop, causing some of the keys to stick, and some not to work at all.

'Why is your computer damaged?' asked his father, finally.

Angel quivered as he attempted to draw even a bit of air into his lungs. He swallowed.

'Um . . .' he said, in an ultrasonic voice.

Both his parents stared in suffocating silence, waiting for his answer.

'Um . . . it . . . it . . .'

Silence.

'He blames his roommate,' said Victoria.

'Um . . . yes! He's . . . he's . . .'

Silence.

Angel lost his voice.

For the next twenty or so seconds, he tried to find it. But no matter where he searched in his throat, amid all the constriction it was nowhere to be found.

'Answer your father.'

Angel swallowed and, moving his lips like a goldfish, searched his throat again. Yet, once more, there was no voice.

'Angel, talk to your father.'

But still, no words were forthcoming.

After another twenty seconds of this, Victoria sighed and said to her husband: 'Angel told me his roommate was the messy one. I explained to him that in that case, he should have said something. And that if he hadn't, it was his choice to live in a mess.'

'This is not just mess,' declared her husband, pointing at the computer.

Putting her fists on her hips, Victoria described everything she'd seen at the dorm. Feeling faint, Angel gripped the counter as he observed his father's visage, analysing his brow microscopically: every line, every pore, every follicle. Angel sensed the fury still growing behind the iron mask of equanimity, but no observer, except possibly Victoria, would have shared this perception.

After listening carefully to his wife's account, Angel's father remained silent for a few seconds. To Angel, whose legs had nearly deserted, each of those felt like months.

His father inhaled to speak.

To enunciate his sentence.

But Angel, unable to hold on any longer, ran to the sink, where he emptied the contents of his stomach.

All he heard, as he recovered and spat into the drain, was silence.

He lingered for as long as he felt it credible, feeling behind him the stupendous weight of his parents' disapproval, and dreading to turn around.

Yet, he had to, eventually, so when he feared that further lingering would only make things worse, he faced his makers, but with his head bowed, staring at the floor.

He heard his father inhale to speak again.

Angel braced.

'Your career placement master will collect you at six. His name is Tom.'

Chapter CXXVI

Angel's alarm clock went off at four.

Now he was waking up at the same time as his father.

He sat up in his bed, spine a curved banana, ribs a xylophone, head a wilting lily. He noticed, like the morning before and like at various times throughout the previous day, the absence of his hair curtain; when he felt his hair, the silly flaps on the sides of his cheeks confirmed once more that this alternate universe he hoped he'd only dreamt, where he was no longer at university and looked like an idiot, was *one hundred percent* real. Like a diver attempting a world record dive, his mood plunged into the abyss, ever deeper, ever darker, under ever higher pressure. The lump in his throat awoke, as did his tear ducts, which irrigated his cheeks for numerous minutes while his nose clogged up with snot. *I just wanted to be a poet,* he thought. But no, his parents' insistence on practicality, finance, and toughness had to take priority. And their irrational suspicion of Madison had to block and thwart him every step of the way. They seemed to relish the prospect of callousing his hands and blunting his intellect. Why couldn't they just let him pursue his own dreams, feel his own emotions, create his own self? Just because his vision was different, it didn't mean it was wrong! If he'd been born in a previous era, the aristocracy or the court would fund him, and he'd be allowed to pursue his muse. He glanced at the poster of Titian's *Man with a Quilted Sleeve*, believed to be a portrait of Ariosto, and asked, 'What wouldst thou have done?' Catching sight of his computer, on standby on his oak desk, reminded him of Amelia crying the day before, of Alba, of Jae, of Vera, of Johannes, of Saïd, of Brad, of Emmanuel . . . If only this was just a nightmare, and it was still Sunday and not Tuesday, and it was afternoon and not morning, and his hair was long and his next task was to pack his suitcase ahead of catching his train back to London. If only he'd wake up in his dorm room, in time for his canteen shift, for his class, for reading . . . But no: his parents would rather he install boilers, and never read, and squander his talent, and not spend money, and break up with Madison.

The lump in his throat grew painful, and the tears cascaded down his face and rained from his chin.

What greater punishment is there than life when you've lost everything that made it worth living?

To avoid encountering his father, Angel waited in his room until he heard him walk past in the corridor. His father had a gym in one of the barns—not the machines millionaire executives had in their homes, but barbells, plates, kettle bells, a pull-up bar, dip bars, kegs, an axle, a tractor tyre, heavy chains, gas tanks with a handle each soldered onto the side, a squat rack, and a bench. He'd spend an hour there before going onto the grounds for sprints, or a run, ahead of breakfast. Angel's plan was to wait until his father was in the barn, then shower, dress, and have finished breakfast, alone, before his father re-entered the house to have his with the rest of the family.

He was willing to wait in the courtyard for this Tom to arrive if it meant avoiding his father. Oil and water, father and son.

After a bite of toast, Angel hid behind the doors giving access to the basement, which were inside the house, just to the left of the service door. He'd chosen to wear jeans, a cashmere polo neck jumper, and brown suede brogues. Nestled under his arm was a hardcover copy of John Milton's *Paradise Lost*, which he intended to read during his lunch hour. Of course, that doleful link to his life as a university student kept the lump in place in his throat and tear ducts open and flowing. He imagined himself a mummy in its sarcophagus, waiting in silent darkness, undiscovered in the recondite depths of a pyramid; or as Tollund man in his peat bog, with the noose around his neck; or as an ice mummy from Sir John Franklin's lost expedition, ravaged by pneumonia, tuberculosis, lead poisoning, starvation, botulism, and scurvy.

He waited for his father to re-enter the house, which he did at quarter till six. With his ears pricked and finely attuned to every nuance of sound emanating from the kitchen, including mention of his name, Angel waited in the dank gloom, ready to leap out of concealment just before the expected knock on the door at the top of the hour.

At two minutes till, he heard a van pull into the yard. Its engine died, a door opened and slammed shut, and approaching footsteps crunched the gravel. Hoping to pre-empt the dreaded knock, Angel squirrelled out, but he wasn't quick enough and the three forceful knocks that followed jolted him like a startled cat. The knocks reverberated down the corridor, amplified by its cold walls, disemboguing in the kitchen.

With the responding voices of his family amplified by his hypersensitised ears, Angel opened the door just enough to squeeze through and stepped into the cold, dark morning. He pulled the door shut before looking at the council worker.

Tom was not quite as tall as Johannes, but he towered over him and spanned the horizon just the same. Thus, Angel was faced with a wall of man. How much Tom might weigh was for Angel incalculable, but he had legs attached to his shoulders. This Gogmagog had a neatly trimmed ginger beard, with a few flecks of grey in the chin. His face could have once been normal, but it had features that would have interested criminal anthropologists.

'Are you Angel?' he said.

His voice was friendly, which was a relief.

'Um . . . yes.'

'I'm Tom.'

Hearing footsteps approaching in the corridor, Angel cast a glance at the door behind him.

'C-C-Can we go?' he said, twitching.

'Yes, just a second,' said Tom, calmly and not moving.

Trembling, Angel took a couple of steps towards the van, disappearing behind his placement master.

He heard the door open.

Angel froze but dared not look. He stared at the ground.

Tom and his father greeted each other and exchanged a few words. Their voices being bassy and nearly inaudible, Angel, E. T.-like, stretched his neck to risk a peek. His eyes met his father's briefly, before Angel quickly pulled back behind Tom. The door then closed, and the gravel began crunching. Angel looked up to find Tom heading towards the vehicle.

'Ready, buddy?' Tom said, looking at him and jerking his head towards the van.

Angel followed him and the two climbed in.

'We'll go get some breakfast,' said Tom, 'and then we'll go do the first job.'

'Okay,' said Angel, eyes wide. The ants were running around again.

'Actually, do you want change? We're dealing with boilers and dusty attics and basements, so you might want to wear some more suitable.'

'Um . . . no . . . um . . . er . . . it's fine.'

'You sure? That's a really posh jumper. You don't want to get muck on it.'

'No . . . no . . . it's fine . . . it's fine . . . er . . .'

'An old hoodie, if you have one, and trainers, would be perfect.'

A hoodie? Trainers? The thought of going back inside the house to face his father and for sartorial degradation was unbearable. 'Um . . . um . . . I . . . I d-don't have one. I don't have one.'

Tom stared at him for a moment, then said, 'Okay . . . It's your jumper,' as he turned the ignition.

For breakfast, the council worker took Angel to a sandwich shop off the A1237.

Tom went up to the counter and the lady womaning it greeted him with a smile.

'Good morning, love.'

'Good morning.'

'What would you like today?'

'Could I have two full Englishes, a portion of chips, a bacon and egg sandwich in a baguette, three large chicken sandwiches on normal bread, two milky coffees, two Oasis orange, and a litre of Lucozade.'

'Orange or original?'

'Orange.'

'Alright. That will be thirty-five eighty-five.'

Tom paid in cash.

'Thanks love.'

The lady brought him the Lucozade and said, 'Just take a seat and I'll bring you the rest.'

Tom stepped aside and the lady turned her attention to Angel.

'And you? What would you like?'

'Um . . . c-c-could I have a cup of Earl Grey?'

The lady looked at him as if he'd just landed from Mars.

'Sorry, what, love?'

'Earl Grey?'

'We don't have Earl Grey.'

'W-W-What teas do you have?'

'Just normal tea. PG Tips.'

'Oh . . .'

Angel hesitated.

'If someone from the office catches you drinking Earl Grey, you'll get the sack,' said Tom.

'Oh . . . okay.'

'So don't do it again.'

'O-Okay.' Angel then turned to the lady. 'I-I-I'll take the tea . . .'

'Okay. That will be one pound fifty.'

Angel inserted his hand into his right-hand pocket, but he discovered, upon exploring its bottom, that the fifty pound note his mother had given him the day before was no longer there. He checked his other front pocket, then his back ones, and his front ones again.

'Um . . .'

The lady stared expectantly. 'Alright, love?'

'Um . . .' Angel steepled his eyebrows and looked around for Tom.

Tom had already taken a seat at a table and was busy checking his phone with one hand.

'Um . . . er . . .'

Angel kept checking his pockets, never finding the money.

'Um . . . Tom?' he called out, but too softly to be heard.

Tom was typing something on his phone.

'Erm . . . um . . . Tom?'

No response.

'Um . . . I'm sorry. Just a moment,' Angel said to the lady, before turning again towards Tom. 'Um . . . Tom?'

But whatever Tom was engaged with on his phone, it was truly fascinating.

'Tom?'

No response.

'Tom?'

No response.

'Tom?'

'Tom, love?' said the lady finally.

Tom reacted immediately, turning towards the till.

Angel indicated with his facial expression and repeated digging into his pockets what the problem was.

Tom got up and joined him at the counter.

'You can't pay?' he said.

'Um . . . no. I-I-I had a fifty-pound note but it must have fallen out . . .'

'No worries. I'll treat you.'

They sat facing each other on the square Formica table.

'Have you done this kind of work before?' asked Tom, before taking a sip of his coffee.

'Um . . . no.'

'What were you doing before this?'

'I . . . er . . . was at uni.' Angel bowed his head. The lump in his throat reared its own.

'What were you studying?'

'Um . . . English literature.'

'That's a bit of a change . . .'

Angel stared at his cup and said nothing, tears welling up in his eyes. He thought about the tea—how *low* he'd sunk already. He thought of suicide.

'Well, don't worry. We'll make a man out of you,' Tom chuckled.

Angel frowned and sipped his tea, keeping his head down. The tea was vile, he thought, nothing that should ever touch the tongue of a gentleman. But he hid his disgust—of the tea and of self.

'Have you read the manual from the office?'

'Um . . . no.' Angel's voice was dispirited, moribund.

'Okay, in the manual, it says that all apprentices must drink their tea with their left hand.'

Angel replied almost without interest. 'Why?'

'Because you are required to operate the tools with your right hand, and if you spill hot tea on it, you could scald yourself and not be able to do the work.'

Angel crinkled his forehead, eyes half lidded. 'Really?'

'Yes. It's one of the health and safety regulations. So you need to drink your tea with your left hand.'

Angel stared at his hands for a moment, considering their softness, now condemned, and grabbed the cup handle with his left one, feeling numb.

A second sandwich shop lady brought Tom his breakfast and he tucked in, while Angel watched, stomach already rumbling. Angel felt like Lemuel Gulliver in Brobdingnag. Yet, the literary image only intensified his despondency.

He observed that Tom drank his coffees with his right hand, but Angel cared little for the inconsistency; he assumed it was because, as the job placement master, Tom had earned the privilege.

Chapter CXXVII

Back in the van, Tom checked his phone. He chuckled at whatever he found there. Angel took it that he'd received a funny message.

Not that it mattered.

'Right. Our first job is in Tang Hall Lane,' Tom said, chuckling some more and turning the ignition.

Angel didn't respond at first, but, suddenly fearing there might be a link between the chuckling and the address, said, 'Is . . . is it a bad area?'

'No. Lovely area. But it's a good thing you're skinny.'

Angel didn't know what to make of this but neither did he care to inquire further. Instead, he listlessly watched the houses, shops, and road signs zoom by, vaulted by lead, drowned by noise. All bounced off his senses like flat pebbles on a water surface—until, that is, Tom turned into Lord Mayor Walk and drove past

York St John University. The Modernist brick, glass, and concrete building, unmissably identified with a black on white sign, broke that water surface like a boulder, to hit his tenderised heart in the fathoms below. The impact concaved his chest; the lump in the throat surged, his lips trembled, and another overflow of tears coated his cheeks.

'You alright, bud?' said Tom, casting a glance at him.

Angel said nothing; he turned his bowed head more towards the window.

The council worker parked the van on the pavement, next to an ominously tall and wild hedge. Ensconced behind the latter stood a semi-detached house with a slate roof, red brick the bottom half, and grey-brown pebbledash above. Its stained and fuliginous exterior surfaces telegraphed neglect. Agrestial weeds spewed forth from the cracks and edges of the uneven front paving, choking the front porch. Various household objects, crates, bags, and junk lay scattered about. Angel noticed that the curtains on the front window were pressed against the glass and that the curtain pole, covered with a thick layer of dust, had collapsed on one side. Rag-like cobwebs hung from the corners.

When Tom jumped out of the van, Angel lingered for a few seconds; then opened the door, dribbled himself onto the pavement, and with even more lethargy than Columbo's basset hound, followed his master.

Tom pressed the doorbell button, but it being deceased, he knocked on the door—with enough force to rattle it in its frame—after which he calmly sat down on a low wall and waited.

'Don't worry, he's there,' volunteered Tom. 'It just takes him a while to get out of the house.'

But Angel was absent. He stood, cold, hands in his pockets, head bowed, staring at the paving stones. At this moment he'd be finishing his canteen shift, with his friends Skinhead, Unibrow, and Emmanuel; he'd be grabbing his notebook and pen, whatever book or photocopies, and heading for his 17th-century Literature class; he'd be crossing the university gardens, with its green lawns, oak trees, eminent statues, and fragrant flower beds; he'd find Jae already in the classroom and they'd compare notes on Jacobean notions of personal responsibility.

For twenty-five minutes, they waited.

A lean, balding, unshaven man of sixty eventually emerged from the side of the house, clad in walking boots, jeans, and an ancient cardigan, buttoned over a square check shirt of indeterminate colour.

'Hello there,' the man said, smiling, the exhaustion in his eyes untouched.

'Good morning, Richard. You've got a broken boiler?' said Tom.

'Yes.'

'Round the back?'

'Yes. Please follow me.'

Richard led them to the back of the house, which brought into view a dark, miniature forest, in the midst of which were all manner of dilapidated household objects, bin liners stuffed with rubbish, PVC crates heaped with junk, plastic containers and buckets, stacks of empty flowerpots, bricks, tubing, wooden beams, water-damaged cardboard boxes, newspapers, and magazines. Partially blocking the rear entrance was a mountain of junk and rubbish, which reached up to the middle of the door. Angel saw in this a metaphor for his soul—his feelings and emotions, his memories and dreams, decaying and decomposing, overgrown by sorrow run amok.

Richard stopped and addressed Tom. 'Okay. I'm sure you'll remember from last time.'

'It's been a few of years.'

'It's a bit more complicated now. Follow me and just do what I do. I'll explain the next steps once inside.'

Unfazed, Tom asked, 'Will there be enough space for me to squeeze in?'

Richard shrugged his shoulders, 'Hopefully. Otherwise I'm out of hot water!'

Gingerly, he climbed up the rubbish mountain, pointing out the exact spots on which they needed to place their feet, and, reaching the summit, crawled inside the house. Tom followed. Angel lagged, eyes sad and dreamy. Tom turned and asked:

'You coming?'

Snapping out of his torpor, Angel got moving.

He put a cautious foot onto the filthy plank that served as the first step and, careful not to tread on wet or glutinous substances, made his way up. However, he stopped once he reached the doorframe, the point where he'd have to get on his hands and knees and enter the black maw of the house, to ingress its digestive system. He looked around for a few seconds, noticing the rotten leaves choking the gutter, the pigeon droppings on the roof tiles, and the plastic bags hanging from hooks on the wall. His skin crawled at the prospect of going in; his mind screamed not to do it. He could almost feel the microbes and bugs marching up his legs, under his jeans. There was still time to run away! But where would he go? The earth offered no sanctuary, no refuge, no welcome anywhere on its surface. He was condemned to martyrdom. With a deep breath, Angel pulled the sleeves of his jumper over his hands, gingerly got on all fours, and went inside.

The interior was a dark cavern of narrow spaces. Angel struggled to breathe as soon as he'd crossed the threshold. The walloping stench was unlike anything he'd previously inhaled, breathing like drawing mouldy lentil soup into his lungs. A bare lightbulb, which was once part of a flush ceiling lamp, the screen of which was long gone, provided the only illumination. The composition of the clutter was impossible to comprehend: a hodgepodge of million-piece puzzles, all jumbled up together, scattered, soiled, and broken. There were stacks of old newspapers and magazines, damaged books, cardboard boxes, items of clothing, bottles, cans, tins, crates, containers, correspondence, plastic bags, board games, framed pictures, timber, coffee mugs, umbrellas, vinyl records, belts, egg cartons, Christmas decorations, extension cords, air fresheners, mouldy tangerine peels, putrid banana peels, broken crockery, discarded food trays, rusty cutlery, chipped cups, and innumerable smaller objects—pens, batteries, markers, copper coins, condiments, blister packs, nasal sprays, expired debit cards, and cupcake wrappers. All this within a short radius; Angel's field of vision ended with Tom's glutes and tractor boots.

Richard, presumably still on all fours somewhere ahead, addressed Tom. 'Right. I don't know if you still remember, but this is the kitchen and we need to get into the garage, which is through that opening. Best way is to get on your back, reach up and grab the top of the doorframe, and then pull yourself in.'

Angel heard shuffling and Tom got moving. When the latter was at the referred-to opening, Angel saw that it consisted of the top fifteen inches of a doorframe. With his bulk, Tom had to suck in his belly to make it through. Angel had oodles of space, but the manoeuvre left his jumper covered in dust, spider webs, and insect carcasses. Moreover, he was unable to complete it, because he lacked the strength to pull himself into the garage.

'Tom?' he piped, staring at the ceiling and scared that he'd be left behind. 'Tom? Tom!'

'Yes?' Tom said finally.

'I can't pull myself in.'

'What's the problem?'

'I can't pull myself in.'

'Okay, just a moment.'

Angel heard shuffling above his head and then felt a fist grabbing the collar of his jumper, behind the neck, and dragging him into the garage with a swift, easy jerk.

Back on his belly, Angel's field of vision was limited to the stacks of yellowing, superannuated newspapers and Tom's tractor boots. With so much sound proofing from the surrounding clutter, Richard's voice had a dead quality to it.

'Are you all in?' asked Richard.

'Yes,' said Tom.

'Okay. So now follow me and try to imitate my movements.'

'Is it all up to this level?'

'No, not the whole house. There are pockets where you can still stand and others where you can duck under.'

'No probs.'

Angel heard more shuffling.

'You need to slide yourself down . . . and there's a place to stand on the other side.'

Tom's boots receded and, as would the stern of a sinking liner, the soles turned skywards, went down, and disappeared into the ocean of clutter below. Angel followed and found himself approaching a cliff, from the top of which Tom's and Richard's heads had become visible. To reach them, Angel had to crawl over the cliff and slide down a steep incline, head-first, arms outstretched, until he reached a layer of clutter that served as the 'ocean' floor. Richard poked his head out from behind Tom to guide him through the rest of the process.

'Okay, now prop yourself against that stack of newspapers on the side with your left hand . . . good . . . turn your hip sideways . . . good . . . now bring up your right knee . . . no, the other one . . . that's it . . . and kick out your foot as you lean back . . . a bit more . . . okay, good . . . and put your foot there on that box . . . there . . . and now stand up . . . mind the ceiling.'

During all of this, Tom had to step forward and partially crush Richard, so that Angel had enough space.

'Right. Sorry it's so cramped. This space is designed for one person, really. I haven't had a tradesman here in . . . ouff . . . maybe eleven years? So . . . anyway, the boiler is behind those boxes. We'll have to move a few things around to access it.'

Richard got started, Tom having to lean against Angel's chest, to create enough room for the man to perform his manoeuvres and re-arrange his clutter. After about five minutes of careful and precise work, the boiler because visible.

It was, not surprisingly, a rusting relic.

Tom and Richard squeezed past each other to swap places. Angel observed while Tom examined the boiler. His nostrils were hit by Richard's musty odour. Having the hoarder so close allowed Angel to see every stain, every hole, every rip in his clothing.

It made Angel think of his own heart, broken and torn to shreds.

Tom turned to look at Angel and, pulling a key out of his pocket, said, 'Angel, can you go back to the van and get the grey toolbox?' Then, to Richard, he said, 'Do you mind passing the key to my apprentice?'

The hoarder did so.

Angel dithered for a moment, fearful of crawling through the stinking, dark hoard alone, but, with eyes on him, and the job pending until he obeyed, he felt compelled to get moving. Careful not to touch more than necessary, he turned around to climb out of the hole, but he heard the man address him. 'You can use that ladder there on the side to get to the top of the pile and crawl from there.'

Angel located the grimy ladder, and, covering his hands with his sleeves, did as instructed. Once outside, he gulped in the fresh air for half a minute, before looking down to inspect his clothing. The grey dust and spider webs covering it blotted the original colours. There were arachnid and cockroach legs, fly exoskeletons, and pupal cases.

But it didn't matter anymore. He didn't even bother brushing them off.

The grey toolbox sat next to six others of varying sizes and colours; Angel grabbed the handle and pulled. But the toolbox might as well have been soldered to the floor. He tried again several times, using both hands and experimenting with foot placements, but all he achieved was to hurt his fingers and tweak his lower back. After five or six minutes, Angel gave up. For a moment, he imagined taking the van and driving down to London—it was early in the morning, so he could, if he sped all the way, still make it to his 17th-Century Literature class. There was no one to stop him. He could stay in his dormitory room, since no one would have claimed it, and carry on as normal until the end of term, provided he avoided detection. Yet, that would be impossible, of course, and he wouldn't get credit anyway because he was no longer enrolled. He was permanently exiled—from the university and therefore from Madison's heart, because she wouldn't respect him. Submission to his fate was all he had left.

Not caring to return inside, he sat on the low wall and stared at the darkening sky. The spirits spat on him with mockery. He bowed his head and, his back a waning moon, allowed the spit to soak him when it turned to rain.

Let me be ta'en, let me be put to death;
I am content, so thou wilt have it so.

Tom found him in this posture twenty minutes later. 'What are you doing?'

Angel made no eye contact, said nothing.

'Oi! What's going on? Where's the toolbox?'

Angel sighed. 'In the van.'

'What do you mean in the van? I asked you to bring it in!'

'I couldn't lift it.'

'And you just sat here?'

Angel said nothing.

'Go into the van and get me the toolbox.'

Angel said nothing.

'You deaf?'

Angel said nothing.

Tom slapped Angel's head. Angel fell on the ground and remained there, indifferent.

'What's up with you!'

Still no response.

'Fuck's sake! You're as helpful as tits on a bull!'

Tom went into the van, ripped the toolbox out, and stormed past Angel, leaving him where he was.

Chapter CXXVIII

When Tom came back, Angel still lay where he'd fallen, among overgrown stinging nettles, Canada thistle, crabgrass, and pigweed.

'Let's go,' Tom ordered.

Sluggishly, Angel stood and walked to the van, head low, eyes far away. He got in and sat, dripping wet, arms by his sides, staring into the distance.

Tom watched at him for a moment. 'Belt up.'

Like a sloth, Angel fastened his seatbelt.

'Next job is a blocked toilet,' said Tom, turning the ignition.

Angel bowed his head. Until forty-eight hours ago, he'd been a cultured man of letters—reading Edmund Spenser in his velour jacket and planning his reunion with Madison. And until only a few months ago, he'd been taking her to the theatre, to Kensington Gardens, to Victorian museums, to fine restaurants, to the capital's most luxurious tea rooms. It had been a time of love and verse, wonder and intellect, romance and refinement. Tears displaced the rain droplets on his cheeks. He'd never be able to take her anywhere again.

He only half-heard the rattle of the diesel engine and daydreamed about high tea with Madison at the Dorchester Hotel. But as Tom drove them to the western part of the city, nostalgia gave way to bitterness: he was now a toilet unblocker, a toolbox fetcher, a peon who dealt in urine and faeces; he might as well be a latrine; his claim to her esteem was gone—torn from him and trampled underfoot.

The blocked toilet was in a semi's upstairs bathroom. The PVC pipe connecting the toilet to the sewer ran externally along a brick wall at the back of the house, first horizontally, and then vertically.

Standing next to Angel before the pipe, Tom said, 'We'll have to cut that pipe, won't we?'

Angel bowed his head and said nothing. He felt the drizzle falling on him.

'Go and get a saw from the van and get started.'

In a daze, Angel took the keys from Tom and went back to the van, where he found several saws in different shapes and sizes—hacksaws, coping saws, jab saws, drywall saws, and then power saws of various kinds. He grabbed a hand saw and sat at the back of the open vehicle, the tool over his thighs, legs dangling over the rear bumper, eyes skyward.

After ten minutes, Tom had to come and fetch him. 'Oi. What are you doing? Get a move on!'

Angel glanced at him and got moving, albeit torpidly.

'Right. So go ahead and cut the pipe,' said Tom, once they were back on site.

Angel stood below the horizontal part of the pipe and, with the speed of a three-toed sloth, lifted his arm, holding the saw vertically to cut the pipe. But in that position, he discovered, what little strength he had, let alone could summon, was expended on just holding the saw upright. The latter twisted left and right, caressing the pipe a few times until he dropped it.

Instead of picking it up to try again, Angel dropped his arms and stood inert, head bowed.

'A ladder might be useful,' said Tom.

Angel began walking back to the van with even greater lethargy than before.

'Today, if you can,' Tom called out.

But Angel's pace remained unaltered. In the van, he found a folding three-step ladder. However, he lacked the strength to lift it, so he again sat, legs dangling over the rear bumper, head drooped, reminiscing about the time he sat with Madison at the university library, reading John Donne.

After another ten minutes, Tom had to come and fetch him.

'Are you taking the piss?'

As before, Angel glanced at him and got moving.

'And the ladder?'

'I can't lift it.'

Tom sighed, went into the van, ripped out the ladder, and slammed the rear doors shut.

Back at the site, Tom plonked the ladder below the pipe and stepped back. 'Go on,' he said.

As if in slow motion, Angel climbed the steps and re-attempted the sawing. This time it went slightly better, but, because of his lack of enthusiasm and grip strength, the saw kept twisting and wobbling. At first, Tom watched, shaking his head, but after ten minutes of Angel getting nowhere, he got bored and sought amusement on his phone.

Finally, after twenty minutes, Angel managed to breach the pipe.

'There you go!' said Tom.

Brown, evil-smelling water burst through the incision, dripping on Angel's jumper and running down his arms. Tom struggled to suppress his cackles at this point, but, when instead of getting out of the way, Angel simply dropped his arms and bowed his head, allowing the foul liquid to continue dribbling on his pate, face, and chest, Tom's amusement was conquered by perplexity.

'Moving aside might be useful,' Tom eventually said.

Angel looked up at the dripping pipe and did as suggested, without re-applying the saw to deepen the incision. The pipe kept dribbling, while Angel stood, chin on his chest, letting the faecal fluid splatter on his jeans and shoes.

'Go on. Finish cutting the pipe,' said Tom, amused again.

Angel obeyed, albeit in a lacklustre fashion, with the saw getting stuck often. Nevertheless, by dint of keeping at it for an eternity, he finally widened the incision enough for the cold, fetid mess trapped in the pipe to arch in the air and splash onto his cashmere jumper.

Yet, even to this Angel was indifferent. Without noticing Tom's gales of laughter, he climbed down the ladder, dropped the saw, and left.

'Oi! Where are you going?' Tom called out. 'Oi! Oi!'

Chapter CXXIX

Angel walked to the front of the van and lay on the ground. He gazed at the heavenly vault of his open-air catacomb, his face like Guido Reni's *Christ Crowned with Thorns*. His life was worthless. Let Tom run him over and spread his entrails on the asphalt. He'd die a martyr for Madison.

'What are you doing?' said Tom, upon finding him.

Angel heard, but neither listened nor answered.

'Oi!'

No response.

'I said, oi!'

No response.

Tom threw his hands in the air and looked at the sky for a moment, fists on his hips.

'I've seen more life in necrophilia porn,' Tom said, finally. He shook his head and left.

Angel spent the next hour watching the clouds sail by. To the cold and the intermittent rain he remained indifferent. The crashes and slams of Tom digging in the van for tools and replacement pipes had no effect. His cranium was a projection room, screening scenes of his moments with Madison. Like the time he'd walked her back to the dorm one evening, after treating her to an Italian dinner and, upon finding a puddle barring her path to the entrance, he'd gallantly taken off his corduroy jacket and laid it down, so she could cross it without soiling her shoes; she'd said, 'Thank you, Sir,' and walked across with an arched eyebrow and her head held high. Or the time they'd discovered Joseph Shipley's *Dictionary of Early English* in the library and spent the rest of the day exchanging messages replete with archaic and obsolete words; she'd shrieked with delight at his polysyllabic curiosities. Or the time when he'd taken Madison to Kew Gardens to have a champagne and caviar picnic breakfast; he'd purchased an old-fashioned wicker picnic basket, complete with monographed green fabric, stainless steel cutlery, and fine china plates, held in place with leather straps. Or the time he'd bought her eight bouquets of the best red roses he could find, adding up to ninety-six individual flowers, one for each day they'd been together; she'd nearly fainted at his romantic gesture. Or the time he'd taken her to the National Portrait Gallery, and explained Hans Holbein's *The Ambassadors* to her, based on his reading of Mary F. S. Hervey's book; she'd listened with great interest, *ohing* and *ahing* at his detailed knowledge. Or the time he'd taken her to see *Henry IV* at Shakespeare's Globe theatre; at the shop he'd later bought her a jigsaw puzzle depicting the bard's world, which they'd built together in her room.

He vaguely heard Tom say his name. But the voice was far away.

'Oi! Time to go!'

But the word 'time' only made him think of *Time Out*, and how he used to browse through the magazine to find fun or romantic outings to enjoy with Madison.

'Oi! Wake up!'

But the word 'wake' only made him think of death and going to heaven, and how heaven was now barred to him because heaven was Madison, and Madison had, in effect, already discarded him, on account of his incomplete education and present occupation.

He'd never behold her face again. He'd never hold her hand again. He'd never kiss her lips again. He'd never hear her voice again. He'd never hear her laugh again. He'd never see her swoon again. He'd never smell her perfume again. He'd never feel her hair again. He'd never spend a moment with her again.

He felt the impact of water splashing his body.

'Fuck's sake!' he heard.

But the water only made him think of the Round Pond at Kensington Gardens, in front of which he'd sat with Madison on a bench one warm afternoon last May.

He'd never sit next to her again. He'd never put his arm around her again. He'd never converse with her again. He'd never declaim to her again. He'd never be elegant for her again. He'd never caresses her again. He'd never take anywhere again.

He felt a large hand clamp around his ankle and his body being dragged. He felt his body lifted and dropped inside the van. He felt a seatbelt clasped over him.

But all he could focus on was his thoughts, his memories, his sorrow, the lump in his throat, the tears. His eyes were open, but they no longer saw.

He heard the diesel engine rattle. He heard it roar for a long time. He heard doors opening and slamming shut. He heard gravel crunching beneath him. He heard knocks on a door. He heard his mother's voice.

'Sorry, madam. I've had to bring him back,' Angel heard Tom say. 'We can't use him.'

He heard Tom's voice and his mother's voice. He heard the door close. He heard the diesel engine coming to life and fading into the distance.

'What's happened to you?' he heard his mother say. 'The state of you!'

His state, he thought, was one of dilapidation, of decay, of decomposition, of disintegration, of dissolution, of dilaceration, of death.

'Angel?'

But Angel was no more; Angel was a corpse, a mummy, a cadaver, a carcass, a skeleton.

'Angel?'

A ghost, an apparition, a phantasm, a phantom.

'Angel? You need to go and clean up.'

A spectre, a wraith, a spirit, a shadow, a mirage, a hallucination.

Chapter CXXX

Questions. Anger. Demands. Confusion. Worry. Coaxing. More worry. Telephone calls. Talking. Pacing.

Angel found himself in the downstairs bathroom and, fully clothed, placed under the shower. The water running off him, he felt like a jamb statue in a Gothic cathedral. This reminded him of when he took Madison to see St Paul's, where he told her about the Old St Paul's and how it had been gutted by the Great Fire of 1666, much like the conflagration of his dreams had since gutted his spirit. Her adorable yawns had prompted him to invite her for lunch at the Coq d'Argent, where she'd asked for a bottle of champagne, 'just because', plus port. This had made her smile.

As if from the bottom of an oubliette, after the water Angel felt his clothing removed, followed by his body in a towelling robe, followed by pyjamas, followed by being put to bed. He heard things being said to him, efforts to obtain a response, but the words flowed around him like breeze around a tombstone.

He lay in bed as if embalmed and in a coffin, like someone deceased, prior to the wake. His duvet a cerecloth. His bed a sarcophagus. His bedroom a mausoleum.

The beams traversing the ceiling above him cast his mind to the time he'd taken Madison to The Prospect of Whitby, the site, it was claimed, of the oldest riverside pub in London and the preferred hostelry of Judge Jeffreys, where Samuel Pepys and Charles Dickens were said to have been regulars. He'd been charmed by how Madison had desired to understand the different lagers, ales, stouts, and porters by sampling as many as possible; she'd been giggly afterwards and needed his gentlemanly arm for support on the sinuous walk to Wapping Station.

Time passed.

How long, didn't matter.

It is silliness to live when to live is torment, and then have we a prescription to die when death is our physician.

Natural light receded, and darkness engulfed the mausoleum. A sign that Death was near. Soon, he would cease to exist.

Vociferation in the corridor. Light floods in. Footsteps. Mourners throng in the chapel, to pay their respects, to weep his passing, to bid farewell.

'Angel?' Destiny, now a necromancer. 'Angel, are you there?'

She shook his body.

'Angel? Angel! Say something! Angel!'

But the corpse was lifeless. His soul already in hell, boiling in excrement.

And she helped send him there.

'Angel, please come back,' said his mother, putting her palm soothingly on his cheek.

His flesh was rotting. Soon maggots would have their feast. And even if they could uneat his tissues, what purpose would it serve? She had stemmed the flow of money, and thereby humiliated him and prevented his ever seeing Madison again. Nothing left on Earth to live for. It'd all been stolen. He'd been despoiled. Picked clean. Pulverised.

O, here
Will I set up my everlasting rest,
And shake the yoke of inauspicious stars
From this world-wearied flesh.

'Angel, tell us what's happening. Tell us so we can fix it,' pleaded his father, in a rare hint of emotion.

But he was the problem, not the solution. He, his father, had erected the barriers to Angel's, university degree, thereby denying him Madison's respect and thereby a reason to ever see her again.

'Angel! Please come back!' Destiny again.

But the oubliette of death only got deeper and deeper, the circle of light above him smaller and smaller.

Dialogue. Concern. Puzzlement. Ideas. A suggestion. A plan. Agreement.

The mourners left the chapel, this time without extinguishing the candles. Perhaps they couldn't be bothered. Perhaps they'd come back to revisit their handiwork.

Time passed.

The atmosphere was one of ending, finality, departure. He remembered his last day with Madison, four and a half months earlier. He'd stayed up all night with her in her room, while she packed her bags. Her friends, all female, all American, had stopped by every now and then to ask for things or chat for a while. He'd been impatient for them to leave each time, for they were stealing his and Madison's moments—although Madison seemed to enjoy the visits, and a gentleman would never block her joy, even when he felt like a fifth wheel. In the morning they'd had an early breakfast at the canteen, which he'd seldom entered at that hour since, being a night owl, he'd always scheduled his classes for the afternoon. He'd had a croissant but had been unable to finish it; he'd been too nervous, too sad. Madison had eaten cereal, bacon, eggs, and toast. He'd then paid for a taxi to Heathrow Airport, since her bags were heavy, and he couldn't have carried them in the London Underground even then. They rode the whole way holding hands, kissing, caressing, and saying sweet nothings. There had been firm promises to write, message, phone, and video call every day. Oaths of eternal loyalty. Vehement plans for their reunion. All the same, Madison had been strangely distant and weird. They'd arrived at Heathrow and Angel had gone with her as far as he'd been allowed. Their final goodbye had prolonged until the last minute. He'd stood, waving incessantly, watching her get smaller and smaller, until she'd finally disappeared in the distance. Even then, he'd lingered, his head bowed, not wanting to leave the spot where she'd last been. The lump had camped out in his throat for hours and visited him often afterwards. The tears had steadily cascaded during his journey back to the university. He'd clung on to the phantom of her touch, the ghost of her scent, the spectre of her presence as they'd grown fainter before finally vanishing, and to this purpose he'd kept the clothes he'd worn to the airport out of the laundry for the following two months. He'd kept his promise to write her traditional letters; he'd chosen Conqueror paper, a Montblanc fountain pen, Edelstein black ink, and good calligraphy. She'd not written back every day and she'd used normal lined paper and a ballpoint pen, but he'd loved her schoolgirl quaintness and her family had probably kept her busy, having not seen her in half a year. To make her smile, he'd varied his calligraphy and the format of his correspondence: a letter in an empty bottle of brandy (Baron de Saint-Fauste), with 18th-century calligraphy; a letter mounted on card and cut into a jigsaw puzzle; a letter in old German script; a very long letter (237 pages); a very short letter (a question mark); and, of course, multiple letters in verse. They'd spoken on Skype or FaceTime or WhatsApp every day in June, but then the calls had become less frequent—again, her family and friends had kept her busy, not having seen her for so long, which was understandable. She'd not posted on her social media very often, and, when she had, the posts had been cryptic, the Instagram posts with no description and her Facebook posts almost non-existent; but this had only made her posts all the more valuable and mysterious—golden riddles for him to decipher and interpret.

Voices again. Commotion in the house. A multitude of footsteps. Mourners, re-thronging in the chapel.

Were there respects they'd left unpaid, tears they'd left unshed, farewells they'd left unsaid? In his mind, Angel welcomed them. Let them see his putrefaction.

Let them witness his martyrdom. Let them observe his decline.

But there was a new mourner present.

A familiar voice.

A comforting one.

Amelia.

Chapter CXXXI

'Angel?'

Amelia put a hand on his cheek. She leaned into him and let him see her face. A picture of kindness and concern.

He considered.

'Angel. I'm here. Please come back.'

Someone cared.

'Angel . . . Don't go away. Please come back. I'm here for you.'

Amelia had never been to his house. How did she find his address? Did she endure a three-hour train ride just to see him? That was surprising. Unexpected. Maybe he could find out. He could talk to her. She'd listen. She could explain to the others. She'd understand his feelings.

'I'm here for you, Angel.'

The maggots lost interest. Death receded. The oubliette got shallower and its trap door opened. His heart pumped again. His lungs breathed in air . . .

For now.

He could die again later if needed. The Prince of Hell would still be there to welcome him.

He turned to look at her. He noticed sister, mother, and father in the room.

'Could you please give us a moment?' said Amelia, turning to the assembly.

Results had given her authority; the family silently vacated his room.

'Welcome back, Angel. How are you feeling?'

He blinked without saying a word. He looked around. He looked at Amelia.

'Hello,' he said.

'You're safe now.'

'You're here . . .'

'Yes, I'm here.'

'Why?'

'I've been desperate to speak to you since I saw you yesterday.'

'Was it yesterday?'

'I was going to visit you this weekend, but Destiny sent me a message a few hours ago saying you were not well. So I dropped everything and took a train.' Tears welled up in her eyes.

'She asked you to come?'

'No. I messaged her this afternoon to get your address. I wanted to surprise you, but she said you were poorly. I couldn't wait.'

'But . . . why?'

Her voice wavered with emotion. 'I knew you were suffering.'

'How?'

'I just knew. I saw it in your eyes yesterday.' She wiped a tear and smiled.

He felt her hand holding his. It was gentle and comforting.

But he looked away.

'Talk to me, Angel. What's been happening?'

He looked at her, opened his mouth, as if to say something, then shook his head.

'You can talk to me. It's just you and me here.'

Still, Angel hesitated.

Amelia squeezed his hand, tenderly.

Angel sighed and looked away again.

She gave him time. Her thumb caressed the back of his hand.

'My parents . . . ,' he said, finally, 'they hate Madison . . . Mastropasqua told them I sleep through my classes . . . and they blame her because I took her out on dates.'

'Are they angry about the money you spent?'

'They don't understand . . .'

'Is that why they withdrew you from the university?'

Tears welled up in his eyes. The latter fixed on her tan shearling coat.

'It's okay, Angel,' she said, caressing his head. 'We'll fix this.'

'Will you?'

'Yes. I'll speak to them.'

'Please . . . I can't live . . .'

'I'll speak to them. I promise.'

Chapter CXXXII

Angel slept.

His mother woke him when she entered the room a while later bearing a tray with dinner.

This almost never happened; in the past she'd only ever done it when he had a blazing temperature—and even then, not always. After all, he had to 'toughen up'!

'We thought it'd be best to let you rest.'

'Thank you,' he said.

Victoria sat on the edge of the bed.

'Amelia's been chatting to us. She's a lovely girl.'

'Um . . . yes.'

'We've invited her to spend the night.'

'Oh . . . really?'

'Yes. We'd thought you'd like that. Plus, it's a long way to come.'

'Um . . . yes.'

'You've never talked about her before.'

'Um . . . she's also . . . er . . . she's studying literature.'

'She said. But we didn't even know she existed. I didn't know until yesterday. And she cares a lot about you.'

Angel looked down at his tray. Roasted trout and potatoes and buttered brussel sprouts filled his plate. More than he could eat.

'She's having dinner with us at the table. She'll come and visit you when we're done.'

'Okay.'

Victoria left.

An hour later, Amelia returned, smiling and her tight black jumper now exposed after shedding her coat.

'How are you doing, Angel?'

'Um . . . okay . . .'

'Your parents are lovely!' she said.

Angel said nothing.

She noticed he still had the tray on his thighs, the food untouched. 'Poor Angel, too depressed to eat. Let me take that back to the kitchen.'

Ten minutes later, she returned with a mugful of Earl Grey.

'Here,' she said, putting it on the black marble coaster on his bedside table. 'Lovely mug!'

'Have you spoken to them?'

'We've been chatting. Your parents are not how I expected them to be.'

'Oh?'

'They're very charming!'

Angel frowned.

'And Destiny is so funny!'

He looked away.

'But they've been very worried about you.'

He looked down.

'They said they've hardly heard from you this year.'

He still said nothing.

'And that you've not been yourself.'

More silence, then, 'Um . . . what else?'

'They don't understand what's happening. They want to help you, but they're finding it difficult.'

'Did you explain?' His eyes pleaded.

'I told them that you loved your degree and that you went to all your classes and that you had a job at the canteen and that you were saving to see Madison in December.'

'Um . . . did you tell them about Madison?'

'I told them you're very much in love.'

Angel started. 'Anything else?'

'Just that she was an American student doing English Lit.'

'Is that it?'

'I didn't really know her, Angel. And . . . they were more interested in me!'

'Did you mention she's elegant? From a good family?'

'I told them she enjoyed going to elegant places . . . and that you were always a gentleman.'

'Nothing more?'

'There was not much more I could tell them.'

'I thought girls spoke to each other constantly in the dorm . . .'

'She wasn't my type, you know? She was with the Americans. And I didn't like her friends.'

'Y-You didn't show them her Instagram account, did you?'

'No, of course I didn't.'

'D-Did they ask?' Angel's eyes were like tennis balls.

'They did, but I said I didn't know her handle off the top of my head.'

'Did . . . er . . . did they try to find her page?'

'Haven't you ever shown them a picture of her?'

'No . . . er . . . no. I haven't.'

'Do you want me to?'

'No! No! Please don't!'

'Oh, Angel. You should tell them about her.'

'Um . . . I-I-I wouldn't know what to say.'

'Tell them how you feel about her.'

'It . . . it's private. They wouldn't understand anything.'

'They're husband and wife, Angel. Of course they know about love.'

'I-I-I wouldn't know where to begin.'

'How do you expect them to like her, then?'

'Um . . .'

'Do you want me to bring them here so you can tell them?'

'No no no! Don't! Don't!'

'Is it because she's a feminist now?'

'Um . . . they'd get the wrong idea. They wouldn't understand she's not like that at all!'

'But why don't you explain it to them?'

'They wouldn't believe me.'

'Why not?'

Angel looked away for a moment, then made eye-contact again. 'W-W-What else did they say?'

'Well, as I said, they were more interested in me. They had a lot of questions.'

Angel thought for a moment.

'What happened earlier?' she said.

'Um . . . what do you mean earlier?'

'Your parents said they found you catatonic.'

'I was depressed.'

'Because of uni?'

'Yes.'

'Why did they withdraw you?'

'They hate poetry . . . they have no sense of beauty of romance . . . they would've preferred me to be a computer scientist and launch an app and wear my hair slicked back and make a billion pounds.'

'But don't you need a university degree for that? It doesn't make sense, Angel.'

'They want me to be a hard-nosed businessman and they think manual labour will shape me into what *they* want.'

'Oh, so it's temporary.'

'So they say. Mastropasqua talked them into it. He hates university students and would rather we all be bricklayers. Do something *useful*, quote unquote.'

'Well, he says that every year. But he does like Jae and Vera. I'm sure he'd like you if you showed him how brilliant you are.' She smiled.

'It's too late. My parents have no time for literature.'

'But your mother's an author. I didn't know she wrote the *Social History of the Penny Dreadful*. That book was amazing!'

'They think poetry is a waste of time. There's no money to be made.'

'Oh, Angel, you gentle soul . . .'

Angel frowned.

'But don't you also want to write novels and plays?' she said. 'Some authors have been hugely successful writing those.'

'It's-it's all about *money* with them.'

'Don't you want people to read your books?'

'W-Well, yes, but . . .'

'Then? Explain it to them.'

'It's pointless.' He looked away and crossed his arms, frowning.

Amelia waited.

'And now I won't have a degree . . . and Madison will never respect me.'

'Why not?'

Angel sighed.

'Why not, Angel?'

'B-B-Because . . . she fell in love with a poet.'

'Are you not still a poet?'

'Yes, but . . .'

'I don't think you any less.'

'But she will. She definitely will!'

'Is she worth it then? If she's that superficial?'

'Yes! Yes, of course she's worth it! It's about standards!'

Amelia paused for a moment, then said, squeezing his hand. 'Angel, don't worry. I'm here until tomorrow. I'll talk to your parents. I'll make them understand.'

He looked at her, dewy hope in his eyes.

Victoria knocked on the door. Angel and Amelia turned their heads in her direction.

'We're going to watch a film,' Victoria said. 'Would you like to join us?'

'What is it?' asked Angel.

'The Count of Montecristo.'

Chapter CXXXIII

Angel joined the family at the breakfast table last. The air smelled of bacon, eggs, coffee, and French toast.

He'd been relieved, although not surprised, he'd not been roused three hours earlier to get ready for his boiler job. It seemed that was now off. But with him out of university, he wondered what would happen next. It all depended on what Amelia said before heading back down.

Amelia had been given a seat beside him, serving as a buffer against his father.

'Aha! Don Giovanni makes an appearance!' quipped Destiny, loudly, the moment he appeared.

'Destiny!'

'Sorry mum,' said his sister, suppressing laugher.

Angel said nothing and sat down.

'Good morning, Angel,' said Amelia, smiling brightly.

Angel noticed that her grooming was immaculate: every hair in place, make-up flawless, clothes without a wrinkle. His parents would approve, he thought wearily.

'Good morning,' he said without vim.

'So. You never told us you had multiple girlfriends,' said Destiny.

Amelia blushed. Angel frowned and looked down at his plate.

'Will you stop?' said Victoria.

'But aren't you surprised?'

'Destiny!'

Amelia looked at Angel for a moment and then addressed his parents.

'I'd like to thank you for letting me spend the night. I've really enjoyed finally having the chance to meet you.'

Destiny replied before her mother could. 'Any time. When are you coming back?' She grinned and wiggled her eyebrows at Angel, who again looked down at his plate and, pretending to rub his forehead, shielded his eyes with his hand.

Victoria said, 'You're welcome to visit us whenever you like.'

'Thank you, madam. I'd love that,' said Amelia, 'Angel is a good friend and he's been so brilliant in London.'

'Well, we're very upset with him,' said Victoria. 'I didn't like what I saw when we went down.'

'I've felt terrible for Angel. The university really let him down with his roommate. He asked repeatedly to be moved but Accommodation would not allow him. They should have stepped in.'

'Not to mention the fact that I was nearly assaulted in the car park by one of his so-called friends.'

'Oh, dear! Who?'

'Johannes,' said Angel, his voice nearly inaudible.

'But, what happened?'

'This savage appeared out of nowhere,' said Victoria, 'screaming Angel's name, hitting my car, and being very aggressive. Thankfully the parking attendant took care of him.'

'Oh, my goodness! I'm so sorry to hear that. But Angel didn't do anything wrong. On the contrary!'

'Is that so.'

'Johannes had been under investigation because of an impropriety on campus. It later turned out he was innocent. But while the investigation was going on, he'd expected Angel to lie in his defence and Angel, of course, absolutely refused.'

'Why didn't you tell me that, Angel?

Angel shrugged, and, without making eye contact, mumbled, 'You were angry.'

'And I'm still angry. For one the lie you told about the laundrette. I still can't *believe* you told me there'd been a *fire* when in fact you *ran out* leaving all your clothes behind.'

'Angel!' said Amelia, surprised. 'You told your mum there'd been a fire at the laundrette?'

He kept his eyes firmly on his plate. He said nothing.

'If I may, madam, that was my fault. Angel later told me that he'd been thinking about a poem, and just as I came to greet him, he'd had a brilliant idea. I was surprised he left so suddenly, but he ran to write it down before he lost it. He's so passionate about his poetry that he sometimes forgets himself.'

'But why *lie*, Angel?' said Victoria. 'If you make a mistake, you need to own it and tell the truth.'

He mumbled, 'You were angry . . .'

'He was embarrassed,' said Amelia, 'and annoyed with himself. But I told him many great literary geniuses have been gripped by inspiration like that. And look at the results! We're still reading their works hundreds of years later!'

'I see,' said Victoria.

'And besides, when they write Angel's biography, this will be just an amusing incident; no one will remember him for his shirts, but everyone will remember him for his poetry.'

'But what about you sleeping through your classes, Angel? We got that straight from the horse's mouth!'

'I . . . um . . . didn't sleep . . .'

'Tell them about your job, Angel,' said Amelia. 'The fact that it's early in the morning.'

'Um . . . yes . . . um . . . I was starting at six . . . I had to get up at four every morning . . .'

'We've had only three classes per module so far since the term started,' said Amelia, 'Angel, bless him, was having trouble adjusting to his schedule at first. But he was constantly reading. He was always telling me about what he'd learnt.'

'Um . . . yes . . .'

'Then why couldn't you answer our questions?' said Victoria.

'Um . . . I . . . er . . . I had the flu . . . I'd been travelling . . .'

'Man flu, more like,' said Destiny.

'Destiny!' warned Victoria.

'It's true,' said Amelia, 'Angel had a terrible flu just before he came to see you. I'd been nursing him back to health, but he was by no means out of it when he left.'

Angel's father probed his son's face; Angel looked away.

His mother said, 'Alright, I understand about the flu, although in real life, as I said, you'll have to learn to function, otherwise it's going to set you back.'

'It was really bad, madam. I found him collapsed in his room on Wednesday night.'

'You'd collapsed, Angel?' said his mother. 'Why didn't you mention that?'

'Um . . . I-I was exhausted . . . and . . . you were angry.'

Amelia said, 'I have no doubt Angel was straining every sinew studying *despite* the flu while that oaf was having parties and filling the room with smoke.'

'Wow, you've really been living up to your name down there!' said Destiny to her brother, laughing. 'We might have to promote you to *Arch*angel!'

'I can see there was context we were unaware of,' said his mother. 'But Angel has been *no* angel. He spent *fifteen thousand* pounds taking that American girl on *outrageous* dates.'

Amelia's eyes and mouth all formed large 'O's. 'Angel! Fifteen thousand! Blimey!'

Angel's eyebrows steepled as he dropped his head, yet again. If he'd dropped it any lower, he would have ended up with butter on the tip of his nose. He said nothing.

'Angel, you're such a gentleman,' said Amelia, placing a hand on his back. 'But you can't be spending your mum's money like that.'

'Uh-oh. Angel is nervous!' said Destiny.

'Destiny. This is serious,' her mother scolded.

Angel hid his head behind his hands, rubbing his forehead, hard, to the point of pulling the skin.

'No wonder she cut you off,' continued Amelia. 'Madam, I had no idea Angel was spending that kind of money. If I had known, I would have tried to stop him.'

'It was not for you to stop him. It was for him to stop himself!' said Victoria.

'Of course, madam. And Angel has told me repeatedly he feels terribly guilty about it.'

'Except, he's yet to tell *me*.'

'Tell your mother how you feel, Angel.'

Angel hesitated, then mumbled. 'Um . . . I feel . . . awful. I'm so sorry.'

'I don't know anything about this girl,' said his mother. And what galls me is that she's clearly taken advantage of you, Angel.'

'Why don't you show your mum a picture of Madison?' said Amelia.

Angel's knees bounced like pistons, but otherwise his posture and forehead-rubbing remained unaltered.

'Go on, Angel. Show your mother.'

Still, he resisted.

Amelia caressed his back. 'Help your mum understand. Tell her what you see in Madison.'

He continued to resist.

'Do you want me to show her for you?'

Angel nodded.

Amelia pulled out her phone, launched Instagram, and, while typing, to maintain the pretence, said, 'Angel told me her handle last night.'

She found a suitable image—one from a few months ago, showing Madison and Angel together.

'There,' she said, handing the phone over to Victoria.

The latter looked at the image for one second and declared, 'I don't like her.'

She passed the phone over to her husband.

Angel's father stared at the image for a second and made to hand the phone back to Amelia without expression or a word. His disapproval, understood, required none.

'Can I see? Can I see?' said Destiny.

Her father passed the phone over to his daughter.

'Woah. Look at those bitchy eyes!'

Angel looked up, forehead crinkled.

'Man, she's taken you for a *ride*, Angel!' added his sister, guffawing.

'C-C-Can I see?' said Angel, extending his hand, and glancing inquiringly at Amelia.

'I chose a picture of the two you together,' she said.

Destiny handed the phone over to her brother.

The photograph was from five months ago. They'd been on their way to a *matinée—High Life*—and the shot had been snapped in the university gardens, outside the girls' dorm. A less angular Angel appeared standing next to Madison—clean-shaven, he, in a pale blue shirt, open at the collar, with a burgundy cravat, and the since-ruined hickory-brown velour jacket.

Angel saw nothing wrong with Madison. To him she looked elegant, stylish, sophisticated.

Puzzled, he asked his sister, 'W-Why do you say that?'

She scoffed. 'Angel, if you can't see it, I can't help you!'

Angel turned to Amelia in a silent plea for understanding.

Amelia smiled kindly and said, 'You always see the best in people.'

'But—'

'Do you want to show your family another picture?'

Desperate for answers, Angel scrolled down Madison's page. He stopped at another image and showed it to Amelia.

'Show it to your mother,' she said.

Angel did as told.

Victoria looked at the image for half a second. 'No. And I don't need to see more.'

'Let me see!' jumped in Destiny, flapping her fingers.

Her mother passed the phone.

'Oh, my! She's *nasty!*'

Angel crinkled his forehead more. He glanced at Amelia.

'It's okay, Angel. This only means you're a really sweet man.'

'But . . . why? How?'

'Because you are kind and you only see kindness in people.'

'B-But I don't see how . . .'

'You love her so much, don't you?'

'Yes. But—'

'Why don't you tell your mum, then?'

He turned to look at his mother. 'Um . . . I . . . I've been with her for nearly the whole year . . . I know her really well!'

Victoria looked away and shook her head, albeit slightly.

'Alright,' said Destiny. 'What was her biggest fear?'

'Erm . . .'

'If she could be an animal, which one would she be?'

'Er . . .'

'What makes her happy?'

'Erm . . . being taken out for dinner! At a fine restaurant. With wine.'

'Of course it does.'

'W-W-What do you mean of course?'

'Every girl likes being wined and dined.'

'But she does!'

'Yea. At two grand a pop!'

Angel looked at Victoria, irises entirely encircled by sclera.

'Yep,' said his sister. 'We all know!'

He looked at Amelia.

She said, 'Clearly Angel was raised to be a perfect gentleman. And he sees beauty everywhere he looks. It's just his nature.'

'Our argument with Angel,' said his mother, 'is that he won't last long out there if that's all he sees. And, clearly, this girl is an example.'

Angel's heart accelerated. The ants began marching.

'Maybe,' replied Amelia, 'Angel needs to see her one more time.'

'To what purpose? So that she can laugh at him some more?'

'He loves her so, so dearly, but sometimes, a bit of distance followed by a reunion can help put things in perspective.'

Angel's knees pistoned away under the table. He stilled them when he saw Destiny noticed him vibrating.

'I'm not going to have this American girl laughing at my son.'

'Sometimes,' said Amelia, 'travel can help a person develop. Many come back with a greater sense of clarity.'

Victoria thought for a moment and exchanged glances with her husband.

'Perhaps,' she said, eventually.

Chapter CXXXIV

'Thank you again for having me, madam,' said Amelia, standing on the platform, next to the London-bound train.

'It's been our pleasure,' said Victoria, clad in an elegant harris tweed purple jacket and skirt. 'But we're indebted to you for your help with Angel. I don't know what we would have done if you hadn't shown up.'

'Don't mention it. Angel is a dear friend. I'll always be there for him.'

Amelia turned to face him.

'Goodbye, Angel.'

'Goodbye,' he said.

She put a gentle hand on his cheek and looked into his eyes, for long seconds smiling with great affection.

He stood, smelling the remnants of her perfume, not knowing what to do with himself. In the back of his mind, he realised she really had beautiful blue eyes.

Finally, she turned and boarded the carriage. The whistle reverberated down the platform, there was a hiss, and the doors rumbled closed. Angel observed Amelia finding a window seat opposite to him and waving as the train got moving. He thought he saw her wipe away a tear, but she was obscured by the reflection on the glass.

And then she was gone.

He and his mother made their way back to her car, the walk punctuated by the metronomic click of her heels.

Once they were moving, she said, 'I'm going to talk to your father about sending you to America.'

'T-To America?' he said, perplexed and hopeful at the same time.

'To see Madison.'

Angel received the news like a bolt of electricity. His neck twitched his head in her direction, eyes like beach balls.

'Really?' he squealed.

'But don't get your hopes up. I'm likely to side with your father, so it's ultimately up to him.'

'Okay!'

Chapter CXXXV

His head a hot-air balloon of anticipation, as soon as they returned home Angel dashed to his room, having promised his mother, of his own volition, to carry on with the university course reading. But, with *Oroonoko* open in front of him, he found himself unable to concentrate.

Perhaps checking his social media first would calm him down.

This time, however, he dared not look at Madison's Instagram. Not only for fear of what he might find, and of how it would upset him, but for fear of jinxing his mother's impending representation to his father. It was absolutely essential that the universal balance not be perturbed by an impulsive act.

To maintain that delicate balance, he lay in bed—although he grabbed a book from his shelf to keep the pretence of reading in case his mother walked in. And, as if on cue, he heard her footsteps approaching. He sprung out of bed, tossing the book aside, and sat behind his computer, adopting a posture of deep study.

The door opened behind him.

He turned.

His mother was holding a small, white box and a plastic envelope. 'I've got you a replacement phone,' she said.

'Oh, thank you!'

'BUT—' she said, pulling the box away from him. 'This time you look after it. AND you pay attention to your surroundings if you need to pull it out.'

'Of course, yes!'

'And if you lose it, or it gets stolen, you tell me *immediately*.'

'Yes, yes, I will, of course!' He nodded fast.

She handed him the box and the plastic envelope. 'Here's also the replacement SIM card.'

'Okay.'

'How goes your reading?'

'Um . . . good! It's going really well!'

'Very good. Keep going.'

She left.

Things were turning around, *finally!*

But he dared not think yet about what *would* be, should his mother succeed with his father, the final piece in the puzzle of normality: his being allowed to return to the university. Although he badly desired to check the university's rules for returning after a withdrawal, he stopped himself, since doing so could also jinx this dream. He resolved, all the same, that *if* and *when* he was allowed to return, he would study the hardest he'd ever studied in his life; he'd allow no distraction to interfere, be it squalid roommates, loan sharks, pub bullies, campus rapists, ecoterrorists, extortionist librarians, or hair-trigger big American girls; he'd live monastically and do all the required reading, plus the suggested, the side, and the optional texts, plus any additional reading he could think of, including all his professors' published essays in the academic journals, so as to leave no stone unturned for a term of straight As. And he'd also do the canteen job, even though he'd probably wouldn't need it anymore, just to strip Mastropasqua of excuses to poison the paternal ear!

Angel unwrapped his new phone—an iPhone 6S—and got it up and running. By now Madison would have got an 11 Pro Max, so he'd have to keep his older model hidden.

He found he had dozens of WhatsApp messages from Amelia, beginning from when he left London. There were a few more from that morning saying she'd enjoyed seeing him and that she'd miss him and to let her know about his visit to Madison.

At the same time, there were no messages from Madison.

Which was strange.

He checked her status and saw that she'd been online an hour ago.

She was staying up late . . .

He considered sending her a message, but, once again, the fear of jinxing the prospective visit dissuaded him.

Since he'd kept his profile private after the fall-out with the climate change thugs, his social media was a morgue. Except, of course, for Amelia's numerous messages from the previous half week.

He thought of Madison.

If it were his fate to see her soon, he'd have to stop by a salon urgently to get his hair fixed. If he could not look like Bernini, he'd have to leap back a century and model himself after Torquato Tasso and Lope de Vega. Pity ruffs were not in fashion . . . He looked through his wardrobe to do an inventory of what he had left: he had two fine corduroy jackets, some okay shirts, three good trousers, a decent pair of jeans. But no shirts worthy of the occasion. His Eton shirts had ended up in the streets of London, and his other good ones had been scavenged by buskers. If only he could get five Eton shirts and a Stefano Ricci for his (possible) arrival! The shoe situation was better: he had brown and black oxfords by Church's—although he'd love to own a pair of Edward Greens, like his father's, or at least a pair of Graziano & Girlings—a pair of Lotusse oxfords in black suede, and a pair of brown brogues by Allen Edmonds. He'd have to make sure whichever shoes he ended up taking were shined to mirror polish; a couple would need to be re-soled—not because they needed it, but because he wanted the soles to be perfect. And of course, he'd want to arrive at O'Hare with his best clothes packed into a Berluti leather rolling suitcase. However, there was little chance of convincing his mother to pay £5,000 for one of those.

He imagined disembarking from his aeroplane at O'Hare, in his best attire, and walking up the airbridge dragging his Berluti case—not fast, like fellow passengers, but at a dignified pace. He imagined handing over his passport at border control and, upon being asked to state the purpose of his visit, proclaiming proudly that it was to be reunited with the love of his life. He imagined walking past the luggage carousels, deeming the scrambling for bags and suitcases beneath him. He imagined the sliding doors beyond opening to reveal Madison standing opposite to him, smiling—not the chubby Madison with green, partially shaved hair and hairy armpits that he'd seen on Instagram, but the Madison he knew, his Madison, the slender one with long, light brown hair and classy, conservative dress; the daughter of the billionaire industrialist and intellectual salon mother. He imagined their bodies colliding into a mutual embrace, and the embrace lasting minutes, hours, days, months, years, centuries . . . He imagined her father having risen to the occasion by sending her in his chauffeur-driven Rolls-Royce Sweeptail, because nothing less would do. He imagined his mother having booked him a room at a five-star hotel near Madison's university, and being taken there to rest, converse, and read poetry to each other, before a romantic dinner in the best French restaurant in the city. He imagined afterwards being driven back to his hotel and inviting Madison to spend time with him in his room. The specifics, however, he dared not dwell on. She was too sacred. And . . . of course, imagining them might jinx his vision.

Chapter CXXXVI

He had lunch with his mother, during which no mention was made of any prospective visit to Madison.

He later had dinner with his mother and sister, since his father was in Berlin. No mention was made of any prospective visit to Madison.

The following day, he had breakfast with his mother and sister again. And no mention was made of any prospective visit to Madison.

Hours later followed lunch with his mother, during which no mention was made.

In the evening, he had dinner with his mother again, since his father was in Prague, and Destiny was training with a record-holding powerlifter. No mention was made.

The morning following, he had breakfast with his mother and sister. No mention was made.

Lunch later that day was with his mother. No mention.

Dinner on the Friday night was with his mother and sister, since his father was still on his way back from Milan. No mention.

Angel was in agony.

But close to midnight, his father finally returned. Normally, Angel would have mourned the occasion, hung around minimally to fulfil filial obligations, and disappeared into his room as soon as he could. This time, however, although he still disappeared, he stationed himself at the top of the stairs, moth-like ears tracking the parental conversation in the kitchen, in particular for any mention of his name, or of Madison's.

Yet still . . . no mention.

When morning came on Saturday, Angel was at the table at seven on the dot, freshly showered and attired in clean, crisp clothes. Although the latter were still many sizes too big and he'd had to rely on the under-jumper and the rear trouser clamp.

'Wow, Angel,' said Destiny. 'I haven't seen you looking this smart since January. What happened?'

Angel frowned and said nothing. He grabbed a slice of toast.

'How goes your reading, Angel?' asked his mother.

'Um . . . good. I've finished *Oroonoko*.'

'Excellent. What did you learn?'

'It's about an African king who is enslaved and sent to Surinam. He is treated badly and eventually murdered. Professor Hynd wanted us . . . er . . . to focus on race and especially gender—'

'Of course she did,' said his mother, derisively.

'—but . . . er . . . I think the book is more about the nature of kingship.'

'How so?'

'Um . . . because *Oroonoko*—you know, the African king—is civilised and has regal qualities, and he maintains them despite his enslavement, while the colonists' behaviour towards him is uncivilised and barbaric.'

'Very good.'

Angel smiled, pleased with himself. He even ventured a look at his father, who nodded in approval. A rare sight.

Thus boosted, Angel buttered his toast with enthusiasm. Angel one, gremlins nil. Madison was one step closer. Yet, the torment of anticipation was exquisite. If only his mother would have that conversation!

His mother's phone rang.

Angel observed her as she picked it up and listened without greeting the caller.

She darted an eye at him.

A chill ran through his body. What now?

She ended the call.

Who was it? asked his father with his gaze.

'Nothing,' she said.

Angel got back to buttering his toast, wondering what the call might have been about. Whether there was yet another undiscovered horror from the university.

His parents discussed Brexit, a topic he was bored of hearing about—including from his professors, who'd endlessly ventilated their views, despite it having nothing to do with literature—and on which he had zero opinions. As he sipped his tea, all he had ears for was two words: 'America' and 'Madison'.

For twenty interminable minutes, the conversation revolved around that topic—Boris Johnson, John Bercow, the EU, Donald Tusk, blah, blah, blah, endlessly. Having to keep track of the conversation was only made worse by Destiny's incessant questions about Amelia.

'So, Angel, how did you and Amelia meet?'
'Um . . . she was in my class.'
'And did you speak to her or did she speak to you first?'
'Um . . . I can't remember.'
'Do you think she's pretty?'
'Er . . . she's alright.'
'Do you go on dates?'
'Um . . . no, no.'
'Have you kissed her?'
'Um . . . no.'
'Why not?'
He fidgeted. 'We're not dating.'
'Why not?'
'I-I-I'm with Madison.'
'Why? Amelia is loads better!'
'Um . . . I-I-I'm just with Madison.'
'If you break up with Madison, will you date Amelia?'
'Um . . . er . . .'
'But will you?'
'I-I'm with Madison.'
'But will you?'
Angel frowned, shook his head, and, dropping his chin, took a bite from his toast.
'So?'
'So what?'
'What's the answer?'
'The answer to what?'
'If you break up with Mad—'
'Please, Destiny! Please!' Angel pushed the air back with his hands as he said it.
Destiny burst out laughing.
Angel chewed his toast, frowning, head bowed.
'That sweet girl likes you, you know.'
Angel said nothing.

'You should look closer to home.'

Angel still said nothing.

'She's very pretty.'

He kept chewing.

'Mum, do you agree that Amelia is pretty?'

Victoria paused her conversation to reply. 'Yes, she's very pretty.'

'And is she prettier than Madison?'

'Much prettier.' She carried on talking about Brexit.

'You see, Angel? Mum agrees.'

'Um . . . c-c-can we talk about something else?'

'No. I want to talk about Amelia.'

'Um . . .'

'So how often do you see her?'

'Er . . . I see her about.'

'Do you have lunch together?'

'Er . . . sometimes.'

'Does she live on campus?'

'Yes, yes.'

'Do you . . . visit her in her room?'

'Erm . . . sometimes.'

'Ooooh! Innnnteresting!'

Angel frowned, shook his head, and took another bite from his toast, his face nearly parallel to his plate.

'Angel, sit straight,' said his mother.

Angel did as told, but still kept his head bowed.

'So, Angel,' pressed Destiny, 'If you weren't with Madison, would you date Amelia?'

'Um . . . she's a friend.'

'But if you weren't with Madison.'

'Sh-Sh-She's a friend.'

'But if you weren't. Would she be more?'

'C-C-Can you pass me the sugar?'

'You already put sugar in your tea.'

'Did I?'

'Yes. So. Would she?'

'Um . . . I-I-I don't know. She's a friend.'

'How good a friend?'

'W-What do you mean?'

'Do you . . . help her with her course work? Does she help you?'

'Er . . . she's not in my class.'

'She told me you took her on two dates recently.'

'Oh? D-Did she?'

'Yes. Once to the cinema and once to McDonalds.'

'Oh . . . er . . . oh, yes, yes. It was her idea. There was a film she wanted to see. F-For her course work.'

'I see. And the McDonalds?'

'Um . . . er . . . she was hungry. It was not a date. I'd never take anyone to McDonald's.'

'But what were you two doing out in London on a Saturday night?'

Angel thought quickly. 'Um . . . s-she had to see a play for one of her modules. I bumped into her.'

'But Oxford Circus is *miles* away from the university.'

'Um . . . I was in the area doing something else.'

'Doing what?'

'Erm . . . er . . . I had to see a play too.'

'Oh, so you went together?'

'No, no. A different play.'

'I see. What a coincidence. Amazing!'

'Er . . . yes, yes . . . it was quite a coincidence.'

'You know what I think? You should have taken Amelia to the fancy restaurants, and Madison to McDonalds.'

Angel avoided answering by taking yet another bite from this toast.

'After all, Madison is American. So McDonalds would've been perfect for her.'

'Destiny. Don't be nasty,' said their mother.

'Okay, sorry, mum. But Madison is nasty! You thought it yourself!'

Victoria ignored her and carried on discussing Brexit.

'So, Angel, when the two of you were sitting in the cinema, did put your hand on her thigh?'

'No, no! Certainly not!'

'And did you walk her back to the dorm afterwards?'

'Um . . . er . . . yes.'

'Ah, so you're still a gentleman. She did say you are a *perfect gentleman.*'

Angel mentally checked his bladder, hoping desperately to find it full and thereby have an excuse to exit the scene. Alas, his bladder was completely empty, since he hardly ever drank anything. He considered pretending he needed lavatorial release, but he feared his mother's disapproving look. This was no time for taking chances!

He chewed in silence.

'Did she invite you to her room, or did you leave her at the entrance?'

'Er . . . entrance.'

'How disappointing. But did she kiss you good night?'

'Er . . . erm . . . no, no.'

'Did you want her to?'

'Erm . . . look, erm . . .'

'She has nice lips . . .'

He stirred his tea a second time, feigning intense concentration on this task.

'You've already stirred it,' his sister said.

He ignored her.

'But, Angel, you have to agree she has nice lips.'

He took a sip of his tea and another bite from his toast the instant he put the cup down.

'I think she has nice lips. I'd kiss her myself!' She closed her eyes and made an exaggerated kissing impression. 'Mmm. So nice!'

He looked up for an instant and, with an exhalation of horror, frowned, looked down, and shook his head while Destiny laughed.

Chapter CXXXVII

Angel's hope that his sister's interrogation would have a silver lining failed to materialise, for there was no suggestion after breakfast that his mother intended to discuss Madison with his father. Had she forgotten?

Exasperated by the suspense, yet wholly impotent, he went to his room. It might be that he'd have to raise the funds for the airfare on his own somehow. And with that in mind he scanned the room for possessions he could sell on eBay, but, although he had a great many valuable items around him, all belonged to his parents, while the ones that belonged to him—old clothes, books, notebooks, pens—had a resale value of zero. Besides, even if he managed to raise said funds, how would he get himself to the airport? He'd have to raise even more just to pay for the taxi to Leeds, which was a long way away. Worse still, a clandestine journey of that nature would incur the parental wrath, which would, in turn, quash any inclination to allow his return to university; it would, in fact, condemn him to two years of *hard* manual labour.

Desperate circumstances demanded desperate measures. He pulled out is phone and began typing a message to Amelia. She might have ideas on how to bring up the subject of Madison with his mother and what to say to induce her to discuss it with his father. Yet, this proved less easy than he'd assumed, for he found himself revising his wording again and again, never finding any that felt quite right.

He was still absorbed in this task when interrupted by a knock on the door. Like a startled cat, he jumped at the sound, and scrambled quickly to oseat himself behind his computer, with a university text on the screen.

'Yes?' he cheeped.

His mother opened the door.

'I need you to come into the drawing room,' she said.

'O-O-Okay,' he said.

It sounded as if he was in trouble. What had she discovered now?

He got up slowly and followed her downstairs, all the while scouring his brain for possible reasons for her being angry or tense. The ants began marching.

At this stage there was nothing he could think of from his university life that remained undiscovered.

Nothing except . . .

the library fine!

Angel's hand flew to his forehead. The ants sped up.

Bollocks! he thought. And how high was it now? He imagined his archenemy, fine-combing the rules and regulations to discover new reasons to slap on additional penalties or bloat existing ones. She would have been notified of his withdrawal, no doubt, interpreted it as a slight or an evasion stratagem, and set her sights on avenging herself through even more aggressive financial depredation. Could she have fast-tracked the penalty escalation process straight through to debt collection? Had a debt collection agency written or rung his parents? Was that why his mother darted an eye at him at the breakfast table when she received that call on her mobile? Had a debt collector shown up at their doorstep earlier in the day?

Angel swallowed.

It was all about to derail.

His assiduous reading, his fastidious grooming, his patient waiting, all been for naught. That one oversight would now cost him everything. The fragile universal balance, so carefully maintained through conscientiousness and an excruciating restraint, had been disrupted. He'd never see Madison again!

As the previous Sunday, he sat on the sofa in the gloomy drawing room. His heart thumped, his chest tightened, his bowels loosened, his respiration shallowed, breaths micron-deep.

His mother took a seat in an armchair. His father was already in the one adjacent, like, as Angel saw him, Ingres' *Jupiter in his Throne*. Angel dared not look at him.

'Right,' said his mother.

Angel's head retracted slightly into his shoulders.

'Your father and I are very disappointed with the choices you've made while at university this year.'

Here it comes, he thought, flinching. He squeezed the armrest to brace himself—although his grip was too weak to dent the upholstery.

'It's cost us a lot of money,' she continued.

Angel's knees began bouncing, but he stilled them almost immediately. His stomach cramped.

'And it's going to cost us more.'

He felt nauseous.

'But your father is of the opinion that you should go and visit this Madison.'

A defibrillator might as well have administered the maximum charge on his chest. He nearly leapt off the sofa.

'Oh, really?' he squealed.

His eyeballs popped out of their sockets and bounced on the floorboards.

'Yes. And I agree.'

'Oh!'

Angel put his hands on his chest and breathed spasmodically, overcome with inexpressible joy and relief.

'Now, as you know, we still don't approve of this relationship. But we think the only way you'll get clarity is by visiting her.'

But Angel was no longer listening, his mind swept off by the unfurling wave of elation.

'So we're going to pay for your flight.'

Angel ran his hand through his hair, smiling with stupefied mirth.

'However . . .' His mother held up a warning finger.

Angel sat up straighter; his posture was of intent listening, but his ears heard the singing of angels.

'You'll have to work within a strict budget.'

'Yes, yes, of course!' he said, with almost hysterical eagerness.

'And if you run out of funds before your return flight, we're just going to move the date forward. We're not going to send more.'

'Yes, of course! I'll stick to the budget! I'll stick to the budget! I promise! I promise!'

'Is that clear?'

'Yes! Yes! It's completely clear!'

'Alright. So go and make the arrangements with Madison and let me know when you've agreed on the dates.'

'Yes! Of course! I'll do it right away!'

'Very well.'

Chapter CXXXVIII

Angel tread on clouds. Suddenly, he saw beauty everywhere. The crisp colours. The joyous morning. The fragrant air. Rather than go to his room, he stepped out onto the grounds to take a moment—to appreciate and reflect on the turn of his fortunes. He revelled in the verdant grass, the bright azure, and the canorous birdsong.

What light through yonder trees breaks
It is the east, and Madison is the sun.

He walked to the mulberry tree and, standing under its canopy, gazed up at the branches. One day he'd bring Madison here. They'd stand together, holding hands and inhaling the fresh aromas of nature. He'd recite to her a poem in the baroque style. They'd sit on the bench, conversing about art history and the cosmos over fino and a charcuterie board. His parents would be away on business, his mother touring America, his father in South East Asia, and Destiny spending the month with a powerlifter in the north of Scotland—or, better, in the Shetland Islands, or, even better, in Norway. Or ideally, in the North Pole.

He wanted to learn the Spanish guitar, so that he could serenade Madison after sunset. And get better at the piano, so he could regale her with Misty, Chopin Nocturne Op. 9 No. 2 in E Flat Major, Liszt's Liebestraum, and Debussy's Clair de Lune. He also wanted to refine his culinary skills, not only so he could prepare the most delicious tapas imaginable, but also so he could cook the most ecstatic dishes that ever passed her tongue.

To this aim, he resolved to sign up for guitar and piano lessons, as well as to take cookery lessons from a three-star Michelin chef.

He also resolved to step up his reading and make an urgent to-read list. For there were a great many classics he'd yet to get to, and he wanted to have read them all before he was reunited with his paramour. And it wouldn't do to just read in vast quantities; the reading would only be worthwhile if he also knew the texts inside and out, so he could impress Madison by quoting random passages with ease, as and when the occasion arose. The texts would need to encompass not only poetry, but also prose fiction and plays from a variety of eras.

Madison made him want to be a better man.

This effervescence of thoughts, plans, and resolutions finally blinding him to his surroundings, Angel headed back into the house. He inspected his visage and hair in the bathroom mirror and thought of what hairstyle he'd adopt to fix Destiny's butchery. He pulled out his phone and began Googling the names of whatever 16th and 17th-century poets and dramatists came to mind, to decide whose portrait he'd show at the hair salon. Christopher Marlowe might still be possible, but Angel's hair wasn't quite that fluffy. John Fletcher was the next option, although that would require curlers, which he wasn't willing to use. Torquato Tasso could be a fall-back, but he worried such a haircut was nothing without a ruff. Lope de Vega was a reliable last stop, but it would look wrong without a high collar. So much to decide!

Of course, looking at the portraits made him think of painting, and painting of painting Madison. It'd be good to arrive at O'Hare with a framed oil painting of her under his arm. No, in a steel case with velvet interior padding. The only obstacle was his inability with the brush. Perhaps he could sign up for painting classes too. That would keep him occupied until he returned to university, at least. When Madison came, he would have her lay on a plaid blanket in the woods and paint her reading, like in the 1875 painting by Gyula Benczúr.

The prospect of a future visit by Madison in turn raised the issue of his ability to drive. He had a driver's licence, but after he drove his Ford Ka into a Grade II listed telephone box two years ago, he'd been met with stern refusals: from his insurer, to reinsure him, and from his parents to buy a new car or find another insurer. Perhaps Destiny would let him practice with her Mercedes. There'd be a price, of course, likely in the form of chores, but any price was worth paying if it was for Madison. If he could get insured, perhaps he could persuade his mother to ask his father if he could collect her from the airport in the Royce. But to get to that point he would need extreme levels of discipline, as otherwise his mother would continue to think him incapable: he'd have to be up at five every morning on the dot; be at the breakfast table at seven without fail, fully showered and attired; be ahead with his course reading and completely on top of the material; keep his room meticulously clean and organised—every surface polished, every item lined up, every part of bedclothing without a wrinkle and in place.

All of this was proof that Madison was good for him, and that his parents, and sister especially, were, as always, wrong.

He'd show them.

Chapter CXXXIX

ANGEL: My dearest and most beauteous damsel whom I passionately love, I come to Your Ladyship's messaging service with tremendous news. I am to visit you, as promised, this month. Please be so kind as to inform this devoted gentleman of yours of suitable days and times for his momentous arrival.

MADISON: Oh yea damn. Forgot. Get back to you

He waited for more, but Madison went offline. After four hours of nothing, Angel composed a new message:

ANGEL: This gentleman eagerly awaits pronouncement from Your Ladyship concerning ideal arrival days and time interval.

MADISON. S'up. Whatever you like

ANGEL: But this gentleman requires the above-mentioned information so that Your Ladyship can make the arrangements to greet him at the airport, since he very much looks forward to being reunited in mutual embrace.

MADISON: Can't you take a cab?

ANGEL: This gentleman can indeed order a coach to convey him to Your Ladyship's presence. However, Your Ladyship's appearance at the arrivals lounge of O'Hare would have amorous repercussions of enormous import.

MADISON: I'd rather you take a cab. It's a two-hour drive.

MADISON: And an hour of my time is worth a day of someone else's.

ANGEL: Of course! Very well, then, this gentleman will order a coach, then. Did your Ladyship say any day would be suitable?

MADISON: Yep.

ANGEL: Extensive preparations are required prior to departure. Would Saturday 2 November be a suitable day for this gentleman's descent upon your university abode.

MADISON: Oh you staying here?

ANGEL: But of course, my paramour!

MADISON: Oh

ANGEL: Is the accommodation not adequate for the intended purposes of romance and adoration?

MADISON: No, sure. It'll be fine.

ANGEL: Because this gentleman doth recall that Thy Ladyship had summoned him to her presence this very month of October, at delightful insistence, and had stated her impatient desire to behold his visage before December.

MADISON: That I did

ANGEL: It will be the most splendiferous and celestial occasion the world has ever witnessed.

MADISON: K...

ANGEL: Very well, then. This gentleman shall then make the necessary arrangements and transmit a message electronically to confirm that the travel dates are in place.

MADISON: How long are you staying for?

ANGEL: As long as your Ladyship desires. This gentleman would be available for your Ladyship's pleasure until December.

MADISON: Can we made it just a weekend thing?

ANGEL: A weekend?

MADISON: Yea. Arrive Saturday afternoon and leave Sunday morning

ANGEL: If the proposed date is unsuitable and Your Ladyship expects to be indisposed, this gentleman would be fully prepared and ready to select a different date more suitable for in-depth romancing.

MADISON: Fine. You can stay the week

ANGEL: What terrible brevity! But this gentleman must be respectful of Your Ladyship's wishes. Arrangements will be made to that effect.

MADISON: K

ANGEL: I leave Your Ladyship now to attend to the necessary business.

MADISON: Sure

Chapter CXL

After communicating the chosen dates to his mother, Angel set about planning the journey with zeal. With Madison a week away, there was no time to waste.

He began by making lists. Beginning with a list of the lists he'd need. After an hour, there were lists of books he needed to have read, of music he needed to have heard, of words he needed to have learnt, of quotes he needed to have memorised. Of clothes he intended to take, of shoes he intended to wear, of accessories he intended to pack. Of tasks that needed completing, of items that needed purchasing, of research that needed doing.

He appeared before his mother in her study to submit his wish list, hoping she would either supply the funds or order the items for him. This time she was sitting at her long desk.

She took the list from him and gave it a cursory glance.

'What do you want leather shirt cases for? Two hundred and twenty-five pounds per case! Are you joking?'

'Um . . . it's so that my shirts don't get wrinkled in the suitcase.'

'No, Angel. No. Research how to pack them or iron them when you get there.'

'But what about at the airport!'

'What about it?'

'I need a shirt to be pristine for when Madison greets me.'

'Lots of YouTube tutorials out there.'

His shoulders sank. 'Okay.'

'And why do you want three pairs of shoes resoled? If they're worn out, can't you choose different ones?'

'Um . . . no.'

'Are they worn out? Bring them here.'

'Er . . . no. It's just that I want the soles to be smooth and shiny on the underside.'

'Angel: no.'

'But—'

'And what do you want a Stefano Ricci shirt for?'

'To be elegant when I arrive.'

'You're not Emmanuel Macron or Vladimir Putin on a state visit. You're visiting an *American girl* you met at *uni*.'

'But it's only one!'

'Which is one too many.'

Angel sighed. 'Okay.'

'And the same with the six Eton shirts.'

'But—'

'When you have your own money, you can get Eton

shirts, but at this point in your life, you don't need them. And I'm not paying for them.'

'But—'

'We've seen what happened to the ones you bought some time ago.'

He rubbed his forehead. 'Okay.'

'Also, you already have a perfectly good suitcase. There's no need to give Rimowa eight-hundred pounds.'

'But—'

'It's not as if you'll be carrying a Rembrandt in your hand luggage.'

'It's just that—'

'We're also not going to the tailor to get you a bespoke suit . . .'

'It's just one for when—'

'You had your chance for your father's birthday. And we know how that ended.'

He scratched his temple. 'Okay.'

'And this Folio Society edition of *The Faerie Queene*—what's wrong with Penguin Classics?'

'It's just for the flight.'

'Again—what's wrong with Penguin Classics?'

'Erm . . . it's not . . .'

'It's not what?'

'Elegant.'

'It's practical. Exactly what you need in an aeroplane cabin.'

'Yes, but—'

'So, if you want a book to read on the plane, we can get you a paperback. Or even better, a Kindle. Amazon has free Kindle classics. But no five-hundred-and-eighty-five-pound Folio Society edition. That's absurd.'

Angel bowed his head. 'Okay.'

'As to the haircut, yes, we can agree on that.'

'Oh, good!' he breathed, smiling.

'But I'm not taking you to Stuart Phillips in London.'

'Oh.'

'I'll take you to the walk-in barber in York.'

'The walk-in barber!'

'Monday afternoon or Wednesday morning.'

'Er . . . Monday afternoon.'

'Good. In that case, we leave at two.'

'Um . . . okay.'

Angel went back to his room.

Mother six, Angel nil.

He hadn't expected her to be cooperative, but it was worth the try. At least he got a haircut.

Said haircut went according to plan the following day, but the barber insisted on tidying up his facial hair while at it, and ended up being too liberal with the clippers, to the extent that he almost obliterated the effect Angel had wanted to achieve. He was back to square one, essentially. He consoled himself with the thought that he still had five days to regrow at least part of what had been shorn.

Left with no option, he followed his mother's diktat to research the optimal ways to fold and pack his garments. He then spent three hours experimenting and practising, fastidiously pursuing geometrical perfection. And, since he still hoped to persuade Madison to greet him at the airport, in all iterations leaving a change of clothes near the top of the case so that he could access it at O'Hare, before the sliding doors at the arrivals terminal unveiled his person to the expectant beloved.

This, in turn, required rehearsing his arrival, beginning with his walk. He desired to appear dignified, yet relaxed; important, yet casual; neat, yet unselfconsciously so. His pace, the tilt of his chin, the swing of his arm, the rolling of his shoulders—all critical details requiring attention. The same with his face: the position of his eyebrows, the tension in his lips, the speed of his blinking, demanded analysis and polish.

To better visualise the scene of their reunion, he did an image search of the airport to reacquaint himself with the interior (he'd passed through it once when he was thirteen). He saw that, because the sliding doors were made mostly out of glass, Madison would see him approaching from a long way off, which made imperative a perfectly executed walk.

It occurred to him that he should arrive bearing flowers. As fresh ones were impractical to carry in the cabin, his best option was to press them. He was annoyed he hadn't thought of it the day before, as his mother might have let him pick up roses from the florist while in York. Not daring to ask his mother, he went to Destiny.

He found her in her room, on the bed, painting her toenails. The walls were covered with posters of Giants Live, the IPF World Championships, and women powerlifters.

'Do . . . er . . . do you think,' he said, 'you could stop by a supermarket on the way back from the gym tomorrow and pick up a dozen roses?'

'Ooh!' She smiled broadly. 'Have you decided to break up with Madison and declare yourself to Amelia?'

'Er . . . no, no. They're for Madison.'

'How are you going to carry them on the aeroplane?'

'Um . . . I'm going to press them.'

'Aren't you leaving in five days? There's not enough time for them to dry.'

'I thought I could dry them in the oven.'

'I see. Well, I can pick up the flowers, but . . .' She held up her index finder.

Angel waited.

'Only if they're for Amelia.'

'Um . . . but I need them for Madison.'

'No can do.'

'W-Why not?'

'Because I don't like Madison.'

'But—'

'No way. No way!'

'But w-why are you so hostile? You've never met her.'

'Well, if I ever do, I'm going to rip her eyes out!'

'Why!?'

'Because of what she's done to you. I won't have *anyone* disrespect my brother like that! I'm going to break her in half!'

'Disrespect? But she loves me!'

She chuckled. 'Well, you'll see soon enough.'

'So . . . er . . . y-y-you won't get the flowers?'

'Never.'

'Please?'

'No.'

Angel's shoulders dropped, and he left with his tail between his legs.

In the absence of flowers, it would all hinge on his choice of poem—the poem he would recite to her, once past the sliding doors. Back in his room, he pulled out Pablo Neruda's *Love Poems*, sat at his desk—on the hard chair, with his back straight, under bright lights—and spent the next two hours leafing through the volume, going back and forth, agonising over half a dozen of the poems, reciting them while imagining himself at the terminal, and trying to divine Madison's reaction to each.

Chapter CXL

Loving in truth, and fain in verse my love to show,
That she, dear she, might take some pleasure of my pain,

Now, along with poetry, Madison enjoyed fine dining and wines. He considered researching the best restaurants in the Chicago area, but, given that his mother had pulled the purse strings so tightly, it occurred to him that maybe he should first inquire about his budget. After dinner, while his mother sat in the parlour reading a novel, he approached her.

'Um . . .' he said.

She looked up. 'Yes?'

'Um . . . er . . . w-what's my budget for the visit?'

'We've agreed to give you a thousand dollars.'

'Er . . . i-is it for the whole week?'

'Yes.'

'And . . . um . . . i-i-is . . . w-w-will there be anything else?'

'What do you mean?'

'Y-Y-You know, for food and taxis . . . and other expenses.'

'That's what the thousand dollars are for.'

'B-B-But the taxi from the airport could be a hundred.'

'Isn't this Madison picking you up at the airport?'

'Um . . .'

'Because if she's not, that's a red flag.'

'No . . . er . . . no . . . er . . . s-she's picking me up.'

'Good. So you'll have the whole thousand for the week, then. That's over a hundred pounds a day. More than enough.'

'Um . . .'

'Anything else?'

'Er . . . no . . . er . . . thank you.'

He went back to his room.

So fine dining was out. Unless, of course, he took her out for dinner on the day he arrived and starved for the rest of the week. Yes, that was more to his liking! More consistent with his aesthetic! Besides, Madison had been doing food challenges, which was gross and absurd, but Destiny had told him, after she did the full English challenge with Leah Shutkever, that if one was successful, one could get the meal for free, so perhaps he could join Madison and have a bite or two if she did one mid-week to tide him over—although he worried seeing her gorge messily would prove embarrassing. Hopefully, Madison still undertook these challenges elegantly and the dish involved would be a fine one, not something grotesque like prawn cocktails, McDonald's, or onion rings.

This reminded him to try and persuade Madison to greet him at the airport.

ANGEL: How farest thee, most beloved damsel? Preparations are apace! I shall be landing at O'Hare aboard flight KL1540 on Saturday 2 November at 15:25. Wilt thou reconsider existing arrangements? This knight in shining armour desires nothing more but to behold thy visage at the terminal on the appointed day and time.

MADISON: I've decided I don't want you to come and visit anymore.

'Eh?' His gasp / squeal was so high it was almost a whistle.

Heart racing, hands trembling, his five-character reply required one hundred and twenty-seven keystrokes.

ANGEL: Why??

MADISON: Meh

Angel rubbed his forehead, his respiration having become rapid and shallow, caged by an aching chest.

He stared at the screen, unable to decide what to make of her answer or how to respond. He'd left it too late. He'd left it too late!

Five minutes passed.

MADISON: You still there?

Angel's fingers hovered over the phone screen, but still his mind was blocked, his cranium overwhelmed by bees.

Another five minutes passed.

MADISON: Hellooo?

Yet, his cognitive function continued to fail him.

MADISON: I can see you're there!

He felt dizzy, weak, out of breath.

MADISON: Well, guess what?

His chest felt as if Johannes had punched it, a tingling sensation developed in his arms and around the mouth.

MADISON: I . . .

MADISON: was . . .

MADISON: KIDDING LOL

MADISON: Of course I'll meet you at the airport, you silly man!

As if the valve on a pressure cooker had been suddenly released, Angel deflated and dropped the phone, his body washed over by an immense wave of relief. He put his hands to his chest and, with steepled eyebrows, sighed rapidly at the glad news, looking at the ceiling, thanking heaven.

After a minute, having somewhat composed himself, he picked up the phone.

ANGEL: It is with cosmic-sized relief that I peruse thy reply. Glad tidings, indeed! I shall then make an appearance for this splendiferous occasion of our glorious and magisterial reunion.

MADISON: . . . but I have one condition

ANGEL: Name thy condition and it shall be done!

MADISON: You have to bring me a present

ANGEL: But of course! Say no more!

MADISON: And you also have to take me out for dinner. Like a gentleman

ANGEL: Naturally!

MADISON: And you also have bring me English treats

ANGEL: They shall be procured this instant!

MADISON: And you also have to bring a guitar and serenade me.

ANGEL: I'd be delighted!

MADISON: And a box of chocolates

ANGEL: I shall find you the biggest and most luxurious one there is!

MADISON: Because I want a chocopology!

ANGEL: I shall be glad to give it!

MADISON: And giant sunflowers

ANGEL: They shall be presented with a bow!

MADISON: And I mean GIANT

ANGEL: They shall be found!

MADISON: Very well, then. I'll consider maybe showing up.

ANGEL: I beseech thee!

MADISON: I'll let you know when I decide

ANGEL: But I thought you had?

MADISON: I'm undecided. We'll see

ANGEL: But I must know!

MADISON: You'll know

ANGEL: When?

MADISON: At a time of my choosing

ANGEL: I have to know before Saturday

MADISON: Gotta go

ANGEL: Already?

MADISON: Speak to you sometime

ANGEL: Farewell, princess of my heart!

Madison went offline.

Angel rubbed his forehead and stared into space, his irises shooting in all directions like bouncy balls.

She must be pranking me, he decided at last, shaking his head and breaking into a smile.

However, that smile faded when he realised he'd now have to bring a guitar and bulky sunflowers. His mother had an old guitar in the house, but the online florists only offered small sunflowers.

He went to his mother again.

'Erm . . .' he began, 'W-W-When I go to America . . . c-c-could . . . erm . . . could I . . . take your guitar?'

'Why do you want to take my guitar?'

'Um . . . to . . . er . . . um . . . to s-s . . . to s-s-serenade Madison when I get there.'

'Oh, for goodness sake!'

'Um . . .'

'No, Angel! You may not take my guitar.'

'W-W-W-Why not?'

'Because no.'

Angel sighed. 'Erm . . . okay.'

Not daring to then ask her for a visit to the florist, he went back to his room. He lay on the bed and stared at the ceiling, his cogs turning.

His phone buzzed.

Amelia had sent him a message.

He put his phone down and continued pondering.

After ten minutes, it occurred to him that the solution was in his phone! Wasn't there an app for everything these days? He could maybe download a virtual guitar and serenade Madison with that. And he could no doubt find a botanical app for the flowers. Or maybe an art app, where he could find a suitable Van Gogh painting.

He dived into the app store and easily located several virtual guitars. An app capable of reproducing the sunflowers he required, on the other hand, proved impossible, and he wasted hours going through dozens of flower identifiers, e-florists, plant trackers and organisers, art software, and photograph retouching tools.

Thus, it was back to physical with the flowers. Yet, the physical, he thought, could be two-dimensional. And for a two-dimensional solution he already had the tools, as he'd dabbled with oils in the past. He could paint the sunflowers and then speed-dry the oils with a hair dryer.

He went to the outhouse where he'd set up his easel years ago, hoping to find a small, unused canvas. One remained. His tubes of oil, brushes, and the turpentine were also still there, so he spent time the following day working on the painting.

This he did after breakfast, with poor results. There was a reason he'd given up oil painting in the first place. All the same, for lack of options, he persisted. Besides, painting with oils suited his aesthetic, so he made sure to photograph himself from behind the canvas, holding a palette in one hand, and a brush in the other. Like in Velazquez's *Las meninas*. The image he uploaded to Instagram and earned him a like and a comment from Amelia.

When he discovered no amount of further brushwork could improve his painting, he left a fan running in front of it and went back to his room. Three hours later, his mother found him there, memorising Nerudan verse.

'Why is there a fan running in the outhouse?'

'Um . . . I'm trying to dry an oil painting.'

'Why can't you leave it to dry normally?'

'Er . . . because I want to take it with me to America.'

'Couldn't you paint with something that dries more quickly?'

He wanted to explain that oil was the only medium that fit his aesthetic, but knew she wouldn't understand. Much less since it had to do with Madison.

'Um . . .'

'Anyway, I've switched it off. It's a bad idea to leave appliances unattended.'

'But—'

'Especially with flammable items around.'

'But—'

'I'm not willing to risk a fire for Madison.'

'But—'

But she left before he could utter his objection.

Later, Destiny found him in the drawing room, practising with his virtual guitar app.

'What are you doing?' she said.

'I'm composing a song.'

'Cool. What's inspired you?'

His eyes bounced around. 'Um . . .'

Destiny sighed and stared momentarily at the ceiling. 'Don't tell me. Madison.'

'Um . . . no . . . no, I just wanted to compose some music.'

'Why don't you ask mum for her guitar? I'd be a lot easier than on that tiny phone.'

'Er . . .'

'It's because it's for Madison, isn't it?'

'Um . . . no, no!'

'It is!'

'Er . . . no, it's not!'

'You should be composing songs for Amelia,' she said, irritated. 'That girl truly loves you.'

Angel said nothing.

'You're deluded. Have you seen Madison's Instagram lately?'

'Er . . .'

'Because I have. What in the blooming heck!'

'Um . . . s-s-she's just pranking people.'

'Oh, yes, of course. So obvious. Silly me!'

'Y-You don't know her.'

'What are you gonna do when you get there? Put your face in her green hairy armpit and go mmm, baby!'

Angel turned away in disgust. 'Agh!'

She burst out laughing. 'You're gonna kiss her and it's gonna feel like a hardware shop!'

Angel crinkled his brow, shook his head, and waved her to go away.

'And what if she's pierced her clit?' She grinned.

'Can you . . . please . . . go away?'

'You might as well put a handful of fifty pee coins in your mouth to get used to tasting metal!' She blasted him with laughter.

Angel bowed his head, frowning, and stared at his phone screen.

'I bet you Amelia is all clean-shaven down there. Probably smells like roses!'

'Can you please stop?'

'And when she goes to the bathroom, rose petals come out of her bum!'

'Please!'

'But Madison? She probably doesn't even bother

with pads or tampons. You know, because of the *patriarchy!*' She bracketed the word with air quotes.

'Please, Destiny, stop! Please!'

'She lets it run down her legs and gets offended if anyone complains.'

'Destiny, please!'

'She might even wear white trousers when on her period, or shorts, just to make a point!'

Angel blocked his ears.

Destiny grabbed his left wrist, forced his hand away, which was easily done, and put her grinning mouth in front of his auricula.

'And I'm sure she stopped shaving her legs! They must be like cheese graters by now!'

'Please! Just stop!' Angel struggled to get away, but Destiny's hold on his wrist was like a vice.

'But if you run your hand over Amelia's leg, I bet you it'll feel like *velvet!* Mmm! Lovely and smooth!'

'Stop! Please!'

Destiny released him and pulled away. 'I'll stop for now.'

Angel dropped his hands, rubbed his wrist, and picked up his phone again.

'But!' she said.

He looked up at her.

'Come next week, you won't be asking me to stop. You'll be *begging* me for more!'

'W-Why do you say that?' he said, sulking.

'Because by next week, you won't love Madison anymore.'

He stared.

She held his gaze, and after a moment, satisfied, she left.

Angel got back to his guitar app, firmly determined

to keep loving Madison no matter what beyond the coming week. Their love was *unbreakable.* It would *triumph* over sceptics and naysayers!

Chapter CXLI

On the evening before his departure, Angel found his mother in the parlour and asked: 'What time do we leave tomorrow?'

'There's no we.'

'Um . . . what do you mean?'

'You're leaving. I'm staying here.'

'But . . . I have to get the airport!'

'You'll have to phone a taxi.'

'Oh. But why?'

'Because I don't like that girl you're going to see.'

'But you paid for the trip!'

'So you can get clarity.'

'But I'm clear!'

'I don't think you are. But I hope you will be by the time you're back.'

Angel looked away, eyebrows steepled.

'I've transferred a thousand pounds into your account.'

'Oh, good!' He smiled.

'The extra is to pay for the taxi to and back from Leeds.'

His shoulders sank.

Victoria continued. 'They'll be about a hundred and twenty each way, so make sure you have enough left at the end of the week.'

'Okay . . .'

'And don't forget the replacement debit card.'

'Er . . .'

'You still have it, right? I only gave it to you yesterday.'

'Yes, yes, I have it.'

'Very well. If I were you, I'd phone to book your taxi now.'

'Er . . . okay. Do you know the number?'

'You can Google it.'

'Er . . . okay. And . . . what time should I book it for?'

'It's minimum two hours to Leeds airport. And you should be there three hours before your flight.'

'Oh!'

Victoria checked the time on her phone. 'I'd hurry. Your flight leaves at six a.m.'

Angel checked the time on his phone. It was nine o'clock in the evening. And there was so much to do still!

He rushed to his room to organise the taxi and pack his bag. The taxi business took half an hour. The suitcase about two, due to last-minute wardrobe indecisions and key items being still in the dryer. Among his luggage he included the sunflowers oil painting, which he'd had to dry with a blowdrier. The most important item in his task list, however, was to obtain confirmation from Madison of whether she'd meet him at the airport. That was essential to fulfilling his vision, but also a matter of practical necessity, since who knew how much a taxi to her flat would cost. A hundred dollars? Two hundred? In the worst-case scenario, he'd not have enough left to wine and dine Madison upon arrival!

ANGEL: My carriage to Leeds Bradford Airport is ninety minutes away. Hath Her Ladyship seen it fit to pronounce herself on the matter of greeting this dignified gentleman at the arrivals' terminal in O'Hare at 15:25 tomorrow?

The message was delivered, but not opened.

Angel waited, staring at the screen for five full minutes.

ANGEL: Doth Her Celestial and Most Serene Ladyship slumber?

The message was delivered, but not opened.

He rubbed his forehead and stared at the screen for another five minutes.

ANGEL: My Lady?

This time the message was delivered and opened, but not answered.

Madison went back offline.

He telephoned her.

But her telephone rang and rang and rang without an answer.

He ended the call and tried again.

Same result.

He tried a third time.

Same result.

Nothing to do but to press on. She'd be there, he told himself.

With an hour and ten minutes to kill, and everyone having gone to bed, he dragged his case to the top of the stairs. At the point of lifting it to carry it down, however, he lacked the strength to get it off the ground. He put his hand on his head and stared at his case, stumped. He stared down the corridor, hoping maybe Destiny was still up, but the space under her door was dark. The only solution he could think of was to stand on the first step down, legs wide apart, facing the suitcase, and with both hands pull it towards him and thereby towards the edge of the top step, until the case dropped onto the step below, between his legs, and repeat all the way down. As the procedure was noisy, after seven steps Destiny came out in her pyjamas to investigate.

'Ah, it's you making that racket,' she said, *sotto voce*, but annoyed.

'Um . . . I'm just getting my case down.'

Destiny sighed. 'Give me that.'

She snatched his case from between his legs and walked it down with ease. Angel followed. Once he reached the foot of the stairs, she said: 'You going now?'

'Um . . . yes.'

She chuckled and shook her head. 'Amelia said to tell you she wishes you a safe journey. She said you haven't replied to her messages.'

'Oh, y-you're messaging?'

'Of course we are.'

'Oh.'

'Anyway. You tell Madison if she ever dares show up here I'm gonna snap her like a *twig!*' His sister underlined her statement with bared teeth and an illustrative gesture.

Angel stared, eyebrows raised.

She rolled her eyes and shook her head again. 'Going to back bed. See you next week.'

He headed for the kitchen and spent the remaining hour practising his serenade song on the guitar app.

The taxi arrived at one o'clock. Having been forced to rise at five the previous morning, Angel was by then exhausted and itchy-eyed, although too nervous to sleep. The reverberated knock on the service door jolted him out of his trance.

When he opened, he found a thin, dishevelled man with long, rusty Brillo-pad hair and demonic eyes. Angel thought of Michel Houellebecq. Behind the man was a dark car, headlights shining into the mist.

'Car for Angel?' the man croaked.

'Er . . . yes, that's me.'

Chapter CXLII

Angel dragged his case out of the house and shut the door. The pebbles crunched as the man carried his suitcase to the car. Angel followed and climbed in as the driver closed the boot. This was it, Angel thought, taking a deep breath, his heart racing; the great moment had arrived.

The driver turned the car around at a glacial pace. Angel looked out the window to seek the moon, but the sky was a black abyss. Once they made it onto the road, Angel straightened himself, holding his head erect in a posture appropriate for the occasion: that of a gentleman on his way to an important meeting. His shoes were shined to diamond polish, every item of clothing was crisp and clean, and his suitcase was perfectly packed, with every item inside precisely folded. He'd wiped the dust off even the most inaccessible seams and corners of its hard carapace with tissues, earbuds, and Dettol. He'd included a variety of colognes and aftershaves, for him to apply depending on the occasion; skin moisturiser and lip balm, for Madison's dermal delight; Nivea and talcum powder, for the same plus olfactory pleasure; finally, eyedrops and spearmint chewing gum, for deploying before disembarkation, to banish redness from his sclerae and any hint of halitosis. And, of course, he'd memorised five different Neruda love poems, to have options at the great encounter, one for each probable mood.

The driver proved as loquacious as a mummy, which suited Angel, since it allowed him tranquillity to contemplate, daydream, and reminisce. He checked his phone while crossing the moors in case Madison had replied; she hadn't. He checked again on the A170; she hadn't. Again on the A1(M); she hadn't. Yet again on the A59; she hadn't. And one more time on the M658; she hadn't. Perplexingly, she'd been online almost as many times as he'd passed Eddie Stobart lorries on the motorway. The Leeds Bradford Airport came into view without her reply appearing on his phone.

'Houellebecq' stopped in front of the building and asked for £116. Angel paid, got out, and checked his phone again while the driver retrieved his luggage. Nothing.

The vantablack above was broken only by the harsh, cold lights around the terminal and adjacent car parks; the silence by the sparse hiss, hum, and rattle of cars passing or idling nearby; and his composure by a frigid, blustery wind that nervously flapped his clothing, with the selection of which he'd placed fine fabrics above comfort. Any residual warmth still clinging to him from the heated taxi was blasted off in a picosecond, leaving him with the shivers, the amplitude of which was increased by anxiety and nerves. In his desire to practice his serenade song, he'd forgotten to eat. He expanded the telescopic handle of his suitcase and dragged it inside, nearly dislocating his shoulder with effort.

There was no need for him to check in, because his mother had already done it online, so he went straight through to security.

And there is where the problems started.

Firstly, he'd forgotten to put his toiletries in a clear bag, so he had to purchase one for £1, which he didn't have. He'd had to find a cash machine, withdraw a tenner, and buy something cheap he didn't need to get change. Secondly, he'd forgotten that there were volume limits to these toiletries, and so the 400ml-tin of Nivea was confiscated. Thirdly, because of the above, his meticulous packing was left in disarray, forcing him to refold and reorganise every item of clothing once past security. The x-ray machine had bleeped because of the clip pinching the back of his trousers, so he had to take it off and put it back on without the help of a mirror. One of his shoes was scuffed after accidentally dropping it while taking it out of the tray. Finally, he discovered, upon opening the suitcase, that the sunflower painting had not yet completely dried and had both stained the inside of his case and been damaged by it.

Thus, a journey that had so far gone without incident was now to resume with imperfections.

With a crinkled forehead, Angel made his way to the duty-free area.

There he encountered further problems, for his longing for Madison's smile made him susceptible to temptation. First to tempt him were the perfumes: Portrait of a Lady by Frederic Malle, Baccarat Rouge 540 by Maison Francis Kurkdjan, Beige by Chanel, Rose Ardente by Givenchy, and Jason Wu's Eau de Parfum. After much vacillation and consulting on his phone, he opted for a 70ml bottle of the Baccarat Rouge, which cost him £140. Second to tempt him were the chocolates: Debauve and Gallais, Amedei, Pierre Marcolini, Richart, House of Grauer, and House of Knipschildt. These were not ordinarily available at airport duty-free shops, he was told by the shopkeeper, but they were running a limited trial. This only gave Angel a sense of urgency, and, again after much vacillation and smartphone consultation, he settled on the box of Debauve and Gallais with the painting of Marie Antoinette. It cost him £200. Third to tempt him was the W. H. Smith, since Madison had asked him for 'English' treats, by which she meant British chocolate bars and crisps—he'd never managed to correct her American habit of calling 'English' anything British, but he'd found it endearing in the end. These treats being cheap, he filled a big bag of them, hoping to impress her. This cost him £24.

My bounty is as boundless as the sea,
My love as deep; the more I give to thee,
The more I have, for both are infinite.

By the time he was done, he had £540 left. He'd have to forgo the wine at the restaurant when he got to Chicago, but he'd cover up by explaining he was tired from the journey.

He thought of having breakfast, but, having already spent half his funds, he deemed it best to wait till dinner with Madison, and then eat as it befit the occasion. A signal day was not one for pedestrian sandwiches or industrial croissants.

He checked his phone for the two-hundred-and-forty-seventh time. Madison hadn't replied. Given that his flight was to depart in an hour, it seemed opportune, or perhaps urgent, to send her another message.

ANGEL: What ensnareth Her Ladyship thus? This distinguished gentleman is now at the airport, his ship due to sail in an hour, and he anxiously and eagerly awaiteth Her Ladyship's pronouncement on the vital issue previously communicated. This gentleman wouldeth be much obliged to receive Her Ladyship's gracious reply.

The message was delivered, but not opened.

He rubbed his forehead.

But he calculated it would be eleven o'clock in the evening in Madison's time zone. Perhaps she'd gone to sleep.

No matter; he had a four-hour layover in Amsterdam, which gave her enough time to sleep, rise, and see his messages.

He trusted her.

When he noticed a nearby screen was already displaying his gate number, he went to it. By the time he got there, however, a long queue had already formed in front. He joined it, feeling elegant, standing straight as a broomstick, and imagined Madison observing him somehow and noticing his impeccable appearance.

Once past the desk, he strolled down the airbridge with a leisurely pace; to walk fast and scramble to overtake each other, like some were doing, was unbecoming. It was also beneath the dignity of such an important day.

Not in keeping with it, unfortunately, were his seating arrangements. His mother had selected for him a middle seat on the starboard side. In row 38—right at the back of the aircraft—which didn't recline. Obviously, the cheapest seat. And a reminder of her disapproval.

However, the flight to Amsterdam was only two hours and twenty minutes, and, besides, the occasion demanded that he travelled with his spine upright, maintaining a couth posture under all circumstances. True elegance manifested in all settings, not just in luxurious ones. This was, therefore, an opportunity to prove his nobility of soul.

His musculature, on the other hand, presented a more immediate problem, proving insufficient to transfer his suitcase from the cabin floor to the overhead compartment. This problem, moreover, confronted him as the person assigned to the window seat beside him, a Brylcreemed man of about thirty in a grey suit, reached his row. Brylcreem waited, taking care not to hide his impatience. Angel waited too, irresolutely scanning the cabin for the nearest crew member.

Brylcreem said, 'Will you please sit the fuck down?'

'Um . . .'

Angel moved aside so Brylcreem could access his seat; the latter elbowed past and sat down.

A female crew member emerged from the galley—a slim, ponytailed blonde.

'Excuse me sir, can I get through?' she said.

'Um . . .' Angel hesitated, finding he could not move in either direction because of the queue behind him.

He also found the case didn't fit in the space between the isle seat in his row and the one in front.

'Your luggage needs to go in the overhead compartment.'

'Um . . .' Angel short-circuited, limbs twitching in antagonistic directions.

'Up there,' said the stewardess, pointing at the compartment and as if he were slow or foreign.

'Um . . .'

He tried to lift his case, but, despite pulling with all his might, was unable to put air beneath it. His whole body trembled with the effort.

'That case should be in the hold,' said the stewardess, her voice raised. 'You need to go back out and hand it to my colleague by the door.'

'In the hold!' he yelped.

'Yes. It's too heavy.'

He was against it going in the hold since this meant the indignity of having to scramble for it in the carousel at the other end.

'Um . . . um . . . it's just my clothes . . . it's just my clothes . . .'

The stewardess refused to believe him, so she grabbed the handle and pulled, as if to confirm its excessive weight. The latter being non-existent, the case flew up and nearly hit the ceiling.

'Oops! Sorry, sir!' she said, after she hit him in the face.

Angel rubbed his cheek and straightened his jacket. Brylcreem, who'd been watching from his seat, sniggered and shook his head.

She added, 'This can go in the overhead compartment.'

Thankfully, she didn't ask him to do the job, and did it herself with ease.

'Please take a seat,' she said.

'Um . . . just a moment.'

He took off his jacket, careful not to brush anything accidentally in case the corduroy picked up dust, neatly folded it in half lengthwise, checking and re-checking for symmetry and alignment, and kept the garment close to him, rather than storing it overhead, where it could get wrinkled as fellow passengers vacuum packed the compartment with luggage, linty coats, and duty-free shopping. Only then did he do as instructed.

His neighbour on the left was a child of about eleven, whose parents sat across the aisle.

Although Neruda's *Love Poems* beckoned from his suitcase, as did Garci Rodríguez de Montalvo's *Amadis of Gaul*, Angel found himself too tired, or wired, to read verse or Mediaeval romance. He should have taken a modern novel, he realised—something easy. But he immediately scolded himself for desiring the path of least resistance—for relaxing his standards. No. If he'd thought of taking a modern novel, it should have been something intellectually challenging. He was on his way to visit Madison, after all! And this demanded that he be at his best on all fronts. Thus, Thomas Pynchon's *Gravity's Rainbow*, Robert Musil's *The Man without Qualities*, or James Joyce's *Finnegan's Wake*, would have been in order. For now, he chose the inflight magazine. He imagined Madison observing him from across the aisle and adopted an air of nonchalance.

Yet, this air was entirely at odds with his feelings. Once settled and with his mind back on Madison, his chest tightened, the ants marched, his heart pounded, and his hands turned to ice. These vectors of discomfort intensified as the craft taxied onto the runway and grew acute as the engines roared and his back was pressed against the backrest. As the Boeing 737 accelerated and became airborne, Angel thought that, from that moment, each second that passed shortened his distance from Madison. Their reunion, once months in the future, was now just fourteen hours away!

A loud crackling and crinkling on his left pulled him out of his reverie. When he turned, he saw the boy had been given a bag of cheese puffs and was scoffing them down, one by one, in continuous and rapid succession, as if by a conveyor belt. The ceaseless crunching was not too much of a nuisance, due to the aircraft's low pressurisation and loud engines; the real nuisance was the rapidly accumulating yellow crumbs on the boy's polo shirt. By the time he began his second bag, the boy's chest had become a constellation of debris, which threatened to fall on Angel's trousers and shirtsleeve.

Angel slid as far away from the boy as the seat would allow. This brought him into contact with Brylcreem's arm, however, who was working on his laptop and burnt holes into Angel with gamma ray eyes. Angel was consequently forced to settle closer to the boy, whose crumbs had already dusted with yellow the edge of Angel's seat. Angel had to pick out a dehydrated corn-based particle from his trouser leg and keep vigilant against future ones for the rest of the flight.

The aircraft landed in Amsterdam's Schiphol Airport at 8:30am. The weather outside was windy and stormy. As he disembarked, he realised that he was now closer in time from Madison, but further away geographically.

He checked his phone.

No reply.

Even though she'd been online since.

Maybe she woke up groggy and decided, in deference to the hallowed day, to reply when she was fully lucid and alert.

But meanwhile, a message from Amelia, wishing him a safe journey.

She also added a bit of university gossip: Camaro had been suspended, having been caught stealing property from fellow students. According to Saïd, Camaro sold the stolen goods on eBay and then used the proceeds to pay clever students to do his coursework and essays for him. Saïd, in turn, had asked her to mention to Angel that he, Angel, owed him £100, but Amelia had told him that Angel was no longer at the university and refused to give Saïd his address. Angel began composing a reply, thanking her and mentioning that one night he'd seen Camaro steal his roommate's Rolex, but then realised that confessing knowledge of the incident, after never having reported it, would reflect badly on him, so he abandoned his reply and put his phone away.

He found a seat near the Mediterranean Sandwich Bar and, gazing at the sign on the giant, green, iron wheel, again considered eating. His empty stomach and icy hands angrily demanded it. Travellers around him, many with greasy hair and stubble, parkas and duffel coats, haggard faces and predatory eyes, all ate and drank voraciously, tired and tense, furtively muttering at or ignoring each other. Yet, Angel worried about already being low on funds for his dinner with Madison, so, instead of buying a sandwich, he pulled out *Amadis of Gaul*, opened it on the first chapter, and readied to read.

But first, he checked his social media.

His last Instagram post had not earned him a like from Madison. Nor a comment. Perhaps, he told himself, the algorithm had hidden it. Didn't posts become less visible after an hour? As to Madison's page, once again he dared not look. Her pranks were amusing, but today was a day for solemnity; a day for the renewal of their everlasting love, for fulfilling promises, for keeping oaths, for re-consecrating himself to Madison. He imagined himself a knight, in coat of armour, on one knee, holding a sword in one hand and bowing his head before Madison, his queen, swearing eternal loyalty. He imagined himself on an epic journey, crossing jagged mountains, ancient forests, and deep ravines; slaying giants, dragons, and cyclopes; overcoming ghosts, apparitions, and sorcery; facing snow, storms, and volcanoes; defeating armies, plagues, and serpents; winning duels, games, and jousting tournaments; escaping witches, labyrinths, and dungeons; witnessing miracles, portents, and magic; surviving wounds, famine, and even death; all in the name of Love, sustained by the memory of his queen, Madison the Beautiful, Madison the Beloved, Madison the Bookish, Madison the Longed for, Madison the Fair, Madison the Glorious, Madison the Perfect, Madison the Precious, Madison the Troubadour, Madison the Wise! He imagined Nicholas Hilliard's portraits of Queen Elizabeth depicting Madison instead, victorious in her regal glory. He imagined entering the arrival's terminal at O'Hare, to find a red carpet, cordoned off on each side, with Mediaeval musicians playing a dignified march, and maidens throwing roses, as he walked towards Madison, with cheers of celebration erupting as the two of them embraced.

He wondered how she would have dressed and done her hair for the occasion. Since her Instagram account, she'd said, was designed to mislead people, to make them think she was a boozer and a glutton so that fellow students underestimated her academic potential, perhaps she'd also intended the account to make her professors think she'd become a feminist, as they'd then give her higher marks. After all, weren't all professors, male and female, feminists these days? Didn't they all take exception at sceptics, like Jae? Mastropasqua was unpopular with the academic staff because he was an outlier, a renegade academic, the demonic scourge of modern trends and ideologies. Yes, it seemed possible that it was all fake. In which case, it'd be the old Madison, his Madison, at the airport, with the long silky hair, the subtle make up, and the understated but expensive elegance.

But what if it wasn't?

In that case, he'd be arriving just in time! A knight in shining armour, riding triumphantly on a white steed, flaming sword in hand, descended from Heaven to rescue his queen from that evil sorceress, Syd, who had bewitched his paramour with vile spells and incantations. He imagined Syd, face lit from below, working over a large cauldron, with rotten teeth and a wart on her nose.

Fillet of a fenny snake,
In the cauldron boil and bake;
Eye of newt and toe of frog,
Wool of bat and tongue of dog,
Adder's fork and blind-worm's sting,
Lizard's leg and owlet's wing,
For a charm of powerful trouble,
Like hell-broth boil and bubble.

Yes, in that case, he'd be just in time to avert disaster. Madison would see him and remember their love, their devotion, their sacred union, and this would break the spells.

Either scenario encouraged him.

He checked his phone for the three-hundred-and-sixty-ninth time.

But Madison had yet to reply.

The time was now 9:00am, which meant it was 3:00 am her time.

Of course she hadn't replied. She was still asleep! At the earliest she'd reply just as he boarded for the next leg of his journey.

He'd wait until then.

CHAPTER CXLIII

When his gate number appeared on a nearby screen, Angel got moving again. His buttocks ached after four hours on razor-sharp bones. The weather had worsened, the sky had become iron, cold rain blasted horizontally across the landscape. The runway workers leaned into the wet blustering wind, eyes squinted, their overalls and high visibility jackets furiously rippling. Inside, midday felt like midnight.

As with the previous flight, by the time Angel arrived at the gate, a long queue had formed. This meant that, once inside the aircraft, the overhead compartment had already been aggressively colonised by hand luggage, coats, and duty-free shopping, leaving almost no space for him. When the stewardess assisted him with his case, she shoved it in violently, scuffing the carapace. She also insisted he put his jacket under the seat in front, despite his protests.

And as with the previous flight, his mother had chosen for him a non-reclining middle seat, in the centre section of the Boeing 787-9, in row 44—dead last, next to the closet, the toilets, and the galley. Only a skinny, quadruple amputee would have deemed it adequate for his circulation.

First to join him on the right was a middle-aged man—grey-haired, balding, with heavy eyebrows, a walrus moustache, and thin, bitter lips. He was with a woman, presumably his wife, who sat across the aisle. She was skinny, haggard, and flinty-eyed, with a map of lines around her lips. Both were well dressed: he in suit and tie; she in a sleeved grape-coloured dress.

'For fuck's sake. Sit down already! My feet hurt,' snapped the woman, while the man leisurely stored his jacket in the overhead compartment.

His voice was a drumful of gravel. 'Well, they wouldn't hurt if you hadn't spent an hour throwing money away in the duty-free!'

'Fuck you!'

'Aw, shut your mouth.'

The woman released a sharp stream of words, but Angel could only focus on the man's responses.

'Shut your trap, just shut your trap,' he said, shouting over her, 'You're giving me a headache.'

Angel observed the scene for a few moments, eyes like cricket balls, then looked down.

He and Madison would never end up like that. Their love was pure, simple, whole.

He imagined their wedding. It would be at York Minster, of course. He'd be dressed in a bespoke morning suit and Madison in a stupendous dress, made of ivory silk, pure taffeta, antique lace, and 12,000 pearls. It would also have a thirty-three-foot-long train, superseding Princess Diana's iconic dress. All his friends would be present: Amelia, Alba, Jae, Vera, Johannes, Saïd, Unibrow, Skinhead, Emmanuel, and Tom. The full Italian contingent would also be there, including Vittorio, Luca, and Archangelo, with his phone and electronic megamix. His parents would bring first-tier entrepreneurs, magnates, investors, bankers, generals, politicians, aristocrats, authors, and academics. Her parents would bring the same, plus actors, composers, and public intellectuals. And he and Madison would bring poets, playwrights, novelists, Nobel Prize laureates. Officiating the ceremony would be, naturally, the Archbishop of York—no other cleric would rank high enough for a marriage of such magnitude. As to the ring, he was disappointed, when he Googled it, that the world's most expensive metal, californium, was highly radioactive; it also cost nearly a billion pounds per ounce; but the next down was rhodium, which was used in jewellery, and was four times more expensive than gold. So the ring would be made of solid rhodium. And, since he expected to have made millions with his writing by then, the ring would be adorned with blue diamonds, the most expensive gem.

His other neighbour now joined him on the left. This was also a middle-aged man, but with dark hair combed back and a couple of days of stubble, clad in worn-out clothes that seemed too big for him. Under his tan shearling jacket and scarf were multiple jumpers in brown and grey, old, and unravelling. The man gave him a weak, tired, half-lidded smile and, without taking off his layers, sat down, head sunken into fleecy lapels.

The man's posture reminded him to maintain a good one. He pushed his buttocks as far into the seat as he could, straightened his back, and held his neck erect. Excellent posture would be his hallmark at the wedding reception. The latter would be held in the grandest venue available—he'd have to research it, but something Mediaeval, in flamboyant gothic—and the catering would be in the hands of Michelin three-star chefs. The food would be served in ornate Kornilov Brother's porcelain plates. The antique cutlery would be in gold-plated solid silver. He and Madison's first dance would be to the tune of one of Girolamo Frescobaldi's harpsichord works, on a bed of roses, with everyone standing in a circle around them. Their kiss at the end of the dance would be greeted with an eruption of cheers, nodding, and clapping. The two of them would graciously bow in acknowledgment. And the whole family and attendees would talk about the wedding for a year afterwards, awed by its sheer magnificence, elegance, and romantic fervour.

'Don't put your shoes there! Leave space for the other passengers!' said the man on his right.

Angel turned to find the Angry Wife was storing her high-heeled pumps in the overhead compartment, the footwear standing neatly next to her hand luggage, coat, scarf, hat, and duty-free shopping.

'Don't tell me what to do, asshole! I'll put my shoes wherever I like!'

'Fuck off. Just sit down and shut up!' replied the man.

The woman yelled back at him, 'I said, don't tell me what to do! Mind your own fucking business!'

'Sit down, woman, will you! And lower your voice!'

She yelled even louder, 'I will not fucking lower my voice!'

'Keep on screeching, then. But take your damn shoes down!' He then muttered. 'Selfish woman.'

'Oh, so I'm selfish! What about you? Disappearing on your fucking hunting trips for weeks at a time!'

'You enjoy the free meat, don't you?'

'You only have time for hunting and your fucking card games!'

'At least I win sometimes. It's all money down the drain with your incessant spending!'

'Fuck you!'

A stewardess now came out of the galley. 'Madam, I'm going to ask you to please keep your voice down and take a seat.'

'Ask her to take her shoes down,' said the man to the stewardess.

The latter checked the overhead compartment and said to the woman, 'I'm sorry, madam, are those your shoes?'

'Yes,' she snarled.

'They need to go under the seat in front.'

'Oh, for fuck's sake!'

With ill grace and jerky movements, the woman removed the offending objects from the overhead compartment.

'I told you,' said the man, laughing.

'Shut up!' she said.

The stewardess made a placatory gesture. 'I'm gonna ask you to please keep your voices down. Madam, please take a seat.'

Angry Wife obeyed, albeit not without giving her husband an acid look.

With a sardonic chuckle, the husband shook his head and pulled out the inflight magazine.

Sight of it reminding Angel of his book, he excused

himself with his left-hand neighbour as he got up to retrieve his copy of *Amadis of Gaul* from the overhead compartment.

When he sat back down, said left-hand neighbour, pointing at the volume, said, 'I used to be an author.'

'Um . . .'

'Didn't do me any good . . .'

Angel said nothing.

'Made a lot of money with my novels.'

Angel said nothing.

'But then I angered the gatekeepers . . .'

Angel said nothing.

'. . . The media went wild . . . campaigners put pressure on my publishers . . .'

Angel stared.

'They all dropped me . . . my agent dropped me . . . my publisher dropped me . . .

Angel stared.

'My bank closed my accounts . . . friends turned out not to be friends . . .'

Angel stared.

'And then my wife left me . . . took me to the cleaners . . .'

Silence.

'You work all your life and then the divorce lawyers take everything . . .'

Silence.

'And the bitch didn't work a day in her life . . .'

Silence.

'Best to stay poor. And avoid women.'

Angel looked down.

The man asked, 'You flying to visit family?'

'Er . . . no'.

'Why are you travelling then?'

'Um . . . I'm going to visit my girlfriend.'

The man chuckled, looked away, then down, and shook his head, a bitter smile on his face.

He said, 'She doesn't love you.'

'W-W-Why do you say that? She does!'

The man turned, one eyebrow raised, his eye half-lidded. 'Really?'

'Yes!'

'How often does she call you?'

'Erm . . . w-we keep in touch by text message.'

'How often does she message you?'

'Er . . .'

'And I mean without wanting something from you.'

Angel thought about it. 'Er . . . well, w-we . . . um . . . follow each other on social media.'

'Does she mention you in her social media?'

'Um . . .' Angel scratched his temple.

'Or is it all about herself?'

'Um . . .'

'Did she ask you to visit her?'

'Um . . . yes.'

'But would she have flown to see you now if you had asked her instead?'

Angel rubbed his forehead. 'Um . . .'

'Does she play up?'

'Um . . . w-what do you mean?'

'Does she get in weird moods and say things that get you riled up? My ex-wife used to do that all the time.'

Angel looked down. 'Er . . .'

'And then claim she's kidding or it's hormones or whatever excuse?'

Angel said nothing.

'Yea. I thought so. Is she mysteriously silent and doesn't reply to your messages?'

Angel opened his mouth but closed it again.

''Cause my ex was the queen of silent treatment . . . she'd say everything was fine when I knew it wasn't . . . would give me this passive-aggressive crap . . . monosyllabic answers . . . sound fake cheerful when she knew I knew it was bullshit . . . expected me to read her mind and then got angry when I didn't . . . she did it on purpose, of course . . . women always want to control their husbands . . . and when we don't do what they say they use emotional blackmail . . . create a toxic atmosphere . . . provoke arguments so they can bring up all this crap from years ago . . . they'll forget all the good things and remember only the bad ones . . .'

Angel said nothing.

'You know what they say, behind every great man, there's a woman rolling her eyes.'

Angel said nothing.

'So she gives you the silent treatment, eh? Acts all weird all of a sudden and you don't know what's going on . . .'

Angel inhaled to say something but stopped himself.

The man sighed and looked forward. 'She doesn't love you.'

'But—'

'Good luck with that.' He scoffed.

Apparently done, the man pulled a battered paperback out of his pocket, opened it at the bookmark, and read.

Angel discretely craned his neck to see what the book was. Louis-Ferdinand Céline's *Journey to the End of the Night*. He'd meant to read Céline—Jae had read *Death on Credit*—but they had not included the author in the university curriculum, neither in the Literary Modernism nor in the Modern European Literature modules. But he'd heard the author was singularly cynical and depressing.

Angel shook his head to shed his neighbour's tar-like poison. No. He was yet another naysayer—another cynic, who disbelieved that Love was possible! Their disappointments were just experiences, not truth, or fate. Madison was not like other girls, nor like the horrible women these unfortunates had been stuck with. She was unique. Special. A freak of Nature. What were the odds? The sceptics were miserable because they regretted their choices, and they regretted them because they'd compromised their standards, because they'd accepted whomever chance had thrown at them, because they were casual and unserious in their relationships, because they lacked poetry and a sense of beauty and instead had fallen prey to fear, fiscal advantage, or boredom. He was not like them, and neither was Madison. And they would never be. They *knew*, and had, *true love*.

Angel clenched his fist, resolved to remain steadfast in his love for Madison, and not let toxic misanthropes infect him with doubt, pessimism, or mistrust.

They got moving.

Angel leaned to glance out the window as the aircraft taxied to the runway. The rain persisted and the sky had darkened to such a degree that, except for islands of artificial illumination, the outside world was a solid mass of onyx. Said illumination occasionally made the rain droplets glint on the outer plexiglass. He checked the time on his phone. It wasn't even lunchtime yet!

After a long interval of suspense, the engines revved up, the giant metal sausage gathered speed, and passengers' backs were pressed against the backrests.

We're finally on our way, thought Angel. Last leg of the journey. On the other side: Madison!

Chapter CXLIV

'Could I have a bottle of chardonnay, please,' said Angry Wife to the stewardess.

'Certainly, madam.'

'There you go drinking again!' snarled her husband, shaking his head.

'I'll drink whatever I want, dipshit!'

'Knock yourself out. At least you'll be quiet.'

'Quiet?! What about your fucking voice! That's all I hear all day! I'm so *sick* of your fucking voice!'

'You only hear it when you nag.'

The stewardess returned, and, leaning between the couple, said in a soft voice, 'I must ask you to please keep your voices down.'

'She started it!' said the husband.

'No, *you* started it! screamed the wife.

The stewardess pushed the air down with her palms. 'Madam, sir, please, keep your voices down.'

'Tell him to stop commenting!' the wife said, crossing her arms and looking away.

The husband sighed and also looked away, shaking his head.

Angel noticed the divorced author observing the scene with the hint of a smirk.

'He'll be bankrupt in two years,' Divorced Author murmured.

Angel glanced at Embittered Husband, then at Divorced Author, but said nothing.

'Her lawyers are already scouring through his bank accounts, I bet. It's what my ex- did . . . she bided her time and then *bam!* Divorce papers! She's now with someone else . . . fleecing him too, of course . . . it's how women build their fortunes . . . none want to work, really . . . feminism is just a way for them to get more . . . they're feminists when there's money to be made . . . but traditional when it comes to sharing the burden . . . it's all double standards with them . . .'

Angel again glanced at Embittered Husband, who had closed his eyes. Angel noticed he wore a hearing aid.

Divorced Author said: 'You ever notice how many men his age get takeaways at night?'

Angel thought about it.

'I used to see them . . . from the back of the limo . . . on my way to fancy restaurants and book launches and five-star hotels . . . I used to laugh . . . now I'm one of them . . . cholesterol through the roof . . . blood pressure same . . . brain fog . . . diabetes . . . kidney stones . . . I've been prescribed medication . . . I don't take it . . . no point . . . I'll be old soon . . . better if I have a heart attack . . . that can't come soon enough, in fact . . . Who knows? Maybe the plane will crash today . . .'

Angel stared at Divorced Author, round-eyed.

'Don't worry . . . death at once is better than in instalments.'

The stewardess returned with Angry Wife's chardonnay. Embittered Husband got the stewardess' attention before she returned to the galley.

'Could I have a bottle of Highland Park,' he said.

'Certainly, sir. Would you like ice?'

'No.'

'Hypocrite,' snapped Angry Wife.

'You drive me to drink,' said Embittered Husband.

'Then you're weak!'

'And so are you, apparently.'

'Go and drink yourself to death!'

'I hope you beat me to it!'

Divorced Author chuckled. 'She's encouraging him of course . . . cheaper than divorce lawyers . . . completely selfish, like all women . . . If he has any sense, he'll gamble everything away quickly . . . that way the bitch won't get anything.'

Angel rubbed his forehead, his mouth opening and closing like a salmon in a fishing net.

But Divorced Author said no more; instead, he got back to his book.

The bees in his brain buzzing too obstreperously for *Amadis of Gaul*, Angel opted for a film. It was a toss-up between *Bohemian Rhapsody* and *Little Women*. After much indecision, he concluded that Madison would have chosen, and preferred him to watch, *Little Women*, which, in any case, was based on a classic novel. Fifteen minutes into the film, however, the woman in front, flipped her long black hair over the backrest, so that it landed on Angel's side, almost entirely covering the infotainment screen. Adding insult to injury, she then fully reclined her seat. The woman's hair being wavy and voluminous, some of it was fluffed out so far that it ticked the tip of his nose, even while keeping his occiput pressed against his backrest. He could smell the woman's shampoo and the sebum from her scalp. To avoid it, Angel was forced to turn his head, either towards Divorced Author or Embittered Husband. But staying turned for long caused neck ache, so he had periodically to turn in the opposite direction, each time brushing his nose against the frizz.

After a while, Divorced Author noticed Angel looking at him and, thinking Angel meant to converse, turned toward his neighbour. But upon registering Angel's plight, and its woman origin, he said with venom, 'Why don't you tell her?'

Angel's irises resumed their game of Breakout. He half-whispered, 'Erm . . . no, no . . . it's okay, it's okay.'

'You can tell her.'

'Er . . . no, no . . . I'm fine.'

'But you *should* tell her.'

'I'm fine, I'm fine.'

Divorced Author shrugged his shoulders, sniggered, and got back to his book. But after ten seconds he turned to Angel again and added, 'That girl you're visiting? She's going to *eat you alive!*'

Angel had no reply; instead, he crinkled his forehead and turned towards Embittered Husband.

Backrest Hair Invader stayed stubbornly reclined, even after they began serving drinks. It was only when the food trolleys reached their rows that she returned her seat to the upright position and the hair disappeared behind the backrest.

Angel lowered his tray.

Chapter CXLIV

The stewardesses distributed the inflight meals.

Pasta, salad, a bun, a packet of crackers, and a granola-based desert.

For the first time in eighteen hours, Angel ate.

But the sky had other plans, for no sooner had he put the first forkful of pasta into his mouth that the turbulence began. At first, it was manageable; within ninety seconds, however, Angel found it difficult to hit his buccal target. He ended up with tomato sauce on his cheeks and both pasta and tomato sauce on his shirt and the crotch of his trousers.

'Oh, bollocks!' he whispered, corrugating his forehead.

He rapidly grabbed the paper napkin to wipe the mess, while the pilot's voice blared from the PA system.

While in the process, the sky upped the ante, and the aeroplane began abruptly dropping at irregular intervals, as if falling off air cliffs. Drinks wobbled alarmingly in their plastic cups. Angel, to stop his Coke from spilling, held the cup aloft, aiming to keep it at the same altitude during the drops. This worked for a while, but then came an unexpectedly drastic drop that sent Angel's beverage flying amid a collective gasp of alarm. The Coke mostly landed on him, soiling his hair, his face, his shirt, his trousers, and his neighbours' sleeves.

'Sorry! Sorry!' Angel said to them, using his napkin to wipe himself dry.

Divorced Author was not particularly bothered, due to being clad in Oxfam finds, and stoically dried his sleeve. Embittered Husband had a spillage of his own to deal with, since the bottle of wine he'd ordered to go with his lunch was now rolling towards the nose of the aircraft, spilling its contents along the aisle.

'Good! Maybe you'll stay sober,' said Angry Wife, while her husband followed with his eyes the bottles' progress.

Embittered Husband turned to look at her. 'You're one to talk. You never make it sober till evening these days!'

'Why would I want to stay sober around you!' she screeched.

'I wouldn't mind it if you stayed quiet!'

'Fuck you.'

'Yea, whatever.' Embittered Husband switched off his hearing aid.

Angel wiped himself until his napkin disintegrated, leaving a myriad tiny paper balls encrusted in his shirt and trousers. He waited until the turbulence subsided, so upset by the stains that he also abandoned his lunch. As soon as the Fasten your seat belts sign went off, Angel jumped up and made his way to the lavatory.

Once inside, he made a detailed examination of the damage. What he found brought tears to his eyes. His romantic journey had been defaced! It's aesthetic ruined. It's purity further contaminated. Madison would take exception at his carelessness and lack of love; at his taking her lightly and for granted; at his disregard for their reunion. She would lose all respect for him. She might even break up with him at the terminal!

The stains screamed in a chorus of abuse, eclipsing the rest of his outfit, devastating its elegance, and commanding focus. He rubbed his crinkled forehead and thought about how best to still the voices. The internet no doubt had a hundred answers. If only there was a signal at 33,000 feet! With critical knowledge beyond reach, he pulled paper towels from the dispenser, wetted one end, loaded it with hand soap, and rubbed the main stain on his shirt. But, instead of the stain vanishing, it was the paper towel that did, leaving a medallion of foam and rolled up tissue behind that screamed more loudly than the stain it was meant to mute.

'Oh, no! Please, no!' he moaned.

It would have been better to leave the stain alone. But in his desperation, Angel couldn't stop. He tried rubbing the stain with a wet hand. Yet, this, instead of clarifying the situation, confused it further, for the medallion grew without evidence of stain erasure. And evidence would require waiting until his shirt dried. Thus, his mind blanking on options, he went back to his seat for the time being, haunted by the raucous laughter of the gremlins in his garments.

By that time, however, Backrest Hair Invader had already flicked her hair over the backrest and reclined her seat, so, reedy as he was, gaining access demanded pretzel-like contortions.

Backrest Hair Invader having made reading impossible, there was nothing left to do but sleep.

When he woke up, the aeroplane was still airborne. But the windows were black. Night had fallen. Weren't they supposed to have landed by half-past three in the afternoon? He checked his phone for the time. It was three in the morning. They'd been flying for fifteen hours. He inspected his neighbours, but they slept, facing away from him, ragged down patchy on their occiputs. The woman's hair in front, however, had grown grey and brittle—or perhaps he hadn't noticed the grey before. It also fell all the way down to the floor. He hadn't noticed that either. He got up, only for his knees to knife him with pain; his lower back, in turn, had become an iron hinge stiff with corrosion. He could almost hear it creaking as he gingerly straightened. Divorced Author failed to stir.

Tapping him on the shoulder elicited no response. Angel turned and tapped Embittered Husband, but Angel might as well have tapped a corpse. While standing, he scanned the cabin. There was something not right about it; the ambiance had changed; the neon fulgor had faded into a subfusc half-light, as if the aircraft were experiencing a brownout—or the electrical systems crushing fatigue. The engines' whine had dropped into a wearied, cavernous drone, overlaid by manic rattling and squeaking. He observed that everyone's hair was grey, white, or gone. He didn't remember seeing only pensioners when he boarded. Their skulls rested at tired, exhausted angles. Divorced Author, he noticed, suddenly looked disturbingly haggard; the latter's clothes were also far more decrepit than he'd remembered, as flaccid and mottled as his skin. When he put a palm of the wall behind his seat to support himself while he squeezed his leg between Divorced Author's, the wall felt wobbly, rickety—soggy, even—and the part where his palm rested gave way. The metal behind it was covered in rust, the electric cabling old and mouldy. Angel looked out for cabin crew, hoping no one had seen. He made it to the aisle and ambled stiffly into the lavatory. The lavatory remained dark even after he latched the door, so he exited it and tried the toilet on the other side. Same result. He walked towards the front of the aircraft, albeit not as sprightly as he might have done; every joint ached. The blue carpeting, he saw for the first time, had faded into a feculent grey-brown; it was threadbare along the centre and had been worn to shreds; in places, it no longer existed. And no one cared? Was the apathy and resignation so great? Whatever it was, it extended to the upholstery, which had been rubbed to ribbons, with foam extruding from ragged holes. The foam crumbled to the touch. Electrical failure had plunged entire sections of the cabin into darkness. The toilets in the economy plus section turned out to be out of order as well. And the same proved to be the case with the ones in front. On the entire journey from the back to the front, he saw no cabin crew except one, seated in the business class galley. The elderly stewardess' ghastly face reminded of cracked earth, her uniform lustreless and loose, her shirt yellowing, her shoes worn out; she stared listlessly into space, as if she lacked the energy even to acknowledge him. Angel returned to his seat. He'd clean up at the airport. But now his neighbours had disappeared. In fact, his section of the cabin was empty. All that was left were defunct seats grey with dust and spiderwebs. He checked his phone again: it was four in the morning, 3 November, but the year was 2069. He launched the photo app and flipped it to selfie: he was old.

He woke up with a start. He'd left too late, he thought. He'd left too late! He'd missed Madison's entire life. She'd married someone else. And she too was old. And sick. And even dead.

But as the dream evaporated, he realised its absurdity.

He unfastened his seatbelt and made to get up, but the FASTEN YOUR SEAT BELTS light dinged on, forcing him into reverse. Another ding prefaced the captain's announcement:

'Ladies and gentlemen, we have begun our descent into Chicago. Please make sure your seat backs and tray tables are in their full upright position, your seat belt is securely fastened, and all carry-on luggage is stowed underneath the seat in front of you or in the overhead bins. Thank you.'

Angel glanced at his clothes, and, although the wet patch had since dried, it was as stained and encrusted with tissue paper as before, except now over a wider area. The tomato sauce elsewhere had dried and formed crusts that couldn't be scratched off without leaving deeper and more intractable stains.

'Oh, balls!'

Chapter CXLV

'Thank you,' said the stewardess, faking a smile by the open plug door.

'Oh . . . um . . . yes, thank you,' said Angel.

He disembarked and made his way to the terminal, heart echoing the thuds of people's footsteps on the carpeted airbridge against the rumble of rolling luggage. He gripped the handle of his firmly; he couldn't afford to leave Madison's presents behind. Chest tight, hands cold, legs like jelly, he shivered. Madison was only minutes away! He imagined her waiting behind the glass doors, fresh and fragrant, in the white knitted dress that he liked, smiling as he approached, and the two of them running into a mutual embrace once he was out. He'd feel her torso, smell her perfume, touch her hair, kiss her lips, hear her voice, be in her presence—for the first time in five months. A lifetime!

Madison was yet to reply, but he now dismissed his concerns. She'd be there, of course. She'd never let him travel all that way and not come to greet him. She loved him. Wanted him there. Had asked him to come. It was obvious she wanted to keep him in suspense in order to surprise him. He smiled at her playful spirit.

His memory of O'Hare was eight years old, but upon seeing its rigid, sterile modernism and super-American grey-and-blue colour scheme, things he'd forgotten became familiar. He followed the crowd through the concourse, scanning for a lavatory in which to change his clothes, but in two minds on whether to avail himself; the terminal was a vast labyrinth. What if he got lost and, by the time he found his way, Madison had concluded that he'd stood her up, or that he'd missed his flight? She'd go home. He couldn't risk it! So, he buttoned his jacket, hoping it covered the stains, and, resolving to keep it buttoned no matter the temperature or the circumstances, continued following the crowd.

The automated passport control kiosk at customs and border protection couldn't recognise him on account of his drastic weight loss, so he was directed to a manned booth to clear Primary Inspection.

The officer swiped his passport and checked the computer screen, his glaring eyes alternating suspiciously between the data and his face.

The officer spoke in a monotone. 'What's the purpose of your visit.'

'I'm . . . I'm coming to visit my girlfriend,' Angel proclaimed, proudly, just as he'd imagined.

'How much money do you have?'

'Um . . . a thousand dollars.' He swallowed.

What if they had the means to check?

Did the screen display his bank balance?
He was waved through. 'Enjoy your visit.'
'Er . . . thank y—'
'Next!'
He was through.
Madison was now only seconds away!
He walked past the crowded baggage reclaim carousels, feeling superior as he dragged his hand luggage, and checked his gait, posture, facial expression, and pace.
The great moment was about to occur!
His heart hammered like a pneumatic drill, his breathing became micron-deep, his hands frozen nitrogen.
Just before the Customs and Agriculture Inspection area, he paused, took a deep, trembly breath, and exhaled. The ants ran close to the speed of light.
'Okay. Here it comes!' he whispered.
And got moving again.
He walked towards the exit in the way he'd practised—though, because hyper-self-conscious, with numerous imperfections in his execution. The chasm between how he felt and how he wanted to appear was so enormous that he doubted whether he was achieving the effect he'd envisioned.
His eyes fixed on the steel-framed glass doors ahead.
The tumult beyond was indistinct and the view blocked by tired air travellers trudging in front. Back glare and reflection denied any glimpses otherwise granted by fleeting gaps.
Therefore, Madison was not visible.
The doors were now five metres away.
Three metres.
Two metres.
They opened for the people in front.

Immediately inside the arrivals hall, said people dispersed, some heading towards transportation options, others effusively greeted by family and friends, others identified by corporate chauffeurs holding signs.

Angel scanned the cordoned area for Madison's face.

There were dozens upon dozens of strange faces, belonging to humans of all genders, ages, races, heights, weights, hair colour, skull shapes, sartorial styles, and physiognomic configurations.

He couldn't see Madison's among them.

He stopped briefly, to scan more thoroughly, but had his ankle bumped into from behind by a man pushing a loaded luggage trolley, so he moved out of the way.

He stood to the side of the cordoned area and scanned it one more time.

Again, all manner of people. Baseball caps, cowboy hats, hijabs, bare heads, bald pates, prescription glasses, mirror shades, big noses, small noses, long beards, short beards, stubble, clean-shaven, light skin, dark skin, fat cheeks, skinny cheeks, square chins, round chins, no chins, piercings, tattoos, dyed hair, dreadlocks, buzzcuts, piecrusts.

But no Madison.

He got nearer.

No Madison.

He scanned the arrivals hall.

A multitude of humans, wildly colourful and diverse.

No Madison.

He noticed that he'd come out of Exit B, so he walked to Exit A, in case Madison was standing there.

He imagined her waiting by that other exit, looking at the glass doors, excited and expectant.

But when he got there, although the entire breadth

and depth of America was represented, Madison was absent.

His irises bounced in all directions.

He pulled out his phone.

It was four o'clock.

It hadn't been that long.

Neither had Madison messaged.

He decided to wait five minutes. Perhaps she had been delayed in traffic and was still in the car park, making her way towards the building. He imagined her walking fast, her heels clicking, her hair flying, her eyes eager.

But the five minutes passed without Madison showing up.

He waited another five minutes.

Same result.

Yet another five.

Same result.

He went back to Exit B.

No Madison.

Where to stand?

He pulled out his phone and composed a message.

ANGEL: This distinguished gentleman hath safely arrived at Chicago O'Hare International Airport and is currently waiting in the arrivals hall, near Exit B. Hath Her Ladyship been delayed in congestion? I trust She is safe and in good health! This gentleman wouldeth be much obliged for an update on Her current location, for he is eager to be reunited and pay homage.

The message was sent and received, but not opened.

Angel waited, staring at the screen until his neck hurt.

Constantly brushed and bumped into by uncouth travellers, he stood against a wall. He set his phone alerts to maximum volume, plus vibrate, and waited, scrutinising the rivers of humans with the most acute concentration, yet also with feigned tranquillity. The lack thereof, however, prompted him constantly to adjust his posture, what to do with his arms or legs or torso never entirely clear.

Another quarter of an hour passed.

And then another.

And then another.

By quarter past five, it growing dark outside, he'd ping-ponged between the two exits a thousand times, and checked his phone a million, despite the alert settings.

His message to Madison remained stubbornly unopened.

Yet, she'd been online.

At last, he telephoned. But the phone rang and rang and rang, without Madison picking up.

He ended the call.

And waited.

Chapter CXLVI

Six o'clock came and went.

Yet, still, no Madison.

Nor replies to his by then multiple messages.

All of which had been delivered, but not opened.

Tired of waiting, and of the feeling of homelessness, yet all the same hesitant, Angel considered hiring a taxi to take him to Madison.

But what if she was on her way?

What if she was stuck in traffic?

What if the reason she could not reply was her telephone having been restricted due to a billing error?

What if she'd been in an accident?

What if she was about to arrive?

What if she was already in the building, racing towards him, anxious, guilty, and profuse with apologies?

What if she mixed up the time zones, and had either already been to the airport and left, or not yet arrived because she thought his flight was still to land?

What if?

Angel pulled out his phone again and checked WhatsApp for the one million fourteen thousand three hundred and seventy ninth time.

If only she'd reply!

He thought of risking a walk to the car park. What car did she drive? He couldn't remember. Or maybe she never told him. Minimum an S-class Mercedes. But maybe he'd see her there, just pulling in, or getting out of whatever luxury car.

Angel got up and dragged his suitcase into the darkness outside. Freezing wind snatched all the warmth out of his body. He crossed the road, clothes rippling, climbed up the grass embankment, gingerly, so as not to damage his shoes, and stepped into the car park. It was, fortunately, not a multi-storey, but a ground-level facility exposed to the sky. Half an hour is all it took to walk up and down every lane, although he wouldn't have been able to hear Madison's voice over the constant roar and whine of aeroplane engines, air vents, and moving land vehicles.

There were a few baseball-capped old men with beer bellies, a middle-aged woman, and a black man with a shearling coat, hood up.

But no Madison.

Trembling violently from the bitter cold and fearing she might have just made it into the building, Angel retraced his steps and went back into the terminal. Nose running, eyes watery, he carefully scanned the crowd gathered before exits A and B, several times.

No Madison.

She was like a mountain that kept receding, no matter how much he walked towards it.

How long to wait for?

If she thought that he was landing at 3:25pm GMT, he reasoned for the thirty-seventh time, she would have been at the airport at 9.25am and left long before he landed. That could explain why she wasn't opening his messages; her feelings were hurt, or she was angry, and was ignoring him. But if she thought he was arriving at 3:25am GMT, she wouldn't be showing up for another three hours. That, however, seemed less likely, since in his message he'd written—and he'd checked and rechecked this—3:25pm on 2 November. Therefore, if anything, she would have come in the morning.

Yes, that would very plausibly explain her non-communication.

In which case, it was a matter of urgency that he went to her flat as soon as possible, so he could explain the terrible misunderstanding.

Yet, that would mean paying for a taxi, which meant eating into the money he'd reserved for the grand, celebratory dinner.

On the other hand, if she was already angry, or sobbing into her pillow, prolonging her suffering was far worse than a more modest menu.

Yes. Whatever the case, it seemed best to go to her now. She'd be yearning for the sight of him more than anything in the world, just as he was for the sight of her.

Before leaving, however, he checked Exit A and Exit B three more times, walking in and out of the crowd, inspecting every face, just to be sure.

But as before, no Madison.

Angel stepped back outside and found a taxi.

A brontosaurian Afro-American man with a shaved head sat behind the wheel of the long, yellow metro cab. He stared, silently awaiting instructions.

'Um . . . can you take me to . . . um . . . just a moment . . .'

Angel pulled his phone out and checked Madison's contact.

He felt the taxi driver's eyes probing him, weighing him.

'Okay . . . er . . . can you take me to . . . er. . .—' He gave Madison's address.

'No prahblem, sir.'

Angel climbed into the vehicle, ants marching. He smelled the air freshener as he noticed the little blue Christmas tree hanging from the rear-view mirror.

The taxi got moving.

He blew up his cheeks and released the air slowly.

For the next forty-five minutes, Angel watched neon-lit motorways, cars, traffic lights, billboards, and tall buildings whizz by. The city was like an extravagant Christmas tree; it was also extremely rectilinear.

This is where Madison lives, he thought, soaking in every detail.

He also watched the back of the driver's head slowly sway at thirty to sixty second intervals. The taxi driver spoke not a word during the entire journey.

Each mile was beset by doubt. What if Madison had finally made it to the airport? What if she was looking for him there? What if, when he arrived at her flat, he'd discover she'd gone to fetch him?

And what if they kept missing each other?

They could spend the whole week like that, and he'd fly back without ever having seen her.

He checked his phone, hoping for a reply, and therefore an answer, but there was none.

His message remained, as yet, steadfastly unopened.

A sudden, mad impulse to instruct the driver to take him back to the airport assailed him. Somehow it seemed more appealing to wait there, because as long as he waited, he was at square one, and it was just a delay, rather than his arrival—their fateful and long-awaited reunion!—not having gone according to plan. Yet, the thought of Madison being angry at him, or disappointed, proved more powerful, and, as unsettled as he felt, the instruction remained unspoken, though ready to deploy in an instant.

The taxi pulled up in front of an older limestone apartment block and the driver stopped the meter.

It read $102.49.

'A hunnert and twenny,' said the driver, his face turned towards him.

Angel looked at the meter and then at his creditor, hesitating. He wanted to query the discrepancy, but, intimidated by the huge black face and the white orbs staring back at him, decided it was best to avoid trouble and just pay. There was probably a tax, he told himself. Or maybe a standard tip.

He handed over his debit card.

The driver charged it and returned it with a receipt.

Angel got out of the car and, staring up at the building, its architecture beautiful to him by virtue of its being Madison's residence, pulled out his phone to check for messages.

He heard the taxi drive away behind him.

As he pushed the receipt into his pocket, it fell onto the pavement.

He picked it up.

It said he'd been charged $130.

He turned to look for the taxi, but it had since vanished.

Maybe I misheard, he told himself.

He reached for his suitcase's telescopic handle.

But his hand grasped air.

When he looked down, he found only pavement.

He'd left the suitcase in the taxi.

'Bollocks!' he whispered, his angry head bouncing with vehemence.

CHAPTER CXLVII

Angel located Madison's name on the intercom panel and rang the buzzer.

He looked through the door's glass panes into the lobby. Warm colours, marble walls and flooring.

No answer.

He rang again.

A frigid wind blew, like knives finding their way into his torso. He flinched and hunched his back.

He waited.

No answer.

He rang a third time.

Waited longer.

No answer.

He checked his phone. It was eight thirty in the evening. No message from Madison.

No one in the lobby.

He phoned her.
No answer.
He messaged her.
Delivered, but not opened.
He rang the buzzer.
Waited.
No answer.
He rang again.
Waited.
No answer.
He rang a sixth time.
Waited.
Checked the time.
Waited.
Looked through the glass panes.
Waited.
Still no answer.
Was the intercom broken?
He phoned her again.
No answer.
He phoned her a third time.
No answer.
The ants got marching.

He stepped away from the green awning above and looked up at the dozens of windows stacked overhead.

Was Madison in any of those rectangles?

Possibly angry with him?

Or not there at all?

The ants sped up.

He glanced at the adjacent tower blocks and wondered whether he'd been dropped at the right place.

But no, the awning showed the address was correct.

Didn't the intercom panel show Madison's name?

Yes, there it was.

He returned to the door and once more rang the buzzer.

No answer.

He rubbed his forehead.

What to do?

He glanced at the street behind him and looked for a taxi, half considering going back to the airport.

Because—what if Madison was there?

He was willing to go no matter the cost.

But—five hours after he landed?

Seemed unlikely.

The hypothermic wind kept blowing intermittently, howling, flapping his garments. No taxi in sight. Just random cars hissing past. The park facing the building was a black cavern, its menacing depth blotted out by moribund tungsten light from decrepit streetlamps. The pavement—or 'sidewalk', as Madison called it—was riddled with cracks, sawtooth weeds growing in between. The red fire hydrant was broken. One of the lamps flickered. The asphalt on the road was like a diagram of the human circulatory system. The whole city was crumbling!

He worried about muggers.

Death Wish, that old film his father liked, came to mind.

Except there was no Charles Bronson vigilante about.

He saw a man approaching.

Facial tattoos and fiercely swaggering.

The ants ran. His heart shifted up a gear.

Angel rang the buzzer.

Phoned.

No answer.

The tattooed beast was now ten feet away.

Angel put his phone to his ear. Swallowed.

Five feet away.

'Yes, of course,' said Angel to nobody.

The tattooed beast walked past.

Angel exhaled.

His heart and the ants slowed down.

He filled his cheeks with air and released it slowly.

He should have stayed at the airport, he thought, shivering. Idiot.

But at that stage, should he go back, or should he wait?

If Madison was at the airport, or on her way back, chances were they'd miss each other. On the other hand, if he waited, chances were she'd eventually decide to come home.

So he opted to wait.

He checked his phone.

No messages.

He phoned her yet again.

No answer.

He tried the door.

Locked.

What if she never answered?

There was nothing he wanted more at that moment but to see her face, hear her voice, touch her skin—to feel she existed.

He lifted his jacket collar and wrapped it tightly around his neck and attempted to huddle deeper into the fabric.

The glacial wind wouldn't stop blowing.

It stabbed his ear drums like an ice pick.

He hopped from one foot to the other, trying to keep warm. Except his feet were frozen and he couldn't feel them.

He waited.

Finally tiring, he sat on the edge of one of the large flowerpots flanking the door, back curved like a banana. The arch of cold earthenware across his buttocks sucked out what little heat he had remaining.

He sat, but with an eye out for police patrol cars, or private security, for fear of being thought an intruder and asked to move on.

Traffic had ebbed away; hardly a car sizzed past.

His knees bounced like pistons, but he let them rip to stay above freezing.

And again he waited.

An hour passed.

He yawned.

No Madison.

By then, the icy pavement had drained all the heat out of his legs, and the freezing flowerpots had numbed his glutes.

His mind reeled with panicked thoughts.

What if she never appeared?

Where would he go?

Where would he stay?

Could he afford accommodation?

Likely not anymore.

Two thirds of his money were already gone, and he'd just arrived!

His only option was to keep waiting.

Ay me! sad hours seem long.

His phone buzzed.

As if jerked by an electric shock, he stood and yanked the device out of his pocket—although not without difficulty: his hands were so numb that he could barely feel it, and his finger so icelike that the Touch ID couldn't at first detect it.

A message!

. . . but not from Madison.

From Amelia, asking if he arrived safely in Chicago.

Battery was at 11%.

And the charger had been in the suitcase, now lost in the huge metropolis.

'Bollocks!'

He fumbled his phone back into his pocket and stamped his feet.

So this is what Robert Scott felt on the Antarctic ice, he thought.

He wondered whether there was a café or restaurant nearby, even a McDonald's, where he could wait in the warmth.

The thought unbolted a colossal rumble in his stomach; he'd only had a bite of pasta in the past thirty-one hours. And his saliva, which had attained the consistence of beaten egg-whites, reminded him he'd barely had a drop of Coke during that entire time.

To this end, he stretched his neck, to scan up and down the road.

Nothing but asphalt, tower blocks, and skyscrapers as far as the eye could see.

A sea of cement without amenities.

Inside each of the thousands of tiny yellow rectangles around him people sat comfortably in their homes, watching TV, reading, listening to music, having a hot meal.

All while Madison was out there, somewhere.

What if she did have an accident?

What if she was indeed in hospital?

If only he could find out! He'd phone a taxi to get him there that instant.

He groped for his phone.

Dropped it as he pulled it out.

Picked it up, to find the screen cracked.

Battery was 4%.

Please stop draining!

What if his phone died and Madison tried to ring him? Or message him? He'd never know!

And without an address, how would he have a new charger delivered?

He heard footsteps behind him.

He turned.

Not Madison.

A guy about his age, with fluffy hair, a long face, and thick-rimmed oval glasses.

Fluffy Hair joined him, took out a key and allowed himself into the building, leaving the hydraulic door closer to do its job.

Did he know Madison?

Could he tell him where she was?

He dared not ask.

In case the guy laughed at him.

Angel watched the closing door for a moment, wondering whether it would anger Madison for him to wait inside, but, unable to bear the cold any longer, squeezed himself into the lobby at the last moment.

Warmth!

He exhaled with overpowering relief, blinking away the tears. Stripped of tissues—they'd also been in his case—he sniffled the built-up snot, producing a gargantuan rattle.

Yet, the lobby was not designed for comfort. It was all hard, shiny surfaces. Cold stone. Cold metal. Two bergère chairs flanking a round, occasional table were the only places to sit.

He felt like an intruder. Like he shouldn't be there.

The lifts were up ahead.

However, Fluffy Hair was waiting for one.

So Angel took the stairs, pretending he was a first-floor resident.

But he stopped on that first floor and waited until he heard the lift come and go, with Fluffy Hair presumably inside.

Angel gave it a couple more minutes before calling a lift.

All along he kept alert to the smallest stirring, the smallest sound.

He didn't want to be seen.

Madison lived on the seventh floor. Apartment B.

The lift came. Fortunately, empty.

He climbed in and mentally urged the doors to close as fast as possible.

He rubbed his forehead.

Was this right? Should he have stayed outside? Should he have gone back to the airport?

He *so* wished he were at the airport.

And that it was three o'clock.

With Madison waiting at the arrivals hall.

The mirror reflected a scarecrow: eyes bloodshot, hair in disarray, shirt a mess.

Before he could fix his hair, a wave of nausea swept over him, bending him in half and scrunching his eyes shut.

A ding announced to Angel the arrival at his destination.

He stepped out into the corridor, goggle-eyed, and sought the door to Madison's apartment.

He heard the lift closing behind him.

A tremendous yawn stopped him for a moment;

when he re-opened his eyes tears blurred his vision.

The floor was vast and there were numerous apartments.

When he found Madison's, he stood before her door for a few seconds. It was wooden, with mouldings, with 7B in brass Italics.

Besides the hum of ventilation, the silence was absolute.

He finger-combed his hair, brushed off his trousers, adjusted his jacket, and pinched the lapels to hide the stained shirt.

He took a breath, chest full of butterflies.

When ready, he knocked, softly.

He waited.

Silence.

He knocked again.

Waited.

Silence.

He glanced up and down the corridor, hoping residents were not observing him through their peepholes.

Then, hesitantly, he pressed his ear against Madison's door.

Silence.

He checked the time. 9:47 pm.

His phone battery was at 1%.

Then it died.

Chapter CXLVIII

'Do you live here?' asked the trim black man in the smart suit, a resident, as he passed Angel, who'd gone back to the lobby. Seldom could anyone achieve his level of neatness: shoes and shaved scalp like dielectric mirrors, shirt as if spray-painted, tie knot with perfect symmetry, cobalt blue suit with impeccable tailoring, golden belt buckle blinding with supernova fulgor.

Angel, who'd decided to wait seated in one of the oak chairs, said, 'Um . . . no, er . . . I'm waiting for someone.'

'Who are you waiting for?' Even the black man's enunciation was flawless.

'Um . . . my girlfriend. She lives in 7B.'

'What's her name?'

'Madison.'

'I don't know any Madison.'
'You sure?'
'I'm sure.'
'I'm just waiting for her.'
'Is she coming down?'
'Um . . . er . . . er . . . she should be back soon.'
'Oh, she's not here.'
'Er . . . no . . . er . . . she . . . she was supposed to meet me at the airport . . .'
'Where's your suitcase, then?'
'Er . . . I-I-I didn't bring one.'
'You didn't bring luggage?'
'No . . . er . . . I keep some of my clothes here.'
'I see. So you visit her often?'
'Er . . . yes . . . from time to time.'
'I haven't seen you before.'
'W-W-We started dating in February.'
'That's eight months. I've never seen you here.'
'Um . . . I-I-I live in the UK.'
'And she didn't meet you at the airport, after travelling all that way?'
'Um . . . no . . . I-I think she got mixed up with the times.'
'Why don't you phone her?'
'My phone died.'
'And you didn't phone her before?'
'Um . . . yes, but she didn't answer.'
The man stared at him for a moment, weighing him, then chuckled, and looked away.
Angel stared.
'Oh, boy,' said the man, shaking his head. 'You should've brought a charger.'
'Um . . .'
'And a clean shirt.'

Angel looked down and saw that his jacket, because it was still buttoned, and because he was bent over with hunger, had splayed open in the chest area, exposing the tomato sauce stains.

'Oh, balls!' he said, pulling the lapels together.

'I'd give you one of mine—but it wouldn't fit you. You'd look like a hot-air balloon.'

Angel, who'd perked up at the mention of a clean shirt, deflated slightly. 'I-I-It's okay.'

'Do you even know what time it is?'

'Er . . . no.'

'Quarter till midnight.'

'Oh . . . really?'

'And you don't know when your girlfriend's going to be back, do you?'

'Um . . . no.'

The man offered him his phone. 'Here, why don't you phone her?'

Angel reached for the phone, but the man noticed movement outside the front door and, his body tensing, suddenly withdrew the phone, saying, 'Sorry, man. My cab's arrived. Gotta go.'

'O-Okay.'

'Good luck with your girlfriend. You'll need it!' The man laughed, looking back at him as he walked out re-pocketing his phone.

Silence.

An hour passed.

Angel's headache beat him down like a piledriver on the top of the cranium—from dehydration—and around the eyes like a battering ram—from stress. Simultaneously, his brain generated colossal intracranial pressure, the questions it threw up multiplying at an exponential rate. The mystery of Madison's whereabouts deepened with every passing hour, with explanations ranging from trivial to tragic, from comical to catastrophic. The implications were all disastrous. If the explanation was simply a scheduling mix-up, and Madison thought he'd stood her up, the lack of a reply, even after he'd messaged, indicated *refusal*, driven by anger of monstrous proportions. If the explanation was that she'd been somehow prevented from replying, it indicated *incapacity*, which summoned a cornucopia of alarming possibilities—from her being injured in a road accident, in which case she'd be angry at him for not showing up with flowers at the ICU, to her being outright killed, in which case he'd never see her again.

But all manner of horror scenarios existed that were potentially worse. What if Madison had been involved in a gruesome car accident, because an outlaw pizza delivery boy, who was swerving in and out of lanes on the motorway—or 'highway', as she'd call it—had startled an elderly couple in a 1980s Jeep Wagoneer, the driver of which had jerked his steering wheel, colliding with a flatbed truck carrying propane bottles, one of which had fallen onto the asphalt, landing in Madison's lane and, only seeing the obstacle at the last millisecond, she had driven over it, releasing a fountain of sparks under her Mercedes that ignited the propane when the bottle exploded, enveloping her car in flames, and leaving her to burn in a cage of twisted metal? And what if she managed to crawl out alive, but with life-altering burns covering eighty percent of her body, including her face and head, and, when taken to hospital, they had to amputate her legs as well, because they'd been too badly fractured in the accident?

Or what if, after waiting for him at the airport all day, she headed back home and, after stopping at a lonely petrol station, was attacked in the forecourt by a group of criminals, who, not content with mugging her at knifepoint, then beat and gang-raped her in the toilets, leaving her unconscious, with a gigantic gash on her face, haemorrhaging until found, hours later, by an attendant, who discovered, upon questioning, that she was suffering from severe amnesia, to the point that she didn't know who she was or how she got there?

Or what if Syd, knowing Madison intended to meet him at the airport, had, on an apparent whim, suddenly taken her somewhere remote, where there was no signal, and no internet, and no phones, but a tattoo parlour, and contrived for Madison to leave her phone behind, perhaps by secretly sequestering it, so that Madison thought she'd lost it?

If only he could find out! He'd go wherever she was, no matter the cost, to be reunited and to save her, to look at her face, hold her hands, tell her that he loved her—wholly, unconditionally, forever.

But with his phone dead, any information was beyond reach. Nothing he could do, except to keep waiting.

Madison, Madison, where art thou Madison?

He pushed the hysterical thoughts out of his mind and told himself there had just been a miscommunication with his time of arrival, and that Madison would understand when he explained.

Another hour passed.

And then another.

By three in the morning, the exhaustion, dehydration, and boredom had defeated the anxiety, hunger, and bright lights, lulling him into a slumber. In this condition he slid down the hard chair, until his head was half-way down the back rest and his buttocks balanced on the edge of the seat, leaving three quarters of him horizontal. Nevertheless, his sleep was haunted by an unrelenting catena of nightmares, each more horrid than the previous one.

When relief came, it took the form of commotion in the lobby. A shrill chorus of shrieks and singing pierced his eardrums, reverberating hallucinogenically against the marble walls. He opened his eyes to find three girls his age stumbling towards the lifts in a state of acute intoxication. The skinny one with the white t-shirt hadn't bothered with a bra, and her long black hair was a rat's nest with a streak of magenta; she had evil pointed eyebrows and her fanged smiling face looked like a black dragonfish. The fat one with the cut denim shorts and fishnets had a blue buzzcut and safety pins in her face, one through her eyebrow and one through her cheek. And the medium-sized one with the ripped jeans and a decrepit zip-up orange hoodie, had green dreadlocks, her head shaved on both sides. The girls walked past him and, after an insufferable minute of clamorous chatter while they waited for a lift, stumbled inside as soon as they dinged open, and ascended to the seventh floor.

So, still, no Madison.

Except . . . Seventh floor? Green hair? Partially shaved?

Angel jumped out of his seat, heart racing, and stared at the lifts.

He'd seen her.

He'd seen Madison.

He rubbed his forehead, eyes like twelve-inch vinyls, irises shooting back and forth like a ball in a squash court.

This was the moment.

This was why he was here.

At least she was well.

Those hideous new friends of hers had sabotaged their reunion somehow. Madison had been deceived. Not been aware of his arrival.

Angel straightened his jacket, ensured it covered the tomato stains, wiped the dust off his shoes, and made his way to the lift.

Once inside and on the way up, he again studied his reflection in the mirror. His irises floated in a scarlet sea, and enough oil coated his hair to dress a large salad. He manually aligned the follicles as best he could and quickly rehearsed his greeting.

A minute later he was once more standing before Madison's door. Silence had been replaced by a rowdy cacophony of young female voices and happy-angry punk music.

He knocked on the door.

But it had no effect. The racket continued unabated.

He knocked again.

Still no effect.

He knocked a third time, louder.

The voices on the other side died down a bit.

He knocked a fourth time.

The voices ceased. The music stopped.

He waited, then knocked a fifth time.

Silence.

Again he waited, then knocked.

Footsteps.

Angel's heart thumped so hard his whole head was throbbing.

A lock turned, several times.

Angel took a deep breath.

The door opened a crack. Behind the chain holding it in place, a fat, double-chinned face with a small, parabolic mouth and dimpled the forehead.

'What?'

His voice failed him for a moment.

Blue Buzzcut glared.

'Um . . .' he said at last, 'Is-Is-Is Madison there?'

'Who the fuck are you?'

'Erm . . . m-m-my n-name is Angel.'

The door slammed shut.

Silence.

Angel waited, eyes twitching, hands freezing, ears pricked. He thought he could almost hear a murmur coming from deep inside the apartment.

Footsteps again.

The clack and rattle of the door chain being removed.

The door opened.

The girl with green dreadlocks stood unsteadily before him, hanging onto the doorframe. She had a nose-ring and a spike through the corner of each eyebrow. There was no bra under her tank top. She eyed him with dimples on her forehead.

'What? No flowers?' she said.

Only the voice confirmed her identity.

It was Madison.

Chapter CXLIX

'Er . . .'

'Also, I said October. It's November.'

'But . . .'

'I think you should go back to the airport and get me the flowers.'

'Um . . .'

'And did you bring the chocolates?'

'Um . . . um . . .'

'Whatever. I'm bored. Just come in.'

Angel hesitated. 'I-I-I hope I'm not intruding . . .'

She turned, sauntered into the apartment, zig-zagging slightly, and called, 'Shut the door behind you.'

Angel blinked, stupefied, but did as told. Then he hurried after her. She turned right at the end of the corridor and Angel followed. It reeked of alcohol and cigarettes, like his old room at the university. Underneath was the sickly-sweet cloying scent of multiple perfumes.

A longer corridor followed. Open doors revealed three bedrooms. All like overflowing textile recycling containers, with unmade beds thrown in and a profusion of bottles and cans of alcoholic beverages and beauty products. Madison had never mentioned she lived in shared accommodation. And how could she tolerate such messy flatmates? They were like incipient versions of Richard the hoarder!

His rehearsed greeting now a dud, he could only manage, 'I-I'm glad you're okay.'

Madison made no acknowledgment.

Angel stared at her occiput, confused.

The hallway carpet was littered with bits of paper, gum wrappers, empty bags of Cheetos, used tissues, hair straighteners, makeup pallets, crumpled clothes, and a thousand unclassifiable items. They passed a dirty kitchen and then continued into the living room, to the right of which a steel-framed glass door gave access to a balcony. The apartment's rigid modernism was offset by the loose profligacy of its occupants.

Blue Buzzcut sat slumped on a sofa with a heavy boot on the edge of a cluttered coffee table, a cigarette hanging from limp fingers, a can of Pabst Blue Ribbon in her other hand, which she rested on her thigh. She stared at him, her forehead still dimpled, her mouth still a sneering parabola. Cross-legged on an armchair across from her sat the skinny girl with the black and magenta hair, her sneakers on the upholstery, a wine-glass wobbly in her hand; she leered at Angel with narrowed eyes. Angel felt like he had walked into a tiger's cage, or a serpent's den. He stood like a lamp post, eyebrows levitating arches of perplexity.

'Okay,' Madison announced. 'This is Angel. Angel,

Taylor'—Madison pointed to Blue Buzzcut—'Syd'—she pointed to Black Dragonfish-Face.

Angel's heart pressed the accelerator. That was Syd! He'd come face to face with the gorgon. And she was Madison's flatmate? She *lived* here and wouldn't be leaving?

He felt exposed. Like his chest would cave in at the slightest pressure. He dared not move.

Neither girl acknowledged him for a moment.

Eventually, Syd grinned, her enormous mouth revealing sharp canines. 'So this is the guy.' She chuckled. Her voice was like a blend of drone doom guitar and a spade scraping stone. 'He's skinny.'

Madison had talked about him with Syd. That bode ill.

'*Anyway*,' Taylor said, loudly, turning back to Syd as though rudely interrupted. 'I still can't believe that fucking guy! *But you're fucking fat*, he kept saying. As if we had no right to send him packing. Fucking douchebag!'

Madison re-joined the conversation, her voice also too loud. 'Yea, he thought he'd get pussy just for buying us drinks. Men are so fucking predictable.'

'I loved your reply: *not my fault you're a dumbass!*' Taylor exploded with laughter, exposing big gums.

Syd said, slurring her words slightly, 'But what if he files charges, Taylor? You shoved him pretty hard.'

Madison dismissed the notion with a wave of her hand. 'He won't. What's he gonna do? Say a girl beat him up?'

'Fuck yeah!' said Taylor, getting up to high-five Madison.

Syd interjected, 'But what if he does?'

'I'll just counter-sue and say he tried to grab my boobs, which is sexual assault, and my friend tried to protect me. He'll spend the next five years trying to defend himself.'

'But it could end up biting you in the ass, Mads. These places have CCTV. And you know how the patriarchy controls criminal justice. You'd go down for perjury.'

'On what basis? We were drinking. I'm traumatized. I couldn't remember accurately.'

'But they'll say you brought it upon yourself for getting trashed and flirting.'

'I have every legal right to get trashed if I want to. And it's not illegal to have a faulty memory. In fact, I'd counter-counter-counter sue him for falsely accusing a victim of lying. So fuck him. I'll make a million bucks!'

Syd grinned, shaking her head. She grabbed a mucky charger cable lying on the floor next to her sofa and plugged in her phone.

'Don't fuck with Mads, motherfuckers. They don't call her Mad Mads for no reason!' said Taylor, cackling.

Angel's exhausted brain short-circuited, stunned, less by what Madison said—because the words mostly bounced off his ears—than by her tone, swearing, and chumminess with the leering gargoyles. What to do, what to say, if anything, was not at all obvious. He was still standing, awaiting acknowledgment, yet he realised he might end up waiting forever. His aching feet eventually directed his next act: he scanned the room for somewhere to sit, but the only available option, an unoccupied armchair, was not exactly inviting: a stained tatterdemalion from the 1980s, with dirty laundry hanging from the back, and a mildewy paperback on an arm rest. Angel got near and examined the seat, worried about crumbs and where to move the utility bills littering the sunken cushion.

'Just fucking sit,' Madison snapped. Syd and Taylor snickered.

He obeyed and heard the crumple of paper under his trousers. He kept away from the smelly laundry by holding his back at ninety degrees; this he did not only because put off, but also out of respect. He was, after all, Madison's guest. The book on the armrest was Shulamith Firestone's *The Dialectic of Sex: The Case for Feminist Revolution*. Almost certainly Syd's, he decided. Once settled, his pupils stayed on Madison. After five months of separation, being able finally to observe her in real life, moving, talking, and reacting to her environment, was simultaneously wonderful and strange, surreal, disconcerting. Those five months might as well have been five years, or fifteen, or fifty. Her altered appearance was difficult to process. Careful inspection still allowed him to glimpse the Madison he'd known: the same lips, the same chin, the same nose, the same eyes, the same eyebrows. But she felt alien, a Martian with green hair. And though desperate to say something, he knew not where to begin.

'Ugh! I feel gross,' said Madison, touching her hair. She turned to Syd. 'Tighten my dreads.'

Madison grabbed a crocheting hook from the table and sat on the floor in front of Syd, who opened her spidery legs to accommodate her. Taking the needle from Madison, she began working on the vile green sausages.

Angel coughed, the acrid stench from Taylor's cigarette like devil thorns in his throat. Madison took no notice of his discomfort; in fact, she hadn't looked at him once since she'd opened the door for him; she was too busy picking at her nails, which were a mess of cracked green polish.

'Fucking starving,' Taylor complained.

'Me too,' said Madison. 'Syd. Order us food.'

'I could have a pizza,' said Syd.

Taylor grinned, 'Dominos. Meat feast!'

Madison frowned. 'No way.'

Taylor's grin vanished. She and Syd looked at Madison, surprised by her tone.

'Meat is patriarchal,' Madison announced.

Stunned silence.

'Vegan?' Syd ventured.

'Okay, vegan. Call Pizza Hut and place the order.'

'Not Dominos?' said Taylor.

'We're having Pizza Hut. Extra large for me. Small for you and Taylor.'

'Small? I'm fucking starving!' Taylor protested.

'Fine. But you have to finish the whole thing.' Madison nodded at Syd to indicate she may now call. She then addressed Taylor again, 'And I challenge you to finish yours before me. Plus an order of garlic bread.'

Taylor sat up and pointed at Madison, suddenly excited again. 'Bitch, you're on!'

Syd picked up her phone from the table, but, before she dialled, Madison turned to her and said, 'Oh. Trigger warning.'

Syd, put her phone down, covered her ears and hummed to herself. Madison turned back to Taylor. 'That pizza delivery guy was looking at your tits the last time,' she said, keeping her voice loud—loud enough for Syd to still be able to hear.

'What the fuck?' Taylor said, frowning.

'Obviously he has a fat fetish.'

'Fuck that. I'm not anyone's fetish!'

'Maybe you should go with it. Might get him to steal some garlic bread for you next time. Maybe a whole free pizza.'

Taylor cocked her head and raised an eyebrow. 'You have a point!'

'Ah, so you're willing to exploit your pretty privilege then?'

'Pretty privilege!?'

'Oh, come on. Don't tell me you're not working it. Look at that cleavage. Look at those fishnets.'

'I wear what I want. I'm not doing it for anyone else. Let alone fucking men.'

'I think you're exploiting your pretty privilege.'

'Oh, like you're one to talk! Look at you last year and the year before! Walking around like a fucking preppie barbie doll!'

'Don't you fucking dare! Of course I'm more beautiful than you and Syd, specially Syd, but I fucking *destroyed* my beauty. And I'm only getting started! That's how committed I am. What have you done? Nothing. Obsessed with fashion from day one.'

'Obsessed with fashion! Have you fucking looked at me?'

'Yeah. I've looked at you. That's why I'm calling you out on it. All this Goth garb you wear—the fucking boots, the fucking fishnets, the fucking black all over, the fucking spiked dog collar. If that's not fashion-conscious, I don't know what is.'

'Oh, yeah, like a fucking blue buzzcut is the standard of beauty. Fuck you!'

'No, fuck *you!* You privileged bitch. You're obsessed with fashion and you walk around in fishnets with your tits hanging out and working it. Ditch your wardrobe, brand your fucking face, and let's see if you're really committed.'

'I was radical before you ever heard of the word, you little princess! I was radical when you were still a fucking Goth with tarot cards and crystals and shit.'

'Deeds not words. You're not what you did. You are what you do *today*.'

Taylor shook her head and looked away, angry.

Syd was still humming.

Madison pressed on. 'You just don't want to admit you're still a slave to the patriarchy, feminist or not.'

'This is sick,' said Taylor.

'It is sick. That's why you need to do something radical.'

'I mean this discussion.'

'We wouldn't be having it if you were honest with yourself.'

'You're full of shit.'

There was a pause.

Then, Madison burst out laughing. 'I'm just fucking with you.'

Taylor looked at Madison for a couple of seconds. The dimples on her forehead vanished and she joined in the laughter. 'You fucking bitch!'

Madison touched Syd's legs. 'Okay, sweetheart.' The sweetheart sounded sarcastic.

Syd uncovered her ears and got back to work on the dreadlocks.

'So when the pizza guy comes,' said Madison addressing Taylor again. 'Kick him in the balls.'

This time Taylor played along. 'Fucking right I will.'

'And don't fucking let any man open the door for you on the way down to greet him.'

'Everyday sexism! Fuck that shit!'

'That's more like it!'

Angel rubbed his forehead. Madison used to adore having, and indeed expected to have, doors opened for her; he'd done it as a matter of course whenever they'd been together, and she'd always smiled and complimented him on his chivalry. That was, in fact, one of the traits she'd most admired about him. Now, whereas he'd hoped that by seeing him again, she'd remember their love and banish Syd's baleful influence, the task ahead seemed nearly insurmountable. Especially if those atrocious quadrupeds lived with Madison. When did they plan to retire? If only he could get some time with her alone!

His eyeballs felt as if encrusted with Himalayan rock salt, his torso like a soufflé prematurely taken out of the oven, his tongue and larynx like cheese graters, his head like an overheated pressure cooker. Intense exhaustion, and the exertion of keeping himself awake, bathed him in cold sweat.

Madison now turned to Syd and said, sharply. 'What are you doing?'

'You asked me to fix your dreads.'

'I asked you to place our order.'

'Oh, damn, I forgot!' Syd picked up her phone, dialled a number, and placed their order—for drinks she added two one-gallon bottles of Pepsi and a twenty-four ounce bottle of root beer. All full sugar.

Starving and thirsty too, Angel lifted his index finger to get Madison's attention, and inhaled in preparation for speech, but she failed to notice him and Syd ended the call without it apparently occurring to Madison to ask him if he wanted anything.

'Forty-five minutes,' said Syd, putting down her phone.

Madison said, 'I hope you really are hungry, Taylor!'

'I'm hungry as fuck. I'm gonna wipe the floor with you, you skinny bitch!'

Forty-five minutes! Plus however long it took them

to eat all that! Clearly, they intended to stay up for another eternity.

'What? You're into body shaming now? I thought you were body positive!'

'Not body shaming. Just calling a spade a spade. Check your thin privilege.'

'My thin privilege is checking out after that pizza! Woooooo!' Madison lifted her tank top, exposed a growing belly, and wiggled her torso. In the process, she also exposed her breasts.

Taylor laughed again. Syd chuckled.

Angel averted his eyes. He feigned decorous interest in the profusion of spiderwebs being knitted near the ceiling.

'Definitely going to SlutWalk in 2020,' said Madison. 'Can't wait. I might be fatter than you by then, Taylor. Then it will be *you* with the thin privilege.'

Taylor chuckled. 'Fat chance you skinny runt!'

'Wait. What did you call me?'

'I called you a skinny runt.'

'Oh, you fucking better be hungry now, bitch.'

'Like you said, deeds not words.'

Madison ignored the taunt. 'Did you hear about what happened to Hannah?'

'Hannah the one with the boobs who does sex work? What happened?'

'Some guy reported her to the IRS.'

'No!'

'Had her Instagram taken down.'

'No way!'

'Yeah. She only posted boob and butt shots there. Just bating. Nothing too explicit. She said there are men on the internet who've made it their mission to report camgirls to the IRS.'

'Motherfuckers!'

'She's gonna be slapped with a huge tax bill. Other girls are fucking furious. If their income's taken away they won't be able to pay tuition.'

'Fucking assholes! Bet you they're incels.'

'Yeah. Apparently some pro-rape guy on the internet has been egging them on. Calls it a thot audit'.

'What an asshole,' said Syd.

Madison addressed Syd. 'By the way, did you ask if the pizza guy is coming by car?'

'Why?'

'Climate change.'

'Shit. Let me check.' Syd telephoned the pizza company. After a brief, tense dialogue, she ended the call. 'S'all good. Electric bike.'

'Good,' declared Madison.

'Is Greta coming to Chicago?' asked Taylor.

'XR Chicago said she'd be at their rally last month, but she didn't come,' said Madison.

'Bummer.'

'Probably some white male in the mayor's office threw a hissy fit and they banned her from the city.'

'Fucking patriarchy.'

'Yeah. Gotta get rid of that shit.'

'Bet you that's why I got marked down in my methodologies class. Professor's a white male. Can't stand a strong woman who stands her ground.'

Madison turned to Syd, 'Trigger warning.'

Syd again covered her ears and hummed to herself.

Madison said to Taylor, again making no effort to lower her voice—on the contrary, she spoke louder—'Professor Smith? He claims to be a feminist, but he ogles all the fucking time.

'Oh my God. He fucking does!'

'And I've heard he's fucked some of the students in exchange for As. He's like Harvey fucking Weinstein!'

'Yeah. But he's only interested in the skinny girls.'

'And only the beautiful ones. So Syd is safe at least.'

'That only proves he's weak.'

Madison touched Syd's leg. 'Okay.' She carried on. 'Can't trust men. Period. Especially male feminists. Everyone I've met is a fucking creep in the end.'

'Too fucking right! Glad I ditched men in high school.'

'You had boyfriends in high school? I thought you were a gold-star lesbian.'

'I dated guys in high school. They were all *shit*. Weak as *fuck*. One came out as *gay*. The other is transitioning. And the last one had a micropenis.'

A long and detailed anatomical discussion ensued, which left no detail out, no word unspoken, no depth unexplored. The more sordid the details, in fact, the better, judging from the girls' absorption. Wincing at the gratuitous excess of scabrous information, not to mention the language employed to convey it, from which he attempted to distract himself by counting the number of stitches in the soles of his shoes, the edges of his shirt sleeves, and the seams of his trousers, Angel could not help but wonder whether he'd ever been the subject of a similar discussion. Surely, Madison, no matter how much under the malevolent influence of these witches, respected his right to privacy, and wouldn't share details gleaned during their moments of intimacy.

At one point, unable to stand it any longer, he cleared his throat, albeit weakly, to remind the girls of his presence and thus hopefully divert them from the subject, but he might as well not have been there at all. He wished he was back at the terminal, waiting for Madison—his Madison—to show up. Or that he'd wake up aboard the aeroplane, still airborne, from this too-vivid nightmare. Or that he'd wake up at the university library and was still planning his visit. Life seemed so much simpler then!

The discussion was only halted by the arrival of the pizzas.

'Finally!' said Taylor, upon hearing the buzzer. But, though excited by the food, she remained seated, and took a drag of her cigarette.

'Well?' said Madison, pointedly raising her eyebrows and pointing to the intercom with her pupils.

'Well what?'

'Go and get the pizzas. Or don't you want us to eat?'

Taylor grumbled, 'Why don't you go and get them?'

'Period pain. My back hurts.'

Taylor got up. 'Man! I didn't wanna get up!'

She went to the intercom, buzzed the delivery man into the building, and went to wait for him at the front door.

Angel stared at Madison, wide-eyed, but she made no eye-contact and within a second Syd monopolised her attention. Syd said, 'I thought you had your period last week?'

'Well, it started again.' The answer was hurled casually.

Syd frowned, but before she could say anything, Taylor called out.

'Mads! Come quick! You've got to come and see this guy. What a fucking dweeb!'

Madison got up and joined Taylor at the door to the apartment, where they guffawed before opening the door, leaving Angel alone with Syd for a minute that felt like a month.

He dared not look at the poisonous viper. Sitting near her felt like sitting next to a cloud of nerve gas. But Syd, at least for the moment, seemed uninterested in him; he registered through his peripheral vision that she'd picked up her phone to scroll through her social media. She did this with the thumb of one hand; with the index of the other she scraped the tartar build-up on her teeth, which she then wiped on her t-shirt.

Madison and Taylor walked back into the living room carrying five pizza boxes, one stacked on top of the other. Along with them came the aroma of hot pizza. The bottom two boxes, presumably containing the extra-large pizzas, were so enormous that to get them inside the apartment they must have had to tip them sideways. Their arms were fully stretched as they held the bottom boxes by the corners. Deciding where to put them proved somewhat difficult, but clearing the coffee table, and using the middle of the long sofa, they found enough space for both. The bottles, cans, nail polish, dirty socks, smelly bras, and overflowing ashtrays they cleared were transferred not into the bins or other appropriate places, but to the floor with arm sweeps. Also added to the floor were the bottles of fizzy drink—the 24-ounce rootbeer for Syd, and the two one-gallon Pepsis for Taylor and Madison.

'Alright,' said Madison, 'Ready?'

Syd interrupted. 'Wait. Your boxes are too neatly aligned. Symmetry is patriarchal.'

'Oh. Yeah, fuck that,' said Taylor. She skewed her pizza box.

But Madison said, 'By doing that you're still a slave to the patriarchy.'

'Why is that?' asked Taylor, dimples re-appearing

on her forehead. Syd glanced at Madison, a sort of question mark.

'Because you're still allowing the patriarchy to decide how you place your pizza box. The best way to fight it is to be indifferent.

'Fuck. You're right.' Taylor unskewed her pizza box.

Syd nodded, granting the argument.

Angel sensed that Madison seemed amused by Taylor's compliance.

The girls opened their pizza boxes.

'Mmmm,' said Syd.

'So fucking good,' said Taylor.

Angel, stomach rumbling, eyed the pizzas and then Madison.

But taking zero notice of him, Madison said to Taylor, 'Okay. Ready? Three, two, one, go!'

Madison and Taylor grabbed the first arm-long slice of their respective pizzas and attacked it vigorously. Observing that Madison paid no heed to the tomato or the mushrooms falling on her chest or lap, Angel could barely stand to watch his paramour's degradation. The times he'd taken her for a pizza back in London, not only had it always been authentic Italian, and in the best restaurants, but they'd always dressed up for the occasion and eaten with knife and fork and a bottle of wine.

It took the girls twenty minutes to discover the limits of their stomachs. Syd finished only half her pizza, which to Angel still looked like a large. Madison and Taylor were leaning back on the sofa, feeling sick. Madison had unbuttoned her jeans and unzipped them all the way down, to give her bloated belly breathing room; she looked five months pregnant. Taylor had tucked her skirt under her abdominal pannus. Both had only managed a quarter of their pizzas and half their Pepsi bottles.

'Fuuuuuuuuuuuuck!' moaned Madison, putting her hands behind her head. Angel noticed she'd not only allowed her armpit hair to grow, but she'd since died it blue—the same shade as Taylor's hair.

Taylor unbolted an epic burp. 'Woman, I'm crashing!'

'Crashing is for wimps,' said Madison.

Syd got up and proclaimed. 'I'm going to bed.'

Angel checked the time on his phone. It was four thirty in the morning. Aside from the nap he took on the aeroplane, he'd been up for nearly forty-eight hours.

'Ugh, I'm off too,' said Taylor, hauling herself off the sofa.

Finally, time alone with Madison! Exhausted as he was, Angel instantly perked up. He stared at his beloved, wide-eyed, waiting for a sign, expecting her to acknowledge him as soon as the flatmates retired, and revert, as if by magic, to her old self. At any point, she'd smile sweetly and throw herself at him to cover his face with kisses, confess how much she'd missed him, and tell him how glad she was to have him in the flesh at last. She might even remove the green hair extensions, rip out the axillar wigs, and peel off the fake tattoo, just so he could witness that his Madison was still there, and that this feminist version was just a ruse, a façade she'd adopted to get maximum marks in her final year. No doubt she hated it as much as he, but, American universities being as they were, so ideological and full of politics, it was an intelligent course of action. Jae's obduracy had, after all, only brought her trouble, and Madison was definitely more perspicacious than Jae.

But Madison simply got up and started making her way out of the living room without so much as glancing at him. He followed her with an uncomprehending gaze. Surely, she meant to grab something from the kitchen and come back. Only when she was almost at the corridor did she turn to address him. She pointed at the open pizza box still in the middle of the sofa.

'Just put the pizza on top of the other and make yourself a spot. You've got this, right?'

'Um . . .'

She waved him off. 'I'm tired.'

Chapter CL

Angel stared at the corridor after Madison disappeared. He stared for five minutes. Madison never returned.

She gave me for my pains a world of sighs . . .

The bright overhead lights having been left for him to turn off, he got up to look for the switches. The lamp next to the sofa had also been left on, so by its light he transferred the pizza from the sofa onto the coffee table and cleared away the numerous items cluttering the cushions: sweet wrappers, crumpled photocopies, hair pins, paper clips, mushroom slices, a bra, a bottle of Tylenol, a nail file, bottles of nail polish, used cotton buds, bunches of hair, fake eyelashes, pens, copper coins, two pairs of knickers, hair bands, three eyeliner pencils, bits of paper, hair brushes, Sellotape, empty Fritos bags, a chicken bone, nail clippings, and a trillion crumbs of variegated provenance. It took him twenty minutes to make his bed tolerable, although nothing could be done about the burns, or the stains, or the smell. With no blankets or equivalent, his jacket was recruited for the creation of warmth.

But he could not yet lie do wn, for he was dying of thirst and concave with hunger. Compounding his distress was Madison's having neglected to grant him permission to grab a slice of her pizza or have a gulp of her Pepsi. Necessary as the calories were, he dared not avail himself; it seemed ungentlemanly to abuse a lady's hospitality through theft. She had indeed hinted that he make himself at home, but did that extend to eating and drinking, or only to borrowing her sofa?

After much deliberation, it occurred to him that he could at least drink water from the tap. Madison surely wouldn't mind that, and the other girls would never know. Thus, he went to the kitchen.

Unfortunately, finding a clean glass proved impossible. The cupboards were bare. All the glasses, mugs, and cups were dirty and either in the sink or on the counters, where they stood alongside stacks of dirty dishes, dried up fruit peals, empty food containers, and used paper napkins; together they covered every available square inch of surface. The dishes were caked with orts, the mugs half-full of caseated almond milk, and any organic matter colonised by mould. White, green, and black varieties were visible everywhere, cohabiting with dust, spiderwebs, stains, mice droppings, and pulverulent grease.

Angel winced. No way he was touching that E. coli lab!

Instead, he waited until all the girls had switched off, which took another twenty minutes, and sneaked into the nearest bathroom, which stood opposite one of the bedrooms. After quietly closing the door behind him, he used his phone torch, intending to locate the sink and drink directly from the tab.

What the circle of light revealed, however, immediately discouraged him. The floor was littered with clothes, beauty products, and soiled sanitary pads. If there was a bin, it was probably under the tall pile of toilet paper and tampon cylinders, sanitary pad wrappers, used tissue paper, empty hair dye tubes, and discarded bottles or shampoo and conditioner. The barbarians—but surely not Madison—had left the toilet lid open. A deep brown film coated the white porcelain below the waterline, and limescale crusted below the rim. As to the sink, a dusty pile of empty hand gel containers, coated in dry vomit, had put it beyond use.

Angel exited the bathroom in a hurry.

It seeming pointless to try another, he returned to the living room.

After five minutes of agonising excogitation with Madison's bottle of Pepsi between his legs, dehydration dictated his decision. Although under cover of rationalisation: he'd come to save Madison, and Syd's brainwashing posed a formidable challenge, so hydration was essential for optimal mental performance. He grabbed the bottle, unscrewed the cap very slowly, to allow the gas a silent escape, and took a tiny sip—enough to wet his tongue. Yet, so urgent was the need for fluids that this sip had to be followed by another, and another, and finally desperate gulps, until the bottle was empty.

Angel exhaled with smiling relief.

Only for it to be chased away by guilt.

And the oily aftertaste of vegan pizza.

The litre of full-sugar Pepsi, moreover, following his involuntary forty-nine-hour fast, produced unwelcome effects, for, while the sugar led to a crash, the caffeine kept him awake. His stomach also protested; the Pepsi, abruptly poured into a cavity so long without content, felt like a glob of melted lead. As a result, he lay on the smelly sofa, hammered by a hypoglycaemic stupor, almost hallucinating, but sleepless all the same and with a stomach ache, until the morning light forced him to rise to close the curtains.

Then, at last, he slept.

But not for long.

He was awoken by a noise in the corridor. When he opened his eyes, he found the curtains open again, showing a dreary plumbaceous sky. The dismal, colour-desaturating light accentuated the mildew on the walls and the mould on the windowpanes. That light made everything look so much worse. The pizzas had gone black. And not a single object lay in view that wasn't somehow damaged or broken. He noticed, for the first time, that what last night he'd assumed was carpeting, was in fact a layer of carboard. It looked as though, when the floor got too dirty, the girls just threw cardboard on top and carried on with their mess. A Formica bookcase, missing two legs, rested tilted on one of its corners. The reek of cigarette smoke and alcohol having grown stale or partially dissipated, had given way to the stench of rotting chicken.

The noise from the corridor recurred, so Angel, thinking the girls were awake, sat up and put his shoes back on. But in the absence of voices, and with the noise persisting, he stood and walked to the corridor.

There he found an anaconda.

The serpent was dragging itself from one bedroom

into another. Madison was in danger! Shaking with fear, Angel ran past the serpent and peered into Madison's room. The anaconda had a black mane with a streak of magenta—it was Syd!—and had climbed onto Madison's bed, opened its jaws, and mostly swallowed his paramour. Incredibly, Madison was awake, and looked at him expressionlessly as she disappeared inside the anaconda's mouth. He could see the contour of Madison's body bulging out of the serpent's, as the latter's stomach released acids to commence digestion.

No!

He awoke with a whimper.

The chill of terror swept over him and he scrunched his eyes shut until it passed.

He opened one eye—cautiously—and then the other.

The living room was still in shadow. The curtains closed. The only sound was the intermittent fizz of cars passing on the road seven floors below and the background hiss of a congested American city.

He sat up.

Inside the apartment: complete silence.

He waited.

No voices. No activity.

He got up and, putting his jacket back on, walked slowly to the corridor.

Silence. Stillness.

He sneaked towards the open door of the first bedroom.

Standing by the door frame, he leaned into the opening, one millimetre at a time, until he could see inside.

An empty bed.

He proceeded to the next bedroom and repeated the procedure.

Another empty bed.

Finally, he snuck up to the last bedroom.
Also an empty bed.
The girls were gone.

Chapter CLI

Madison would, surely, not have left without leaving him a note. She would have signed it and added a few hearts and kissed it for good measure. And she would have left it somewhere he could easily find it when he woke up.

So he looked around. First in the living room, on the coffee table and in the vicinity of the sofa; then on the living room window sills; then on the balcony door; then near the corridor; then in the kitchen, on the fridge and cupboard doors; then in the corridor; then on the front door; then on the bathroom doors; then on the bedroom doors, in case he went to find her; then in the living room again, anywhere and everywhere.

No note.

He checked his phone, but it was still dead.

He glanced at Syd's charger and hesitated. However, after reasoning that Madison could have sent him messages, and that she'd want him to receive them, he plugged in his phone. After an eternity, it came to life.

The time was 3:22 pm.

And there was a message, but not from Madison. From his mother, asking to confirm that he'd arrived safely.

He checked his social media.

No messages.

He checked Madison's social media.

No updates.

He checked, after taking a deep breath, Syd's social media.

Only a drunken selfie on Instagram from the previous evening, with Taylor and Madison pulling stupid faces at the camera.

As Taylor had been tagged, he checked Taylor's social media.

Set to private, so he was locked out.

Thinking Madison might have gone downstairs to check her mailbox, he thought of going down to the lobby. But what if she was already in the lift, heading towards him? And, moreover, if Madison had not left him a note, it seemed unlikely she'd left him a copy of the key.

But no, of course she did! If an urgent errand had rushed her off her feet to the point that she'd had no time to scribble him a note, she'd certainly never have left him in the apartment without the means to re-enter should he need to fetch breakfast from a coffee shop. He felt bad for doubting her.

With that in mind, he looked for copies of the keys—by the door to the apartment, in the kitchen, in the living room.

Nothing.

Could it be that Madison had an extra set in her bedroom?

He went to the corridor and stopped at each door to scan the contents of each bedroom, hoping to identify Madison's without intruding in her flatmates' private space.

All the bedrooms were incomprehensible in their clutter. Each a riot of artificial colours. And if he thought that he'd be able to tell Madison's possessions by their superior quality and elegance, he was instantly disabused, for there was not *one* object in any of the bedrooms to which those descriptors would apply. Cheap and nasty was king. Quantity reigned over quality. And conscientiousness was a trait universally disdained, for, like in his nightmare, every single item—be it clothing, or furniture, or books, or mugs, or lamps, or posters, or whatever—was somehow damaged or broken. All three girls seemed to be marching in lockstep, aesthetics-wise. To approach something resembling an educated guess, he had to go back and forth between the three bedrooms to narrow the options down to two, the sizes of Taylor's clothing, and her choice of footwear, finally ruling out the bedroom in the corner of the L-shaped corridor.

Surely, Madison would keep pictures of him in her bedroom, enabling him to identify it. But no such pictures were visible. She clearly relied entirely on her iCloud. Nevertheless, surely, Madison would display the postcards he'd sent her, on a corkboard, or her wall, or her mirror, or a picture frame. But no such postcards were visible. Nevertheless, surely, Madison would still have the souvenirs they'd collected during their time in London: there was a pebble he'd given her in Kensington Gardens, to memorialise an afternoon walk near the Round Pond, when they'd held hands and talked about their dreams and the future; there was the lock he'd given her outside the Odeon, in Leicester Square, to symbolise their eternal union, two days before she left; there was the flower he'd stolen from the table of the Céleste at the Lanesborough, the time he took her there for afternoon tea, in celebration of their seventeenth weekieversary; there were countless cinema, theatre, concert, and ballet tickets, each of them a memento for a glorious occasion, an unforgettable moment, a unique atmosphere, a snapshot in their relationship, full of wonder, poetry, and romance. But no such souvenirs were anywhere on display.

In the end, Angel was forced into a method he found shameful and distasteful: he crossed the threshold to the room nearest to the living room and, stepping carefully over the belongings scattered on the floor, went to the bed, where a laptop sat covered in feminist stickers—'fight like a girl', 'girl power', 'feminist as f@#$', 'fuck your patriarchal bullshit', 'the future is female', 'that's ancient herstory', and 'pro-choice, pro-feminism, pro-cats' they vociferated. He opened the lid. The wallpaper was solid pink with text on one side in black Helvetica bold: 'You go, girl', it screamed. When he clicked on the mail app, the password prompt popped up, barring him access. The user picture, in addition, only showed a hand giving the middle finger.

'Bollocks', he whispered, closing the lid, and carefully putting the laptop down in exactly the same spot.

Next, he picked up a notebook, which had been dropped on the floor, on top of a green hoodie. Alas, whoever owned the notebook had not been a conscientious student. A date had been scrawled at the top of the first page, plus the name of a module—'Women in Western Literature'—but, instead of class notes, the rest were bored doodles. Pages and pages of it.

He tried the desk drawers.

All empty, except for one with a dildo.

None of the books scattered about, all angry feminist rants, judging from their titles and cover designs, had an inscription.

And of the messy stacks of paper here and there, none included a letter bearing the addressee's name. The papers were all photocopied course materials that had been collected, brought home, dumped wherever they may fall, and allowed to get crumpled and stained with coffee, beer, and Coca-Cola.

With a perplexing absence of identifying items in this room, Angel went to the one adjacent, praying he'd have better luck there.

And this he had.

But the luck was balanced by disappointment.

He found a postcard he'd sent Madison in August, showing Hans Holbein the Younger's *The Ambassadors*, under the bed. A despicable vandal—surely not Madison!—had drawn John Lennon glasses on George de Selve, and a huge circumcised penis, ejaculating, on Jean de Dinteville. The corners were bent, the middle was creased, and the reverse, where he'd written her a sonnet memorialising their visit to the National Portrait Gallery, was soiled by a brown stain, pink chewing gum, and a dark shoeprint.

For the next hour, Angel sat in the living room, stomach churning, elbows on his knees, head in his hands, staring at the carpet. Surely, Madison wouldn't treat their love that way. Surely, she respected their memories. Surely, she wouldn't let anyone come near the sacred relics of their union—let alone deface them in a wanton and juvenile fashion. It had to be Syd. Or perhaps even Taylor—albeit led by Syd, of course. The demon Syd had to be behind it. Because there'd been no indication that Madison felt anything other than reverence for their London romance. She treasured it. She'd sworn fidelity. She'd said their love was forever. And hadn't she begged him to come? Hadn't she asked him to hurry? Hadn't his visit been urgent and desperate?

Syd had corrupted her far more than he'd imagined.

Of course, Syd held her captive, cooped up in the apartment, where she could poison her ears, censor her speech, direct her reading, shape her vocabulary, influence her dress, police her friendships, warp her thoughts, restrict her visitors, inseminate her dreams, trick her psyche, manipulate her emotions, condition her responses, regulate her habits, ruin her beauty, punish her elegance, impoverish her experiences, and cultivate her worst instincts. Whereas he, Angel, had been thousands of miles away, sighing, weakened, invisible, muted, at the end of a tenuous digital tether that had constantly been eroded and interfered with.

He had to put a stop to this.

He had to save Madison.

Or she'd be lost.

As would he.

Back in her room, he rummaged through her possessions, rifled through her papers, and went through her notebooks, drawers, and cupboards, timidly at first, but ever more boldly as the distressing discoveries piled on. She'd made a wedge with another of his postcards to stabilise her desk. She'd stuffed some of his letters into a pair of boots, so that they wouldn't lose their shape. She'd made a paper airplane with her *Phantom of the Opera* ticket and set it in on fire, then splashed Coke and stomped on it to put it out. She'd used a set of photographs of them together, taken at the photobooth of the High Street Kensington Underground Station the previous March, as a place to stick her used chewing gum—which she did not do on the reverse, but on the image side. She'd used books he'd given her, all first-edition hardbacks, signed and inscribed, to prop up her bed, which had collapsed on one side; some of the pages were wavy from water damage, or stuck together by food drippings. She'd used the Deutsche Grammophon vinyl pressing of Hector Berlioz's *Symphonie Fantastique* he'd given her for their second monthaversary as a makeshift ashtray—she'd been smoking!—leaving the empty sleeve on the floor, to be walked over, ruined by a wine spillage, shoved into a bin, and buried under a tall pile of used makeup wipes, empty bottles, waxy Q-tips, discarded Cheetos bags, plastic wrapping, balled-up paper, blackened banana peels, ripped envelopes, dead batteries, oxidised apple cores, crumpled shop receipts, chicken bones, fast food containers, Starbucks cups, chocolate foil, balls of hair, and a dried-up half-eaten hamburger.

'No!' he wailed, with steepled eyebrows.

He fell to his knees.

And wept.

Chapter CLII

Madison returned at 8:29 pm. Exasperatingly, she returned accompanied by Taylor and Syd.

The three of them entered the apartment engaged in noisy conversation and ambled into the living room in a cackling gaggle.

None acknowledged Angel, even though he stood up to acknowledge them. Or, rather, to acknowledge Madison.

Madison and Taylor carried brown paper bags, which they plonked on the coffee table, on top of the two pizza boxes from the previous evening. Each bag held a bucket of KFC, plus carboard boxes, presumably containing burgers or wraps or burritos or whatever, and three one-gallon bottles of Wild Cherry Pepsi. Sight of these allowed Angel a sigh of relief, as they made it less likely Madison would notice he'd finished the rest of her bottle without her authorisation. The buckets made their analogues in Britain look like thimbles. An eight-year-old child could have bathed in one of them.

Angel had sat back down at one end of the sofa, so, when Taylor dropped herself on the other end, she nearly sent him flying into the ceiling. She wasn't as big as—what was her name?—Betsy, the Big American Girl from university, but she was still massive, and her sitting down felt like an asteroid impact, complete with a foam tsunami rippling through the cushions.

Syd sat in the same armchair as the previous evening, and Madison in the armchair he'd occupied when he first arrived. They both crossed their legs, oblivious to their sneakers on the upholstery.

Angel kept his eyes glued to hers, eyebrows raised, waiting for even the briefest eye-contact, or the smallest gap in the conversation, to get her attention. But the girls' jabbering was constant; not even a laser-thin crevice appeared into which he could insert a word. And not once did Madison glance in his direction. Her eyes were either on Syd, Taylor, or the fried chicken.

The latter the girls attacked with gusto, their appetite equalled by their lack of manners. Sounds of mastication, heavy breathing, and loud swallowing offered Angel a nauseating symphony of greed and avidity. Syd picked at her chicken like a bird, as did Madison. Taylor ripped the pieces apart directly with her teeth. Angel wondered what happened to their veganism.

'Oh my God! I forgot to mention,' said Madison, her mouth full. 'I spoke to Emily the other day. She says her sister's gone full trad wife.'

Taylor said, 'Really? The fuck is wrong with her?'

'She's an anti-feminist, apparently.'

'What the fuck?'

'Yeah. And pro-Trump.'

'Fuck me. That's fucking insane!'

'Tell me about it. Women are *dying*. And this chick's pro-fucking-Trump.'

'I hope she gets punched in the fucking face!'

'Emily's tried to talk to her but it's like talking to a brick wall.'

'She's been brainwashed.'

'Yeah. She's full of conspiracy theories too. Thinks feminism is a fraud concocted to destroy Western civilisation.'

Taylor rolled her eyes. Syd snorted with derision.

'*And*,' Madison continued, a piece of chicken flying from her mouth, 'she says she doesn't want to end up a menopausal forty-five-year-old cat lady.'

'So she's gonna slave after some dude,' said Taylor, 'who's gonna keep her barefoot and pregnant. Cleaning and cooking all day for a man who'll rape her every fucking night. Fuck that shit!' Taylor shook her head.

'Yeah, that dumbass been promoting that shitty film about the men's rights movement.'

'What do they need a fucking movement for! They have all the power! The whole of society is their fucking movement.'

'She describes herself as *red-pilled*.'

Taylor screamed. 'Of course she does. Blue-pilled fuckwits always think they're red-pilled. That's why you're fucking blue-pilled, you assholes!'

'Yeah. Duh!' Madison put her tongue behind her lower lip and pushed it out to look simian.

'I know we're perpetuating the patriarchy right now by eating meat, but, woman! This shit makes me so fucking angry!'

Madison finished a piece of chicken. 'Fuck trad wives and fuck the patriarchy!' She tossed the bone across the living room; the bone flew in an arch and landed on the carpet, near the corridor.

'Yeah. Fuck the patriarchy!' Taylor, who'd just finished a drumstick, emulated Madison's act of defiance. The bone hit the wall and landed on the bookcase below, on top of a paperback.

Syd grinned, observing Madison and Taylor—with, was it calculating eyes?—while keeping quiet.

Given this turn in their conversation, Angel was momentarily grateful of being unnoticed. He took his eyes off Madison and stared at his trouser legs, keeping still as a mannequin, waiting for the expressions of rebellion to pass, wanting to disappear. Amelia wandered into his mind. This corrupt version of Madison would despise her; Amelia likely represented everything they abhorred. He made a mental note not to mention her to Madison in conversation.

Taylor opened one of the bottles of Pepsi and took a gulp.

Madison, noticing, grabbed another bottle and said to her, 'Bet you can't chug that whole bottle down in one go.'

'Fuck you. You're on!'

Taylor pushed all the air out of her lungs, put the bottle to her lips, and begun gulping down the Pepsi.

Madison and Syd chanted, 'Chug! Chug! Chug!'

Wincing at the thought of 'chugging' down a cold carbonated drink, Angel observed the Pepsi make its way down the bottle at lightning speed. Todd or Josh or whatever his name had been, would have been in awe.

'Ahhhhhh!' Taylor exhaled, grimacing with eyes scrunched up while she waited for the burn to pass.

'Wooooooo!' screamed Syd.

Madison stared with amusement, but kept silent.

Taylor now unbolted a stupendous burb, which rattled the windows and was greeted with rough laughter by her flatmates. She raised the empty bottle like a trophy in the air. 'Yeah bitcheeeeeeesssss!'

Syd whooped again.

Madison, however, did not join in.

Instead, she unscrewed the cap, threw it at Taylor's face, and said, 'Pathetic. *I'll* show you how it's done!'

She put the bottle to her lips, tilted it decisively, and began gulping down the liquid of pain.

Taylor and Syd chanted, 'Chug! Chug! Chug!'

Gripping tightly the cushion he was seated on, Angel, eyebrows arched, head slightly retracted into his shoulders, followed the Pepsi's downward progress. He worried about her precious organs—her pancreas, her liver, her blood!

After five seconds of visible agony, however, Madison removed the bottle from her lips, leaned forward, and sprayed Taylor and Angel with fizzing Pepsi.

'Fuck! That hurts!' said Madison, her chin dripping.

Taylor and Syd, the latter dripping too, found her reaction hilarious and exploded with cackles.

Angel didn't, and methodically wiped the Pepsi off his face and clothing with his hand, not daring to reach for the paper napkins scattered on the coffee table.

'Oh, fuck!' murmured Madison, head bowed, amidst the ongoing cachinnation.

She jumped to her feet, ran to the balcony, and hurled the contents of her stomach into the night.

More cacophonous laughter rang from her flatmates' undulating tracheas.

Angel stared, distressed and horrified.

For the next few minutes, Madison kept her body bent over the veranda, spitting down onto whatever lay seven floors below. Taylor and Syd high-fived and carried on laughing.

Worry overcoming horror, Angel got up and joined Madison on the balcony. He dared not put a hand on her back, so he stood next to her and piped, 'Are you okay? Are you okay?'

Madison said nothing; she continued to spit, green dreadlocks over her face. A frigid wind had the dreadlocks dance like rags on a clothesline.

'Madison, are you okay? Are you okay? Madison?'

She still made no reply.

He waited a few seconds and tried again, 'Are you okay, Madison? Um . . . do you want water? Do you need a paper napkin?'

No reply. Just continued spitting.

'C-C-Can I get you anything?'

No reply.

'A-Are you okay?'

No reply.

'Ma-Madison, I'm worried. A-Are you okay?'

As if he weren't present at all, Madison straightened and walked past him and back into the living room.

'Fuck, woman. That didn't go well,' she announced to the others, detonating another payload of cackling.

Angel followed and sat back down on the sofa, crestfallen.

'Taylor one, Mads zero,' said Taylor.

'Hell no. Mads one, Taylor *zero*.'

'I won!'

'No you didn't. Look at you. You're four times my size. I drank a third of a bottle, so pound for pound I drank more and *faster*.'

'That's fucking bullshit!'

'No it isn't. Syd. Who won?'

Syd hesitated. 'Wasn't the challenge . . . to drink the whole bottle?'

'The challenge was to see who drank faster,' Madison asserted, without even a modicum of doubt.

'But . . . you said . . .'

'I bet her I could drink from the bottle faster.'

'You bet me I couldn't drink the whole bottle in gone go. I did. You couldn't. End of,' said Taylor.

'I didn't say that. I said I bet you couldn't drink from the bottle in less time than I did. And I wiped the fucking floor with you.'

'Are you fucking real?'

'But Mads . . .' began Syd.

Madison interrupted, 'Say I won.'

'Fuck you!' shouted Taylor.

Madison raised her voice. 'Syd, say I won.'

Madison's tone made Angel nervous and sad at the same time. He couldn't remember what she'd said. But Syd was clearly provoking her. He stared firmly at the carpet. The imp was truly awful. No wonder Madison was erratic and angry—her mental health!—that's how Syd weakened her defences!

A tense silence.

Even louder, 'Syd. Say it!'

Taylor looked away and muttered. 'Fucking bullshit.'

Syd stared, paralysed.

Madison stared her down.

Then exploded with laughter. 'Ha haaa! Gotcha!'

Sighs of relief from the other two girls, followed by reluctant chuckles.

'You really got me,' said Syd, awkwardly.

Taylor responded with sarcasm, 'Yeah, very funny.'

'Alright, snowflake, you won,' Madison declared.

Angel's gaze remained on the carpet. He was somewhat relieved, however. Madison had not lost her sense of humour. Ever the prankster. She was still there. Evil, devious Syd had yet to swallow her whole. There was hope!

Chapter CLIII

Taylor yawned, her open maw like a hippopotamus'. 'Bitch, I need a fucking nap!'
'Ugh, I need one too,' said Madison, standing up. She addressed Syd, 'Come to my room.'

No . . . no . . . no!

Ignoring Taylor's waddling exit, Angel closely observed Madison as she towed Syd away.

This is how it happens!

He inhaled to say something, hoping to hold Madison back so they could finally converse, but Syd commanded her attention, keeping Angel out of her line of sight.

Bollocks!

Unsure of how to proceed, Angel repeatedly stood and sat down, wanting to follow Madison, but not daring. She might get angry!

His stomach cramped.

Ten minutes later he heard Madison open her door noisily and walk to Taylor's door while talking on the phone.

'Hey Taylor,' she shouted. 'Ashley is throwing a party tonight. You wanna come?'

Angel heard Taylor mumble something in the affirmative.

'Awesome. Start getting ready then!'

Confirming their attendance to her caller, Madison went back into her room, out of which, a minute later, blasted hyperactive American female voices—YouTubers yammering continuously without taking a breath.

Out of Syd's room, a similar stream of hyperactive YouTube yammering flowed moments later.

And out of Taylor's room exploded angry punk music, sloppily played and pierced with female screeches.

Angel cringed at the racket. But it occurred to him that, since Madison was at last alone in her room, presumably getting ready, this was his chance finally to talk to her. He made his way to her open door and knocked, albeit so softly that the pappus of a dandelion seed landing on a cotton bud would have been more thunderous.

Seated at her desk, with her back to him in front of a mirror, an open make-up pallet on the right and an open laptop on the left, Madison continued to cake her face with foundation.

Angel could see his own reflection in the mirror. He knocked again.

No response.

He knocked a bit louder.

No response.

'Madison?' he piped.

No response.

He knocked a fourth time. 'Madison?'

No response.

He knocked yet again, louder than before. 'Madison?'

She sighed, stabbed the space bar on her laptop to pause the video, and turned with an eyebrow irritably raised, 'What!'

Taken aback, he hesitated. 'Um . . .'

'Hurry up. What is it?'

'Um . . . c-c-can w-we talk for a bit?'

'Can't you see I'm busy?'

'Um . . . er . . .'

'Look. I haven't got time. Later. Okay?'

'Er . . . o-o-okay.'

Angel withdrew and returned to the living room.

An hour passed.

The YouTube videos and Taylor's punk rock blared without a break.

Angel thought he could at least ask Madison when she expected to be back. Surely, that wouldn't inconvenience her too much; it would only take a second to answer the question. He went back to her door and knocked as before.

Madison, now in a tank top, was rummaging through a pile of dirty laundry.

'Madison?' he said.

No acknowledgment.

He knocked again. 'Madison?'

No acknowledgment.

'Bingo!' she said to herself, pulling out a mauve zip-up hoodie.

He knocked. 'Madison?'

She turned and snapped, 'Angel, can't you see I'm getting dressed?'

'Oh, I-I-I'm sorry . . . I-It's just that . . .'

'I'm *busy*. Later. *Okay?*'

'Y-Y-Yea, of course. I-I'm sorry. I'm sorry.'

He withdrew and returned to the living room. He heard Madison slam her door shut behind him. A sharp click followed as she pressed the lock button.

Another hour passed.

The YouTube videos stopped, as did the punk rock. They were replaced by Madison's, Syd's, and Taylor's voices.

Angel could smell a blend of perfumes and cigarette smoke wafting in from the corridor.

Madison's voice: 'You ready? Let's go partyyyyy! Woooooooo!'

The other two replied with whooping of their own.

The front door opened and closed. The girls' voices faded.

He was alone.

Chapter CLIV

A day and a half had passed already and he'd only been able to exchange precious few words with Madison. There were only five and a half days left. And if he ended up waking up at three in the afternoon, as he had today, there'd be only four left—ninety-six hours. His time with her was slipping through his fingers.

He ran to the balcony and looked down.

A green head, a blue head, and a black head with a streak of magenta. The girls were standing by the kerb. If he rushed down right then he could maybe join Madison—ask her if he could go with to the party. But before he pulled away to act on this impulse, a taxi stopped, and the girls got in. Within seconds, the taxi pulled out, snatching precious hours with Madison away.

Lips tight, Angel banged the veranda, and went back inside.

He sat on the sofa, head in his hands, and thought.

Perhaps he could ask Madison the address and take a taxi to wherever the party was being held.

He pulled out his phone.

ANGEL: I would like to offer my most sincere apologies for the earlier interruption. I hope Her Ladyship will forgive this gentleman's eagerness to hear her melodious voice in conversation, particularly after months of excruciating separation and an arduous journey of nearly four thousand miles. Subsequent events having taken place at great velocity, it hath only occurred to me now that I could join Her Ladyship at the party. Would Her Ladyship be amenable to such an outcome?

The message was sent and received.

But not opened.

The ants were marching.

Angel waited.

Checked his phone.

Message unopened.

He waited some more.

Checked his phone.

Message unopened.

He waited ten minutes.

Checked his phone.

Message unopened.

He waited another ten minutes.

Checked his phone.

Message unopened.

And so on for the next two hours.

Despite the ants, Angel forced a smile. Madison must be having a great deal of fun. He loved her, and loved her deeply, so how could he begrudge her enjoying time with her friends? On the contrary, it made him happy.

But the falsity of that happiness made it unsustainable, and a corrosive cocktail of anger and jealousy gradually overwhelmed it.

After checking his phone one more time, he threw it across the room.

It landed next to the chicken bone near the corridor.

He remained seated with his head in his hands, staring at the carpet, for what felt like an hour, the anger mounting all the while. His breathing grew fast and his jaw tight. The memory of the day's discoveries flickered in his mind. How could she treat their love that way? How could she be so callous? How could she be so disrespectful? Each time he thought about a memento she'd ruined it was like a knife to the heart. Yet, instead of on Madison, he focused his anger on Syd. *She* did it. *She* was responsible. He loathed her already, but he now hated her with trembling vehemence. He thought of her tacky hair, her crooked teeth, her stupid eyebrows, her cheap clothes, her nasty tattoos, her revolting thinness, her insufferable accent, her infuriating smugness, her idiotic feminism, her filthy habits, her odious laziness, her repulsive voice, her vile fishface, her vulgar stickers, her abominable clothes, her contemptible suspicion, her monstrous skull, her detestable books, her grotty Instagram, her hateful mindset, her intolerable presence, her sick disposition, her clumsy doodles, her heinous—

His phone buzzed.

Turning towards the phone, he considered ignoring it. But after twenty seconds he became conscious of time slipping by, and the thought of wasting his visit without Madison was too painful to bear.

He jumped to his feet and retrieved his phone.

No reply from Madison.

Instead, messages from Amelia.

He opened them.

She asked him whether he was enjoying his visit in Chicago and his time with Madison. This made his stomach cramp again. She added that she'd seen he'd read her message the previous evening and had taken his lack of a reply to mean he'd been extremely busy, probably spending every possible second with Madison and taking her everywhere, like a gentleman. This made him even more anxious. To this she appended another instalment of university gossip. Apparently, his roommate had suddenly dropped out, or been expelled; no one knew anything about it, including his American friends, who were surprised to find him gone. She'd found out from Saïd, who'd inquired to see if he, Angel, had come back because he, Angel, owed him, Saïd, two hundred pounds; Saïd had told her he'd gone to knock on the door to his room only to find it open and the contents cleared out. Saïd had again asked for his, Angel's, address, but she had refused to give it to him. She had later told Alba, Jae, and Vera to do the same, just in case. Jae, incidentally, had been suspended by the university. Incitement to hatred, it was claimed. But Jae had told her she'd simply taken issue with Professor Hynd's view on the gender pay gap and that the discussion had degenerated into an argument that had ended with Jae being told to leave. Jae had said that she had debated the professor calmly and logically, but the professor had lost her temper and called her a conspiracy theorist. Jae had also told Amelia that a petition had been launched to ban Professor Mastropasqua from teaching at the university. The professor, according to Jae, was laughing about it and saying he was going to teach them—the administrators and the students pushing the petition—'a lesson they will never forget'. In addition, there'd been chaos in the canteen, because Emmanuel had unexpectedly given notice and not bothered to show up from the day following.

Angel tapped the reply field, but the bees in his cranium had disabled his language centre, so he put the phone back in his pocket.

Another hour passed.

He went back into Madison's room. It smelled of perfume. When he opened her laptop, he found it password protected. When he rifled through her notebooks, he found no diaries or journals. When he examined her books, he found half a dozen feminist rants, some of which were not even borrowed from the university library but owned outright. When he went through her laundry, he found no elegant outfits. When he drilled through her receipts, he found only bars, Walmart, Amazon, and fast-food restaurants. When he searched her bed, he found crumbs, dandruff, and period stains. When he inspected her bedside table, he found an ashtray and packets of cigarettes. When he looked under the bed, he found a bong.

Next, he went back into Syd's room. It stank of cheap perfume and he was amazed she used any. Every object he found he hated on sight. Her sheets were tacky, her posters obnoxious, her t-shirts rank, her desk filthy, her shoes ridiculous, her carpet squalid, her books idiotic, her calligraphy atrocious, her stickers childish, her coats absurd, her mugs gaudy, her unguents laughable, her furniture nasty, her photographs repellent, her laptop inferior, her dildo farcical, her handbags gross, her jumpers offensive, her underwear nauseating, her jeans comical, her socks annoying, her curlers infuriating, her tank tops foul, her hoodies abominable, her backpack putrid, her suitcases daft, her hats moronic, her notebooks cretinous, her pens rubbish, her highlighters shoddy, her class notes jejune, her lamps silly, her medication predictable, her knickknacks puerile, her pyjamas tawdry, her flip-flops disgusting, her coins bacteria-ridden, and her nail clippers badly designed.

Revolted, he returned to the living room.

No updates on Madison's social media.

Syd's he didn't even want to look at.

He made a new attempt at replying to Amelia, but he couldn't find a way to spin developments since his arrival, didn't have the energy to do so anyway, and wasn't sure he wanted to in the first place, so he put his phone back in his pocket. His sister came to mind . . . *by next week, you won't love Madison anymore*, she'd said. Wrong. No, he was not happy with recent discoveries, but they were all the work of Syd. Madison was not at fault. She'd been bewitched. The Madison he knew was still there; he only had to break Syd's nefandous spell. How, he was yet to ascertain. But break it he would! Evil would be defeated. Naysayers proven wrong. Sceptics convinced. Their love would triumph! He'd find the way to reawaken it, she'd realise her delusion, evict Syd and the other one, comb out the dreads, tidy up her flat, clean up her diet, replace her wardrobe, ace her course, and move to the United Kingdom, so they could be together forever after.

The struggle he faced, however, seemed insuperable. Just the thought made him nauseous. For a mad moment, he considered going back to the terminal to wait for Madison. Maybe, if he did, the old Madison would show up and re-set his visit from zero. There was nothing he desired more at that moment.

His phone buzzed.

Several missed calls and another message from his mother, asking he confirm his safe arrival.

Madison had yet to open his message.

He threw his phone down onto the armchair opposite.

And for the next three hours, with his stomach churning and knees bouncing, he ruminated about what to do.

Chapter CLV

By the time the girls got back from the party, it was five o'clock in the morning. His stomach had not allowed him to either sleep or eat, and the additional Pepsi he'd drank to keep dehydration headaches away had proven gastrally unhelpful. Upon hearing the girls' entrance, he instinctively stood up, only to sit down and stand up again, ants marching, uncertain as to what would look best. As Madison didn't call his name, and her flatmates were suspiciously quiet, he went to the corridor. Syd turned the corner first, her hair a mess and her head down. Taylor followed, carrying Madison slung over her shoulder. Madison's body was limp.

'W-What happened?' he asked.

Both Syd and Taylor ignored him and disappeared into Madison's room.

When he reached the door, he saw Taylor dumping Madison like a rag doll onto the bed.

With unsteady feet, Syd pulled the duvet over Madison.

'Madison?' He said.

No acknowledgment.

'Madison?'

'What's your fucking problem?' said Taylor, lasering him with angry irises.

'Give him a break,' said Syd, slurring her words.

Angel addressed Taylor. 'But . . . w-what happened?'

Taylor ignored him; she watched Syd tuck Madison in.

'W-What happened?'

No acknowledgment.

'I'm worried . . . w-what happened? Is she okay?'

No acknowledgment.

When Syd was done, the girls left the bedroom, pushing past Angel as if he didn't exist, Taylor pulling Madison's door closed in his face.

'W-What happened?' he moaned one more time, stepping back.

No answer.

Syd and Taylor went into their respective rooms, closed their doors, and locked them from the inside.

Angel stood in the corridor, frozen with bewilderment.

He reached for the doorknob on Madison's door, but pulled his hand away at the last millimetre and returned to the living room.

There, he sat, staring at the wall. Should he wait until Madison got up? Should he go to her room and try to talk to her? What if she had class early tomorrow and he again woke up after she was gone? And what if she didn't return until evening? Another entire day could pass without seeing her! That would make it three days. Nearly half his stay already wasted.

This cinched it. He returned to Madison's room. She was still dead to the world, in the same position she'd been left. The ghostly light a residue from the living room. He watched her breathe.

See how she rests her cheek upon her pillow
O, that I were a pillowcase upon that pillow
That I might touch that cheek!

He leaned over the bed and shook her shoulder gently.

'Madison?' he whispered.

No response.

'Madison? Are you awake?'

No response.

Angel put his hand on her head, to caress it, but jerked the hand away as soon as the palm touched the dreadlocks, wincing. They felt like Scotch-Brite.

He stared at the vague, inert form. Madison's breathing was steady. At least there was that—she was alive. His phone told him it was 5:31 am—nearly a quarter into day three of his visit.

'Madison?'

Nothing.

He went back to the living room, head bowed.

Chapter CLVI

Angel woke up with a start.

His hand searched for his phone, which he found near his hip.

4:57 pm.

'Oh, for God's sake!' he whispered, with enough vehemence to bounce his head.

He jumped to his feet, put on his jacket, wiped his furry teeth with a paper napkin, finger-combed his greasy hair as best he could, and stepped into the corridor.

Taylor's door at the end was closed.

Syd's door was open. Her bed empty.

Madison's door was open. Her bed also empty.

'Hello?' he piped.

Not a sound.

'Hello?'

Stillness.

He went to Taylor's bedroom door.

'Hello?'

Nothing.

He knocked, softly. 'Hello?'

Nothing.

Carefully, he pressed his ear to the door.

Silence.

Keeping his ear pressed, he knocked again.

Silence.

He looked at the knob for a few seconds, doubting, then slowly turned it and opened the door a crack.

Taylor's bed was empty.

'Hello?'

Nothing.

He opened the door a bit more and looked inside. No one.

'Bollocks!' he whispered.

He launched WhatsApp. Madison had seen his message from last night but chosen not to reply. There were no other messages. Her social media contained no updates. Syd's, on the other hand, had one, showing Madison 'chugging down' a bottle of tequila. The description read 'Mad Mads being badasssss'.

He shoved the phone into his pocket so angrily that the clip pinching the back of his waistband came off, sending his trousers to the floor. Even more angrily, he yanked them up almost to his chest, and held them on his way back to the living room. It took ten minutes for him to calm down enough to re-clip the waistband.

'Okay,' he whispered to himself. 'Um . . .'

The way forward seemed nebulous. Yet, he knew that, unless he acted, unless he seized the initiative, the week would slip by sans even ten words with Madison. Syd was winning. Things going her way. No wonder she was relaxed about his visit; the abysmal sorceress knew how to psychologically manipulate Madison, how to orchestrate situations, so that he wouldn't have access to his paramour, no matter the physical proximity. He had to break the spell! Wield his trusty sword and cut through Syd's smoke and mirrors!

The clock was ticking.

In a burst of resoluteness, he pulled out his phone, consulted the internet, and, finding what he needed, send Madison a message:

ANGEL: This gentleman wonders when he will enjoy time alone with Her Ladyship. For the second day running, he hath found himself abandoned in Her Ladyship's castle, without news of her situation or whereabouts. This gentleman respectfully requesteth an audience to confer on this and another important subjects.

Not including a skin-crawling bathroom visit, composing it took him forty-five minutes, as the battle between desired brevity and impulse to express grievance clouded his judgment, preventing certitude as to appropriateness and optimal tone.

She replied immediately, for once.

MADISON: *sigh* had class and now appointment. Speak later.

Her tone and brevity like a boot to the stomach, Angel began composing a reply. But, if the initial message had proven difficult, this one proved impossible, and Madison was back at the apartment, together with Syd and Taylor, before he'd decided on the definitive wording.

Upon hearing the girls entering, he stood, ants running, waiting for them to appear in the living room. This, however, they failed to do; in a variation to the weekend's routine, they all disappeared into their respective rooms.

Yet, this was not unwelcome.

On the contrary.

This was his chance!

Angel went to Madison's door. He found her lying in bed, scrolling through her phone, with the same zip-up hoodie she'd worn the day before, which had acquired stains. Still unacknowledged after several seconds, with his bowels loosening and his hands growing cold, he knocked gently.

'S'up,' she answered, without turning to look at him.

'C-C-C-Could I come in for a second?'

Madison shrugged. 'Sure.'

He approached the bed but kept a respectful two-feet's distance.

'Um . . . um . . . I . . . er . . . I-I-I haven't seen you much.'

No answer. Instead, she began typing something.

'And . . . I've really missed you,' he continued.

She kept on typing.

'So,' he carried on, 'I . . . um . . . I thought maybe I could . . . um . . . take you out f-for dinner.'

Madison laughed.

'I-I-I'm sorry?'

'Sorry, what was that?'

'I-I was saying that . . . I thought . . . maybe I could take you out for dinner . . . you know, at a restaurant . . .'

'Oh, cool. When?'

'Um . . . tonight . . . if . . . if you're not too busy?'

Madison got typing again.

Angel waited.

'Um . . . did you hear me?'

Madison kept typing.

'Madison?'

Madison kept typing.

'Madison?'

Madison finished typing. 'Yeah. What were you saying?'

'Um . . . I . . . I . . . er . . . I-I was saying that I could take you out for dinner . . . tonight . . . if you're not too busy . . .'

'Uh-huh.'

Madison scrolled down.

'Did you hear me?'

'Sorry,' she looked at him. 'Did you say you want us to go out for dinner tonight?'

'Yes, yes. Tonight!'

Madison sat up, 'Awesome! I'm starving.'

Angel smiled. 'Um . . . Excellent. I-It will be like in the old days.'

By this he'd meant to suggest she should attire and beautify in an elegant fashion, in keeping with the types of restaurants he'd taken her to in London.

'Suits me!' she answered, which suggested to Angel she might not have taken the hint. She went back to scrolling.

His irises twitched as he thought of a tactful way to underline the hint. 'Um . . .' he began. 'There's a-a-a very elegant restaurant I'd like t—'

A knock on the door.

Angel turned to find Syd standing at the threshold.

Madison put her phone down and pepped up at the sight of the witch. 'Hey. Angel is taking us all out for dinner!'

Syd smiled with her Mariana-Trench fish mouth and drawled. 'Alriiight!'

Angel arched is eyebrows and lifted his palms at Madison. 'Um . . . um . . . no . . . um . . .' he said, not looking at Syd.

'Go and tell Taylor,' said Madison to her flatmate.

'Hey Taylor!' she shouted down the corridor. Angel cringed at her horrisonant, razor-like voice. 'Get ready. Madison's friend's taking us out for dinner.'

'Awesome!' Taylor bellowed.

Angel rubbed his forehead. 'Um . . .'

Madison asked, smiling, 'When do we leave?'

'Um . . . um . . . er . . . eight? Er . . . eight o'clock?'

'Great. I've got time to clean up a bit then.' Madison took off her hoodie, revealing a brand-new tattoo on her upper arm.

Angel's eyeballs nearly rolled out of their sockets; his arms jerked and froze, hands clawed; his jaw dropped and bounced on the carpet, tumbling all the way to the balcony and down the seven floors.

The tattoo was huge, dark, and ugly. It was wrapped in film. He scrunched his eyes shut before he could grasp the design, the ink's mere presence on her once pure skin feeling like a baseball bat to his solar plexus. A knife to the heart would have hurt him less. A sudden shortness of breath, followed by incipient hyperventilation, momentarily prevented speech.

'Do you mind?' asked Madison, pausing in her denudement in a way that told him to leave.

He squeaked. 'Um . . .'

'Yes?'

'Um . . . y-y-y-you got a-a-a-a t-t-t-tattoo?'

'Yea. This afternoon. What do you think? Awesome, right?'

'But . . . um . . . um . . .'

'What? Do you have a problem with it?'

'No! Um . . . um . . . it's just th—'

'My body my choice. So *fuck* you.'

'No no . . . um . . .'

'But I'll forgive you this time because you're taking us out for dinner.'

'Um . . .'

'Fuck me! I haven't had fine dining since my mother's fiftieth birthday in August. I can't *wait* for some fucking delicious wine!'

The fact that it wasn't even since he took her out for dinner in London only salted his wounds. 'Um . . .'

'Now. Do you mind? I need to undress.' She pointed to the living room with her head.

Angel rubbed his forehead, his eyes wild, his breathing fast.

Madison waited.

Walking slowly, head bowed, he made his way back into the living room.

Taylor's room exploded with screeching feminist punk, Syd's with YouTube blather.

Angel sat on the sofa, elbows on his knees, head in his hand, mind reeling.

Chapter CLVII

Angel spent the next five minutes mentally cursing Syd. She'd ruined everything! The whole point of the dinner was to woo Madison; to converse with her, to remind her of their love, to awaken her from Syd's hypnosis, to resuscitate the real Madison. He'd imagined that *that* Madison, currently dormant, would respond to his offer, like the sleeping princess receiving the princely kiss, motivating her to don an elegant dress, comb out her dreads, undye her hair, put on fine jewellery, step into a pair of high heels, discard the coarse language, pull the hardware store out of her face, and rediscover her love of classical poetry. But that would be impossible with Syd and the other one present, intruding on their moment, impeding their dialogue, diverting Madison's gaze, monopolising her ear, lowering the tone, debasing the evening, wasting the little time he had left. What was worse: even if Syd and Blue Buzzcut had declined to come along, Madison had now tattooed herself. At Syd's instigation, no doubt. Madison had been permanently damaged, her pure skin defaced, her beauty mutilated. It was official. Irreversible. Embarrassing. A vandal might as well pour hydrochloric acid on the Monalisa, graffiti the Sistine Chapel, build a multi-storey carpark on the roof of Notre-Dame. Could he stand the humiliation of going to an elegant restaurant with a *tattooed* woman? And not just tattooed a little bit somewhere discrete, but with an ocean of black ink pushed into her skin, visibly, confrontationally, daring elegant citizens to say something, yelling to be noticed. Everything else, she could fix—but her tattoo? No coming back from that.

Or was there?

He pulled out his phone and consulted the internet about tattoo removal. To his immense relief, he saw that places able to do it did exist. Both in Chicago and back home in Yorkshire. It took multiple sessions. And it was expensive. But cost was no object. He'd find the money somehow. Any which way he could. The tattoo could be removed. That was the important thing. So, perhaps, there was hope. He'd only have to persuade Madison, and as soon as he got a chance to speak to her, to remind her of their love, she'd come around. Love conquers everything, and it would conquer the tattoo!

Yet, for now, the tattoo was a reality. And he faced navigating a costly dinner that had lost its purpose, not to mention its elegance, thanks to the unwelcome addition of mannerless moochers. They probably wouldn't be allowed into the restaurant, which would perhaps save the evening, but it seemed unlikely that Madison would leave her flatmates at the door; she'd insist they find a cheaper establishment with a more relaxed dress code instead. She, thanks to Syd's interference, would make it even more pointless.

It suddenly occurred to him that this would have never been an issue with Amelia. On the two dates she'd instigated, she'd arrived at her best, elegantly attired, made up, and perfumed.

'Okay,' he said to himself, rubbing his forehead, thinking.

Perhaps he had to lead by example.

He'd been in Chicago since Saturday, not showered since Friday morning, and it was now Monday evening. He'd been sleeping on a dingy sofa and not changed clothes once. It was strange that Madison hadn't noticed he'd arrived without luggage. Or toiletries. Nevertheless, the least he could do was to make himself presentable. If he rose to the occasion, rather than sink into depression, perfection would materialise. Madison was bound to respond to his appearing before her clean, pleasant-smelling, and with freshly ironed clothes. The scales would then fall from her eyes, she'd remember their time in London, and she'd ask her flatmates to stay at home, so that she and he could re-connect with a romantic date—the way it was meant to be.

Therefore, the correct course of action was to ask her whether she'd mind his using the shower, whether he could borrow her iron and ironing board, and whether she had dishwasher fluid and vinegar so he could remove the tomato sauce stains. He'd then stand at her bedroom door, where he'd be seen by Madison, and break Syd's malignant spell.

He went to Madison's room to execute his plan.

But, as he approached, he heard Syd's voice. Syd

was inside, and the two were chatting. Angel inwardly cursed. However, hoping to gather information, he stood close to the doorframe, pressed against the wall, and listened.

'I've already booked my next session to get more work done,' said Madison.

Syd asked, 'What are you planning to get?'

'I want to get started on a sleeve.'

'Have you decided on the design?'

'Who cares. All I know is I want to get sleeves on both arms, and then do my back, my chest, and my legs. And I'd love to get some facial tattoos too.'

Facial tattoos! Angel's hand shot to his forehead. This felt like a punch in the stomach.

'Wow. Well, think about the design carefully. Make sure you really like the art.'

'You know what? Fuck the art. I'm gonna go for a blackout. Straight for a blackout.'

'Maybe it's worth starting slow, you know? Not rush it. Make sure you're gonna be happy long-term.'

'I always wanted lots of tattoos. But now that I think of it, why stop there? A blackout makes a much bigger statement. I'm not gonna be like these wusses who get a fucking butterfly somewhere invisible. Fuck that!'

Angel's eyebrows steepled. Nausea bent him in half.

'I'd never have thought a few months ago.'

'You should do the same. In fact, I *dare* you. Get your skinny ass blacked out. Including your face. Which, let's be honest, it's not exactly an oil painting anyway.'

Silence.

Madison pressed on, 'You know about the patriarchy, so why be chicken? You should be saying, I'm fucking done with being oppressed. I can do whatever the fuck I want! I'm gonna drink hard, eat like a pig, swear, be rude, and get tattoos if I want to. This is a free fucking country!'

'Which is great, if that's what you want. All I'm saying is, make sure you're gonna be happy with whatever you do. Me personally I'd prefer some art.'

'Well, if I decide I don't like it, fuck it, I can always tattoo art on top. White on black.'

Tears welled up in his eyes.

'Just remember that there's no going back after that.'

'I might even tattoo my eyeballs black. I'd look like a demon. Truer to my nature! Argh!'

Syd laughed.

A tear ran down his cheek.

Madison: 'In fact, I might go all out and do cam work.'

Angel pricked his ears.

'You mean like Hannah and those girls?'

'Yea. She told me how much she's making today and, woman, she's raking it in! And I'm thinking, there she is wearing designer clothes and driving a fucking BMW, and I'm fucking two hundred thousand dollars in debt! And I'm way better looking! Fucking goddess next to her!'

'If you think it will be empowering, go for it, but weigh the risks. There's a lot of creeps out there.'

'Nah. Hannah showed me some of the messages she gets in her DMs. She shares the funny replies on her stories. Woman, she's fucking brutal. It's hilarious! These fucking men are getting their asses handed to them. She probably gets paid for that too! I love it!'

'I'm not sure. Creepy men are not always so easy to handle.'

'I can handle it. I can handle anything! Hannah told me about this site, OnlyFans, where men pay you to do stuff. A hundred bucks to show your boobs *per guy!* That's fucking awesome. Imagine! Making thousands a day just by waving my ass around!'

'But you said your ass was only for me.'

'Bah. It's only fucking men ogling. If you're obedient, and keep paying tribute, my ass is still for you. Until I get bored, of course. This is just me laughing at those creeps by taking all their money.'

'I'm not sure.'

'What happened to sisters supporting each other? You should be *encouraging* me to express myself in whatever way I want, not limiting me or deterring me!'

'I suppose you could be debt free in a year or two.'

'Yeah. I'm strong and beholden to no one. Fuck college debt. I'm gonna fuck the patriarchy in the ass! Uh uh uh uh!'

Syd cackled.

Angel covered his face, now awash with tears. He collapsed against the wall and slid to the floor.

It was hopeless. She was lost.

Slothlike, he stood and, head drooping, returned to the living room.

Chapter CLVIII

N*o!*

Madison was *not* lost!

She was *still* there.

And so was *he*.

And so was he, sitting on the sofa, with his head in his hands, staring at the carpet, not thousands of miles, but just a few yards away from the love of his life.

Inert, but not for long.

While there was proximity there was hope!

He wiped away his tears.

He just had to figure out a way. If only Syd would leave her alone!

But then he realised: this was a test.

A test of his love for Madison.

A test of his commitment to that love.

A test of his devotion.

A test of his fealty to his Queen.

Hadn't they sworn eternal loyalty? Absolute fidelity? Hadn't they'd given their lives to each other?

Love would conquer!

Love would impel him to victory!

As he scoured his brain for ideas, he remembered—hadn't he memorised a selection of poems by Pablo Neruda? Yes, he had! Verses that expressed the magic of love. Verses of amorous magic. Verses that touched the soul and awakened the deepest and most profound romantic sentiments in existence. *They* would break the spell!

He'd appear at Madison's door and begin reciting. The verses would banish the witch, who'd flee like a vampire from daylight. The cursed Madison might initially resist, but the ringing words would enter her ears all the same, they would end her affliction, dissolve her hate, warm her heart, weaken her knees . . . she would reawaken, and swoon, and run towards him, and cover him with kisses. The real Madison would inevitably respond. She'd drink the verses like a plant long deprived of rain. She'd welcome the light like a prisoner long confined to a dungeon. She'd break the chains of confoundment, exit the torture chamber of ideology, and come to him, her saviour and liberator, to reaffirm their perpetual love. Syd would wither into a desiccated carcass. Blue Buzzcut would run for her life. The witches vanquished by love triumphant.

He checked the time. It was 7:29 pm.

There was no time to waste!

He jumped to his feet and returned to Madison's door.

Chapter CLIX

This time, he did not hide.
He stood in full view of Madison and the accursed witch.
They turned their faces toward him.
He took a deep breath, and declaimed:
'I love you without knowing
'how, or when, or from where.
'I love you straightforwardly,
'so I love you because I know
'no other way than this:
'where I does not exist, nor you,
'so close that your hand
'on my chest is my hand,
'so close that your eyes close
'as I fall asleep.'
He waited for the response.
Stares.

Silence.

Angel blushed.

Madison snorted, a pressure cooker of hilarity.

The sound detonated a payload of feminine laughter.

He watched the girls, paralysed.

Their eyes were scrunched shut, their mouths open, their tracheas undulating, their heads tilted back.

Then, after seconds that felt like years, Madison, recovering, regarded him with mocking eyes and said, 'Ooookaaaaaayy . . . ?'

To which Syd contributed by addressing Madison. 'He's so weird!'

Angel stood, waiting for more, his face hotter than an iron, pins pricking through his pores; he resisted the impulse to run.

And because he lingered, the atmosphere in the room began to shift—from amusement to irritation.

Madison raised her eyebrows. 'Anything else?'

Tears welled up in his eyes.

The girls stared at him, Syd with confusion, Madison with an unchanged expression.

'Anyway,' she eventually said, waving him off and turning to Syd. 'So if I get to a grand a day, I can use half of it and pay the whole thing off in six months.'

Angel remained at the door, frozen.

Madison and Syd kept discussing money, cam work, and men being 'assholes', as if he weren't there.

A full minute passed.

Madison stopped talking and irritably turned to him again. 'Do you fucking mind? We're *talking*.'

Momentary silence.

Madison screamed, 'I said: do you fucking mind!?'

Angel went from frozen to petrified. His heart accelerated.

Madison pointed in the direction of the living room. 'Just go in there and wait for the fucking taxi or something, *okay?*'

Angel retreated, his humiliation complete.

Chapter CLX

But instead of into the living room, Angel retreated in the opposite direction: past Taylor's room, through the front door, and into the corridor outside.

He gently closed the door behind him as tears again welled up and ran down his cheeks.

For a moment he hesitated; he turned to glance at the door, surprised to find himself there. He contemplated asking for re-admittance, but the thought of it proved intolerable. There was nothing for him on the other side.

Madison no longer lived there.

Perhaps she never had.

His legs started moving, Angel vaguely conscious of their transporting him towards the lift. When it came, he avoided the mirror, entering with his head bowed.

A column of buttons; a finger presses one.

Doors close. Within a minute, doors open into the lobby.

Zombielike, he walks towards the entrance. A door with glass panes and a handle. His hand pushes it down.

His legs move him forward.

He finds himself outside, in the night.

Fresh air—relatively speaking.

The fizz and hum of passing vehicles. Moving lights, white one way, and red the other. Darkness before him, suspended constellations of tungsten, neon, and light-emitting diodes to the left and right.

His hand checks the front pocket.

Relief as the phone is there.

A screen before his face. A search term. Digits tap on numbers. A high-pitched voice emanates from his throat, giving out his location.

Buttocks rest on the edge of a large, frigid flowerpot. A familiar feeling, from three nights ago.

Ten minutes elapse.

The wind blows cold.

A car pulls in by the kerb.

He ambles towards it, gets inside—it's warm—and the vehicle moves.

Tears cascade.

The lump visits his throat.

Nausea.

The apartment block where he'd stayed recedes, gets smaller and smaller.

But he doesn't look back.

Madison is dead.

Chapter CLXI

The car stopped in front of Terminal 5.

The North-African driver informed Angel the fare was forty dollars.

Angel handed over his card.

The card was returned to him, along with a receipt.

But the driver continued to look at him expectantly.

Angel, however, poured himself out of the car without a second thought, closed the door, and faced the front of the terminal.

He heard the taxi pull away with angry, screeching tyres.

It would only be a year later that he'd realise the driver had been expecting his tip.

He ambled into the building and stopped by the arrival's exit. Exit A and Exit B.

No. She was not there.

She truly was dead.

His eyelid dam overflowed once more, coating his cheeks with a running sheet of tears.

His lip trembled.

The lump in his throat swelled to the point of nearly bursting his throat.

Angel walked away.

At the KLM ticket counter, in the departures area, he spoke to a uniformed lady.

Yes, he could change his departure flight.

No, there were no more flights to Leeds that evening.

Yes, there was one the following day.

Yes, there was a seat available.

The flight would depart at 14:42.

Was he alright?

No there were no direct flights. The flight at 16:00 also had two layovers.

Yes, there was a fee in both cases.

No, it couldn't be waived or reduced.

No problem to book him for 14:42.

He'd land in Leeds at 9:30 the following day.

Was he sure he was alright?

'Enjoy your flight.'

The time was now 8:45pm. An 18-hour wait, during which he would not lack time to ponder and reflect.

And, most importantly, to conjure up a non-humiliating explanation for his early return.

He went through security and into the Air France / KLM lounge, where he fell into a grey armchair next to the window.

For a long time, he stared at the aeroplane stationed on the other side of the glass, tears raining down his cheeks.

But his lachrymal glands gradually flagged, as dejection gave way to anger.

Because he remembered.

He remembered taking her to the Ritz for breakfast back in March and her crass insistence on ordering the £180 caviar omelette, *in addition* to a Full English, which she'd then been unable to finish. He remembered her relishing what his money bought, grinning from across the table, gawking, like an uncultured tourist, at the Versaillesque fantasy decorations. She'd manipulated him into showing her Green Park, the Victoria Memorial, Buckingham Palace, the lake at St James Park, and finally the Household Calvary Museum, despite knowing he had to be in class. Afterwards, she, always insatiable, had wanted to see *Dumbo*—and not in any cinema, but in the Odeon Luxe in Leicester Square, just so she could lazily order food from her seat to gorge on during the film. Had she for even a moment considered what film *he* wanted to see? No, of course, not. And she'd then even complained they didn't have her favourite American snacks. As if access to American snacks was a human right and the British didn't have their own tastes to consider first.

He remembered the time he'd walked her back to the dorm after treating her to an Italian dinner and how, upon finding a puddle barring her path to the entrance, he'd laid down his expensive corduroy jacket, so she could cross without soiling her shoes—even though they'd been cheap and beneath the occasion; she'd stomped across, as if merely getting her due. And not once did she express surprise, or later show concern for his jacket, or offered to have it dry-cleaned.

He remembered the time they discovered Joseph Shipley's *Dictionary of Early English* in the library.

They'd spent the rest of the day messaging each other using as many of the obscure words as they could, but the nupson had only chosen the stupidest ones and misused every single one of them.

He remembered the time when he'd taken her to Kew Gardens to have a champagne and caviar picnic breakfast—even though she couldn't tell the difference between caviar and couscous; he'd wasted his money on an old-fashioned wicker picnic basket, which she'd then broken while using it as a stool. Again, not once did she apologise or offer to buy a new one.

He remembered the time he'd bought her eight bouquets of red roses; not only had she received them lukewarmly, but she'd failed to put them in water, allowed them to die in her room, and then thrown them in a skip, without respect for his heart. She didn't even think of pressing at least one to preserve the memory. She'd cleared out his love from her room like a piece of rubbish.

He remembered the time he'd taken her to the National Portrait Gallery and tried to explain Hans Holbein's *The Ambassadors*; she looked bored out of her mind and her oohing and ahing had not only been grating and dumb, but fake. Her brain was like a sieve. She only cared about food and expensive wine, and the latter so long as he paid for it.

He remembered the time he'd taken her to see *Henry IV* at Shakespeare's Globe theatre; at the shop he'd later bought her a jigsaw puzzle depicting the bard's world. He'd chosen it thoughtfully. They'd built it in her room, but she'd lost pieces before they'd even finished it and later ruined it with a careless spillage of Cherry Coke.

He remembered the time he'd taken her to St Paul's. He'd tried to tell her about the cathedral and its gutting by the Great Fire, but she'd yawned so incessantly that he hadn't seen the point in continuing. Yet, she'd woken up fast when he'd invited her for lunch at the Coq d'Argent, where she'd ordered the most expensive dishes, a bottle of champagne, 'just because', and port to boot, heedless of the cost. Why bother, after all: *he* was paying!

He remembered the time he'd taken her to The Prospect of Whitby. She had guzzled down pint after pint of every kind of lager, ale, stout, and porter that had struck her fancy; she'd got so drunk she could barely stand afterwards and then made a scene in public, guffawing, whooping, and staggering from one side of the street to the other, hardly able to walk at all as they made their way to the Underground station. An embarrassment.

And he remembered their last day together in London. He'd stayed up all night with her while she packed her bags, ignoring him while she chatted to her horrid American friends, jabbering on without saying anything at all, squandering their last hours together, even though she was never going to see the garrulous harlots again anyway. In the morning they'd breakfasted at the canteen; she'd been perfectly fine, polishing off a bowl of cereal, bacon, eggs, and a stackful of toast. On their way to Heathrow, in the taxi he'd paid for, her hand might as well have belonged to a corpse, her kisses lukewarm, his caresses taken for granted, and his sweet nothings rewarded with plastic smiles. Her firm promises to write, message, and phone every day had been barefaced lies. His oaths of eternal loyalty reciprocated with lassitude, his plans for their reunion with platitudes. She'd been distant and weird throughout. At Heathrow he'd gone with her as far as he'd been allowed, but she'd left eagerly, dying to get away from him. He'd stood, waving, watching her recede, until she'd finally disappeared in the distance. And she'd kept her back arrogantly turned the entire time. Not once did she look back. Later, for two months he'd kept the clothes he'd worn to the airport out of the laundry; she probably dumped hers on the floor and used them as a carpet—because she'd grown too *fat* to wear them. He'd loyally kept his promise to write her traditional letters, using the best inks and papers, varying the format and applying this creativity; her replies, in turn, had been tardy, boring, slapdash, shallow, narcissistic, scribbled on lined paper with ballpoint pen and atrocious spelling. And after June she'd found ever more clever reasons to be unavailable on Skype.

And those Instagram posts? Her 'transformation'? Planned from day one. To hurt him. No question about it, looking back. How could he have been so stupid? He'd been fleeced and made a fool of. Taken in by an outright psychopath.

O serpent heart hid with a flowering face!

It'd not been *she* who had been bewitched by a third party, but *he* by *her*.

Well, *never again!*

And to think of the money he wasted on that vamp! To the point of not being able to afford basic necessities—food, drink, laundry. Of being cut off by his mother because she couldn't trust him. Of being reduced to wearing rags.

Idiot!

And the money was the least of it! She'd cost him his university education! The respect of his parents! Forced him into manual labour! A life of excrement!

And even if he ever convinced his parents to enrol him again, he'd now waste his life re-doing modules he'd already done and graduate late . . . months behind everyone else. They'd be starting on their Masters' and their PhDs, while he remained a lowly undergraduate, repeating material he already knew, being thought of as thick and a failure! All because of *her!*

Blockhead!

How different it would have been if he'd spent that money—even a tiny fraction—on someone who deserved it. Someone who respected him. Someone who appreciated him. Someone who wanted to spend time with him, not because of his debit card, but just to be with him. Just to hear him talk. Just enjoy his company, even if saying nothing or not going anywhere. Someone who would enjoy any kind of date, even if at a McDonalds, so long as they were together. Someone who sought him out, who cheered his presence, who mourned his absence, who cared when he was silent, who nursed him when sick, who fed him when hungry, who shielded him when threatened, who dropped everything when needing help, who'd move heaven and earth to find him if he disappeared.

Someone . . . like Amelia.

Amelia!

That sweet girl.

That beautiful person.

And how had he treated her?

Like a doormat.

He'd avoided her, vomited on her, forgotten their dates, disappointed her, caused her to fall, embarrassed her, ignored her messages.

And yet, not once had she begrudged him.

Not once had she diminished him.

She'd kept coming to him with big eyes, a trusting face, and an open smile, and he'd kept knocking her down, punching her, kicking her, treating her like rubbish.

He imagined her chest collapsing at each of these blows, air whooshing out of her lungs.

He imagined her eyes looking at him and asking why.

He imagined her laughter dying.

He imagined her hair in a loose bun, her back receding as she walked away, her head low, defeated.

He imagined her soul bruised and bleeding, covered in cuts and wounds that he'd inflicted.

It was monstrous.

How could he have been so blind?

There she was, right in front of him, all along, giving herself freely.

A beautiful girl, clever, pleasant, romantic, kind, generous, refined, stylish, funny—everything he could possibly want. A girl who loved him, who put herself in harm's way to protect him, even if he was the last person to deserve it, who went out of her way to help him even if it broke her heart.

Her precious heart.

He suddenly wanted to kiss it to help it heal. To hold her occiput in his cupped hands and caress her forehead, to smooth all the hurt away.

The tears began raining again, but this time not on his own account, but on Amelia's.

When he got back, he was going to make things right.

He pulled out his phone to message her, but upon tapping the reply field he stumbled. Of course, she had no idea that he was on his way back. She still thought that he would be away until Sunday. That he was with . . . that other one.

He wiped away his tears.

Before messaging, he'd have to think of what to say. Especially since Amelia was in touch with his sister, who would relay any and all information to his parents. Destiny was probably raring gleefully to have her views confirmed. And his mother would, of course, feel satisfied that she'd been right too. And his father would take him even less seriously in future for the same reason. And so would Vera. And Alba. And Jae.

He decided to wait.

Chapter CLXII

Finally, Angel boarded the plane for the first leg of his journey. This time he had a window seat. His favourite. But he had no eyes for the baggage dollies, hydrant trucks, service stairs, or station agents brutalising people's luggage; he only had eyes for Amelia's WhatsApp messages, which he now read in reverse order, carefully for the first time, and for the first time at all in many cases. He scrolled past the most recent ones and began reading from the last time he saw her.

Wed 23 Oct

> I was so sad to see your figure receding on the platform as the train pulled away. But I really enjoyed meeting your family. As I said, they're not what I expected at all. Very

strong, disciplined people, but very charming too. Beautiful house! And it seems they were receptive to my arguments re: letting you visit Madison. Let me know how that goes!

9:03

Mon 21 Oct

It was so surreal to suddenly find you on campus, after all that happened over the weekend. Friday feels like a month ago! And I can't lie, Angel, I'm devastated that you're leaving the university. But we have WhatsApp and social media. Let's stay in touch. Perhaps you'll let me visit. I've been wanting to see the Yorkshire Dales and visit the Brontë Parsonage. I'd love it if you were my guide!

14:15

Destiny tells me you were mugged at the train station on Friday and that they took your phone! OMG are you okay?? At least you're safe, that's the most important thing. But why didn't you reply from your computer at home? Were you still ill? I have so many questions. I hope we can chat soon. I'm dying to see you and give you a hug.

11:01

YAY! Destiny just replied to my message and tells me you've been at home all along! I'm so relieved! I'm not even angry. That you're whole is the only thing I care about. Oh, you precious precious poet! Such good news! So you went to see your parents? Why didn't you tell me? Why didn't you reply to my messages? Did you lose your phone?

10:57

I'm sorry for the delay, but I fell asleep and Alba didn't wake me! She said I needed to rest and that the matter was now in the hands of people who can help. I'm back on duty now!

9:29

I'm feeling a bit tired now, but I'm soldiering on. Refreshing the news sites constantly on all feeds for any developments. Keep hanging on. Help is on its way.

7:15

Lots of news sites carrying the story. Wow. It seems your parents are very prominent. You never said! Your mother wrote The Social History of the Penny Dreadful? I had no idea! Awesome book. Anyway, this all helps.

6:20

Okay! The news is out! This should get the police moving, finally. Clearly, money talks, but today it will be talking for a worthy cause. Hang on tightly, Angel! You WILL be found!

6:01

Won't be long now until the news websites are updated! I'm refreshing every five seconds!

5:37

Alba has joined me now to help keep me awake. Early riser! So you need not worry. You can count on me.

4:45

I'm drinking loads of coffee to keep myself awake. I won't abandon you, Angel! With you until you're found, one way or the other.

4:02

Still here!

3:36

Just a few more hours before the papers come out. Keep hanging on. I'm right alongside, wherever you are, every minute, every second.

2:59

I'm thinking of you every minute. I'm right here with you. We're going to see this through, Angel. Everything will be alright.

1:47

I'm here for you. All the way to the end. Checking my phone constantly. Alarms and alerts at full volume. You're not alone! Help is coming!

00:25

Sun 20 Oct

Alright. I've contacted a few newspapers and told them about you and the fact that you've gone missing. I wasn't optimistic, after the experience with the police, so I was surprised at how interested they became after I told them your name. Or rather, interested in your parents. Are they important people? Anyway, they'll be running the story in tomorrow's papers. I'm praying this will help. You will be found, Angel, no matter what! I'll make sure. I won't give up. Hold on a while longer!

23:22

Okay, I've now gone to the police station and filed the missing person report. I'm so upset! They seemed so blasé about it. As in, they'll 'keep an eye out'. What's that going to achieve? I tried to explain it was urgent but they seemed to be laughing about it and not taking it seriously. I got angry and I cried and that only made things worse. But don't fear, Angel, I'll make sure you're found, even if they won't lift a finger!

21:17

I'm leaving for the police station now. I hope it will all be a false alarm. But if you are in distress and you see this, don't worry! I'm coming to your rescue!

19:40

Missed call at 19:34

As a last ditch attempt I've gone for a long walk around the campus. Looked everywhere. Spoke to security again. Alba has come and she and I combed the entire perimeter of the campus. Looked in every alley, every ditch, every hedge. It seems there's nothing else I can do but file a missing person report.

19:21

Missed call at 18:59

Angel?

18:58

Missed call at 17:03

I don't want to cause trouble, but if I don't hear from you soon I'm going to report you missing with the police. The nearest station is not far, so I'll go in person.

16:19

Angel, this is serious now. If you see this please please please reply. I can see my messages on Facebook and Instagram have been read. Why don't you reply? Are you hurt? Is that why? Are you incapacitated somehow? I keep imagining you in pain in a ditch by the road where no one can see you, suffering and unable to get help. I've messaged your sister on Instagram but she's not replied. I can't find a way to contact your parents.

14:44

Angel, I'm begging you. Please reply. I'm really worried something has happened to you. I've asked everyone and no one has seen you or has any idea of where you might be. Let me know you're okay

10:27

Missed call at 10:26

Missed call at 9:55

Missed call at 9:31

Missed call at 8:56

Sat 19 Oct

Please, Angel, wherever you are, please reply. I'm really worried about you

22:19

Missed call at 21:38

Missed call at 20:57

Alba tells me she hasn't seen you. And neither has Jae. Angel, where did you go? Please. I just want to know that you're okay

19:42

Okay. I've asked campus security about you and they haven't seen you. I explained the situation and at first they didn't want to show me the CCTV, but I insisted and it seems you left the campus last night. Where did you go? Are you okay? Do you have your phone with you? I've messaged Alba. I'm hoping she took you to her flat. We know what she's like!

17:51

Missed call at 17:20

Where are you? I didn't see you at breakfast or at lunch in the canteen today. I went back to your room one more time and no Angel. I see my messages are not being opened and I fear that you went to get fresh air last night and fell and you're incapacitated somewhere. If you see this, please respond

14:38

Missed call at 13:52

Missed call at 12:19

I still haven't heard from you and I worry something has gone wrong. Are you okay? I've just been to your room again this morning and it didn't look as if you've been in at all. Saïd told me he's very surprised because you're good friends and you had promised to pay £25 last night that you owe him. I saw Camaro entering the building as I left and he doesn't know anything either. I still hope the reason is that you're feeling better. I'm DMing this on your social media, in case your WhatsApp is down

9:13

Missed call at 9:06

Missed call at 8:55

Fri 18 Oct

I've stayed up as long as I could, but I can't keep my eyes open anymore, so I'm going to sleep now. But please do send me a message as soon as you see this, no matter the time. Even if you don't want to wake me up. I just want to know you're safe

23:29

Missed call at 23:27

Missed call at 23:01

Missed call at 22:29

I stopped by your room again. Saïd still hasn't seen you. You must be feeling loads better! I hope so. All the same, for my peace of mind, drop me a line as soon as you see this. I'm glad I've been able to help

21:48

Missed call at 21:47

Missed call at 21:46

I'm a bit nervous, Angel, but I hope you're feeling better. I've gone back to my room now, after waiting twenty minutes. I've left you dinner on your bedside table. A BLT—your favourite!—and a prawn sandwich, in case you felt like something different. Please message me when you're back so I know you're okay

19:27

Missed call at 19:25

Missed call at 19:23

Missed call at 19:18

Missed call at 19:14

Missed call at 19:11

Missed call at 19:05

Angel, where are you? I've come to your room (the door was open) with some dinner but you're not in. Saïd hasn't seen you and says he's been looking for you. No one in the corridor has seen you either. Are you feeling better? I'll wait for you here

18:59

Thu 17 Oct

I'm worried about you

22:01

Missed call at 20:43

Please, if you see this, send me a message so that I know you're alright

20:12

Missed call at 19:02

Angel?

18:44

Are you okay, Angel?

17:47

He couldn't continue. Tears welled up in his eyes. Such a sweet girl. They'd all been right about her, all of them, all along! He just couldn't see it, or wouldn't see it, because his mind was too busy hallucinating about that . . . distraction.

Fool!

But he was going to make things right this time. He was going to do what he should have done from the beginning.

His immediate neighbour was a businesswoman, clad in a maroon, figure-hugging, two-piece outfit. She was slenderer than Amelia but with the same hair colour and just as meticulously groomed. Angel smiled as she sat down, but she remained serious and unacknowledging. Next to her was a middle-aged woman, possibly an academic or website editor, with closely cropped green hair. He hated her instantly.

Under normal circumstances, his face would have been glued to the windowpane, watching the take-off and receding landscape as the aeroplane gained altitude. This time, however, he hardly noticed the craft was in motion, and only realised they were airborne when the Fasten your seatbelts sign dinged off, so replete was his mind with thoughts about Amelia and their time at the university.

One time, before he got distracted by . . . that other, she'd brought him from Moscow an ushanka hat; she'd visited Russia over the Christmas holiday with her parents, whom, she said, had always been avid Dostoyevsky readers. The hat? He'd put it on once, when he first got it, and maybe one other occasion, at Amelia's prompting, during a bitterly cold evening, and then stored it away. And she'd also brought him a nestling doll—'matryoshka', she'd said it was called—depicting Russian writers—Leo Tolstoy, Fyodor Dostoevsky, Anton Chekhov, and some others. Which ones? He didn't know where the hat or the matryoshka were. At home, at the bottom of his armoire somewhere? He resolved to dig them out the moment he got back.

Another time, at the beginning of the year, also before his distraction, she'd insisted they revise for their exams together one evening and brought a large pizza to his room for them to share. It blew his mind that he'd once been able to eat two whole slices. His then roommate had been atypically absent. Angel wondered whether Amelia had contrived that absence, and whether she'd had other aims in mind besides revision.

Another time, around Christmas, he'd bumped into her in Covent Garden, wearing a bobble hat, matching scarf, and mittens. She'd been buying presents for her mother. He'd been bobbing about like driftwood in a tide of humanity, bereft of ideas. Right away she had volunteered to help. She'd asked what his mother did for a living, her cheeks rising with an enthusiastic smile. He'd replied she was a writer. 'Oh, really? What does she write?' she'd asked. 'Um . . . oh, j-j-just . . . boring stuff,' he'd replied, thereafter stubbornly refusing to give out further details. She'd suggested they visit the Mulberry shop, where she'd identified a brown Congo leather glasses case as a possibility, which, after much nahing of other suggestions, he'd accepted, having finally remembered that his mother's case was falling to pieces. The gift had been well received, but he never thanked Amelia afterwards.

Another time, she'd invited him to join her for Guy Fawkes' night near where her parents lived. She'd met him at the Guildford train station and driven them to Cranleigh. They'd walked from Notcutts, where she'd parked her car, a Fiat 500, and enjoyed the fair, having hog roast sandwiches before the torch-lit procession. It'd been a frigid night, and, despite making a matryoshka of himself with endless layers of wool and corduroy, he'd still been shivering, to the extent that Amelia had taken him to the Costa on the High Street and bought him the largest cappuccino available, to which she'd then added 14 sachets of sugar. It'd had to be ordered to go, because all the chairs and stools had been put on the tables. At the Benson Fun Fair, they'd ridden the waltzer, but their chair had been spun so fast that afterwards he'd been completely disorientated, needing Amelia's help to find his bearings. She'd clung to his arm the whole evening. Did she give him a flier? Did he have to buy a ticket? He couldn't remember. And now regretted throwing them away thoughtlessly if he did. He resolved to check every pocket in every coat he still had at home in case they'd survived. He hoped fervently they had.

Out of these recollections the aeroplane pulled him by hitting the runway in Detroit.

Chapter CLXIII

His connecting flight to Amsterdam—the second leg of his journey—was eighty minutes away, so he allowed the stream of fast-walking air travellers following the same route to carry him to his destination, his wide-open orbs twitchily registering under arched eyebrows the signs overhead, anxious for the security of being at the gate.

As soon as he got back home, he would contact Amelia, he'd resolved. What he'd say or how he'd say it, he was yet to figure out. Reconnecting with her having acquired tremendous importance, he worried about phrasing his message incorrectly, thereby producing adverse results. He feared a sudden change in the dynamic between them would spook her into withdrawal, awkwardness, weird silence. How did it suddenly become so difficult to send her message? He checked his phone while still walking, hoping she'd messaged him, thereby making it easier, but she had not. She probably assumed he was busy with . . . busy in Chicago and wanted him to enjoy the visit without injecting herself into it.

The concourses at the McNamara Terminal were long, and the airport's Americanness was everywhere emphasised through its white, blue, and red colour scheme. The LED lights mounted on the ceiling had already declared supremacy over the fading daylight from the flanking floor-to-ceiling windows.

As he approached his gate, he began to relax. He was in the right area and there was plenty of time; he wouldn't miss his flight.

It was this relaxation that allowed him to spot an anomaly ahead of him.

A man.

A tall man.

A tall man in a black suit.

A bearded man.

In an outmoded suit.

Professor Mastropasqua!

About twenty yards in front, the professor sat at a gate, reading a book, presumably waiting for the boarding announcement.

Angel couldn't resist.

He had to stop.

'Um . . . P-P-Professor Mastropasqua?'

Mastropasqua looked up, his satanic eyebrows rising as he put his book down.

'Yes?'

'Um . . .'

Recognition in the professors' face, but not a smile. 'You're Angel, aren't you? From my Food and English Literature class.'

'Yes, yes, that's me.'

'What brings you to Detroit? Or . . . De-twah, as the French used to call it.'

'Er . . . I-I'm just catching a connecting flight.'

'But what brings you to the colonies?'

'Erm . . . I-I was just . . . er . . . v-visiting someone.'

'I see. Did you know that the Cadillacs that were once made in this city were named after the city's founder?'

'Er . . . no, I-I didn't'

'Antoine Laumet de La Mothe, sieur de Cadillac. He founded the city in 1701.'

'Oh.'

'We throw names and terms about every day, but so few people know their history.'

'Er . . .'

'Anyway. I'm so glad you dropped out of the university. Your father told me he'd found you a council job.'

'Um . . . yes, but . . . er . . .'

'Good. You'll learn more useful skills there than at the university.'

'Um . . .'

'I know you didn't want to leave the uni before graduating but you'll be grateful you did. You'll see.'

'Er . . . okay . . .'

'And you can always finish your degree elsewhere. At a better university. It's only a term for you, isn't it?'

'Yes . . . um . . .'

'Right, so you might as well finish. But if I were you, I'd stay away from universities. Don't ever become a university professor. At least until they're reformed. A lot of bad people and bad ideas.'

'Erm . . .'

'But all the same: learning is a life-long pursuit. It doesn't begin or end in those wretched places. You learn more outside of them. In fact, a university education might well stop you from learning! It might even turn you into a bad apple.'

'Oh.'

'So keep on learning. But above all *think*.' He tapped his temple. 'Be sceptical of fashion. Things are seldom what they seem.'

'Erm . . . yes . . . um . . .'

'What seems good is often evil, and what seems evil, may in the end turn out to be good. Remember that.'

Angel said nothing.

'And often, the good is right in front of you, might have been all along—might even be obvious!—but you haven't been able to see it because your mind has been cluttered with nonsense. Universities today are very good at that.'

Angel said nothing.

'You flying to Heathrow? Manchester?'

'Um . . . Leeds.'

'You going back home then.'

'Yes.'

'Taking a taxi or is your mother collecting you.'

'Er . . . taxi.'

'I tell you what. Is there a girl you care about at the university?'

Angel smiled. 'Yes, yes, there is one.'

'Why don't you ask her to take the train and meet you at the airport. Drop everything. Just go. Be spontaneous. Spend the day together in Leeds. You won't regret it. I guarantee it.'

'Er . . .'

'Don't you want to be a poet? It's what your father

tells me.' He chuckled. 'He's ripping his hair out about it, but what does he know?'

Angel said nothing.

'If you want to write poetry, you need to start with *love*.'

'Er . . .'

'So ask the girl to forget about her lessons for the day—she won't learn anything useful anyway—and have her spend the day with you.'

'Erm . . . o-okay.'

'You'll thank me later.' Mastropasqua patted him on the shoulder, albeit with such force that Angel nearly fell over.

The gate's PA system suddenly exploded with a flight announcement in cabin crew sing song. Both Angel and the professor turned toward the gate to find a uniformed female cabin crew member standing behind the counter, speaking into a microphone.

The professor stood up. 'Well, it's been a pleasure, Angel, but it's time to go. Please send my regards to your father.'

'Erm . . . okay, yes, I will.'

Mastropasqua took a couple of steps towards the exit, only to stop and address Angel one last time. 'And please tell your father not to worry about me. I'll be fine.'

'Okay.'

'Good luck.'

'Thank you.

The professor joined the queue forming in front of his gate, and Angel resumed his walk towards his.

Chapter CLXIV

Angel made his way into the cabin so impatiently that he kept stepping onto the heels of the person in front.

'Sorry, sorry!' he said, for the second time, after the person gave him an evil look.

This time he was in an aisle seat in the central column at the rear—the least bad option among what had been available. But he didn't care. He nearly pushed his way into it as soon as the person walking in front had allowed him sufficient clearance.

Seven hours and thirty-six minutes. Then another ninety in Schiphol Airport; a last, one-hour flight to Leeds; and finally a taxi home. He'd then contact Amelia and ask her to take the train to York that instant. It had to be York, because she wanted to see the Dales and the Brontë Parsonage. Hopefully, his sister would take him to the station. Or, failing that, his mother; she seemed to like Amelia too.

It no longer mattered that they'd laugh at him for his early return. In fact, he was already willing and eager to accept that they'd been right all along.

. . . often, the good is right in front of you, but you haven't been able to see it because your mind has been cluttered with nonsense, the professor had said.

How right he was!

He wasn't even angry that the professor had talked his father into yanking him out. He now remembered that he'd hesitated between taking Mastropasqua's module and taking another class with a different professor, worried initially about joining the many who'd been failed. But the cosmic purpose had since been revealed. It was as if fate had ordained his choice! It all led to this. To clarity!

The aeroplane could not take off soon enough. Could not fly fast enough.

Knees bouncing uncontrollably, orbs tracking passengers as they boarded, fingers tapping rapidly on the arm rests, Angel mentally pushed the passengers to move faster and the pilot to take the aeroplane onto the runway. Alas, his fellow air travellers moved like snails, taking years to remove coats, decades to fill overhead compartments, and centuries to get settled into their seats.

Come on!

He pulled out his phone. Amelia had last been online on WhatsApp at 17:46, or 23:46 her time. Thirty-one minutes ago. She'd probably gone to sleep for the night.

Good! That would give him time to think how best to phrase his message. Perfect wording was key. He'd draft it in Notes and polish it throughout the flight. But he'd get started later. When in the right headspace.

Meanwhile, to speed up the passage of time, he thought of music, but, upon scrolling through his iTunes, he discovered every song he'd loaded on his phone was associated with . . . a certain Chicago resident, now deceased. No songs even tangentially linked to Amelia, therefore none that he could repurpose. He sighed. Twit. Well, the existing songs were no longer needed or welcome. He block-deleted the entire library. New sources of inspiration would emerge. In fact, what were they playing in Covent Garden last year? Gene Autry—'Rudolph the Red-Nosed Reindeer'. Wham!—'Last Christmas'. Maria Carey—'All I Want for Christmas is You'. He couldn't remember more. Never mind. It was enough. He added them to his library quickly, before being asked to switch off his phone, stuffed his headphones into his hears, and listened, paying attention to every note, thinking of Amelia, and remembering their Christmas shopping in Covent Garden.

He remembered she was wearing UGG boots. And the same three-quarters suede jacket she'd worn two weeks ago. And he remembered how her kisses had felt on that latter occasion. Rapturously pleasant. Why hadn't he paid attention? She *did* have nice lips! Of course he'd known Destiny was 100% right when she'd shared her views on the matter, but he hadn't wanted to acknowledge it. He hadn't, because his mind had been *cluttered with nonsense.*

And wasn't today the fifth of November? Guy Fawkes' Night! He ripped the phone out of his pocket to message Amelia suggesting that they go to the event in Cranleigh. They'd eat hog roast, bear torches in the procession, bake their faces before the bonfire, watch the Guy burn, holding hands and never letting go. He smiled.

Remember, remember the fifth of November,
The Gunpowder Treason and Plot,
I know of no reason
Why the Gunpowder Treason
Should ever be forgot!

But, realising it was Tuesday, and that the bonfire would normally be lit on a Saturday, he checked the date for Cranleigh's festivities. They had already passed: 2nd November, the day he flew out. *Damn!* If he'd known better, *that's* what he should have been doing. Pillock!

He put his phone away.

He wouldn't be making that mistake again.

In fact, he'd make sure the next Guy Fawkes Night would be the most romantic, atmospheric, and unforgettable they'd ever experienced.

He pulled out his phone and went on Amazon to search for books about Guy Fawkes and the Gunpowder Treason Plot. By next year, when they went again to Cranleigh, he'd know everything there was to know on the subject. He'd blow Amelia's mind with his detailed and comprehensive knowledge.

'Sir? I'm gonna have to ask you to switch off your phone or put it on flight mode,' said the stewardess.

Angel was jolted out of his reverie. 'Oh, sorry!'

He did as instructed.

He went back to remembering the Christmas shopping in Covent Garden. There'd been had a green Morris parked there, with decorations on the roof. He resolved to find an insurer willing to insure him and get a green Morris as his next car, in homage to that memory. He'd take Amelia everywhere in it! The Yorkshire Dales. The Brontë Parsonage. Castle Howard. If only he could go back! He'd been an absolute *wanker* to underappreciate those moments. He'd give *anything* for a time machine. Faster-than-light travel. A wormhole. And not just to go back two years—he'd go back to when he first met her. It would have been in September 2017, but what day exactly? What hour? What minute?

He punched his leg.

Dunce!

Which reminded him of another occasion when he'd been one. Because sometime between the night in Cranleigh and the afternoon in Covent Garden, Amelia had suggested, several times, that they go to a 1950s diner she liked—what was it called? Joe? Big Joe? Big Moe! Big Moe's dinner! That was it. She'd wanted to take him there, but he'd waved her off, rebuffed her grumpily even, because at the time it didn't suit his aesthetic. He now remembered the disappointment in her eyes.

Her lovely eyes!

He punched his leg repeatedly.

Moron!

Via his peripheral vision, he caught his neighbour, a man with a beany hat who looked like Ron Swanson from *Parks and Rec*, turning to stare at him with disapproval, but Angel thought it best to ignore him. He realised he'd been mumbling angrily to himself. Too long to explain.

To compensate, he'd take Amelia to that diner as the first order of business. He'd buy her everything on the menu. He'd be ready with flowers. He'd take her to the cinema afterwards. The Electric Cinema, the oldest and one of the most luxurious in London. He'd make sure not to eat anything that might upset his stomach beforehand.

And he'd then take her to *every* one of the French restaurants he'd tried to get them into on their more recent date. The other one he'd ruined. He'd come dressed in his most elegant clothes. Shoes shined to such fulgurant reflection that even his father would wonder how he did it. Trousers so perfectly pressed that its pleats would cut diamonds. Shirt so impeccably tailored that it might as well have been spray-painted on his torso. He'd bring a dolly, in case there were no taxis available, so that she wouldn't have to walk a single step more than necessary.

And he'd buy her the flowers, the chocolates, and the bottle of dessert wine that he owed her. This time with his own money, not someone else's. With gold sovereigns, if that's what it took. Juliet roses. To'ak chocolates. Riesling, Beerenauslese, Kiedrich Gräfenberg dessert wine by Weingut Robert Weil.

Yes, he'd do all that, and much more.

Chapter CLXV

Amelia collided with him, nearly toppling him onto the platform with the force of her embrace. He encircled her in his arms as they held each other, feeling her soft flesh pressed against him—her enormous breasts against his chest, her belly against his belly, her thighs against his thighs, her face nestled in his shoulder, his lips kissing her fragrant neck. In this posture they remained until their feet hurt—forty five minutes perhaps—oblivious to the commuters flowing around them, or the trains coming and going, their love like a rock islet, standing timeless and unperturbed in the midst of a raging ocean—Rockall in the North Atlantic; Bishop's Rock, off the coast of Cornwall, Elliðaey, off the coast of Iceland.

They took a taxi home, which was free from sister and parents. The former was up in Scotland, attempting those Dinnie Stones she'd talked about, and the latter were away on business—his father in St Petersburg and his mother down in London for the day. Angel and Amelia went to his room, and she lay on top of him, fully dressed, still wearing her UGG boots, kicking her feet in the air, holding his face in her hands and covering it with velvety kisses. She was heavy, but her softness was overwhelmingly pleasant, plush, comforting; he caressed every swell, every curve—a giant, cool, fluffy pillow in a freshly washed case that smelled of lavender and perfume. But she was also much more. He couldn't stop holding her, exploring the contours of that novel landscape, her physical mass welcome evidence of her presence in the world. No girl he'd ever been with had ever felt this good. Any other woman was now inconceivable. And why would anyone ever consider it? Amelia was impossible not to love. And she loved him so deeply it hurt her. They hugged each other tightly, their closeness never enough.

'Sir? Any drinks?'

Angel opened his eyes to a lanky sun-kissed stewardess with blonde hair in a tight bun, standing in the aisle behind a trolley loaded with bottles of wine, spirits, beer, water, cartons of fruit juice, cans of fizzy drinks, plastic cups, and a bucketful of ice. She smiled, awaiting a response from Ron Swanson.

'San Pellegrino,' he croaked.

'With ice?'

'Yes.'

'Certainly, sir.'

Angel observed the stewardess drop ice cubes into a cup, pour water until the fizz reached the rim, and hand it over to his neighbour. This she followed up with a napkin and a bag of barbecue-flavoured salted almonds.

She moved on without asking Angel whether he desired a drink.

'Um . . . excuse me . . . madam?'

But she was already past him and asking someone in the row behind. 'Any drinks, madam?'

Angel gave up. He wasn't thirsty anyway, he told himself.

But any thoughts of thirst were quickly displaced by the vapours of his dream. His head was filled with Amelia—her soft kisses, her caresses, the feeling of her body on top of his, or rather, how he'd imagined it would feel, her smile, her voice, her hands, the scent of her hair, her huge blue eyes . . . Azure, or royal blue, or sapphire, depending on the light. Precious atolls. Seeing her again had become urgent and desperate.

He reached for his phone, intent on sending her a message, until he remembered there was no signal at 33,000 feet.

He'd message her from Schiphol.

The moment he landed.

The instant the wheels touched the Tarmac.

He'd tell her to forget about her lessons and take the train immediately to meet him at Leeds-Bradford Airport.

Professor Mastropasqua's idea was the right one. He knew it in his bones.

He'd spend the whole day with Amelia.

He'd likely go down to London with her.

He'd sleep rough on a park bench for the rest of the week if he had to and bring her back to York for the weekend on Friday afternoon. Straight from her last lesson or seminar to the train station.

They could stop at Guildford on the way up so she could grab her car.

And they'd go and visit the Brontë Parsonage, the Yorkshire Dales, York Minster, and whatever else she wanted to see.

They'd be inseparable. Glued together. Siamese twins.

Because they'd be joined at the soul.

Forever and ever.

Landing still hours away, and craving her company, he attempted to sleep again so he could continue the dream.

But he was past the point where he could.

Therefore, instead, he deep scanned his brain for memories in which to indulge.

And there were some, long sunk into the quagmire of nonsense but now resurfacing.

He remembered how he'd come to know about The Prospect of Whitby. Amelia had told him about it! She'd suggested they visit it around the time he was reading Dicken's *Barnaby Rudge*. *She*'d been the one who told him Dickens used to frequent this pub, where Pepys had also been a regular. But, while he'd been interested in the idea in principle, he'd avoided making concrete plans, deflecting Amelia's suggestions to go the following weekend every time. Barmen could never hear him when he ordered. It was embarrassing. Which is why he generally didn't like pubs. Somehow that . . . other person he'd ended up taking there had heard about it too and bullied him into making it a date. And he'd obeyed because at the time that other person wore Cartier and Louis Vuitton.

Pfff! *Mind cluttered with nonsense.*

And he now recalled that Amelia, upon hearing he'd been there with someone else, had smiled faintly and wiped away a tear.

The thought of it summoned the lump in his throat.

Bellend!

And apropos of books, he remembered how, after hearing him talk of his desire to read it, Amelia had found him a leather-bound edition of Alexander Pope's translation of *The Odyssey*, by Homer. An 1805 edition, no less, in excellent condition. An early Christmas present, she'd said. And what had he done with it? He'd left it on a shelf in his room, untouched, until, months later, during the Spring, he'd given the volume to . . . that other person, on the spur of the moment. At the time he hadn't given it a second thought, because he'd forgotten that Amelia had gifted him the book. Because his mind had been *cluttered with bloody nonsense!* In the shock of realisation, he hoped she'd never found out. The thought of the hurt it would have caused her hurt him even more.

Wanker!

He resolved to track down a copy of the exact same edition, in the exact same condition, and put it in his room, visibly on his bookcase, where she could see it next time she visited. If it later turned out she'd known about the re-gifting, he'd explain he had only loaned the book, or that his aunt had later given him a copy of the same edition, which was the re-gifted one.

Or maybe he'd get on his knees and *plead* for forgiveness.

But the worst thing he remembered was how, when Amelia had suggested in the early days of January, just ahead of the beginning of term, that they sneak into a park at night to watch the Quadrantids meteor shower, he'd agreed to it, only to fall asleep and never show up. When she'd seen him the following day, she'd smiled and said, caressing his cheek tenderly, without a hint of malice, 'Poor Angel, you must have been exhausted.' He'd later found out, via Alba, who'd been angry at him, that Amelia had brought an inflatable mattress, fleecy blankets, foldable pillows, binoculars, and a picnic basket full of snacks and beverages for them to enjoy while they chatted and sky-watched. And that she'd brought his favourite snacks—bread sticks, cashew nuts, pimento olives, maraschino cherries—and made him a serrano ham sandwich on crusty baguette. And that she'd also brought an adapter, so they could plug their headphones into the same iPhone and listen to music together. And that Amelia had not posted pictures of her carefully arranged set-up on Instagram in order not to make him feel guilty. Alba had known because she'd been the one helping her!

And that picnic basket that he'd later bought to take that . . . other person to Kew Gardens? Where did he get the idea? From Amelia, of course! He'd discovered they existed when he saw *her* basket in *her* room, neatly tucked away under her desk. It had looked brand new, indicating she'd purchased it especially for the occasion.

'Oh, Amelia!' he mumbled, wiping abrupt tears from his eyes. 'I'm so sorry. I'm so, so sorry.'

For you had eyes and chose me.

He bowed his head and, hands covering his face, stung by horror and shame, wept in silence for a long time.

Chapter CLXVI

Back in Schiphol—but under what changed circumstances!

Amelia had not yet been online that morning, and he'd been unable to even begin his message. When he wasn't staring at the blank text field on WhatsApp, unable to decide on the first word, he wrote two or three and immediately deleted them, always dissatisfied. He wanted his message not just to convey his feelings, but, because it was to define a moment that would be forever remembered, that would be etched in their hearts, that would remain an everlasting monument to the beginning, he wanted it to be impactful, poetic yet authentic, not forced, genuine, honest, free of purple prose. It had to be a declaration worthy of being printed or framed or engraved in marble. Yet, because unable to see her, he was unable to gauge her mood, and therefore to determine the optimal opening sentence.

Never mind. He had a ninety-minute layover before the final leg of his journey, which gave him enough time to load up with presents from the duty-free area. He had a great deal to atone for. Pity about the chocolates he'd lost in Chicago. Those had been truly worthy of Amelia. However, Schiphol was vast and the Netherlands a hub for international trade. They'd founded the Dutch East India Company, hadn't they? One of the most influential companies in history. He'd be able to find anything he wanted. He'd get her the most sumptuous chocolates, or the most luxurious perfume, or the most . . .

No. Wait! He was doing it again!

Amelia wouldn't care about such things.

Of course she appreciated them.

But what she really cared about was *him*, Angel.

This time he was not going to clutter his mind with materialist nonsense. The occasion demanded that he *un*clutter, that he focus on what was truly important. Which was him and her. Angel and Amelia. Coming together at last.

That had to be the focus.

So he would meet her free of encumbrances.

As he was.

He walked breezily past the duty free and went straight to the gate.

Not even caring about his rumpled and stinking clothes.

Once there, he pulled out his phone, and got working on his message.

By the time boarding was announced, she's still not been online. Her status remained: 'last seen yesterday at 00:46'. The clock had adjusted to local time, but it was the same as before: 23:46 GMT.

All the better. His message would be the first thing she saw that day. It would be received on a clean slate. And it would therefore have the centrality it demanded. It would define the day, and every day thereafter.

Zombielike, Angel remained focused on his phone all throughout boarding, handing over his passport and boarding pass, ambling through the airbridge, and settling in his assigned seat, barely registering the cabin crew, fellow passengers, or his surroundings. Free of luggage, he could devote both hands to the task.

He failed to notice take off and had only the vaguest sense of being airborne. His neighbours he blanked out completely, so afterwards he'd have no recollection of what they'd looked like.

Before he knew it, the aeroplane had already landed in Leeds and its engines been switched off.

It was 9:35 am.

And his message remained as far from completion as when he started it.

His heart raced.

The ants marched.

His hands became ice.

Except this time, it was for a pleasant reason.

He'd not acted on Mastropasqua's suggestion in the end because he'd needed to focus on his epic declaration of love. But whatever. As soon as he'd sent it, the wheels would be in motion. Amelia would arrive in York, today, hopefully in three hours or less, and she would collide against him at the train station, and she'd be in his arms, and they'd hold each other tightly until it got dark outside, never wanting to let go, just like in his dream.

That moment could not come soon enough.

Chapter CLXVII

Angel had barely noticed fellow passengers jumping out of their seats like as many jacks-in-the-box when the FASTEN YOUR SEATBELT sign pinged off.

Indeed, he was the last person to stand and the last person to leave the aeroplane.

And not because he'd become less impatient to see Amelia, but because he was still battling with his message.

Somehow, neither the declaration of love, nor the prefatory remarks, were coming.

He kept writing, then deleting; writing, editing, then deleting. Endlessly.

He made his way into the terminal without taking his eyes off the phone screen.

'Do you mind?' said the Border Force officer, harrumphing.

'Uh?'

A pair of blue eyes burning under a heavily lined brow. 'Put your phone away when going through border control.'

'Oh, sorry.'

Angel did as instructed.

His passport was swiped, and the contents of its data sheet and the computer screen gone over with a fine-tooth comb.

The Border Force officer seemed disappointed not to find anything he could detain him for, so he slapped Angel's passport down and jerked his head to indicate he should clear out.

Putting away his passport and retrieving his phone Angel executed as a single movement.

He drifted past the luggage carousels, past customs, and through the glass doors into the arrivals hall.

Needing to get his bearings, he followed the signs to the exit.

The plan was to take a taxi home and hopefully send Amelia his declaration while *en route*.

But then it occurred to him that it'd be better to go to York Station instead. It'd be an hour and a half to wait until Amelia arrived, if she left immediately after receiving his message, but any wait would be worth the reward.

His phone buzzed in his hand.

His arm bent as if jolted by a lightning bolt.

It was not Amelia.

It was his mother.

VICTORIA: Can you explain why a bailiff just showed up at our door demanding £1,726.13? He said it was a library fine owed to the university! The original fine plus penalties, interest, court fees, and bailiff fees.

Why didn't you mention the fine when we went down last month? I've had to pay it, but when you're back in the UK we are going to have a conversation about how you're going to pay me back. Your father is furious.

Angel swallowed, heart thumping.

He put his phone away.

He stepped outside and got into the nearest available taxi.

'Um . . . Leeds Station,' he said, before he realised what he'd done.

Forget York.

Forget waiting.

He'd go straight to Amelia!

The car got moving.

Angel resumed drafting on his phone, while the radio jabbered on about the weather, the news headlines, a terror attack, Brexit, and the forthcoming general election.

It seemed only seconds passed before he found they'd arrived at the railway station.

His drafting had yet to get him anywhere.

Chapter CLXVIII

Angel scanned the bank of screens overhead.

There was a train to London King's Cross at 11:15 am.

Forty-five-minute wait.

Enough to craft his message.

He bought his ticket, ordered a coffee at the The White Rose, and sat at the indoor terrace, facing the timetable displays.

He worked on his message.

For the next half hour, the neon-lit sea of humanity flowed past him on a bed of tiled flooring; pouring onto or off the platforms; eddying briefly around Burger King, Boots, M & S, The Body Shop, or W. H. Smith; laden with suitcases, handbags, briefcases, duffel bags, backpacks, or shopping.

But, in the end, the time elapsed unproductively.

Angel headed for the platforms and boarded his train.

Once seated, he resumed his work.

He now had a further two hours and sixteen minutes within which to complete it.

And that was likely his last chance, because afterwards he'd be in the London Underground, riding its tightly compressed trains, changing lines, staying alert on the platforms, paying attention to the stops, constantly interrupted by actions or announcements.

And, as the clock ticked, the pressure mounted. And not only did fatigue and awareness of minutes passing disrupt the composition of his text, but so did an accumulation of fears and doubts.

One impediment was the thought, which had only occurred to him when he boarded the train, that Amelia might disdain his declaration on the basis that it was coming after things hadn't worked out in Chicago, suggesting that to him she came *second*, that he was using her to fill a gap, that he was rebounding impulsively. How to prove that the scales had fallen from his eyes? That his feelings were genuine? That she was *first*, and not an afterthought?

Angel paused and rubbed his forehead.

'I hope Boris wins with a decent majority so he can get Brexit done for once and for all,' said a man in the adjacent aisle seat.

The man's companion replied, 'Do you think Farage's party will steal his votes?'

'Nah. Boris has successfully deflected blame towards Parliament. And Bercow, of course.'

Angel refocused on his phone screen, the rest of the conversation fading into a murmur.

'How could anyone do such a thing?' said a sharp-voiced lady seated behind him. 'They were just kids!'

Angel sighed and pinched his nose.

The lady's male interlocutor replied, 'I've only once heard of such a thing before. But that was in Kenya. Never here.'

Angel plugged his ears with his index fingers and stared at his phone, resting on his knee.

Of course, that solved the problem of surrounding conversations, but not of composing the message.

He unplugged his ears.

'. . . it's neither going to be the paradise of freedom and economic prosperity that the Brexiteers promised, nor the catastrophe that the remainers prognosticated,' said the man beside him. 'Honestly, I don't think much will change.'

'But if we're out, we'll be free to make whatever trade agreements we want,' said his companion.

'They can't ignore the biggest trading block. They'll have to comply with EU standards, like it or not.'

Angel craned his neck to see if there were unoccupied seats elsewhere in the carriage. He needed peace and quiet!

The carriage was full. Moreover, some commuters were standing.

The lady behind him said, 'You could understand if it'd been an embassy or a bank, but this doesn't make any sense.'

'It's also been shopping centres and public transport in the past. And like I said, they did it in Kenya.'

'But these young people. It's madness!'

'It is mad, isn't it? These things aren't rational.'

Angel stared at his phone. Attempted for the thousandth time to compose the opening sentence.

His neighbour said, '. . . and the other trade agreements will take years to negotiate.'

'And what about the deal with the Americans? Trump seems keen.'

Angel's neighbour chuckled. 'If they negotiate it with Trump, it will be a deal favourable to the Americans. Unfortunately the UK is the junior partner in these negotiations. We need them more than they need us.'

'Well, I think it'll be good when we're out. We can't have unaccountable bureaucrats in Brussels framing our laws and telling us how to live.'

'And you don't think they're not going to frame them anyway? You're dreaming if you think we'll be able to do whatever we want. The world is completely interconnected. The only difference is: we won't have a seat at that table! *And* everything will cost more.'

'You're so negative!'

'Well, we'll just have to wait and see. Nothing we can do anyway!'

Angel stood up and stepped over his neighbour to look for empty seats in a different carriage.

He had to walk through six of them to find one that wasn't packed like a tin of sardines.

He took a window seat unflanked by commuters and got back to drafting.

But five minutes later, the train began to lose speed.

He glanced out the window.

The train kept slowing, down to a crawl.

Cables. Poles. Houses. A bridge passing by.

And finally: a platform.

Peterborough Station.

Already!

The train stopped and the doors opened with a hiss.

Within seconds, he had neighbours again.

And not just neighbours, but chatty middle-aged mothers to boot.

'. . . he did apply to that university, but in the end he went to the University of the West of England.'

'My youngest will be finishing his A levels next year. I do worry whether this is going to start happening now. What did the mayor of London say? That it was part and parcel? Useless.'

'You might have to put your foot down and tell him to find a place up north.'

'Yes, but he wants to get into finance and work in the city.'

'Oh, dear.'

'And I don't quite fancy more thoughts and prayers or candlelight vigils.'

Angel got up again and weaved his way around the forest of standing commuters through to the last carriage.

Full.

He reversed direction and weaved his way towards the front carriage.

When he arrived there, he found a smattering of empty seats.

He chose one by the aisle, next to a headphoned man in a suit watching a film on his iPhone.

Angel got back to work.

Chapter CLXIX

What seemed like seconds later, Angel felt the train relent.

He glanced out the window.

Vegetation gradually gave way to man-made structures as the train slowed to a crawl.

Numerous posts.

Three modernist high-rise bocks.

Then a sea of houses.

Then a series of tunnels.

More railway tracks.

He was in London.

And his message remained unfinished.

Or, rather, not even begun.

'Bollocks!' he whispered.

Conceding defeat, Angel put his phone away.

He'd simply show up.

That was it. He'd simply show up and explain in person.

It was the best way.

Face to face.

The way knight errants did it.

The way Amadis would have done.

With this, the ants received their marching orders.

He was going to see Amelia!

After the train stopped and the doors opened, he was among the first to disembark. His chest tightened, his stomach cramped, his legs turned to jelly.

Regardless, he accelerated, weaving his way past the ambling commuters and coppers standing in high visibility jackets, catching up even with the impatient, stressed-out businessmen in blue and grey suits.

In less than twenty seconds, he was in Kings Cross Station's main foyer.

It'd been two and a half weeks since he'd last been there, but it felt like two and a half months.

He'd been delirious with the flu. Amelia had been nursing him, bringing him food and medicine. She'd supplied clean sheets. She'd checked on him regularly. She'd interceded with the canteen supervisor. And, by way of thanks, he'd left without even the courtesy of a message, abandoning the sandwiches, the Panadol, and the tissues she'd taken the trouble to procure.

He thought of her, seated on the side of his bed, caressing his forehead, checking his temperature, smiling kindly at him.

And he remembered staggering out of his room, focused on his snot, and not once thinking about her feelings.

Blockhead!

The time was 1:30 pm.

He headed for the escalator leading to the Kings Cross St Pancras Underground station.

At the noisy ticket hall, he purchased his ticket.

But, as he approached the bank of escalators leading down to the platforms, standing like a twig that got caught in a rock before the human waterfall, he noticed a scrawled sign informing commuters that the station he was intending to travel to, the one nearest to the university, was closed.

'Oh, for goodness' sake!' he whispered.

What to do?

The next nearest station was ages away from campus and involved onerous line changes, plus a bus ride.

And he hated riding the bus.

He could never tell where the stops were, or where he was, or when to press the button.

Therefore, since he had funds remaining, he headed for the exit.

He'd take a taxi.

It'd be more relaxed, and he wouldn't arrive windblown or sniffling from the cold.

He'd make a dignified entrance, worthy of the occasion.

He imagined himself being driven.

It felt right.

Because he was, indeed, about to declare love to his future wife.

There was a taxi rank directly outside the station, beyond the throng of slow-flowing commuters and, today of all days, the heavy presence of Metropolitan Police.

He got into the first available one and gave the name of the university.

'Sorry mate, that whole area has been cordoned off. No one can get in at the moment.'

'Oh? Really? Why?'

'Because of the terror attack this morning.'

'Oh, bugger! So you can't get to the university?'

'Nah, mate. Can't get through.'

'Um . . . can you take me as close as you can?'

'I can take you up to the diversion.'

'Okay.'

'But the police won't let you through.'

'Um . . . yes, just . . . um . . . take me up to the diversion.'

'Okay, mate.'

The driver set the car in motion.

Angel punched his leg. 'Bugger!'

All these delays. All these impediments!

The gremlins were determined to bar him from Amelia.

But he'd not let them win.

Arcalaus' sorcery would fail.

Love would triumph!

Angel would conquer!

He'd burst through the obstacles, squeeze past the blockages, and pierce through the occlusions.

He'd claim his damsel!

Amelia!

Chapter CLXX

The taxi pulled over some twenty yards ahead of the diversion.

Up ahead, Angel found a hallucinogenic kaleidoscope of blinking blue lights and yellow and orange neon. A forest of road cones, thronged pedestrians, policemen in high-visibility jackets, police patrol cars, fire engines, a dozen ambulances, media vans with satellite dishes, and thickets of cameras on tripods, connected to generators by tangles of cabling.

Angel paid and got out of the car.

Besides police, emergency services personnel, gawking onlookers, nervous residents, exiled shopkeepers, evacuated office workers, inconvenienced motorists, and angry delivery men, there were reporters speaking in urgent voices, their breaths steaming in the cold. That part of London seemed to have ground to a halt.

To get to the university, Angel had to get past the cones and police cordon. He decided he'd pretend, if asked, to be a student. The university would have certainly told students to stay on campus until further notice, so Amelia would be in.

He approached the nearest police officer, who was talking to a handful of pedestrians.

'Sir?' Angel said.

The policeman ignored him.

'Sir?'

The policeman finished talking to the pedestrians.

'Sir?'

A couple approached the policeman and got his attention.

'Sir!'

The policeman answered the couple's questions.

'Sir!'

No acknowledgment.

'Sir!'

The policeman went to speak to his colleague. Angel waited.

The policeman came back.

'Sir?'

The policeman's walkie talkie came alive.

Angel waited while the policeman communicated with a colleague.

The walkie talkie fell silent.

'Sir?'

A pedestrian approached the policeman and got his attention.

Angel sighed.

Glancing past the cordon, past the emergency vehicles and personnel, all of whom seemed preoccupied with tasks, Angel decided to walk in.

And he did. Unnoticed.

It was an eight-minute walk to the campus. From the two minute mark, ash and dust covered every surface. The asphalt. The pavement. The lamp posts. The letter box. The naked trees. The wrought iron fences. The adjacent parkland. The cars parked along the road. Emergency vehicles and personnel were everywhere, in ever greater numbers as he approached, but visibility was poor. Everything was grey. The foggy air reeked of burnt wood and rubber.

He covered his nose with a lapel.

His eyes watered.

No one saw him.

As he walked past the Atlantis launderette and the Arnude Windera Merchants off-licence. The former had closed for the day, the latter had closed down altogether. The premises had been vacated and an estate agent's TO LET sign had appeared next to the fascia. Probably went bankrupt after his roommate left, he thought, shaking his head.

As he walked, massive plumes of smoke became visible, rising overhead. He became aware of car alarms wailing in the distance.

The terror attack appeared to have taken place in the immediate vicinity of the university.

He hoped Amelia was okay.

He pulled out his phone and checked her WhatsApp status.

Last seen yesterday at 23:46.

He still wanted to surprise her, so, although worried, he put his phone away.

It'd be best if he simply showed up at this time of peril.

To rescue her.

To make her feel safe.

As he turned the corner, to approach the campus, he found the road blocked by ambulances and fire engines. Large hoses snaked on the ground like pythons. So densely packed were the vehicles, the firemen, the paramedics, and the policemen, that they formed a barrier of activity, blocking the view.

The temperature went up in a steep gradient as he approached.

So did the sound of the car alarms, and of the voices shouting and bellowing around him. These were set against a pervasive low rumble, the oscillating hiss of pressurised water, and a penetrating whine, like the sound of a turbine or the engine of a 747 waiting to take off.

Enormous billows of toxic smoke intermittently wafted across the street, blotting out everything, obscuring the view, and darkening the scene.

The smoke came from the university campus.

'Oh, my God,' he whispered.

Angel walked past them, still undetected, to get a view from the edge of the campus.

And then he saw it.

Where there'd once been buildings, statues, green laws, trees, and flowerbeds, was now the site of a cataclysm. The buildings had collapsed into smoking hills of rubble and twisted iron. The lawns were rivers of mud. The trees had vanished—splintered or burnt to ashes. The only colours were grey, brown, and black.

Amelia!

He wanted to run into to the site but knew he couldn't. There was nowhere to run to. So instead he scanned the ruins, searching for the girls' dorms.

He couldn't see it.

It was at the back of the campus and therefore not be visible from his current vantage point.

Heart racing, Angel crossed the road and followed the perimeter of the campus, his legs like jelly.

The sights of devastation were difficult to process. Didn't seem real.

Gradually, the girls' dorm came into view.

Or what might have been the girls' dorm—it was hard to make sense of the site. Every landmark had disappeared.

One thing was clear, however.

The dorm was a ruin.

A wet hill of concrete, brick, and twisted metal.

It was also emitting a great deal of black smoke, which, thankfully, was blowing away from him.

Anyone trapped inside would have long suffocated.

All the same, firemen in masks attempted to dig out survivors. Or dead bodies. Body bags had been lined up on the ground and were being removed one by one.

The only buildings left standing were the Gothic humanities library and the gym, although both had sustained window damage.

A colossal wave of anguish swept over his body.

He pulled out his phone and, with trembling digits, typed a message to Amelia, hardly noticing he was breathing fast. This time, he had no difficulty. All doubt and confusion had dissipated.

ANGEL: I'm back in London. I've gone to the campus and found it no longer exists. Please tell me you are okay. Please tell me you are safe. Please tell me where you are. I must see you. I must.

He pressed the Send icon.

One grey tick.

He waited.

One grey tick.

He waited more.

Still one grey tick.

'Oh, please, oh please,' he mumbled.

He telephoned.

Straight to voicemail.

He telephoned again.

Straight to voicemail.

His voice a thin thread. 'Please, Amelia, please.'

He glanced at the mountain of rubble. Was Amelia under it? Was she trapped, waiting to be rescued? Was she injured, unable to call out for help, to tell the firemen she was there? Was she . . . ?

'No!'

Tears welled up in his eyes.

The impulse to run towards the rubble, climb it, and start frantically digging, was strong. Every second counted.

But he knew he'd be thrown out of the site.

He telephoned a third time.

Straight to voicemail.

He checked her WhatsApp status.

Last seen yesterday at 23:46.

Chapter CLXXI

The policeman escorted Angel back outside the cordon.

He'd finally been spotted climbing the ruins.

The heat had been immense.

It had damaged his shoes and his trousers, and he'd scorched his hands.

None of the rubble could be moved, except for a pebble here and there. It'd all seemed so hard, so rough, so heavy.

The memory of it now seemed like a dream.

His blackened face showed skin on the cheeks, where tears had washed away the ash.

Once outside, while detained pending examination by a paramedic, he spotted among the onlookers two familiar faces.

Jae.

And Johannes.

Of course, having both earned suspensions from the university, they had escaped the attack.

Angel asked the policeman watching him whether he could speak to them, explaining they were fellow students.

Permission was granted and Jae and the Swede were sent to join him.

Jae was not her usual self. Gone were the Olympian calm, the superior eyebrow, the halcyon mockery; she looked shaken, fragile, vulnerable—things Angel had never imagined possible. She was also draped around Johannes. Also, until now, unimaginable. It had previously seemed she'd never condescend to date anyone. It wouldn't be until about a year later that he'd realise the Swedish strongman made sense—he was probably the only one manly enough for Jae.

Johannes said, 'Angel buddy, what happened?' In the trauma of events, their dispute had been forgotten.

'Um . . . I . . . I-I went in.'

'Why?'

'To see if Amelia was there.'

Johannes looked away, eyes haunted and distant.

'Why did you want to see her?' said Jae, her voice trembling.

'I . . . I wanted . . . to tell her that I love her.'

'You didn't even know her!' she screamed.

Jae burst into tears and sought comfort from the strongman, nestling her head in his chest.

With his leg-sized arms, he held her tightly against him. Johannes glanced at him. Shook his head.

Angel observed the scene for a moment, resisting the conclusion.

And then he crumbled.

Chapter CLXXII

Two days later news of the first arrests linked to the London attack made the headlines.

Contrary to initial speculation, the attack had not been masterminded by an Islamist group.

The mass murderers had been home-grown.

This knowledge convulsed the nation. The trauma was worse than 9/11. In the latter attack, Islamist terrorists had destroyed the World Trade Center in New York, killing thousands of people. But in the 5/11 attack, the terrorists had not been foreigners and they had not targeted bankers or stock traders or finance professionals, but young university students. People who'd just become adults. Who'd yet to live their lives.

The inhumanity was incomprehensible.

And yet, it happened.

It had to be investigated so that it may be understood.

Faces were shown.

Angel would have recognised them immediately.

But, at the time, grief at the events of the fifth of November had rendered him catatonic.

And this time there had been no Amelia to pull him back.

He was admitted into a psychiatric hospital for treatment.

It took months for him to re-emerge.

And it took a year before he was fit enough to speak to the police, to help them with their ongoing investigation.

The reasons for their interest became apparent soon enough.

They still had no clear idea of what the terrorists' motives had been.

But they suspected a friend of his father.

A man who'd since disappeared from the face of the earth.

The two faces first shown in the press belonged to Babyface, the maintenance guy at the university, and a British man. And this British man had been Angel's roommate.

His American roommate.

Chad or Brad or Josh or Todd or whatever name he'd gone by.

His actual name was James.

Born in Sussex, from British parents.

An expert with explosives.

They'd since arrested another man.

A man who operated the off-licence near the university. Arnude Windera Merchants.

They'd found evidence of tunnels leading from the shop to various university buildings, under which the terrorists had built 'wine' vaults where they'd placed their bombs.

They'd also arrested yet another known to Angel—a large, tattooed man with a beard. A convicted rapist.

He'd dealt with transportation.

Additionally, there were suspects still at large.

One was Emmanuel.

Although it was thought he'd vanished into bedsit-land, where he'd lived under an assumed identity until last year, when it was thought he'd died of COVID-19.

The other suspect who was still at large was his father's friend: Professor Orlando Mastropasqua.

Now the world's most wanted terrorist.

Angel had been among the last known persons to speak to him.

After that, it was as if he'd never existed.

Comparisons to the Gunpowder Treason Plot had been inevitable.

Conspiracy theorists speculated that he was in the pay of Habermas—not the philosopher, but the grand conspirator behind all conspirators. 'You think George Soros is the puppet master?' they whispered at fringe meetings and murky pubs. 'Hah! He's just a stooge! A false flag operation! The real power lies with those behind him. The ones you don't see or ever hear about. Tell me, have you ever seen a picture of this Habermas? Do we even know what he looks like? There! Irrefutable proof, if any was needed!'

Of course, Angel's father had already been extensively interviewed. And so had Angel's mother. And Angel's sister.

The revelations had rocked the entire family.

All of this had been reported in the press.

Sensational articles had also appeared, telling of his

'heroic' and 'desperate' attempt to save his sweetheart from the inferno.

Johannes had come to enjoy a period of minor celebrity, his feats of strength and hypercaloric diet having received coverage in Lad Bible and similar online publications. He'd even done a collab video with Eddie Hall.

Jae had caused a stir with a series controversial declarations and amassed a large Twitter following, on the back of which she'd been given a column in the *Daily Mail.*

The police were especially interested in a message Amelia had sent Angel while he was in Chicago. When faculty and student activists had begun pushing for Mastropasqua's removal from the university, Amelia had told him the latter had laughed about it and said he was going to 'teach them a lesson they [would] never forget'.

Angel remembered overhearing the professor cryptically promising to his father that he was going 'to destroy them all'. And he also remembered seeing the professor conferring with all of the suspects at different points—with Beard at the park; with Babyface outside the main building; with James, outside the Jenni Murray Hall, when his supposedly American roommate got out of the Royce and bid the professor goodbye with a Sussex accent; with the wine merchant in the off-licence's cellar, which did have a long tunnel and where he'd seen spades as well as wooden crates that could have contained items other than wine; and, finally, with Emmanuel in the kitchen. 'Doing manual labour, eh?' the professor had said to Angel, approvingly.

The professor had been known for hating the university and for urging students to drop out and take up menial jobs. Or become independent scholars, without a degree. He'd even encouraged Angel's father to withdraw his son from the university, telling him that Angel was sleeping through his classes, which wasn't true, at least with Mastropasqua's classes. But he'd also encouraged Angel to keep learning. So he was not against education. He was against the university and modern universities in general.

But there might have been a personal motivation too. In the profiles of him run by the news organisations, it was mentioned that he'd once had a daughter, who had attended the university nine years earlier; that she'd got involved with student activists; and that she'd ended up taking her own life. His marriage of fifteen years had in consequence fallen apart. His ex-wife, an accomplished Mediaevalist, had not had contact with him in years. Hadn't Jae mentioned the rumours about it last year?

Much that hadn't made sense, began to make sense during the interviews.

Of particular significance had been his last conversation with the professor in Detroit. *Is there a girl you care about at the university? Why don't you ask her to take the train and meet you at the airport? Drop everything. Spend the day together in Leeds. You won't regret it.* 'You'll thank me later,' he'd said.

This was hours before the bombs were detonated.

Mastropasqua had tried to save her. Because Angel's father was Mastropasqua's friend.

But Angel had not heeded his advice.

He'd delayed.

Amelia had been alive then.

She would have jumped at the chance to spend the day with him.

And now she was gone.

Alex Kurtagic is not a New York Times best-selling author and has never appeared on the Sunday Times Best Seller list. He has not published numerous books nor sold sixty-eight million copies worldwide—and he is yet to be nominated for the Nobel Prize in Literature. He does live in a region where the sky is always grey or black, and where it rains almost every day of the year. For no good reason, his prose remains untranslated in 170 languages.

Lightning Source UK Ltd.
Milton Keynes UK
UKHW040658040123
414815UK00001B/109

9 781999 357382